Pelion Preserved

Other books by Anna LaForge

The Marcella Fragment
Agave Revealed

Pelion Preserved

by

Anna LaForge

Book Three of Maze

All rights reserved.
Copyright © 2015 by Anna LaForge

Cover design and illustrations by Jeff Raby: Creatis Group
creatisgroup.com

Cover art: *Parting of the Sea King and Princess Volkhova*
by Mikhail Alexandrovich Vrubel
© Fine Art Images / age fotostock

No part of this book may be reproduced or transmitted in any form or by any means, electronic or mechanical, including photocopying, recording, or by any information storage and retrieval system, without permission in writing from the publisher.

Newcal Publishing
newcalpub.com

Trade Paperback Edition
ISBN 978-0-9850168-8-3

All of the characters in this book are fictitious.
Any resemblance to actual persons living or dead
is purely coincidental.

This book is set in Palatino Linotype and is printed on acid free paper.

Yet a third time for Bob
(Who makes all things possible)

My river runs to thee:
Blue sea, wilt welcome me?

My river waits reply.
Oh sea, look graciously!

I'll fetch thee brooks
From spotted nooks,—

Say, sea,
Take me!

Emily Dickinson

Contents

Prologue		The Last Day	1
The Clansmen of Endlin			
	Chapter 1	Nativity	9
	Chapter 2	The Once Sacred City	23
	Chapter 3	Land's End	36
	Chapter 4	The Citadel	51
	Chapter 5	The Tehran of the Kwanlonhon	68
What Shall I Be If Not A Stranger?			
	Chapter 6	The Gauntlet	88
	Chapter 7	Chance Encounters	104
	Chapter 8	Rough Passage	118
	Chapter 9	Night Watch	138
The War Within			
	Chapter 10	The Bronze Doors	155
	Chapter 11	Interiors	169
	Chapter 12	The Iron Door	185
	Chapter 13	Deception	203
The War Without			
	Chapter 14	Days of Choice	219
	Chapter 15	Crooked Paths	233
	Chapter 16	The Gift to the Giver	249
	Chapter 17	Battle Cry	261
The Prodigal's Return			
	Chapter 18	Letters in the Flame	275
	Chapter 19	A Dog Howls	287
	Chapter 20	Sacrifice	300
	Chapter 21	The Sign of the Gull	320
	Chapter 22	Beacon of the East	341
The Equerry Of Endlin			
	Chapter 23	Always and Forever, the Sea	357
	Chapter 24	Judgment Day	379
	Chapter 25	Testament	395
	Chapter 26	The Last Tehran	410
	Chapter 27	The New Age	420
	Epilogue	Pelion Preserved	431
Appendices			
	Appendix I	The Rise of the Eastern Republic	452
	Appendix II	Excerpt from *Tyrants Among Us*	454

Cast of Characters

The Council of Pelion
    She-Who-Was-Magda, Nineteenth Mother
    Esslar, Master of Mysteries, Master Healer
    Galen, Commander of the Legion
    Symone, Head Archivist of the Greater Library
    Evadne, High Healer of Pelion, healing partner to Japhet
    Japhet, High Healer of Pelion, healing partner to Evadne
    Anstellan, Instructor of the Maze, Master of the Hetaera Guild

Citizens of Pelion
    Aethra, mate to Manthur, daughter of Magda
    Adrastus, President of the Guild Assembly, Master Engineer
    Remy, Secretary to the Nineteenth Mother
    Dictys, Lieutenant of the Calvary; Head Trainer of the Maze
    Briseis, Master of the Printer's Guild
    Pentaur, Monitor of the Maze
    Labicus, Master Trader of the League of Independent Traders
    Macris, Apprentice to Labicus

The Sarujian Mountains
    Altug, Headman of the Sarujian stronghold, mate to Valeria
    Valeria, Teacher of the Sarujian stronghold, mate to Altug

The Province of Cyme
    Gwyn, former ernani, mate to Temenus
    Temenus, former candidate of Pelion, mate to Gwyn

The City of Endlin
    Falal, sponge dealer of the Abalone District
    Oman, tea merchant of the Abalone District, father of Ridha
    Ridha, sa'ab to Oman, concubine to Shakar Kwanlonhon
    Lampon, agent of Pelion, mate to Phanus
    Phanus, agent of Pelion, mate to Lampon
    Olimpoor, agent of Manthur
    Cassis, agent of Olimpoor, disguised as a Kwanlonhon clansman

The Province of Cinthea
    Latona, Dreamsayer of Cinthea
    Alyssa, daughter of Latona, Bard of Cinthea

Clan of the Kwanlonhon
    Manthur, third son of Linphat V, Tehran of the Kwanlonhon
    Rahjid, sa'ab to Linphat V, abdicates in favor of Manthur
    Shakar, second son of Linphat V
    Tasir, fourth son of Linphat V, guardian to Sandur
    Sandur, sa'ab to Manthur
    Pischak, playfellow to Sandur, father of Bonhur
    Bonhur, sa'ab to Pischak Kwanlonhon
    Fawaz, Pilot of *Sea Horse*, flagship of the Kwanlonhon
    Kasovar, brother to Linphat V, guardian to Manthur

Clan of the Synzurit
    Balafel, Equerry of Endlin

Clan of the H'ulalet
    Nayeem, Tehran of the H'ulalet
    Rassad, Pilot, son to Nayeem

Clan of the Onozzi
    Yodhat, Tehran of the Onozzi
    Vavashi, sa'ab to Yodhat, concubine to Shakar Kwanlonhon

Clan of the Assad
    Djaras, Steward, chosen as a candidate for the Maze

The Ernani
    Kokor of the Painted Caverns
    Tibor of the Marsh-Dwellers
    Yossi of Dragon's Tooth
    Eddo of the Smoking Mountain
    Jincin of the Northern Wastes
    Pharlookas of the Western Ridge
    Ulkemene of New Agave
    Vlatla of the River People
    Becca of Botheswallow
    Zuniga of the Serpent People
    Hanania of Beymouth
    Draupadi of Droghedan

Acknowledgements

Robert Fitzgerald for the use of his excellent translation/adaptation of Homer's *Odyssey,* and Emily Dickinson's ecstatic poem, *The Outlet* (162). Stephen Sterns, who is single-handedly responsible for authenticating every nautical detail to be found here, not to mention his guidance when it came to actually shaping the book. Meghan Found, my touchstone in the process of writing this trilogy, and Beth Snyder, my queen of grammar. And lastly, thanks to Kathryn Johnson Cameron, who contributed much appreciated financial support to this book through the *Pelion Preserved* Kickstarter Project.

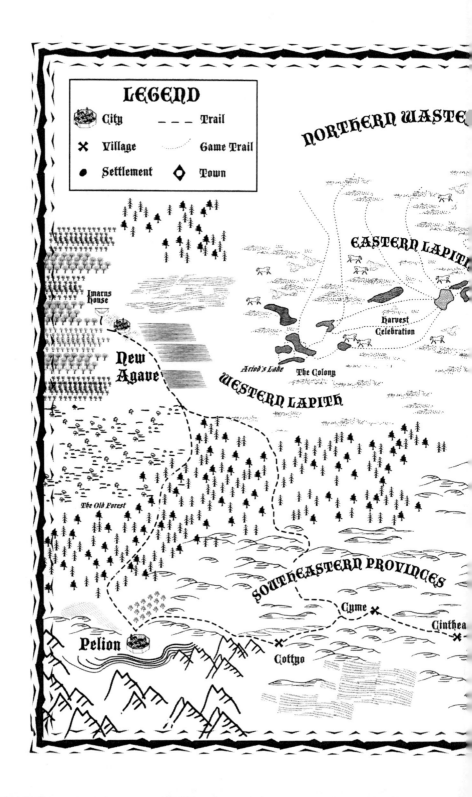

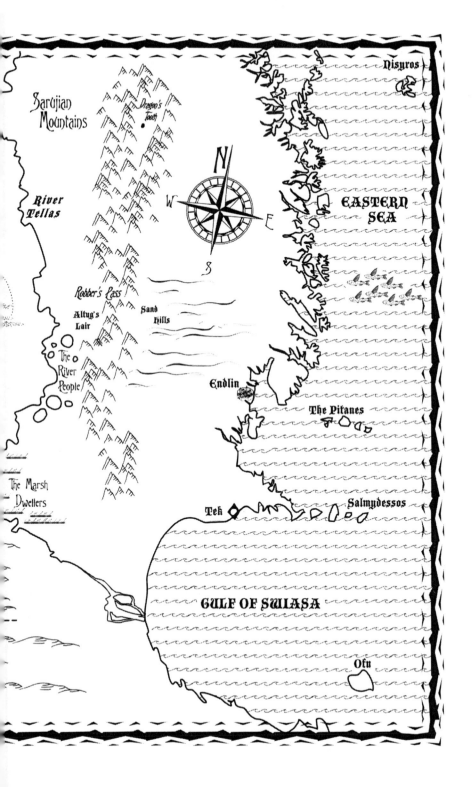

Prologue

The Last Day

SHE WOKE FOR the last time. She napped most of the day, but now, as dusk fell, she paused with eyes open to consider her much-extended life. It struck her as odd that she had walked on two planets in her lifetime, Old Earth, and this one, the one with no name.

"We have named it."

Of course you have, she thought without bitterness. You've plucked us from a dying planet and planted us here. You are Sowers, beings whose purpose is to scatter seeds across the universe. It's right and proper that you should name our world, for we are entirely yours, our genome gradually changed by you, each succeeding generation genetically bound to this planet in the hope that we will not destroy it as we did Old Earth. I made this bargain with you long ago, and I keep my bargains.

"It is our name for this world, devised for our use. It need not be yours."

She heard the apology contained in his flat, uninflected mental voice. He had been with her since the first day, this Sower who called himself "Singer." Part of his physical being stood at the entrance of her tent, part lived with his fellow Sowers on the ships they plied across the universe, part existed someplace beyond her imagination. He glimmered as he shifted in and out of phase, wings folded, a serene warden, eternally present and (it seemed to her) eternally young. In her early days on Old Earth, she'd seen images of Horus, the Egyptian falcon-god. If the Sowers resembled any life form that had ever lived and breathed on Old Earth, they reminded her most of those bird-headed figures with their unblinking gaze.

"What is your age?" she asked him that morning, considering her own age, which was incalculable.

"What age would you have me be?" he answered in that preternaturally calm way of his, a manner that never varied, not once, not a single time, in their thirty years of conversation.

Not even when a horde of wild men attacked them one terrible night, killing a dozen of their best people and stealing their herds—sheep and goats—did he alter his tone. That loss left her furiously bereft, mourning not just the piles of bodies that must be burnt, but the loss of milk for the children and wool for the weavers. The bodies of three Earthers and nine planet-born were fed to the flames at dawn, leaving no evidence of the crime committed against them. This death ritual was her invention, conceived when she remembered the countless acres devoted to the dead of Old Earth, miles upon miles of graves that served no purpose, housed no families, grew no crops, pastured no animals. We must learn to consecrate the act of living, she reminded herself, instead of worshipping the dead.

Still, she was angry.

"I'll send out our best scouts to track them, take back our herds, and kill each and every one of the raiders," she announced, feeling ruthless and absolutely justified.

"That would be satisfying."

He never disagreed with her. Even so, the wording of his reply brought her up short, causing her to reconsider.

"We must protect ourselves from these roving bands. As we've grown larger, we've become a richer target. A fortress, I think, will make a difference. On a hilltop. With stone walls and a moat."

"Moat?" he repeated, eyes shut as he accessed the meaning of the word, before fixing her again with his fierce raptor stare. "A dry moat," he countered, "where animals may graze and orchards may grow."

Instead of sending out searchers for the missing sheep, she supervised the burning of the bodies, said the rite of remembrance, and sent out calls for suggestions for a likely site on which to build a permanent home. For the first twenty years since departing the ship, they crisscrossed a section of land they came to call the Southern Province, known for its temperate climate, fertile soil, and long growing season. They made maps as they went, searching for (and finding) small islands of humanity, for the Sowers, true to their word, cast human beings and books (and songs) in a wide swath across the new world. Some they encountered chose to join their nomadic community; some did not. Shared languages made associations easier, although the emerging common language was to her practiced ear a polyglot of the tongues of the mountain-dwelling peoples of Old Earth, from the Alps to the Himalayas, from the Rockies to the Andes. As much as they could, at her insistence, they traded for books of all kinds. Now, having surveyed the territories around them and doubling their original population, they were finally ready to put down roots, raise yet another tent city, plant orchards and crops, and begin to build.

They chose a valley not far from where she'd found herself on her second day of consciousness. On an escarpment that jutted out into a larger, deeper valley to the south, a geologist discovered a deposit of granite capable of forming the foundations of a group of buildings which, when complete, would resemble the walled fortresses that once dotted the blue hills of Tuscany.

Among the congregation of books they carted about as if they were ingots of silver and gold was one promising to teach them how to build a medieval castle. We have books, she thought for the umpteenth time, and all of us are literate. We have everything we need. It would take many decades beyond her death to complete, yet still she saw it in her mind's eye, looming high on the hill outside her tent, castellated stone gleaming in the twilight.

"Pelion," she murmured to herself.

"A mountain on the peninsula of a country called Greece. A well-watered place known for its greengage plums."

"Mount Pelion, legendary home of Chiron the Centaur. The center of learning in ancient Greece. Boys were sent to study and grow to manhood—boys like Achilles, Jason, Theseus, Heracles."

"Heroes of your legends?"

"Princes trained to be warriors and kings. Learned centaurs, mythic beings half-men, half-horse, taught them poetry, geography, herb-lore and healing."

"Males only?"

"We will change that."

"Are you a centaur, then?"

"It seems I am!" she said, enjoying their banter. "Part human and part something else. Linked to the old world but hopeful of the new. Like Chiron, we will teach any and all who journey to Pelion."

Singer spoke, or rather, sang his approval. He sang rarely, but when moved to vocalize, his eerie compositions brought camp activities to a standstill. Today he favored high *Bel Canto* style, all runs and trills, with liberal use of *portamento* as he descended to the lowest notes of his four octave range. She shivered a bit as she listened to the words. He'd chosen as his text a nineteenth century African-English phrase taken from the Book of Joshua, "And the walls came-a tumblin' down."

Copying down these words in her book, she remembered the day he insisted she begin recording all her impressions and observations. "Why?" she'd asked, somewhat impatiently, for there was much to do and little time to write. To which he'd replied:

"You are the First Mother. You will not be the last. Perhaps you will encourage others to write."

Perhaps not, she remembered thinking, not interested in pursuing that particular line of inquiry since the subject of her death was not a popular one with her. That was a decade ago, before the building site was cleared and the engineers began their work constructing the quarry. Today, she found herself interested.

"Care to explain why you're singing about walls coming down when we've yet to build them up?"

"You imagine the beginning. I anticipate the end."

It was a promise. Singer would be present when the walls came down.

"This being is older than this planet."

Startled, she cast about for meaning before remembering her question from the morning. What's happening to me, she thought, half-frantic that she could no longer keep track of a simple question and a simpler reply. These days, my happiest hours are spent napping in the sun. Food no longer tastes good to me. My eyes and ears fail me more often than not, as does my memory. Even as she strung these thoughts together, she understood finally, unequivocally, that she was near her end. All was shadow now, the evening stars twinkling on the eastern horizon.

"Are you ready?"

It came as a shock that she was, indeed, ready. Would it have been better if she'd realized it this morning and lived her last few hours savoring life instead of napping? Of course not, she thought, disturbed at how easily she fell into sentimental thinking, she who disliked sentimentality above all things, who prided herself on her dry eyes when Singer informed her of the final death of all life on Old Earth. I did not cry then. I will not cry now.

"What must I do?"

"Send out the call."

She assembled her message, instilling in it a sense of urgency, a yearning for a mind that would meet and match her own until, gradually, her consciousness would slip the constraints of her body and fly free. Not to be alone, but to join Singer on the darkling plain where other adepts would join them in time, all of them gathered under a single sun and a crescent moon, symbols of a search that brought the Sowers, explorers of countless galaxies, to a quadrant of the universe foreign even to them.

Having rescued the inhabitants of Earth mere hours before their planet became uninhabitable to humans, the Sowers discovered something they had not known before. As each of the rescued folk fell into the deep sleep of time travel, they began to dream. Sharing the consciousness of those dreamers, the Sowers discovered song. Not birdsong, or whale calls, or the sound of waves and wind, but the sound of human-constructed melodies, rhythms, and rhymes. This was song, called "The First Art" since no instruments were necessary, something absolutely unique to the race who called themselves "human." Thus was the name "Singer" adopted by an alien being whose travels spanned countless universes, but had never before heard the simplest of songs.

The first gift of the Sowers to humanity was life itself – rescue and transport to a new home. The second gift, adeptness, was recompense for the gift of song given to the Sowers and thus, to every corner of the universe.

This, Singer promised her, oh, so long ago. Her body would die, but her consciousness would live on in a place that existed outside the fixed rules of three-dimensional time and space. There she would watch, as Singer watched, as the grand plan, to which she had devoted her entire being, began.

She slept, her dreams untroubled. Sometime near dawn she woke to find a strange woman kneeling at the foot of her cot.

"What are you called?"

"Anara. Daughter of Evelyn."

She did not know this woman, dark-skinned and sloe-eyed, but she knew her mother.

"I assisted at your birth."

"My mother told me."

"She was so proud of you, the firstborn of our community."

"My mother never traveled beyond the mountains where she was born, yet she let herself be pulled up into the Sowers' ship, so determined was she that I be born, that we not be left to die in the great conflagration."

The elder woman took the young woman's hands in hers.

"Why have you come?"

Anara answered calmly, matching the tone of the old woman who was known by everyone in the settlement as "Mother."

"Because you called me."

"So I did. For a great thing is going to happen, Anara. Something that has never happened before. Hold tight to my hands, close your eyes, and open your mind. You know how, don't you?"

"I do. My teacher taught me."

"Then you know there is nothing to fear."

Her eyes shut tight, Anara nodded her head.

"She's ready, Singer, as am I. Shall we begin?"

Before the First Mother could prepare herself in any way, the transfer between them began, the old woman's memories streaming into the mind of the Second Mother, who would, from that day forward, identify herself as She-Who-Was-Anara.

"Shall we go?" asked Singer, who waited by her side. This time, however, he spread his wings, revealing to her for the first time his feathered breast.

Strange as it was to leave her body behind, she did so happily. It was, after all, her last day, but also her first. The settlement spread out before her, the encampment of tents and beyond that, the fields, orchards, herds. Four hundred souls and growing. Her people, the majority of them now planet-born. Hardy people, who worked long hours, delighted in song and dance, and learned to read even as they learned to walk. A few, like Ansara, were being born adept, just as Singer promised, but that was the long battle others must fight. This was her creation, her idea of what the world should be. This was Pelion.

She would put up the walls. Let others take them down.

Pelion Preserved

"And the First Mother said: "Stay, for we are nothing without you."
"We have tarried longer than we intended," said the Sower known as Singer, a favorite of the First Mother as she was to him.
"What of the gift you promised? One that will prevent us from destroying this world as we did the one called Earth?"
Singer went silent until it seemed he might not speak again. Then he said:
"Build a maze. There will your descendants go to be transformed. There they will learn to speak heart to heart, mind to mind, unto the thousandth generation."
"How should we build it? We know nothing of mazes."
"You have books, do you not?"
The First Mother, a lover of books, nodded and said: "We do."
"Build it," Singer said, "and all will be as I have promised. Build it," he repeated, "and we will come again."

        from *The Book of Mothers*, attributed to the First Mother

"What of the sons who dream of safe haven?
What of the daughters who dream of the sea?"

        from *The Book of Mothers*, attributed to the Fifteenth Mother

Chapter 1

Nativity

SPRING STUMBLED ON sluggish feet that year, reluctant to be born. A feeble sun delivered light without warmth, sinking into quick oblivion as heavy-bottomed clouds gathered low on the horizon. Once the sun retreated, the rains began in earnest, drenching the already moisture-packed earth, the wind kicking up as the evening wore on, whipping leafless branches into a frenzy, the naked trees swaying under the lash of midnight storms. All in all it was a wretched spring as springs go, dismal and damp, a bleak reminder of a cruel-edged winter one would prefer to forget.

This particular evening began no differently. Pelting rains, wind-driven, pounded with such force on the city streets that gutters overflowed their boundaries, drain-pipes spouted rivers, and ditches churned and foamed like miniature seas. The dusk of a peculiarly greenish hue cast an eerie, otherworldly light over the hushed city, as if the world was once again awash with primordial oceans. At any moment, flying fishes or porpoises out of legend might appear, their sleek, silvery forms guiding wayfarers like drowning sailors to an unseen shore.

A single hardy soul braved the elements, muttering to herself as she braved the horizontal sheets of stinging rain, her cloak a dripping mass of stinking wool, wondering (for the tenth time that evening) what the founders had been thinking when they prohibited horse travel within city walls. No doubt they held some ancient prejudice against conveyance, a fear, perhaps, that wagons and carriages might make the city-dwellers lazy, or, worse, threaten the egalitarian ideals of which they were so fond. "Certainly we're equally miserable in this damnable wet," she grumbled to herself, shivering all the while, anxious to escape the storm, to shut fast the door against this weeping world, to warm damp fingers and toes before a blazing hearth. What will be my welcome, she wondered, before thrusting that thought aside as one shoves aside a gem whose cost is so dear that even to contemplate its purchase is a questionable indulgence.

Wet to the skin, with every step her toes squelched in her soggy stockings. The residential side streets, cobbled with the same grey stones that formed the outer walls of the city, were laid in a slightly concave configuration, causing water to run in currents down their centers, making certain flattened sections into moats that could only be forded by jumping from stone to stone, making her look, she was certain, like an over-sized rat escaping a scuttled ship. The uneven height of the stones made them doubly treacherous, with the result that she kept her attention on her ruined, water-logged shoes, trying not to hear the voice inside her head, its monotonous drone reminding her she might come too late.

Turning onto a broad, tree-lined promenade of evenly laid paving stones, she found her stride. Picking up the pace, she fell into a more natural rhythm, hurrying past the buildings and shops, vacant now and unlit, their blank windows reflecting the oily shine of the rain-slick streets.

She gauged her progress by counting plane trees as she passed, their broad, stubby branches thrusting up like so many fat fingers, the willowy secondary branches seeming the offspring of some other kind of vegetation, one that admitted no kinship with the parent plant. A hybrid, she decided after some deliberation, bred for deep shade and longevity, planted centuries ago by those who passed their lives within fortress walls but forever dreamt of shady groves. Barren as the branches might be, they offered a natural windbreak, preventing the stinging rain from slamming against the exposed skin of her face. Thankful for their protection, she hugged the portion of the walk closest to their trunks, her splashing footfalls defying the tedious repetition of the rain.

The number and variety of trees multiplied as the boulevard gradually narrowed to become a flagged path wending its way through the park that lay at the center of the city. Holly trees, their leaves sharp-tipped as they guarded their newest of berries, stood sentinel around a fragile-limbed cherry tree bedecked with the pink bounty of too-early blossoms, sagging now under the heavy downpour, moping for the return of a suitor who had left it to languish, relinquishing its petals like so many discarded love letters on the saturated ground. Alongside the walkway, scattered among the trees and the rising fog, stone benches lurked like crouching hounds lapping at their bowls. These were stopping places for folk who had need of rest or reflection as they traveled to and fro, from which spot they could see the sharply-pitched roof of the House of Healing rising high above the tallest trees, its curved clay tiles shedding rain in wind-swept sheets of crescent ripples.

Here, nestled amongst the dripping trees and shrubberies, the mulched beds of hibernating roses and nascent bulbs, stood a building of white stone, its exterior corridors of arches and columns decorated with hand-carved traceries of branch, seed, and flower—each of them unique, rivaling each other with their makers' persistent attempts to duplicate the seemingly random perfection of nature. It was as if the stone carvers sought to freeze the world in mid-summer, hoping to stave off the dead moons of winter, the time of chilblains and chapped hands, so their carvings might generate heat enough to warm the hands chipping away patiently at the smooth stone blocks. Four centuries had passed since the last carver brushed away the last chips of stone, but their dream of summer's bounty survived unchanged except for the encroachment of the gardens and the height of the trees.

Her feet heavy with the last few steps, she paused for a moment outside the great oaken doors, running her hands over the brass latch, fingering the bell cord, which once pulled, would necessitate entering a place she still might avoid. Steadying herself, she lifted her eyes above the door, finding a lintel which bore no name. Instead, etched deep into the hard tablet of stone hung cascades of sun-warmed grapes, carved by the hand of a master whose artistry had long since outlived his name. Overhead the gnarled branches drooped with the weight of the fruit of the vine at its plumpest and most succulent, ripe for a harvest which would fill new wineskins to bursting—a promise carved in stone.

She pulled the cord.

Light spilled out over the threshold, engulfing her. Out of the brightness emerged two figures, their hands outstretched in welcome.

"Welcome, Magda, to the House of Healing. You are in time."

The names of the healers were Didion and Lara, she discovered as they ushered her into an empty room, offering a warm drink and a seat by a brazier. After a brief greeting, Lara, the woman healer, slipped away. Magda turned her attention to Didion, who walked with a slight limp, yet seemed too young to suffer from rheumatism or a like complaint. When he caught her watching him as he returned from hanging her sodden cloak on a nearby peg, he proffered an easy explanation, seemingly unflustered by her stare.

"My legs were broken four years ago. I usually manage not to limp. This dampness makes it difficult."

He eyed her for a moment, anticipating questions. When none came, he sank down beside her on the bench, grimacing as he straightened out his legs in front of him.

They sat in silence, the woman wary, the man unsure of how to proceed. Finally he spoke, slowly and with great care, choosing words as one chooses fruit from a basket, trying to avoid any that are bruised.

"Aethra rests. The babe comes slowly, too slowly, we fear. Everything went well, much better than we hoped, until a few hours ago."

Magda nodded, knowing her rightful place was at her daughter's side, but just as sure she was not welcome. She forfeited those rights a year ago when Aethra lost her first child, Magda's first grandchild. The taste of that loss was bitter in her mouth, but she would not confess this to a stranger, no matter how kindly he informed her that tonight she might bid farewell to her only child.

"The cord is wrapped around the babe's neck. We must open her womb." When Magda flinched at the thought of a knife slicing her daughter's flesh, the healer continued undeterred. "We have told her she may not survive such a birth."

Magda lifted her eyes from her hands, pinning the man with a heavy gaze signaling the weightiness of her disapproval.

"And Manthur?"

Didion shook his head.

"You misjudge him. He is nearly mad with grief, yet he convinced Aethra you must be called despite what passed between you. Surely you realize that it is Aethra who . . .," until, sensing her reaction, he broke off what he had thought to say and tried another tack. "I know you think him haughty and proud. In his native land he is the prince of a powerful clan. His family traces its lineage back to the First Days, before Pelion was founded. This is no ernani from the hinterlands, but a cultured, learned man who finds our ways as unfathomable as we find his."

"Yet despite the cost, he must have a child."

She spat the words at him. Refusing to engage her in debate, Didion rose and straightened his robes, his eyes hooded, his bearing dignified and slightly remote.

"Lara and I have been their healers since they lived in the Maze. If you cannot believe that Aethra conceived this child of her own free will, then you hide from truth in a way I can only pity. Mayhap your daughter dies tonight. If so, Manthur loses the woman with whom he underwent Preparation and with whom he shares his every thought. Can you set aside old grudges for the sake of the child they have made? Can you remember the death of your mate and find it within yourself to comfort Manthur as others comforted you?"

Receiving no answer, perhaps expecting none, Didion departed. Magda sat unmoving, dying again at the mention of her mate, resenting the empty place inside her mind he once had occupied. Tonight she might lose Aethra, the last link with one who had been her other half, for in his daughter lived his firm mouth that could soften into a smile of such sweetness that she could see him again, if only for a fleeting moment. Aethra of the chestnut hair, a mirror of her father including the air of fragility that clung to her since childhood. Strong of spirit she might be, yet betrayed by a body too easily tired, too often prone to illness and always slow to heal. As Aethra would die, her mate had died, smiling to the end, sending out his love as if it could part the darkness and disperse the lingering shadows of Magda's grief.

Suddenly she was furious with them both. How easy it is to die, to slip away quietly with a healer's help, abandoning those who must live on. For the first time she could almost believe what the healer swore was true. It would be just like Aethra, warned not to risk another pregnancy after delivering a stillborn daughter and almost bleeding to death in the process, just like her tender-hearted father to decide that a babe, this "sa'ab," this first-born child of a foreign prince, was worth the loss of her own dear life. Magda blamed it on Manthur and his ridiculous proverbs. What was the one Aethra had recited to her once?

"A man's luck is his sa'ab."

Was it possible that her darling daughter loved so deeply that she would risk everything to give Manthur a child? That she had purposefully placed her life in jeopardy so her mate might wear the second earring that declared him a father, and thus, in his native land, a man of measure? It was a tradition so incomprehensible, so patently absurd that she had laughed outright, offending Manthur and angering Aethra. The price exacted for her contempt was the loss of her daughter's affections. Aethra closed their home to her, forbidding her to visit and returning her gifts unopened. Worst of all, she concealed this second pregnancy. Better no mother at all than one who scoffs at a daughter's dreams.

Much as she disliked this scenario, she feared it contained the grains of truth. It was too easy to blame Manthur, or for that matter, to blame everything connected with the Maze. How she hated the grim ugliness of its sprawling form, its windowless walls and guarded turrets. For six moons her daughter was interred in its bowels, willfully pursuing a choice her mother could not support, emerging from its labyrinths newly adept with a stranger by her side. That Manthur was not native-born was of little consequence. If he had been pleasant, or merely polite, she might have gradually accustomed herself to his presence. But Manthur—arrogant, imperious, patronizing—possessed no quality she admired. Yet, she reminded herself, struggling to be fair, Aethra found in him something of value.

At that thought a memory rose clear and strong within her. Allowing its power to claim her, she found herself standing outside the doorway of a healing chamber not far from the room in which she presently waited. It was early morning, a single hour past dawn, and a man leaned over a bed to patiently brush aside locks of wildly disordered chestnut hair surrounding a pale face. Smiling, he drew from behind his back a full-blown rose still wet with dew and placed it gently in the woman's hand, then knelt beside her, running his forefinger lightly over the bridge of her nose, following the track of a light spray of freckles.

"Shalt thou lie abed again today? Who will tend me if thy laziness persists?"

The woman smiled at his teasing tone, a feeble smile that held within it tears.

"What need have you of me?" Her smile faltered, tears dripping slowly down wan cheeks. "Another might serve you better . . ."

His face grew stern, almost cruel, his black eyes flashing in sudden anger.

"Thee wilt not mention this again!" And then, more softly, "Thinkest thou I have the patience to teach another thy skills? Shall I be forced to endure the shame of hair unbraided?"

"But your luck, Manthur . . .!"

Obviously moved by her distress, he mastered himself, saying, "Thou art my luck, Aethra. I need no other."

He inclined his head, intent on kissing the woman's lips. Hearing someone approach, he settled for stroking the hand that clutched the thorny rose so tightly that the eavesdropping mother saw a drop of purest crimson stain the purity of the crisp white bedclothes.

"PARDON ME FOR disturbing you. Are you Magda?"

Irritated at the untimely disturbance of her thoughts, Magda raised her eyes, emitting an audible gasp of disbelief as she did so. In front of her stood a woman robed in deepest black, and so, the Eighteenth Mother of Pelion.

"Again, I ask pardon, for if you are Magda, mother of Aethra, my message will not wait."

Summoning her manners, Magda rose to face her questioner. Quickly she noted the triangular face, the grey-green eyes with their sparse lashes and a deep crease permanently etched between her eyebrows. That she stood a few feet away from the fabled Prophetess of Agave sent a shiver down Magda's spine. If the tales were true, this woman had braved the slave-market of Agave alone and brought about a miracle still on the lips of the entire citizenry of Pelion. Even those who doubted the truth of the rumors were careful with their tongues, for who would knowingly bring the wrath of the Mother of All down about their ears?

"I . . . I am Magda," she stammered, unsure if protocol demanded a bow of the head or a curtsey, suddenly awash in feelings of foreboding, wondering why this powerful personage should search her out, positive her message did not contain welcome news.

The younger woman gestured politely toward the bench. Magda moved quickly to obey, suppressing another gasp as the Eighteenth Mother, after lowering the plain wooden box she held in her arms to rest on the floor next to her feet, took her place beside Magda.

"The High Healers asked me to . . ."

"High Healers?"

The Eighteenth Mother evidenced no affront at the interruption.

"Didion and Lara, who greeted you."

Surprised that her daughter was attended by the highest-ranked healers in Pelion, Magda's jaw dropped open, then clenched tightly shut as the Eighteenth Mother continued.

"When they summoned you, they hoped you might see your daughter. Since your arrival there have been complications. She's been moved to another room, and the procedure has begun."

Her eyes searched Magda's face.

"I thought you might be in need of company."

Flinching at the thought of surgery, Magda's first impulse was a primal need for solitude. What could this childless woman know of her grief? And then, even as she thought she must demand privacy, the image of her daughter confronted her, her tender flesh sliced open by a surgeon's blade, her life leaking away in a trail of bright blood. Reaching out, begging without words, Magda found her hand grasped by a small palm of surprising strength.

Leaning her head back until it rested against the plastered wall, Magda strove to clear her mind, struggling to find some meaning in her daughter's death. In this house Aethra had been born. In this house she would breathe her last. Gradually the ugly vision of futility and waste faded, erased and vanquished as Magda recognized the rightness of birth and death and yet another birth. Bowing to what she could not change, conscious of the possibility of continuity held within the cycle of mortality, she bid her daughter farewell, finding within that timeless span of waiting the exact moment of Aethra's death and, at long last, was able to honor her daughter's dreams.

Hours must have passed as she sat in the half-trance of reflection. At last her hand was released and she reentered the waking world. Not until that moment did Magda understand that the Eighteenth Mother of Pelion had offered her much more than the comforting touch of a human hand. Never, even with her mate, had she experienced such power and clarity of inner sight, for her adept gifts were meager at best, allowing her to receive another's thoughts, but denying her the ability to influence another mind. Touched by the generosity of this woman, who did not shirk away from death but accompanied her on a journey that must have wrenched her emotions as strongly as Magda's were wrenched, she sought for some means of expressing herself. Shy, yet thankful, she struggled to find the words.

"I . . . I had not thought to meet you here. I . . . I give thanks that you came."

The Eighteenth Mother's head shook slowly from side to side, the heavy patter of rain on roof-tiles fading away, bringing with it a lightening of mood and an end to the tension between them.

"If truth be told," the Eighteenth Mother replied, "I was summoned for a different matter entirely." The wooden box was lifted and cradled on her lap, a hand with a silver ring on the third finger resting lightly, protectively upon the lid. "This is one of my happiest duties, for I must offer each newborn babe its gifts."

An answering smile appeared on Magda's face as she remembered another Mother, the seventeenth of her line, robed entirely in black, apple-cheeked and smelling of freshly laundered clothes dried in the sun, reaching down to lift a sleeping infant from Magda's arms.

"I had forgotten."

Sitting side by side, they waited patiently for their summons, each woman lost in private thoughts. The Eighteenth Mother seemed to dream, motionless and withdrawn, while Magda wrestled with a guilty conscience.

"What's become of Manthur?"

The Eighteenth Mother roused herself, her eyes blinking rapidly as if to clear them of too-bright visions.

"They sedated him after Aethra was taken from the birthing room. Their parting was," she frowned, seeming to run through a mental dictionary in order to choose the exact word, "painful." She frowned again, seemingly dissatisfied with her choice, adding, "A friend of mine watches over him now."

"Has he no friends of his own?"

It sounded like an accusation, although she had not meant it as such. The Eighteenth Mother either understood her curiosity or refused to comment on her rudeness.

"His closest friends were the ernani with whom he underwent Preparation. By now they have returned to the lands of their birth. He has not yet forged friendships with his cohorts in the League of Independent Traders. He has felt isolated during this last year," she continued sadly, "and now is doubly alone."

"He will have her child."

A deeper frown crossed the Eighteenth Mother's face.

"True. He will have his sa'ab."

Her face cleared and a spark seemed to light up her eyes from the inside, turning them more green than grey. "The High Healers are ready for us. Shall we go together to greet this newest child-of-the-city?"

"Will she . . . will my daughter's body . . .," Magda struggled to control her voice, hearing it break despite her efforts. "Will I be able to see her after all?"

The Eighteenth Mother nodded, adding quietly, "It was her wish that her son be blessed in her presence."

"It's a boy child then?"

Sensing Magda's surprise, the Eighteenth Mother hurried to explain.

"It's often the case with transformed women that they can discern their child's gender long before birth. It was so with Aethra." A fond smile lit her face, bringing a suggestion of beauty to her plain features. "Once the child quickened in her womb, she gave him his name. She held many conversations with him in the moons that followed," she paused, adding thoughtfully, ". . . many conversations . . ."

Jealousy hit Magda hard. That her daughter's newly acquired gifts surpassed her own was surprise enough, that this stranger was party to Aethra's pregnancy while she had been excluded seemed doubly unfair.

"I had no idea you knew my daughter so well."

The words themselves were not offensive, but the spirit with which they were delivered cast a pall over them both. For the first time the Eighteenth Mother appeared uncomfortable. Rising to her feet, she cradled the box in her arms as she regarded Magda.

"I do not judge you," she stated simply, "but neither will I indulge you. I sympathize with your loss, but cannot find it within myself to condone your behavior."

Yet despite her beliefs, she offered her aid without hesitation, helping a guilt-stricken mother take the first difficult steps toward acceptance. Humbled, Magda lifted two empty palms toward the younger woman in the ancient gesture of supplication.

"What shall I do, Mother?"

The Eighteenth Mother squared her thin shoulders and lifted her chin.

"First, you will witness the child's Blessing. Second, you will forgive the father. Third, you will guard the child as Aethra would have guarded him, keeping him safe within the circle of your arms."

"So be it," whispered Magda.

"THESE ARE THE gifts of those-born-of-the-city."

As the swaddling clothes fell away, the babe kicked mightily, emitting a bleating cry to convey his displeasure with the proceedings. Spared the ordeal of a passage through his mother's body, he had been freed from his watery world to emerge into a place of dry air and bright, blinding light. His protests were sharp and fierce, his delicate skin dyed a deep shade of rose, his clenched fists striking out angrily against the cold.

The wooden box lay open at the foot of the bed, its interior divided into four compartments, each lined with soft velvet. The handle of a knife, the blade buried in a leather sheaf, was all that remained in the discarded container. The former contents of the box, two vials, one of polished silver and the other of dull gold, were held in the hands of the healers. A statuesque woman with hair of a distinctive reddish shade, the newborn's grandmother, stood by her daughter and her grandson's side, in her hands the sacred oil.

The Eighteenth Mother held the child with practiced ease, smiling down at him, uttering none of the cooing sounds with which mothers quiet a peevish infant. To those who watched it seemed that she encouraged his cries, daring him to raise his voice to the heavens, demanding he announce his arrival to all those assembled. Content at last, she lifted him on high, one hand under his black-fringed head, another under the tiny buttocks, and cried out joyfully:

"A child is born! Sandur, son of Aethra and Manthur, we welcome you to Pelion."

A rush of sudden laughter from the onlookers met her proclamation, for the babe started at her cry, then added his music to hers, the mingling of their voices producing an oddly haunting harmony, two trebles joined in the celebration of life kindled anew.

One inhabitant in the room did not join in the laughter. He stood apart from the others, leaning against the frame of the open door, swaying from time to time as if uncertain of his balance. His garb was unique and in complete contrast with the plainly dressed citizens of Pelion. Luxurious robes fell to his ankles, arranged in multiple layers of finest silk dyed in colors of emerald, topaz, turquoise, and brilliant vermilion, flowing freely from beneath a richly embroidered sash knotted at his waist. Others in the city might be as dark-skinned; none wore such elaborately distinctive accessories, a golden hoop swinging from his pierced left earlobe, a gemstone embedded in the crease of his right nostril, and most curious of all, a full head of hair as black as a raven's wing arranged in tiny individual braids looped together at the nape of his neck and falling in a thick cluster to the middle of his back. From time to time he fingered the earring, a nervous, distracted gesture unconnected with the ritual at hand.

Nothing registered on his face as the ceremony proceeded. He seemed insensible to it, his gaze fixed on Aethra's linen-wrapped body, still and unmoving on the narrow bed. From time to time a tremor shook him, and a facial tic convulsed the muscles above his jaw. The woman in black seemed most aware of his presence, for she turned to him as each gift was offered, perhaps hoping the ritual would remind him of a day in the recent past when he, like his son, had been sprinkled with the water of life, drank the sacramental wine, and was smeared with the sacred oil. Her hopes were in vain, for he gave no indication that he saw anything but the stillness of his mate's body beneath the shroud, heard nothing but the absence of Aethra's heartbeat.

The babe's skin glowed where it was anointed with oil. The woman healer offered a blanket in which to wrap him. The Eighteenth Mother turned to face the man poised in the doorway, walking purposefully toward him, the child held out the full length of her arms.

"Will you hold your child, Manthur?"

Blank eyes lifted to her, bleary and reddened from tears shed privately in the empty room where he was imprisoned after they stole Aethra away from him, restraining him, ignoring his request that he accompany her to the place where she would be delivered of the child. Turning deaf ears to his protests, refusing to honor his wish that they not be parted, they forced noxious fluids down his throat, leaving him to scream out his fears alone, drifting in the poisonous fogs of a drugged and dreadful sleep. Their treatment of him was the worst in a long line of indignities. For this last and greatest cruelty he would never forgive them, since in their haste to quiet him, their potions robbed him of his last minutes with his beloved. His thoughts disoriented, his senses reeling, fighting against the terror of losing her, the drugs prevented him from honoring the promise she had wrung from him that morning when the pains began, a promise that Manthur would not let his Aethra die alone.

"He is your long awaited sa'ab, Manthur. Have you not a single word for him?"

Called back to the present, he peered down at the screaming thing that had killed its mother.

"My sa'ab?" he managed to croak, and then began to laugh, his shoulders shaking as he gasped for breath, ironic laughter aimed at this stupid, thoughtless woman who used a word beyond her comprehension.

"Indeed," he rasped out harshly, "I have a word for him."

With her back to the other inhabitants of the room, no one noticed that the Eighteenth Mother stood rooted to the wooden flooring, her eyes opened wide in horrified recognition, unable to move or to scream for the help that lay within easy reach of the open door. Here were the frothing mouth and mad, mad eyes that had haunted her since the miracle in Agave.

Time stopped as Manthur's gaze left the squalling infant to survey the room, a hazy vapor enveloping him even as the room receded, diminishing in size and form at the same time that every object, every texture, all lines and colors crystallized into a hard, flat picture without dimension. As the room congealed about him, he discovered he could move. Effortlessly negotiating a path toward the bed, he found the waiting knife, the hilt cold in his sweating palm. The knife sprang up of its own accord.

"Murderer!" he screamed at his newborn son.

A white-hot arrow of pain caught him between his eyes, his head pounding as a single thought drilled a burning hole through his mind even as his arm began the downward swing. Everything around him burst into life: the child's wails jarring against his ears, shouts of alarm, and a sudden lion's roar of all-too-human fury. The knife carved its deadly, unstoppable path as his head throbbed with an agony so intense he could do nothing but obey the overpowering command of that single, indomitable presence. In the last instant, his wrist twisted the knife away from its intended target and sank it smoothly into the black-covered breast heaving above the screaming child.

Another form streaked across Manthur's blurred vision, her chestnut hair and features vaguely reminiscent of someone he once had loved. In slow motion, the madman watched the long descent of the black-robed woman and screaming child into the arms of Aethra's mother, who caught and held them before they struck the floor.

MEMORIES FADE, BUT one memory Lara would retain to her dying day. She would forget the mad stare of Manthur, his lips parted in a gaping grimace of lurid hate, saliva foaming out of his mouth and dripping down his chin, his upraised arm trembling as it clutched the sacrificial knife. She would forget, too, the slender body of the Eighteenth Mother crumpling slowly toward the floor, the hilt of the silver knife catching the light from the tallow candles and reflecting coldly against the black cloth in which its length was buried. Even the heart-stopping vision of Prax flying through the doorway and with a soldier's quick eye understanding that he came too late, his grief turned to rage as he attacked the man in his charge. This, too, she would eventually put to rest. But to the end of her days she would remember the sound of Magda's scream. Ripped from her throat as the Eighteenth Mother's body collapsed into her arms, her cry contained such frightful agony that Lara's first confused thought was that the knife must have passed completely through the Eighteenth Mother's body and pierced the heart of Magda.

Manthur's life was saved by Magda's scream, for even Prax's killing rage could not ignore the force of that agonized wail. No one moved or even seemed to breathe; like statues they stood, caught as if in a trance or held by some invisible presence willing them to immobility and silence.

And then, as a dancer moves to music unheard by human ears, Magda lowered the Eighteenth Mother's body to the ground. With no hint of hurry or distress, each gesture a caress, she straightened and smoothed the mussed robes, pulling them down to cover the dead woman's legs. Next, she turned her attention to the babe, hushed now, big-eyed and solemn, as if despite his infancy he sensed the importance of this moment. Disengaging him from the dead arms that held him still, Magda lifted him up to her lips. A single kiss was deposited on his crown of dark fuzz. At her touch, he gurgled, then rested contentedly in her arms.

Magda broke the silence, speaking without any trace of self-consciousness. "Prax, you must not harm Manthur."

The rope-like veins in the Commander's thick forearms twisted like waking vipers, and a gagging sound issued from Manthur's open mouth. As Magda spoke, Prax's smooth, dome-like head jerked up, a fearsome snarl on his lips.

"I know you not, lady."

"I know you," Magda countered quickly, "and I tell you Manthur must not be harmed. You, above all the people in this room, know that Hesione would not have wished it."

At the mention of the name of the woman lying dead at their feet, Prax started and frowned. The pressure of his hands must have eased a bit, for Manthur drew a single gasping breath.

"Who are you to speak her name?" Prax growled. "And who are you to issue orders to me or to anyone?"

Rocking the sleeping babe, Magda matched him stare for stare. In a quiet voice that belied the magnitude of what she revealed, she said:

"I am She-Who-Was-Magda, Keeper of the Flame, Bride of Agave," she drew a shaky breath before adding, "and Nineteenth Mother of Pelion."

Didion's arm circled Lara's shoulders as the High Healers understood what had just transpired in their presence, something no one had ever witnessed before, the greatest wonder of their world accomplished here, in the humblest of healing chambers.

A wary look came over Prax. With a mumbled curse he thrust aside Manthur's body, which slumped to the floor, and faced Magda with forearms clasped across his chest. With a knowing smile, Magda shook her head at him.

"You would ever demand proof, would you not, Prax?"

Sighing, she closed her eyes for a moment, as if, Lara thought, to locate a memory. Opening them again, she looked him squarely in the face. "Once you took a silver band from the finger of a dead woman. Now I ask you to perform this same task for me. Give me the ring that must abide with Pelion forever."

And so it was that Prax, the Commander of the Legion of Pelion, a slave's son who witnessed the translation of Agave, became twice-blessed. Dropping on one knee beside the body of She-Who-Was-Hesione, he lifted her small limp hand to remove the silver band, slipped it onto the proffered finger of the newly ascended Mother of Pelion, and doubted her no more.

The Nineteenth Mother issued her first commands.

"Lara, find a wet-nurse for the child. Didion, gather your helpers and accompany Manthur to a healing chamber. I put his treatment in your hands, for he must be returned to health."

She-Who-Was-Magda surveyed the room. At the sight of two lifeless bodies, her daughter and her predecessor in the black robes, her lips trembled and her eyes filled, overcome by the realization that life had been preserved even as life was extinguished.

"I say the rite of remembrance at dawn."

* * *

AND SO IT was that the chain of nineteen generations remained unbroken. As the dying She-Who-Was-Hesione reached out to touch the mind of Magda, there was no time for niceties, for call and response, for request and acquiescence. With but a few moments to transfer the wisdom of the ages, Hesione recognized the touch of Magda's human flesh. Her mind leaping out to touch Magda's thoughts, she sensed the limits of Magda's adept powers, but trusting that in this, the final heartbeats of her short-lived life, she must not retreat, but push forward as she had done in Agave, trusting instinct rather than intellect.

Later, much later, Magda would remember the agony of Hesione's assault as the most terrible and glorious moment of her life, experiencing the violent expansion of her mind, understanding that she was becoming something other than the woman she had been. It was all a jumble now, these memories and identities of the eighteen women who lived inside her now, but somehow she held onto her sanity, understanding that there was no one else to receive Hesione's final gift. It was a strange nativity, for not once, but twice, birth sprang out of death, and all who witnessed that transformation were by its action in some way transformed.

A clear bright dawn broke over the valley of the castle, for the spring storms wandered off to water more distant lands. Twin plumes of smoke rose from the vicinity of the Sanctum to be rudely scattered by a playful morning breeze.

Gardeners would long recall the spring that began that morning as one of the loveliest in memory. And an elderly woman scratching out her memoirs some thirty years later would remember it, with fondness and regret, as the day her life began.

Chapter 2

The Once Sacred City

A SLENDER CRACK APPEARED as a head pushed forward past the doorframe, a round head fringed by thinning hair combed up and over a balding crown to end in three well-oiled curls spaced evenly across a curiously unlined forehead. Situated as the head was, stuck between solid wooden boards that masked any suggestion of neck or shoulders, it appeared to float, a disembodied orb, rather like a full moon hanging low on the horizon.

The man in the moon studied the solitary figure within the tower chamber for a long moment before interrupting her with a politely cleared throat and a disapproving frown.

"Forgive me, Mother. Adrastus is early. I pointed out that the appointment is not until noon, but . . ."

A derisive sniff signified his opinion of her over-anxious visitor. Magda swallowed a smile, all too aware that if she gave even the slightest indication that her secretary's assessment of the current President's character matched her own, his airs of self-importance would be unbearable for at least a week.

"Remy," she began sternly, watching as his frown became a pout, "you must treat the President of the Guild Assembly with the respect his office merits." On a more conciliatory note she added, "You know our relations with the Guild Assembly are not what they should be. Would you increase the tension between us?"

As always, he offered up sincere protestations of innocence, assuring her that he lived only to serve her, and, as always, she listened patiently to his passionately delivered speech, reassuring him (when at last he ran out of breath) of the value she placed on his services.

For twenty years they had exchanged this dialogue on a regular basis. It held no surprises, a comforting regularity when she considered the chaos of the first ten years of her reign. In that first decade, the number of inhabitants of the Maze doubled, then doubled again, causing numerous breakdowns in a system constrained by procedures and regulations made obsolete by the passage of time. Overcrowded and understaffed, the building badly in need of repair and maintenance, the Maze became a monster-child, consuming ten, fifteen, twenty hours of her days, threatening her ability to fulfill her many other responsibilities.

One particularly hectic afternoon, Esslar, a newly appointed member of her private Council, threw up his hands, disgusted by the reams of paper she was frantically arranging and rearranging, and gave her the best advice of her life.

"You may be the Mother of All, but you're only human. A century ago, the Fifteenth Mother retained a council of four, thirty monitors, and a staff of a hundred to assist exactly fifteen couples. Presently there are over two hundred ernani in the Maze and twice that many assorted personnel. Even so, you insist on managing as she did, alone and unaided. Please, I'm begging you, find some help! If I possessed any talent with files and record-keeping, I'd offer my services. Since I've none, you must find someone who does."

That someone was Remy, a non-adept with remarkable skills of organization who managed her affairs with the ease of a juggler who keeps three balls in the air while balancing a plate on the tip of his nose. From the moment he took up residence in the anteroom of her chamber, not a paper was mislaid or an appointment missed. In a matter of weeks, the bureaucracy of the Maze became his pet project and martyrdom of choice. Fastidious to the point of mania, he brooked no fools and suffered no infringements on the petty kingdom he ruled with a legion of pens and an army of inkpots. The single irony of Remy's appointment? Esslar disliked him on sight. The result? A running battle of slights and insults: Esslar detesting Remy's officiousness, Remy resenting Esslar's trespasses on territory he considered his own, namely, anything and everything to do with the Nineteenth Mother of Pelion.

"Offer the Guild Assembly chairs and assure Adrastus I will be with them momentarily."

Remy's eyebrows shot upward. In a subdued voice, he confessed a sin even more unthinkable than a lack of punctuality.

"No one accompanies him. Adrastus came alone."

Hiding her apprehension as to what this turnabout might bode, she considered what ploy might best procure her enough time to compose her thoughts.

"Assure Adrastus that I am delighted to see him, but I rush to finish a letter that must be posted. Admit him in a quarter of an hour." As he withdrew, she bestowed on him a dazzling smile. "And Remy, make sure you emphasize my delight."

With a sniff to indicate his grudging compliance, he shut the door behind him. Alone again, she began muttering to herself, an old habit growing worse with age. So much subterfuge, she mumbled to herself, wiping her pen and tightening the ink-stopper. So many games between city and provinces, stuffy guilds and independent traders—delicate negotiations demanding patience, humor and tact. She was party to all of them for one simple reason; she was good at it. No one expected that her talents lay in this direction, nor could she have predicted the outcome herself. Once a widowed owner of a small fabric shop grinding out a modest yearly profit on imported threads and locally-woven cloth, she became the master-mind behind revisions of countless outdated procedures and antiquated institutions, although she retained an inordinate fondness for what had once been an object of profound dislike, namely, the Maze.

In the past thirty years the original Maze had been renovated and enlarged to encompass a steady stream of pilgrims from the north and southeast as well as the rapidly expanding territories to the west. New lands were charted in several directions, from the Gulf of Swiasa to the south (the so-called Flowering Lands, long thought to be a myth) to Droghedan some six hundred leagues west of New Agave. The colony at Ariod's Lake never failed to send its yearly contingent of ernani, and the villages and towns to the southeast— Cinthea, Cyme, and Cottyo—yielded up their finest youth to the beckoning arms of the sacred city. In the course of her reign she had interviewed, counseled, and participated in the Transformation of thousands of ernani and their mates. In addition, she oversaw the dissolution of the Trial, revised the Legislation of Preparation, supervised the foundation of the Agavean Session, and instituted yearly tours throughout the surrounding villages and towns to keep her abreast of developments outside the city.

Despite her many achievements, her life still lacked the joy that accompanies a job well done. True, she tired more easily these days, and her journeys were shorter of late, but even when she reminded herself that she approached her seventieth year, making her the oldest woman she knew, having outlived all her friends and siblings, such excuses did little to erase her belief that she had not yet achieved her mission and that her term of office, the longest in memory, was somehow incomplete. It often seemed to her that everything accomplished was merely a completion of plans begun by another, and as an interloper thrust into the black robes purely by chance, she simply finished the duties of one ripped untimely from the earth.

Lately, her feelings of disquiet had increased. Claimed by what could best be described as a sense of futility, she often found herself brooding, disturbed yet unable to pinpoint the exact cause of her disturbance, uneasy yet reluctant to put a name to her fears. Was the prologue finally over, she asked herself, and the moment of her entrance approached? Or was the drama played out and the time grew near for her final exit from the stage?

For the past four years, the exact length of the current President's tenure, she watched and waited, unsure of anything except her growing belief that the cherished plan of her predecessors existed in disastrous conflict with the city chosen as the site of the miracle of Transformation. Most disturbing of all was her inability to act. Several times she thought to interfere with Adrastus and his supporters; each time she had been restrained, curbed by some unknown but forceful presence as a spirited steed is broken to saddle and bit. Like a newly-tamed filly, she fretted for a free head and a hard gallop over a distant plain, but the voices inside her head whispered, "Not yet."

It was Symone, the official Archivist of her Council, who furnished some of the more logical reasons for her uncomfortable relations with the major source of her worries. The citizens of Pelion knew Adrastus as a highly-respected engineer chosen to oversee the reconstruction of Agave. Symone revealed him to be one of the male candidates selected through that most wretched of by-gone institutions — the Trial. Unable to complete the Path of Preparation for reasons unknown, he departed the Maze by his own volition, abandoning his partner in the process. The Records of Transformation offered nothing but a single column linking his name with that of his one-time mate. Yet that same experience, the one from which he had fled, provided him with a first-hand understanding of what remained a mysterious process to the rank and file of the citizenry.

His election to the presidency was unanimous, a feat never before achieved in a Guild Assembly election since its founding in the third century of Pelion's existence. His platform worried Magda more than she dared confess, if for no other reason than from the day of his first public address he trumpeted his distrust of everything connected with the Plan of Preparation. Proudly, he announced himself to be non-adept, a remark not troubling in and of itself until one considered the ethics in which every adept, both born and transformed, was schooled. "In no ways shall you proclaim your gift," proclaimed the first unbreakable rule of adept life, preventing any adept from making a comparable admission and thus muzzling a substantial proportion of the population. One might think that such a position would have alienated adept Guild members from this brash Master of Engineers, but Adrastus was far too wily a politician to disenfranchise himself from any single group.

Once word of his campaign began to spread, he won adept support through a series of brilliantly waged public debates. Pitting himself against ill-prepared rivals, he produced as if by slight-of-hand an exhaustive list of statistics which proved beyond the shadow of a doubt that for the past thirty years Pelion's resident population had decreased in inverse proportion to the growth of the Maze. To hear Adrastus speak was to envision the demise of the proud city of Pelion, an entire generation lost to the wilderness, its highly-skilled artisans and teachers shoeing horses and teaching the alphabet to outlanders when they might have refined metals and edited books at home. Not even that bastion of research and learning, the House of Healing, escaped his portrait of decay. "Where are the healers of tomorrow?" he would demand. Then, while his opponent stood dumb, Adrastus would inform those assembled that although there might appear to be an excess of apprentices undergoing the rigors of that program, fully half of them would leave after their five years of training. If that was not enough to sway them, he would add (in tones hushed with ill-disguised horror) that he himself had visited Imarus House, a new center of healing near Agave, to find it staffed by former healers from Pelion, deserters (and thus betrayers) of the city of their birth.

No facet of life in Pelion escaped his investigation. Everywhere and in all things he found cessation and entropy. Upon hearing his sermon of doom, adepts and non-adepts alike, who sensed that their world was changing and were unsure if they approved the onslaught of the new, hurried to cast their votes accordingly.

The result of Adrastus' election was an outwardly cordial and covertly insidious attack on the Maze. Without ever putting the idea into words, he caused a rift between born and transformed adepts by hinting that the former were superior because their gift came to them naturally. Soon those transformed adepts who might have remained found it increasingly more difficult to gain acceptance into the guilds as apprentices, their subsequent departures serving to worsen the statistics Adrastus was so fond of quoting.

The latest assault was financial. Although life within the Maze had never been luxurious, the vast influx of ernani increased expenses three-fold and more. Since the entrance of the Novice class a century ago, the Guild Assembly consistently provided the bulk of supplies and services necessary to Preparation on the grounds that its participants would eventually enter their doors as apprentices. For eighty years that mutually beneficial relationship had endured. With the end of the Agavean slave trade, Pelion lost its monopoly on freedom, and with it, the assurance that everyone who entered by the northern gate would reside there permanently. Contributions from the guilds dwindled while apprenticeship programs for natives of the city were made more lucrative.

If all this was not bad enough, Adrastus came alone to a meeting scheduled a fortnight ago with the understanding that the entire Guild Assembly, composed of a Master from each House, would attend.

Her meditations complete, Magda shut her journal. Smoothing her robes and straightening her veil, she pondered how best to greet a man whose actions threatened what she held most dear. At the sound of footsteps in the hall, she rose to her full height, unbent despite her years, and stretched her facial muscles into a semblance of a smile. Grace in the face of adversity had ever been her strategy. No one, least of all Adrastus, would sway her from her course. If this was to be her final battle, no one would ever say of her that she faced it with anything less than aplomb.

". . . THAT YOU SHOULD have no illusions as to our decision. The vote was all but unanimous. Once the people have made their will known, there can be no appeal."

She took it calmly, if for no other reason than to rob him of the sight for which he had hurried to her tower chamber, the Mother of Pelion receiving the news that her activities were deemed worthless by the populace. The child, having matured, had no further use for the mother.

"Might I know who voted against the referendum?"

He slowed his pacing at her question, the lines around his mouth deepening into chasms of disapproval. She discerned in his movements around the room proof that he had once been a gifted athlete. The body had thickened with age, and his once dark hair was grey around the ears, but there was untapped power in his stride.

"There were no surprises there: the healers, the hetaeras, the League of Independent Traders, and," his voice hardened, "the Printer's Guild."

Ah, she thought to herself, there is an upset here! You've little love for the intangibles of life, health and the celebration of the body which the healers and hetaeras espouse. The traders work outside the city and thus concern you not. But the printers are a craft guild. You thought to win them all to your side, did you not, Adrastus? Have you forgotten that we teach first of all the love of learning? Were you unaware that our ernani take with them in their packs and bundles, on their wagons and hand-pushed carts, a multitude of precious books? Or did you overlook the fact that the Printer's Guild is two years behind in current orders, many of them sent to that same Healing House in Imarus you visited not long ago?

But she said nothing, merely nodding in reply, watching as he continued to mark off the dimensions of her tower chamber. For nearly an hour she listened, asking only a few mild questions, never challenging the authority with which he reeled off a list of demands forged, no doubt, by himself and his supporters over the past few weeks. With a start she realized that she had lost the thread of his argument and hurried to attend him.

". . . although we've not decided if it should be razed or adapted to some other purpose. The location is somewhat distant from the shopping district and might best be converted to residential property. . ."

Interrupted by a low chuckle, the President of the Guild Assembly turned to find the Nineteenth Mother shaking her head at him as one might scold a backward child.

"But that's absurd! Surely you realize the impossibility of what you suggest! Destroy the Maze?!"

Momentarily perplexed, he groped for the reason behind her unexpected and unseemly mirth.

"Of what possible use is the building if it lies empty? Or had you thought to . . ."

"But the Maze will not be empty!"

Now he was stammering, obviously convinced that senility had claimed her.

"But . . . but . . . there will be no . . . no funds for operation, no more candidates supplied by the city . . ."

"I understand your position, Adrastus. Will you hear mine?"

With a gracious gesture she indicated a backless bench against one of the stone walls, hiding her smugness as he sank heavily upon it. *Did you think victory would be so easy? That the old woman would weep and wail? Think again, engineer!*

"If the citizens of Pelion no longer choose to participate in the Path of Preparation, then the way will be closed to them."

Adrastus' head shot up at her ominous tone, but she was undeterred. *If the child spurns the mother, let the child learn what it means to be cast adrift in a perilous world.*

"Know this, Adrastus, and engrave it on your heart. The Maze will endure. I make my pledge to you and to all who have shut the door. On the eleventh moon of this year, after the harvest is stored, as has happened every autumn for a hundred years, men and women will gather at the bronze doors seeking entry. And the door shall be opened to them and to their descendants unto the thousandth generation."

When a flood of angry protests sprang to his lips, she silenced him curtly with a raised hand.

"This interview is concluded. Pelion is done with the Maze and everything connected with the Path of Preparation. No longer will I seek the Guild Assembly's approval, explain my plans, or allow you to peruse my records. Make this abundantly clear to your followers. I will continue to honor my duties to the city—the blessing of the newly-born, the rituals and observances which only I may perform, as will I counsel anyone who seeks my guidance. But remember, Adrastus," her voice took on a steely edge, "the workings of the Maze are no longer Pelion's concern."

A face tight with animosity met hers. A pang of guilt brought her up short. It might have been her face so many years ago as a much beloved daughter announced her intention to enter a place where for six moons she could neither receive nor send any message to a widowed mother left lost and lonely by her defection. Magda's question was posed before she could consider its consequence.

"Why did you depart the Maze, Adrastus? Why did you leave the cell you shared with Gwyn of Cyme?"

He stiffened, his florid complexion losing color. Magda felt a burst of shame. She might dislike the man; she hadn't intended to wound him. Executing an almost military about face, he headed for the door. Again, she reached out, calling after him:

"She left the Maze with the gift she sought, freeing you of blame."

Without any indication that he heard her, Adrastus passed out of the chamber.

Magda slumped into her chair, defeated not so much by his efforts to destroy the place he once inhabited as by his refusal of her offer of help. Someone else had looked at her with that same wintry stare. Even as she flinched against a memory that had haunted her for thirty years, Manthur's face rose up to confront her.

DEEP-SET EYES, BLACK as polished onyx, stared fixedly at her, a gaze of frigid indifference that shed no light as to feelings or thoughts, nor did their dull sheen indicate that, indeed, Manthur felt anything at all. His hair—thick, blue-black, luxurious—no longer braided, fell freely down his back. A second golden earring dangled from his left earlobe. Beyond these changes, he might have been the ernani she'd met four years ago. Ignoring the chair she indicated upon his arrival, he planted himself directly in front of her desk, dwarfing her with his breadth of body and the majestic ease with which he wore the elaborately codified dress of his homeland. A resident of Pelion might think his apparel odd, even eccentric. Anyone living east of the Sarujian Mountains would recognize him as the third son of Linphat V, Tehran of the Kwanlonhon clan. Why has he chosen to make formal what should be informal, she wondered, and why does his formality disturb me?

For disturbed she was, facing him for the first time in half a year, unsure of the reason behind his sudden request for audience. For the full duration of those six moons he had been detained in the House of Healing under Didion and Lara's care. Weekly reports made their way across Magda's desk, reports which spoke of complete withdrawal, a lethargy of mind and body that left him staring blankly at the walls of his chambers for hours and days on end. Then, three moons ago, a sudden awakening, violent and vocal, and from that time forward, a gradual re-entry into the world. Throughout his stay she pressed the High Healers for details, offering her new powers to aid his cure. But they were adamant that she stay away and, trusting in their expertise, she put her energies into other tasks, curbing her impatience.

"His mind is badly damaged," Lara explained. "We've brought him back to sanity. Even so, his injuries are such that he has locked away any feelings which might trigger the memory of his loss. The result is two-fold; he avoids the painful reminders of the murder he committed, but neither does he experience any of the gentler emotions. In time he may come to trust himself again. For now, he seeks an existence without emotional connections of any kind."

Didion spoke a warning. This was why they thought it necessary to prepare her.

"We urge you not to enter his thoughts. He has come to trust Lara and me. To enter without his permission might cause irreparable harm. We ask that you honor our recommendation."

Her promise given, she sat at her desk, fiddling with the papers strewn haphazardly over the polished surface of the scarred wood, wondering how best to break this uncomfortable silence, relieved when he spoke first.

"The High Healers have given me leave to depart the House of Healing. I came today to ask your permission to return to the land of my fathers."

Afterward she would wonder why neither Didion nor Lara had hinted that this was his plan and, after questioning them some days later, would think it odd that in the merging of their minds they had guessed nothing of his purpose. That morning her reaction was one of sheer relief. Only her Council knew the manner of her predecessor's passing. No one had died by violence in Pelion for generations, and the presence of a murderer in their midst brought with it a disturbing sense of failure on all their parts.

"You have my permission, Manthur, although you have no need of it. You have always been free to stay or go."

The unblinking gaze never wavered. So cold he is, she thought to herself, self-possessed and yet distant, and then her intuition took its accustomed leap.

"My sa'ab must accompany me."

Even her intuition could not soften the blow. He had not seen nor asked to see his son in all these long moons. She had come to think of the child as hers to raise, to hold in the circle of her arms as she had promised She-Who-Was-Hesione. Now Manthur claimed a right of blood that would take her grandson far beyond her powers to protect him, across the leagues that stretched between Pelion and the sea.

"I do not contest your right to raise your son, but I strongly question your judgment. The child thrives, but he is over-young to endure the hardships of such a journey. Perhaps in a year or two, when he is . . ."

"Two wet-nurses accompany my caravan. A woman of my people, chosen by my father, will serve as his ayah. Every care shall be taken for his well-being. If necessary, we'll stretch the journey into four moons or five."

Magda heard only the repetition of that single telling phrase—"a woman of my people, chosen by my father." Those words, spoken casually and with perfect equanimity, were undeniable proof that Manthur must have hired the fastest messengers available to speed his message east immediately upon his awakening. All this time he had waited for the caravan, and not once had he visited the child. Did he think to put her off the trail of his decision to depart, or was there another, more frightening, reason for his avoidance of his son?

She moved her hand toward the bell which would alert the wet-nurse waiting to bring the child to her.

"You have not seen your sa'ab as yet. Shall I send for him?"

A wave of something like pain danced across his features, vanishing as quickly as it appeared.

"That will not be necessary. I trust that he is well since you have said it."

She rose to her feet, her weight resting on her palms held flat against the table. Dropping her pleasant demeanor, she lashed out at him with the full force of her fears.

"Why do you avoid his presence? Can it be you hate him still and think to harm him once you pass the northern gates?"

Her accusation was cruel, but how could she grant a father who had almost murdered his child complete power over a tiny, helpless babe? Inside herself she made a vow that unless he could convince her of the child's safety, she would do everything in her power to deny him. She had only begun to explore the true nature of those powers, but she held no doubts as to her ability to prevent the loss of her grandchild. To her surprise, he stood his ground against her, replying with equal force:

"You forget he is my sa'ab. You know nothing of our customs, but for a parent to mistreat a child is an unconscionable act, the greatest crime imaginable, and the only one for which the punishment is torture and death. I . . .," his voice wavered, then held firm, ". . . I understand the reason for your fears, but my sanity has returned and with it my sense of duty."

"You speak of duty. What of love?"

His lips tightened as the tic she remembered from the night of Aethra's death reappeared over the skin of his jaw.

"I will raise him as my sa'ab. He will learn obedience and duty and take his place as a member of my clan. He will want for nothing. Of this I give my word."

"And if he is adept?"

Realizing she had caught him unprepared, she moved quickly to press her advantage.

"Surely you realize the possibility exists. Many transformed adepts have passed the gift to their children. If this is so, Sandur must be trained. You have not the experience to undertake his education, nor does anyone in Endlin."

"My sa'ab must accompany me."

Impressed by his stubbornness, she nodded slowly and resumed her seat. He had convinced her he would not harm the child. It remained for her to guarantee her grandson's future.

"Yes," she agreed, "I will give him over to your care."

Sensing his quick surge of victory, she added a single stipulation.

"This you must promise me. When my grandson reaches manhood, I will send for him. Once here he will be tested. If he proves adept, he will be trained. If not, he will enter the Maze," she paused before adding softly, "for this, I believe, would have been his mother's wish."

She did not mentioned her daughter by name. Even so, her thoughts were suddenly filled by Aethra of the chestnut hair, who came to her out of a place she was allowed to visit only in her dreams. Silence hung over them in the tower chamber, and the man bowed his head. When he lifted it, she wondered if he, too, had experienced Aethra's presence.

"I give you my word."

"I require more than your word."

Later, she would wonder at her hardness; at the same time she blessed her powers of foresight. Even though her inner sight was curtailed by her promise to the healers, she sensed something devious in his reply and guessed he hoped that by the time the boy grew to manhood, another woman would occupy Magda's place. As if caught in a lie, he frowned, studying her silently for a moment.

"In my father's house, a clansman's word is his bond."

"In Pelion, we have found that a document is less easily forgotten or subject to a change of heart by one or both parties."

"And if my sa'ab refuses to obey the summons?"

"You've boasted that obedience is the first rule learned by every child of Endlin. You will have ample time to prepare him for the time when he must obey. Teach him well, Manthur."

Their eyes locked. For the briefest instant, as quickly over as it began, she saw what lurked behind that unblinking stare. There, beneath the layers of silken robes and studied normalcy, lay an all-consuming hatred of the world. Oblivion was all he sought, an oblivion much like death, for he had died one rainy night in early spring only to find himself unaccountably alive. My life is counterfeit, his mind screamed, a sham of existence; and then his face assumed again the rigid mask of indifference.

The rest of the interview was a jumble of impressions: the scratching of her pen as she forged the terms of their agreement, the silent hatred of Manthur as he waited, the thick drops of sealing wax imprinted with her seal, and the blotting of the single line of ink which comprised his signature.

As he turned to go, it struck her that she might never see him again. Casting aside the history of their wretchedness, she searched within herself for charity. Finding it, she bid Aethra's beloved farewell.

"Manthur, I ask your pardon for all the difficulties between us. I never doubted your love for Aethra . . ."

But he was gone, as the child would soon be gone, and she would hold in her memory the sight of that stiff and unforgiving back.

MIDDAY PASSED AND evening approached, the shadows lengthening in the tower room as she sat weighing the causes of her despair. From time to time the door cracked open to be pulled shut again, the ever-watchful secretary judging that her mood allowed no interruptions. After a time she seemed to rouse from her trance and opened her journal to check several entries against her memory. An hour later she produced a key from a drawer and unlocked a wooden box, drawing from it a single piece of wrinkled yellow parchment. As the afternoon wore on, she turned to an enormous leather-bound book of obvious antiquity and thumbed through the pages rapidly, seeming to browse, from time to time uttering an exclamation of something that sounded like success. Not long after, in a sudden burst of activity, she grabbed paper and pen and began to produce rows and columns of figures, making continual adjustments as she worked her sums, checking her tabulations from time to time against a well-thumbed book residing in the top drawer of her desk.

As she wrote, her mood evidenced a subtle change. Where once she had been grim and solemn, occasionally she would bark out something approximating laughter, a low cackle that echoed and re-echoed against the stone confines of the chamber walls. Satisfied at last with her equations, her attention turned to a large map mounted on the north wall of the room. Lighting a single candle, she held it up to view the territories of the known world, squinting a bit in the dimness of the rapidly darkening chamber. Occasionally her frequent mumbles became distinguishable, at which time one might have heard certain names being repeated, the order never varying, a litany of routes, fordings, passes, and landmarks. Seemingly content to rest from her labors, she used the candle to light the tall tapers of a massive brass candelabra and lowered herself stiffly onto an armchair outfitted with cushions, pulling over another chair nearby to serve as a footrest.

The candles burned steadily, flickering occasionally as a particularly strong blast of winter wind forced its way through the cracks around the high northwest window. The stone-walled room grew chilly, but the woman in black appeared oblivious to the cold as she sat with head bowed, her chin resting on the two upheld fingers of her folded hands. Animation gave way to repose as she rested, sending her thoughts toward the place of inner tranquility. There, in that pregnant moment between reflection and action, the Nineteenth Mother of Pelion found her path.

How others of her ilk had found their road she did not know. Her mission came not from prophetic visions or voices whispering on a darkling plain, but from a well-spring of human sadness. Alone and unaided, in the course of a single afternoon she stumbled upon a plan which would consume her to her dying day. No one would say of her reign that what began as an accident ended in resignation, and for that surety she offered up fervent thanks.

To the outside world she would appear unchanged, a model of urbanity and charm, for she understood this to be her greatest strength, just as she understood that the past thirty years had been a schooling of sorts. The time of her matriculation was upon her. If Pelion was to be preserved, the task was hers to perform.

"*Be content,*" voices whispered from the shadows converging around the brilliant clusters of candlelight. Like a prodigal returned from an extended voyage, they welcomed her into their fellowship, affirming both the ripeness of the time and the rightness of her course.

And in her heart of hearts, She-Who-Was-Magda knew joy.

Chapter 3

Land's End

IT WAS A modest shop with a tendency to disappear. Not that it ever actually vanished from its place, snugly lodged between a tea merchant and a sponge dealer, an action which would have been frowned upon by the landlord, who disliked foreigners without the necessity of additional provocation and who reluctantly agreed to lease the shop only after a full year's rent was offered in advance.

This tendency to disappear was far subtler than any magician's machinations and took the form of giving the distinct (or more correctly, indistinct) impression of concealing itself between its larger and more imposing neighbors, much as a person given to shyness clings to those more bold. Only the most discerning and curious of observers spied the humble, hand-printed sign placed on the inside ledge of the single, salt-encrusted window. More often than not the shop was quickly passed by in favor of more exotic emporiums, its drab and uninviting facade seeming to prefer seclusion and even to enjoy being ignored.

This preference for obscurity seemed particularly odd when one considered the location of the shop, a site central to the Abalone district, which is to say, the heart of the export trade. Here, on the angled streets running up and down the slope of Abalone Hill (one of seven such hills that made up the greater metropolis of Endlin) could be found all the bounties of the east and the faraway isles floating dreamily on an undulating sea.

An old saying had it that a stranger to the seven hills might find their way to the Abalone district by smell alone. It was not far wrong. The off-shore breezes blew steadily, kissing the well-protected harbor with the gentleness of a lover, with the result that the market air seemed an elixir of exotic fragrances—scented oils of almond, camphor, eucalyptus, cinnamon, sandalwood, and precious vanilla; incense of olibanum, agalloch, calambac and linaloa; oil of myrcia, pungent balsam and bergamot. And then there were the flowers, their petals dried for sachets or stored with fixatives that ensured they would bloom forever as perfume or aromatic waters: essences of lavender, heliotrope, lilac, sensuous jasmine, heady fuchsia, sweet alyssum, lemon verbena, and attar of roses.

Not all odors were heavenly scents: rank fish-oils of tuna, whale, and porpoise, the livers of halibut, cod, shark, refined and traded as lubricants, medicines and unguents. Wood tars and turpentine, gums of juniper, labdanum, and shellac offended the nose and brought tears to the eyes, as did the smoky fires drying the numerous varieties of fish, gutted, boned, and hung to cure on countless racks open to the sky.

The fabric market alone commanded an entire block, for here could be found delicate Cinthean lace, each piece unique and unequalled in intricacy of design, silks, baize, and batiks, hand-painted with vegetable dyes and (for the richest patrons) embroidered with flecks of precious metals, linen, flax, and cotton from the provinces to the south, and such specialty items as Lapithian wools, angoras, fleeces and felts, plus a multitude of leathers tanned and cured, suitable for all-weather boots or the thinnest dancing slipper ever to grace a female foot.

For the more modest purse there was homespun and muslin, sacking or shoddy, twill and ticking. Tarpaulins, netting, sailcloth, webbing, and all the tackle associated with fishing did a steady stream of business, not to mention the sellers of grommets, twine, hemp and net-weights. Dealers in pearls, polished shells, and corals hawked their wares as freely as did the sellers of the humble sponge, filling the humid air with a cacophony of cries rivaling a confederacy of migrating birds.

Food for the senses as well as the stomach, the innumerable provisions of the sea and the warm gulf breezes that grace the eastern shores and bar the icy rule of winter, all these were offered up for sale. Only when storms hammered the coastline for days on end, causing smaller vessels to founder or capsize, trapping schooners and frigates as they fretted and tossed against their moorings, only on those days of punishing wind and pummeling rain, did the tradesmen of the Abalone district close their doors.

In keeping with long-established customs, local merchants announced their intention to do business with doors flung wide, luring potential customers inside by displaying samples of their wares on carts covered with multi-colored canopies to protect them from the bleaching glare of the sun. Despite the neighbors' hope that one day the wretched foreigner with his strange notion of merchandising would bow to the inevitable and follow their example, the shop's door remained firmly closed, nor was a single sample of its contents offered up for inspection by the browsing passersby.

Yesterday, Oman the tea merchant, a voluble man of decided opinions, announced to Falal the sponge dealer (who resembled his sponges in that while he readily absorbed opinions, he needed squeezing to produce his own) a prediction that the shop must surely fail by the end of the week, the result of shocking mismanagement and a regrettable lack of manners. It reflected badly on the street as a whole, Oman insisted (with the ponderous air of a man who was a stranger to doubt), since only a fool would enter a shop that purposefully concealed its wares. To Falal's diffident suggestion that the sign might possibly offer that exact information, Oman snorted his disbelief, obviously offended by the thought that lines and squiggles painted on a placard could ever take the place of a properly arranged exhibit of imported teas.

Having bowed to Oman's authority on all matters concerning the Abalone district for the past twenty years, Falal withdrew his suggestion with an embarrassed shake of his head, concurring with his host that foreigners evidenced little understanding of the finer points of trade. Taking another sip of the fine black tea sweetened to the consistency of syrup reserved for Oman's closest friends and business associates, Falal returned the discussion to neutral ground by offering up the mild suggestion that the rains seemed rather late this year . . .

No one would have been more surprised than Falal to learn that he was correct on both counts: the rains were most decidedly late, and the message announced by the block-printed letters was all the invitation necessary to assure the initiated shopper that here, inside the narrow portal and behind the moisture-warped door of a shop which tended to disappear, lurked enchantment.

CANOPIES FOLDED AND carts wheeled inside the shops lining the streets of the Abalone District (named for one of the finer delicacies of Endlinese cuisine) as the few stragglers who remained rushed to complete their purchases and hurry home. By the time the watch called the sixth hour after midday, the last shopkeeper had long since barred and locked the front door, ever mindful that city nights differed from city days. In the daylight hours the streets were safe to all. Once the sun descended beneath the low clouds that seemed to rest like rumpled pillows on the bed that was the sea, night-rule governed, and the harbormasters of that province were the seamen of Endlin.

Stabbings were commonplace, drunkenness a preferred state of being, and brawls a badge of honor in the many taverns and brothels stretching along the docks and piers. The Tehrans of the six clans ensured the safety of their citizens by erecting a limestone wall separating the Abalone shopping district from the businesses nearer the shore that catered to a seaman's tastes. The clansmen might furnish their sons as guardians of the gates, but they turned their collective backs on what occurred along the shoreline between dusk and dawn, ever-mindful that the bulk of their fleets were manned by these reckless patrons of the inns, taverns, and brothels. If anyone was so foolhardy as to venture south of the limestone wall after dark without at least one dagger worn in plain sight and another secreted in a boot or a hidden pocket stitched inside a vest or jerkin, it was the Tehrans' joint opinion that they forfeited their rights to health and property, with the result that robbery became a lucrative way of life, or, as the saying went, "What the paymaster sows by day, the thief gleans by night."

One such incident was in the making that particular night on the unlit road leading up out of the shore district on a steep grade, climbing into the hills that surrounded the harbor on three sides. The intended victim trudging up the crushed shell pathway appeared an ordinary seaman, his worsted cap pulled low over his forehead, his leather jerkin much-patched and the worse for wear. Nothing in his appearance promised much of a reward to the gang who was tailing him. Their leader (a certain Dax) was something of an optimist, with the result that he imagined even the humblest of his prey carried something of value hidden on their person. Every so often, perhaps one robbery in ten, he was proven right, with the result that this meager modicum of success awed his cohorts, convincing them that Dax had a "nose" for plunder.

Two men worked up front in the shadows, gliding soundlessly in and out of the deserted storefronts that sold trinkets by day and sheltered beggars and inebriates by night. The remaining two, one of them Dax, trailed their quarry by five or six paces, their arms wrapped around each other's shoulders, singing an off-key drinking song with fine raucous abandon while keeping a sharp eye on their mark. Once he was confident that the prey had dropped his guard, having dismissed his followers as harmless drunks, Dax gave the signal to attack.

What followed made a life-long impression on this gang of four and caused Dax to switch professions late in life, becoming a ship's cook of such unrelenting cynicism that he was dubbed "Dour Dax" for the remainder of his days.

All these things transpired because instead of running, screaming for help, or begging for mercy (the behavior any respectable robber expects from a lone victim who suddenly finds himself surrounded by four armed men), the seaman came to an abrupt halt. A dagger appeared from nowhere and was shifted expertly from hand to hand as the seaman turned in a tight circle to survey his assailants. Unaccountably, he flashed them a grin.

"Well met, lads! Who's first?"

Ever the professionals, they jumped him at the same time.

The youngest of the four got there first, finding nothing to stab save air. When a body whirled to attack him, his second slash met flesh. The victim's scream sounded vaguely familiar, causing him to realize, to his everlasting chagrin, that he had unwittingly slashed his elder brother across the belly. Dax's experience was less intensely personal, but considerably more painful.

His right hand was grabbed at the wrist, the pressure of the grip causing him to drop his weapon as a single blow from a well-aimed dagger hilt broke his arm below the elbow. The fourth man suffered the greatest indignity, taking a sturdy boot full in the groin with enough force to reduce even the most stalwart of thieves to a retching, gasping, shadow of his former self.

The fracas over in perhaps ten heartbeats, the sole uninjured member of the party took to his heels, probably considering how best to evade his elder brother's wrath. Kicking away the knives glittering faintly against the pale surface of ground-up shells, the seaman puffed a bit as he crouched down to inspect those who remained. Rolling the victim of the knifing over on his back, he squinted at the wound, the trickle of blood shining blackly in the wan moonlight, and settled back on his haunches to offer a well-meaning observation.

"Not so deep as it might have been, I reckon. Ye must forgive the lad; he's young yet and a bit quick on the draw. Fast on his feet, though, that's for certain."

Proffering Dax a helping hand, the seaman heaved him to his feet, gesturing toward the injured arm.

"A clean break. 'Twill heal in no time, mark my words."

His expression sobered as he considered the agonized moans of the man who could not seem to remove his hands from his crotch.

"'Tis a cruel blow, but ye gave me no choice. Yer balls may ache, but I spared yer life."

Receiving not a single response (although, in fairness to the robbers, it must be mentioned that the seaman spoke a language unknown to them), the doughty sailor sheathed his knife inside the waistband of his wide-legged trousers, brushed off his pants for no appreciable reason, and resumed his path up the road, humming tunelessly to himself.

His humming ceased as the wall came into view. Cut from the limestone cliffs on the north shore of the harbor, the stones were absolutely sheer, offering no toeholds and defying any but the most tenacious of rock-climbers. The signs of human habitation thinned and fell away as he mounted the last rise, his breath coming faster as the rate of incline increased with each step he trod.

As he approached the gate and joined the line of those who sought night entrance into the more civilized districts, he pulled his cap even lower over his forehead and stuck his hands in his pockets. The line was fairly short, perhaps ten people in front of him, due no doubt to the lateness of the hour. Even so, his progress was slow, and he cursed under his breath only to draw himself up short, remembering how many times he had counseled patience to his men, muttering:

"Slowly and softly, old lad, slowly and softly. The race to him as never rushes."

The bodies in front of him either passed through the gate or were refused entry, causing them to slouch back down the hill, their heads tucked between their hunched shoulders like dogs responding to a severe scolding.

As his line of vision cleared, the seaman got his first good look at the guardians of the gate. With the strict attention to detail that helped him survive in a profession not known for the longevity of its members, he began ticking off the information their appearances offered him. Some twenty foot soldiers stood at attention, their pikes dug deep into the crushed shell to help reduce the strain of keeping them vertical. Their eyes moved as they surveyed the line, alert for a sudden move, a hidden weapon, anything out of the ordinary.

Between the phalanx of guards, directly in front of the gate, stood a pair of clansmen, robed and braided, arrogant as only Endlinese clansmen were arrogant, looking down their pierced noses at the motley crew assembled to seek entrance into the city of their fathers. Noting the single earring hanging from each man's earlobe, the seaman breathed a little easier. "Two rings mean trouble," was the proverbial wisdom of those who sailed the eastern seas. Trouble was the last thing Galen (for that was the seaman's name) needed tonight, so a single ring was a welcome sight.

A frown creased his brow as he tried to figure out the puzzle of the robes. After a full moon spent among these clansmen of Endlin, Galen remained a novice when it came to distinguishing a Synzurit from an Onozzi, let alone the difference between a sa'ab and a lesser sibling, either mistake enough to make a mortal enemy in less time than it took to wipe his bum. The fish-oil lanterns mounted on the gates offered precious little light by which to study the colors and patterns of the different layers of silk. Squinting, he searched for a particular shade of red somewhere between rubies and flames. Finally deciding they weren't Kwanlonhon, he stood quietly, fingering the pass and trying not to stare at the growing pile of confiscated weapons. An impatient nod ordered him to step forward.

Offering his pass, he immediately retreated the proscribed three steps and waited as they discussed it among themselves. Both men were typical natives of Endlin, brown-skinned with luxuriant black hair and dark eyes ending in an upward slant, shaped much like the fruit of the almond trees blossoming on the hills beyond the gate. As their conversation progressed, it became clear that the one with the opal embedded in his right nostril was in charge. Galen's guess proved correct when Opal Nose waved him forward with a ring-bedecked hand.

The first sentence spoken ended on a slightly rising inflection. Other than guessing it was a question, Galen could grasp nothing of its meaning. With a shrug of his shoulders and a shake of his head he indicated his confusion. Opal Nose frowned, then tried again in another language, more hesitantly spoken this time, continuing his probing and insolent inspection of the ragged seaman.

"What business have you beyond the wall?"

The words were strangely accented with an extremely nasal delivery, but at least they were comprehensible.

"I'm a tradesman, lord, in the Abalone district."

The clansman's eyes widened slightly, signaling his disbelief, narrowing again as they swept over the poorly-made clothes of cheapest homespun and the oft-patched leather vest.

"You do not appear so, foreigner."

The last word was spat, as if it left a bad taste in the speaker's mouth, indicating that he disliked Galen's place of birth even more than he detested his fashion sense.

"Yer eyes are keen, lord," Galen admitted, trying on an affable grin.

Opal Nose was not amused.

"Waste not my time, foreigner. Explain."

A sudden rush of anger almost got the best of Galen, the imperiousness of the command putting his teeth on edge. Still, he swallowed it. Slowly and softly, he reminded himself, or it's back down the hill and the whole night wasted.

"I value my skin, lord, and I've found I've a better chance of keepin' it if I'm thought to be a seaman."

"If that skin has value," the clansman's tone indicating that it did not, "why visit the harbor after dark?"

Galen smiled inside himself, finally hearing the question he was hoping for.

"I've a doxy there, lord."

Opal Nose looked quickly to his companion for enlightenment. Finding no help there, he repeated the unfamiliar word, stumbling a bit over the pronunciation.

"A ... doxy ...?"

"Aye, and a stunner she is! A regular beauty and as lively a bedmate as a fellow could want."

Indicating that both men should move in closer and lowering his voice so they wouldn't be overheard by the soldiers, Galen added with a slight leer, looking up into confused faces, "Perhaps the young lords would like her name? She's a handful, she is, and enjoys two twice as much as one."

Galen registered the horrified shudders, heard the gasps, watching with inner amusement as the clansmen retreated a step from him and then from one another, more repulsed by the immorality of the act being described than they were by the unseemliness of his offer. His pass shoved into his hand and the gate opened in response to a command more sharply spoken than was necessary, Galen was waved through the gate without further ado.

* * *

BEYOND THE GATE, inside the shop with a tendency to disappear, a single inhabitant turned a page and read on, the glare of the oil lamp making his task an easier one since the writing was small and closely spaced. He bent over the book spread open on a planked table, occasionally moving a hand toward a wooden trencher to retrieve what looked to be morsels of dried fish, or to a green-glass bottle to take a swig of sour wine, both of these gestures accomplished neatly without necessity of lifting his eyes from the page.

The shop was extremely narrow, far longer from front to back than from side to side, and made narrower still by the shelves running along both sides of the longest walls. From the smell of newly sanded wood inside the shop, the shelves appeared to be recently constructed. There was another smell, faint but undeniably present, and one not quite so easily distinguishable, although familiar to those who frequent libraries. Dusty and slightly musty it was, a singular smell containing the reminders of the pastes, rags, and pulps necessary to the fabrication of paper and the animal glues of the bindery, for the shelves were lined with books.

There were maps as well, many of them hand-colored in the palest of pastels, some of the largest ones hung like colorful kites on specially constructed racks mounted on the rafters, to be swung aside for purposes of examination and then stored neatly against an adjoining wall. Pamphlets were arranged in an orderly fashion underneath the counters running horizontally from left to right while on their tops resided neat stacks of blank paper, ranging in quality from that suitable for sketching or for childish scribbles to the finest watermarked cotton rag, which would endure for centuries longer than the writers who inscribed their thoughts upon it. Leaded pencils, assorted grades of chalk, fragile charcoal, quills of mallard, pheasant, humble goose and stately peacock, all the implements of writing, too, lay waiting for the touch of the writer's hand.

A wide expanse of canvas divided the shop from the living quarters where, beside the table, were arranged a few sticks of secondhand furniture. Two narrow cots stood side by side on the opposite wall from the hearth, an overturned packing crate between them topped by a basin and ewer of the cheapest grade of pottery. The three chairs were mismatched, as was the meager amount of crockery arranged on packing boxes near the hearth. Food-stuffs (and there was little in evidence besides day-old bread, the remains of a smoked fish, and a few pieces of dried fruit) were stored in more boxes stacked on top of one another to take up less space. Everywhere and in everything was a sense of economy, of making do with as little as possible, of simple living and modest means, as if the inhabitants could live on books alone, eating words and drinking ideas with no thought given to bodily comfort or fashions that might better please the eyes.

The reader lifted his head abruptly, although not a single sound disturbed the hush of the room, and reached for the lamp. Shortening the wick until the faintest of gleams issued from the glass chimney, he rose to his feet, rubbing the back of his neck for a moment to relax its stiffness, and hurried to the back door. Again, without any of the signals one might expect, a rap or scratch or the low murmuring of a password, he waited perhaps three heartbeats before briskly shoving aside the sturdy crossbars fitted at the height of his shoulder, waist, and knee, turned the latchkey, and stood aside as a shadowy figure entered from the alleyway, stepped nimbly into the room through the narrowly cracked doorway, and quickly and quietly eased the door shut, locking it fast.

No greeting was spoken, neither did hand clasp hand, as men are like to do when first they meet. They might have been strangers to the unschooled eye. A closer look revealed the warmth of their regard for one another as they exchanged glances and without wasting time, set about their tasks. The reader, a slender man of medium height and perhaps forty summers, somberly dressed in a high-necked tunic and wide-legged breeches dyed a serviceable and nondescript brown, turned up the wick and set about preparing a light supper for his guest.

Galen, older and stockier than his host, but possessing the flat stomach of a much younger man, moved toward the beds, removing the hidden dagger from his waistband and stripping off his seaman's garb. Wrapping the weapon carefully in shirt folds, he stored the cast-off clothing in yet another of the packing crates. Reaching for a sponge purchased from the shop next door and a thick cake of yellow soap, he poured tepid water into the basin until it threatened to overflow and proceeded to wash himself vigorously, slapping happily at his back and shoulders with the water-logged sponge, sending water and suds flying.

The reader made no complaint, but rather smiled as he tore apart a wheel of bread and arranged fish and dates on a platter, his brown eyes laughter-filled as they turned over his shoulder from time to time to observe the bather's antics.

"Why this merry mood? I haven't seen you so light of heart since the day the bandits attacked the rear wagon on the outskirts of Tek."

A bark of laughter was his answer. The reader's face sobered as he turned worried eyes on the man who was drying himself with a flour sack, rubbing his back and flanks against the rough cloth with all the contentment of a bull scratching against tree bark.

"Galen, what have you done this night?"

"Ah, lad," the older man sighed as he tied a length of cloth about his loins and pulled on a pair of clean breeches, "ye worry for naught. 'Twas only a few robbers on the far side of the wall, ill-trained and over-anxious. I've had worse fights with angry women." Not hearing any response, he looked up from his buttoning, his deep-set eyes twinkling. "Sure, Esslar, do ye think I'd fight unless there was no other way round it? I've not picked a fight in thirty years. Rest assured I've not begun today. Fightin's for the young, laddie, not for an old codger like me."

Even this meekly spoken appeal could not soothe the troubled face of Esslar. Running a hand through brown close-cropped curls, the temples showing a bit of grey and more grey in his neatly trimmed beard, he shook his head as he set the platter on the table and uncorked a bottle of wine.

"Perhaps, as you say, I worry for nothing. Still, I'm uneasy every time you set foot beyond that wall. I understand that you must go, that Phanus and Lampon need to see the face of their commander from time to time, and that some things are difficult to judge without observing them with your own eyes. Understanding does not make the wait any easier."

The Commander of the Legion pulled a chair from underneath the opposite side of the table and sat down heavily, resting his hairy forearms on either side of the platter as though guarding the food from those who might steal it if he was not wary. They were the habits of a lifetime, the product of poverty and ignorance in the lands of the far west, yet despite his education, his career, and the acuity of his inner gifts, he had set aside neither accent nor manners, as if to remind himself daily that as a peasant he had been born and that to be a peasant was not entirely a bad thing. Galen had no need of inner sight to know what troubled Esslar, for it had troubled him as well. In between mouthfuls of food, he tried to put it into words.

"There's no denyin' it's hard. Hard for us all. To live as we've always lived, with easy access to those like us, and then to find ourselves alone, surrounded by nothin' but minds with whom we can find neither companionship nor solace. She warned us, tried to prepare us, but the loneliness runs deep. It's not so bad for Phanus and Lampon. Their gifts are slight, and it's for that reason they were chosen. It's worse for me, but for ye, Esslar . . .," he shook his head, "it must be well nigh unbearable."

Esslar closed his eyes as the Commander began to speak. Now he spoke without opening them, his forehead creased with strain.

"The truth is I worry not for you, but for me. It's selfish, I know, but what would I do without you, Galen?" When there was no response, he murmured softly, "I think I should go mad."

Knowing the truth when he heard it, Galen resolved to go less often below the wall. Across the table from him sat the most sensitive adept he had ever known, perhaps the most sensitive adept who had ever lived. Here was a mind remarkably receptive to the subtlest of suggestions, pliant to impressions and intuitive beyond imagining. Esslar was that greatest of rarities, a born adept who had practiced his gifts since childhood, perhaps since birth, needing no one to instruct him in his ability to touch a body and know where the sickness lay, to read in objects the history of their making, and to fashion subtle adjustments in the thoughts and memories of others, enabling him to achieve the position of Master Healer before his twentieth year.

There was more to Esslar than these special abilities, of that Galen was certain. If someone asked him the definition of a visionary, he would have been hard-pressed to supply one. If asked to point one out, he would have indicated Esslar without a moment's hesitation. There had been many private conversations between the Nineteenth Mother and her Master of Mysteries before their party left Pelion three moons ago. After each of them, Esslar emerged a trifle paler and more dreamy-eyed than usual. Even his title, Master of Mysteries, was shrouded in secrecy. Symone of the sharp tongue, Galen's favorite intellectual, told him once that no one had held that particular title on the Council for over a century, the last one being a certain Beal of Pelion.

However much doubt there might be about the exact function of a Master of Mysteries, there was not a single doubt that their journey across the southeastern provinces and up the southern shore, the book-laden wagons so heavy that the wheel rims left deep indentations on the packed, hardened earth, the mule teams spelled after three hours of pulling, four Cavalry patrols working round the clock to ensure they kept on schedule to arrive in Endlin by late spring, the leasing of the shop, the construction of the counters and shelving, and the laborious process of unpacking accomplished in only a few days, and, indeed, their entire stay in Endlin, revolved not around money to be made in the book business, but around Esslar of Pelion.

What Galen learned in the days since they'd been left alone (the Legionnaires returning via the southern route with the exception of Phanus and Lampon, who worked the harbor district for information until the time came for them to manage the book shop), was that the reason for their speed was Esslar. Tonight Galen obtained proof of what he'd long suspected to be true. How long could Esslar endure without breaking under the strain, the multitude of minds pressing in, some of them sick and deeply troubled, yet unable to assist them without their consent and unable to request that consent since to make himself known as an adept would necessitate breaking his vows and endanger his life in the process? No wonder he worries, thought Galen, and immediately regretted his escapade with the robbers although they had been the happiest ten heartbeats he'd spent in many a moon.

"Come, man, think no more on it. I'm safe and sound, dagger and all, and I've good news to boot!"

When Esslar managed a smile, Galen was encouraged. It wasn't necessary that they communicate with the spoken word since they kept their minds open to one another at all times (a safety precaution the Nineteenth Mother insisted upon and something Galen had never experienced with anyone other than his mate.) After returning from the rush and bustle of the harbor district, he'd found the silence of the shop oppressive and judged that a spoken conversation might lessen Esslar's melancholy.

"They didn't search you?"

Further urging was unnecessary. Galen poured out the story of the gate, embroidering it a little as was his wont, hearing his success in Esslar's hearty laughter.

"Shame on you, Commander! What would Lucrece say?"

A slow, sensuous smile spread over Galen's weathered face.

"My Lucrece would say that the shame lies in the fact that they've never laughed in bed." The smile faded. "I've studied 'em as you have, Esslar, but I'm no closer to understandin' 'em. What must it be like to never know your mother, to have many concubines but no mate?" He paused and frowned. "It's no wonder they're downright unfriendly to man and beast."

"Yet we've never seen them with their children."

"Ye're right. I was forgettin' the children ."

"Kazur wrote that the harems are like gardens, glorious places of light and fountains, tame animals and perfect peace. The ayahs attend them, and the fathers visit daily. No child is unwanted, and daughters and sons are loved and indulged equally . . ."

" . . . except for the sa'ab," Galen added, to which Esslar replied:

"Except for the sa'ab."

A timid scratch on the door broke their reverie. In the next moment, Galen grabbed the trencher and bottle and disappeared behind the canvas wall. Only then did Esslar slide back the bars and turn the latchkey.

"H'ESSLAR?"

She whispered as she slipped into the cramped, ugly room where the kindly foreigner lived without even the simplest of comforts. Her black eyes, long-lashed and carefully lined with kohl, swept over the room, searching for the old man with the grizzled beard who helped H'esslar with the heavy boxes and the arrangement of the oddly-bound papers. When she found no evidence of his presence, she let out her tightly-held breath. Of the purpose of the papers and goods that littered the store she understood nothing at all, but accepted them without reservation, as she accepted this foreigner of vast understanding and inner peace.

She unwound the dark gauze carefully from her head and shoulders, mindful that she not mar the elaborate ropes of waist-length hair already arranged for the festivities that commenced at dawn, uncertain if he understood the risk she took for his sake, but determined that H'esslar and no other would first behold her in her formal robes.

He said nothing as she pulled away the veil and turned to face him, the brilliant vermilion over-robe of the Kwanlonhon clan catching fire and glowing hotly in the light of the oil lamp.

"So," he observed quietly, his perfect accent fluid in her ears, "tomorrow your father's sa'ab brings him his luck."

Ah, he understands everything, she thought, this foreigner with the pale face of one who hides from the sun!

"They come at midday to escort me."

She wandered around the room somewhat aimlessly, her silken slippers whispering against the woven mats covering the floor, and lightly touched the bound papers covered with miniature rows of black spiders, noting that he ate the simplest of foods and that the table wine was not fit for drinking. How came he to this place and from what strange land, that he could understand what tomorrow meant, the life-long dream of her father and her father's father, that one day their family would link its name to a clan, and that tomorrow she would enter the citadel of the Kwanlonhon? She would not be her lord's second concubine, or even his twenty-second, but she would bring honor to her family, a red robe to her children, and in doing so, would fulfill her destiny by assuring her father's good fortune.

Even though she sensed the admiration of H'esslar's gaze, she took little pleasure from it. No one knew better than she, Ridha, sa'ab of Oman the tea merchant, concubine-elect of Shakar, prince of the Kwanlonhon and brother to the greatest of the Tehrans, that her beauty had no meaning in and of itself. She was born a sa'ab, the luck of her father and the vessel of Shakar's child-to-be, and she embraced her fate as she would embrace Shakar tomorrow night, as a stranger who made all things possible.

"May your child bring honor to the father."

This was the ritual response, one she had heard many times in the last few days. To hear these words from H'esslar's lips brought joy to her heart since she knew he had never said them to anyone but her. Smiling at him as he stood in his drab clothing of the worst quality homespun and the poorest craftsmanship, she brought him a gift that might have equal value to his words of blessing.

"The Tehran will not attend the ceremony since my entrance brings riches but no honor to the clan. The princes Rahjid and Tasir will escort me to Shakar. My father said that in the place where he waited with the dowry, many . . . 'books,'" she pronounced the foreign word carefully, having practiced its strangeness on her tongue in the privacy of her bedchamber, "lined the walls. Perhaps, if you set some out on a cart, the great ones will see and buy."

He accepted her gift (as the rules of polite behavior demanded) with a formal bow of his head. She turned toward the door, rewrapping the cloth about her to shield herself from prying eyes. It was a difficult choice to risk shaming her father on the night before her bringing-in, but she had made it freely and with good conscience. Somehow she could not bear the thought of leaving H'esslar without so much as a final glance. Even less could she bear the thought of the shop closed and H'esslar left destitute and begging in the streets.

They said no farewells. She was glad he spared her the ordeal of doing so. She left richer than when she came, for H'esslar's esteem was far weightier than the gold and jewels with which her father had purchased his dream.

"OMAN'S SA'AB?" Galen asked upon the barring of the door.

"Much more than a sa'ab, old friend."

A condensed translation of the conversation ensued.

"Shall we put out a cart then, and draw them in?"

"We shall not." The surety of Esslar's directive carried with it absolute authority. "We must continue to avoid anything which might attract attention."

"But if Tasir comes . . ." Galen added slyly, a twinkle in his eyes.

"If he comes, I'll wait upon him."

"And if he informs his Tehran about a newly-opened shop, and this same Tehran happens to drop by . . ."

"Then I'll wait upon the Tehran, although I think it far more likely that I'll be summoned to the citadel."

"So," Galen stated, his relief profound, "it begins."

"Yes," the Master of Mysteries echoed softly, "just as the Nineteenth Mother said it would, everything put into motion by a woman of Endlin."

"The girl loves you, Esslar," the commander remarked after a thoughtful pause.

"She wouldn't understand the word. She understands only the honor of her family and the duties of a sa'ab. She'll put my memory aside and bring it out on the days she is happiest. My fondest wish is that those days are many and blissfully spent."

The subject was closed. Galen understood it was never to be mentioned again.

"Now, Commander, as to the good news you boasted of earlier in the evening, what have Phanus and Lampon to report?"

Galen cursed himself roundly.

"Damn me for a blabberin' fool, here I'm forgettin' the best news of all! *Seahorse* was sighted along the northern coastline yesterday. The runner said she's headin' out toward Nisyros, the last jaunt to pick up a shipment of spice before her holds are filled and she flies for home."

"How many days?"

The older man shifted in his chair, frowning a bit.

"Hard to say. Twenty if the winds blow true; thirty at most. If the westerlies kick up, she'll have to tack her way in."

"Her pilot?"

"Uh . . ." Galen searched the mine of information he absorbed daily from his spies, latching onto the name with a gleeful shout. "Fawaz!"

"A good pilot?" asked Esslar.

"A great one if the tales be true. The harbormaster told Lampon there's none can rival him. Did ye ken a Tehran would trust his sa'ab with anyone less?"

A mask slipped over Esslar's face as he replied serenely, "Of course not."

Galen wasn't fooled. Here was yet another subject not to be discussed.

"I'm for bed," Galen announced, feeling the ache of muscles he'd strained in the fight and cursing the fact that this leisurely life was fast turning him into an old man. When Esslar made no move to follow, Galen turned back to him, frowning slightly as he examined the pale face and too-thin body of his charge. Hell and damnation, Galen thought angrily to himself, he takes everything too hard! Worrying about the fate of a girl he barely knows. The girl has what she wants, thought Galen, prancing in her red robes like a filly being led to her first race.

For once the sagacious Commander misjudged his man, for Esslar's thoughts had left the girl in the scarlet robe and were rapidly overtaking a schooner skimming over moonlit waters toward a remote isle off the north shore of Endlin.

"Bring her home, Fawaz," he urged silently, the dusty air of the bookshop growing black and heavy as he turned down the wick of the oil lamp.

"Bring her and all who dwell within her safely to shore."

Chapter 4

The Citadel

HEADS TURNED ALL along the pier at the uncommon sight of a boy making his way down the dock to a newly arrived ship being unloaded. Children of clansmen were a rarity here. The roughness of the wharves were deemed unsafe for a precious mite whose slightest misstep could bring about an event for which there was no possible excuse and for which no father would ever be forgiven—the untimely death of a child.

The morning was a particularly busy one, and the dock where the *Seahorse* berthed was a near riot of frenzied activity. Perishables were unloaded in the coolness of first light, the clerks checking inventories against actual goods, the scales swinging to and fro as baskets were weighed and numbered and then lifted again with a hearty grunt by the porters whose half-naked bodies ran with rivulets of sweat as the sweltering heat of the day neared its peak. By the first hour after the break for the midday meal, only the heaviest items remained to be raised from the depths of the steaming holds by the day-laborers (hired on the spot that morning by the clan's chief steward). Their ringing calls of all-clear signaled their helpers above that another crate was ready to be pulled up by the wrist-thick hemp ropes running over a pulley block and swinging over onto the surface of the main deck.

A porter, his enormous basket brimming with cinnamon bark balanced precariously on his head, risked upsetting his load by removing one of his hands to point out the unusual sight of the boy to his fellow worker, both of them clucking their tongues at the carelessness of a clansman who would permit his son to run unescorted along the pier.

The boy seemed oblivious to the attention his presence created among the dockworkers. Traveling on winged feet, he dodged people with an alarming lack of prudence. His long, coltish legs jumped awkwardly over the bales and boxes blocking his way, and his robes and hair flew wildly. His face aglow with perspiration and nearly breathless from his exertions, he fought his way up the gangplank through a dull roar of curses, grunts, and shouted orders, coming to a halt on the forward deck.

Looking as face after face passed him by and standing on tiptoe and craning his neck in all directions, he searched in vain for a likely-looking clansman. The workers acknowledged his presence with several curious stares, giving him wide berth so as to avoid brushing against his robes. This was his first time aboard a ship, and he was a stranger to its protocol, although his uncle had taught him that in every situation in life there was a right and proper way to proceed. His bottom lip trembled a bit, for his message was important and his uncle severe. Struggling not to cry, for the shame of tears shed in public would be far worse than any punishment his uncle could devise, he felt the pressure of a hand on his shoulder.

"Here, boy," a gruff voice ordered. "No one weeps aboard the *Seahorse* without permission from the Tehran himself."

Relief overcoming shyness, the boy almost blurted out his thanks for being noticed before remembering his purpose. Drawing himself up to his full height (which brought him eye-level with a piece of polished pink coral dangling from a silver chain resting against a broad expanse of silk-draped chest), he announced with all the self-importance he could muster, "I bring a message to Sandur Kwanlonhon from the Tehran!"

A muttered curse startled him, for surely the sender of this message deserved the greatest of respect! Stepping back, he bumped into something solid, hearing as he did so a sharp cry of "'Ware!" Losing his balance as the crate behind him shifted, he would have fallen backward but for strong hands that grabbed him, lifting him into the air by his shoulders at the exact moment he heard the ominous thud of the crate falling heavily on the spot he had so recently occupied.

His face pressed against silken robes, the rapid pounding of his heart rivaled that of his rescuer, who held him tightly for a long moment. Held safely in the clansman's arms (for so his manner of dress proclaimed him), the boy heard his rescuer reprimand someone sharply, his voice crisp with authority.

A hand touched the crown of his head, and a kinder voice asked, "Are you hurt, boy?"

His cheeks flushed hot against the cool silken folds as he murmured a denial. Now he was being lowered so that his feet touched the deck again. The clansmen gently but firmly disengaged himself, pushing him away, reminding him that only his father had the right to embrace him in so intimate a manner. Regaining his footing, he kept his eyes focused on the wooden boards of the deck, awaiting a rebuke without resentment, knowing it was the duty of all clansmen to correct the faulty conduct of a boy being trained for manhood.

"You are . . .?" the clansman prompted, recalling him to duty.

"Bonhur, sa'ab of Pischak Kwanlonhon."

"When did you leave the harem, Bonhur?"

"Two moons ago tomorrow, sir."

"Two moons . . .," the clansman repeated, no louder than a sigh. The boy shifted uneasily, wondering what punishment was meted out for the crime of clumsiness. The clansman cleared his throat.

"What's your message, cousin?"

It was a kindness to be addressed in such a manner since the closeness of their blood relation was almost nil. Encouraged, Bonhur replied, "I . . . I ask your pardon, sir, but . . .," his voice cracked, causing him to wish his voice would change and change quickly, ". . . but I may not deliver it to anyone but Prince Sandur himself."

An open palm appeared in front of his down-turned face.

"Then do your duty, Bonhur Kwanlonhon. Deliver it into Sandur's hand."

As the boy's eyes flew up to meet those of the Tehran's sa'ab, an audible gasp escaped his lips. How could he not have noticed the elegant over-robe of amethyst overlaid with its telltale pattern of gold, especially when his uncle explained exactly how he was to recognize the Tehran's firstborn? Brought sharply back to attention when he realized that Prince Sandur held his hand patiently outstretched, he fumbled for the rumpled paper hidden inside his robes before placing it squarely in the middle of that leathery palm.

The Prince accepted it without comment. Remembering his manners and the lesson just learned, the boy looked around carefully before retreating the three steps tradition demanded. Breaking the seal of red wax, the Prince's eyes ran quickly down the page. It seemed to Bonhur that something in the message disturbed the Prince, for his jaw set and he looked up, beyond the dock and up into the hills toward the citadel. A long silence followed, during which the Prince appeared to have forgotten his presence. Bonhur grew increasingly uncomfortable, certain that he should not interrupt an elder's thoughts, but worried that his uncle would scold him for loitering. His problem was solved when a shout followed by a loud crash sounded from the forward hold. The Prince jerked to attention, following the direction of the resulting commotion, almost stepping on the boy in his hurry to investigate.

"My duties call. You are excused."

These were the formal words of dismissal, but his uncle had told him to wait for a reply.

"Is there an answer to the message, Prince Sandur?"

In that split second between question asked and answer given, Bonhur looked up into a face grown suddenly haggard, the face of a man called to a duty he dreaded. Bonhur's answer was a brusque shake of a princely head. In the next instant, Prince Sandur disappeared, his robes swirling about him in a violent rush of vivid color.

The boy scampered off the way he came, hurrying back to the place where his uncle waited, for the porters' assumptions that the boy was unsupervised were incorrect. For the goodly part of an hour a clansman paced nervously at the edge of the wharf, anxiously scanning the milling crowds for the face of his nephew, worried that the boy was over-young for the Tehran's task and might come to harm. Locating his slight form among the bigger-bodied men, he gestured for Bonhur to hurry.

As his feet carried him down the gangplank and onto the dock, Bonhur's mind was every bit as busy as his legs, wrangling with his first adult decision, the first time he had ever been called upon to make a judgment based on a code of ethical conduct he had only just begun to learn. By the time he caught sight of his uncle's upraised hand signaling him to proceed with all speed, he had already decided that his report would dutifully include mention of the near disaster for which he alone was to blame.

The boy's decision was twofold, for one detail of this day's happenings would be purposefully omitted from the account of his first meeting with the Tehran's sa'ab. With the natural sensitivity of youth, he resolved that no one would ever learn from Bonhur Kwanlonhon that on the second moon after his thirteenth birthday he had looked into the face of a man as far above him in rank as the stars are above the ocean depths, and pitied him.

FAWAZ THE PILOT stood watch on the quarterdeck, his legs spread shoulder-wide, his fists planted firmly on his hips as he regarded the furor around the forward hold with a mixture of disgust and relief. His contracted duties ended with the docking of the Kwanlonhon flagship last night, although it was his custom to stay on board until the holds were emptied. Or at least this served as a convenient excuse for not leaving the ship. If truth be known, he always felt a bit lost at the end of a voyage and needed time to readjust his thinking. For six moons he had been lord and master, his judgments never questioned, making life and death decisions for the crew delivered into his care. Now he was merely Fawaz, a lesser son of a lesser son who must obey until the Tehran offered him another contract and he made his escape by way of the sea.

The crowd around the hold parted at the arrival of Prince Sandur, who immediately began to restore order, gesturing and pointing as he delegated responsibilities, his voice carried away from the quarterdeck by the easterly breeze, his air of authority unmistakable.

No one would guess Sandur is exhausted, thought the pilot. Having learned to nap at any time of day or night in his early years in training as a ship's helmsman, Fawaz had snatched a few hours of sleep between midnight and the fourth bell. Now he was tired, but not so tired that he wasn't planning a night of extended celebration in the harbor district before making his way up the hill to the citadel tomorrow morning. Sandur, on the other hand, worked through the night, checking and re-checking the inventories he'd handed over to the Tehran's chief steward at first light. The rest of the day was spent overseeing the unloading of the cargo with the same diligence with which he began his duties half a year ago.

Half a year, mused Fawaz, watching as the work started up again. An almost perfect voyage, and certainly the most profitable one he had piloted in the five years since he completed his apprenticeship and received his first commission from the Tehran. They'd had their storms, weathering them with no loss of life and little damage, broken up a few shipboard brawls, a common occurrence on a voyage of this length, and suffered a single incidence of theft from the hold.

Stealing was the most serious of crimes since it was an offense against the entire Kwanlonhon clan. Fawaz was glad it was Sandur's problem, since as the clan's trading representative he was responsible for all trading ventures, the behavior of the seamen on shore, and the profitability of the entire voyage. It had been a hard judgement, but Sandur made it calmly and without undue cruelty, offering the thief the choice of losing his hand or banishment from Endlin. To everyone's relief, the thief chose banishment and was put off on a remote but habitable island.

Other than that single unpleasantness, they'd been luckier than most. Fawaz would make it his business to catch up on all the gossip concerning the trading fleet that night, but he had compiled a private inventory upon entering the harbor, noting that an Onozzi ship, the *Cormorant,* was undergoing extensive repairs, probably the result of storm damage, and the Effrentati flagship had lost most of her quarterdeck to fire. These were the lucky ones, however, having limped safely back to Endlin. Others would either be lost at sea or captured by the pirates who worked the far points of the trade routes, hiding in inlets until they spied a ship heading inbound, her holds full, running slowly in heavy seas and responding clumsily to the rudder, and take her and her crew as booty. Goods were sold to smugglers who ran a flourishing business up and down the coastline while the crew was killed outright or kept on board as slave labor.

But we're home, Fawaz reminded himself, home safe and sound with a fat profit guaranteed to bring a smile to the Tehran's face, especially since his sa'ab returns to him uninjured and in perfect health. That had been Fawaz's main worry from the day he was offered the contract—life was difficult enough at sea without shouldering the extra burden of a Tehran's sa'ab. His initial reaction to the offer was to refuse it, although to do so might damage his reputation with the clan elders and hinder the advancement of his career. When the Tehran added the additional lure of piloting the maiden voyage of the *Seahorse,* the finest flagship in the fleet, he sent up a prayer to the gods of the four winds and accepted without additional delay.

Six moons at sea was usually enough time to bring about either friendship or enmity. Strangely enough, he felt neither for the Tehran's sa'ab. Not that he had any quarrels with a man who never complained, accepted Fawaz's shipboard authority without a hint of the resentment he expected from a clansman of much higher rank, and fulfilled his duties with a strict regard for fairness and discipline; but neither had he come to love him.

When it came to the subject of Sandur Kwanlonhon, Fawaz was more puzzled today than he was at the outset of the voyage. In his five years at sea, he'd never met anyone as coolly correct or quite so humorless. The sight of that same man rescuing a boy from near disaster gave him second thoughts. He'd never wondered at the fact that Sandur didn't wear the second ring, although he was well past the age when a sa'ab usually settled down to father a family. There was something desperate in Sandur's headlong rush to pull the boy to safety, fury in his usually expressionless face when he reprimanded the deckhand responsible for the poorly balanced stack of crates, tenderness in his touch as he smoothed the black head buried in his robes.

Perhaps he's not so bad after all, Fawaz considered grudgingly. Interrupted by Sandur's polite inquiry, "Permission to approach the quarterdeck?" Fawaz waited as the Prince took up his accustomed position on Fawaz's right.

"What's amiss in the forward hold?"

"Someone pulled the wrong line and the rope left the sheave. The entire load fell. Several crates were smashed in the process."

"Anyone hurt?"

"Bruises only. I had the injured ones carried up and called for an apothecary."

"How close are they to finishing?"

Each of Fawaz's questions was answered with perfect poise and a certain sense of detachment, as if Sandur were an observer rather than a participant. The last one, however, brought a slight crease to the Prince's brow. Instead of answering Fawaz's question, he ventured one of his own.

"It's for that reason I took the liberty of disturbing you. It seems I've been summoned to the citadel and must leave the ship before the unloading is complete. I wondered if . . ."

" . . . if I would agree to stay on board until the chief steward releases the inventories and bring your copy to the citadel tomorrow morning."

A crooked smile appeared on the Prince's face, perhaps the second or third Fawaz had witnessed in their time together. When he nodded his appreciation of Fawaz's quick humor, his free-flowing black hair with its strange reddish cast was set afire in the afternoon sun.

"Will you have time to prepare yourself?" Fawaz asked, running his eyes over the tangled cords of unkempt hair, the robes darkened by patches of sweat under the arms, the dust and grime embedded in the skin around the Prince's eyes and mouth. For the first time, Fawaz sensed hesitance, even indecision, from the Tehran's sa'ab.

"I'm not sure of the urgency of the summons."

It was Fawaz's turn to frown, and frown he did, with a sense of impending doom as he remembered his training at the hands of his uncle. Nothing was so important to that training as instant and unquestioning obedience to any command by an elder or a clansman of higher rank. At the same time haste was necessary, to enter the Tehran's presence without proper regard to manners of dress might be construed as an insult. Propriety demanded that a sa'ab be groomed to perfection in the presence of the father.

"How was the message phrased?"

For the second time that day the Prince took him by surprise by handing him the summons. While Fawaz skimmed the handwritten note, the Prince turned away to contemplate the citadel situated on the northern cliffs, the highest point of land in Endlin and the ancient seat of the clan of the Kwanlonhon.

> Your duties on *Seahorse* are ended.
> Attend me in the hall of audience.
> Manthur, Tehran of the Kwanlonhon

A strange message from a father deprived of his sa'ab for six moons, mused Fawaz. Terse and unwelcoming, the signature as formal as the one that graced the contract Fawaz was offered from that same hand, he began to understand the Prince's quandary. Still, there might be some emergency of which they were ignorant.

"It's not my judgment to make, Prince. Even if we had a woman on board it would take hours to prepare you. Surely the Tehran understands what constitutes life aboard ship."

Even as he said it, Fawaz questioned his reasoning. Unlike his predecessors and the Tehrans of the other clans, Manthur Kwanlonhon never served his mandatory apprenticeship on board a trading vessel. This deficiency in his education was something of a mystery, as was the fact that the present Tehran was not the sa'ab of his father. Linphat V's firstborn, Prince Rahjid, abdicated the position he'd assumed after the death of his father in favor of Manthur, a third son, an event that shook the foundations of the Kwanlonhon clan. Fawaz could remember his father's dismay at finding his clan headed by a lesser son, although those anxieties were quickly quelled by the brilliance with which Manthur ran the business affairs of the clan. In the past three decades the Kwanlonhon had surpassed the Synzurit in wealth and currently enjoyed the highest credit rating in Endlin. Certainly a man as far-seeing as the Tehran would understand that his sa'ab must enter his presence unbraided, having been denied the presence of a woman for these six moons.

The Prince echoed his words, muttering vaguely, "Yes, surely he will understand," although Fawaz thought he sounded unconvinced. Another thought struck the pilot.

"Who was the boy?"

Without lowering his eyes from the citadel, which glistened on the white cliffs under which the waves churned and foamed, the Prince answered him distractedly, his thoughts busy elsewhere.

"The son of a playfellow of mine."

"Rather young to be delivering messages in the harbor district," Fawaz observed dryly, as shocked as his crew at the presence of one so small.

"Only two moons out of the harem," the Prince murmured, "and in tears because he could not find me. Who would require such a thing of him?"

The question lingered on the breeze as Fawaz considered the first year of his training, ripped from the security of the harem to live in a world ruled by instant obedience, swift punishment, and total isolation from the father he adored.

"You must hurry, Prince," Fawaz reminded his companion.

It struck him that finally, in these last few minutes of their voyage, he had come to like Sandur Kwanlonhon. Sadly, his realization came too late. Tomorrow they would meet in the citadel and everything that had passed between them would be erased; Fawaz would resume his role as the lesser son of a third cousin to the Tehran, while Sandur would become the man who would one day rule the Kwanlonhon clan. If Fawaz was fortunate and the Prince proved generous, the success of this venture might procure him the commissions that would ease the financial responsibilities of his old age. For unlike Sandur, Fawaz would never father a family, having given up that option when he chose his profession. No father could leave his family for any reason. Thus, to begin fathering children meant that one must live forever in the citadel within the tightly closed confines of the clan.

Acknowledging his advice, Prince Sandur bowed his chin to his chest with a gesture that indicated a command understood and accepted, and took his leave of the *Seahorse*. Fawaz watched from the quarterdeck, following the figure garbed in amethyst-colored robes until he vanished into the surrounding crush of dockworkers. With the far-reaching gaze with which he measured the progress of his ship against the stars when the cool night breezes rifled through his hair, the pilot traced the path of the Prince's journey by memory, imagining him hurrying up the shell path that led to the gates surrounding the harbor district, through the winding market streets of Abalone Hill, and up the north road to the Kwanlonhon citadel.

As he surveyed that fabled vista, taking in the magnificent spread of the cliffs as they rose above the crashing waves, Fawaz recalled the music of the citadel's many fountains, its sunlit plazas with their elaborate mosaics, the luxurious foliage of the exotic plants and trees which made the harem the loveliest garden he had ever seen or hoped to see again, and breathed a sigh of pure relief. Not for him the life of the citadel. He would live alone to the end of his days, denied the luxuries of that legendary palace by the sea, but he thanked the gods that he would be amply compensated by the glory of the west wind, the sails rising taut and full-bellied as they bore him out to the seas where freedom and solitude held hands like lovers.

It is not every man's choice, but it is mine and it will suffice. With that thought, Fawaz the pilot resumed his watch.

FOUR PALAQUIN BEARERS clutched their poles tighter as they began the final ascent to the citadel, their toes spread wide to grip the earth as it passed beneath their hardened, leather-like soles, their breath coming in pants as they hurried onward. A fat purse awaited them if they made their trip in record time, and each man jogged with that thought in mind. The closed sedan chair swayed gently from side to side, its single occupant resting his head against the cushions, lulled by the rhythm of the bearers' strides.

Their pace slowed as they approached the gates. A guard in scarlet robes waved them through without bothering to inspect the contents of the chair. They trotted on, their breath coming in deep gasps now, their strength nearly spent from the hard pace their leader (the eldest of the four cousins) set from the outset. Their passenger had ordered them to deliver him to the main door which led to the public halls and meeting rooms. Unbeknownst to the inmate of the chair, they followed the crushed shell path as it curved around to one of the many wings thrusting out from the center of the citadel, each wing the site of the private apartments located on the fringes of the massive hall.

Choosing an entrance on the far west side, the door over-hung with a silk awning against the strength of the afternoon sun, they lowered the chair carefully, so as not to disturb the clansman within, and sank to their knees, their heads bowed in exhaustion.

The door beneath the awning opened immediately, as did the door of the sedan chair, and the bearers watched their passenger emerge at the same time a silver-haired clansman in a magnificent over-robe of sapphire blue appeared in the doorway, exclaiming, "At last!"

In the flurry of activity which followed, the respectful bow from the passenger to the elder clansman before he was ordered into the apartment with almost frantic haste, the quick distribution of monies that appeared as if by magic from inside the robes of blue silk, and the resulting joy of the four cousins that their labor had not been in vain, not a single man amongst them thought to question the necessity of their rush from the harbor district to the citadel. No one questioned it since the reason was perfectly clear to even the most backward of observers. The palanquin bearers were witnessing the reunion of a loving father with his weary, travel-stained sa'ab, and all four men made their way back down the northern road with a sense of deep satisfaction. Having earned three times their usual fare, they had also been instrumental in returning a wayfarer to his father's house.

"HE HAS SUMMONED me, uncle. I dare not delay," Sandur protested as he was propelled forward into the cool darkness of the interior by a hand placed firmly in the middle of his back.

"You made good time through the city, and the bath is already prepared. My steward obtained clean robes from your apartment. Hurry, now, and waste no time."

"Even if I bathe, my hair . . ."

" . . . will be braided by my concubines, who attend us in the great room."

Having reached the baths, Sandur came to an obstinate halt, trying again to reason with his favorite uncle.

"He must know I've arrived."

"He knows nothing. The guard at the gates was bribed, the bearers think you are my son, and my steward cleared the apartments of any eavesdroppers."

Prince Tasir Kwanlonhon, the fourth son of Linphat V, drew himself up to his formidable height, topping the younger man before him by several inches, and frowned down at him.

"Listen to me, nephew, and listen well. His temper is near the breaking point. For the past moon we have lived in fear that he will bring the citadel crashing down around our ears. He banished three clansmen in as many days, demoted a steward who displeased him to the rank of street-sweeper fourth-class and insulted Shakar so cruelly and with so little cause that he has not left his apartments for a fortnight. Rahjid is in hiding as well, lost among his storybooks and content enough with his birds and frequent visits to the harem to visit his grandchildren."

Tasir's harangue was producing its desired effect. The prince he had trained to manhood stood white-faced and grim, the old look of terror haunting his eyes, the same look he wore as a youth when word arrived that his father requested his presence. Still not content that his orders would be obeyed, Tasir continued, for there was danger in what he did today. He judged it best that Sandur should understand exactly why he was countermanding the orders of the Tehran.

"I may be ignorant as to the cause of his black mood, but this I know. A visitor has been summoned for the sixth hour after midday. Judging from the time Manthur sent for Pischak, I surmise that he expects you in attendance at nearly the same time. We have, then, nearly two hours to prepare you. With my concubines' help, your hair will be wet, but decently braided. I leave the decision to you. Will you risk his displeasure by rushing to him in your present state of disarray, knowing it will infuriate him, or shall you make yourself presentable and arrive at the exact time he expects you?"

In answer, Sandur pushed open the door to the bath. Sandalwood-scented steam drifted out into the hall, the tiled walls within dripping with moisture. A white leisure robe lay arranged on the massage couch along with a clean challah and new sandals placed neatly beside a stack of drying cloths. As he passed over the threshold, Sandur asked the question for which Tasir could supply no answer.

"Who is this visitor, uncle?"

Tasir gestured for him to close the door.

"I've been unable to discover his identity. Time spent worrying is time wasted. Don't dawdle, nephew."

With that, Tasir departed, his silver braids slapping against his broad back as he hurried off to gather the women.

SANDUR CLOSED THE door and bolted it from within, a precaution against any untoward interruption by a wandering servant or concubine, although the rules of modesty were most strictly maintained between adult males. Up until the age of twelve, the year he left the harem, he bathed and played with children of both sexes without restraint. Upon entering training, the formal rules of manhood came into effect. It was forbidden for anyone but a woman to look upon the nakedness of a clansman. There were certain provisos for such things as swimming, a favorite pursuit in this city by the sea; but as a rule men avoided other men under such circumstances and tended to swim in private or in the company of concubines. Even when aboard the ship, living in the cramped cabin he shared with Fawaz, not once did either man break this taboo, but maintained the codes that ruled them from the first day they left the harem.

Stripping off the foul garments that stank of sweat and fish oil, Sandur stepped into the tiled bath and lathered himself from head to toe with a cake of milled soap. This done, he ducked himself in the waist-deep water, soaped himself again, and rinsed away the last traces of lather. Rising from the bath, he descended several steps into the soaking tub, built of fragrant woods and heated from below by a charcoal-fired brazier, sinking as quickly as the heat of the water would allow until only his head emerged. Leaning back against the wood, his hair floating loosely around his shoulders, he closed his eyes, relaxing for the first time in twenty-four hours, letting the hot water soak out the last of the impurities from skin that had known nothing but sponge baths and sea water for the past six moons.

Assuredly his uncle was right, and he let that thought calm his dread of what waited for him in the hall of audience. Nothing angered his father more than impropriety.

Now, at least, he would be decently groomed and attired. This had ever been his uncle's way, he thought gratefully, shielding him from shame and setting him on the proper path of duty. Other men looked back on their training with hatred, but those seven years spent under Tasir's rule were blissful, the happiest days of his life as he was schooled under a hand of iron, but a hand that knew fairness, restraint, and best of all, forgiveness.

From his uncle he learned the proper behavior of not only a clansman (for so all sons were taught) but the responsibilities of a Tehran's sa'ab. There could have been no better teacher than Tasir. His other uncles, Rahjid and Shakar, were as different from each other as the east wind from the west: Rahjid, his grandfather's sa'ab, a natural hermit with the tastes of an aesthete, and Shakar, a second son of a decidedly hedonistic bent whose concubines numbered nearly forty and whose ruling passion was horse racing, a sport adored by clansmen and commoners alike. Tasir, however, resembled his father in looks and manner to the degree that Sandur had often wondered if the same concubine served as the vessel for his grandfather's seed, although to ask such a question was unthinkable. Like his brother Manthur, Tasir was a man of modest tastes and great learning, his library reputedly rivaling that of Sandur's great-uncle, Nazur Kwanlonhon, a former Equerry of Endlin and a man whose life had been devoted to the search for manuscripts for his library and fine horseflesh for his stables. More than any other clan, the Kwanlonhon had long been known as learned men. Only recently had they become wealthy, a fact due, Sandur knew from first-hand experience and his ten-year apprenticeship in the trading fleet, to the efforts of his father.

It was for this reason that Sandur rejoiced as *Seahorse* sailed into the harbor, bringing one of the richest cargoes in recent memory to the treasuries of the clan, sure that at last he had found a means whereby to please his father and ask of him the favor he carried like a night-blooming orchid that wilts and shrivels in the light of day.

Sitting in the bath, the steam rising from water scented with precious oils, he conjured Vavashi's face. Her sloe-eyes glowed at him, promising him the second ring and the life he desired above all others. He met her through her brother, a lesser son of Yodhat Onozzi and a frequent visitor to the Kwanlonhon citadel for the purpose of exchanging messages between the clans. Invited to visit the Onozzi palace for a dinner party, Sandur found his attention captured time and time again by a woman who wore the gilt patterns of a sa'ab on her over-robe. To his amazement, she returned his interest. Their words were few, uttered in the public domain of the dining hall. In a voice softer than the silk reserved for newborn infants, she made her position clear. If an offer came from the Tehran of the Kwanlonhon, her father, the Tehran of the Onozzi, would accept it.

This question of rank had always been the failing of the other women he suggested to his father as fitting vessels for the first child of his body, but how could his father refuse the sa'ab of another clan's Tehran? Vavashi would achieve her destiny, bringing her father the honor of a strong link to the richest clan in Endlin, and Sandur would at last know the joy of holding his child in his arms.

Rushing home that night to the citadel he shared his news with his uncle, confiding in him the glad tidings. Tasir counseled patience, offering a disappointed Sandur his pledge that when he returned from the voyage his father arranged for him on the flagship of the fleet, Tasir would add his considerable support to Sandur's plea.

Now, instead of preparing his case over the span of the next few days, days in which the cargo reports would be examined by his father, proving Sandur's ability to trade with acumen and thrift, he was summoned peremptorily into his father's presence with not even enough time to dry his hair.

Rousing himself, for he found himself nodding as his muscles were loosened by the intense heat of the water, he reluctantly left the tub and went about drying and dressing, tying the challah about his loins and donning the white cotton undergarments. The breeches were of a cut peculiar to the clansmen of Endlin, tight-legged yet cut full from well below the crotch and tied around the waist with drawstrings. The matching tunic with its billowing sleeves fell loosely around his torso. The white robe of thin silk came last of all, and he knotted it tightly about his waist.

Now he was decently attired in the leisure robes which might be worn in the presence of concubines without necessity of the four additional robes whose colors represented his clan (the Kwanlonhon vermilion), his lineage (his grandfather's topaz and his father's emerald), and his position as sa'ab (amethyst traced with gold).

As he rubbed his hair with a cloth, combing through the tangles with his fingers, he considered the import of Tasir's recital and felt his stomach knot as it had not done in the past six moons. Those cautionary words revived the old fear, the fear Sandur kept hidden even from his faithful uncle, for to speak it would be the most appalling sin a child could commit against his father. Even to think it filled him with revulsion. Try as he might, he found himself thinking of nothing else as he reclined in the sedan chair, surveying Endlin through the black gauze which shielded occupants from the stranger's gaze and transformed the city into a grey haze of spectral bodies and buildings.

Why had that particular boy been assigned to deliver him the message? Why should one so young and inexperienced, who had left the harem only two moons ago and by rights should not begin his duties outside the citadel until the sixteenth year, be asked to brave the dangers of the docks? What if he had not seen the crate shift and grabbed those thin shoulders in hands that shook with fear at the thought that such a young life had been put into danger for his sake?

The answer was too awful to consider. It must be a coincidence that Bonhur was the child of his favorite playfellow in the harem. For if it was not, then his father — who loved him as all fathers must love their sa'abs, their firstborn, the favored child from whom all luck sprang — sent Bonhur to mock him, placing an innocent boy's life in jeopardy for no other reason than to taunt him with a reminder that Pischak, five years Sandur's senior, had fathered a sa'ab twelve years ago.

Refusing to contemplate such calculated malice, Sandur tossed the drying cloth to the floor and pulled the bolt.

No father could be so hateful. It was impossible, as illogical as it was objectionable to any clansman trained in the ways of manhood. His father might be less involved in his care than most, but he was a Tehran, responsible for the well being of an entire clan, his time claimed by duties few other fathers performed. He might be strict, but Tasir was stricter, grooming Sandur for a position that demanded a level of discipline few men could attain. Think on that, he cautioned himself, when your thoughts turn ugly and you malign the one whose seed gave you life. It is the way of a father that he loves his offspring. If yours seems demanding, it proves his belief that you can achieve more for the clan than any of his other children. You are his sa'ab, and a man's luck is his sa'ab. What man would be so unwise as to destroy his luck?

His faith restored, he broke into a trot, heading for his uncle's great room and the ritual of braiding which would allow him to enter his father's presence as a respectful and obedient son.

TASIR WATCHED FROM under half-closed lids as the women went about their work, nimble fingers with lacquer-tipped nails flying as they braided the hair of the Tehran's sa'ab. Since their hands knew no other employment, they were experts at this most intimate of tasks, for only a woman could braid a clansman's hair. Tasir's concubines had braided this particular head many times, just as they had enjoyed the delights of Sandur's bed, for the proper training of a boy included instruction in the begetting of children. Tasir himself selected Sandur's first partner, a mature concubine of perfect beauty and mild temperament who schooled him in the ways of pleasing a woman since it was common knowledge that a perfect child most frequently results when the vessel which nurtures it is brought to the moment of ecstasy.

All this Sandur learned, but above all Tasir taught him that most important of lessons: the first duty of a clansman is to control conception. Children represented a clansman's stature, his worth, and the immortality of the clan. To father a child without proper thought given to the worthiness of the vessel or the permission of his father (if he lived) was considered a reprehensible act. It was for this reason that a boy's training concerning women was given the highest priority, second only to his memorization of the rules of the clan. Lessons, languages, hunting in the neighboring hills, study of the sea and everything to do with the clan's trading fleet, all these things were worth nothing if a boy could not learn the one great lesson which was the cornerstone of a clansman's life.

To control conception separated man from beast, and on this principle rested the endurance of the race. Let others breed indiscriminately, without attention paid to the quality and longevity of their descendants. In the clans, breeding children of beauty, health, and intelligence was a way of life. It was for this reason foreigners visiting the citadel would often comment on the size and stature of the clansmen in contrast with the commoners who bred without a thought for tomorrow.

It was a hard rule, Tasir conceded, but there was justness in it. A single flaw was enough to deny a clansman progeny—less than perfect vision, deafness, recurring sickness, a tendency to bleed, impaired memory, difficulties in learning, melancholy, repeated bouts of drunkenness, noisy breathing, poor digestion, corpulence, rotten teeth. Any of these would be enough to cause a father to forbid a son the right to breed. Concubines were selected in much the same manner. If the first child produced was anything less than perfect, the child was not allowed to draw its second breath, and the concubine would be dismissed from the clan, since, unlike a man, she possessed no other talents that might add to the clan's wealth.

Only when Sandur proved his understanding of this rule had Tasir allowed his nephew access to his concubines. Those desirous of sampling Sandur's newfound skills sought entry to his rooms in the darkness of night. Like all uncles who first offer their concubines to their nephews, Tasir waited with some anxiety for those who bedded with the Tehran's firstborn to resume their monthly flows, keeping far from their beds in the meantime, ensuring that any issue from their bodies was his and his alone. As time passed he grew to trust this most honorable of nephews, for not once had Sandur brought on Tasir's head the shadow of shame.

In his studies he proved brilliant, mastering the language of the southern lands, the tongue of the Lapith, and the dialects spoken on the islands to the far east. His knowledge of geography, especially that of a coastline that spread a hundred leagues to the north and south of Endlin, was unsurpassed. In the years after training he distinguished himself repeatedly as he apprenticed with clan stewards, traders, ship-builders, and pilots, making his way from his first post as messenger to that of a highly respected trader to whom the Tehran had entrusted a six-moon journey to the farthest reaches of the eastern seas.

As to his form and figure, he was without blemish, healthy, and according to the whispered accounts confided to Tasir's ears alone, an accomplished and considerate bedmate.

Reaching his full height well into his twenty-second year, he stood shoulder to shoulder with his father. Whereas his younger brothers and sisters inherited the coarse blue-black hair of the majority of clansmen, Sandur's thick mane took on a distinctively reddish cast when lit by sun or torchlight, an omen some clansmen took as living proof that he would bring glory to the clan of the red robe. Everything about him declared his right to father the next Tehran of the Kwanlonhon, yet he wore the single ring of a childless clansman.

A peal of unseemly laughter drew Tasir's attention to the group of women surrounding the young man who lay sprawled on the woven woolen carpet, fast asleep, his neck propped up against several floor cushion so as not to hinder the concubines' task. At Tasir's frown, hands flew obediently over reddened lips to beg his pardon. Voices lowered to the merest of whispers, they arranged the pattern of the hundred braids that announced, as did the red robe, that this clansman was a member of the Kwanlonhon. Tasir witnessed their joy at Sandur's return without jealousy; they deserved the delights of a younger body, he admitted with a grunt, especially since his own days of frequent beddings were past. His youngest concubine, taken into his household as a favor to her father with the understanding that she would never bear a child of his body, massaged Sandur's temples as he slept, smoothing away the lines of tension and worry etched into his forehead. Noting the wistfulness of that caress, Tasir resolved to encourage her to visit his nephew's apartments tonight. Six moons without a woman, Tasir wondered to himself, when for thirty years I have never slept anywhere except these rooms.

Gesturing for the women to hurry, he turned his thoughts to the audience awaiting both Sandur and him, for he had not told Sandur that he, Rahjid, and even sullen Shakar had been summoned, as well as the entire clan. To what purpose, he worried, should my brother gather the clan before a stranger? What does he plan and for what reason did he dispatch Pischak's sa'ab, a boy of barely thirteen summers, to the docks? To this question he added one that perplexed him with more and more frequency. Why does my brother deny his sa'ab the right he deserves above all others? And why, ye gods of the four winds, am I becoming increasingly convinced that this brother of mine, this greatest of Tehrans, is unworthy of this sa'ab, who I have trained with utmost care to wear the golden robes?

More questions arrived unbidden. How can it be that Manthur, a younger son, reappears without warning after an unexplained absence of five years with his sa'ab sleeping peacefully in the arms of an ayah? And what of the elder brother, Rahjid, who resigns the post for which he trained for a lifetime in favor of a lesser sibling? What can explain the fact that Manthur knew nothing of the trading business, having abandoned his apprenticeship after a single year, vowing to travel the world and saying his farewells to our father as if he would never return, but has managed our business affairs with an uncanny ability to confound our competitors? And how can it be that I, who loved Manthur as I loved none of my brothers and received the proof of his affections when he entrusted me with the training of his sa'ab, have grown to fear him to the point that I avoid his presence whenever possible?

Gazing steadfastly at this nephew who never laughed, rarely smiled, and had not a single friend of long-standing, Tasir made a private vow. He swore not on the wind gods, on the heads of his children, nor on the good name of his clan. It was a simple vow, and one that might destroy him, but he made it in tribute to the nephew who slept exhausted on the floor of his great room, groomed by the hands of women not his own.

"I will not assist my brother in this madness. The gods help me, but I will not be a party to the shaming of this sa'ab."

Chapter 5

The Tehran of the Kwanlonhon

MANTHUR, TEHRAN OF the Kwanlonhon, stood with his back to the shopkeeper, sublimely indifferent to his presence, his interest riveted on samples of merchandise spread across the table. His forefinger, square-tipped, manicured, adorned with an emerald of impossible size, played among the items on display, pushing aside one, hovering briefly over another, the richness of the items offered up for his consumption making it nearly impossible to select a first course. Sunlight streamed down from the window directly above and behind the table, a thousand motes of dancing dust turned a shimmering, incandescent gold, matching the over-robe which proclaimed his rank and status as the first lord of the Kwanlonhon, which is to say, the most powerful being in Endlin.

Etchings, woodcuts, collections of plays and poetry, essays, diaries, dialogues, prefaces, treatises, were offered up meekly for his inspection. One handsomely-bound volume, the color of aged claret, caught the Tehran's attention. The restless forefinger circled back to it, paused for a moment, then lowered to stroke the calf-skin binding with something akin to reverence. Having studied the correct behavior of commoners toward clansmen, Esslar waited as was prescribed, eyes lowered yet discretely attentive, willing himself to immobility, stifling a smile when the Tehran, having made his selection, began to leaf slowly through the contents of the claret-colored book.

The private domain in which Esslar found himself was severe in its lack of ornamentation, contrasting sharply with the glories of the audience hall through which he had passed before being motioned through a low door and into the Tehran's presence. Always sensitive to his surroundings, Esslar inspected the room under lidded eyes, realizing with an inner jolt that they contained the unmistakable signs of frequent, if not constant, habitation. The upholstered lounge, with its matching pillow, bore signs of indentation, while the low-backed chair, covered in fine cowhide and pulled near an oil lamp, seemed a perfect place for reading. An ottoman shoved hurriedly to one side of the chair bore depressions indicating regular use. Books lined the walls, all of them revealing signs of hard service. A cloth map of considerable size, stretched and mounted on the wall opposite the table, traced the routes of trading vessels with wooden pins inserted at various points. A glazed canister in the corner held bamboo rods of different lengths used, Esslar guessed, to point out delays or changes in itinerary to those high-ranking elders who were party to the inner workings of Kwanlonhon trading ventures.

The Tehran's initial greeting, while formal, was not unfriendly, due no doubt to Prince Tasir's description of Esslar as a modest tradesman who hoped to make his fortune in the book trade and needed the support of a well-placed patron. This was exactly the impression Esslar intended to make. The summons to the citadel arrived exactly three days after Tasir's initial visit.

Esslar made his preparations with care, his decisions prompted by his many sessions with the Nineteenth Mother, whose reminders sounded continually in his ears.

"You must be ordinary, posing no threat. The slightest suspicion and he will dismiss you from his presence."

Frowning, she remembered other messengers denied even the courtesy of an audience.

"It is vital that you come near enough to touch his thoughts before he has time to erect barriers of any kind."

To that end, Esslar wore a tunic and breeches purchased in the markets upon arrival, adding a slightly more expensive robe of dull, third-grade silk. The Tehran's first appraising glance weighed the message of the newly-purchased robe, classing its wearer as someone willing to spend a few hard-earned coins if it meant he might curry the favor of a high-ranking clansman.

The Tehran turned away from the window, the book open in his hands.

"Your stock is as impressive as my brother promised."

The Tehran's off-hand delivery made Esslar breathe easier. This was her hope and his, that he might be admitted to the Tehran's presence without undue suspicion. The paleness of Esslar's skin might proclaim his foreign birth, but his garb and manner were identical to the commoners of the city, his accent like that of a native speaker.

"Your brother is kindness itself, great lord. He honored me with several purchases, each selection made with the keen eyes of an avid collector."

My praise of Tasir rankles him, Esslar noted, using his intuitive powers to sense what this expressionless face concealed.

"Perhaps a collector, but hardly a connoisseur. Why else would he have let this treasure escape him?"

An impatient forefinger tapped the page.

Esslar allowed himself the slight shrug of an expert.

"Few are acquainted with Dorian's work, the audience being limited for such an esoteric subject. This is a special edition, printed eight years ago and already something of a rarity. My compliments on your taste, great lord."

The Tehran's eyes found the book again, ignoring the flattery he heard continually and for which he had no use. As he turned a few more pages, stopping from time to time to examine the meticulous etchings of the flora and fauna of the Eastern Isles, Esslar made his first tentative probe, by-passing the Tehran's conscious mind and moving directly into the chambers of memory, finding himself inside the Maze, specifically, in the Hall of Gathering . . .

. . . WHERE THE POLISHED wooden walls gleamed with torchlight, fiddles and fifes wailing to the beat of a high-pitched drum. Manthur held a woman in his arms, a woman who smiled as they danced across the crowded floor, her pale face radiant, lit from within, cascades of chestnut hair floating freely around her frail shoulders as she swayed to the beat of the drum. Glorying in her gaiety, Manthur watched as Aethra danced on air, her head thrown back as she laughed up at him, exposing the slender column of her throat.

"Shall we dance forever, Manthur, until we grow so old we cannot lift our feet?"

His answer was to swing her up into his arms, waiting for her shriek of surprised delight to subside before whispering in her ear.

"Thou, my beauty, shall dance forever in my heart."

He paused, his excitement growing.

"Tonight we dance no more."

Sensing her disappointment, he rushed on, anxious to issue the invitation he had denied her for so long.

"We must hurry back to the cell."

As roses bloomed in her already flushed cheeks, he marveled as he always did at the fairness of her complexion.

"What sayest thou? Wilt thou untie my challah?"

With a blissful sigh she snuggled close, resting her head on his shoulder as he carried her toward the door, careless of the onlookers who smiled knowingly as he brushed past them.

A wiry man with a mischievous grin blocked his path.

"Not so fast! I promised to dance with every woman here! Would you have me disappoint Aethra?"

Manthur smiled down at Dorian, inclining his head toward the moon-faced woman who sat with the musicians, her lithe hands making the two-headed drum sing with the rhythms of her native land.

"In no way shall Aethra be disappointed. On this you have my word. Fenja awaits you, Dorian. Dance with her instead."

His burden was light, and he carried it with a heart so full his chest ached under the rough fabric of his blouse. A freckled hand stole up to stroke his braids and he broke into a run, wanting nothing else than to hear the bolt slide shut on the cell door . . .

ESSLAR WITHDREW GRADUALLY, the Tehran's private dreams continuing unabated. *So it is as we hoped,* the healer rejoiced; *his memories are intact!* Steeling himself for what would follow, Esslar spoke the next lines of the script.

"Pardon my boldness, great lord, but how did you become acquainted with the work of Dorian the Chartist?"

In his struggle to free himself from so powerful a memory, the Tehran replied without thinking.

"I knew him long ago."

"He's a native of Pelion, I believe. Was it there you met him?"

The Tehran's head shot up, the black braids sprinkled with grey striking against his neck, his gaze suddenly intent.

"What do you know of Pelion, tradesman?"

Even with his suspicion aroused, the Tehran believed the charade of the bookseller. Not once did his thoughts jump toward Esslar, who answered him with precision, careful not to be caught in a lie.

"Much of my initial inventory came from Pelion, although I've traded in the towns and villages along the southern route and found several treasures there. Among them was this rather fine catalogue of gemstones compiled by a jeweler from Tek."

Mollified by his explanation, the Tehran accepted his offering and began leafing through the pamphlet. As he lowered it to rest on the table, freeing his fingers to separate some pages that had stuck together as a result of humidity, Esslar sprang the trap.

"This, too, might interest you," he suggested mildly, spreading the document he had removed from its hiding place in his robes on top of the opened catalogue. This done, he prepared himself for whatever might follow.

The Tehran's attack was instantaneous and brutal, his thoughts leaping out at Esslar, expecting easy entrance and a quick assessment of whatever information this bookseller's mind might hold. Instead he found an impassable barrier which yielded no reward.

It was for this moment that Esslar had prepared, and perhaps, he sometimes fancied, the moment for which he had been born. No one except a Mother of Pelion could have withstood this mental barrage, denying Manthur entry or the slightest glimpse of what lay within. And then, without observing a single principle of the ethics he had sworn to uphold, ethics that required him to respect the walls of privacy erected by another adept, Manthur neither retreated nor offered his apologies as custom demanded, but doubled his efforts.

The Master of Mysteries stood adamant against a mind striving to penetrate his thoughts. Time hung suspended as they waged their bitter feud, a battle fought with hatred and enmity by Manthur and with implacable composure on the part of Esslar.

Behind the barrier, in the private realm of his inner thoughts, Esslar grieved over what had become of this former ernani. Here was uncontestable proof of what the Nineteenth Mother had long suspected; Manthur had misused his gift for years, forcing his way into non-adept minds with no care for the damage he left behind. In his encounter with the princes in the book shop Esslar found Rahjid's mind badly scarred, yielding the explanation for his unexpected abdication, and Tasir's less damaged, although to an expert such as Esslar the signs of tampering were readily apparent.

Beginning to understand how thoroughly the trap was set, Manthur erected a barrier of his own, shielding his thoughts from Esslar. The time was ripe to proceed.

"I am Esslar of Pelion, Master Healer and member of the Nineteenth Mother's private Council. I bring this message to Manthur of Endlin. Three times has the Mother of Pelion asked you to honor this contract. Three times you have ignored her summons. I am the final messenger. The time has come for your son to return to the city of his birth."

"He does not have the gift."

The Tehran dismissed the entire matter with a shrug.

Esslar stiffened. This was the Nineteenth Mother's worst fear—that Manthur had harmed her grandson's mind.

"Have you treated him as cruelly as you did me?"

This accusation brought a brief flare to the impassive black eyes, a reaction lending credibility to the Tehran's next admission, grudgingly made, but containing the ring of truth.

"I touched his thoughts once while he slept. Nothing more."

Privately resolving to examine Sandur's memories on this point at the first opportunity which presented itself, Esslar plunged on.

"This changes nothing. The contract stipulates that even if he proves non-adept, he must be allowed to enter the Maze."

Esslar sensed the Tehran's confidence, his absolute belief that he was impregnable to attack.

"What care I for a contract signed under duress, the terms forged by a witch who hates me? And of what use is this paper in any case? Shall you bring Legionnaires to storm the citadel and ride at their head, waving this in the air?"

A sneer appeared on Manthur's still handsome face.

"Are you simple enough to believe I would allow anyone to rob me of what is rightfully mine? Does she think me still an ernani, to be ordered about by underlings, obeying rules drafted for cutthroats and murderers, treated like a prisoner without rights?"

He smiled, a cold smile that did not reach his eyes, dismissing Esslar with a wave of his hand.

"Leave now and I'll ensure your safe passage out of Endlin."

Ignoring the unspoken threat, Esslar kept to the script, thankful that the Nineteenth Mother had foreseen the need for a plan which had become so much a part of him that he could speak his lines at the same time he kept his attention on the subtle details of Manthur's response.

"A copy of this contract has been filed in Equerry Court. Should you refuse to honor your pledge, copies will be delivered to the Tehrans of the other clans."

The Tehran shrugged again, unimpressed by what he considered to be an empty threat.

"So they discover I break a pledge made thirty years ago. You forget that every one of them would consider the promise to surrender a sa'ab null and void under any circumstance."

"You miss my point. They might disregard the terms of the agreement, but questions will follow: 'What is an adept?' 'What is the Path of Preparation?' 'Where is this place called Pelion?' Would you risk having such questions answered in open court? Do you want them to discover the true reason for your rapid rise to power? And most importantly, will you suffer the name of the place you have kept hidden these thirty years, preventing potential ernani from making their way south as is their right, to rise to the lips of every clansman and commoner in Endlin?"

They were but guesses, her guesses shrewdly posed after years of interviewing free traders and caravan leaders. Nothing else could explain the dearth of ernani from the east—exactly two since Kazur's entry fifty-five years ago—and none since Manthur's return to Endlin.

The Tehran's face revealed nothing.

"He is not here, in any case. He sails the farthest fringes of the eastern seas."

"The *Seahorse* was spotted along the northern coastline ten days ago and will dock by the end of this moon."

For the first time the Tehran registered surprise.

As Esslar continued to outline the boundaries of the trap, he sensed the Tehran's increased respect for his adversary.

"I am prepared to wait, as are those who accompany me. We have left nothing to chance. You will find no legal grounds on which to banish us from Endlin. Our business is duly registered with the Equerry, our rent and taxes for the year paid in full. Nor will the document registered with the Equerry be made available to you. My instructions are clear on this point. Upon my death or disappearance, it is to be circulated as I have described."

A tense silence stretched between them. Not even the Tehran of the Kwanlonhon dared oppose the power of the Equerry, the highest rank attainable by a clansman not a Tehran. Elected by clansmen and commoners alike, he ruled the courts, arbitrating and enforcing municipal laws with a rotating force of single-ringed clansmen. Esslar's threat carried additional weight since the current Equerry came from the Synzurit clan, ancient rivals of the Kwanlonhon.

The Tehran's forefinger tapped lightly on the table.

"And if I let him go to Pelion, what if he chooses not to stay? You cannot hold him against his will; as an ernani he may depart the Maze at any time."

"Why would you deny your son this greatest of gifts, a gift for which you yourself undertook the same journey?"

A shadow flew over the Tehran's face.

"My reasons are my own."

The Tehran's mask descended. Esslar continued.

"Then understand what we propose. The contract demands that you surrender your sa'ab so that he may enter the Maze. Once there, it will be his decision to stay or go."

Esslar paused, letting his warning float on the moist, sea-scented air.

"Make no attempt to contact him. He will be protected by his grandmother, who will tolerate no interference."

The Tehran lowered his eyes to the contract.

"Tell the black hag I shall send her my son. I'll summon you when all is prepared."

Without lifting his gaze from the signature scrawled at the bottom of the page, hoarse with barely controlled fury, the Tehran rasped from between frozen lips, "Get out!"

Esslar's conquest yielded no sense of victory. Some things he had learned; others remained hidden behind the inscrutable countenance of the Tehran of the Kwanlonhon. Now he must wait, guarded day and night by Galen's dagger, for the Mother of Pelion judged this to be the most crucial time of her plan, unsure if even the threat of the Equerry would prevent an act of retribution. Esslar remembered his disagreement with her on this point, arguing that Manthur would by necessity agree since he had no other choice.

"Many choices remain," she insisted, her wise old eyes peering out at him from beneath her black veil. "In our ignorance of what he has become lies our greatest peril. We can only hope that our innocence does not cause us to underestimate what his choice might be. In the evil we cannot imagine lies our deadliest foe."

* * *

AS THE SUN commenced its leisurely descent toward its final resting place behind the western hills, the Tehran's guests began to arrive. By the sixth hour the great hall of audience resembled nothing so much as a gathering of tropical birds. Silks of every hue and tint, the quintessence of the dyer's art, clashed and complimented one another, complex patterns and ornate designs forming an ever-changing kaleidoscope of such extraordinary intensity that it made one question what the eye beheld. Marigold met magenta, aquamarine acknowledged apricot, chartreuse saluted saffron, cobalt confronted carnelian in a glorious spectrum of riotous, frenzied, tumultuous color.

Like the winged creatures they resembled, the guests preened and struck elegant poses, arranging their flowing plumage with seemingly casual disregard, yet self-conscious and smugly satisfied with their beauty, for they were undeniably beautiful. From the elders, unstooped and vigorous, their once dark heads turned to silver, grey, or purest white, to the youngest of the sa'abs, plump and sturdy with brilliant black eyes soberly considering a new and remarkable world peopled entirely by adults, the clansmen of Endlin embodied male privilege and physical superiority.

That this was a gathering of the Kwanlonhon rather than the Assad or the H'ulalet could be determined by the dress of the women, each of them attired in the glossy folds of vermilion silk which constitute the formal over-robes of a Kwanlonhon concubine.

The sa'abs among them were distinguished by diverse patterns of gold woven into their scarlet draperies. Always mindful of their rank, these first-born daughters took their place immediately to the right of their fathers, while the concubines lingered a few paces behind, chattering gaily among themselves. Their gaiety sprang from the fact that they had been chosen to attend so important an occasion, and they whispered excitedly behind their hands, the wide sleeves of their robes falling away to reveal plump arms and pumiced elbows, their dusky skin lustrous with expensive oils, their elaborately arranged ropes and tresses of black hair gleaming blue in the horizontal shafts of afternoon light streaming in from the western windows.

Certain high-ranking members of rival clans had been invited, causing Kwanlonhon fathers to eye Effrentati or Synzurit youths as they strutted by, weighing their merits, considering what prestige might result if a formal offer arrived for their daughter. The most eligible of these rival clansmen, easily identified by a single earring, received special attention since they offered that most desirous of advantages, the chance to produce a sa'ab. Celebrations such as this one were vital to the health of the clans since inbreeding was forbidden. There was little doubt that several offers would be made and accepted before the new moon appeared. It was of this that the concubines whispered behind lacquer-tipped fingers (remembering the day when they had left their fathers' houses to become Kwanlonhon), as well as that most recent of events—the long-awaited return of the flagship *Seahorse* and its reputed hoard of treasure.

The buzz and clamor of the crowd rose to an ear-shattering pitch, bouncing off the glazed mosaic tiles whose patterns covered every conceivable surface of the hall. A double row of columns running along the circumference of the grand rotunda supported the central dome where, underneath its lofty canopy, four wide steps led to the raised dais, the ancestral seat of the Kwanlonhon clan.

Long tables arranged along the eastern wall groaned under the weight of the evening's repast. Long fronds of drooping palm held by serious-faced boys of no more than fifteen years, their guardians eyeing them from time to time to ensure that manners remained flawless and behavior exemplary, fanned the delicacies. The menu pronounced the proximity of the sea, offering salty anchovies and cucumbers in yogurt sauce, sardines served with hot mustard, turtle eggs pickled in vinegar, smoked filets of snapper and sea bass sprinkled with paprika and the fresh juice of lemons, plus octopus and squid quick-fried in batter. Stacks of freshly-baked wheels of unleavened bread, trays of ripened fruits, and the sweet desserts so dear to the residents of Endlin—almond paste layered between flaky tiers of pastry and sugary concoctions of dates and nuts baked to a honey brown—tempted the most discriminating of palates. Samovars held reservoirs of the hot black tea that was a staple of life along with porcelain jars of delicately flavored rice wine. Servants ran to and fro, adding last minute garnishes, for no one was so impolite as to partake of food or drink before the appearance of their host.

Unobserved by the guests, a steward directed a stranger to a place by a low door on the far side of the dais. He had donned his best robe of dull green (the color of oak leaves in high summer) in tribute to the importance of the occasion, although amongst this cotillion of egrets he appeared a lowly wren, unmistakably common and easily ignored. Not a single soul acknowledged his presence with so much as the flicker of an eyelash. If he noticed their snubs, he gave no sign that he was bothered and stood observing their ceremonies with interest.

Three blasts of a conch shell brought a sudden hush to the proceedings, and as the prow of a ship parts the waters, the throng split and receded as the Tehran sailed past them. In the wake of his passing strode his brothers, the Princes Rahjid, Shakar, and Tasir. Behind the four sons of Linphat V walked the Tehran's sa'ab.

As the Tehran mounted the dais, his brothers took their places around his chair, Rahjid to his right and Shakar and Tasir (as lesser sons) to his left.

Pelion Preserved

The Tehran's sa'ab lingered below them on the second step, bowed deeply to his father, and after a brief wave of the Tehran's hand, straightened and turned to face the assembly. As he was recognized, a wave of appreciative murmurs approached the shore of the dais, crested, and broke, returning to silence as the Tehran greeted the assembly.

"Welcome, kinsmen and honored guests! We are gathered to celebrate the first voyage of our flagship, the *Seahorse*, returned to us undamaged and on schedule, her cargo enriching us a hundredfold over our initial investment."

Concubines gasped while male heads nodded in silent approbation, the clansmen understanding what the women did not. The success of the *Seahorse* was not just a matter of finances, but a question of honor. Designed, built, rigged, stocked, and piloted by members of the clan, her achievements were a tribute to Kwanlonhon efficiency and skill. It was only right that the Tehran considered this a just cause for celebration so that every clansman's contribution might be acknowledged.

"I have additional cause for celebration since today my sa'ab is returned to me."

Many a sentimental sigh was heaved at the earnestness of this speech, every heart touched by Manthur's pride in his firstborn. Eyes flew between father and son, marking the similarities of their height, the likeness of their features, and the majesty with which they stood — one in the burnished gold reserved for Tehrans, the other in spotless amethyst silk overlaid with gilt. Only the stranger noted that the sa'ab's posture relaxed upon hearing his father's praise while the father's eyes remained cold even as his lips spoke a message of warmth and affection.

"The success of his venture has caused me to make a decision concerning his next duty for the clan. I have no doubt but that he will continue his service on our behalf with the dedication taught him by my excellent brother, Prince Tasir."

This unexpected announcement gave rise to scattered applause and a round of speculative whispers, most of them concerning the long-awaited news that an offer had been made and accepted by a fellow Tehran on behalf of his daughter. As the Tehran waited for them to settle, his sa'ab fingered a piece of polished coral suspended from a slender silver chain. Prince Tasir stood immobile, his eyes seeming to pierce the back of his brother's braided head.

"My sa'ab leaves tomorrow at dawn for points west. There he will study opportunities to expand our trade along the inland routes and consider what goods will best ensure a profitable return. Too long have independent traders robbed us of our profits. It has long been my dream that the Kwanlonhon be the first to negotiate formal trade relations with the west. Soon we will take our rightful place as the leading clan of Endlin, extending our enterprises to the far reaches of the world!"

A full-voiced shout signaling the clan's endorsement greeted the Tehran of the Kwanlonhon.

As the clansmen began to chant his name, Manthur stood with squared shoulders and lifted chin, receiving their homage as was his due. When the chant showed no sign of lessening, he raised bejeweled hands to quiet them.

"Food and drink await, and musicians have been summoned! Rejoice, kinsmen, and continue your good and devoted service to the clan!"

As the festivities erupted, no one but the stranger saw the Tehran's sa'ab clutch the pink jewel from the sea so tightly his knuckles turned white. As the lute player took up his twelve-stringed instrument and began to pluck out the haunting melody of a song dating from ancient days, not a single participant in the revelries observed (as did the stranger) that twin fires ignited in Prince Tasir's deep-set eyes. And only the chief steward, whose position depended on his careful observance of everything to do with the Tehran of the Kwanlonhon, saw his master command his brothers and his sa'ab to accompany him to the low door where the stranger waited.

"I HAVE LITTLE time to spare. I must return to my guests."

Esslar was invited to approach with a careless, almost insolent wave of Manthur's bejeweled hand.

"Sandur, this is Esslar, who guides you to Pelion."

Despite the burning stare of the younger man, Esslar kept his composure. I will give you no cause to hate me, the healer promised silently, sensing the prince's resentment. The Tehran was busy with some notes, refreshing his memory of the many details he had overseen today.

"Your trunks were brought up from the ship this afternoon. Additional items suitable for the journey have been selected and packed. My steward has procured letters of credit as well as a generous amount of coinage, the stable master has selected a dependable mount, and the kitchen staff has been instructed to prepare food appropriate to your tastes. Your apartments have been cleaned and aired . . ."

"Father," the prince interrupted, "who is this stranger?"

A frown gathered between the Tehran's eyebrows.

"This *stranger*, as you so rudely put it, is my guest, which is reason enough for you to treat him with respect." A thought seemed to strike him as he added with a chilly smile, "If you must know, your uncle Tasir brought him to my attention."

Tasir stiffened, worried eyes flying to his nephew.

"He was introduced as a simple bookseller, brother, not as a guide to foreign lands."

"Then you were fooled, brother," the Tehran observed frostily, "for Pelion is his home."

"Pelion?" the young prince repeated, looking to his elders for enlightenment.

Surprisingly, it was Rahjid who answered.

"A city far to the south and west, thought to be a legend. A walled castle in a fertile valley, if the tales be true, where the streets are paved with precious stones and where those who dwell are rumored never to die."

"Hold your tongue," the Tehran replied testily. "As usual, you babble of things beyond your comprehension. What does it matter what Pelion is or is not? It is enough that I say my sa'ab will go there."

"But father, I . . ."

"Enough!" the Tehran thundered.

Esslar braced himself against the gathering storm. The three brothers turned to stone. Out of desperation, the prince found the courage to continue.

"Father, with all respect to you and your guest, I know nothing of this Pelion. Should you send me there without preparation?"

As soon as the question was asked, Esslar guessed the direction of the Tehran's thoughts. In that instant, he acknowledged the Nineteenth Mother's wisdom. Manthur's choice was one they had never considered. He meant to poison his sa'ab against everything to do with Pelion, thus ensuring Sandur's quick return to Endlin. An unwilling witness, Esslar readied himself for disaster.

"Preparation," the Tehran murmured, seeming to consider his son's request. "So be it. I know something of Pelion and its ways. Your first lesson concerns their custom of greeting visitors."

Leaning back in his chair with studied nonchalance, he announced, "You will disrobe."

The prince paled as his uncles exchanged horrified glances. When no motion was made to obey him, the Tehran dropped all pretense of pleasantness.

"You will disrobe!! Have I ever denied my sa'ab anything he desires?"

Wincing under the lash of Manthur's tongue, Tasir broke in, trying to placate a brother who had lost his reason.

"Brother, think what you ask of him! This is not our way!"

"Nor is it our way that a Tehran's order be ignored," Manthur observed, "or that an uncle interferes with a father's relationship with his sa'ab. Too long have you spoiled him, brother. Now you will stand silent while he executes my command."

Like a swimmer underwater, the prince moved to obey. With fumbling fingers he untied the embroidered sash, freeing his robes to hang loosely about him. The first layer of amethyst was placed neatly across the lounge, to be followed with those of emerald, topaz, and vermilion. Next, his fingers worked at the knot of the leisure robe. Raising his eyes to his father, he begged wordlessly that he not be asked to continue, meeting a merciless stare offering no reprieve.

The white silk was laid next to its discarded mates. Gathering the hem of the tunic, he took an audible breath before lifting it over his head. At the first glimpse of bare flesh, all three uncles lowered their eyes resolutely to the floor, refusing to break the taboo against witnessing another clansman's nakedness. The pink coral swung against the prince's chest as he untied the breeches and pulled them off, standing in the narrow challah with his fists clenched at his sides.

Helpless to interfere lest that interference bring about even worse reprisals to be suffered by the hapless prince, Esslar closed his eyes, wishing he could close his ears to what followed.

"Continue," came the Tehran's implacable command.

His son pleaded in a low voice, "Father, do not ask this of me."

An icy silence filled the confines of the Tehran's private study and lingered there awhile.

"You will look upon my sa'ab, bookseller, and judge his worthiness to enter Pelion."

Esslar opened his eyes on the son who stood naked in front of the father. He had seen many bodies in his time as a healer, touched them and treated them, soothing away aches and pains, probing and palpitating organs and muscles. Always he had marveled at the human body's precision of form and complexity of function. This body was that of a man full-grown, clean-limbed, smooth-skinned, broad of shoulder and slim of hip. The coral swung gently against his chest, a pendulum measuring out the sentence of the prince's humiliation. Face, neck, and forearms were darkened by constant exposure to sun and wind; the rest was the color of seasoned teak. Tight dark curls covered his chest, running in a straight line down his belly to surround his genitals. As was the custom among clansmen, he was uncircumcised. His height came from the length of his legs rather than from his torso. The muscles of his thighs and calves were highly-defined yet elongated—the legs of a swimmer, Esslar decided. And then, because he feared that not to do so might be considered the direst of insults, Esslar looked directly into the prince's face.

The resemblance to his father was uncanny, almost a mirror image except for a slight reddish cast to the thick hair which grew straight back from a heavy brow, the intricately woven braids falling well below his shoulders. The almond-shaped eyes, too, were his father's, more brown than black, perhaps, but equally commanding as they stared back unblinkingly at Esslar. The nose was slightly flattened, the nostrils arched and flaring, the chin held at an arrogant angle, suggesting that he surveyed the world around him with considerable disdain. As was the fashion, he was clean-shaven, the skin over his cheekbones and jaw pulled tight and seamless. It was a stern face, schooled to immobility, all planes and angles with no trace of a curve. The mouth might have been generous if his lips had not been folded together into thin lines of what must have been disapproval.

Esslar thought to find more than disapproval, expecting nothing less than hatred for what his presence had brought about. Hatred would have been preferable to the prince's stare as he gazed with haughty indifference at the stranger responsible for his disgrace, refusing Esslar any insights, indeed, preferring to disavow Esslar's presence in the room.

"He is as you promised—unblemished and obedient," said Esslar with a respectful bow.

"Then take your leave. Be outside the front gates at dawn."

As Esslar departed the Tehran's private office, pushing his way past clansmen and concubines, his ears burned with the chatterings and prattlings of that mindless crew.

"Ah, what love he shows for his sa'ab!"

"The prince is his luck, after all!"

"How graciously he honors him!"

"What good fortune is Sandur's, to be born to such a father!"

Sick and saddened, Esslar increased his pace, suddenly frantic to escape the citadel of the Kwanlonhon and its cloying, fractious beauty. Love, luck, honor—what did they know of such things? Their idea of love was a child reared by a hired servant in a supposedly protective but ultimately stifling environment, their luck an excuse to barter away their daughters and sons without a thought for their happiness, their honor measured by riches amassed due to learning denied anyone not born a clansman.

It was as she had told him, a city built on sand, fortified by a dedicated and uniform masculinity: collective, conventional, and profoundly enclosed. In its pursuit of obedience and duty, it denied its residents the essence of human potential: independence, diversity, and creative thought. Esslar's flight from the citadel took him down the steep winding road that led toward the heart of the city. From his elevated view of the harbor the flat grey sea shone like a pewter plate glazed by twilight. Elated that the long-awaited journey approached, he sent his thoughts racing forward to the coming dawn.

As the Nineteenth Mother predicted, Esslar's innocence proved his downfall, for in his sudden burst of excitement at what he had accomplished, this gentlest of healers forgot those who, unlike himself, could not so easily escape the sickness which grows like a chancre on the souls of the dispossessed.

* * *

SANDUR HAD NO feelings left. He had passed through them all: disbelief, outrage, injury, and shame. Worst of all was the sure and certain knowledge that his father despised him. This day had taught him that his life was to be a series of journeys devised to keep him far from the citadel. It was this knowledge that drove him now, forcing out a politely-phrased question from between rebellious lips as he retied his challah.

"May I ask, father, if you intend to let me wear the second ring?"

"It would be inappropriate to discuss that now. I must attend my guests."

As the Tehran rose from his chair, a growl rumbled deep in his youngest brother's chest.

"Answer him, Manthur."

If the Tehran was surprised by Tasir's interference, he gave no indication of it, but resumed his chair and looked up thoughtfully at his son.

"We have had this discussion before, I recall, and each time we have been unable to agree on the suitability of the woman. Have you someone to propose?"

Sandur tried not to stammer as he made haste to reply.

"There is a woman of the Onozzi clan, father, Vavashi, the sa'ab of Tehran Yodhat Onozzi. We have met and she indicated her interest. If an offer is made, her father will surely accept."

Sandur waited, silently willing his father to approve, confident of his ability to endure yet another journey if, after his homecoming, he could attend the bringing-in of his first concubine. Unexpectedly, Shakar uttered his first words of the evening.

"I . . . I am grieved to hear of this, nephew. Had I known I would never have . . ."

Still not lifting his eyes from the floor, Shakar's face darkened with what might have been rage or shame. Before he could continue, the Tehran interrupted with an icy observation.

"Your uncle blushes, as well he should. It seems his gambling debts have already cost him more than his yearly allowance, and it was necessary to acquire additional funds. To this end, he's accepted yet another concubine into his household, a commoner," the scorn in Manthur's voice was lethal, "the daughter of a tea merchant, I believe. An additional contract was signed a few days ago for Vavashi, sa'ab of Yodhat Onozzi."

His most cherished dream fading around him, Sandur looked into the void. He had thought to find meaning in the duties of a sa'ab; now he saw them for the punishments they were. Despite his efforts, he was judged as wanting, exhibited like a piece of horseflesh and banished to a distant land.

"Since my presence displeases you, father, might I refuse this journey and request instead that you allow me to return to sea?"

"Refuse?" the Tehran repeated, as if unfamiliar with the word. With comprehension came a sudden fit of rage. Leaping to his feet, he shoved back the chair and approached his son, his face less than a handbreadth away. The hair on the back of Sandur's neck rose as he witnessed the malice contained in those flashing black eyes.

"You forget yourself, sa'ab!" Spittle sprayed Sandur's face, making the last word a curse. "I have just given my word to the entire clan that you will go, and go you shall even if I must tie you to the horse myself! You will obey because you have no choice but to obey! Perhaps your days at sea have brought on a loss of memory. It is time for it to be refreshed!"

Striding to the map, he grabbed up a bamboo rod from the canister, then hit it sharply against the table, wood cracking against wood as the end of the rod split. Turning to Tasir, he proffered the instrument of discipline.

"I blame you for this, brother, for assuredly his training leaves much to be desired. You will give him twenty cuts."

Tasir crossed his arms across his chest.

"I'll not shame him, Manthur."

A stunned look crossed the face of the Tehran to be replaced with one of cunning.

"If you do not perform this task for me, the righteous request of a father whose disobedient child must be disciplined according to our laws, I will have my steward summon one of the common guards. Would you prefer a public flogging," he taunted, "that announces to every resident of the citadel the failings of the sa'ab you yourself prepared for manhood?"

Their eyes locked.

Ever so slowly, as if his hand moved against his will, Tasir accepted the rod.

"Ready yourself, nephew."

Sandur studied the rod held in his uncle's firm grasp. Too sick at heart to trust his voice, he knelt on the rug. As he drew aside the heavy mass of braids to the side of his neck, Rahjid and Shakar turned their backs, a formal announcement of their refusal to condone so harsh a punishment. Their courtesy in performing this simple act of charity almost made him weep. Bending over to rest his weight on his forearms, Sandur placed a fist in his mouth to prevent himself from crying out.

Many times Tasir's belt had bitten into his back during the days of his training, yet never once had his uncle hit him in anger. Punishment was the duty of all uncles who accepted the guardianship of their nephews, since law forbade a father to raise his hand against his children. It was Tasir's custom to postpone a beating until his hand and eye were steady, at which time he would explain exactly why and how the punishment would proceed. Never had he left a lasting mark on the smooth skin of his nephew's body.

The first blow caught Sandur squarely between the shoulder blades. He had readied himself for pain, half-expecting the bite of leather, but nearly screamed as his flesh was split open by the razor-sharp edges of the split bamboo. As a warm trickle of blood ran down his back he bit hard into his fist, trying to control the shudders passing over him in waves. As his uncle worked the rod with a steady beat, Sandur became his drum, his body vibrating with each stroke. Soon he lost count, nothing penetrating his mind except the whistle of the rod as it sliced through the air and the awful force of its impact against his back and shoulders. In time he passed into a kind of stupor, hearing himself moan as each blow landed. Only the pain was real, that, and the blood dripping down his lacerated back and onto his ribs and flanks. He was not kneeling anymore, the agony of the beating driving him down to the floor where he lay with his head buried in his arms, tears of pain leaking out of the corners of his eyes. At last there were no more blows, only the sound of his ragged breathing and finally, his father's voice.

"Cover yourself."

Understanding came slowly. Struggling to his knees, his arms shook as he tried to rise, bringing on another wave of searing pain. Crouched on the blood-spattered rug, he shuddered helplessly, all the time horribly aware of his nakedness. Sandals appeared at his right and left and two sets of hands lifted him to his feet. Shakar and Rahjid dressed him as if he were a child, the elder man muttering under his breath as he knotted the draw-strings of his breeches.

"Lift your arms."

Sandur bit his lips against the agony of movement. A muffled groan escaped him as the tunic was pulled down over his head, the fabric rubbing against the open wounds. The robes followed, layer upon layer of pristine silk concealing bleeding flesh. As Rahjid bent to tie the embroidered sash around his waist, tears trickled down his withered cheeks.

"My brothers will accompany me to the hall. You are excused from attending the festivities. If you need anything to further prepare yourself for your travels, summon a steward. A servant has been instructed to wake you before dawn."

The golden robes disappeared behind the low door.

Rahjid and Shakar murmured words of farewell, and they too were gone.

Through the haze enveloping him, Sandur heard a sharp crack as Tasir broke the rod over his knee and hurled the pieces to the floor.

"Forgive me."

Sandur nodded his head, unable to reply.

"Shall I summon an apothecary?"

Sandur shook his head, as unwilling as his uncle to risk gossip generated by a loose tongue.

"I didn't know about the contract with Vavashi. I should have spoken to your father earlier."

Again, Sandur shook his head, sure it would have made no difference. Suddenly he swayed, to be caught by his uncle's hands on his upper arms, holding him firmly upright.

"Listen to me, nephew."

The fog around him parted as Sandur observed Tasir's ravaged face.

"You have no choice, as I had none. Go west with this foreigner and try to forget. Send me word when you arrive. And know this," Tasir said, his voice rough with tenderness, "the greatest failure of my life is that I love thee more than my own children."

A crooked smile rose to Sandur's lips.

"You are not at fault, uncle."

"Nor art thou, nephew."

"But still I am unworthy."

His uncle's mouth opened as if to speak. No words were forthcoming. Sandur had thought it impossible for his misery to increase, but his uncle's silence spoke volumes. Never could he reclaim the honor he had lost today.

Tasir released his hold gradually until he was convinced Sandur could stand unaided. With a quick nod of farewell, he ducked under the low door, pulling it shut behind him.

Sandur risked a few steps, testing his legs. Finding that they supported him, he staggered over to the map tacked on the wall. Leaning his cheek against the stiff cloth, with his forefinger he traced the coastline he knew better than the streets of the city, fingering each island and reef, each inlet and cove, finally coming to rest on the sand hills west of Endlin. For the first time in his life, he considered what lay in the direction of the setting sun. Most of the map was unmarked, huge blank spaces on which a hand had lettered names empty of meaning.

A vast expanse to the north was labeled "Land of the Lapith." He felt a tug of regret that he must travel south rather than north. In the harem, one of his ayahs told stories of winged horses who flew above the northern plains. He had loved her tales as a child since she was easily the best storyteller in the harem. She had been dismissed not long after, as all his ayahs had been dismissed, none of them living up to the rigid standard of perfection demanded by his father. It had been the same way with his friends. Too late he learned not to mention their names in his father's presence. Now he lived without friends; tomorrow he would begin to live without family.

His back throbbed as he stumbled toward the door. It will be a short night, he reminded himself dully, and you must sleep. His stomach was empty, for he had eaten nothing all day. The effort of finding a steward and ordering food brought to his apartments was more than he could perform. Summoning what little strength was left him, he departed his father's chamber.

* * *

THE CELEBRATION HAD spread from the hall of audience to several of the adjoining public rooms, including one of the leafy plazas open to the starry night skies. Torches blazed, attracting hordes of insects who contributed their buzzes, whirs, and hums to the conversation and laughter of the guests. A drummer of some repute had replaced the lute-player, his palms dancing over the drum pressed between his thighs, adding its pulsing descant to the night sounds of the citadel. One solitary figure picked his way gingerly through the groups of three or four, shaking his head at requests that he join them. A few found him even more remote than usual, only to be reminded that the Tehran's sa'ab had never been given to gossip or gambling, the only two recreational pursuits (other than luxury) that made life in the citadel worth living.

Pischak, who counted himself Prince Sandur's oldest friend, called after him, received a brief nod of recognition and an even briefer refusal to an invitation that he share a glass of wine. Much later that night, as his concubines undressed him and helped him find the bed, Pischak would recall that Sandur was paler than usual and a trifle unsteady on his feet, but dismissed it as the result of imbibing too large a quantity of rice wine.

Prince Sandur was also remembered that night by Tasir's youngest concubine. Finding her way to his apartments, she scratched softly at his door. When the handsome sa'ab failed to appear, she slipped away on bare feet to sob out her loneliness in her pillow. The sixth child of a H'ulalet trader second-class, she knew her father could never offer a large enough dowry to attract a high-ranking clansman. Prince Tasir's offer was an act of pure kindness, a tribute to an ailing father who died less than a moon after her bringing-in. As her tears wet her pillow, slipping down a cheek softer than swan's-down, she fell asleep believing herself to be the most miserable member of the Kwanlonhon clan.

She would never know that the Tehran's sa'ab heard her timid scratch as he lay in the darkness and breathed a relieved sigh when he heard her receding footsteps on the tiles.

With a bitterness that almost canceled out the pain that left him sleepless, Sandur considered that this youngest concubine of his uncle (for he recognized her perfume and remembered how she had stroked his brow) would have shrieked at the sight of these marks of shame he would wear forever on his back.

As he closed his eyes, desperate for sleep, a familiar voice rose out of the darkness, a voice he had heard since earliest childhood, yet a presence to which he could put no name or face. She came to him as she always did, as fresh and vibrant as the eastern breeze seaman prefer above all others, full of warmth and promises of the glories life held in store for him. She told him stories, sang him songs, and whispered secrets he could never remember upon waking. And always, always, she pledged her love for him. Her visits confused him upon awakening, and he often puzzled over their meaning.

Even so, tonight he welcomed her. The pain lessened, and in the next moment he was floating in a tidal pool, the water sun-warmed and fragrant as it washed away blood and fatigue. As his thoughts sank under the surface, he surrendered himself to dreams, hearing the steady beating of a heart. Soon he knew only her and her secrets, and was rocked to sleep on the sweet waters of repose.

THE CITADEL OF of the Kwanlonhon slept while the night breezes rippled the waves and black tides broke against limestone cliffs.

The city by the sea slept as well, with the exception of a tiny shop where a light burned deep into the night. A burly man with white hair and beard snored on a narrow cot, a hand flung up over his head in close proximity to the dagger hidden under his pillow.

The shop's other resident sat by an oil lamp, his elbows resting on the table, his head buried in his hands, his meditations broken by a mind-shattering scream careening up and out of the depths of the citadel, then quavering in the night air above the city, a wail of self-loathing and despair, infinite regret and undying devotion.

For in his prison-house of memory, which acknowledged no passage of time, the Tehran of the Kwanlonhon mourned the loss of his Aethra and raged against the coming of yet another futile dawn.

Chapter 6

The Gauntlet

TO EYES ACCUSTOMED to the repetitive motion of waves, the sand hills west of Endlin seem a continuation of the sea, a series of mounds rolling smoothly toward infinity, many-layered and shrouded in a beige haze of indolent stillness and suffocating heat. Given the poorness of the alkaline soil and erosion in the rainy season, the hills themselves were unsuitable for farming and barely fit for grazing. It was a mist-tinged landscape, colors bleached of energy, pastels of muted greens, pale yellows, and creamy tans better suited to a water-colorist's brush than to the task of supporting human life. Between the mounds, in sheltered valleys humid and lush with vegetation, could be found the sparsely scattered populace of the sand hills, who avoided the ancient road winding serpent-like around the knolls and through the dells, for they are, and have always been, suspicious of the stranger's ways.

At the summit of one of the highest mounds, a bay gelding cropped occasional patches of grass, grazing lazily under slack reins that let him wander as he chose. A swarm of gnats settled around horse and rider, drawn by the moisture of their sweat, to be lashed by a coarse black tail. With a disgruntled oath, Galen slapped them away. Picking up the reins, he nudged the bay forward with a booted heel.

"No rest for the likes of us. Gee up, lad. Time to be gettin' on."

Black-tipped ears flicking back to listen to the rider's burred speech, the bay shook his head in silent agreement and settled into an easy walk.

Galen had thought to escape the heat hovering over the valley road. Lured by the prospect of an open sky and the promise of coolness in higher altitudes, horse and rider climbed steadily, only to find a fiercely unforgiving sun, an orange stone glowing in the surrounding haze, beating down unmercifully on hills and valleys alike. He checked their progress, marking the route they'd take tomorrow, his blouse soaked through with perspiration, his eyes smarting from the sweat dripping down his forehead. Wiping it away with a large square of serviceable cotton suitable for a bandage, blindfold, or gag, he gave the sure-footed gelding his head, letting him pick his own way down the slope.

He left his companions at midday, figuring they'd eat and take a short rest in the hottest hours before continuing on, reaching this point about three hours into their journey. He half-expected to meet them where the bottom of the hill met the valley road. Clucking to the horse, he worked the path forward and back, checking for tracks in the sandy loam, finding nothing but the shod hooves of the bay.

Pulling up, he eased himself in the saddle and considered his options: either to backtrack in order to check on Esslar's progress by re-tracing the path he'd traveled earlier in the afternoon, or ride on toward the watering place he'd spied from up above, a likely camp for the night. Grumbling a bit, he found himself remembering the instructions that sent him off on his present course.

"*Possess yourself with patience! I know you fret that our progress is slow, but it cannot be helped. Leave us now and find a place to rest tonight. And Galen,*" the healer's thoughts prodded him, not unkindly, "*we'll need running water and ample shade.*"

With a decisive grunt, the rider reined the horse around and kicked him into a trot. As the pair moved off toward the west, Galen's thoughts raced backward, remembering both the cause of their delay and the reason this night's camp must by necessity include a source of spring-fed water.

The Tehran's sa'ab proved to be exactly as Galen expected, nay, dreaded — a perfect match to the arrogant dandies who roamed the market district, looking down their pierced noses at the common folk and expecting by right of birth the fawning attention of merchants who hung on their every word. Although this prince might be dressed more soberly than most (for he'd put aside the gaudy robes and jewelry and donned more sensible traveling gear), he was as unfriendly and unapproachable as any clansman Galen had ever met. Since leaving the grounds of the citadel, he had spoken perhaps ten words to either of his companions.

His mount was magnificent, a blooded grey stallion dappled with silver, as high-strung as his rider and flashy to boot. Clearly, the prince knew how to sit a horse, although neither horse nor riding ability explained his first directive, issued as they approached the western-most borders of the city. Chin up, jaw set, he announced his intention to take up a position at the rear of the party, commanding that the pace be set at a sedate walk. Convinced he was being tested, Galen called the prince's bluff, letting it be known in no uncertain terms that he, and he alone, would determine the speed of this tiny caravan. For the first time, and assuredly not the last, Galen felt the considerable weight of his lordship's displeasure.

"If you have objections, let us part now."

Esslar provided the translation, moving easily between the two languages, offering not the remotest hint as to how Galen should respond. Even though the healer was sticking to the plan they'd forged long ago, his refusal to take sides left Galen feeling unaccountably abandoned and distinctly annoyed.

"All right, lad, we'll give it a try. But mind ye keep up! I'll not be comin' back to find ye if ye lose yer way or that fancy horse of yers pulls up lame."

His warning met with a hostile nod, from that moment onward it was war.

His lordship would eat nothing out of the common provisions, nor did he eat anything at all as far as Galen could see. At rest stops he disappeared into the dense foliage lining the road, returning when Galen shouted for him, mounting his stallion and taking up his position at the rear. When they made camp at dusk by a stand of acacias, he immediately disobeyed Galen's orders that he arrange his sleeping robes near the campfire and carried his gear to a site as far removed from them as possible. When Esslar translated Galen's request that everyone help with the preparation of the evening meal, the Tehran's sa'ab didn't even bother to argue, but gave a terse shake of his braided head and headed off in the direction of the brook. To Galen's complaints Esslar made no response, going about his tasks with his usual efficiency, unpacking the foodstuffs for the meal.

"Let him be," he advised silently, and Galen held his tongue.

The second day began poorly, the prince sore from a full day astride a horse after a half-year at sea and ashen-faced as he mounted the grey. At the first rest stop he vanished again, forcing Galen to call for him repeatedly before he reappeared.

That afternoon the weather turned beastly hot; the horses lathered after a single hour on the road, while the prince lagged further and further behind, his figure shrouded by waves of heat radiating off the sandy soil and clouds of dust swirling around the horses' hooves. Tired of looking back over his shoulder, Galen called a halt a few hours after midday and dismounted, his patience at an end. When the prince pulled up beside him, he let loose a volley of ear-burning abuse, every word dutifully translated by Esslar.

The Tehran's sa'ab listened, then, without uttering a word, dismounted stiffly and stalked away, shoving a path through the tangled vines and creepers growing along the roadside.

Galen made to follow him, but was held back by a restraining hand.

"Come, Galen, let's stop for the day. The horses could use a rest, and for once I'll have time to write in my journal."

"We've three hours of daylight left!"

"He needs time alone," the healer replied, looking off in the direction the prince took, then smiled at Galen, the sand gathering in the fine wrinkles under his eyes, "and you, my friend, must regain your peace of mind."

Knowing when he was beaten, Galen shrugged. Both men made camp, Esslar gathering twigs and branches for the evening fire and Galen taking up his accustomed duties with the horses. After unpacking the gear, he removed saddles and bridles, gave them each a brisk rub-down and tied on the hobbles that would prevent them from straying too far, leaving them to graze in the tall grasses. Esslar spread his sleeping robes under a cypress tree and settled down to bring his journal entries up to date. Galen decided he could benefit from a little privacy of his own. Setting off in the direction the prince had gone, he chose a shady spot under a cassia tree.

Soon he was nodding, the drone of insects and the sweltering heat making him dream of crisp autumns and snow crunching underfoot. His thoughts were far away from this land of perpetual summer when his ears caught the sound of something moving off to his left. Dismissing it as proof that his lordship, too, was settling down for an afternoon nap, Galen was almost asleep when he heard a noise not so easily dismissed.

It came from the direction of the stream, sounds that were low-pitched, muted, and distinctly human. Galen made his way on his belly, crawling through the thick undergrowth, somehow sure that he must not alert his quarry. Freezing as something purple flashed in front of his eyes, he lowered himself behind a bed of ferns, trusting their fronds to provide good cover.

An article of clothing adorned a kalmia bush a few yards in front of him, a sodden mass of purple fabric spread over the shrub's waxy foliage dripping water over a profusion of star-shaped flowers. Beneath the bush lay a pair of sturdy riding boots, a pair of stockings strewn haphazardly a few feet away. A leather belt with knife sheath and money purse still attached, as well as an expensive silver chain, lay discarded nearby, their positions suggesting that they were tossed aside in the wearer's haste to reach the stream. As someone whose life often depended on observing other people's habits, it struck Galen as odd that the fastidious prince hadn't taken the time to stuff his stockings into his boots and odder still that he would leave his purse and jewelry in plain sight. His curiosity aroused, he turned his attention to the beach.

Pushing away a frond blocking his view, he located Sandur, who knelt at the edge of the sluggish stream, rubbing what looked to be another piece of cloth against the sandy bottom and then rinsing it, inspecting it from time to time before repeating the procedure, his braids shielding his face from Galen's view. Stripped to the waist with the band around his breeches darkened by the rivulets of sweat running freely down his chest, he seemed younger and more vulnerable, a man rather than a prince, and a tired man at that.

Seemingly satisfied with the results of his scrubbing, he struggled to rise, grabbing at an overhanging branch with his free hand to haul himself to his feet. Having regained his balance, he let out his breath and closed his eyes, swaying slightly as though overcome with dizziness. Wiping his hand over his brow, he seemed to revive, then turned away to spread the cloth over another kalmia bush.

There, in the crusted welts across his back and shoulders, dried blood smeared over his ribs and fresh blood seeping from half-formed scabs, was writ the parting gift of the Tehran. Here was the reason for the continual delays, the unexplained disappearances, the lack of appetite, and the preference for solitude at all times and in all places. No longer did Galen need to puzzle over heavy, dark-colored clothing worn in such unbearable heat. Nor were the muted sounds of misery a mystery. This was the Tehran's sa'ab's daily ritual, to bite back groans as he pulled away the garments adhered to his flesh by a mixture of blood and sweat, then wash away the tell-tale traces of gore, all in the hope that his companions would not discover he had been scourged.

Returning to the stream, slump-shouldered with weariness, the prince waded slowly toward the center and knelt, the brackish water barely covering the top of his thighs. Cupping his palms, he lifted them to his shoulders, seeming to brace himself before releasing the water to trickle down his back. Each time he lifted his arms the motion elicited a soft moan, a visible tremor running through him as the water coursed down his lacerated flesh.

Galen retreated the way he came.

Esslar looked up at his approach. Closing the journal as Galen plopped down beside him, Esslar endured Galen's accusing stare until the older man could keep silent no longer.

"Why didn't ye tell me?"

"Tell you what?"

"That they beat him half-senseless once ye took yer leave."

Esslar set aside the journal.

"How bad is it?"

"Bad enough," Galen growled. A thought struck him. "Are ye tellin' me ye had no knowledge of it? And all this time I thought ye were readin' him! That's the plan, isn't it? I keep my distance while ye figure out how best to reach him?"

He might have been talking to a stone since Esslar gave no indication he was listening. When Galen paused for breath, Esslar spoke up, that faraway look in his eyes again.

"I know he's in pain; there's little else in his mind. Even so, I've kept away from his memories. She thought I should know him better before I rush blindly into the unknown. So, to answer your question, I didn't tell you because I thought it best if you treated him as you would if he'd not been injured."

Galen chewed on it a while, testing the logic and finding it sound. When a hand touched his forearm he started, then looked deep into Esslar's eyes.

"Show me."

With the ease of a practiced adept, Galen took Esslar to the stream, reliving the memory in vivid detail, feeling Esslar's inner wince as he viewed the bruised and swollen flesh oozing pus and blood. Esslar broke the connection, sitting silently in the afternoon haze, his mood bleak.

"It grows worse and worse. He's already been shamed in my presence; if we reveal we know about his condition, he'll wonder how we come to know, and if we offer unwanted assistance, we'll strip away the last remnant of his pride."

"Pride be damned!" Galen bellowed. "Yer a healer, man! How can ye let him go another hour without easin' his hurts? Can ye imagine the agony of sittin' a horse, let alone the sting of sweat in open wounds?"

"I don't need to imagine it."

At that mild rejoinder, Galen was instantly humbled. A healer was trained to experience a patient's pain. It was madness to imagine Esslar building a barrier to shield himself from his patient's suffering.

"Ye have my apology."

"You gave me no offense."

A cicada began its whir. They sat quietly, listening to the sounds of summer, jointly considering this mission for which they'd both volunteered. For the past four months they'd learned each other's methods of reasoning and judgment, forging the bonds of trust necessary for bringing what might be the last class of ernani to Pelion. And so they sat side by side, near a deserted road two day's ride west of the eastern sea, wondering how best to bring the Tehran's sa'ab to Pelion.

"He's woeful proud," Galen mused aloud, "and we've only a few days of easy ridin' left us. Once into the foothills we'll start climbin', and if the tales be true, it's a rough passage up to Robber's Pass. We've a need for clear heads, keen eyes, good spirits and stayin' power. She used to laugh, teasin' me about my age, jestin' that the young might have to carry the old. Instead, I've got an invalid on my hands."

"He can't last much longer. He's taken no nourishment, and the wounds are festering. Soon he'll become feverish."

"It's likely Manthur planned it from the start. Shame the lad, then beat him senseless. What a world!"

Galen wagged his head, scratching his beard as he always did when puzzling over the vicissitudes of life lived outside Pelion.

"We've one thing in our favor, I suppose. The taboo of modesty has already been broken; perhaps it won't be so difficult a second time. If only Manthur had named me healer . . ."

"Then ye'll say naught?"

"No," Esslar sighed, "and you must continue as before."

Galen nodded, not relishing his role but understanding its purpose. Esslar continued.

"It need only be a small step, but he must come to me of his own volition. His dignity is all that's left him. I'll not be the one to strip it from him."

Galen heard the resolve and chanced a question, even though it trespassed on territory not his own. It was never part of the plan that he enter the prince's thoughts, or even that the lad come to like him. Galen's mission was to escort a group of ernani to Pelion by the end of the tenth moon. Yet at the same time, he understood that this prince was much more than the Nineteenth Mother's grandson.

"Why did Manthur do it? Why would a man torture his own child?"

The healer seemed to retreat into himself. Galen had almost decided that there was to be no answer to his question when Esslar began to tell a story.

"Once a man took a pup to raise. He was a poor man, living by the sweat of his brow, and he needed a dog to protect his flocks. He was a harsh man and taught the pup his duties with many a cruel blow. Yet still the dog loved his master, for he knew nothing else. He and the dog lived together for many years, through drought and famine, working side by side, the man always unkind and the dog always affectionate."

"One night a wolf attacked a lamb, carrying it away to devour it. The man punished the dog the next morning, cursing and kicking him, for to his mind the dog had failed in his duties. That night the wolf came again. This time the dog killed the wolf in a great battle that left the dog badly injured. The man, overcome with joy, reached down to pet the dog for the very first time. When he did so, the dog leapt at him and ripped out his throat."

The story told, Esslar opened his journal and lifted his pen.

"I dinna understand," Galen grumbled, irked by Esslar's fondness for riddles.

The healer regarded him affectionately.

"The only thing to understand is that the story must be rewritten."

"I THOUGHT YOU might like some tea."

The prince considered an outstretched hand holding a tin cup from which a spiral of fragrant steam arose. A storm front from the northwest moved over them in late afternoon. Although no rain fell, the air cooled. For the first time since leaving Endlin, a fire was necessary for warmth as well as protection from night-roaming creatures.

"It's a special brew of my own making,"

It was a long day, but a good one, and Esslar's hopes were high. Once Galen left to scout a location for tonight's camp, Sandur's tension eased. He'd purposely slowed the pace, stopping several times along the road so Sandur might wander as he willed, writing in his journal until he reappeared. The prince seemed to relax his wariness and dozed in the saddle, allowing Esslar a respite in which to consider how best to proceed.

The camp was ideal, a half-league or so off the main road in a low dell near a clear-running stream meandering under mossy branches—a private place in which to treat a patient whose brow was beaded with perspiration despite the coolness of the gathering dusk.

By the time they arrived, Galen had caught and gutted a good-sized trout and was broiling it over coals. Esslar gathered dandelions and wild leeks while Galen cared for the horses, both men avoiding the stream and tending strictly to business. When Sandur returned, shivering in his damp clothes, he surprised them both by accepting a small portion of fish and swallowing a few mouthfuls before wrapping himself in a blanket and making his customary retreat. As always, he chose a spot removed from their own sleeping places and rested with his head propped on his saddle, his eyelids half-closed.

Rolling slowly over onto his left side, lips stretched in a grimace, he reached out a hand to take the cup.

Receiving no thanks, a discouraged Esslar rose to go.

"It . . . it's good."

Esslar smiled into the night air.

"It will help you sleep."

Black eyebrows drew close together.

"Why should I need help in sleeping?"

"Because you are feverish and have slept poorly these past two nights."

Like a horse that shies at a piece of flapping cloth, the prince reared back his head.

"How do you know this?" the prince demanded.

"I'm a healer."

His announcement met with a suspicious glare, Esslar shrugged and turned away, only to be called back again.

"And . . . and what exactly is a 'healer'? Are you some sort of apothecary? Lancing boils, applying leeches, pulling teeth?"

The first step was taken, for these were more words than the prince had strung together in three days. Esslar lowered himself to the ground and sat cross-legged, noting that his patient was shivering now, his body trembling with chills.

"A healer sets broken bones, stitches wounds, assists in childbirth, and treats all manner of diseases. I'm also trained to prepare medicines against pain and infection."

"Why, then, did you become a bookseller?"

It wasn't the question Esslar anticipated, although he answered it as honestly as he could.

"There came a time when I could no longer practice my craft. I became unhappy, melancholy . . .," he chose his words with care, aware that the prince was scrutinizing him closely, alert to the slightest hint of falsehood,". . . a kind of sickness of the soul. A friend helped me understand my calling, and I began work of another kind."

Everything he could say he had said. Apparently satisfied by his answer, Sandur took another sip of tea, warming his palms against the cup.

"How would you cure a fever?"

Esslar took his time, conscious of the fragility of the moment.

"It's not a question of curing the fever itself. The tea I prepared has the power to lessen fever and ward off chills. But fevers return unless their cause can be discovered and treated."

The prince took another sip.

"And how would you make such a discovery?"

"It would be necessary to examine the patient."

"To touch him?" the prince inquired, a single brow lifted over a calculating eye.

"I know of no other way," Esslar replied, troubled by the direction the conversation was taking.

"And there is no other reason you might wish to touch a patient? No other reason you might watch him as he slept?"

"None that I know of."

In a muted voice that not even Galen's sharp ears could have heard, the prince asked with absolute frankness, "Do you mean to share my sleeping robes?"

Aware that his shock must be readily apparent, Esslar made no effort to conceal anything, but blurted out the first words that came to mind.

"Why do you ask?"

The prince shrugged, unembarrassed, seemingly amused.

"It's a common thing among those denied the second ring. So it is among seamen on a long voyage."

"Is it a common thing with you?"

A crooked smile appeared on the prince's lips.

"It is not."

"Nor is it with me."

A brooding silence grew between them as the prince searched his face with doubtful eyes.

"Yet you have looked upon my nakedness, watched me as I slept, and without my asking, brewed medicines for me."

"I'm a healer," Esslar repeated helplessly, beginning to realize the enormous chasm separating their cultures. He had memorized Kazur's journals, read everything Symone could locate in the Greater Library concerning the customs and traditions of Endlin, and had lived among the commoners of the Abalone district. But commoners are not clansmen, he reminded himself sharply. As a prince reared among princes, Sandur was a highly educated aristocrat, well-traveled, urbane, a man of the world in every sense of the phrase. To one such as Sandur, Esslar and Galen must seem a pair of rustic clowns. There's much to learn here, Esslar thought, and much to be taught.

The prince shifted position, clearly uncomfortable. Dark circles under his eyes and sunken flesh around his nose and mouth made him appear older than his actual age. After another sip of tea, he announced:

"I give you leave to examine me with these provisions: the other one must keep away, and on no account will you touch my hair."

Some time later, when Sandur lay in a drugged sleep, Esslar would reflect on this first of many conversations and admire how neatly the prince turned the tables. Swiftly gaining the upper hand, he hadn't begged for Esslar's help so much as granted a stranger the privilege of treating him. It was a lesson in statecraft Esslar would never forget and one worthy of Sandur's maternal grandmother, ample warning that this prince was assuredly no fool.

At the current moment, listening as the prince outlined his requirements, Esslar realized he must refuse to enter into this exchange as anything less than the prince's equal. If he was to break down the system of hierarchies by which Sandur was raised, he must begin now or forever be thought of as an underling.

"I have my own conditions which you must meet before I accept you as a patient. You must follow my orders in all things: taking medicines as I prescribe them, resting whenever I say you must rest, and curtailing your activities until I judge you fit. As to my friend," Esslar added smoothly, "it may become necessary for him to assist me."

"Of what help could this . . .," Sandur searched without success for the name of his antagonist " . . . this foul-mouthed horseman be? He's not a healer, and I like him not."

Esslar swallowed a smile at Sandur's assessment of the Legion Commander, for outwardly they were as different as two men could be: a prince and a self-styled peasant, a suave negotiator and a rough-tongued man-at-arms, a humorless patrician of elegant tastes and a ribald prankster who enjoyed nothing better than a good brawl. Yet both men would die rather than admit weakness.

His amusement fled as he considered how best to prepare Sandur for what would follow without revealing that he knew exactly what injuries lay beneath the damp purple blouse and cotton tunic.

"There are potent herbs in the tea I prepared, yet it's possible your fever may worsen. If so, you might rave and thrash about, hindering my ability to treat you."

When a curt nod cut off Esslar's explanation, he completed silently what must remain unsaid.

"And so the 'foul-mouthed horseman' will restrain you while I clean the wounds, and hold you down when I must use the knife. While my hands are busy elsewhere, he'll mop your brow. When you scream, he'll remind you that it's almost over, and when you faint, he'll sigh out his relief as if they were his wounds and not yours."

Breaking the silence that fell between them, the prince of Endlin announced, "I am in agreement, healer."

"As am I."

Esslar paused, deciding that both he and the prince needed time to ready themselves for the ordeal to follow. "Loosen your garments while I make preparations." Rising to his feet, he looked down at Sandur's elaborately arranged braids. "Tie up your braids, prince, so I'll not brush against them by mistake."

As dark eyes lifted to meet his, he saw gratitude underneath the pain and exhaustion.

"And so, my prince," Esslar promised silently as he walked back to the campfire where Galen waited, *"when you wake tomorrow, the fever gone and the pain eased by my salves, you'll know these things to be true: my word can be trusted, and though you may dislike the 'other one,' he deserves to be called by his name."*

THE RAUCOUS SHRIEK of a kaka jarred Sandur awake. Bleary eyes opened on a sun-drenched landscape. A flash of olive brown, grey, and red winged past him, the parrot repeating its screeching cry. Squinting against the glare, his first thought was that he must have overslept. His head cleared and he remembered.

He inched his right hand toward the nape of his neck, preparing himself for the pain of movement. His fingers found the strip of cloth he'd wrapped around his braids undisturbed. Although a slight twinge ran through his shoulder blade, it was nothing like the agony of the past few days.

His fingers worked at the knot and pulled away the cloth. He lay still for a while, panting a bit from the effort of movement, dismayed by his weakness. They had arranged some kind of pallet for him to lie upon and must have removed the saddle he gripped until his fingers cramped, placing a folded robe under his head instead. He lay flat on his stomach, his back and shoulders bare, a scratchy blanket covering his lower body.

When he could locate neither healer nor horseman, he began a careful inventory of his surroundings, noticing that although it must be nearly midday, he lay in shade. Puzzled, he looked up to find a cloth rigged to shield him from the sun, a clumsy sail dangling between two sturdy saplings. A low fire burned nearby, and steam issued out of a metal container with a strange handle growing out of its side. Someone had placed dates and raisins on a tin plate and what looked to be smoked eel, a favorite food since childhood. Wondering idly how these poor tradesmen could afford such an expensive delicacy, it came to him with a jolt. While he slept, unaware of their activities, they had rummaged through his gear, stealing his purse and letters of credit, rifling his packs to carry off what they liked, and had stolen his horse, leaving him to fend for himself, no doubt laughing over the gullible prince who had trusted them.

And then the memories he pushed away upon waking overcame him, and he was screaming into the twilight, half-maddened by the pain of the fiery stripes burning on his back, the white-haired horseman holding him down, the sad-faced healer running the silver blade of the knife through the flames before cutting open another infected place. Stripped to his challah, his skin sticky with sweat and gore, his fevered thoughts muddled and confused, never once had he doubted the healer's skill. Calmly, the one called H'esslar would warn him that he must probe for yet another sliver of bamboo, and when the worst was over, would assure him he could rest awhile. In those brief respites when he was insensible to anything except his bone-deep weariness and the labored sound of his breathing, a cloth held in work-roughened hands would wipe away the mixture of sweat and tears blinding him while a gruff voice muttered in a thick dialect he could barely understand:

"Aye, yer a brave lad, and that's the truth! Only a wee bit longer now, and then it's a good night's rest."

As the mist lifted from his eyes, he saw the contents of the plate for what they were—the healer tempting him to eat, hoping the food from his personal stores might better please him. Inside the container boiled another of the healer's draughts, and the horseman was doubtless responsible for the tarpaulin that kept the sun's rays off his back. They had not touched his hair nor asked how he came to be beaten, but treated him fairly and in accordance with their agreement. Rough mannered and uncultured they might be, lacking any understanding of the niceties of polite behavior, yet they understood something of honor. It was a comforting discovery. He need worry no longer that he might be robbed, beaten and left for dead, murdered outright, delivered into slavery, or any of the countless scenarios drifting through his thoughts as he followed two strangers down a seemingly endless road.

The sound of splashing water and hoots of laughter floated up from the direction of the stream. His stallion, Seal, wandered into view, the sunlight glazing him silver as he grazed, the dapples on his flanks shining like sea foam, his tail in constant motion against the flies. Hunger rumbled in Sandur's stomach simultaneously with a sudden urge to relieve himself. Just as he was considering how best to go about crawling toward the bushes, for he was doubtful he could stand, he heard voices.

"There's no chance ye'll ever find work washin' clothes," the elder man grumbled.

"And for that I'll be eternally grateful," laughed the healer, striding up the bank through the tall grasses, his arms full of dripping laundry, his gaze restless until he found Sandur.

The white-haired man appeared behind him, both men wet-headed and wearing clean clothes. Their identical brown tunics and breeches caused Sandur to wonder if they might be uniforms of some sort. It shocked him that they had bathed together, especially since the healer had no interest in male coupling. Sandur could imagine no other explanation for their conduct. As they drew closer, he grew increasingly uncomfortable about his state of undress.

"You're awake!" the healer cried, indicating to his companion that he should take the laundry from his arms. The transfer made, the healer approached and knelt by his side.

Shyness overcame Sandur. The healer took no notice as he brushed a palm over his patient's brow and bent to inspect his back.

"It goes well," he mumbled, intent on his handiwork. "Yes, it goes better than we have any right to expect." His expression softened as he asked, "How do you feel?"

"I . . . I'm hungry," Sandur admitted, more surprised by the return of his appetite than the healer's quick burst of laughter.

"Those are welcome words! I'll help you dress, and then you may eat the midday meal."

"I am no child . . .," Sandur began, hating the idea of anyone dressing him, to be silenced by a stern rebuke.

"That was our agreement, and I'll hold you to it. You'll not budge from this pallet until I say so. I took several stitches. If you pull them out . . ."

The healer's threat had its desired effect. Nothing on earth would move Sandur from the pallet if it meant a repeat of last night's agonies. Miserable at having to discuss the private functions of his body with a commoner, he confessed the fullness of his bladder. A pottery jar was pressed into his hand.

"I'll help you turn onto your side," the healer promised. "If you've no objection, might I search for some clean clothes among your gear?"

Inwardly lamenting his helplessness, Sandur gave grudging consent. True to his word, the healer helped ease him over onto his side. Left alone with the clay jar, he listened as they spoke among themselves. His reading comprehension of the southern language was excellent, his proficiency at speaking not quite so advanced. He kept it secret on purpose, in case he might overhear any plans from which they thought to exclude him. The horseman's speech was often incomprehensible, the healer's less so, although in the past few days his ear had become accustomed to the plump vowels and sharply pronounced consonants.

"How fares his lordship?"

"Sore but hungry. His color is better, and his brow is cool to the touch. Some of the cuts still ooze, but they're less angry than they were. I must help him dress and get some food and medicines down him." A short pause. "Grab that saddlebag and toss it here."

The saddlebag landed with a thud and was duly unstrapped.

"Something that opens at the back," the healer mumbled to himself. A low whistle from the horseman.

"Surely there's not so much money in the world! One of them would keep the Maze open for a year, and damn me if there aren't two!"

"Hush, Galen!" came the healer's warning hiss. As Sandur rolled back onto his stomach, he caught a glimpse of the letters of credit being stuffed back into the bag.

Never thinking to check the amounts, he was unsurprised to learn of his father's generosity. It had always been the Tehran's way to lavish gifts upon his children, tokens, Sandur thought bitterly, of benign neglect. Fingering the coral pendant, he fought against a sudden onslaught of memory, unwilling to go back . . .

" . . . if you're ready?"

Startled by the sudden appearance of the healer and unsure as to the nature of his question, Sandur mumbled something indicating agreement, unable to rid himself of the feeling that in some mysterious way the healer had helped him put aside the ugly thoughts that sometimes threatened to overcome him. Sneaking a quick glance up at him, Sandur searched the healer's face for evidence of his suspicions. H'esslar's eyes were placid pools, lacking even a ripple to disturb the calmness of their waters. Putting aside his misgivings, he offered no resistance as the healer knelt and began dressing him.

"We've already eaten, and Galen wants to spend the afternoon exploring the area. He's more than willing to hunt for the evening meal and asks if you'd prefer fowl or rabbit?"

Sandur preferred fish, but considered the request. Had he been too quick to judge the one with the sharp tongue and impatient air who seemed unaware of his bad manners? Perhaps the horseman was not so much disrespectful as ignorant. If this was the case, then it became a clansman's duty to teach a commoner the ways of civilized behavior. First he must call a truce.

"Tell Galen," Sandur pronounced the name carefully, "there's a certain pheasant that nests amidst the underbrush of these hills. The cock is redheaded with a white band around the neck. They're excellent sport and a favorite delicacy in the citadel."

The healer nodded without comment, busily slitting open the back of a cotton tunic and nodding his approval when the garment slid easily over

Sandur's outstretched arms. Clothed again, Sandur felt his dignity restored. A whimsical smile played about the healer's lips.

"I'll inform Galen about the pheasant. Rest now, and I'll bring your meal."

NOT UNTIL NIGHT crept over the dell, spreading its moist blanket of tranquility, did the healer pick his way soundlessly around the sleeping bodies and head down the bank toward the stream. The moment he called for her, she found him, the vast distances crossed with the blinking of an internal eye. Their thoughts merged, a joining of her maturity and his genius, and she gleaned from his memories all thoughts and impressions. He offered no resistance, letting her harvest where she willed, secure in his knowledge that this farmer would sow where she reaped, content to be the fertile lands in which she planted. At last the farmer rested, her baskets full, her bushels overflowing, bathing him in the radiance of her gratitude.

"You are right to help him keep the past at bay."

"Yet we've so little time . . . "

"Thirty years of abuse are not easily forgotten. You've made a good beginning; he no longer believes you might harm him."

"Galen says we'll reach Robber's Pass by the end of this moon."

"You are expected. All is in readiness."

"What of your search, Mother?"

The wind sighed over the waters.

"The time is not yet ripe. I wait for a sign."

A star shot across the horizon. She was gone.

He stood, refreshed as if from a full night's rest, his mind cleansed of the residual memories of his patient's pain. So she had healed him twenty years ago when the melancholy took him and he was cast adrift in a welter of anxieties for which he could find no remedy. Iolas, daughter of Surnan, described the ailment from which he suffered two hundred years before Transformation. His self-diagnosis, confirmed by his colleagues at the House of Healing, brought no cure, but rather despair.

Somehow she found him that interminable night as he waged a losing battle with himself, a healer who could not heal himself being sucked into the vortex of madness. As he plummeted down into that whirling maelstrom, he was swooped up into the cradle of her mind to emerge as one newly born. His sanity restored, his gifts unaccountably strengthened, he became her Master of Mysteries, an ancient title for a prodigy of barely twenty years of age.

Taking his place on his sleeping robes, he noticed that his patient slept fitfully, lips mouthing words, hands clutching frantically at nothing. Brushing his fingertips across the prince's brow, Esslar wished away the nightmare, dispersing it into the heavy dampness of the night air.

"*Pleasant dreams will be yours until we delve deeper. When that time comes, we'll go together.*"

His promise given, the Master of Mysteries slept.

Chapter 7

Chance Encounters

UNDER THE GNARLED branches of an ancient olive sat the sentinel, pink tongue lolling over ivory incisors, panting slightly in the oppressive heat. Another, less dignified cousin of his breed might have stretched out full on the ground, enjoying the feel of cool grass on hairless underbelly, and likely would have dozed with eyes half-closed, surrendering to the laziness of the afternoon, lifting a head now and then to bite at a flea and collapsing with a contented sigh. But other dogs had not the responsibilities of this one. Intent on his duties, he sat sentry under the lone patch of shade to be found in the busy marketplace.

Several townspeople threw sidelong glances at his formidable presence, quickening their pace as they passed by the olive tree, although he favored them with not so much as a glance. Their caution was understandable. Deep-chested and thin-flanked, his head reached higher than a woman's waist as he sat on his haunches, his open mouth revealing an impressive row of sharp teeth set in a powerful jaw. Eggs and oil must have found their way into his food, for his coat shone with good health and frequent brushing. A long, curving tail, free from tangles and burrs, lay quiet in the grass. His size and confirmation suggested the great wolfhounds of the north, with a high-domed head and a square, rather than a pointed, muzzle. His waterproof coat was iron-colored, a brindled grey intermixed with silver, his ears pointed and tipped with black.

A single child approached him during the course of the afternoon, although since this was a market day, many children were in evidence, their hands grasped tightly by mothers and fathers who rushed them quickly past the sentinel under the tree. This particular child, a boy of perhaps three, fearless and independent as only three-year olds can be, had either strayed into the marketplace from a nearby residence or was somehow separated from his parents.

Whatever the cause, he walked boldly up to within an arm's length of the dog and, planting his stubby legs wide apart, regarded him solemnly for a moment. When no hackles rose and no growl rumbled, the child ventured two steps forward and waited again. The long tail swept through the grass from side to side, granting him permission to touch.

A chubby hand reached out to stroke the dog's shoulder, the small dirty fingers gliding smoothly over the thick coat. The dog inclined his head, rather like a monarch receiving homage, and the child slid his hand up behind a cocked ear. The great beast closed his eyes as the child scratched him. Very slowly, and with great dignity, the dog turned his massive head and licked the child's cheek.

This gentle swipe of the tongue surprised the child into laughter, causing an elderly woman to lift her eyes from the fabric she was inspecting in order to consider the source of that almost indescribable sound—the spontaneous and unaffected laughter of a child.

She laughed so once, on summer days not so different from this one, the sun white-hot as it blazed a path across the cloudless sky, the dust rising from the ground with every step. Yet, try as she might, she couldn't remember ever feeling as hot or as dusty as she did today. As a child, the dry, scratchy heat of high summer was nothing less than a condition of delightful existence, to be experienced wholeheartedly, either by flinging herself face-first into a snow bank or stomping in a luscious puddle of mud. So it is with the child and the dog, she thought to herself, a first contact of sorts.

Mumbling under her breath, as old folks tend to do, she left the fabric booth and hobbled over toward the olive tree, her vision still sharp even if her arthritic knees ached, and her backside was sore from her recent travels on horseback. Her robes were dusty, bone-grey at the hemline and the bottom of her veil. In this village of Cyme her appearance lost its uniqueness, allowing her to venture freely among the market-goers, stopping here and there to examine a particular ware or overhear a conversation in progress. In Cyme, no one thought to lower their voices when she approached, with the result that she heard it all—the complaints about the lack of rain and worry that the grape crop might be affected, the news that the night watchman had surprised a thief three nights ago as he broke into a village wine store, escaping with a wineskin tucked neatly under each arm, that a girl child had been born to a local couple at the new moon. She listened as much to what was not said as to what was gossiped about freely in the market square, and was relieved when she heard not a single rumor touching upon the problems she wrangled with daily in the northwest tower.

Her discomfort eased almost immediately as she passed under the branches of the olive tree, the welcoming shade enveloping her in coolness she had not enjoyed since dawn.

As she moved, so moved the Legionnaires, flanking her on all sides, careful to blend in with the villagers who roved from booth to booth. It amused her that her escorts often made purchases, a favorite one being wine, for Cymean vineyards were the best in the southeastern provinces. In the thirty years since she had instituted regular visits to the villages and towns neighboring Pelion, the job of accompanying her had changed from hazardous duty to a welcome break in patrol routine. Bands of slavers were occasionally sighted along the farthest fringes of the patrol areas, but from the western bank of the Tellas River to New Agave, the Legion ensured the safety of the roads, and Magda traveled as freely as did her people.

The wolfhound acknowledged her presence with a brief motion of his tail. When she made no move to approach him, he resumed his watch. Leaning her back against the thick trunk (for the tree was at least three centuries old and located in the exact center of the market place) she let her gaze wander over the crowd until they found the object of the dog's attention.

A sudden burst of giggles and shrieks erupted from a group of children gathered around what, after careful consideration, Magda identified as a woman. The rounded hips beneath the baggy breeches were unmistakably female, although she stood as a man does, pelvis tilted forward, knees locked, hands on hips. The cap was a man's as well, a kind of pie-wedge with a short brim, which was removed with a sudden flourish, and a wealth of hair tumbled down her back. A wispy scarf was tied deftly around her waist to serve as an apron, and she began to mince and flounce, flirting with her unseen suitor. The performer's back was to the olive tree, the audience surrounding her in a tight semi-circle, stair-stepped rows of children arranged in front with adults in the back. Magda decided she was viewing a storyteller of some kind. The woman's words were inaudible since the crowd around her responded loudly to her antics. Now the scarf was ripped from her waist, wrapped quickly about her head to make a turban, and she was a man again, an overprotective father fat with food and self-importance, waddling from side to side and scratching his non-existent beard in woeful dismay.

The children's laughter was almost continual now, carefree trills of pure hilarity; more contained adults smiled and nodded their enjoyment. Then it was over, the woman bowing to the crowd as they clapped and whistled their approval, the adults tossing coins into the cap she held outstretched in her hands. The crowd dispersed reluctantly, several onlookers stepping up to converse with her. As if obeying a prearranged signal, the dog rose, yawned and stretched, and trotted over to the woman's side. Without a break in her conversation, the woman's hand reached down, found the dog's head, and then slipped down to his back, her fingers grasping the rough coat easily since his shoulders stood only a little lower than her hip.

Magda looked around for Dictys, locating him five paces to her right, lounging against a food stall. At her silent directive he relayed her orders that her conversation was not to be disturbed or overheard. This was a procedure of long-standing, and the other Legionnaires gathered more closely around the woman and the dog as Magda made her way toward them.

The storyteller knelt, gathering up her meager properties and arranging them carefully in a kind of pouch with a wide strap attached to it. Next, she unbuttoned the top two buttons of her blouse and pulled out a leather pouch. The drawstring loosened, into the pouch went the copper coins. Sensing Magda's approach, the dog whirled, growling low in his throat. Still on her knees, the woman raised her head, holding the pouch tightly against her breasts with both hands.

"Come no closer and stand very still!"

Magda froze, sending out a warning to the Legionnaires, forbidding them to interfere. The dog stalked stiffly toward her, hackles up and lips pulled back in a ferocious snarl. He sniffed her robes and her hands, no doubt identifying her by scent as the woman who had shared the shade tree with him, then circled back his mistress, content that Magda meant no harm.

"What do you want?" the woman demanded as the dog returned to her side.

"To congratulate you on your performance. Such mastery is rare and I wondered . . ."

Magda recovered from one shock to be faced with another. Slowly, her voice died away.

". . . how long I've been blind."

That was not at all what Magda wondered. She chose this woman as she had chosen hundreds of ernani—always alert to qualities like independence and industry. Now, as she looked into the storyteller's face, she gauged anew the nature of her character. Admiration grew and with it an urge to know more.

"On the contrary, I had no idea you were blind. My question concerned how you came to learn your craft."

The woman's face was pleasing even when gathered into a frown. That frown replaced by a contrite smile, she became fair to the point of loveliness—a high brow with a distinct widow's peak, a pert nose ending just above a gently curving mouth, and a firm chin. The eyes gazing sightlessly back at Magda were her most remarkable feature, twin orbs of a distinctly mutable grey, the color of the rarest of star-sapphires, each eye ringed with sooty lashes, opened wide and staring fearlessly at a world she could not see. Next to the silvery curls of the dog, her hair appeared more gold than red—the color of amber beads. Reaching up a hand to push the heaviness of her hair away from her neck, she laughed, a low-pitched ripple that held within it self-reproach.

"Pardon me for misjudging you. It's a common question, and I mistook your intent. In truth, I learned my craft from my mother, who was a famous dreamsayer. Perhaps you've heard of her? Latona of Cinthea?"

Her voice was a resonant contralto with the slightest trace of a provincial accent. The tinge of sadness in her question caused Magda to wish she could answer with something other than the truth.

"I know her not, nor am I acquainted with dreamsaying. Is that what I just witnessed, a dream of yours being performed for the enjoyment of the crowd?"

This laugh was quite different from the first one, rich and full-bodied as she rose to her feet and shook her head, color rising to her cheeks.

"You must not compare dreamsaying with the simple tale I acted out for the children. Dreamsaying is an adult art, and few have the gift. My mother was one of these," the colors in her eyes seemed to swirl and eddy as the tears rose, like a sea change coming on, "but I fear I lack her mastery."

"The children felt no lack," Magda reminded her, and was rewarded by a heartfelt smile. "Since you come from Cinthea, I suppose you travel widely with your companion here. What is your route, so that I might write to friends in villages along the way and tell them of your arrival?"

It was only a minor fabrication, for indeed Magda kept close contact with many former residents of the Maze who resided in the provinces. Her purpose, however, was far more serious than assuring the storyteller a large audience and a full purse. With such knowledge in her possession, she could alert the Legion to watch for a blind woman and a dog who walked the public roads. The dog had proved his ability to guard his mistress, but sickness or a single arrow could fell him, and the girl would be lost, without direction and helpless to protect herself. Somehow Magda could not part from this plucky wayfarer without assuring herself of her safety.

"My thanks for your thoughtfulness, little mother."

The honorific was spoken in the Cinthean dialect, a term of affection applied to the elderly lace makers who were that region's living treasures.

"The road is long between towns, and word of mouth travels slowly. Often I arrive too late for market day and must delay my travels. Rauros and I," the dog's ears perked as she spoke his name, "take the southwest road, the one which leads to Pelion."

She spoke her destination with a distinct quaver in her voice. Again, Magda sensed an overwhelming sadness.

"To Pelion?" Magda repeated doubtfully. "Have you friends there, or relations of some kind? So large a city is oftentimes unfriendly to visitors."

The woman knelt in the dust, her face hidden behind her hair, and began to search with her hands for the pouch containing her belongings. Finding it, she laced a strap though a buckle and pulled it tight, her nimble fingers working the leather with easy confidence. She spoke as she worked, the dog standing rock still as she placed the pouch over his back and tightened the straps across his chest and under his belly.

"I know not a single soul in Pelion, and as you say, we may find no welcome upon our arrival. But this journey is a promise I made, and regardless of the cost, it's a promise I intend to keep."

She tugged at the girth straps until the dog grunted a mild protest, then rose to her feet, brushing off the knees of her well-worn breeches. A bit of string appeared from the breast pocket of her blouse with its dirty collar and frayed cuffs, and she tied up her hair. This done, she extended her hand in Magda's general direction.

"Well met, little mother. If you write your friends, you'll have our gratitude."

Magda took the proffered hand quickly, unwilling for it to remain outstretched and empty as it searched for the location of an elderly woman whose face she could not see.

"By what name are you known?"

"I am Alyssa, daughter to Latona."

A low command brought the dog around to her right side, and she took hold of a leather handle woven between the saddlebags hung over the dog's ribs. He started off confidently in the direction of the inns and stables, the woman keeping step with the dog's loose-limbed strides.

Magda watched their departure, her hand still tingling from its contact with the blind woman's flesh. The dog's name, Rauros, meant "rushing waters" in the Cinthean dialect. And those eyes, grey as the sea at evening tide . . .

A shiver ran between her shoulder blades.

Could this be the one she had searched for since the winter thaw, plying the roads through the sleepy villages and hamlets surrounding Pelion? How many times had she looked into a stranger's face, her mind probing into private thoughts, searching within the chambers of memory, her touch cautious, discreet, respectful of their secrets, considerate of the mysteries she found within but always sensing that this was not the one.

Her weeklong journey was a whim of sorts, a much-needed break from the drudgery of days that crept by tortoise-like, waiting for news from the searchers who ventured where she could not go herself. Could it be that her sudden urge to visit Cyme was more than a whim? Was it a call, perhaps, a summons of some sort?

"Mother?"

"Yes, Dictys."

"We, uh, we wondered if you wanted her followed. I know it's procedure, but, uh, but I wasn't sure if . . . ?"

There was no need to explain his confusion. Dictys was a product of the Maze, a transformed adept who knew as well as Magda did that only the unblemished could walk the Path of Preparation.

"What are you thinking of?" she asked herself silently. *"Already you play with ideas that may end in catastrophe. What you undertake is experiment enough. Shall you add another element of the unknown to something untried, something that may yield no reward?"*

Aloud, she said, "Nay, Dictys, let her be. Alert the area patrols to watch out for her on the southern road."

The obviousness of his relief brought a lump to her throat.

"We enjoyed her performance."

"Yes," she said, more coldly than she had intended. "Yes," she repeated more kindly, "she is extraordinary."

As they headed for the stables, a pang of regret struck her. Her eyes moved tirelessly through the crowded streets, hoping for another glance of a woman and a dog walking to Pelion, begging for coins with which to pay for their bed and board, sleeping under the starlit canopy of the heavens when the drawstring purse was emptied of its coppers.

How heartlessly she had behaved, offering no words of hope or encouragement, not even pressing into that outstretched hand a silver coin to ease their way, affording them a room rather than a hovel or a week's worth of food they could share among themselves. Why hadn't she thought to offer them a place to stay once they reached the city? Or, best of all, invited them to return with her to Pelion? What would have taken five days on a good horse could last as long as a fortnight on foot. What would it have mattered if she discovered that her benefactor was the Nineteenth Mother?

No bright head emerged from among the milling crowds. Cursing her uncharitable spirit, Magda mourned for the storyteller as she mourned for another bright-haired girl lost to her these thirty years.

Like Aethra of the chestnut hair, Alyssa of Cinthea had disappeared.

"A SMALL HOUSE, Rauros, with a well-swept walk and a neatly-kept garden. A place where they'll be glad of a few extra coins."

The dog's soft whine indicated agreement.

"A henhouse would be nice with a chicken on the boil. I'm famished, and you must be, too."

A single woof answered her in the affirmative.

She trudged along, trying to match the pace he set, conscious that she keep her grip on the handle light so as not to hinder him. He always shamed her with his tireless gait, his endurance in the face of hunger. I must feed you better, she worried, conscious that he was thinner than he should be, his ribs like barrel staves under the thick coat of hair. She was thin as well, her belt in the last notch, the waistband on her breeches gathered around her like a flour sack. Thirty days on the road between Cinthea and Cyme, a journey that would have taken ten if she'd not been robbed at the first inn, a thief cutting her purse loose from her belt while she slept in the common room. If only I'd spent a few extra coins on a private room, she lamented for the hundredth time, or slept with Rauros in the barn.

From that night forward they avoided inns, depending on the kindness of the folk who lived on the outskirts of the villages. Once their fear of the dog was overcome, most of them were generous to a fault, letting her sleep on a makeshift pallet on a kitchen floor or on a bed of straw in an outbuilding with their animals. They were several miles southwest of Cyme by now, put on the right road by a young man with a cultured accent who stopped to offer assistance when he saw her kneeling by the dog, unsure as to which route led out of town. Hearing the admiration in his voice change abruptly to pity, she hid her hurt, thanking him with all the politeness she could muster and nudged Rauros to walk on.

The air was cooler now, with a refreshing hint of moisture. As tired as she was of the unremitting heat, she dreaded the thought of rain. Neither of them must risk sickness, for she had no money for medicines, and a rainy spell would mean hard coin spent on living quarters that brought her no closer to her destination. She measured the distances in her head—Cinthea to Cyme, Cyme to Gebron, Gebron to Cottyo, Cottyo to Pelion. The village teacher helped her plan her route, drilling the names into her skull, figuring out the distances she must travel. But that was in Cinthea, when her purse was heavy with her inheritance. Her mother's legacy lost, her sole resources were Rauros, the contents of her pack, and her skills as a storyteller.

How her mother would have enjoyed her performance this afternoon! How pleased she would have been that her daughter was practicing her craft! Not that she wouldn't have been concerned over her poverty, but Latona, famed dreamsayer of Cinthea, would have been delighted that her daughter had come into her own.

"You can do anything, child, be anything! Your work is inspired, your gestures clear and well-defined, your voice flexible, your characters unique and wonderfully creative!"

"And my face, mother?"

"Your face is lovely, daughter."

"It's not grotesque?"

That fear was her barrier, the picture she carried in her head of the poor blind girl making ghastly faces at the crowds, her vacant eyes frightening the children, making them run from her.

"Alyssa, surely you know that as much as you are my daughter, I would never suggest that you pursue this course unless I thought you could uphold the finest traditions of the Cinthean bards. The league approved your audition, twenty bards voting unanimously to admit you. Did they lie as you accuse me of lying?"

"You would not lie on purpose, but perhaps you are over-fond . . ."

"I'm nothing of the sort!" her mother sniffed, aghast at the insinuation that she might love her daughter more than her craft, although both mother and daughter were equally aware her protestations were made only for show. This refusal to indulge in displays of emotion had been Latona's defense since the morning her eleven-year-old daughter woke from the fever that raged through Cinthea, killing one child out of every four under the age of twelve. Alyssa's eyesight was the price of her survival, but Latona's determination never wavered. Untiring in her efforts, persistent in her demands, she refused defeat in any form.

"It will not do! You must move your eyes to the right as you spy the lamp and then look around warily for the thieves. Again!"

"Lower your chin, child! It pulls your neck out of alignment and puts a needless strain on your vocal cords. Let your head float on the column of your neck."

"Of course you can roll your eyes! Your muscles will remember how! Good, that's a much better choice for the giant's wife . . ."

Every story was taught her—the boy and the lamp, the girl and the wolf, the peasant and the fish, the king and the nightingale—each one a precious resource held in the vast communal memories of the bards. Written language came to Cinthea only recently. The oral tradition remained strong, and no celebration was considered complete without the appearance of a bard. Once her mother was satisfied that she'd mastered the folk tales, she studied the epics, the long poems recited annually by the hearths in the moons of winter: tales of journey and romance, mythical beings and mysterious gods, stories of love and duty, revenge and reconciliation.

Latona shared with her daughter the mastery of everything except dreamsaying, and that, too, she would gladly have shared but for the fact that dreamsaying could not be taught. More valuable than diamonds, more revered than lace makers, rarer than sun dogs in a winter sky, Cinthean dreamsayers came into the world only once in several generations. Their deaths were mourned as a tragedy affecting the entire province, for until another dreamsayer appeared, no one could read the dreams of the populace. In men and women's dreams lay their destiny, desires, fortunes, and defeats, and without a dreamsayer the code remained unbroken. Matches would be made without assurance of their success and longevity, journeys undertaken without knowledge of the dangers to be faced, decisions made without consideration of future affects. In short, with the death of Latona came the end of an era. In the oral histories of the Cinthean bards, the years of her life would forever be designated as "The Age of Latona."

A wasting sickness came upon her a year before her death, allowing mother and daughter time to prepare themselves for separation. Each woman ached for the misery of the other, but as Latona lived, so she would die, and expressions of remorse were not allowed. Until the last day of her life, Latona read the dreams of her people, ever-conscious that with her death Cinthea would pass into the dark times which ran in cycles between the ages of the dreamsayers.

On the day of her death she saw no one but her child, and for the last time, Latona read her daughter's dreams. It was her parting gift, along with the heavy purse she placed in her daughter's palm, wrapping the sensitive fingers around her life's savings. The girl whispered her dreams into her mother's ear, the mother lying still and silent under the heavy coverlet, seeming not to listen but hearing every word, every pause, every nuance, her eyes as sightless as those of her daughter.

As the whispering voice ceased its recital, the mother spoke in the trance-like tones of the dreamsayer, "Your destiny lies in the realm of water, in things that float on the surface of the sea. But first you must search for sight, a search to the south, to the valley of the castle."

After a long silence, Latona spoke for the last time, not as a dreamsayer, but as a dying mother to her only child.

"I ask of you a promise, daughter, and with this promise I take my leave. One thing will content me and allow me easy passage into your dreams, where I will live forever, as dreams of your father live on in me. Promise me this—you will undertake the search."

The daughter murmured her consent. As she had foretold, the mother passed easily into the realm of dreams, and the Age of Latona came to an end.

RAUROS TOOK A gradual swing to the right and came to a full stop. Alyssa's hand brushed against wooden planks as she fumbled for the gate-latch. Her ears caught the sounds of running water, the lowing of a cow, and a woman's voice crooning a song that sounded like a lullaby. The scent of fowl cooked with rosemary wafted by her nose, and she worked impatiently at the latch with both hands. The gate swung open with a rusty squeak, and Rauros led her forward, stopping again to give her the signal that steps lay in front of her. Her toe finding the rise and measuring its height, she stepped onto the threshold. Lowering a hand to meet the wetness of his nose, she pushed him behind her, having learned from past experience that her initial request for food and lodging would be met more warmly without Rauros straining forward against the harness, sniffing eagerly at what he hoped would be his evening meal. Tucking in her blouse and pushing back the wisps of her hair, she found the door and knocked.

The hinges creaked, and a woman's voice spoke, low and melodious and without fear, "Good eventide."

"Good eventide, mistress." Alyssa ran her tongue over her lips, readying herself for the speech she'd perfected over the past moon. "I wondered if you might have a night's food and lodging for a blind woman and her dog? I can pay, and neither of us will be a bother. We're used to sleeping in the barn and will eat anything you can provide."

She ended on a hopeful note and what her mother had always told her was her most winning smile. In the silence that followed she prepared herself for rejection. One night it had taken four tries until a reluctant soul finally gave them permission to sleep in a muck-filled cowshed and offered a rind of cheese, a boiled egg, and a cup of milk, all of which she'd given to Rauros.

"Will a place by the kitchen hearth serve?"

"'Twill more than serve, mistress!"

Remembering her companion, she motioned Rauros forward and heard the woman chuckle to herself.

"Faith, he's more horse than dog! Does he like chicken scraps?"

To Alyssa's chagrin, Rauros emitted a loud woof that signified his excitement at the mention of chicken (one of the many words he recognized). The woman's chuckle became outright laughter.

"Come in, both of you, and rest while I finish the meal. I'm alone tonight, and your company is welcome."

A hand grasped Alyssa by the upper arm, and she was led inside. Rushes rustled beneath her feet, and a fire popped and crackled as the grease from the cooking fowl spattered against the coals. She heard the sound of something being scraped against a wooden floor, and the hand on her shoulder pressed her down into what proved to be a chair. Rauros crouched at her side, licking his lips in anticipation.

"My mate was called to Gebron and returns tomorrow night. I can't remember how to cook for one, so there should be more than enough. There's rice with mushrooms, carrots and onions, sharp cheese and olives. Our hives yield sweet honey, or there's gooseberry preserves. I baked today, so you've a choice of yeast bread or raisin scones."

"Might I help you, mistress? If you show me where to wash my hands, I could lay the table or slice the bread."

Her offer was refused, but Alyssa took no offense. She could sense when someone was uncomfortable with her blindness, and this woman was most decidedly not. She chattered as she worked, honestly glad for the company, and Alyssa warmed to her almost immediately. When a bowl of congealed porridge was set down in front of Rauros, he devoured the contents in three bites before licking the bowl clean, rolling it noisily around the floor with his nose. The edge taken off his hunger, he was soon snoring, dreaming no doubt of the chicken that loomed in his future.

"Where do your travels lead?"

"We journey to Pelion."

"Pelion," the woman repeated, her hands stopping their busy preparations.

"Do you know it, then?" Alyssa asked, always anxious to learn anything she could about the city to the south. The elderly woman who had accosted her in the market seemed disturbed to hear her destination. Her warning frightened Alyssa, who knew only that she must go and knew not what to do when she arrived.

"I've visited there in my time."

No information seemed forthcoming. To her surprise, a palm was placed gently on her shoulder.

"Have you a name you'd share with me?"

"Alyssa of Cinthea."

"You're welcome here for as long as you'd care to stay, Alyssa." The woman added quietly, "You must call me Gwyn."

THE RAIN BEGAN an hour before dawn. Wrapping herself in a robe, Gwyn closed and latched the bedroom shutters, proceeding on tiptoe into the kitchen. The dog was instantly alert, his glowing eyes reflecting the redness of the coals. When Gwyn made no move to approach the pallet by the fireside where the girl slept, the great head lowered again to the blanket. Pulling the kitchen shutters inside, she latched them shut and stood for a moment listening to the rain.

Her sleep had been restless, her dreams troubled as she tossed and turned in the bed, reaching out for the empty place beside her. At last she gave up hope of sleep and lay awake, playing with the notion of sending out her thoughts to Temenus before discarding it as selfish and unwarranted. He would be fast asleep in Gebron, tired after a full day of meetings with the village elders.

The rain pattered lightly against the roof, the soft rain farmers covet, soaking into the crusty soil instead of running off in rivulets. This was no fickle shower, here tonight and gone on the morrow, but a steady deluge of two or three days that would plump the fruit of the vines and assure a plentiful harvest. Enjoying the music of the rain on the roof, Gwyn pulled the rocking chair nearer the window and settled herself to wait for dawn. The girl's form lay in silhouette, black against the pale glow of the hearth, her cheek pillowed on the dog's flank as he lay curled up beside her.

Gwyn gazed into the dying coals, seeing there another girl of twenty summers undertaking a journey of her own. Thirty-five years had passed, but she remembered her loneliness, her fear of the unknown, the disbelief of her family at her insistence that she make her way south, the sorrow of her leave-taking. Her children were grown now, with children of their own, but the memories of youth came thick and fast, brought on by the visitor who knocked at her door and spoke the name of Pelion.

As a log crumbled into ash, the dog lifted his head again, ears perked. Born and raised a farmer's daughter, Gwyn wasn't sentimental about animals and forbade her children's pets entry into the house. Something about the dog's behavior, half-starved but mindful of his manners, not snapping at the food in her hands but waiting politely for it to be dropped into his bowl, touched her heart. She'd intended for him to sleep in the barn, but could not bring herself to separate them, the dirty-faced girl whose hair was a mass of tangles and the dog who sighed his contentment as his mistress took a well-worn brush to his coat and groomed him until he gleamed in the firelight.

Gwyn asked no questions of her guest as they partook of the evening meal. With a single touch of her hand on the girl's shoulder she sensed all that was necessary: the recent loss of a loved one, a promise to be kept, worries about the lightness of her purse, hunger and wretched weariness. Her observations throughout the meal and afterward, when the girl helped her dry the dishes, filled in the missing details. The unkempt hair and scruffy clothes belied her upbringing, for although she might be poor, Gwyn was positive she had not been raised in poverty. Neither timid nor bold, entirely self-assured, the girl went about her business without fuss or bother, asking where the food lay on her plate, nodding her understanding, and eating with grace and skill. She spoke little but listened intently as Gwyn related a description of the room in which they sat. Afterwards, when she rose to ready herself for bed, it was clear she'd memorized the geography of the kitchen. With scarcely a bump or a misstep she found the pitcher and basin in its stand, the linen cabinet on the wall next to the sleeping chamber, and obtained a glass from the third kitchen shelf and filled it from the water jug on the woodblock under the kitchen window. Gwyn found herself forgetting the eyes within that mobile, expressive face were blind as the girl sorted through the items in her pack and arranged her pallet neatly on the floor.

The decision that had floated in her thoughts all evening and disturbed her rest tonight was put into final form as Gwyn watched the room lighten about her. With the coming of the dawn came the certainty that her resolution regarding Alyssa was a right and proper one. Her initial intention was to house them until they both were rested and well fed, sending them on their way with clothes cleaned and mended and a full basket of provisions. Her dreams taught her this could never be. She would enjoy no peace of mind as long as Alyssa walked the road to Pelion as Gwyn once walked it—alone and afraid.

What will Temenus say, she wondered, although she knew exactly what he would say. "My dearest ernani," he would begin, the accent of Pelion still strong after thirty years in Cyme, "if nothing else will content you, then to Pelion we must go."

The lines around his eyes would crinkle as Gwyn deposited herself in his lap. As always, he would hold her close, his big frame dwarfing the chair, his hands roughened from labor, his joint-swollen fingers stroking her plait of greying hair.

"I'd a mind to visit there myself, but thought you'd not leave the grandchildren for so long a time."

It was a half-truth, but she would love him all the more for not mentioning the reason she never returned to the city in the south. He visited there regularly in the early years of their mating, taking each child to be blessed and continuing his work with the experts in agriculture. With the death of his parents he went less often, his reputation as a surveyor spreading throughout the provinces, his services in constant demand as the roads became safe and farmers became willing to venture farther away from the villages, putting tracts of wilderness to the plow. The intimacy with which they lived, the continual sharing of their thoughts, made it impossible to hide what kept her in Cyme, enduring his absences and the emptiness of the bed. Nor would she have chosen to hide anything from Temenus, the man they brought to her cell in the Maze one evening after weeks spent in tears and desolation, grieving over the man who left her without a word, disappearing from her life and never seen by her again. She thought herself unlovable; Temenus proved her wrong.

The time had come for her to give Temenus the reward he deserved, having given her the courage to try again, to risk her heart with another stranger, to welcome one who bore no grudge at being a second choice. Tomorrow she would tell him her decision, and he would rejoice in the knowledge that she no longer feared a chance meeting in the streets of Pelion with a certain Master Engineer. Together they would walk the streets of that glorious city, their hands clasped like young lovers rather than the old couple they had become. And if in their travels Gwyn encountered a man with whom she'd once shared her life, she would pass him by with nary a glance, hand in hand with the mate of her heart. For her sake, Temenus made his home among her people, bringing them his diligence as well as his skills. For his sake, Gwyn would put the past to rest, taking her rightful place beside him in the city of his birth.

"*What miracle have you wrought, Alyssa of Cinthea?*" Gwyn demanded silently of the sleeping girl. "*Why did you stop at my door this evening, and why can't I bear the thought of sending you away? Have you bewitched me, child, or have I passed into my dotage, contemplating a journey when I should be napping in the sun?*"

The girl slept on, the dog snored, and the woman rocked as the day was born, bringing with it a liberation of sorts—the fields watered, the dog fed, the girl succored, and the woman content.

Chapter 8

Rough Passage

"HALOO THE HOUSE!"

Insistent pounding rivaled the thrashing of tree limbs and the driving gale of the wind. When the door of the hut cracked open, a frightened face, seamed and cracked like the parched leavings of a river bed, peered out at three hooded wayfarers. An ear-splitting crack of thunder, a jagged flash of raw blue lightning illuminated the night, and the man at the door stepped back a pace, his mouth agape at the sight of two bearded strangers whose unnatural coloring—a ghostly shade of pasty white—indicated a sickness of which he wanted no part. Moving quickly to shut the door and barricade it from the inside, he was stopped by a voice shouting at him in his own language:

"We seek shelter! We're prepared to pay!"

A fat purse appeared from under a rain-drenched cloak. After peering closely at the face under the hood, the farmer swung the door wide, retreating into the hut while frantically motioning for his woman to move away from the entrance.

The strangers entered hastily, pushing their shoulders through the narrow frame, the tallest one forced to duck in order to clear the low entrance, the one with the white beard and colorless eyes shouldering the door shut against the force of the wind and dropping the bar into place. Despite their cloaks, all three were drenched to the skin and covered with mire, their boots and breeches muddied well past the knees, rivulets of dirty water forming pools at their feet.

The long-awaited rains arrived from the northwest in late afternoon, the cloud-tossed skies breaking open with a tremendous clatter, releasing a torrential downpour which would flood the farmer's rice fields. A stickler for details, the rice farmer (perpetually bent and bow-legged from his work in the fields) sent up the traditional prayer of thanks to the west wind, grateful that his livelihood was secured for at least another year. Now, as he watched the hoods being pulled away, feasting his eyes on one particular head covered with elaborate braids, he sent up an even more fervent prayer.

Bowing low, he motioned his woman to do likewise, anxious that she obey him without delay. Maintaining his obeisance out of respect for one of the fabled clansmen of Endlin, he managed to stammer out a greeting.

"Welcome, lord, to my humble home."

Neither the rice farmer nor his wife witnessed the glances exchanged between the bearded foreigners, nor did they notice the expression of considerable irritation fly across the features of the clansman as he cleared his throat and formally acknowledged their presence.

"You have our thanks. The storm caught us on the road, and your light is the only one we've seen for miles. We tied our horses outside your barn and wondered if we might stable them and take our rest among your beasts?"

The rice farmer's protestations spewed out of his mouth as his woman shoved him forward.

"Of course your companions may use the barn, but such a lowly bed would be unfitting for a clansman of . . .?" The farmer raised his head, sucking in his breath expectantly.

"Of the Kwanlonhon," was the reluctant reply, causing the farmer to puff out his cheeks at the monumental good fortune that was his. Never before had any clansman of Endlin, let alone a member of the rich and influential Kwanlonhon clan, knocked on his door, or the door of any of his neighbors. Surely this was no accident, but an act of providence that must be embraced.

"Please accept our hospitality, lord. My woman was just preparing the evening meal. I would consider it an honor if you joined me in my humble repast."

Thus began the formal ritual of insistence and denial, each persisting with equal politeness, both men aware that the privilege of rank demanded the clansman's eventual acceptance of the commoner's offer since not to accept would insult the farmer and dishonor the clansman. When the exchange of formalities ended, the clansman turned back to his attendants. They spoke at length, the older servant gesticulating energetically with his hands.

"My companions ask if they might sleep here as well. The floor will suit them if there are no other beds."

The farmer's dreams crumpled around him until his woman poked him urgently in his backside. He took a hesitant step forward. As he stepped over the invisible barrier of three paces, the clansman stiffened but made no move to brush him aside, as was his right. Lowering his voice to a whisper, the farmer spoke the ancient formula and watched the clansman's eyes close as if in thought. He made no other sign, but nodded slowly.

"I'll honor your request, but lest you misunderstand, I give fair warning that I'll not return to my father's house for many moons. I make no promises."

The rice-farmer sputtered out his thanks to empty air, for the clansman was already striding to the door, past his open-mouthed servants, and out into the storm.

THEY FOLLOWED HIM out of the farmer's hut and into the rain, mystified by his behavior as he grabbed up the stallion's reins and led the grey into the sagging barn. Once inside, he untied his pack and retreated to a stall where they could hear the sounds of furious activity.

"*What's amiss?*" Galen asked silently as they worked over the steaming horses, rubbing them down with handfuls of straw.

"*Something that disturbs him mightily. A task he must perform, I think, and one he does not relish,*" the healer replied, his concern clear.

It was Sandur's third day on his feet. He tired easily, causing Galen to curse the storm that welled up out of nowhere, the sky changing from blue to black in a matter of minutes, the winds and torrential rains proceeding to blow them nearly off the road, the horses foundering in mud up to their hocks. Busy with the task of squinting through the lashing rain as the road washed out under the horses' hooves, Galen barely heard Esslar's triumphant shout above the howling of the wind. Following the direction of the healer's arm, he'd sent up fervent thanks for the flickering light that promised shelter, fire, and a mug of tea to warm the shivering Prince.

Once inside the farmer's hut, Galen might not have understood the conversation, but he understood greed, for that was what lit the farmer's eyes as he bowed and scraped to Sandur. Stubbornly refusing to be separated from his charge, Galen watched as his request was translated, and the bow-legged farmer and his half-starved mate reacted with nervous fits. Whispered words made the prince's shoulders tense under the wet cloak. He'd responded with the voice Galen disliked, the one that barked out orders to underlings with every expectation of instant obedience, then fled the room without a word of explanation.

Galen's musings were interrupted by Esslar's silent warning. Looking up from the horse's withers, he beheld a clansman attired in full regalia, his amethyst over-robe wreathed with gold shining in the light of the oil lamp the woman pressed into Esslar's hand before they made their way to the barn. Four layers of silk, although badly wrinkled, were gathered in neatly at the waist by an embroidered sash. What looked to be a diamond glittered in the indentation above his right nostril. With the ring in his ear and the silver chain around his neck, he was no longer the injured man Galen had known on the road, but an arrogant prince flaunting his wealth and prestige. Galen kept his mouth shut, trusting Esslar to provide a silent translation.

"What's happened?" the healer asked.

"Nothing that concerns you. You will stay here while I accept the hospitality of the house." With that brusque response, the prince started for the door.

"We deserve an explanation," came Esslar's mildly-spoken rejoinder. To Galen's relief, the prince slowed and turned back to them.

"It's impossible for you to come inside," he began evenly, his impatience clear. "In all probability, the farmer and his wife will join you in a few hours."

"They will leave you alone in their home?" the healer queried, unsure as to what this particular information signified.

The prince sighed, raising his eyes heavenward at yet another breach of decorum, annoyed that they insisted on discussing something for which no discussion was necessary.

"I will not be alone."

When this tastefully-chosen hint was met with puzzled frowns he swore softly under his breath, frustrated by their ignorance.

"There is another person in the house, the farmer's sa'ab," he explained slowly, as if to someone lacking their wits. "Her father has asked that I . . .," he paused, ". . . that I fulfill the ancient oath of the clansmen."

He seemed to expect some reaction. Galen could tell Esslar was totally at sea.

"What oath is that?"

Sandur's nostrils flared.

"Is it possible that with all your knowledge you can be uninformed of such basic matters?"

"Forgive me, prince, but as a stranger to your lands I beg for enlightenment."

Galen ground his teeth at the idea of Esslar humbling himself before this arrogant prince. After a moment in which he seemed to gather his thoughts, the prince offered an explanation.

"In the years of before, my ancestors made their way across the ocean in ships. According to our legends, their journey lasted many moons before they found the eastern shore. Another race inhabited the coastline, a sickly and illiterate people who were not thought suitable to breed with the ship-dwellers. Since it was necessary to populate the new land, each man fathered many children with the women in the ships. In this way, the clans were duly founded and named after six leaders—Effrentati, Synzurit, Onozzi, Hulalet, Assad, and Kwanlonhon."

"They brought with them something of the old learning, and as the clans grew in strength and wealth, bad feelings erupted between the natives and the clans, the first century marked by bitter feuds and much loss of life. Finally, one of my ancestors, the first Linphat Kwanlonhon, made a compact between the clansmen and the commoners. It's almost forgotten within the city. Here in the wilderness, memories are long."

There was a break in the translation, as if Esslar's concentration was broken, then quickly restored.

". . . that any commoner might request his daughter be serviced by a clansman. If judged suitable, she might be accepted into the clansman's household. The custom is an old one, and one I may not ignore."

"Even though you've informed your host that you," Esslar chose his words carefully, warned by Sandur's glower that he was venturing onto dangerous ground, ". . .that you seek no women for your house, he still insists you honor his daughter with your . . . your services?"

"Doubtless he's convinced his sa'ab's charms will seduce me," the prince snorted his disdain, "or he's listened to too many ballads of yesteryear."

"Forgive me, prince, but what of your injuries?"

Always the healer, Esslar searched for some polite way to broach the subject of the as yet unhealed wounds. The prince folded his lips tightly together, a sure sign that he was furious.

"Do you suggest that I would disrobe in the presence of a commoner?!"

Esslar stood his ground as the prince seethed.

"What if the woman should conceive? Surely her father would not . . ."

"Enough!" the prince thundered, startling the horses and the other livestock in the barn, one of the hens squawking in alarm. Grim-faced, he fixed them both with a stony stare.

"For a clansman of my rank to consider a commoner a fit vessel for his sa'ab is ludicrous. For you to question my behavior in this matter is almost as insulting as your lack of manners. I have forgiven much in our travel together, but you go too far. Never speak to me of this again."

Turning on his heel, he strode out into the storm.

Esslar and Galen collapsed onto a bale of straw. They sat for a while, each lost in his own thoughts. Galen spoke first, piecing together what he'd just heard, trying to make sense out of something he feared might be beyond his comprehension.

"So now he's off to join with the lass, but he'll not disrobe or release his seed?"

Galen shook his head, appalled by the coldness of it all, a woman offered by a father with no thought as to her wishes, a man bound to pleasure her but taking no pleasure himself.

"I dinna ken how he'll manage it."

Galen shook his head again, weary of strangers and strange ways, tired of everything foreign and the sheer effort of understanding difference.

"It's no wonder he's bad-tempered—forced into a bargain five centuries old, his wounds still tender, and the lass probably a virgin to boot."

A look of pained recognition crossed Esslar's face.

"What is it, man? What ails ye?"

"We never thought, never considered, what it would mean," Esslar whispered.

Galen leaned closer.

"Neither Kazur nor Manthur were sa'abs. They were lesser sons who left home with their father's blessings, free to mate as they chose, never thinking they would return. But Sandur . . .," Esslar paused, lifting anxious eyes to Galen. "She couldn't have foreseen this. Only now do I begin to understand."

"Understand what?"

"What are the gifts a male ernani offers along the Path of Preparation?"

Galen swore aloud.

"Worse and worse it grows," Esslar said gloomily, "a slim chance growing slimmer with each passing day. Kazur wrote nothing about this custom, either because he considered it common knowledge or thought we might not understand."

"He thought aright," Galen added bleakly.

Esslar rose and began to pace back and forth between the walls of the cow stalls, running his hand through his wet hair until it stood on end, a gesture Galen interpreted as a sure sign he was reaching the limits of his patience.

"What else did Kazur omit, and why? How can I prepare Sandur for the Maze if I can't predict how he'll react to a given situation? He trusts us to deliver him to Pelion and allows me to tend his hurts. Even so, he merely endures our presence. He has no curiosity about us, has never even asked me why I chose to leave Endlin. I can find nothing in his conscious mind except duty, a duty he hates but never questions."

"Freedom comes hard to slaves."

The healer's head shot up.

"Slaves?"

"Maybe not a slave as my folks were, but a slave to duty all the same. It's sure he's ne'er been truly free."

The healer stopped pacing. A look of rapt concentration appeared on his face as he stared at the wall in front of him. Accustomed to his trances, Galen settled down to wait, picking his teeth with a piece of straw, content that a subtler mind than his was at work. At last Esslar regarded him, the glimmer of a smile floating about his lips.

"I know that look, Esslar, and it bodes naught but trouble!"

A hearty laugh was his reward, the healer suddenly young again, the harried look gone and a plan gleaming in his eyes.

"Say rather that it bodes ill for our charge."

"Do ye ken we two can charm the likes of a Tehran's sa'ab?"

"I doubt it not, Commander. We begin tomorrow—tit for tat, no quarter asked and none given. We'll pry open the cage doors and force him out whether he will or no."

* * *

THE SARUJIAN MOUNTAINS filled the horizon. Ridge piled upon ridge, jagged peaks rising up, pushing their way into the clouds, as if the earth, experiencing a violent paroxysm, had jutted forth knees and elbows, the sharp protuberances from its body forming a mountain range which split the world nearly in half. Late summer might reign in other lands, but on the snow-capped summits winter held court throughout the year. Soon autumn would make its fleeting but resplendent appearance, the hardwood forests touched with tongues of fire, then mercilessly stripped to the bone, ransacked of their festive coverings by the jealous winter winds until they stood naked, defenseless against ice storms and brutal cold.

As they climbed, the weather grew chillier, the breeze brisk, the sunlight hard-edged. At dawn a fragile coat of frost dusted the leaves and undergrowth, and the horses could be found frisking playfully on silver-tipped grasses. By midday the travelers put aside cloaks and wrappings and exulted in the warmth of the sun; by late afternoon the cloaks reappeared. At night they huddled together around the campfire, each taking their turn at feeding the blaze that must on no account be allowed to burn itself out before first light.

Sandur had never known such cold. Once the sun went down, he donned every piece of clothing in his pack (with the exception of his formal robes) and bundled himself in his cloak. Even so, he shivered and shook, his fingers and toes frozen and his face numb. His companions, on the other hand, seemed as invigorated as their steeds. The horseman, especially, appeared to revel in the crisp, dry air, striding about in his great boots, slapping his arms about his shoulders, his breath vaporous in the early morning light. Both men had pulled sheepskin vests and sturdy leather breeches from their packs this morning, along with what looked to be fur-lined cloaks and gloves. Neither man offered Sandur so much as an extra pair of worsted stockings.

Today's journey passed like a dream, Sandur busily sorting through a jumble of impressions and events as Seal followed the healer's mare over the timbered foothills and up the rock-strewn paths. Past thickets and glens, down banks to ford icy mountain streams and then up again to the next rise, the stallion grunting as he picked his way up a particularly steep grade, Sandur pondered the events of the past fortnight. One thing was certain—since the night of the thunderstorm his relations with his guides had undergone a complete and undeniable reversal.

He'd felt it for the first time upon entering the barn to change his clothing after a sleepless night spent with the farmer's sa'ab. Admittedly he was not at his best, his temper shortened by an awkward exchange with the farmer, the little man insisting he accept the girl into his household, the girl drooping in the doorway to the tiny bed chamber, her expression morose and woebegone.

At his entrance through the sagging doors of the decrepit barn, neither man looked up from their cold meal of bread and cheese. At the time he'd been grateful for their lack of interest. Only lately had he come to resent their indifference.

Many explanations presented themselves; none seemed entirely satisfactory. The horseman had always been brusque, the healer more civilized and certainly the friendlier of the pair. Since that morning, it was as if Sandur ceased to exist. At first he put it down to the weather, steady downpours that slowed their progress and dampened their spirits. Next he considered his behavior, but upon reflection decided he'd treated them fairly, instructing them in the manners they so sorely lacked, correcting them when their questions bordered on impertinence, keeping himself separate from them as custom demanded. Somehow, his plans to teach them went awry. Their questions ceased, and more and more they talked only among themselves, pleasant conversations he overheard and might have joined if it had not meant revealing he understood their language. The healer never inquired as to his health and stopped translating, cutting him off from any contact with the horseman. No longer did they offer him food from their stores or urge him to join them beside the campfire each night. Although he'd consistently refused their offers in the past, it bothered him that they no longer asked, especially since his provisions were sadly depleted.

Camp routine changed as well. The evening after leaving the rice farm, Sandur dismounted and led Seal to the horseman, proffering the reins. Unaccountably, the horseman refused to take them. Esslar joined them, discussing something with the white-bearded elder in a low voice before turning to Sandur.

"Since your wounds are healed, your horse is your own business from now on."

Sandur's protestations were met with a half-smile and a shrug.

"We agreed to escort you to Pelion, and so we shall. We are not servants. If you need help, I'll be happy to translate Galen's instructions."

"I need no instructions in the care of horses," Sandur replied stiffly, "although I understood you were employed by my father to guide me to my destination and serve me along the way."

As the healer translated word for word, the horseman stroked his beard, shaking his shaggy head from side to side. This time the healer spoke more forcefully.

"You've been misinformed. I offered our services freely and without stipulations; your father accepted on your behalf."

Sandur was stunned for a moment until he remembered the horseman's comments concerning his letters of credit and divined what lay behind this sudden turn of events. Reaching under his cloak, he untied his purse and held it aloft, bouncing it once in front of the healer's nose before making his offer, the coins jangling noisily against one another.

"Then let me purchase your services. Name your price."

The healer's face hardened.

"You mistake my meaning. Our services are not for sale."

It was on the tip of Sandur's tongue to inquire as to exactly what professions they represented—a healer who sold books abandoning his business to escort a Tehran's sa'ab south, an elderly man skilled in horses and trails who might have excelled as a caravan leader yet seemed content to ply his trade for no reward—but he said nothing. Today, a fortnight later, he struggled to discover the reason for their drastic change in attitude and more importantly, sought to understand why the indifference of two commoners could so completely disturb his peace of mind.

The sun sailed across the skies. By late afternoon Sandur arrived back where he started, the night they questioned him concerning the farmer's sa'ab.

THE ENTIRE AFFAIR was doomed from the start. A voice inside his head whispered that he should refuse, that no one need ever discover he'd broken a custom begun by his forefathers, that his injuries alone would be more than enough excuse to avoid a wretched bedding for which he felt nothing but distaste. Still he went, resentful and ill at ease, to be faced by a timid virgin unschooled in even the most commonplace niceties of bedding a man.

Her mother had taught her nothing—the graceful art of disrobing, the shedding of transparent silks that Tasir's concubines performed like so many butterflies emerging from their chrysalises, freeing their soft-skinned, perfumed bodies in a tantalizing dance that whetted the appetite and heightened the senses, the enticing display of their beauty offered up for his delight, demanding he forego his own needs in order to concentrate solely on theirs. Instead, all the carefully orchestrated steps ensuring a woman's pleasure became a tawdry joke, a tasteless experiment in degradation.

Not only was she untrained, she was terrified, her eyes enormous with fear, her lips trembling as she fought the knot tied around her waist. He had no desire to watch but found himself unable to look away, fascinated and repelled by the crudeness of her clothing, the dirty hair, reddened hands, broken nails and scraped elbows. When at last the cheap robe fell to the floor, she made a pitiable attempt to cover her nakedness, backing away from him to the low bed, her knees knocking together and tears streaming down her face. He felt nothing, not the faintest hint of arousal. If she'd denied him with a single shake of her head, he would have returned to the barn without a moment's regret. But she was a sa'ab, and for that reason alone he persevered, respectful of her father's rights, determined that this lowliest of commoners should enjoy at least a moment of pleasure at a clansman's hands.

It took an hour before he could touch her without her flinching, another hour until her whimpering stopped and she was able to concentrate on what he was doing with his mouth and hands. Thankfully, she made no attempt to touch him. It was his custom to strip to his challah so as to enjoy the sensation of a woman's skin against his, for although the rules denied a clansman entrance into a woman's body unless he intended to breed, other pleasures could be enjoyed. A trained concubine would have been incensed at his refusal to disrobe. The girl knew no better, and he had no intention of revealing the stripes across his back.

After hours of patient labor his efforts were rewarded by a sharp shudder and a thin mewling cry. Exhausted, he sank into a fitful slumber until the sound of a cock's crow. After the session with the crestfallen farmer, a one-sided conversation as far as Sandur was concerned since he'd made his position clear from the outset, he'd finally fished out a golden coin and pressed it into a grasping hand, sickened at the thought of paying for one of the worst experiences of his life.

Through it all he blamed not the father nor the girl, but himself. In some ways it was if he stood naked in his father's chambers again, unable to mount a protest, caught in a trap not of his making. Esslar responded to the girl's plight, questioning Sandur's right to bed her. What the healer didn't understand was that it was Sandur's plight as well, forced into a situation that made a mockery of his dearest wish. Yet what could a foreigner know of bedding customs? Did they think him a rapist, spreading his seed indiscriminately with violence and abuse? Stricken by the thought, he realized why they shunned him. He'd behaved like his father, refusing to grant needful information, using his rank to silence inferiors, answering questions by shouting out commands. He, who at the tender age of seven had sworn never to treat others as he had been treated, had exactly duplicated his father's conduct.

"I am not my father," he proclaimed, speaking the words out loud in the hope that someone might hear and believe. Seal's ears flicked back. Patting the stallion's shoulder, the muscles gliding smoothly under dappled skin, Sandur lifted his eyes to the mountains.

"IT'S NINE DAYS past the eighth moon," Galen observed, poking aimlessly at the fire with a pointed stick.

Esslar sighed and nodded, taking a sip of tea as he considered the sparks shooting like stars out of the flames.

"They know we're here. If we wait much longer, they'll bust a gut and ruin everythin'."

Galen scanned the surrounding shadows.

"They've ne'er been long on patience."

"A few more days . . ."

"So ye said two days ago."

"Perhaps if you went on ahead . . ."

The Commander snorted rudely, jamming the poker deeper into the fire.

"I can feel a change. He's been struggling with himself for days. He just needs more time."

Never enough time, fretted Galen. Nine days behind schedule—six spent tending his hurts, three more lost to the rains and bad roads, the nights growing colder the higher we climb and his lordship shivering under his flimsy blanket, too proud to ask for a thicker one. Sighing, Galen tossed another log on the fire.

He'd played this role before, having served his stint as Head Trainer of the Maze for nigh onto seven years. Still, studied cruelty didn't come easily, even when he understood its necessity. He might not like the man, but it troubled him to watch this thin-blooded easterner suffer from the unaccustomed cold and listen to his stomach rumble noisily in his sleep. Hunger was no stranger to the son of former slaves; the difference was that Galen had never chosen to be hungry.

If these difficulties weren't enough, he had to contend with the watchers. The day the road gave out, he located the correct trail easily enough and sent up a prayer that Altug's messages had reached each and every stronghold. He'd half-expected an arrow in his back until two days ago, when he'd caught his first glimpse of a scout and identified the bird-whistles the mountain people used to signal the presence of intruders. Relieved though he was to learn they were expected, he kept his guard up round the clock, ever mindful that not even a respected leader like Altug could fully control the wildness of the mountain folk. They lived like the goats whose milk gave them cheese and a fermented liquor rumored to resemble liquid fire. Untamed, clannish, and absolutely ruthless toward any stranger foolish enough to trespass their borders, their skills with a bow were legendary, as was their reputation as trackers. Galen figured out their system in a matter of hours, noticing with professional pride that they were using a Legion tactic—swing shifts with relief scouts spelling their cohorts every two hours.

Esslar sensed their presence without actually seeing them, while the prince seemed oblivious to the figures gliding soundlessly through the undergrowth, their rags of dark greens and earthy browns nearly invisible among the forest shadows. Robber's Pass was a day or so away, their first stop among many. Regardless of Esslar's wishes, the time for a serious conversation with the prince was upon them.

Galen's head shot up as a high shrill whinny broke the silence. In the next instant he was on his feet, running hard toward the picket line he'd rigged at dusk, his dagger freed of its sheath. Over the sound of a scuffle he heard the prince shouting at his assailant. With his next breath he smelled horses. Then he saw Sandur.

He was standing next to the stallion, one hand on the halter, the other stroking the great silver head rising and plunging as the horse snorted his distress, his hooves pawing nervously at the ground. The prince crooned softly to him in the nasal, sing-song language of Endlin, his face hidden by a mass of unruly braids. Hearing Galen's approach he tensed and looked up, squinting into the darkness.

"He ran that way!" the prince offered immediately, pointing due west. "I grabbed him but he . . . he . . .!" Searching vainly for the appropriate word, he pantomimed someone wriggling away. Not until then did Galen realize he was being addressed in the southern tongue. Before he could react, the prince held out a piece of cloth.

"This came away from his clothing."

"Was he armed?"

The prince shook his head.

"Where's yer knife?"

"In my gear."

"Ye thought nothin' of yer own safety, but went after him bare-handed? Did ye not ken he might be armed?"

"I thought only of Seal."

"Aye," Galen grunted, "so ye did. He's a fine beast, but not worth yer life."

The prince made no answer, but continued stroking the stallion's mane.

"Ye've a knife in yer gear, then. Do ye ken how to use it?"

"Aye," came the confident reply.

Galen struggled not to smile at the sound of his lordship's broad west country accent.

"Well, ye must wear it from now on. The blame is mine for not warnin' ye. Come to the fire, now, or Esslar will worry."

"Shouldn't we post a guard near the horses? I would gladly take first watch."

Galen chuckled as he sheathed his dagger.

"Nay, lad, the mountain people need no horses. They're likely curious."

The prince looked doubtful, but gave the stallion a final pat and, to Galen's surprise, accompanied him without further protest.

"Ye speak our tongue well."

"I was taught to read and write it, but had no practice speaking. Many words are difficult to pronounce. Often, I fail to understand you," he hurried to add, "or the healer."

"That's as it should be. We come from different lands."

Galen waited hopefully for the next question, giving an inward shout of thanksgiving when it came.

"Where are you from, Galen?" asked the Tehran's sa'ab with unfeigned interest. The Commander of the Legion smiled up at the starry night, calling down a blessing on the head of the nameless night-stalker who hurried homeward through the dark forest, his torn blouse flapping in the night breeze.

Side by side, former peasant and exiled prince walked toward the glow of the campfire where the healer waited.

ON THE APPROACH to the stronghold at Robber's Pass the path widened enough that three might ride abreast. At Galen's command, Sandur moved up from the rear, Esslar taking the middle position flanked by Galen on his right and Sandur on his left.

"Keep yer hands in plain sight and a smile on yer lips."

Before Sandur had time to wonder at the absurdity of smiling into an empty landscape, a body dropped from a tree limb, landed lightly on two feet, and without a word or even a glance at the three riders, a mountain man garbed in forest green slung his bow over his back, took hold of Galen's bridle, and fell into step beside them. In the next moment, two more figures appeared from behind the trees lining the path. A hand flashed out to grab Seal's bridle. The stallion shied and reared, the mountain man dodging flailing hooves, Sandur fighting to control the high-strung animal while Galen cursed steadily under his breath.

"They'll gladly cut his throat. Settle him or lose him."

The stallion's eyes showed white, his ears flicking back and forth as he listened to the steady stream of his master's reassurances. This time he suffered the stranger's hand on his bridle.

"Calm yourself as well, prince. They are a hasty people, quick to anger and slow to forgive," Esslar advised in a low voice, his smiling lips barely moving and his hands resting easily on the pommel of his saddle.

Sandur took a deep breath and forced a smile, trying not to stare at the man walking beside Seal. Soon he had other things to occupy his attention, for a mile down the path, as if summoned by magic, men began to emerge from behind trees and boulders, all of them dressed in a motley assortment of tunics and breeches dyed in shades of nut brown, slate grey, and deep forest green. In a matter of minutes the riders were surrounded by perhaps thirty escorts, all of them armed with bows and quivers, dagger sheaths dangling from wide belts strapped around their waists. Their forearms were protected by wide bands of leather and they were shod in soft boots reaching nearly to their thighs. Sandur had never seen such men, compact and swarthy like the commoners of Endlin, dark-haired and dark-eyed, but there the resemblance ended. They did not so much walk as swagger, shoulders back and chins held high, their long hair upswept into top-knots with shaggy mustaches drooping down on either side of their mouths.

As the silent procession moved on, some of the tension dissipated. Sandur's first impression was that they were being pointedly ignored. As he looked closer, he noticed a group of young men walking directly in front of Esslar's mare. From time to time they looked back over their shoulders at the healer, long burning glances sent by black unblinking eyes. Catching sight of a neighbor involved in the same activity, they would quickly jerk their heads forward again, seemingly embarrassed at being caught staring. From time to time Sandur felt their eyes on him. In time their odd behavior became clearer; they envied Sandur's position rather than his horse. It was a strange sensation to discover that their rapt regard of him resulted from his proximity to the healer. Sandur eyed Esslar askance, but the healer seemed blithely unaware of their stares.

The last few rows of trees lining the trail fell away as they rounded a bend, replaced by rows of people, many of them seated on rocks and tree stumps, all of them silent and, Sandur thought, almost reverent as the cortege passed by. Women stood in groups or by the sides of men, some of them holding nursing infants to their breasts. Sandur had never seen ayahs like these, young women with skirts hitched up and stuck into their waistbands as they suckled their charges in public. Elderly women best suited to the task of rearing children were seamed and wrinkled with weathered skin that spoke of long hours spent out of doors. Tame goats wandered among the crowd. Chickens squawked as they hurried out of the way of the forward guard. Here and there long-eared donkeys munched on grass, some of them loaded with bundles of kindling. To the side of the trail, half-hidden among the boulders and tall stands of pines and firs, squat huts fashioned out of logs or stones nestled in groups of two or three, their stone chimneys spouting wood smoke into the clear mountain air.

The pace slowed and then halted, the mountain men fanning out on either side of the riders, clearing a space in front of an elderly man who stood at the summit of the trail, his legs spread wide and his hands planted firmly on his hips. His iron grey hair was swept up into a top-knot, the twin tails of his moustache reaching the middle of his broad, leather-vested chest. He appraised them silently for a long moment, surveying Galen and the healer before coming at last to Sandur. A flicker of something like recognition crossed his face. Sandur blinked, and it was gone.

The crowd held their breath, everyone intent on this man who wore not a single emblem of office but was instantly identifiable as their leader. Sandur, raised in a culture which valued appearance almost as highly as it regarded character, sensed in this plainly dressed mountain-dweller the same qualities that marked his father—a keen intellect, a strong will, acute powers of judgment, and unshakable confidence. Even as he marked these similarities, a slow smile spread over the leader's face. Any resemblance between this man and his father vanished. Never had his father's face lit with such a heartfelt smile; never had he shouted out so warm a greeting, his hands raised high above his head in a cordial salute.

"Well met, friends of Pelion! Abide with us awhile and accept the hospitality of our stronghold!"

A tremendous shout rose from the throats of the men to be swelled by a strange trilling sound, high and warbling, from the women. The trance broken by the leader's words, Sandur was immediately surrounded by curious faces, hands stretching up to help him dismount, more hands reaching out to stroke the dappled stallion, to release the ties of his pack and loosen the strap on his saddlebags. He was borne forward by the crowd, trying not to mind that they touched him, fighting to keep the smile on his face, fearing it was becoming a grimace. When a stray hand brushed against his braids, fury rose within him to be met with a calm voice that seemed to speak in his mind as much as his ears.

"They mean no insult. They've waited many moons for our arrival and are understandably excited."

Sandur turned his head to find Esslar's dark eyes shining in his pale face and felt a firm hand grasp his upper arm as Galen appeared out of nowhere. Flustered as he was, unnerved by people who knew no better than to crowd him, shocked that someone had been so impudent as to touch his braids, he allowed the horseman his presumption and let himself be led forward.

"I am Altug, headman of this stronghold."

For the first time it became clear that the headman knew Sandur's guides since he neither sought nor offered introductions to anyone but Sandur.

"I am Sandur Kwanlonhon, clansman of Endlin."

Again the headman seemed to take his measure before gesturing for his guests to accompany him. A path cleared before him as he led them through the crowd, chatting sociably as they walked.

"Valeria awaits us. She intended on greeting you herself, but there was a ruckus among some of the youngsters only she could quell. We've visitors aplenty, and every home is full to bursting. Even so, she insisted that classes continue despite the uproar."

Altug paused in front of what looked to be a piece of rock cloven by a bolt of lightning and swept aside a heavy deerskin hung from iron pegs embedded in the stone. A dark hole was revealed. Altug stepped through, beckoning them to follow. Sandur walked forward into total blackness, the darkness a solid presence, cold moist air licking at his face. He followed the sound of Altug's footfalls, hearing those of Esslar and Galen behind him, uncomfortably aware that they were walking down a steeply raked path. Just as he was about to panic at the strangeness of this place, light glimmered in front of him, and he heard the sound of treble voices raised in a kind of chant. Another hide was brushed out of his path, and he caught his breath.

Light from a multitude of braziers arranged at different points throughout this underground cavern bounced off smooth walls of glistening pink rock. Slender pyramids of stone rose from the cave floor; others hung down from the natural stone ceiling. The air was warm and dry, the scent of burning pine filling his nostrils. But it was not the splendor of the cave (an enormous room larger even than the audience hall of the Kwanlonhon citadel) that caused Sandur to gaze in wonder about him. What made his heart leap up and a gasp escape his lips was the sight of children, boys and girls ranging in age from three to sixteen summers, all of them bright-eyed and alert, their half-sung, half-spoken chant stilled as they looked with curious eyes at the visitors.

Foreign as the setting might be, Sandur recognized it immediately as the stronghold's harem. Here were no tame beasts or playthings, no pools or fountains, but the warmth and light and sense of peace hovering over this place was unmistakable. Several ayahs and fathers were in attendance; one elderly woman approached them with hands outspread, her plump face beaming like a full moon. Unlike the women he had seen outside, her eyes were blue, her skin like milk and her hair, braided and arranged on the crown of her head, was a rich brown streaked with grey. As she drew closer, her full skirts brushing against childish hands reaching out to touch her, her hands smoothed each dark head as she passed, rewarding them, Sandur sensed, with a blessing of some kind.

"Welcome!" came a husky voice of surprising strength and authority, "I am Valeria."

Altug's pride in a woman called Valeria caused Sandur to assume she was his sa'ab, yet this woman was far too old to be the headman's firstborn. Sandur mumbled out a greeting, watching her closely as she welcomed Galen and Esslar and turned to acknowledge Altug. Then, in an unseemly and brazen fashion, unsuitable to both her age and rank, this elderly ayah who might have been a concubine in her youth (for Sandur guessed she had once been fair), reached her arm out to hug Altug's waist and leaned slightly against him, her head lodged companionably against his shoulder. If this was not enough, the headman made no motion to brush her aside but planted his lips firmly against her dimpled cheek.

They were speaking of festivities, contests, feats of skill, feasting and dancing and other things which held no interest for him. All Sandur could see was the woman called Valeria. She seemed unconscious of his gaze, so engaged was she in a conversation in which she took a leading role, explaining boldly instead of deferring to Altug, once even interrupting to correct him in front of his guests, a fault for which she should have been dismissed no matter how skilled she might be in the care of children. Even a valued concubine or a female sa'ab would never be indulged to this degree, flaunting her knowledge in front of strangers, shamelessly caressing a man in the presence of other men. If her age had not made her ridiculous, Sandur would have found her behavior unforgivable. As it was, he found her merely repugnant.

The sound of tramping feet and voices raised in shouts of hilarity echoed in the stone passageway. Into the harem flowed a stream of women, the young ayahs he'd seen on the trail. The children erupted into sound and movement, the youngest ones running with arms lifted up to be swung onto their hips, the older boys exchanging jests and swatting each other playfully, the girls skipping and pulling each other's braids. Above the noisy clamor rose Valeria's voice.

". . . announced we should end classes after your arrival. The mothers were grateful for another half-day of freedom for last minute preparations."

She used a word Sandur didn't know, but it wasn't the word that unsettled him so much as the queasy feeling that something was wrong.

". . . and meet our daughter's child. Quarig! Come here, young rascal, and greet our guests!"

The boy who ran towards them could have been no more than three years of age, his fat legs pumping, his ayah following a little behind him, another child at her breast. Altug crouched down, grabbing the boy by the waist and lifted him straight up into the air, the child screaming with delight, then swung him about so that he might perch jauntily on his grandfather's shoulder.

"This is Quarig, our first grandchild," announced the woman called Valeria.

Sandur's head pounded, his ears rang, his stomach knotted, his sole thought that he must leave quickly or risk bringing shame on his head and those of his companions. Forcing out a lie about caring for Seal, he excused himself and hurried through the horde of children, shrinking away from the women who weren't ayahs at all, but the concubines who had borne these children. "Mother" was the word Valeria used, a term signifying a woman chosen to rear a child jointly with the father.

Finding the deerhide, he pushed it aside, the daylight freeing him from unclean thoughts and unnatural longings, for no one had ever laid such a loving hand upon his head. Cold air poured into his lungs and he breathed deeply, pushing away ideas that frightened him, shaken to the core by the voices in his head that kept asking questions he could not answer.

"SHOULD I GO after him? He's sore distressed . . ."

"He has Aethra's mouth. I had the sense that if he smiled, I would see her there."

"Like Manthur, but sterner, stiffer. . ."

Esslar opened himself to the jumble of their thoughts, denying permission for Galen to follow Sandur, hearing with interest Valeria's description of Sandur's mother, and advising Altug that the Manthur he once called friend no longer existed.

As the cavern emptied, they took their places on several abandoned stools, Altug sending his grandson off with a pat on his rump. The child ran out, and they were alone. There was no need to exchange pleasantries since they had been in communication for several days. Altug began the conference with an apology.

"I told them not to come too near, but it's clear they upset him. When you missed the appointed day, a rumor spread that you weren't coming. Other strongholds have sent prospects for selection, and I can barely control them since they owe me no allegiance. I put our sons in charge of your escort, and it seems they were able to keep order well enough on the trails, although I fear you had an unexpected visitor two nights ago."

"Aye," Galen admitted, although he was quick to add, "but we've reason to bless the lad, whoever he might be."

"His name is Yossi, and a more pig-headed youth I've never met," grumbled Altug.

Valeria sent a fond look at her mate.

"Say rather that he reminds you of yourself at his age: hard-nosed, cynical, and ambitious to boot."

Altug growled out something in the mountain dialect, and she laughed out loud, her plump body shaking with merriment.

"He's vexed because Yossi has been a pest since the day he arrived. His stronghold is unknown to us, far to the north, a place that translates into the southern tongue as Dragon's Tooth. He came alone, arriving a moon ago and making a grand entrance, having eluded the watchers at every turn. He's been here in the hold every day, learning as fast as I can manage to teach him. I didn't ask him why he felt it necessary to visit you. My guess is he wanted to reassure himself you were truly coming."

Esslar spoke as if in a dream.

"He heard of the gift, but feared we might be wizards, spirits made of dragon smoke who steal away human souls. The stallion seemed to him a ghost horse, pale

and silvery in the moonlight. Not until Sandur attacked him did he believe we were flesh and blood."

The headman and his mate exchanged glances. Rousing himself, Esslar took a more business-like tone.

"How many have come, Altug? And when do I begin?"

"Nine men and two women so far, although there might be some late-comers in the next few days. The end of summer celebration begins tonight and continues tomorrow with the archery contests and a victory feast. I thought you might begin the day after."

Esslar nodded, a tiny frown appearing between his eyes.

"How many may you choose, Searcher?"

Valeria's question hung in the air between them, for all present understood that this class would be like no other, and if it should fail, none would follow. The Nineteenth Mother's call went out in the third moon of the new year. For five moons, in every colony and province where ernani made their homes, they waited for the Searchers sent forth to glean their youth for what might be a last chance at Transformation. To the four points of the compass she sent them—to the Western Ridge and Swiasa in the south, to the northern tundras beyond the Land of the Lapith and the eastern shore. Four Searchers entrusted with a precious mission, trained by the Nineteenth Mother herself. Her cautions had been strongly worded, her demands stringent; no ernani would be admitted beyond the bronze doors without a Searcher's full endorsement.

"I can say only this; if I find within them what we need, they'll accompany us south."

Esslar shared their concerns, for these were the best of their people. The Nineteenth Mother was adamant on this point. He recalled her final thoughts as the wagons rumbled out of the northern gate:

"Let no entreaties move you, however heartfelt. It will be a small group, the smallest since the Novice class. It would be irresponsible to involve too many in what might prove a failure. Remind them that if we are successful, the doors will re-open to all who seek entrance."

Esslar spoke aloud, willing them to understand and accept.

"Galen says we must not linger. For this reason I'll begin tonight, meeting them as a group so they'll be relaxed and confident when the time comes for the individual sessions. Have you explained that I must examine their bodies?"

Altug twirled the ends of his moustache and caught his mate's eyes. Valeria nodded.

"They've been told, although most of them are unfamiliar with the healing arts. We thought, if you've no objections, that Altug might be present when you examine the men and me with the women . . ."

Galen made his first comment on the proceedings, lightening the atmosphere with his ribald sense of humor, "Give way on this, healer, or ye'll be a pincushion the first time yer foolish enough to step outside the hold."

Altug guffawed. Esslar could not help but laugh while Valeria literally shook with mirth. As the laughter ebbed, Altug rose and made for the exit to the cavern, Galen following. Esslar was unsurprised when Valeria lingered.

"He found me repellent. A loud-mouthed shrew clinging desperately to her youth. Is that who I am, Searcher?"

"His first impression was one of beauty, a gifted ayah blessing her charges. He sensed your tender regard for your pupils and your love for the child and the grandchild of your body. I warned you this would happen," he reminded her, "yet you insisted on assisting me."

He sensed she was comforted although the hurt had gone deep. Her youth was gone, but to see herself reflected in Sandur's judgmental eyes, a mirror magnifying every flaw as he fought to arrange the world as he had been trained to understand it, this had brought misery to one whose loving heart contained room enough for every soul who roamed the Sarujian Mountains. Valeria was a mother to her adopted people, and so they had named her thirty years ago when she taught them to read and write and cured them of rickets, worms, and goiters, her donkey's back loaded not with the luxuries that might ease her life in this harsh mountain outpost, but the books and medicines with which she would teach and heal them. "Mother of all mothers" she was to them from the moment of their birth.

She nodded slowly and turned to go. Esslar called her back.

"Send me Yossi."

Her eyes lit, for he spoke her dearest wish.

"No promises," he warned, but she had already fled, her small feet carrying her heavy body with surprising swiftness.

Alone in the cavern where the fires of the first inhabitants burned throughout the cruel moons of winter, Esslar cleared his mind, pushing away worries—Valeria's hurt at the reminder that her youth was gone, Altug's fears that his grandson might never enter the Maze, Galen's reminders that the road before them stretched long and hard—and concentrated on the voices in Sandur's head.

"Do we ask too much of him?" the Master of Mysteries inquired of the empty air.

His answer came out of the south, a sentence quoted from an ancient book of prophecy.

"And what of the sons who dream of safe haven?"

Chapter 9

Night Watch

THE NINETEENTH MOTHER'S private council assembled at dusk. Symone, Head Librarian and Archivist, a scholar of extraordinary talents whose specialty was the ancient lore of Pelion, couldn't provide a factual explanation of the custom's derivation. Once, when questioned about this very matter, she stared down her nose (a considerable span given its length) before replying: "What better time to fight the darkness?"

Council members were summoned in a similar manner, a mental call reaching them wherever they labored: the High Healers, Evadne and Japhet, examining a patient in the House of Healing and Anstellan, Master of the Hetaera Guild, reviewing third-year apprentices. On this particular occasion, Briseis, Master of the Printer's Guild, was summoned as well. Bent over galley sheets, proofing the typesetting before approving a first run, he lifted his head to check the time and dove back to work with renewed energy.

The call found Symone on her hands and knees, struggling to retrieve an obscure volume from a bottom shelf, the knot of her thinning hair threatening to come awry with the force of her exertions. As the finger of the Nineteenth Mother's thoughts reached out toward her, beckoning her to the tower chamber, she hauled up the heavy book and staggered toward a nearby alcove, brushing aside offers of help from her assistants before lowering it onto a table. Pulling a pencil stub from its accustomed resting place in the middle of her meager bun, she lifted her eyes to the high windows of the Greater Library, noting the progress of the sun across the afternoon sky, then went about her business, taking rapid notes that resembled the fine tracery of cobwebs or the tracks of bird's feet in wet snow.

Remy, too, was busily engaged with paper and pen, copying out the pages the Nineteenth Mother requested that morning, all too aware of the sands running through the hour glass. Every so often he frowned, twisting one of his eyebrows with his left hand as his pen raced across the surface of the paper.

In time they finished their tasks, the healers washing their hands and drying them on the cloths stacked in readiness beside the examination table, Anstellan finishing his session with a good-natured reminder of the examination scheduled for tomorrow to a chorus of polite groans, the printer storing the corrected galleys in his desk and bidding his co-workers a pleasant goodnight. Symone finished the last sentence with a flourish, using the pencil to anchor the lop-sided bun in its rightful place at the same time Remy was smoothing his tortured locks over his baldpate after wiping his pen and tightening his inkwell.

Crossing the open square as citizens hurried home to prepare the evening meal, they made their way to a private side entrance guarded by a pair of Legionnaires. Up five flights of stone steps they climbed, Japhet and Evadne arm in arm, progressing at a sedate pace (for they were well past their middle years), Anstellan taking the steps two at a time, Briseis huffing and puffing, reminding himself that in the future he must forgo that extra helping of bread pudding, and Symone, late as usual, bounding up the stairs like a harried rabbit, a roll of papers stuck haphazardly under her arm.

Another matched pair of Legionnaires met them at the top of the stairs and ushered them on without delay. At the end of the hall stood an open door leading to a large antechamber. Inside Remy waited, handing each of them the papers that represented his work for the day before making his departure. Cloaks were removed, garments straightened, disheveled hair put to rights, and they entered the inner sanctum of the Nineteenth Mother of Pelion.

IT WAS THE Nineteenth Mother's custom to speak aloud in Council sessions although everyone present was either a transformed or born adept. Symone, ever inquisitive, once asked her why she refrained from using inner speech in the privacy of her chambers. Far from being affronted by the question, the Nineteenth Mother offered this reply.

"Remember my origins, Symone. I've always feared that if I become too dependent on these gifts, which came to me late in life, I might forget how to talk."

Upon hearing this admission, a region of Symone's crusty heart warmed and swelled. From that moment on she adopted a protective attitude toward the woman who chose her for the task she had aspired to since meeting Kazur Kwanlonhon, the former Head Librarian. An expert in the lore of Agave, this transformed ernani from the eastern shore became her mentor, shepherding her through her training in the Greater Library. To him she owed her choice of scholarly expertise. She'd thought to establish her reputation by investigating newly discovered cultures, the Flowering Lands perhaps, or the Western Ridge. In a single afternoon, Kazur changed her mind.

"History must always be rewritten. The time approaches when Pelion must be reexamined. Strip away the blinders, the false assumptions and complacency. See Pelion as a stranger sees her. Walk through the northern gates for the first time."

And Symone walked.

Manuscripts untouched for centuries, the parchments stiff, their brittle edges crumbling with age, the vegetable inks fading, old-style language and bizarre spellings—these were her guides. Having mastered the past, she considered the present, finding the seeds of discontent, the unheard warnings of disaster, yet buried them deep inside herself, unwilling to be a prophet of doom for the city she adored.

Fourteen years ago, on a gloomy afternoon when the darkened interior of the Greater Library made it impossible to read without the aid of candles, a voice broke the silence, asking:

"How long until we pass away?"

Symone recognized the speaker, having overheard conversations between the Nineteenth Mother and Kazur many times among the stacks and alcoves reserved for researchers and scholars.

"Two more generations, perhaps three."

"How shall we fail?"

"Through civil strife."

"Can you elaborate?"

The Nineteenth Mother seated herself in the empty chair across from Symone. The severity of black suits her, Symone thought idly, an elegance of line that drapes her tall figure in simple majesty. As the Nineteenth Mother continued to regard her, she was brought up short. Organizing her argument as Kazur had taught her, Symone proposed a thesis.

"The spread of adept powers grows disproportionately. In another generation there won't be enough candidates from Pelion to match the influx of ernani. Pelion's legacy is one of leadership, pride in the old knowledge the founders brought with them, and because it's been a closed city for almost six hundred years, a profound distrust of outsiders. As the transformed adepts spread that knowledge and begin to make their own contributions, competition will arise."

"I see two possibilities; Pelion will either severely limit the number of ernani who seek entry into the Maze, charging high fees for admission in order to control the supply of talented adepts or, more probably, the Maze will simply be closed. When either of these events occurs, the ernani will unite against the city."

"If this comes to pass, and the ernani prevail, must it spell doom? Isn't it likely that the Maze will endure, changed somewhat, but still be a viable place for Preparation?"

Symone frowned, unwilling to continue, unable to stop. For years she'd dreamed of holding this exact conversation, of sharing her views rather than keeping her findings to herself.

"The problem, as I said, is disproportion. At first it was gender-based because of insufficient female ernani. That lack led to the Trial, our greatest folly since Surnan's attempt to breed adepts, and was partially solved by the creation of New Agave. The newest disproportion is primarily geographical. Up to this point the ernani have consisted of the finest specimens of the nearby populous—the most intelligent, ambitious, and aggressive inhabitants from the surrounding provinces. The peoples of the fringes, the most removed and the least informed, remain untouched. If the balance of power tips too strongly in any single direction, to the adept colonies in Lapith, for instance, or the growing contingent of adepts residing in the southeast provinces, the plan will fail."

"And what is that plan?"

Symone had wrestled with this question for years. It lingered, unwritten and unspoken, beneath every decision and development concerning Pelion since the day the First Mother led her people into this valley and lit the fire on the altar rock. Symone lifted her eyes from the manuscript spread out before her and answered.

"Total enlightenment. Everyone who walks the earth must receive the gift, speaking heart to heart and mind to mind."

"Yes," said the older woman, and again she whispered, as if in benediction, "Yes."

An overpowering sense of relief flooded Symone, for in that precious moment of confirmation, the value of her life's work was affirmed.

"You are everything Kazur promised and more. His place is empty now, and I have grieved these many moons. It's time to put grief aside. Will you aid me in that plan?"

"Yes," said Symone, and their pact was made.

"YOU HAVE BEFORE you a list of expenses for the next class. Remy assisted me with the figures, basing them on a class size of thirty. As you can see, our coffers fall far short of our needs."

From anyone else this pronouncement might have been greeted with sighs and much shaking of heads. Instead, it was met by a quick surge of energetic thinking. No problem was so large that it could not be faced with perspicacity and wit. She-Who-Was-Magda's Council, hand-picked by her over a thirty-year tenure, rose to the challenge.

"How go the book sales?" asked Anstellan with his usual forthrightness. Trim and lithe, a famous runner before entering the House of Hetaeras, he was the youngest member of the Council. Like Symone and Esslar, he was born adept, while Japhet, Evadne, and Galen were former residents of the Maze. When the Council sat in its entirety (a luxury not enjoyed for these eight moons) its appointed members were evenly balanced, although the Nineteenth Mother always insisted with a laugh that she, too, should be counted among the Transformed.

"We received the first profits from Endlin only recently; Phanus and Lampon assure me that sales continue strong. The success of the shop in New Agave is beyond all our predictions."

The Nineteenth Mother beamed at the Master Printer, who ducked his head, his cheeks dyed a mottled red.

"It is for this reason I summoned you, Briseis. Both shops write that their inventory is sadly depleted. May we depend on you for more stock?"

Despite his shyness, for he was far more comfortable with presses than with people, Briseis found the wherewithal to address the Nineteenth Mother directly, his adoration shining behind thick spectacles that seemed to be forever sliding down his nose.

"We've already donated our entire back stock. The vote was heavily in your favor, and there's been nary a complaint from the membership since it's all we can do to fill our present orders. If I push for more recent publications, I may have a riot on my hands. Adrastus has his followers . . ."

"Say no more," the Nineteenth Mother cut him off pleasantly, although it was clear she preferred that the President's name not be mentioned in her presence. "We appreciate your efforts and sympathize with your dilemma. Not for the world would I ask you to jeopardize your position in the guild. We have need of friends, and your friendship will always be remembered."

"I was thinking," Briseis ventured timidly, "you might have back stocks of your own."

"How so?" she asked, eyebrows lifting heavenward.

"Why, the libraries, of course!" Breseis blurted out, wincing as he caught sight of Symone's horrified expression.

"The libraries?!" Symone squeaked, aghast at the thought of her priceless stacks being pilfered. Bashful though he might be, Briseis was also tenacious by nature. Refusing to be intimidated by this over-bearing Archivist, having tangled with her many times in the past, he hurried to defend himself.

"You know as well as I do that you've duplicate, even triplicate copies in the Greater and Lesser Libraries, especially now that we've put so many handwritten manuscripts into print. If you combed those stacks, it's my guess you'd find twice as many volumes as we donated."

"Is this so, Symone?" the Nineteenth Mother asked.

Japhet spoke up before Symone could form a reply.

"Evadne and I could order a review of all texts in the House of Healing's reading room and surrender any duplicates. As long as we've one copy of everything in the Greater Library, we'll survive. Symone's staff will have to contend with an influx of healers among their sacred haunts, but the change of scenery will do us good. I find myself enjoying my excursions here; the walk clears my mind."

"Don't forget the holdings in the Maze," added Anstellan. "Most of them are basic texts, but with so small a class we should be able to get along with single copies of everything."

Much as she hated parting with so much as a pamphlet, Symone felt the rising tide of enthusiasm and observed, with a sinking feeling in her stomach, the avid glow in the Nineteenth Mother's eyes. It didn't help matters that the original idea for the bookshops was Symone's. Groaning inside, she put on a brave front.

"We'll begin tomorrow. If I put every apprentice to work and halt all cataloging and restoration, it should take a fortnight or so."

Privately, she vowed that not a single volume would be surrendered without her personal supervision, this final thought easing the blow of separation.

"Symone, don't grieve over the loss of your books. They go to be treasured elsewhere. And if that's not enough, I give you my word that if we are successful, we will make acquisitions a high priority and fill your shelves to bursting once again."

A happy lull fell over the tower chamber. With further expressions of gratitude, the Nineteenth Mother dismissed Briseis. As the door closed behind him, she spread her fingers over the pages in front of her.

"The next item on our agenda is not so easily dealt with. The second sheet comprises a list of our staff within the Maze. Given the size of the incoming class and the limitations of our budget, we must greatly reduce the number of personnel. This is a sad reality, but one we may not ignore."

They knew it would come to this. Even so, they shifted uncomfortably in their chairs. The ninth moon was upon them. In less than sixty days the bronze doors would open has they had for a hundred years. Each of them had pledged their support to the Nineteenth Mother's plan, sharing with her a determination that the Maze continue to function. Still, these financial constraints were new to them, and they worried over the dismissal of people with whom they had labored, Japhet and Evadne for over twenty years, Symone for fourteen, and Anstellan for the last five.

"I don't know how you'd like us to proceed, Nineteenth Mother," Evadne began, "but it seems reasonable for each of us to consider those areas for which we are personally responsible. If so, then Japhet and I will evaluate our fellow healers and those who prepare and store food."

Something of Evadne's equanimity in accepting this burden passed on to the others. "I suppose the staffs of the Halls are mine," offered Anstellan.

Symone chimed in, "I'll review teachers and library personnel."

The Nineteenth Mother might have ordered them to comply, or simply told them what she expected, but this had never been her way. For thirty years she had overseen the working of the Maze; none knew it or loved it more than her. Even so, her touch on the reins of power remained unfailingly light. Hers was a delicate dance to music unheard by anyone but herself.

"Remy offered to review the laundry and sanitation workers. Since Galen is unavailable, I asked Dictys to evaluate all trainers and monitors. In regard to Dictys, he has agreed to assume the position of Head Trainer."

"Dictys?" Japhet inquired with a puzzled frown. "He's young for such responsibilities, isn't he? Galen promoted him to lieutenant just a year or so ago. Surely a more seasoned veteran would be better suited for such an important post."

"As you say, he's young, but he has one qualification I consider more important than age or experience. If you will recall, he is mated to the first female ernani from Droghedan. We sent the Searchers into the wilderness; thus, many of the ernani they select will come from lands hitherto unknown to us. I urge each of you to consider this when you evaluate your personnel. Be sensitive to their ability to cope with oddities, with the unexpected."

Anstellan loosed an audible groan, shaking his gleaming head of close-cropped curls.

"Do I hear what I think I hear? Must I prepare for the worst?"

She-Who-Was-Magda laughed out loud, for he was a favorite of hers, always ready with a quip or a jest, a clown with the face of an angel.

"I suggest only that they will be superstitious and most probably offended by what you teach. Customs concerning joining are highly sensitive matters. We've been spoiled of late, most of our classes coming to us from places where former ernani have prepared the way. Many of these will be first-time representatives of their people, as was Dictys' mate."

The laughter left her face.

"Yours may be the most difficult task of all, Anstellan. Always before, one member of each couple has been native born, taught during adolescence by Masters of your House. This time, no one will know our ways."

Her comment brought silence to the room. Here was the crux of her plan, a deviation from all that went before. Cut off from the population of Pelion by the Guild Assembly's referendum, the Nineteenth Mother proposed that ernani join with ernani on the Path of Preparation. At first they thought her mad. Esslar alone remained silent in the face of their rejection of her proposal. The debate raged for hours, Symone reminding her that the Sixteenth Mother, faced with the lack of female ernani, had tried without success to join citizen to citizen. Japhet and Galen, as former ernani, voiced their belief that without the help of their native-born mates they might never have adapted to life within the Maze. Through it all she listened carefully, posing inquiries, probing suppositions, soliciting advice.

When there was nothing left to discuss, she said, "Shall we use the past as an excuse, confident in our beliefs that what has never been attempted must surely miscarry, or shall we proceed on faith alone? Have all our forbearers labored in vain? Shall you be the last caretakers of the Maze? Shall I be a Mother without a cause, thirty years of my life ended in ruin, the Maze abandoned, wrecked by prejudice and senseless fears?"

The measure of their trust was such that not once since that certain night nine moons ago, a night when the Council members searched their hearts before voting unanimously to proceed with her plan, had they voiced their doubts.

After a somber silence, Symone asked, "What news from the Searchers?"

"They come, Symone, they come. Even now they undertake the long journey home."

The Nineteenth Mother spoke with eyes closed, fists clenched.

"One from the frozen tundra beyond northernmost Lapith, another from the southern lands where mountains smoke, one from a place called Dragon's Tooth, another from the marsh-dwellers of the river Tellas. One man is tattooed, his skin a living record of his exploits with a spear, and a woman whose arms are scarred with the bites of the serpents who are the gods of her people. Twenty they have found, out of which a mere handful have ever heard of Pelion. Strange are their ways, even stranger their gods: the four winds, the smoke of the dragon's breath, spirits who reside in trees, ancestors long returned to dust, all the forces of the natural world they worship. Some believe in nothing save the power of their weapons."

"What of Esslar and Galen?" Evadne asked with some urgency, ever mindful of absent friends.

"They came down out of the mountains without mishap and are building a raft to carry them downriver. They are seven now: Yossi and Kokor of the mountain strongholds, Tibor of the marsh-dwellers, Vlatla of the river folk. Vlatla supervises the building of the raft, for such is the craft of her people. She teaches them to use the long poles while she stands at the tiller."

A shadow passed over her face. Sensing her weariness and the lateness of the hour, they slipped away until only Symone remained. The Nineteenth Mother, lost in thought, looked up as the thin, waspish figure of the Archivist approached her chair.

"What have you found, Symone?"

"Tidbits and hearsay, nothing of fact."

A smile tugged at the Nineteenth Mother's lips as she considered her hard-headed compatriot. Symone and Esslar were the opposites by which her Council was balanced—Esslar the dreamer, intuitive, mysterious, often cryptic in his pronouncements, and Symone the pragmatist, sharp-eyed and shrewd, unfailingly rational with a tongue capable of slicing steel.

"Even so, what do you conjecture?"

Seating herself, Symone consulted her notes. Taking a deep breath, she began to do what she did best, sifting through the stuff of legends to find the truths buried beneath.

"Cinthea's history is oral, as it is everywhere with the exception of Endlin and Pelion, yet Cinthea is different, primarily in the existence of their bards. We would consider them storytellers, but they are much more. To join their league, you must have a prodigious memory and a talent for recitation. Although they live far-flung throughout the region, at the winter solstice they gather in Cinthea proper to begin the chanting of the epics, each member responsible for specific passages, all of them actively engaged in correcting details and adding new sections that constitute the events of that particular year. It's a remarkable system, communal in nature, each bard passing memorized sections on to a chosen successor."

"And the dreamsayers?"

Symone frowned.

"More difficult to unravel—too much hocus-pocus and silliness. They're not exactly gods; in fact, I can't find any mention of gods in Cinthean culture, but they're almost worshipped. They come along every few generations and are reputed to read the dreams of the populous," the scholar sniffed her disbelief, "no doubt with appropriately chosen conjuring tricks."

The Nineteenth Mother appeared to mull the information over in her mind, her eyes closed as she concentrated.

"What is the purpose of having your dreams read?"

"Predictions of events, although the bulk of it is better described as personal advice or suggestions for future actions." Symone shrugged. "What we would call counseling, I suppose."

The Nineteenth Mother's eyes flew open.

"Could they be latent adepts?"

Symone blinked rapidly for a moment. Despising superstition in any form, her mind raced as she sought to bring the unexplained into cogent form.

"It's possible, more than possible," she agreed slowly, "especially when you consider our own history. The Tenth Mother instituted a search for adepts beyond Pelion. According to the records, her Searchers were successful. Without training, cut off from others like themselves, they often went mad or committed suicide. If adepts were born into a culture that valued prophecy and believed wholeheartedly in dreams, they might find a way to channel their gifts. It wouldn't be dreams they read so much as the thoughts and emotions of their subjects."

She paused for a moment, chewing on her pencil.

"They'd be better suited to the work if they were limited adepts, able to read but unable to send and thus less likely to inspire fear."

"Is there any record of inheritance? A dreamsayer who gave birth to another dreamsayer?"

"None that I can find, although we've little information. Two Searchers writing in the first quarter of this century recorded the phenomenon. Another mention comes from a former ernani from Cinthea who evidently remained in Pelion. Some of the early Chartists who mapped the area contributed observations of the winter solstice ritual but nothing more. The only way to test your hypothesis would be to journey there and attempt an interview with their current dreamsayer."

"I fear that's impossible. She died not long ago."

No explanation for the Nineteenth Mother's remark was offered. With unusual tactfulness on her part, Symone asked for none. Rising to take her leave she asked something which concerned her far more than the research she'd just presented.

"Why are you troubled by the river woman steering the raft? Do you fear an accident of some kind?"

The Nineteenth Mother started, taken unaware. Examining that thin face with its long, aggressive nose and almost non-existent chin, she read protectiveness in those piercing eyes and unvoiced concern for the Council's missing members.

"Sometimes I underestimate you, Symone, and for that I beg your pardon." She hesitated, seeming to weigh something in her mind before continuing. "I fear no accidents. Such is Vlatla's expertise in these matters that her raft will bring them south much faster than they could ever travel with three on horseback and four afoot. My sadness stems from the fact that one among them might help steer the craft, but keeps himself aloof, unwilling to contribute his talents to the group."

When the identity of the recalcitrant ernani was not forthcoming, Symone decided not to pry. After rolling her papers into a tight cylinder, she took her leave.

Only the walls were party to the Nineteenth Mother's sigh.

"When will you join us, Sandur? Why do your eyes remain closed?"

A half-formed idea drifted across her mind, but she was too weary to pursue anything but sleep.

Five stories below her window the watchman called the hour before midnight. The Nineteenth Mother never heard him. She was fast asleep, her dreams filled with the sonorous chanting of the Cinthean bards.

* * *

AT THE RAP on her door Gwyn placed her knitting in the basket on the floor beside the bed and rose from her chair. She evidenced no resentment at the interruption but moved swiftly to the door and swung it wide. A well-loved face was revealed, the girl's hair clean and shining, her scrubbed skin smelling of soap, her dress fresh from the laundry, the full skirt stiff with starch.

"You're early! Was the audience not to your liking? Did you find the new comb by the basin? Where is Rauros?"

Pulling the girl inside, Gwyn shut the door behind her. By the time she resumed her chair, Alyssa had already claimed her accustomed place on the side of the bed near the window, poised expectantly for their afternoon chat.

"Yes. No. Yes. Sleeping in my chamber," the girl answered pertly, then burst into laughter, her mirth so contagious that soon Gwyn was laughing too, both of them reflecting the brightness of the autumn sun filtering through the filmy curtains of the modest inn.

Alyssa's chamber next door was a twin to this one, a small but cheery room with white-washed walls, the wooden floors swept daily by the staff and scattered with rag-rugs, the hearth already laid for tonight's fire. The furnishings were simple: a goodly-sized bed, two wooden chairs with reed-woven seats, a writing table, a sizeable chest, and a bed-stand with basin and ewer. It was the second inn they'd tried, the first one deemed unsuitable because of the owners' dislike of the dog. Alyssa wilted under the innkeeper's disapproval, but when he forbade Rauros his accustomed place beside his mistress' feet in the common room where they took their meals, Temenus slapped the money for that night's food and lodging into the palm of the owner (who quailed before the ham-fisted farmer's anger) and stated his position in no uncertain terms.

"We didn't sneak the dog into our rooms, but announced plainly at the outset that he was her companion. Would you have her stumble and fall while he sits locked upstairs? What harm does he do, sleeping quietly beneath the table? Be assured we'll vacate our rooms in the morning and secure more hospitable quarters. Things have come to a sorry state in Pelion when visitors are treated with such rudeness. Make no mistake; I'll lodge a formal complaint with the Innkeepers Guild on the morrow!"

It took Gwyn several hours to calm him, unused as she was to such fits of temper. Normally he was the mildest of men, soft-spoken and slow to anger. Not until late that night, while they snuggled together in bed, did she discover the reason for his outburst.

"I'm troubled by the way things here have changed. My friends at the experimental farms are the same, older and stiffer in the back and shoulders, but just as willing to demonstrate a new technique of grafting or offer me seedlings that show promise of hardiness during dry spells. The young ones give me nothing but stares and cold shoulders, as if I was a freak of some kind."

He turned his head toward her on the pillow they shared, the moonlight playing over the nooks and crannies of his weather-beaten face, worry etched into the deep folds on either side of his nose and new creases in his brow. When she reached out to smooth them away, he took her hand, holding it fast in his callused paw.

"Today was the last straw. I can overlook rudeness towards me, but I can't allow such behavior toward Alyssa. Just when she's coming into her own, finding an audience, paying back every copper I've lent her and beginning to fill that purse of hers, a simple lack of courtesy ruins everything."

"We cannot fight her battles for her, my love, and you mustn't try. Her mother gave her backbone and trained her carefully to make her way in the world."

Sensing Temenus' trouble ran deep, Gwyn continued to whisper softly into his ear, disengaging her hand to stroke the temples where the grey hair glinted like silver threads in the moonlight.

"You cannot fight single-handed what Pelion has become. We're strangers here, and nothing is as I dreamed it would be. The shopkeepers treat me politely enough until they hear my accent. Oh, my love," she sighed, all her plans gone awry, "it's no longer your city, and now I fear 'twill ne'er be mine..."

"Hush, Gwyn. If you cry, I shan't bear it."

He pulled her into his arms, cradling her against his bulk. His lips moving against her cheek, he spoke the words she dreaded to hear.

"My business is nearly done. Soon we must return to help the children gather in the harvest."

She nodded her head against his stubbled chin, torn between her longing for home and hearth, children and grandchildren, and her feelings for the girl they must leave to the mercy of a city grown suddenly unfriendly.

"A few more days," Gwyn promised.

A kiss was his thanks, and she fell asleep in his arms.

In their dreams they walked hand in hand though the city, a different city from the one in which they slept, a place born out of dreams, a city without walls.

"... AND OFFERED THE portico for me to use when it rains! At first I thought she meant to send me away. Her voice is unpleasant, shrill and grating. Then, instead of shooing me off, she complimented me on the story!"

Gwyn scrutinized Alyssa's mobile features and flying hands, trying to find in this sun-lit face the starved waif who once knocked at her door. The girl had bloomed in the past few weeks, her figure filling out with good food, the dark circles under her eyes vanishing as she slept nightly on a good mattress in a room free of drafts. Gwyn helped in the selection of a new dress, chosen for comfort and versatility more than fashion. Temenus provided a map of the city and helped Alyssa trace the route with her fingers, pointing out the sites he thought might best supply her with a steady stream of onlookers. For the first few days Gwyn accompanied them, helping Rauros and Alyssa learn their way. Now girl and dog traveled alone, roaming the plazas, parks, and market streets from mid-morning to mid-afternoon, searching for the best places to tell stories to the people of Pelion.

". . . the best place yet since children come there every day. She said she'd use me a few days a week to begin, then, if the staff agrees that my stories are worthwhile, I'll work more and be paid a salary! Just think, Gwyn, a regular salary instead of tossed coins!"

Since the first day of travel on the road to Pelion, Alyssa kept careful records of the funds Temenus lent her. Expressing his delight that Gwyn would not be left alone while he worked, he offered to cover Alyssa's expenses if she would undertake the role of companion. Alyssa would have none of it. She would pay her own way, or they would part company. In the face of her mulishness, he could do nothing but agree.

Her debts paid and her purse heavier every day, the inn a familiar place and the family who ran it fond of both girl and dog, this latest development was all Gwyn could have hoped for. There was no doubt of the girl's talents. Gwyn witnessed firsthand her daily miracles with the crowds, watching as they reacted first to those unseeing eyes only to come under her spell the moment her beautifully modulated voice began the telling of the tale, her hands describing the setting, a castle or a forest glade, a cottage or a riverbank thick with bulrushes. By the time the characters emerged—a spoiled princess, a gawky youth all elbows and knees, a cantankerous wolf or a benevolent grandmother—they saw nothing but the pictures she painted, transported by her to the landscapes of their imaginations.

". . . although she seemed surprised when I told her I come from Cinthea. Not anything I could put my finger on. A kind of curiosity, I think. In any case, I'm to return tomorrow the hour after midday."

"What is this place, Alyssa?"

"She called it the Lesser Library, although I'm not quite sure what that means. Is it a small building, or are the people who go there less intelligent than others?"

Gwyn smothered a laugh.

"I think not, although the name seemed odd to me, too, the first time I heard it. There are two libraries, one for scholars and researchers and another for casual readers and younger students. You can borrow a book from the Lesser Library while the books in the Greater Library are never removed from the building."

The girl shrugged, her interest dwindling. Suddenly, it struck Gwyn that Alyssa couldn't read. For a moment she couldn't quite fathom it, the thought of this girl of vast memory and obvious intelligence never reading a book or sitting in a classroom seeming to her a shameful waste of talent. Gwyn had been taught to read and figure in the Maze. Although she never waxed brilliant in the classroom, she kept the account books and read nightly to Temenus, whose eyesight for small print was not what it used to be. Her thoughts were interrupted when she realized the girl sat brooding, her blank eyes staring out the window.

"What is it, child? Why this sudden change of mood?"

Alyssa sighed before turning to the place from which Gwyn's voice reached her ears.

"It's just that . . . that I know you'll soon be leaving."

Gwyn moved to the bed and placed her arm around the girl's shoulders, reminding herself she must not indulge in private sorrows.

"We've had this conversation before. Each time, you say you must remain in Pelion. You know you've a home with us if you want it. Cyme might not offer the riches to be made in the city, but you'd not lack for an audience on market days, and you'd be a great help to me on the farm. If you're intent on staying here, you've a place to live, a decent wage, and friends will surely follow."

"I didn't come for riches or to make new friends. I've friends aplenty in Cinthea and respectable work as a bard."

This was the place where every conversation foundered, the girl turning inward and Gwyn unable to pierce her reserve. Prevented by her vows from reading a non-adept's thoughts except under conditions of dire emergency, she relied on skills of persuasion.

"Well, you've guessed aright. Temenus' work here is finished, and the crops are waiting." The girl bowed her head. "I'll never be easy in my heart unless I know what you plan. Is there nothing you can tell me," she pleaded, "nothing to send an old woman home free of worry?"

The girl tensed and closed her eyes. Tears leaked out from beneath her eyelids to be trapped by the thickness of her lashes.

"There's no plan, Gwyn, no reason except I promised I'd come."

Gwyn pulled the bright head to her breast, wordlessly stroking her hair. She was never able to explain what happened next. Without forethought, without even a conscious decision on her part, she broke a rule that was as much a part of her as breathing. A tingling sensation ran through her fingertips, and her thoughts leapt across the darkness to enter a chamber of

Alyssa's memories. There, in what she quickly identified as a sickroom, a body lay beneath a thick coverlet, a skeletal hand reaching out, a quavering voice rising from the heap of bedclothes . . .

The contact ended abruptly, catapulting her back into the waking world. Not with a word or a gesture did Gwyn betray herself to the one whose tears wet the bosom of her dress. Inside, her mind reeled, for she was only Gwyn of Cyme, a former ernani of little consequence, an ordinary woman come face to face with the extraordinary.

FEARFUL AS GWYN was as she entered the Nineteenth Mother's antechamber, the round-faced clerk, or secretary (for so he introduced himself), put her at ease. Here was none of the rudeness of the city-dwellers; a slight briskness on his part as he offered her a chair and asked her business, but nothing in his manner revealed surprise at her presence or offense at her request. She stumbled over her tongue more than once, painfully aware of her provincial accent and her second-best skirt patched twice over the knees. All the while he nodded pleasantly, a genial moon bobbing over the sea of papers covering his desk.

Soon Gwyn found herself repeating her story to someone who bore no resemblance to the Eighteenth Mother she'd known in her youth. This woman was old, almost ancient, the ivory skin of her cheeks covered with a tracery of fine lines like so many veins in a grape leaf. Her forehead and eyes shadowed by veils, her chin resting upon two fingers of her clasped hands, she seemed to sleep, her face expressionless, offering no clues. The story told, Gwyn's request humbly but urgently stated, the Nineteenth Mother nodded, a firm nod indicating both understanding and the termination of the interview.

"Rest easy; from this day forward Alyssa will live under my protection. Her position in the Lesser Library is assured, and my secretary will keep me informed of her progress. You have my thanks, Gwyn. Go now, and say nothing to Alyssa."

No promises were given other than the girl would not be left friendless. Nor was any mention made of broken vows. Not once did the Nineteenth Mother give any indication as to her thoughts or feelings, yet strangely, a sense of finality came over Gwyn, a feeling that her duties were finished. Satisfied, she withdrew, hurrying back to the inn, to Temenus, eager to take up her life where she had left it before the rains came to Cyme.

"AH, GWYN!" WHISPERED the Nineteenth Mother as the patched skirt disappeared behind the door, "what have you brought me?"

Magda was an old hand at wrestling with adversity. Still, after thirty years of victory, she prepared herself against defeat, always mindful that her opponent might have mastered a new hold since their last match in the tower chamber. Now she gathered her powers as she paced, her arms locked under her breasts, her head bowed, walking the stone floor, opening herself to the visions and voices that brought her to this moment.

Gwyn began the contest, a former ernani defending the right:*"Her mother spoke the words! They were my words, Mother, the ones that brought me here from Cyme. 'A search for sight . . .'"*

Latona the Dreamsayer took up the cause, her voice echoing in Gwyn's thoughts, a mother speaking beyond death through the agent chosen to escort her daughter to Pelion, *"Your future lies in the realm of water, in things that float on the surface of the sea."*

Images took over: Rauros of the rushing waters, the tingle of her flesh when she touched the girl's outstretched hand in the marketplace at Cyme, the same tingle that caused Gwyn to leap inside and solve the mystery of Alyssa's presence in Pelion.

Her opponent girded its loins, loathe to surrender without a fight.

"Without blemish shall be the ernani," proclaimed the Legislation of Preparation, the rules by which selection was bound, rules Magda had sworn to uphold.

"Only a perfect vessel is worthy of a clansman's seed," warned Kazur, an old man writing what was to be his last book, a journal written explicitly for Magda's use so she might imagine more truly the life her grandson lived in a faraway land.

Now her own words were turned against her, a powerful strategy against which she had little defense.

"What you undertake is experiment enough. Shall you add another element of the unknown to something untried, something that may yield no reward?"

Weakened, she twisted in her opponent's grasp, her limbs pinned, her shoulder resisting the mat. Her imagination became her next enemy, the voices of her council upraised in alarm. Rebellion stirred among them, resentment that she augmented their difficulties with yet another constraint.

"What shall we do with her? She can't be taught to read or write, nor can she participate in the arena!"

"A wolfhound in the Maze? A guard dog trained to attack any stranger who approaches her, who almost attacked you? Unsuitable, unsanitary, and dangerous to every resident!"

Last of all came Esslar's report from Altug's stronghold. Sandur grim, unsmiling, rejecting overtures of friendship from Yossi and Kokor, passing his time among the mountain children, not minding the small hands that fingered his earring and tugged at his braids, enjoying their games, their songs, their chanted alphabets, a rare smile on his lips as he surveyed them at play. A vision gleaned from the Master of Mysteries rose up to confront her—Sandur playing with every child save one, a boy brushed aside to be gathered up into Valeria's lap, a bright-eyed, cheerful lad whose only fault was a withered leg.

Strangely enough, it was Symone—flinty, unsentimental Symone—who came to her rescue, a surge of energy filling her being, enabling her to break the hold of despair.

"Everyone who walks the earth must receive the gift, speaking heart to heart and mind to mind."

Wrestling the darkness into submission, Magda willed it to disperse and trouble her no more. Her predecessors joined her in the struggle, pushing away doubts, sending them back to the dark lands where they would reside until the next match, nursing their wounds, altering their tactics, gathering their reserves for yet another foray against the light.

Victory was hers. Her body sagged, sending her stumbling for a chair on which to rest her aching bones.

The watchman sang out the hour as night took up residence in the valley of the castle. In a window of the northwest tower a single light blazed. The citizens of Pelion, scurrying home by way of the central square never looked up. In the old days, many would have remarked upon its brightness, confident that someone toiled on their behalf. In these sadly modern times they never marked the brilliance of that light, nor dreamed of the battle waged within. None heard, as Magda heard, the final confirmation that her struggles were not in vain. It came in the form of a question, the answer supplied by her heart.

"What of the daughters who dream of the sea?"

Chapter 10

The Bronze Doors

ESSLAR'S EYES MOVED leisurely across the page, lifting to stare into space from time to time, his attention focused on a point distant from the placid landscape around him. The book, well thumbed after frequent (if not daily) readings, had been committed to memory long ago. Having exhausted the pleasure of the narrative, his process of reading altered. Where once he read from paragraph to paragraph, sentence to sentence, now Esslar read from word to word, stripping away the skin of the writing to find the muscle below. He read in a half-dream, lulled by the regular snores of his companion and the occasional cries of waterfowl, the lapping of waves against the shoreline, the buzz of swarming insects, and intermittent splashes as the fish rose to feed on the smooth surface of the Tellas.

A snort, a cessation of snoring, and an abrupt exhalation that might have been either a groan or a sigh disturbed his concentration. Beside Esslar, Galen lay stretched out on the grassy bank, his handkerchief arranged like a tent whose side-flaps billowed in the breeze, the bridge of his bulbous nose serving as the center pole, his white beard peeking out from beneath the bottom of the faded fabric. When the snoring resumed, Esslar shook his head, envying Galen's ability to fall instantly to sleep, a talent developed over years of guard duty and irregular hours. Certainly the Commander had every right to enjoy the rare indulgence of an afternoon nap, something Esslar intended for himself before finding it impossible to sleep, worries nagging at him despite the bucolic atmosphere in which he found himself. He used the book as the next best thing to sleep, shutting out the presence of the ernani, refreshing his spirit rather than his body, for his spirit had been sorely tried.

Putting the book aside, he yawned and stretched, then pulled his knees up under his chin and wrapped his arms around his legs so as to scan the sandy beach some ten feet below his perch on the highest point of the riverbank. The abandoned raft rested near the water's edge, its duty done and its logs drying in the afternoon sun. The cork floats of Tibor's fish lines bobbed as the waves lapped the shoreline, proof that the fish-eaters were determined to eat their fill tonight before heading overland with the rising sun.

At this point, the great river Tellas widened and lost some of its depth. Several narrow, tree-covered islands in the middle of the channel blocked Esslar's view of the opposite bank. If he craned his neck to the right and squinted down the gleaming swath of water, he fancied he could make out the cascades a half-mile south of camp. The sound of the falls warned them of danger long before reaching the rocks and shoals. The narrow beach drew them to this site, a slight bend in the river where the current lost its strength. It was Vlatla who insisted they disembark near a proper swimming place.

Esslar understood her need to cleanse herself, for her monthly flow began during the last days on the raft. Even though they put in to shore every evening to make camp, it was a difficult time for her, the sole woman in a band of men, unable to take her accustomed place in the lodge where the women of the River People isolated themselves during the days of ritual pollution. She bore it gamely, as he knew she would, keeping to herself and shying away from the others, hurting Tibor's feelings more than once when he sought her out after the evening meal to converse in their language of hisses and clicks only to have her move away from him, drawing her blanket around her head and shoulders to protect herself from his advances. Like Tibor, Yossi and Kokor were obviously confused by the change in her behavior, the mountain men as oblivious as the marsh-dweller to the cycles of a woman's body.

Only Sandur reacted to her plight, a remarkable occurrence until Esslar gave it proper consideration. Once he did, everything fell into place—Sandur's abrupt offer to take the tiller after a fortnight of virtual idleness on the raft; his new habit of accompanying Vlatla when she sought out a private place to bathe, not asking if she desired an escort, following her all the same and choosing a spot nearby where he could ward off others if they ventured too close. Nothing else in his manner changed, certainly not the marked reserve or the air of condescension with which he regarded her. Oddly enough, Vlatla seemed comfortable in his company, relieved, no doubt, at the cessation of hostilities between them.

From the day Sandur stood among the mud and wattle huts of the river people, watching with silent disapproval as Vlatla oversaw the lashing of the logs and the application of the tarry pitch that would render them impervious to rot, he categorically refused to share his wealth of shipbuilding experience in the construction of the raft. Nor did he contribute his skills as a navigator in its passage downriver, choosing instead to monitor the horses. For almost a moon Sandur looked through Vlatla as if she was not there, yet somehow the onslaught of her menses sparked an instinctual response from him, perhaps a reminder that she was, in fact, a woman, although there was not the slightest resemblance between hard-working Vlatla and the indolent concubines Esslar knew from the citadel. Still, the healer judged it a step in the right direction, if not an overture of friendship, at least an action that bound Sandur closer to his peers.

When an audible sigh escaped him, Esslar glanced at his companion, guilty at the prospect of disturbing his rest. Although Esslar might bear the spiritual burdens of the ernani, Galen bore the brunt of their constant squabbles and misunderstandings, breaking up arguments on a daily basis and dispensing his unique brand of justice with an iron will and a seemingly endless fount of patience. The source of that patience was his experience as an ernani, an ability to understand their difficulties as if they were his own combined with the knowledge that he must bring them safely to the Maze.

Adjustments came slowly, each ernani clinging desperately to former ways, frightened of the changes demanded of them, changes which challenged time-honored beliefs as the river's currents sped them past lands no longer recognizable as home. Some problems were laughable: Tibor's affront at the suggestion that he cleanse himself with water rather than coating his skin with mud, the mountain men's complaints at the steady diet of fish, and Yossi's nightly chanting sessions that kept the others awake long after they took to their sleeping robes, no one able to sway him from his unique and decidedly noisy religious practices.

Other occurrences were far more troubling: Kokor pale with fright, every muscle in his body resisting the first tentative step onto the gently rocking raft, and the misery written in Yossi's face as his beloved mountains disappeared from view as the Tellas bore them relentlessly south. Then there were the first few days of Vlatla's presence among them when she ate nothing, growing visibly weaker each day. Esslar tried to charm her appetite until he realized it was not the food, but the communal nature of the meals that prevented her from eating. Partaking of food and drink in the presence of males was a completely foreign notion to her since the river women ate their meals apart from men. Vlatla might steer the raft, but it took almost a week before she could bring herself to eat a meal in the presence of the men who served as her crew.

Despite these difficulties, Esslar remained confident of his choices, alert to their strengths and weaknesses, sure of their inner rectitude, a resolve that would carry them through the bronze doors and beyond. Day by day he monitored their progress, watching as they persevered, marking their halting steps toward kinship with their fellows, sympathetic of their fears and the deep, abiding loneliness that grew as every mile distanced them from family, friends, and the only lives they had ever known.

"Worry gaineth naught," Galen offered over a gaping yawn, putting an end to the stillness of the afternoon, "or so my dam was known to say."

"Your mother was a wise woman."

"She was and no mistake. Book learnin' she may have lacked, but she ne'er spoke without teachin'."

"Her son seems to have inherited her talents."

To that observation Galen made no reply, but stretched until his joints popped and cracked. Jamming his cloak into a roll under his neck, he stared up into the cloudless autumn sky.

"Eight days and twenty and we'll reach the northern gate."

This observation, offered simply and without need of comment, sent each of them into private meditation. The older man smiled his contentment, well-pleased at their rapid progress downriver and anxious to see his beloved Lucrece as the younger man frowned, new anxieties pushing their way into his thoughts, dispelling the tranquility of the afternoon. That tranquility was further broken by several male shouts, a woman's shriek, and a loud splash.

"What are they up to now?" Galen grumbled, pulling himself upright, his keen blue eyes traveling quickly to the site of the disturbance. His disapproving frown turned into a delighted grin. With a loud guffaw, he slapped his thigh. Esslar's laughter was more muted but equally as heartfelt. The men were ducking a fully clothed Sandur. Splashing her way knee-deep into the water to enjoy more fully this unexpected turn of events, Vlatla urged her companions on.

"Should I go down and rescue him or let him fend for himself? There's little doubt but that it's Tibor's revenge."

"How so?"

"One too many sneers, anger at bein' ignored, his lordship's refusal to join them in the evenin' swim, the usual complaints." Galen paused to reflect. "A wee bit of jealousy where Vlatla's concerned, I reckon."

Sandur came up sputtering to be dunked again by a half-naked Tibor, Yossi and Kokor stripped to their breeches and waist-deep in the water, resisting Sandur's struggles to free himself while Yossi showered what the observers assumed were highly personal insults rendered in the mountain dialect on the prince's submerged head.

"Your decision? They hurt nothin' but his pride, and it's true he's in rare need of a bath."

"Leave him be."

The Commander dropped back down to his former position.

"They've trapped him without knowing it," Esslar mused aloud, his gaze fixed on the river. "His preference would be to bathe with Vlatla or by himself, yet he understands that the former is impossible, and every time he tries to sneak away, they follow him. The scars don't help matters."

"Has he let you see them?"

"Not since the day he took that fall coming down the western slope, and I saw traces of blood on his blouse. I gave him a salve to keep the scars soft and pliable, but he's resisted any further offers of assistance. He's always polite but absolutely insistent that I keep away."

"Look! They've let him go!"

Esslar held his breath as Sandur's head emerged from the water, hoping that what began as a prank would not end as a war. The prince's sodden garments ballooned about him, his face covered by dripping ropes of braids as he coughed up water and struggled for air. Once he recovered his breath, he tossed his hair away from his eyes and stood quietly, considering his tormentors one by one, all of them retreating slowly toward the shore, backing away from the threat of reprisal. Then, with an energy Esslar had never suspected the elegant heir to the Kwanlonhon clan possessed, Sandur began to strip, throwing each piece of clothing at the men, who leapt forward eagerly to catch them, Vlatla applauding his performance with shrieks of laughter, all the ernani caught up in the fun of the unexpected. When the last boot was pried off and tossed into Tibor's waiting arms, Sandur, clad in a narrow challah, turned away from the shore, executed a deft surface dive, and disappeared underwater.

When he appeared again, some thirty feet away from his original position, another, less self-conscious performance began—an unexpected exhibition of his swimming expertise. Moving effortlessly, gracefully, at one with the river, he glided smoothly through the waters, rolling from his back to his stomach, diving deep to reemerge like a porpoise leaping out of the ocean's depths. Sandur swam as seals and otters do—joyful, confident, utterly at ease, water his preferred medium of existence. Yossi and Kokor, who never ventured in water deeper than their knees, stood slack-jawed and open-mouthed. With a glad shout, Vlatla plunged headlong into the shallows and began to stroke out past the point, Tibor close behind her, the mountain men sulking as they waded back to shore.

Esslar turned to find Galen gazing steadily at the three swimmers whose wet heads glistened as they swam and dived, their laughter carrying to shore, their words indistinct and their enjoyment palpable.

"I ne'er thought to see such a sight—his lordship playin' with the commoners!"

Galen observed the breaking of one tradition, Esslar counted the others: ignoring the taboo of modesty around other males, the decision not to attack those who dared touch his hair, and finally, and perhaps most importantly, revealing his scars to others, proof, perhaps, that the ones inside were beginning to heal. It was three moons since the beating. Esslar feared the damage ran too deep, that the cycle of abuse could not be broken. Today, thanks to a prank engineered by the ernani, Sandur refused the role of victim.

Twenty-eight days. One more moon to convince Sandur to enter the Maze. One more moon to ease his way.

* * *

THE EVENING MEAL was nearly finished when Yossi dropped to his knees, motioning them to be silent, his left ear pressed to the ground, his eyes closed. In the next moment Kokor was beside him in a similar position, Galen strapping on his sword, Tibor grabbing up his fishing spear, Sandur unsheathing his knife.

"How many and how close?" Galen demanded, kicking out the fire and cursing softly under his breath. To be attacked this close to Pelion was an ignominious fate and one that enraged him almost past endurance. In another three days they'd reach the first outpost, at which time they'd be escorted to the northern gates by a sizable cavalry patrol.

The mountain men muttered to one another in their own language, seeming to debate a moment before Kokor announced, "Three horses running hard." And then, more grimly, "Close."

"Could it be our own patrols?" Esslar asked over his shoulder as he searched frantically for the knapsack containing his medicines, feeling the tension rising in Galen and guessing the answer almost before it was spoken.

"Impossible. A standard patrol is six riders."

"Only three. Good odds," Yossi observed.

Galen glared at him.

"Ye know the drill. Ye'll stay safely hidden 'til I give the signal."

Yossi sulked while Galen pointed out the best positions for defense.

"Yossi and Kokor, take to the trees. Esslar and Vlatla, head for the beach and take cover. Tibor, Sandur, toss all the gear into the bushes while I douse the fire."

The mountain men vanished, taking up their positions as the forward guard on the far side of the trail. Esslar wrapped a cloak around Vlatla, hurrying her away, the river woman sending a worried glance after the men who were busy scattering belongings this way and that, clearing the campsite of all signs of habitation. That done, Galen motioned impatiently for them to take their position in the bracken. In the next moment the camp stood deserted, a wet pile of ashes shining dimly in the moonlight.

Hooves pounded against the trail. While the ernani waited, Galen gauged them individually, sensing their excitement, their willingness to fight, their shame at hiding from a clearly outnumbered foe. None of them understood, as Galen did, that bone knives and hand-made spears were as nothing against iron-forged swords wielded by professionals on horseback; nor did they realize that while Galen himself was expendable, each of them was a precious resource, brought from the east to complete a plan that might change the course of history. Yossi spoke of odds; for Galen, a single death was unacceptable unless it was his own.

A fearsome cry rang out of the darkness, a falsetto wail that raised Galen's neck hairs. He'd heard it before in equally dangerous circumstances, shrill and wild, piercing the night sounds of the woods, the eerie, unforgettable sound of a Lapithian warrior keening for the death of a kinsman in battle, a sound which, once heard on the wide plains of Lapith, can never be forgotten.

"Hold yer positions! Make no move!"

Galen fought his way out of the undergrowth. The trail lay before him, the rocks and pebbles glistening in the blue light of the new moon. Off to his right, a doe broke cover and darted across his path, a ghostly wild-eyed stag in close pursuit sprang gracefully into a shaft of moonlight and away again into darkness, the warrior's cry setting the sleeping forest into motion.

A cloud passed across the moon, plunging the trail into darkness. The pathway lightened again momentarily, revealing one rider well out in front, the others streaming far behind. Galen heard the rhythmic grunts of the lead horse it as it pounded down the trail.

She rode bareback, clinging like a burr to the broad back of her flying steed, her flaxen hair streaming out behind her, hands and knees working the sweat-darkened shoulders and flanks of her exhausted mount. Again she lifted her head, screaming out her hatred and her grief, fear and desperation equal partners as she fled her pursuers.

Galen stepped into the trail, his sword sheathed and his empty palms upraised. Her head shot up, her face set as she bore down on him. Closing his eyes, he sent her a silent command. At the last possible moment, the horse came to a shuddering halt directly in front of him, showering his boots with gravel. Grabbing the rider by her shoulders, he pulled her down off the horse, praying she understood the southern tongue.

"Safe! Do you understand? Safe!"

She nodded vigorously, peering up at him as she babbled in a broken mixture of southern and Lapithian. Covering her lips with his palm, he indicated silence.

"Go there. No sound."

Pointing off to the right-hand side of the trail where Tibor and Sandur waited, he shoved her away. She stumbled forward as an opening appeared in the undergrowth, a single hand reaching out to assist her. The hole closed behind her, and she vanished.

Shooing the blown horse off with a slap on the rump, Galen turned to face the riders who were bearing down on him at a dead run.

They were furious, enraged by her escape and headlong flight into the night, maddened by the loss of so rich a prize. Galen hadn't marked her appearance, but they were aflame with lust for their captive. The sliced ear of one man was testimony to her struggles; the other bore four bloody scratches running from his cheekbone to his jaw. Breathing hard, they glared down at Galen, their horses fidgeting restlessly under tight reins.

Fifty years of hard living told Galen exactly who they were. Former slavers turned bandits, they worked the fringes just outside the Legion patrol routes, robbing and murdering anyone foolish enough to travel alone, living off the land and the plunder their victims provided. Galen tasted the bile of hatred and swallowed hard.

"Give her back and we'll let you live."

Galen let an amused smile play over his lips as he settled on a strategy. He chose the game of foxes: confuse and misdirect.

"I fear ye've lost yer booty, friends. As to lettin' me live, ye'd best look about."

His whistle pierced the night. The bandits' hands moved instinctively to their sword hilts as Tibor and Sandur stepped out from behind the bushes and Kokor and Yossi dropped down out of the trees. They stood at stalemate, two swords on horseback against a larger but poorly armed force on foot. Praying the ernani would understand the nature of his gambit, Galen grinned pleasantly up at the riders.

"Leave now and ye can keep yer horses. Stay and I'll not answer for yer lives."

He gestured to the men hovering about him, grateful for Tibor's square-built torso smeared with river mud, the topknots and fierce mustaches of the mountain men, Sandur's mass of unruly braids. A note of apology entered his voice.

"They call me leader, but as ye can see, they're half-wild and as bloodthirsty a band as I've ever known."

Quick-thinking Yossi was first to take the hint. Jabbering noisily in the mountain dialect, he mounted an immediate protest, Kokor joining in with matching fervor. By the time Tibor started up with the clicking noises of the river tongue, the robbers were surrounded by the babble of seeming madness. Sandur maintained his silence. Sensing the robbers' growing nervousness, Galen decided to push the bluff a mite further. Fastening an irate gaze on Yossi, he shook his finger at him, feeling a rush of gratitude when the mountain man's eyes lit with instant understanding.

"Nay, man, I've said we mustn't eat the horses!"

Yossi wailed out his disappointment with a string of senseless gibberish and moved toward the nearest horse, running his hands greedily over the muscled hindquarters and smacking his lips.

The man with the sliced ear gulped.

"They, uh, eat horses?"

Galen heaved a tired sigh, the sound of a beleaguered man faced with an impossible task.

"Aye. They're near ravenous, and horseflesh is a rare treat. But it's those two ye should worry about," he gestured alternately to Tibor and Sandur, shaking his head regretfully. "That one is a fish-eater who uses human flesh for bait." Brandishing his spear, Tibor capered madly in the dust, his performance rewarded by two pairs of raised eyebrows and dropped jaws. "The quiet one, well," Galen scratched his beard, "he eats whatever and whoever he kills."

A woman's scream ripped through the night. Heads jerked up all around while Galen blessed Esslar's ingenuity and Vlatla's pluck.

"That must be the rest of them," he offered by way of explanation. "She's not so pretty as she once was, I'll wager, but it's been a long time since we shared a woman."

"The rest of them . . .?"

His chest swelling with paternalistic pride, Galen surveyed his flock of miscreants.

"Aye, these be the night sentries. The others are down by the river, skinnin' and guttin', preparin' our meal." He added as an afterthought, "Would ye care to join us?"

Muttering excuses, the men turned their horses, backing away from Yossi and Kokor, who continued to yowl their complaints at being robbed of their prize. After trotting a way down the trail, booted heels dug into ribs, and they broke into a gallop.

Sandur spat in the dust at Galen's feet, his upper lip curled in a sneer.

"I hadn't thought you a coward."

Galen sheathed his sword, a familiar lightheadedness creeping over him as it did after every battle, finding himself loathe to fight yet again with an outraged prince.

"Two choices, laddie. Fight or frighten them away. 'Twas my choice and I made it."

"You made us play the fool!" Sandur sputtered, "A band of mindless savages! Cannibals! Surely they laugh at us as they ride away!"

Galen studied him a moment, keeping a tight rein on his temper.

"I'd think by now ye'd have guessed that none of us is playin'. What would ye have me do? Risk precious lives to protect yer dignity?"

Galen warmed to his task, finally able to tell this Tehran's sa'ab exactly what he thought of him.

"If ye'd stop broodin' and look about, ye'd guess why I'd rather play the role of bandit than risk a single injury! But no, ye've closed yer eyes and ears, blind and deaf to everythin' ye've seen and heard!"

Galen was roaring now, unable to stop himself.

"Ask them!" he thundered, pointing to the others who shifted uncomfortably under his gaze. "Ask them why their lives are precious! Ask them why they leave family and friends to make this journey, not because their father ordered it, but of their own free will!"

When the prince paled at the reference to his father, Galen's conscience blunted his anger. Sandur's Preparation was not his business, but he'd not allow anyone turn what was a solid victory into a shameful defeat. The ernani performed bravely and with a willingness that gladdened his heart. In each of them resided a selflessness this selfish prince would never understand. Regaining control, Galen offered the only apology he could manage.

"Tired men speak careless words. Get some sleep. We leave at dawn."

As Galen strode away, he worried what harm he'd done. Esslar's mission was to instill in Sandur a desire for the Maze. In a fit of temper, he might have destroyed what little gains he'd made. Stricken to the soul, he made his way back to camp, his step heavy, his shoulders slumped, feeling every one of his fifty years.

SANDUR COUNTED STARS until the others slept. Yossi's nightly chant, incantations against the drifting demons who haunt the mountaintops in the guise of clouds and fog, slowed and was finally silenced, to be followed by the regular snores of those pious few who, having made peace with their gods, go to their rest unafraid. Pulling his blanket around his shoulders, Sandur picked a careful path around sleeping bodies, stopping for a moment to observe the women nestled together under one blanket, Vlatla's dark head pillowed next to one of gold.

The autumn nights grew colder, and already he'd donned the wool breeches and leather jerkin he'd been given in the mountain stronghold. His hair was still damp from this afternoon, his body pleasantly tired from his swim. Even now he couldn't explain what had possessed him: disrobing in front of strangers, then playing as he hadn't played since leaving the harem, splashing Vlatla and wrestling with Tibor. He'd taken a special dislike to the marsh-dweller from the first, hardly able to believe someone could live in such filthy surroundings, the bogs and marshes noxious with the fetid stench of decay. How could he explain the unexpected civility of this mud-covered savage, who, when Sandur paused on the beach, searching for his missing clothes with a sinking heart, passed Sandur his own blanket without a word, indicating that he should wrap it around his shoulders before walking into camp? There was no doubt that Tibor had seen the scars, as had Vlatla, but neither betrayed by a word or a look what they thought of someone who merited such a vicious flogging.

If this was not surprise enough, there followed Vlatla's tongue-lashing of Yossi. The rules of the camp as established by Esslar required everyone to speak the southern tongue, but once the river woman discovered Sandur's clothing buried in the sand, she went after Yossi with murder in her eyes, hissing at him with hands on her hips, the prankster wilting under her steady stream of abuse while Kokor laughed in that quiet way of his at an increasingly sheepish Yossi. Sandur could not quite fathom it—Tibor's generosity, Vlatla's anger on his behalf, Kokor's warm-eyed regard, or Yossi's halting apology. He'd done nothing except forgive them the dunking and join in their play, yet everything was changed.

Bewilderment turned to anxiety as he looked in vain for the healer, finding an empty pallet near Galen's sleeping form. By instinct he chose the path leading down to the beach and was rewarded by the sight of a moonlit figure skimming stones across the water. At his approach, the healer turned to regard him for a moment before observing, "Sleep eludes me as well. Come and sit for awhile."

Motioning to the raft, the healer picked up a robe from the sand and, wrapping himself in its folds, took his place beside Sandur. The silence between them was easy; Sandur was mindful of the peace that always seemed to envelop Esslar, a quality he could never find within himself. How long had it been since he'd felt anything other than hurt or betrayal? The answer came to him with a jolt. This afternoon, he thought, this very afternoon. I was angered by their attack, furious at being treated so rudely. Then, in a single moment, I freed myself.

"I didn't know you swam so well. Who taught you?"

It should have been my father, Sandur thought bitterly, remembering all the other fathers who taught their children to swim in the harem pools. Instead, he answered with a careful half-truth.

"No particular teacher. My playfellows and I swam in the harem. My uncle's concubines taught me how to dive."

A memory caught him unaware, his uncle's women calling up to him where he stood balanced on a ledge of a limestone cliff, their floating hair writhing like starfish as they beckoned to him with rounded arms kissed by the sun, inviting him to join them below, promising ample rewards for his first leap into nothingness. His body split the waters. As he swam up toward the light he was surrounded by their fulsome nakedness.

He remembered a question he wanted to ask.

"What of the woman? There was blood on her skirt."

The healer's profile shone as the moonlight reflected off the slow-moving waters of the Tellas.

"They raped and beat her, sparing her face although her body is covered with bruises. She cleansed herself, and I tended her hurts. Sleep came when Vlatla sang to her."

Only the abuse of a child by the father was a worse crime than rape. To rape was to set aside every notion of civilized behavior, to ignore the carefully discriminating practice of breeding. Among the clansmen it was unknown, although Sandur heard rumors of rapes in the seamen's district. As he pulled the woman toward him into the bushes, the sight of the blood on her skirt sent him almost mad with rage. It hurt that Galen (whose opinions he respected almost as much as Esslar's) misunderstood him so completely. Once again he'd been helpless to defend himself, standing mutely by as he had so many times before, biting back the protests beaten out of him at an early age.

"Galen said he lost his temper. Don't judge him too harshly. His responsibilities weigh heavily on him."

Sandur had already forgiven the white-haired horseman who stood alone and fearless on the moonlit trail, braving the onrush of flying hooves and the cruel-eyed men with swords. Another question grew up around the image of the woman on horseback.

"Why was she so foolish as to travel alone?"

"She wasn't alone until today. Her cousin traveled with her, her mother's sister-son and her playmate since birth." The healer's voice threatened to fade away, then returned with greater force. "He neither understood nor shared her desire for the journey south. But Lynsaya needed escort, and escort he would give," he paused, "and did give, until he could give no more."

They weighed his death between them, a stranger lying unburied and unmourned in a land not his own, fodder for the carrion that dwelt along the banks of the supremely indifferent river.

"So she came as the others do to enter this . . . Maze?"

A curt nod was his answer. Somehow he expected more, a smile or a glance to reward him for finally naming what hung between them since their arrival at Altug's stronghold, the long-awaited explanation of why in each place they visited a constant stream of suppliants waited to be interviewed by this humblest of booksellers. Sandur witnessed it from afar, hiding his curiosity under a mask of disinterest, watching as they disappeared with the healer, sometimes for hours at a time, to return elated or, more often than not, chastened and downcast, feet dragging and heads bowed. Nothing was forthcoming save that single nod.

"I spoke to Kokor tonight . . ."

Kokor of the Painted Caverns, a stronghold near Altug's, its proximity allowing Kokor to walk ten miles each day to study with Valeria, who taught him to read and write and figure in her underground school room. He was Sandur's age, a man whose eyes saw much and whose mouth spoke little. To Kokor he turned for much-needed information, certain that the close-mouthed mountain man would not betray his trust.

"He told me about . . . about his interview with you."

Stumbling and stammering, embarrassed by the private nature of the mountain man's session with the healer, Sandur tried without success to put modesty aside, remembering that Kokor did so when asked to share what the examination entailed. Just when he decided to say no more, to leave off questioning and retreat into silence, it came to him that he had already experienced a similar session on the night of screams when he had surrendered his body to the healer's hands. Relieved, he forged on.

"He spoke about a place called the Maze and a gift of some sort, but he . . ."

". . . but he couldn't answer all your questions," the healer interjected, still gazing intently at the river before them.

Grateful for a response of any kind, Sandur took heart.

"I . . . I wondered if you . . . if you might tell me more."

For the first time the healer turned toward him. A measuring stare followed, sober and reflective.

Sandur felt his merits and flaws assessed, his entire existence called into question, as if the totality of every decision he ever made, every action ever performed, was aligned along the measuring stick of Esslar's gaze. No wonder so many emerged from those sessions pale and shaken, for who could face such scrutiny and escape unchanged? And then, when it seemed impossible for him to endure that uncompromising stare a moment longer, Esslar looked off into the darkness.

"You ask and I answer."

The healer settled himself deeper into his robes.

"The greatest of gifts may be found in Pelion, in a place of Preparation called the Maze. If you so choose, you may pass through the bronze doors, for I have found you worthy."

They talked together until dawn unfurled its bright pennants above the floating islands of trees, the prince's forehead wrinkled with concentration, his elbows on his knees, his chin resting on two upraised fingers, a posture so like his grandmother that Esslar wondered anew at the mystery of kinship. As he had promised her, Esslar revealed nothing of the past, speaking instead of difficulties and deprivations, of challenges and the possibility of failure. The bronze doors might open, but the Tehran's sa'ab must consider seriously what lay within before he undertook a task designed to test his mettle. There would be no special favors for an eastern prince, no excuses because of rank, no relaxation of the strict rules by which all ernani lived and worked within the Maze.

Sandur sat lost in thought.

Esslar bided his time, waiting for a decision that must be freely made, his thoughts many miles to the south.

"When the time comes," she insisted, "you must set him free. Everything we propose hinges on his ability to choose. For thirty years he's been trained to obey, forced to hide his resentments beneath filial duty. We offer him an escape from servitude, an end to abuse. Even so, given his upbringing, self-determination may be more frightening than the rod of obedience."

A trout leapt up from the deep, mouth open and silvery scales shining, hanging suspended for a breathless moment in time, life vaulting up out of the dawn-colored waters of the Tellas.

The prince stood, shrugging off the blanket.

"I will enter the Maze."

Sandur's fingers worked impatiently at the clasps of his jerkin, at the buttons of his breeches, at the ties of his challah. Standing naked and unashamed in the crisp morning breeze, he ran toward the shoreline, diving headlong into the river, his body the bronzed shaft of an arrow loosed by an unseen hand.

As the Tehran's sa'ab baptized himself in the cold waters of change, the Master of Mysteries sat in quiet meditation, hopeful for the first time that the story might be rewritten.

Chapter 11

Interiors

LANGUID TENDRILS OF sound floated by, whispering with hushed voices, muted conversations of the long-departed seemingly embedded in the very stones over which Alyssa trod, their mortar mixed not with the common stuff of masons, but the sands of time and waters of eternity. Footsteps sounded in emptied halls, hob-nailed boots marching to the rhythmic clink of chains, thin leather soles tripping hurriedly past her, in search of she knew not what. Often she would turn, disoriented by a passing ghost pushing by her, busily pursuing an errand begun some hundred years ago, made impatient by her slowness. "We remember," the stones reminded her as she ran her fingertips over their rugged surfaces. "Our memory is boundless, nothing forgotten, every memory of every soul locked inside us, stored up for the future, for those who come after, for those like you."

Her guides called it the Maze, a place of confusion with its interlocking corridors twisting and turning back upon themselves, its dead ends and sudden reversals designed to baffle those who put their trust in what their eyes beheld. To one such as her, unseduced by architects' schemes, the Maze became the single place on earth where others must be led and she, alone, could walk unaided. Whether others heard the phantom voices and muffled footsteps or held private conversations with the talking walls, she never learned, perhaps because she did not think to ask. Mystery, after all, was part and parcel of her craft. Unafraid, she yielded herself up to it, sure to the marrow of her bones that if she surrendered herself to its all-encompassing memories, her story, too, would never be forgotten.

Alyssa let the Maze possess her, just as she allowed the Nineteenth Mother entry into the substance of her dreams. A single phrase leapt out of the Nineteenth Mother's mouth and lodged within her heart. "A search for sight," the old woman promised, revealing a door in a wall she thought blank. Through this door she was determined to walk.

Over the past moon they engaged in frequent conversations, the earliest concerning her life in Cinthea, although more recently the subject switched to another, more difficult, topic. To Latona alone did Alyssa confess her thoughts and feelings concerning blindness, although, to be fair, no one ever sought to question her frankly and without sentiment. Gwyn, who she missed daily, accepted her blindness simply and without question, caring for her as she might have nursed a motherless lamb with a finger dipped in milk or splinted the wing of an injured bird.

The Nineteenth Mother was not Gwyn of Cyme, nor was she Latona the Dreamsayer. She was, instead, the single person who could further Alyssa's quest for sight. As such, Alyssa granted her the right to quiz her.

The surprise came not so much from the Nineteenth Mother's questions, but from what the answers taught Alyssa about herself. She'd thought her inner self, the substance of her character, unchanged by her loss of sight. In conversation with the Nineteenth Mother, she came to understand this as a denial of sorts, an illusion fostered by the panic of a girl of eleven who wakes to find her world unaccountably altered. She discovered as well that she'd overcome almost every obstacle in her path. Granted, her mother's obstinacy was a major force in her development, yet alone and unaided, she'd traveled a road many sighted people would have thought far too dangerous.

There was also considerable relief in voicing what annoyed her: people who grabbed her hand or arm to guide her without asking her permission; those well-meaning but thoughtless few who would open a door for her but forget to inform her of the raised threshold; the proprietary air people assumed when she was forced to ask for help, as if she owed them life-long friendship for performing a basic act of courtesy.

As the Nineteenth Mother probed deeper, Alyssa made the monumental discovery that although she'd always considered herself a timid person, she was, in fact, brave to the point of foolhardiness. Not only this, but she, who once feared children might run from the sight of her empty eyes, was proud and even vain of her abilities as a storyteller.

With the Nineteenth Mother by her side, she mourned over the loss of color, confessing her sometimes overpowering need to see her reflection in a mirror, a desperate longing to replace the face of an adolescent with that of the woman she had become. Last and most painfully of all, she revealed her recurring nightmare, the illogical fear that she might lose her way in a strange place with no one to guide her, wandering forever without direction, abandoned and alone under an empty sky.

A few days after a particularly painful session in the tower chamber, the Nineteenth Mother made this pronouncement.

"I've given it careful thought, as has my Council, and we've decided you must learn your way about the Maze on your own." Alyssa tightened her grip on the mane of Rauros' coat. "Monitors assist the other ernani, so I thought Rauros might serve as your guide. You, however, have convinced me otherwise."

"I . . . I convinced you?"

"My plan is for you to enter earlier than the others, undergoing the ceremony of Blessing a fortnight before they arrive. During that time you will learn your way and thus need never worry that you might become lost." She added slowly, "I would not have you fear the Maze, Alyssa. Despite what you may hear to the contrary, it was meant to teach as much as it was designed to confuse. Within its patterns you will find that chaos yields to order."

"But Rauros . . .," her voice broke, and the dog growled low in his throat, a warning that he was aware of her unhappiness and liked it not. Worried that he might misbehave and shame her in front of the Nineteenth Mother, Alyssa strove to keep her voice even and free of distress.

"Rauros is more than my guide; he's been my friend since the day he was weaned. I cannot abandon him, for if I did, I fear he would grieve."

"No one suggests that you abandon him. The innkeeper's son agrees to care for him during the first moon. He'll bring him to the Maze everyday an hour after midday, the time the women frequent the arena. During those hours, you'll be together."

"And after the first moon?"

There was a pause while a chair was scraped across the floor and leather-shod feet walked away from her, a measured tread indicating thoughtful contemplation.

"We've not spoken of this, but I fear we must."

Alyssa's stomach knotted into a hard lump.

"There are no guarantees of immediate success within the Maze. For the first moon you will live in the Hall of Women, a pleasant experience for most ernani and one that gives you ample time to reaffirm your decision. However, the first moon of joining is . . .," she hesitated, ". . . is often difficult."

The old woman ceased speaking, allowing time for Alyssa to interpret her meaning. *She thinks I will be rejected by this stranger they choose for me,* Alyssa thought, flinching away from the idea before facing it squarely as her mother taught her.

"Yet listen closer, daughter," Latona the Dreamsayer seemed to whisper in her ear.

"As I have explained to you, two must walk the Path together. During the first moon of joining it sometimes comes to pass that a couple finds themselves at odds. When this happens, the couple is separated, new partners are assigned, and the process begins again."

"And you think this will likely happen to me . . .," she swallowed hard, "and. . . and I may be in the Maze for much longer than five moons. "

The Nineteenth Mother walked toward her. A dry palm rested lightly on the bare skin of her forearm.

"I think this—that you should be prepared. If I doubted your chances for success, you would not be here. Whether it be five moons, ten, or twenty, I believe your search will not be in vain."

Comforted by the feather-light touch of the hand on her arm, Alyssa regained her composure. The hand was removed, and Alyssa reached down to fondle her dog.

"So, Rauros will join me when . . . when I'm sure he'll be welcome."

She could not see the Nineteenth Mother's smile, but she heard it just the same.

"Just so. When Rauros is welcome, he will take his rightful place by your side."

MAGDA'S LONG-AWAITED SUMMONS came at mid-morning, a tap at her door rescuing her from her desk, her heart in her throat as she undertook the hundred steps that would take her to the battlements, her aches and pains forgotten as she hurried toward her first encounter with her grandson. Esslar assured her it would come to pass, counseling her to contain her excitement, a friendly warning that she must wait and watch, but a warning all the same.

Her first glimpse of Sandur came as she searched the milling crowds gathered at the northern gates on that day of days for a tall, dark-skinned man dressed in the clothes of Altug's people. She knew from her frequent contact with Esslar that the braids were abandoned after the final swim in the Tellas, a good omen she ventured to suggest, although Esslar seemed doubtful.

There, in a commotion of angry citizens, many with fists upraised against the ranks of Legionnaires arranged in a protective wedge around the newcomers, she located him, walking between two men whose top-knots proclaimed them to be natives of the Sarujian mountains. Her hands grasped the stones so tightly that by the time he passed beyond her field of vision, tears came to her eyes with the pain of returning circulation.

The first day of the eleventh moon was unending: twenty-two Blessings, twenty-two repetitions of the ritual words, twenty-two new faces. With each meeting she whispered to herself, "These shall be my grandson's friends." Eddo, his skin marked by blue tattoos; Zuniga, her forearms scarred by the serpent's tooth; Jincin of the Northern Wastes and Becca of Botheswallow; silent Vlatla and impertinent Yossi. Mindful of the weightiness of her task, she searched their minds one final time before offering the gifts, finding within each of them what the Searchers had sworn to provide. Elated by their success, still she yearned for the sight of that lone ernani, who among all those gathered outside the bronze doors that autumn morning, would not be ushered into her presence.

The second day passed, then a third and a fourth, Magda fretting under the restrictions that prevented her from seeking out Sandur's company, dependent on reports from the personnel of the Maze, frustrated at every turn by the meagerness of their news.

"He seems to be settling in as well as most."

This from Pentaur, a monitor selected for his calm and unruffled manner. That Pentaur's serenity, so much like the sense of peace that hovered over Esslar at all times and in all situations, was becoming a particularly irritating trait, was an irony not lost to her.

"A handy man with a knife," Dictys drawled, a decided twinkle in his eyes as he added, "although I doubt he'll ever be much of a wrestler. Too much temperament."

"He's thin but fit," Japhet offered helpfully. "Like most fish-eaters, he tolerates fowl, but won't touch lamb or goat. The spices Esslar brought from Endlin seemed to spark his appetite, and the kitchen has sworn to please."

She bore their teasing without comment, bridling at Galen's rude guffaw.

"They dinna ken his lordship, or they'd ne'er swear to please! I'll ne'er forget the look on his face when Yossi offered him a spoonful of tasty squirrel stew!"

Not even the faintest glimmer of a smile crossed Esslar's lips.

"Nothing comes easy to him." A different note entered his voice, one that brought Magda up short. "There'll be no quick victories where Sandur is concerned, only a succession of miserable defeats. Then, when all of us are close to despair, he'll reverse our every expectation."

Esslar's surety disturbed her greatly, as did his prophecy of disaster. Today brought with it Sandur's request for an interview, and she hurried to the library which stood vacant until the newly-arrived ernani were ready to begin their daily lessons.

Selecting a spot that allowed her to stand in shadow while he would be illuminated by the sunlight streaming in the windows, she smoothed her robes and arranged her waist-length veil. Footsteps echoed on stone, the door opened and shut, and Magda looked into the face of Aethra's child.

Flesh of her flesh, bone of her bone, half of the blood flowing through his veins came from her and her beloved, the remainder sprung from Linphat V and a nameless concubine. Her eyes searched his face for what seemed to be an eternity, desperate to find somewhere in those brooding features the babe that once gurgled happily in her arms or, even more yearned for, the sweet smile of a long-dead daughter.

Despite Esslar's repeated warnings, disregarding years of schooling in the pitfalls of false assumptions, Magda waited for a spark of recognition, proof of a blood-bond that would admit no barriers of time or place. Instead, her image was reflected back at her by appraising eyes that might have been

Manthur's some thirty years ago, two unforgiving mirrors that reflected her pasty skin, sagging at the jowl and under the chin, marred by deep wrinkles and broken veins, a face grown old beyond count of years. Recoiling from this unwelcome vision, her hurt was compounded as she watched him look away from her in order to master his repulsion. Dreams of reunion shattered around her, broken fragments of folly littering the stone floor. Damning herself for a fool, unwilling to reveal her upset, Magda took hold of herself. No more fantasies, she instructed herself grimly, no more illusions. Erase everything and begin again.

Taking a deep breath, she cleared her mind. Careful not to invade his thoughts, she concentrated on outward signs. None of the awe with which the ernani usually regarded her was present. Having been told she was the highest authority, he treated her accordingly, standing at attention and waiting respectfully for her to begin. Other facts were quickly noted and stored away: his curiosity about the room in which he found himself, his eyes flicking briefly over the maps hung on the walls and the shelves of books; the care with which he dressed this morning, his boots cleaned and polished, the freshly-washed hair combed back straight from his forehead to fall loosely below his shoulders, the scent of soap still clinging to him. He wore the uniform of the ernani, a full-cut blouse tucked neatly into baggy-legged breeches made of rough fabric suitable for rough usage, yet it seemed to her that he wore them with a touch of majesty, standing tall and slim-hipped, a single golden ring shining in his earlobe. Despite the blank eyes and expressionless face, she sensed the anger in him, a life-time of pent-up fury concealed under a facade of perfectly wrought control. Her preparations made, she began the interview.

"How may I ease your way, Sandur of Endlin?"

His stiffness matched hers.

"In the past few days I've discovered that the other men underwent some sort of ceremony. Why have I alone been treated differently?"

Hearing irritation beneath those crisply pronounced syllables, she smiled inwardly, glad he'd risen to the bait. Now she must make her way carefully, mindful that the only thing holding him here was his bond with Esslar.

"You are mistaken. It is customary for anyone not born in Pelion to undergo the ceremony of Blessing before entering the Maze."

She watched as his world went momentarily upside down. Straight black eyebrows knit at this incredible news. Doubting his ears, he demanded further clarification.

"Are you suggesting that I was born in Pelion?"

When she nodded her head by way of a reply, he nearly choked.

"Clearly, that's impossible! I'm a stranger to your city, a first time visitor from Endlin, the land of my fathers and the city of my birth."

Magda turned to the library table and opened a leather-bound book to a page marked by a strand of ribbon. Running her finger down the column, she read the entry in question aloud.

"You were blessed at the third hour after midnight on the fifteenth day of the third moon, at which time you were given the name Sandur."

A voice thick with menace rose from behind her back.

"Do you insinuate that I am not my father's son?"

Ignoring his rudeness, fully aware that she had just offered him the direst insult possible to a clansman of Endlin, she turned page after page, moving backward in the book until she found the desired heading.

"Your father underwent the ceremony of blessing at midday on the first day of the eleventh moon, four years before your birth. You may check his signature if you doubt my word. He wrote his full name: Manthur Linphat Afaf Kwanlonhon."

Pointing out the line in question, she stepped back to allow his approach. A curtain of hair fell between them as he bent over the table. Purposefully granting him privacy, she moved directly behind him. Straightening abruptly, he slammed the book shut, standing with his palms resting on the tooled leather cover.

"My father was an ernani."

"As you see."

"And he received this gift Esslar told me of?"

"He walked the Path. I can say no more."

A curt nod acknowledged her evasion. The next question took her by surprise, a sudden flush rising to her cheeks.

"Were you present at my blessing?"

The memory of that night smote a mighty blow. She weathered the tempest passing over her, grateful he could not see her face.

"Several were present, including myself."

"My father as well?"

"And your mother!" her mind screamed. Instead, she said: "Your father was there."

He walked toward the window, looking out over the small garden littered with leaves, the bronze and gold chrysanthemums still untouched by frost. His voice drifted back to her over his shoulder.

"I have no memory of this blessing, although I no longer doubt your word. I . . ." his voice caught, "I wonder if you would describe it for me."

His change of mood brought him suddenly closer to her, not as one who shared her blood, but as a badly-shaken man requesting that she provide the details of his birth. Something of his melancholy touched a like chord within her, so much time wasted, words unspoken, secrets maintained.

"Everyone who would be blessed comes naked and alone. So the ernani were blessed five days ago. So you were blessed in the House of Healing, held aloft in my predecessor's arms, your name pronounced for the first time."

He listened intently, stiff-backed, his fists clenched at his sides. Allowing the poetry of the well-beloved words fill her, her voice swelled and lingered over the rich cadences of blessing.

"These are the gifts of Pelion to its people. First, water, the wellspring of life. Second, the wine of the grape, the source of ecstasy and freedom from pain. Third, the sacred oil—to the head it brings richness of thought, to the heart, strength of purpose, to the sex, hope of creation rekindled."

He turned, the light from the window illuminating him from behind, his silhouette ringed with fire.

"These gifts are given to all, but to one who would walk the Path, we ask that they be returned. Before you leave Preparation, your gifts must be offered."

She paused, wondering if the timoe was ripe. The Prince of Endlin stood crowned with light as if shedding the darkness of his childhood years. She could delay no longer.

"No one walks the path alone. Our way is the joining of one to another, and so you will be joined with a woman. With her you will offer your gifts. They are three in number: your beauty given with the hair of your head, your strength given with the blood of your body, your fertility given with the seed of your sex."

She hesitated for the space of one heartbeat, then set her grandson free.

"If you cannot bring yourself to offer these gifts, you must leave the Maze."

For the first time she saw herself within him, and in that moment, felt her spirit quicken as once her womb had quickened with Aethra. Surrounded by that brilliant aura, haloed by the light, he was revealed to her as the man he might become, a blending of two ancient cultures, the savior of Endlin and the hope of Pelion reborn. She shut her eyes against the completeness of her vision, understanding that the price of his Transformation might be his precious self.

Every gift they asked of him would cost him dearly; every day within the Maze would try his spirit to the breaking point. Here was the truth of Esslar's warning, for he was Sandur's sword and buckler, Magda's weapon forged on a night of near madness, honed and sharpened to assist her with this most perilous of Transformations. For Aethra's child they must risk everything, for if Sandur should fail, then all would come to naught, and the light would flicker, dim, and die, a candle gutted by the cruel winds of upheaval.

A shiver ran through her. Opening her eyes, she found herself pinned by the power of her grandson's gaze.

"Before I make my decision, I have two questions."

"Ask them."
"Who is my ... my mother?"
"Aethra of Pelion."
When he repeated the name, tasting its strangeness on his tongue, she found herself trembling. She wondered if she should inform him of Aethra's death. An inner voice cautioned, *"Not yet."*
"Will I see Esslar again?"
"He asks that you remember his words at parting. You must make your way on your own."
His chest raised and lowered although she could not hear his sigh.
"I will persevere."
The door opened at his knock, and he disappeared behind it, leaving her alone and inexplicably content. It was not the reunion of her dreams, but she heard him speak his mother's name. Somehow, it was enough.

MEMORIES CAME IN fits and starts, catching him unaware, sending him off-balance, reeling under the force of the resentment they called up inside him. The routine of the Maze saved him. Without it he would have foundered in deep waters and drowned. As it was, he clung to the habits drilled into him over the past week as a storm-tossed mariner clings to the mast, welcoming the morning bell that freed him from the tyranny of dreams, grimly grateful for the activities that measured out his days. Moving through space like a sleepwalker, following Pentaur wherever he was led, his body went through the motions of training while his mind grappled with the past.

Most painful of all was his surety that the old woman had not lied. Years spent around negotiating tables where men traded falsehoods without a qualm had taught him the signs of deception: the smile that never reaches the eyes, the hand offered too eagerly to cement the bargain, the subtlety of the swindler, the apparent guilelessness of the professional poseur. She was none of these. Truth hung about her like a mantle, the same cloak Esslar wore. They were of a breed, truthsayers in a world of liars and hypocrites.

When the rage overcame him, fury burned so deep he felt his insides smolder. At first he could not think about his father, but spent his wrath on all the others who aided him in the great deception. The procession of ayahs who must have known or at least suspected the truth, yet never revealed by a word or a glance the reason for the difference in hair color which set him apart from his siblings. The concubines, too, must have been party to the details of his birth in a foreign land, all of them privy to the underground chains of gossip and speculation that sped through the citadel like grass fires on the great plains to the north. Even Tasir, his foster-father, his beloved uncle, concealed the truth at the same time he spoke words of love.

All those years spent in misery, seeking the reason for his father's indifference, the purposeful neglect, the punishments for imagined faults, the hatred . . . and then he was lost again, feeling the bite of the belt against his back, listening to the snickers of the other children . . .

"ANOTHER STROKE, ONLY one more stroke," his ayah whispered through tears that must on no account be shed in the presence of the Tehran.

Bent over as he was, he could see the hem of his father's golden robes, a sandaled foot tapping out the rhythm of the beating. His back smarted under the blows of the strap as he listened to his playfellows' nervous laughter, all of them gathered to watch the unusual sight of a child being punished. No one was ever beaten here. No one save the Tehran's sa'ab.

His ayah was crying outright now, tears rolling down her wan cheeks as she folded the strap. A stolen glance at his father's face revealed that she would be gone tomorrow, replaced by yet another stranger, another cast-off concubine relegated to duties within the harem.

"Do you understand your failing?"

There would be no forgiveness for his error, no lessening of parental displeasure despite the harshness of his punishment. He nodded mutely, still hopeful that the interrogation would be quickly ended to be further chastised by a sharp rebuke.

"You insult my presence with your sullenness! A sa'ab addresses his father respectfully at all times. Now, repeat the lesson you have learned so all may hear."

Frightened, he searched for a cause, trying to avoid those black eyes staring down at him with avid dislike. What had he done this time? What had provoked his father's anger on this, his first visit to the harem in two moons?

He was playing, he remembered, playing with Pischak's dog, rolling on the ground and tussling with the silky-eared spaniel pup, laughing as it strove to lick his face, the pink tongue warm and wet on his cheek. Pischak didn't mind that the pup preferred Sandur's company. He had pets aplenty, while Sandur had none. And then, without warning, a frosty voice issued a command just as the pup gave him another lick, causing him to laugh again, finding, when the laugh was finished, that the harem was strangely silent.

"I failed to honor your presence, father."

"Continue."

"I . . . I laughed when I should have been silent."

"And?"

"And . . . and I played with Pischak's dog after you forbade me to do so."

Sandur braced himself before lifting his eyes from the floor. A terse nod indicated he had answered correctly.

"The dog will be removed from the harem lest you be tempted again to ignore my command."

An ear-splitting wail rose from Pischak. Sandur swallowed hard, tasting the bitterness of having unwittingly betrayed his best friend.

"Your ayah seems unable to keep order. I will furnish you with a suitable replacement. See that you honor my wishes in the future. One day you'll take your place in the world of men. If you cannot learn obedience here, in the company of women and children, what hope have you of success outside the harem walls?"

"I will try harder, father."

"See that you do."

The golden robes vanished. The other children drifted away, unwilling to risk being in his presence. Sandur stood alone by the gilded gates, wiping away the salty tears running down his cheeks.

"THE TRUMPET CALLS us to the baths."

Sandur opened his eyes on the arena. Panting, covered with sweat, he felt the muscles in his legs tremble from the race he'd just run. The other ernani filed out of the gate, the air filled with their jibes and banter. Wiping the stinging sweat away from his eyes with the sleeve of his blouse, he looked over his shoulder at the track, wondering how he'd managed to find his way around it.

"You finished second; Jincin overtook you in the straightaway," Pentaur reported matter-of-factly, ushering him into line.

Sandur took a morose pleasure in the fact that he'd nearly beaten Jincin, a red-haired wild man from the northern wastes whose legs ate up distances like a starving wolf pursuing a hare. Ever since his interview with the old woman, Sandur excelled in everything Dictys threw at him, even managing to pin Yossi in the wrestling bouts he despised, hating the necessity of writhing on the ground with a sweating partner who smelled of garlic or worse.

Pentaur headed through the swinging doors toward the baths. Sandur quickly gave up trying to learn his way in this warren of passageways. Falling into step beside his monitor, he progressed at an easy pace as Pentaur took the many turns and sharp reversals of direction without a break in stride. Sandur found himself at ease with Pentaur's silences, relieved that there was no necessity of making pointless conversation with a menial. Just when his mind began to wander, Pentaur pointed out a door on the right-hand side of the hallway.

"Tomorrow you'll be tested. I'll escort you here after the midday meal."

"What sort of test?"

"Reading, writing, figuring; nothing to concern you. Once the tutors decide your placement, you'll go on to more advanced work. History, perhaps, or the sciences."

"Why do you assume I read and write? Would you make the same assumption about Tibor or Jincin?"

"Tibor and Jincin are not natives of Endlin."

A pang struck Sandur somewhere in the vicinity of his breastbone.

"What do you know of Endlin?" he asked gruffly, to be answered with a non-committal shrug.

"Only that they, too, keep the old knowledge alive."

Sandur recalled the maps covering the walls of the room where the old woman met him. hey were extremely detailed, he remembered, and piqued his interest until everything fled his mind except the certain knowledge that the shores of Endlin were not his native land. Lied to since the moment of his birth, it struck him that somewhere in this vast fortress of grey rock rising from the floor of a fertile valley, lived a woman he must call mother.

"I'll wait for you in the wardroom."

Jolted back into existence, he found himself in the showers. The other ernani were noisily engaged in washing off the grime of the day's labors before heading toward the inner room where copper tubs of steaming water waited. Weariness hit Sandur hard. Bone-tired, he stripped to his challah and picked up a sponge. Eddo stood beside him, using a scrubbing brush on the blue-black tattoos covering his hairless chest, grunting with pleasure like a horse rolling in sand. Long ago Sandur gave up his modesty, becoming inured to the sight of male bodies in various states of undress. He'd worked up a lather and was running a sponge over his shoulders and under his arms when Eddo spoke up from behind him.

"Who did this?"

It was the first time anyone had ever asked him about the scars. A lie rose to his lips almost without necessity of thinking, a lie devised to protect his honor and that of his father. And then, unaccountably, Sandur spoke the truth.

"My father ordered me beaten."

Eddo blinked hard before growling, "He's a coward. Also a fool."

Five moons ago, five days ago, Sandur would have slit the throat of anyone who dared insult the Tehran of the Kwanlonhon.

Today he said simply, "Yes."

* * *

"HOW DOES HE fare?"

Esslar's sympathy went out to her, a grandmother grieving over a grandchild she barely knew. Should he increase her burden with the day by day, moment by moment account of a man being torn apart? Should he reveal what he had learned during the last few days with Sandur, forced to witness sessions of soul-shattering abuse, watching as a boy of five, of seven, of twelve, was ridiculed and taunted, his naturally high spirits beaten into submission, his small body quaking as he muffled his sobs with his pillow?

Each day the hatred grew, unfettered by chains of duty. Sandur relived each episode of abuse, working through the puzzle of his life, still unsure of the answers, yet certain that in the secret of his birth lay a key that would unlock the bonds of servitude. His revolt was total, sparing no one, not even people like Tasir, who struggled on his behalf, protecting him from his father despite the risk of incurring the Tehran's displeasure.

Esslar helped where he was able, silently prompting Pentaur to interrupt Sandur's thoughts when they bordered on the murderous or the suicidal. Yesterday a worried Esslar advised Dictys to end a wrestling bout, the Head Trainer dragging Sandur away from Yossi, who regarded the eastern prince with almost childish surprise, not understanding what he had done to bring on such a killing rage.

Sandur's moods swung too violently for Esslar to influence them since interference would necessitate direct control. Helplessly, he walked the corridors of Sandur's memories, finding chambers dark and dreary almost past bearing, no light within them, an endless succession of horrid places where a lonely child dwelt, unwanted and unloved.

Worst of all, in the moments when Sandur was thrown back into the waking world, the single thought that drove him was revenge. It was unformed as yet, but as the hatred grew, so grew the need for reprisal. As Esslar learned in the first few days of their journey, Sandur was no fool. The pieces were coming together: his father's almost supernatural abilities to guess what lay in the minds of his competitors, the whispers circulated throughout the citadel that Manthur dabbled in sorcery, Rahjid's unexplained abdication. Even if Sandur was unsure as to the exact nature of the gift, he knew his father had walked the Path of Preparation. A plan was forming even now. If he could become his father's equal, if Sandur, too, walked the Path, he could match his father word for word, blow for blow. Soon there would be not one, but two dark lords in Endlin.

This was the chance they took, an enormous gamble that in their attempt to rewrite history, they might compound their mistakes. If this Preparation should fail, the gift would eventually pass away, a distantly recalled memory of an all too brief golden age. If it should succeed, Pelion might endure, but without the one city which, in many ways, surpassed its achievements.

For five centuries Pelion existed in seclusion, its founders suspicious of outsiders who once had persecuted them for their special abilities, choosing instead to turn inward in an attempt to study more thoroughly the interiors of the human mind. In that same span of time, Endlin mapped the eastern boundaries of the known world, their tall ships plying the seacoasts, their helms manned by a constantly curious merchant class who delighted in the new, the extraordinary, the unexplored. Even if the miracle came to pass and ernani joined with ernani, how long would they survive if the entire eastern seacoast and the uncharted lands beyond dwelt perpetually amongst the shadows?

Lost as he was in private worries, Esslar heard the Nineteenth Mother's quiet musings.

"My daughter could have charmed him. It was a gift she had, a legacy from her father. His same sweet smile."

So strong was Esslar's relief, he laughed out loud. She turned to him, a question in her ancient eyes.

"Why do you laugh?"

"So as not to weep."

"Just so," she smiled back at him. "We've no time for tears. Let others weep for the world; we must set it right."

"You've just given me the means."

"Have I?" she asked, a pleased expression passing over her tired face. She'd grown smaller during his absence, her frame stooped as if from perpetual exhaustion.

"Would she ever find rest?" he asked himself, then answered, *"Not in this world."*

"I will deliver him into his mother's care."

If she was surprised, she gave no sign.

"Would you like to accompany me?" Esslar asked, knowing how difficult it was for her to be excluded. She shook her head, a faraway look in her eyes.

"Name it not. I've learned my lesson and will not soon forget. He's not to be touched by anyone but you. I am too fond to be of help, grown foolish in my old age. In a single minute in his presence I cast away the lessons of a lifetime and became a doting woman delinquent in my duty."

"Yet stay by me."

"As long as I have breath."

Her care-worn face his anchor to the waking world, he left her, taking the well-worn path into Sandur's thoughts, leaping the chasm with practiced ease and landing lightly in the darkened corridors. The Tehran's sa'ab hovered in that delicate state between sleep and full-fledged dreaming. As a dream

began to form, Esslar recognized Manthur among the shadowy forms gathering to plague Sandur's rest. A voice spoke out of the past, the voice of one whom, against his will, is forced to speak the truth.
"*I touched his thoughts once while he slept. Nothing more.*"
Startled, Esslar considered his course, weighing intuition against the formidable presence of the Tehran of the Kwanlonhon, then led Sandur into the fog of memory.

THE BOY SLEPT fitfully, tossing and turning, his hair tousled on the pillow. The night was warm, and he slept unclothed, pushing away the silken sheet impatiently as if it, too, conspired to disturb his rest. The candle beside his pallet, placed there by a compassionate ayah who knew his fear of the dark, flickered in the sultry sea breezes creeping into his chamber. Other children of the Kwanlonhon harem slept with siblings or playfellows, brown-skinned bodies curled up beside one another like so many kittens. The Tehran's sa'ab slept alone.

The nightmare came all at once, the boy's ten-year-old mind invaded by a restless, searching presence. Sifting through memories only to cast them away, the presence turned hungry, insatiable, searing the boy's soul. Secrets were probed, innocent secrets of childhood—a harmless prank played on an unsuspecting ayah, a hiding place for favorite treasures, whispered confidences among friends, a spaniel pup to be grieved over nightly, a pink tongue wet against his cheek, the unaccustomed delight of being loved.

Unsatisfied, the presence grew brutal, demanding. The boy could hide nothing, think nothing, do nothing but quiver as his every fault was magnified a thousand times, the all-seeing, all-knowing power condemning him without hope of appeal. He was a bad boy: sullen, uncooperative, disobedient, spoiled, a disappointment to everyone who met him. Helpless to resist, cowed into submission, he implored forgiveness, begging for mercy, anything to appease the shadowy figure that assured him his cause was hopeless.

A woman's voice pushed away the shadows, combating his fears:
"*You are his long-awaited sa'ab, the bringer of good fortune. You are our hope, the proof of our blessing.*"
A choked cry dispelled the voice, the nightmare ended, and the boy awoke.

His father stood in the doorway, his hands covering his face. Clutching the sheet to cover his nakedness, the boy lay tense and shivering. His ayah appeared, her grizzled hair unbound, her face puffy and swollen with sleep, shuffling forward to freeze at the sight of the golden robes shining faintly in the candlelight. At the sound of her approach, his father ordered her out in a strangled whisper more frightening than a screamed command. The ayah fled.

The shadowy figure of his father stood still and silent, a phantom of the night sprung to life. The candle flame flickered violently and went out, plunging the chamber into darkness. Out of that darkness came his father's voice, pensive and strangely contrite.

"I'll not disturb your rest again. Sleep now."

Just before the boy sank into oblivion, he thought he heard his father speak, but could make no sense of the words.

"If thou comest to him, why not to me? Awake and asleep, I search for thee. Shall we never dance again, my beauty?"

Sweet visions wrapped around the boy like a watery embrace. A woman sang, her voice floating back to him as he sailed away on a ship of dreams.

"YOU FOUND HER?"
"She came of her own volition."
"Does he know her?"
"She is always with him, but he knows her not."
"She's with him now?"
"Aye, a song on her lips."

Night deepened around them, soft night, gentle night, the only sound the sputtering of the candles and a mother's lullaby to her unborn child.

Chapter 12

The Iron Door

"How fine it is! Like a flake of snow! Teach me, Alyssa! Teach me how it's done!"

Responding to a gentle but insistent tug, Alyssa loosened her grip on the piece of lace. Soon she was surrounded by expressions of wonder. The tiny scrap must have been passed from hand to hand, for each woman who fingered it issued an enthusiastic response. Alyssa, always on her guard against expressions of false admiration or patronizing forbearance, detected nothing but honest appreciation. Gratified that her skills with thread, hook, and bobbins were appreciated by her new companions, she basked in their praise.

It was typical of Ulkemene (a former worker in the orchards of New Agave) to draw attention to Alyssa while the others worked on their copybooks. A tutor came every morning, teaching her to work sums on the abacus. Once the lessons in reading and writing began, Alyssa retired to a quiet corner and made do with listening, learning the alphabet through countless repetitions and memorizing the spelling of words.

"What do you call it, Alyssa?"
"Have you a pattern I could borrow?"
"Who taught you?"
"Is it something only the blind can do?"

She managed to reply with what she hoped was an air of calm serenity. "Lace-making is an ancient craft practiced throughout my province. No patterns exist. Each piece is unique, created by the invention of the lace-maker. Mother teaches daughter. When a child is old enough, she begins by learning to spin thread. The greatest lace-makers are the old women, 'little mothers' we call them, for we have a saying in Cinthea: `Cheese, wine, and lace improve with age.'" She paused a moment before adding, "As to your question, Draupadi, many, but not all, have lost their sight."

The tiny piece of lace was returned to Alyssa's empty, outstretched palm.
"I meant no insult."
"I took none."
A roughened hand squeezed her forearm in wordless apology.

"Of what use is this 'lace'?" demanded Zuniga, her voice booming across the room from the vicinity of the study tables.

"Why does it need to be useful? Can't a thing have worth just because it's beautiful?" protested Ulkemene, troubled by the serpent woman's pragmatic approach to life.

Becca, who came from faraway Botheswallow, a name derived from the flocks of swallows who migrated yearly to those far-off climes, spoke up in her typically thoughtful manner, posing a solution calculated to cancel the debate.

"It would seem that here in the Maze, a thing must be both useful and beautiful. Evadne teaches us the healing ways even as she instructs us in cleanliness and grooming. Symone helps us appreciate the beauty of a poet's words, but insists that we learn to read and write so we may compose poems of our own."

A few sighs drifted through the air of the dayroom, for it was difficult to learn the stranger's ways, until a wry voice asked mischievously, "And what of Anstellan's lessons, Becca?"

Lynsaya's jest caused Ulkemene to giggle behind her hand. Zuniga's raucous laughter rose to the raftered ceilings.

"Aye, what of joining, Becca?" Zuniga demanded when she'd recovered the power of speech, calling out over the sound of general merriment. "Should our beddings be useful or beautiful? Perhaps a better question is why you're in such a rush to finish that gown? Do you want your partner to notice the evenness of your stitches or the fact that it clings in all the right places?"

Another wave of hilarity overcame them, part of it due to Zuniga's wit, a greater part springing from the relief they all felt at broaching the subject of tomorrow night. The thought of sleeping for the last time on the narrow cots lining the dormitory walls, of entering the subterranean cells on the morrow, all the worries and concerns of women facing strange men in locked rooms, were contained in the laughter that met Zuniga's gibe.

Rather than Becca, it was Vlatla who gave answer. Slowly, deliberately, the river woman recited the words each of them knew by heart, "There need be no joining in the first moon. The Nineteenth Mother promised."

"And if we're forced?" Draupadi asked, her voice as harsh as her work-roughened hands. Alyssa heard Lynsaya catch her breath and hold it for a long moment, releasing it gradually when Becca replied.

"Shouldn't we trust our caretakers? Shouldn't we remember the Searchers who brought us safely to Pelion? All of us traveled here in the company of men. Were any of us raped or mistreated?"

Silence affirmed the truth of her reasoning, and peace entered their collective souls.

When Ulkemene spoke up, Alyssa found herself wondering if her face could possibly match the sweetness of her voice. Over the past moon she'd formed a picture of each woman, sometimes helped along by a stray comment or a private disclosure. She knew of Lynsaya's hair (the color of sun-ripened wheat and the object of much discussion among the other women) and of Draupadi's apprehension that no man would appreciate her boyish frame, just as she could tell that Zuniga towered over her while the top of Ulkemene's head barely reached her shoulder. The majority of her pictures remained works of pure imagination. Becca she imagined as a prophetess of yore, statuesque and full-breasted with a noble brow and far-seeing eyes. Dismissing Draupadi's dissatisfaction with her appearance, Alyssa knew her to be wiry and immensely strong, and imagined sharp eyes underneath ebony brows which rose like wings when she laughed and drew together in a horizontal line when her feelings were hurt. Vlatla was the most difficult one to imagine since she rarely spoke and seemed most comfortable on the fringes of the group. A month or more since their original meeting on the road to Pelion, Lynsaya remained Vlatla's closest friend. Alyssa imagined them as complete opposites, the long-legged daughter of eastern Lapith and the compact, quick-moving woman of the River People, one blue-eyed and quick-tongued, the other sloe-eyed and moody. Ulkemene she imagined as a petite beauty with a dreamy expression, her dulcet tones like the cooing doves who nested in the eaves of Gwyn's barn.

"Let's play the game one last time, shall we?" Ulkemene suggested, clapping her hands together to alert the others. "We've hours to spare before the evening meal, and I'm too nervous to study."

"We mustn't ignore the rule of privacy," came Becca's immediate objection, although she sounded only half-convinced.

"Not until tomorrow," Zuniga pronounced with satisfaction. "Once we're joined, we'll keep our secrets. What's the harm in learning something useful tonight?"

A wave of agreement passed over the group. Alyssa heard chairs and benches being drawn towards her. She didn't deserve to be at the center of the group, for she alone had nothing to offer when it came to playing the game, but she appreciated their generosity in not excluding her. In time they were settled, and the buzz of activity gave way to hushed anticipation. As was her habit, Zuniga functioned as organizer.

"You talk for the south, Becca, Draupadi for the west, Hanania for the north, Vlatla for the east."

"Lynsaya is a better speaker," Vlatla countered quickly.

"But she joined your party much later," Zuniga pointed out quickly. Having been a leader of her people, the serpent woman was unaccustomed to having her wishes contradicted.

"Lynsaya will tell it best."

"Very well, but only if you promise to add anything she forgets or some detail she might not know."

Becca spoke up again, still worried at the prospect of breaking a rule despite the fact that it didn't take effect until tomorrow evening's trumpet blast.

"Remember to speak no ill. Think how you might feel if the men were gathered together as we are, telling each other our faults."

"Agreed. Who will begin?"

Hanania volunteered and the game commenced.

No one could remember how the game first came about. From a chance remark or an amusing anecdote shared among two or three women, it grew into a formalized event, a designated speaker describing the men with whom she'd traveled on the long road to Pelion. The fun came in comparing stories and impressions, although as time passed they began to listen more intently, eager for a hint as to a prospective partner's character or appearance. If the caretakers knew of the game, they never indicated disapproval. Only in the last few days had Anstellan explained the rule of privacy that forbade any discussion of what occurred behind the iron door.

At first they thought he was teasing them, for by now he was both friend and confidant, entrusted with their most intimate secrets. It would not be stretching a point to say that they loved him, for who could resist his physical beauty coupled with a cheerful disposition and a strong intellect? Still, they kept their distance as he kept his, always mindful that the Path lay before them and that Anstellan of Pelion would not walk by their side.

He was more serious than usual the day he explained the rule. The women gathered near the fireplace on the western wall of the dayroom, an early snow turning the outside world white and necessitating extra layers of stockings and woolen shawls draped around the shoulders of the thin-blooded southerners. Dressed in the immaculate saffron-colored robes of a Master Hetaera, his short curls shining with good health, his chin smooth, his figure trim and upright, more than one woman sent up a silent prayer that her partner might be as clean and well-groomed. He began the session as he always did, greeting each of them in turn, satisfying himself that they were alert and in good spirits before taking up the subject for the day's discussion.

"For many reasons, some I may not discuss, the Nineteenth Mother has evoked the rule of privacy. It will be strictly enforced during the first moon of joining. To break this rule will mean immediate expulsion from the Maze, without exception and without appeal."

He surveyed them soberly for a moment, letting the warning ring in their ears, before breaking into a smile.

"The good news is that you may speak to me at any time. In fact, I'll be insulted if you don't request counseling sessions with me on a regular basis."

No one was surprised when Becca posed a question with her usual tact.

"You said there were reasons you can't discuss. Might you tell us what you can?"

"It's our belief that you'll benefit from the rule since it will prevent you from comparing your lives within the cells with those of your friends."

It seemed a hard rule after all they'd shared. Their days would continue as before, but their nights would be forever altered. The name of their partner must not cross their lips, for to speak it, however innocently, meant that the gift for which so much had been dared would be denied them. Twelve women made twelve promises. Eleven of them lowered their eyes to their laps. One stared blindly into the fire, wondering how many first moons of joining she must endure.

BECCA FINISHED HER recital to a round of appreciative applause. Everyone had their favorite, but the story of Eddo's tattoos grew with the telling, and Becca was undoubtedly the best storyteller from the southern lands. With expansive gestures and a credible attempt at a bass voice, she mimicked Eddo's elaborate explanations of each and every feat memorialized on his chest, back, and shoulders, sending the entire room into gales of laughter.

Perhaps because it was the last time the game would be played, the oft-times sullen Draupadi rose to the occasion, providing the first really detailed description of Pharlookas, a reputed giant of remarkable height and girth (although Lynsaya was quick to remind everyone that the warriors of Lapith were the tallest men in the world). Jincin, too, was greatly admired, and Hanania did him proud, recounting his daring when their party was attacked by slavers on the farthest boundaries of northwest Lapith. He spoke a language only the Searcher understood, but had no trouble communicating his feelings for their attackers when he pulled a slaver from a running horse and drove his spear through the man's chest and deep into the blood-soaked earth. Since the majority of the women were dark of hair and eye, with complexions ranging from olive to ebony, few of them could imagine Jincin's flaming hair or ruddy beard. Lynsaya and Alyssa's people tended toward lighter hair and blue, green, and grey eyes, but, they, too, confessed never having seen anyone approximating the reports of Jincin's coloring.

Lynsaya spoke last, spending most of her time describing Yossi of Dragon's Tooth. Her spirited rendition of his nightly chant to ward off dragon's breath made Zuniga hold her sides and roll to and fro on the floor, although this former priestess would have been the first to fly into a rage if anyone ridiculed her snake-gods, who reputedly lapped milk from the bowls of their worshippers.

As Lynsaya's tale drew to a close, Ulkemene asked dreamily, "What of the prince from the eastern shore?"

Lynsaya snorted, a uniquely Lapithian sound not unlike a horse clearing its nostrils. Vlatla offered a quiet translation of her friend's response.

"She likes him not, and so says nothing. He gave her insult by refusing to breed his stallion to her mare."

"But you liked him, Vlatla?"

"My likes or dislikes are unimportant," the river woman responded, her vagueness indicating her unwillingness to elaborate.

"Speak no ill, then, but tell us what you can," Becca urged, the group adding their pleas. Slowly, reluctantly, Vlatla began.

"He's a hands-breadth taller than Lynsaya, dark-skinned and well-formed. At first he wore his hair in many braids, so many I could not count them. On the morning after Lynsaya joined us, the braids were gone." Seeming to gather her thoughts, she continued more rapidly. "He's a fine swimmer, better even than Tibor or myself. In the water he's different somehow, younger and at peace. It's the only time I ever saw him smile."

"What of the scars?" Ulkemene asked eagerly.

Vlatla started, then turned to Lynsaya, who hung her head, refusing to meet her best friend's accusing gaze.

"Lynsaya has no right to gossip of what she never saw."

"But, Vlatla, you told me!"

"I erred by telling you. All of us have scars, although we may not wear them on our back. You know the truth of this, Lynsaya, as do we all."

A trumpet sounded, calling them to the evening meal, the game ending in a flurry of activity as they returned their benches to the tables and replaced their books and papers on the cupboard shelves. Lynsaya looked around anxiously for Vlatla. Seeing that she lingered by the windows and stared out over the fallen snow, Lynsaya hurried away in the direction of the refectory, resolving to ask pardon tonight after the torches were put out.

When the others departed, Vlatla sighed, running her hands through her hair, remembering it hanging wet and curling after an evening swim. *A full moon without a swim,* she thought sadly, *and so many moons remain.* When a cupboard door swung shut, she gasped, startled to discover she was not alone.

It was the blind woman from the southeastern province they'd skirted on the road to Pelion. Having stored away her threads and hook, she stood facing the closed doors, her posture alert, her expression guarded.

"Who's there?"

"Vlatla."

"I ask pardon, Vlatla. I didn't mean to frighten you."

She must have heard me gasp, Vlatla decided, *but did she hear me sigh?* "I thought myself alone for once."

To her surprise, the blind woman laughed aloud.

"Ah, to be alone for only a small space of time! Sometimes I yearn for the cell, for a place of my own. They are wonderful women, very different from my cousins and friends, yet I grow tired of this endless waiting. Tomorrow we'll meet the men face to face, and I fear we'll discover they bear little resemblance to their descriptions. Stories are so much more interesting than reality."

Strange, thought Vlatla, she speaks my thoughts exactly, until she realized they must be everyone's thoughts. Suddenly, she regretted her treatment of Lynsaya. She's as restless as we all are, her long legs freed of her skirts for a few short hours after midday when she runs in the arena, hair flying in the breeze. No wonder she tried to impress Ulkemene, whispering secrets no one else knows. The blind woman is right; we're bored with waiting.

"You came alone to the Maze, did you not?"

"Not quite alone," the blind woman smiled, "but not like the rest of you. I can offer nothing when they play the game."

"Would that I had a like excuse."

"You did well, standing up for him as you did."

The blind woman, having turned away from the cupboard, stood facing Vlatla across the dayroom. How can she pinpoint my exact location in this large room? Sharp ears, Vlatla decided, sharp enough to detect a sigh at thirty paces.

"In truth, I . . . I didn't like him" Vlatla stammered, unwilling to take credit for defending anyone other than herself.

"Him?"

"Sandur. He's like the stinging nettles we harvest for flax. The slightest touch raises a welt on your palm."

"Yet, as you say, nettles yield flax," the blind woman observed mildly. "In some ways I'm thankful I came by myself. Whomever they choose will be like a tale told for the first time."

"I prefer the old stories," said Vlatla, "the ones I know by heart and can welcome like long-lost friends."

Vlatla wondered if the blind woman sensed her secret. What would she do if, when the iron door opened, and a man stepped over the threshold, it wasn't Tibor's face she beheld? The Searcher cautioned her against becoming emotionally involved with the men with whom she traveled, but what was she to do? With Tibor, she shared a common language, a similar heritage, a love of the river, and most importantly, a common goal to better their folk. How strange it was to discover that although Tibor's home lay less than a week's journey downriver, they would never have met save for the Path.

"They will eat everything if we don't hurry," the blind woman said as she turned toward the door, reaching out her hands to make sure the way was clear.

She moves gracefully, Vlatla thought, like cattails ruffled by a stray breeze. I wonder if she knows how beautiful she is? Don't be a fool, she reminded herself. How could she know what only a looking glass would tell her?

"Would you like to take my arm?"

The blind woman hesitated, then smiled.

"Yes. Let's walk together."

ANSTELLAN TOOK A swig of wine and choked, grimacing at the sour taste of the lees. Setting down the goblet, he wiped his mouth and looked down for the fiftieth time at the list in front of him. "The Night of Groans" he'd dubbed it five years ago. Tonight he was considering adopting a new title: "The Night of Unmitigated Disaster." Two hours past midnight, everyone was exhausted, Anstellan was fast losing patience, and they were still at an impasse.

Twelve couples! All this effort for twelve couples! According to Symone, this was the smallest class in the history of the Maze, the Novice Class consisting of twenty couples, fifteen in the class of the First Transformation. His first year as Instructor he'd joined ten times this number before the watchman called the eleventh hour! Of course, he'd overseen a staff of eight hetaeras with several fourth-year apprentices keeping track of the records, and now he was working alone. Even so, nothing, not even the Nineteenth Mother's frequent warnings, prepared him for this!

"Let us review," he ground out between gritted teeth. "Nine couples have been selected; three remain. The men: Kokor, Pharlookas, and Sandur. The women: Alyssa, Ulkemene, and Vlatla."

No one made a sound. The Nineteenth Mother appeared to be sleeping, her eyes closed and her chin resting on the tips of two fingers. Galen stifled an enormous yawn while Symone turned the page of a book she'd been reading all night. The High Healers were busily involved in contemplating the table top. Esslar alone seemed attentive, which increased Anstellan's irritation.

"Let me repeat my recommendations: Sandur and Ulkemene; Kokor and Alyssa; Pharlookas and Vlatla."

Anstellan waited, without much hope. Just as he'd feared, Esslar took up the debate where it broke off.

"He'll treat her like a concubine."

It wasn't the fact that Esslar disagreed that annoyed Anstellan so much as his seeming inability to suggest a plausible solution. Nine partners had been suggested for the Tehran's sa'ab; nine were summarily rejected.

"Vlatla?" he suggested hopefully, watching those hopes die as Esslar shook his head.

"That would be less satisfactory than Ulkemene. If anything, Vlatla is more withdrawn than Sandur and suffers from a lack of self-esteem. At best, he'll treat her like a commoner. At worst, he'll make her life a misery."

Galen spoke through another cavernous yawn.

"The healer's right."

Groaning inwardly, Anstellan offered the only name they had never discussed in relation to Sandur.

"Alyssa?"

Galen hooted aloud.

"His lordship and a blind woman? Remember what happened in the stronghold? He'd not come near the crippled lad!"

Lifting her eyes from her book, Symone uttered her third pronouncement of the evening. The other two lectures had been equally as daunting, phrased in crisp, exacting language against which it was nearly impossible to argue.

"If I understand Esslar correctly, he fears two things. First, that a woman of any lesser strength of character than Sandur might allow him to resume former patterns of behavior. Secondly, even if a woman should earn Sandur's respect, there's a strong possibility that he'll simply disengage. It would seem, therefore," she flipped a page for emphasis, "that we need a woman of independent spirit who will refuse to be ignored."

Esslar extended his thanks to the Head Librarian with a single, resonant thought. Symone blinked rapidly before continuing to read further down the page.

"I must admit," Evadne interrupted, "that I'm concerned with the direction of this conversation. A successful joining is a matter of balance, of give and take. What will Sandur offer this woman in return for her strength and forbearance?"

Now we're getting somewhere, rejoiced Anstellan. Evadne was the most tenacious of women. Once committed, she'd never rest until an acceptable solution was reached. If the Nineteenth Mother insisted on maintaining her silence, perhaps Evadne could put Esslar on track.

"It's difficult to put into words," Esslar leaned back in his armchair, staring raptly at the ceiling, "but this I believe: Sandur will prove himself a partner of endless devotion and unswerving loyalty. There's nothing miserly about him. Once he loves and is loved in return, his capacity for giving will know no bounds. No stranger will go away empty-handed; no friend will ever live in want. His mate will be showered with unimaginable riches; more importantly, she'll be rewarded with the knowledge that it is she, and she alone, who tapped the natural generosity of his spirit."

Symone shut her book, Galen straightened in his chair, Evadne leaned her head against Japhet's shoulder, and Anstellan smiled. For the first time in nearly seven hours, the Nineteenth Mother spoke aloud, reciting two lines of what seemed to be poetry:

What of the sons who dream of safe haven?
What of the daughters who dream of the sea?

Esslar's response was instantaneous.

"Alyssa dreams of the sea?"

"Since she was a child, long before she lost her sight."

"Then you've chosen her?"

"That is the task of this Council," she demurred.

Without warning, Esslar went into a trance. They'd witnessed it before, Galen more accustomed to these episodes than the rest of them, but still it was unnerving. One moment he was with them, the next he was gone, lost inside himself and unapproachable until he was ready to rejoin them.

"How fares her confidence, Evadne? She'll need full measure of it for the first moon," the Nineteenth Mother asked matter-of-factly, seemingly not bothered by the fact that Esslar sat vacant-eyed and barely breathing.

"She teaches lace-making and tells her stories, although the constant noise and confusion of the dayroom wearies her. Her grasp of the Maze is astounding, immense powers of concentration for one so young. She moved her things into the cell yesterday and seemed reluctant to leave."

"If anyone's interested, the First Transformation took place in that exact cell," Symone announced without fanfare. "In fact, there's never been a failed joining inside those four walls."

"Have you grown superstitious?" Japhet asked. "I thought you despised that sort of thing."

"I report facts. Make of them what you will," Symone replied acidly and retreated back into her book.

"His lordship can be cruel when he's a mind to be."

This observation came from the Legion Commander, who roused himself from his former lethargy to regard the Nineteenth Mother with a worried frown.

"Alyssa's known cruelty aplenty. The world is never kind to those with different gifts. For that reason this city was founded."

"I dinna envy her. In four moons, I ne'er heard him laugh."

"Ask yourself this, Galen. Did your cell ring with laughter during the first moon?"

A crimson tide rose to Galen's hairline as he stroked his white beard, trimmed now and carefully groomed out of deference for his Lucrece.

"Nay, yer right. Laughter came later."

A sudden movement from Esslar brought them to attention. His face remained blank, so concentrated was he on describing the images passing in front of his unseeing eyes.

"Crooked paths. Letters in the flames. A dog howls. And the sea. Always and forever, the sea."

The scratching of Symone's pen could be heard.

Esslar returned, accepting the goblet of wine handed to him by Galen. "I do not see Alyssa. Neither do I see any other woman."

The Nineteenth Mother nodded curtly and took over the meeting.

"We've known from the outset that there will be failures. For this reason I've reinstated the rule of privacy. In another moon, we'll have to repair what damage we've done tonight. We've grown lazy, my friends. Now we must go to work. I want staff members to make regular reports on such things as appetite, personal hygiene, excessive fatigue, alterations in study habits, and performance in the arena for both men and women. No detail, no matter how insignificant, must escape us."

"As to Sandur, Esslar does not speak for Alyssa, neither does he speak against her. If the Council should approve their joining, Anstellan, what would be your recommendation for those who remain?"

"Kokor and Ulkemene; Pharlookas and Vlatla."

"So, have we reached a consensus?"

As they opened their minds to her, she tallied the votes.

"We are agreed."

The Council would long remember the words with which she dismissed them. She was not given to speeches or high-flown rhetoric. First and last, she remained the limited adept who once owned a fabric shop. Still, thirty years in the black robes worked their charms upon her. Tall and stately she seemed to them that night, although they knew her to be thin and a trifle stooped, an ancient wraith held together by skin and gristle. With the maturity of a woman who has led and continues to lead, she buoyed up her flagging strength and taught them a lesson they had nearly forgot.

"This night, the moon rises full and heavy in the evening sky. Eighty years ago, another class began, their caretakers working with nothing to sustain them but a promise. That promise has never failed. Ernani and candidates alike have fled the Maze unchanged, wearers of the black robes have broken their vows, council members have shirked their duties, and the city of Pelion has bargained away its obligations; yet not once in all those years have those who offered their gifts failed to receive what was promised."

"Hold it fast in your hearts, the pledge that one day we shall be as One. The iron door opens and shuts. The miracle begins."

LIT BY AN occasional torch set into a series of brackets lining the stone walls, a shadowy hallway stretched before him. The doors were identical, blank and featureless, each one a solid sheet of iron mounted on sturdy metal hinges. Pentaur slowed his pace and turned to survey his charge, his hand resting on a sliding bolt.

"I'll come for you after the morning bell."

Sandur wondered if his nervousness showed, then shrugged away the thought. Why should he care what a servant thought? This was merely the means to an end, a necessary step toward a future time when he might face his father on an equal footing. Whatever, or more rightly, whoever resided within was merely another trial to be endured, no different from his apprenticeship with the clan shipbuilders or his first trading venture to Ofu.

The hinges ground as he stepped forward into darkness. The bolt slammed into place, its metallic reverberations punctuating the finality of his choice. A shiver ran down his spine. He hated the dark, had hated it since childhood. Holding his hands in front of him, he took a tentative step forward, barked his shin against something solid, and swore aloud.

A voice of surprising depth and clarity spoke out of the darkness.

"I stumbled as well the first time I entered this cell. Could it be an omen?"

"Damn you, woman," he thought to himself as he rubbed the bruised place. *"If you're worried about bad omens, why not light a lamp?"*

"Are there no candles?" he demanded, more rudely than he intended since he'd imagined a less clumsy beginning and feared he'd lost face. The woman was either dense or lazy, for she replied simply: "I didn't think to light one."

He grimaced, glad the darkness hid his exasperation. His intention was to win her affection in record time, train her to her duties by the end of the first moon, and render these so-called gifts with all possible speed. If she was truly as dim-witted as she appeared to be, his plan might take longer than anticipated.

As his eyes adjusted to the darkness, he could just make out her form. She stood beneath a high, narrow window, a slender shaft of moonlight falling over her shoulder turning her gown a silvery shade of grey. More details of the cell were revealed as he moved toward the hearth and knelt, feeling around for a tinderbox. Someone had laid a fire. Once a spark was struck the bone-dry tinder ignited and spread swiftly to the larger sticks of kindling.

Sandur brushed off the knees of his breeches, watching her out of the corner of his eyes. She made no move, nor was she involved in a like examination of him. Instead, she stood as if carved from stone, a caryatid robbed of speech. Deciding that shyness might be the reason for her silence, he took the initiative.

"I am Sandur Manthur Linphat Kwanlonhon, a clansman of Endlin."

He thought he heard her sigh.

"I am Alyssa," she said quietly, "a bard of Cinthea."

"A bard?" he repeated uneasily, unsure of her meaning. His vocabulary was improved, but he was certain he'd never heard this word before.

"A teller of tales. The bards of Cinthea are an ancient guild of my province. Between us we hold the memories of our people as well as the stories of those who came before."

Relief flooded him, accompanied by grudging approval. He'd feared a kitchen wench or worst of all, a tattooed barbarian, a proper match for Jincin or Eddo, but totally unacceptable for a Tehran's sa'ab. Guild membership suggested training and even some status within her community, although the practical side of his nature scoffed at the idea of offering stories in exchange for goods. Certainly she sounded educated. After listening to the hodge-podge attempts of the male ernani to speak the southern language, her flawless diction and elegant phrasings were a tonic to his ears.

Although his initial anxiety was somewhat abated, something about her stillness bothered him. She seemed content to wait, but for what? The fire burned more brightly, revealing more of her appearance, and again he found confirmation that she was no drudge or slattern. Her face lay in shadow, hidden by a waterfall of hair. What he could see of her figure pleased him. The gown was ill-fitting, the shoulder seams cut too wide, the bodice darts uneven and the waist too large and unevenly gathered. Despite the poor skills of her seamstress he could discern the graceful line of her neck and shoulders and the curve of her breasts under the shoddy homespun fabric. Perhaps grown uncomfortable with his silent inventory, she opened her mouth to address him, closed it almost immediately, and turned away toward the wardrobe, her hand reaching out to grasp the wooden knob.

"You must forgive me for staring," he began smoothly. "I was unprepared for your loveliness."

Flattery rose easily to his lips, the same flattery that made him a favorite with his uncle's concubines and insured a steady stream of bed partners whenever he took up residence in the citadel. He knew every move by heart—the provocative glance, the soulful sigh, the burning stare—each of them a necessary step toward a satisfactory bedding.

"Am I lovely?" she asked with a kind of fierce intensity. He smiled inside, at ease and in control for the first time since entering the cell. Refusing to answer until he could see more of her, he selected a piece of burning tinder and lit the candles along the mantelpiece, making his way around the bed to the narrow ledge beneath the window. As he passed behind her, his nostrils flared at the faint scent of lavender.

His hand shook slightly as he touched each wick with fire. So long without a woman, so many days spent in the company of men, almost a year since his last night of pleasure with one of Tasir's concubines, who didn't sneer at the Tehran's sa'ab, but came willingly, even joyfully, sure of his talents and hungry for release.

The cell gleamed about him, the candles flickering, and the fire blazing, vertical shafts of moonlight flooding into the tiny enclosure now bathed in light. Her hair burned like newly-minted coins, a ribbon of reddish-gold streaming down her back, straight and fine, a few wisps dancing about her profile. As he stood transfixed, holding his breath at her nearness, marking the rush of color suffusing her cheeks, stifling his impulse to reach out and touch that glorious hair turned to flames, she wheeled to face him.

Her eyes were pools, grey pools of incalculable depth. How many times had he stood on deck as the prow cleaved its way through the waters, the heavy seas churning as they were split and forced apart by the force of the ship's onward rush, the gulls screaming, the west wind blowing him out to sea, sky and water one color, one wash of pewtered silver, one vast, boundless, shining entity . . .

"Am I lovely?" she repeated, her voice tinged with sadness.

In one brief spasm of time he nearly cried "Yes!" but bit his tongue until it bled, seeing in those pools no movement, and whispered instead, "You . . . you are . . . blind?"

The color drained from her face.

"I am as you see me."

She was lovely no longer. Beauty fled the room, leaving it cold and damp, a dreary cell without life, without promise. Loathe to look at her, he brushed past her without a word, his anger growing as he paced the narrow causeway between bed and wall. Unthinkable, it was unthinkable that such a one as she was thought a suitable partner for a prince of Endlin! A shudder ran through him at the thought of living in eternal darkness, bleary-eyed and stumbling, dependent on a few coins thrown out of pity for stories describing sights she'd never seen.

Panting with rage, he cursed aloud, damning Esslar with every breath he drew, damning the old woman and her wily ways, calling himself a thousand times a fool.

"You need not fret, Sandur Manthur Linphat Kwanlonhon, nor accuse those not present to defend themselves."

His name rolled expertly off her tongue, her intonation matching his, parroting back his lineage in a cruel parody of his original introduction.

"They meant no insult, no affront to your dignity. Nor, I'm sure, did they intend me to be hurt by your . . . your obvious disappointment."

It was not the words themselves that stung him, but the heavy irony with which they were delivered. She was walking now, confident and assured, her right hand brushing the wardrobe as her left reached out to find the back of the chair. After seating herself and arranging her skirts, she continued quite calmly, as if lecturing a sullen child.

"According to the rules, we must remain together until the next full moon, yet there's no necessity for strife between us. You've made your position clear. Rest assured I'll not force myself upon you. We'll make no joining, on that you may rely."

If she heard him mutter his relief under his breath she gave no sign, continuing as she began, coolly and deliberately.

"I've several requests to make of you if we are to pass this moon in harmony. As you might guess, I would appreciate tidiness on your part. A chair moved out of place or items of clothing strewn on the floor might cause me to stumble or fall. Also, since we are to prepare our meals together, you must be careful to replace knives and utensils to their proper places."

He nodded his agreement until he realized she could not see him. Grudgingly, he growled out a reply.

"I've no wish to cause you harm."

Much as he would have preferred to spend the next moon with one of his uncle's concubines, it struck him that no concubine would have reacted quite so unemotionally to an outright rejection of her favors. He was accustomed to tantrums and tearful pleading, screamed threats and sly maliciousness, yet this woman seemed unmoved, even uncaring. Irritated by her unwomanly behavior, he resolved to put her in her place. If she thought to govern this cell for the next moon, she must learn that a Tehran's sa'ab would not be ruled by her or by any woman. Seating himself in the empty chair across the table from her, he half-expected her to turn her head. Never altering her position, she continued staring into the fire burning in front of her sightless eyes.

"I require," he stated forcefully, "that you refrain from touching any of my possessions or my person."

He thought he saw her lips tremble. Since he could only see her profile, he couldn't be sure if she laughed or wept.

"How am I to avoid this when we lie abed?"

Casting his eyes about the cell, he searched for another place to sleep, finding only the enormous bed with its thick mattress, down-stuffed pillows and quilted coverlet. Promising warmth and sweet slumber after many moons of hard ground, narrow cots, weird chanting, reverberating snores, and the ever-present bone-chilling cold, he couldn't bring himself to reject its invitation. Yet fair was fair.

"I'll hold you to our bargain except when we sleep."

As the words passed his lips, he was suddenly and uncomfortably aware that he had never actually spent the night with a woman. Clan tradition specified that once pleasure was enjoyed, the concubine returned to her chamber so each partner might take their separate rests.

She nodded, apparently unsurprised by his reply. A huge chasm opened up between them. What must have been a cart being wheeled down the outside corridor could be heard. A grate slid open at the bottom of the iron door, and a tray slid through the opening.

"What is it?"

Sandur was already on his feet and kneeling down to inspect the steaming offering.

"Our evening meal: steamed fish, rice and lentils, pickled cabbage and pudding."

He didn't think to hide his revulsion at the sight of the overcooked fish, mushy rice, bland lentils and lumpy pudding, the same wretched fare he'd forced himself to eat day after day since his other choice was starvation. As he eyed the tray, wondering if she'd be willing to trade her portion of pickled cabbage for the pudding he despised, a rueful voice interrupted his thoughts.

"It would seem that Pelion's cuisine is not to your taste, nor is it mine, I confess." She continued dreamily, "Oh, for crisp cucumbers in yogurt sauce, salty black olives, trout grilled over a charcoal fire, freshly-baked yeast rolls and sweet dates . . ."

Her enthusiasm grew with his hunger, her recital setting his mouth watering and his stomach growling.

". . . grouse rubbed with sage, dandelion leaves tossed with sweet onion, squash blossoms fried in golden batter, cauliflower relish, and plump dark raisins! Wine aged in oaken casks, Cymean wine, filling the mouth and nostrils with the taste and smells of high summer . . ."

"Stop!" he ordered, amused against his will, "lest I throw this tray in the fire, and we both go hungry until tomorrow morning . . ."

". . . when we'll be summoned to yet another meal of tasteless porridge!" she finished triumphantly before bursting into laughter.

He shook his head at her foolishness, yet found himself in sympathy with her and even entertained. She seemed transformed in that moment, neither cold nor unfeeling, but youthful and vibrant, her mirth a welcome diversion after the awkwardness of their meeting.

"Alyssa," he began tentatively, setting the tray down on the table between them and placing her plate within easy reach, "the healer is always after me to eat, but I've no appetite. Have you recipes for some of the dishes you described?"

"Can you cook?" she asked pertly, her eyebrows lifting like a bird's wings spread for flight. "I would have thought a prince unused to laboring at a kitchen hearth."

"Who told you I was a prince?" he growled, decidedly unamused by her levity now that it was at his expense.

"Lynsaya and Vlatla," she answered quickly, "although I myself am unfamiliar with princes, having never met one before today. In the old tales they are a useless lot, raised in luxury and ignorant of anything except making war and slaying mystical beasts lurking in the forests."

His lips quirked at her description.

"I've defended myself against those who've attacked my ship and hunted since boyhood in the sandhills west of Endlin. I would hardly call that making war or slaying mystical beasts."

"But can you cook?" she insisted stubbornly, her face alight with fun. Against his will, he laughed aloud.

"Despite what the bards of Cinthea may say about princes, I can cook a plain meal, sew a straight seam, saw a board, drive a nail, read a map, navigate by the stars, and design and oversee the building of a sea-worthy vessel. My people are merchants and sea-farers. I was trained for work rather than play."

A soft smile clung to her lips.

"Then I have every hope our meals will improve, Sandur of Endlin, and that we can live amicably together. Shall we be friends, then, and part as friends on the Day of Choice?"

A hand was extended toward him, a slender hand with tapering fingers and oval nails. It hovered in the air between them as she reached out blindly to seal their pact. In Endlin she would never have been allowed to draw a second breath. In Altug's stronghold he could not bear the sight of the boy with the shrunken leg. Now he reached across the table to take the hand of a blind woman in his.

SHE WAITED PATIENTLY until his breathing slowed and deepened. Sleep came hard to him, as if he fought it off to the last possible moment. He was dreaming now, muttering disjointed words in a strange language. Deftly, delicately, she freed herself from the strands of hair that had fallen across her shoulder as he tossed and turned and slid out from beneath the bedclothes, careful to tuck them in so as not to awaken him with a draft of cold air. Finding the thick woolen cloak where she'd left it on the chest at the foot of the bed, she wrapped it snugly about her and tiptoed to the hearth, feeling the heat from the dying embers, and resumed her place in the high-backed chair.

Only then did she let the tears come. She wept soundlessly, unwilling that a sob should betray her. The tears rolled down her cheeks unchecked, tears she refused to shed in front of him.

He'd cursed the Nineteenth Mother, but Alyssa blessed the old woman a hundred times over, for without her warning she would have faced him unprepared. Cruel he was, like the stinging nettles the river woman likened him to, cruel and angry and imperious of manner . . .

Yet he had laughed.

It was a fleeting moment, abruptly begun and quickly over, yet as she mulled over its memory, her tears dwindled. Again she heard him assure her that he could build a ship and sail the seas with only the stars to guide him. Since the days of her childhood, when first her mother taught her to remember her dreams, she'd dreamt continually of the sea. Blindness did not change those dreams, although the fear of drowning kept her far from the shores of the village stream where the other children played and dived among the rocks and standing pools . . .

"Alyssa."

Startled out of her reverie, she feared he'd awakened until she heard him utter a low moan and resume his steady, rhythmic breathing. Do I haunt his dreams, she wondered bitterly; am I the nightmare that disturbs his rest? Wiping away the last of her tears, she stood as one of the logs hissed and another crumbled into a pile of ash.

She crept under the covers, grateful for the heat radiating from his body. As her head touched the pillow, he turned toward her, his moist breath warming her cheek, and uttered a plaintive sigh.

Tired now, but cleansed of hurt, she sighed as well. Her last thought before sleep claimed her was to hope that when the next man who shared this bed with her called out her name, she would be to him neither freak nor demon, but the welcome muse who journeyed with him toward the shadow lands and into the realm of dreams.

Chapter 13

Deception

THE REVIEWING STANDS, carpeted in dirty white, rose like so many building blocks toward a leaden sky. The oval track was a gaping wound, a reddish incision in the pale crust of the arena's flesh, the edges swollen by drifts blown against shoveled piles of snow. Attacked at dawn by a row of shovelers slogging their way through knee-deep snow, the cleared track bespoke a wistful optimism that the winter storm had dissipated its energy, hopes dashed by a timorous sun hiding behind low-lying clouds, refusing to show its face and by its inaction promising yet another snowfall by evening.

At mid-morning, a few of the hardier male ernani dragged one of the straw targets from the far end of the field to the shoveled area just inside the gate. Their attempts with the long bows were half-hearted at best, their fingers aching with chilblains and their bowstrings frozen. Sadly, they bade farewell to the open sky, retreating to the brazier-warmed training rooms where an exhibition by several expert swordsmen from the Legion Infantry was underway.

Neither Lynsaya nor Hanania, fleet of foot and inured to freezing temperatures, ventured forth from the dayroom after the midday meal to take their accustomed places at the starting line. Draupadi, too, forsook her beloved climbing ropes in favor of a lesson with a member of the Potter's Guild. Becca of Botheswallow, swathed in numerous shawls, three petticoats, and two pairs of worsted stockings, was safely ensconced in front of the fireplace where Symone conducted an advanced class in reading. The windows in the dayroom rattled as the icy breezes whipped around the triple-thick walls of the Maze, the drone of the shuttle, the low rumble of the pottery wheel, the paragraphs read aloud in clear treble voices, and the roaring of the four hearths raising a bastion that staved off winter's dominion.

Despite the ernani's retreat to warmer climes, the arena had its inhabitants. There, on the straightaway of the oval track, a cloaked, hooded figure stepped lightly over the frozen cinders, a gloved hand grasping the harness of a large, loose-limbed dog whose iron-grey coat matched the clouds looming overhead. They walked aimlessly for a time, the dog's ears cocked, listening to his mistress' voice over the whistling of the wind, commiserating with whatever secrets she confessed. Some signal passed between them, for the dog came to a halt while the woman searched inside her cloak pocket and produced a tooth-marked ball. The dog tensed, barking excitedly, and the woman threw the missile in a long curving arc toward the wrestling pit. The dog was in motion before her fingers left the ball, his legs a blur as they bore him past the track and onto the fields of grass where his paws left great rents in the snow. With a bounding leap he caught the ball in mid-air, then trotted back to the figure waiting patiently for his return, dancing a little to keep her toes from freezing. Upon his return, she praised him mightily, stroking the great head and shoulders while he teased her a bit, refusing to relinquish the ball until she scratched behind his ears. It was an old game, one that never lost its charm with repetition.

Their play continued until the woman felt the first flakes of snow skip against her eyelashes and melt on her cheeks. The dog was halfway across the arena busily engaged in marking his scent on an upright timber supporting the climbing ropes, when she whistled. At her signal, he scooped up the ball and ran to her side, thrusting his nose against her hand to announce his return. The pair stood for a long moment together, the dog's head uplifted, searching her face with dark, trusting eyes, whining low in his throat. And then, with a quiet word, she pocketed the ball and took hold of the harness, following him toward the wardroom where the innkeeper's boy waited.

They passed through the swinging gates and to their separate destinations, the dog to the inn and the woman to the interior of the Maze. Once they passed inside, another cloaked figure rose from his place on the southernmost reviewing stand, a site downwind of the dog's keen nose. The reviving wind must have buffeted the silent watcher, for it sent snow swirling over the arena, blanketing the track in white, reestablishing the dominance the shovelers had questioned. He seemed oblivious to the temperature, icicles forming on his moustache and beard, his face drawn and his expression frozen. Only his eyes held the spark of life, brown eyes set in a pale face, eyes that never once left the woman as she made her daily pilgrimage around the track of the snow-covered arena.

EVADNE PULLED HER shawl fast around her shoulders as she limped down the corridor, her knees aching and the joints in her fingers stiff and sore. Never had she known such cold. Snow came occasionally to Pelion in the winter moons, usually melting away in the course of a single sunlit day. Unfortunately, this early winter storm showed no signs of dissipating. For almost a week the city was held in winter's thrall, the libraries and schools closed, the side-streets impassable, the fuel merchants hard-pressed to meet unprecedented demands for candles, lamp oil, charcoal, and kindling, the ranks of workers depleted by a respiratory illness that had half the city coughing and the House of Healing under siege. Japhet bid her farewell this morning at dawn, amused by her worried reminders to keep his feet dry.

"This is the weather of my youth," he reminded her as he wrapped a muffler round his throat and stuffed his hands into fur-lined gloves. "Besides," he added, kissing her lightly on the cheek, "one of us must go, and I'll not have you slipping and sliding on the ice."

Irked by his tone, she reminded him that youthful escapades in Lapith were no guarantee of an old man's safe passage to the House of Healing. Instead of sparring with her, as she'd half-intended, he'd grown solemn and placed his hands firmly on her shoulders.

"Since you won't look after your health, it seems I must. Even the shoveled streets are treacherous; one misstep and you'll sprain an ankle or break a hip. Your joints are swollen, and I'll not let stubbornness bring you to harm."

She buried her head in his cloak, hating the thought of his departure, fearing he might catch whatever disease this was that demanded his presence in the House of Healing. She apologized silently, wrapped in arms that had held her for forty years. Just as silently he promised her he would take precautions against contagion, and lastly, that he would make every effort to keep his feet dry.

At least the Maze is free from disease, she comforted herself, having spent the last few days thumping chests and listening to lungs. She and Japhet had been on the alert since the first cases were reported, watching for flushed faces and dilated eyes, listening for the dry hacking cough that characterized the early stages of the disease. They were an embarrassingly healthy lot, these ernani, with scarcely a sniffle or a complaint between them despite the draftiness of the hallways and the dampness of the underground passageways. The southerners suffered the most but put a good face on it, while the northerners were clearly invigorated by the cold.

Certainly their spirits are high, she decided after a moment spent reviewing her healing sessions of the past few days, then frowned as she began comparing past classes with this one as they neared the Day of Choice. Twenty-five years of memories assaulted her, and her frown deepened. Where is the tension that usually approaches as they consider the magnitude of their choice? Where are the doubts and fears, the quarrels and frequent requests for counsel? A new and more disturbing thought struck her as she recalled her first moon with Japhet, a time of difficult adjustments for a formidable, barely literate warrior from Lapith and a highly-educated young woman who'd never stepped outside the city walls. Are we the victims of a hoax or witnesses of something foreign to our experience? Have we been fooled by what seems to be a remarkably easy transition by twenty-four ernani to the rigors of the Maze, or is this class embarked on a new Path, and one for which we have made no provisions?

With these possibilities firmly implanted in her thoughts, she arrived at her destination and pushed open the door to the solarium.

She found Alyssa where she thought to find her, sitting by one of the braziers on an upholstered couch, her agile fingers hooking lace, spools of cream-colored thread spread out over her full skirts. She raised her head at the sound of the door being opened, her expression intent, a welcoming smile on her face.

"Evadne! How glad I am you've come!"

"Have you need of me, child?"

Wondering how she'd been recognized so easily, Evadne decided not to press the matter. Keep your small secrets, daughter of Latona, she pleaded silently. Let us help you with the large ones. The girl shook her head, her smile even more beguiling, and patted the empty place beside her.

"No need except for company."

Taking the place indicated, Evadne executed a quick survey of her charge's heightened color.

"Your cheeks are flushed, Alyssa. Are you fevered?"

She touched the smooth skin of an ivory brow as the girl chirped out her answer.

"Chapped from the wind no doubt. Your hands are always so warm! That must be a useful thing for a healer."

The girl prattled on, Evadne listening with half an ear.

"What of your menses, child?" she interjected when the girl paused to take a breath. "You experienced no initial discomfort, but I've wondered how you've fared for the past few days. If you remember, I asked you to visit me again."

To Evadne's sharp eyes it seemed the girl's smile froze. Then, with a careless shrug, the girl substituted a cheerful reminiscence.

"I must have forgotten. I've never known any pain; in fact, if it weren't for the calendar I'd never know when the bleeding begins. My mother was one of seven sisters, and none of them ever experienced discomfort. My mother's mother says the women of our family excel at breeding children. I'm the only child of my parents, but I've twenty-six cousins on my mother's side. 'A quick tongue makes for quick birthing,' my grandmother used to say, and my aunts would laugh while my uncles groaned."

Evadne listened intently this time, always eager to learn a patient's history, especially in matters concerning childbearing. Yet even as she listened she was reminded that her original question remained unanswered. My inquiries are being ignored, she realized with a start, every question willfully misunderstood, redirected, or answered with a flow of information that has nothing to do with my original intent. Deciding to test her theory, she introduced a new subject, resolving to watch rather than listen.

"How fares Sandur?"

The flush deepened, the sightless eyes blinked, and Evadne thought she detected a quiver at the corners of the girl's mouth before she blurted out an answer that must have been rehearsed hourly, so easily did it fall from her lips.

With gestures and abundant laughter she described their cooking ventures together, patting her stomach as she assured Evadne she was putting on flesh. Recreating their first meal together with detailed accounts of the menu, embroidering the event with several comments attributed to Sandur, she closed her tale with a spirited description of the washing-up.

The story ended and, a few more pleasantries exchanged, the healer made her departure, leaving the girl to whatever comfort the solarium offered since it was clear she would accept none from Evadne. Essler had sent her a single probing thought only an hour or so ago, an enigmatic suggestion that Alyssa needed her. For once, his seemingly infallible intuition failed him. Evadne held no doubts as to Alyssa's need, but neither did she doubt that her presence was unwelcome and that Alyssa's fiction was purposefully designed to deceive.

THE HEALER LEFT at last. With a violent sweep of her hand, Alyssa relegated the contents of her lap to the floor and collapsed against the cushions.

Three more days. Three more days and this will end.

A few hours ago she'd stood in the arena, ready to follow the innkeeper's son beyond the bronze doors, past the northern gates and home to Cinthea, when a voice inside her head whispered, *"Not yet."*

It was odd that Evadne arrived so unexpectedly, stepping out of a dream Alyssa wove in the empty arena, a dream of divulging everything, of freeing herself of the burden she carried, the coldness of the weather nothing to the coldness of her heart. And then, her tongue poised to blurt out the truth, she'd found herself unable to speak anything but lies, desperate for the healer's advice but unwilling that anyone should be party to what began seven days ago and ended this morning at dawn.

A WEEK AGO, not long after the morning bell sounded, she'd traveled the ten paces between the bed and the wardrobe when Sandur announced, "There's blood on your shift."

He spoke so rarely she was momentarily startled. There was no time to be embarrassed since he spoke again almost immediately from behind her right shoulder, proof that he'd left the bed and followed her to the wardrobe.

"Have you everything you need?"

"I . . . I hadn't thought to . . .," she stammered, unwilling to admit she'd forgotten the passage of days lest he think her somehow foolish. "I'll go to the healer before breakfast."

"Have you any discomfort?"

For twenty days their conversations revolved around the planning and execution of the evening meal, which, once consumed and cleared away, dissolved into nothingness as he settled to his studies and she took up her lace. Now he'd posed two questions in as many minutes, each one concerning a highly personal matter. Mystified by his curiosity, for she'd thought him indifferent to anything except his private pursuits, she decided to put aside her shyness.

"I've never any pain, just a slight headache for the first few hours. After some exercise and a hot bath, I'll be fine."

Donning a robe, for she had no wish to flaunt her blood-stained nightshift in front of him, she pulled the sash tight and knotted it, hoping her answer contented him.

"Are you a virgin?"

For a moment she doubted her ears. Nothing of a private nature ever passed between them, not a word as to his background, no offers of anything even approaching companionship, which for the first few days, she'd hoped would be the basis for their relationship in the close confines of the cell. Her repeated attempts at conversation were met by polite diffidence, a word or so exchanged for form's sake before he retreated into the books and rolls of paper he kept stored in the chest with his other personal belongings. The unfairness of his question struck her hard. What right had he, someone who clearly found her company undesirable, who avoided her at every opportunity and cared less than nothing for her, to ask such a thing?

"Of what possible interest is my virginity, or lack of it, to a great prince of Endlin?" she flung back at him, her temper flaring. "Why this sudden concern? Or should I be flattered by your attentions after twenty days of being ignored?"

She waited for a muttered curse or a pompous rebuke.

"I suppose I deserved that," he began slowly, "and so must beg your pardon. I didn't mean to insult you. It's just that . . ." he broke off, obviously struggling to explain himself, ". . . that in Endlin no one would give such a question a second thought."

"You speak freely of such things with strangers?"

"Strangers?" he repeated blankly. "I didn't think you considered us strangers."

"What would you call us?" she asked impatiently, unplaiting the two fat braids she wore each night to prevent her hair from becoming a tangled mass of snarls by morning.

"I thought we were friends."

Her laugh was cheerless, her fingers tugging at her hair as it unfurled to fall loosely about her shoulders.

"Friends? On what do you base that conclusion? I hoped we might become friends—sharing our experiences, discovering common ground, discussing the day's events during the evening meal. Perhaps you use the word differently in Endlin."

"But we live easily together," he protested, "preparing the meals, cleaning the cell, working at our different tasks before retiring . . ."

She cut him off, unsympathetic that he sounded so thoroughly confused.

"What you describe is not friendship, but self-preservation. We eat to fill our bellies, keep the cell clean so the rats have no cause to enter, and study and work for purposes of self-interest. We keep to the letter of the pact we made the first night and have made no progress since. I've spent countless hours in your company but know many people much better with whom I've shared an afternoon's conversation."

Her hand found the brush near the small metal tray that held her hairpins. Soon her hair crackled and flew about her face.

"These other people, are they members of your family?"

"I have no immediate family. My father and mother live in the realm of dreams and I have no siblings."

"Then who . . . ?"

"Aunts, uncles, cousins, neighbors," she shrugged, "although my closest friends in Cinthea are my fellow bards. We trained together during our apprenticeships, mastering the epics and preparing our auditions for entry into the league."

When he made no further comment, she decided to pose a question of her own.

"What of your friends?"

Waiting for his reply, which seemed a long time in coming, she made herself a promise, a selfish promise perhaps, but one she intended to keep. For twenty days she'd been ignored but kept on trying, if for no other reason than she felt she owed the Nineteenth Mother at least the semblance of an effort. If he dodged this question, or retreated into another one of his haughty silences, she'd wash her hands of him and never try again.

In a tone of voice she'd never heard before, one that suggested he was being strangled, he said: "I've none."

Too shocked by his response to curb her tongue, she blurted out the first thing that came to mind.

"None at all?"

"None," he repeated woodenly.

A pounding on the iron door caught them both unaware. With a quick curse he was undressing hurriedly, stripping off his nightclothes and donning his training gear. Out of habit, she turned away, granting him the same privacy she required of him, although she had only his word that he turned his back when she disrobed.

The chest lid lowered with a dull thud. Expecting him to exit without bidding her farewell, she jumped when his voice sounded close to her ear.

"I . . . I want to be your friend, Alyssa. Will you teach me how?"

What a lonely prince he must be, she found herself thinking. A second, and more impatient, pounding spurred her reply.

"We'll begin tonight," she agreed.

It seemed to her that something brushed against her hair. A breeze from his hasty retreat, she decided, thrusting any other possibility firmly out of her mind.

THE WONDER OF it was that friendship came so easily. It began without fanfare and with no trace of awkwardness.

The meal was one of their finest creations—a dried fish unfamiliar to either of them, soaked overnight in a marinade of onions, garlic, and wine, grilled to perfection and served up with fried rice and fresh ginger. Sandur's contribution was a tart relish of pickled cucumbers, shredded cabbage, and hot peppers. Dried figs and strong black tea ended the meal, Sandur drinking his after adding what seemed to her an inordinate amount of sweetening while she took hers with milk.

He surprised her by being the first one to introduce a topic of conversation, describing his progress with the short sword.

"I'm beginning to understand the artistry of it. Knife fighting has no rules, or at least no rules anyone obeys. There are feints and parries to be sure, but certainly no formal attempts at footwork."

"Who's the best?" she asked between mouthfuls of rice, grateful that this dish was customarily eaten with the fingers. He took his time in answering, no doubt because he was eating just as hungrily.

"That's hard to say. Yossi is quickest to experiment with different combinations. Pharlookas is immensely strong. He knocked a shield out of Tibor's hand as if it were a child's plaything." He ruminated for a moment before adding, somewhat grudgingly, she thought, "I suppose Kokor is best."

"And Jincin?" she asked eagerly, remembering Hanania's description of the man with hair and beard the color of flames.

"What do you know of Jincin?" he demanded with a trace of his old haughtiness. As she struggled not to smile, the means of his first lesson came quickly to mind.

"I know all the male ernani. Besides the ones you mentioned, there's Eddo, Zorab, Thunander, Salaris, Karn, and Pwyll." She ticked off her fingers, delighted with her success in remembering their names and decidedly glad the women had included her in the game. Sandur did not share her delight.

"I had no idea you were so well-acquainted with . . ."

He was so stiff, so formal, she feared she could hold her mirth no longer. Nearly bursting with laughter, she waved a greasy finger at him.

"Has no one ever teased you? Friends do such things, you see, and delight in playing tricks on one another. If you'd reflect for just a moment, you'd realize I've had no opportunity to meet any of the men since entering the Maze, just as you've not met the women."

"This teasing," he asked after a short pause, "is its purpose to make me feel a fool?"

Straight-faced, she nodded her head vigorously.

"Then it seems you are good at it."

Laughing so hard she nearly choked, she gasped, "Sandur, you made a joke!" to which he replied, quite smugly:

"I hoped you would notice."

The next lesson came after the meal was cleared away and the dishes were washed and stacked. They worked neatly together, Sandur scraping and washing, Alyssa drying and putting everything away in its proper place. This done, Alyssa stripped the bed and remade it with fresh linens while Sandur swept the hearth and stoked the fire. As she tied the soiled laundry into a bundle, she heard him open his chest and remove his study materials. The chair scraped against the floor as he took up his usual position at the table.

"What is it you work at with such diligence? The papers rustle and your pen scratches, but it doesn't sound like the penmanship exercises the women practice in the dayroom. Sometimes I hear long strokes, other times a kind of rubbing."

It was the first time she'd referred to her blindness since the night they met. To her relief, he made no mention of it, but endeavored to answer her question. In the process, he gave her the first substantial bits of information about his former life.

"I studied with the finest scholars in Endlin, who taught me to read and write several languages. All clansmen are literate and study such things as history, geography, mathematics, law, and literature."

"Are the clanswomen literate as well?" she asked, for to read and write seemed to her the most valuable of skills.

"There are no clanswomen."

Something about his tone should have warned her not to proceed.

"There must be women!"

"There are women, to be sure, but they are not schooled as clansmen are, nor are they called clanswomen. They are concubines."

The last word was spoken in a different language and pronounced with a slight nasality.

"Concubines," she repeated, trying the word on her tongue. "What exactly is a concubine?"

"A concubine is a woman who belongs to the household of a clansman," he replied testily.

"Belongs? Do you mean she's the mate of a clansmen?"

A snort signified disgust.

"I mean that if he deems her worthy, she may become a vessel for the children of his body."

"What makes a concubine worthy? Is there some kind of test she must pass?"

For the first time he seemed hesitant to answer.

"The only test is that she be perfect."

"In what way perfect?"

"It's difficult to explain. Perhaps in time I . . . I can make it clear to you."

He was evading the question, as well he might considering the barbaric customs he described. Still, she kept her own secrets, and on that basis she decided to respect his right to curtail a conversation if it risked revealing what he preferred to conceal.

"I interrupted you, Sandur. You were telling me about your studies."

Perhaps guilty over his unwillingness to discuss the customs of his people, he waxed eloquent, his slightly nasal baritone filling the cell. As he spoke, she warmed herself by the hearth, toasting her face and outstretched palms in front of a fire that crackled and popped as though applauding the fact that at last Sandur had found his tongue.

"I'm copying maps, Alyssa, maps of the known world. In Endlin we have detailed charts of the entire eastern seacoast, the trade routes, shallows, reefs, and harbors, but almost nothing west of the Sarujian Mountains. A Master of the Chartist Guild teaches me every afternoon, a fellow called Dorian. The maps in the library are enormous, so I copy them using a smaller scale. Once I settle on the correct dimensions, I rough out the topography and sketch in details. Colors and lettering come last of all."

"Which one do you work on now?"

"A map of Lapith," he announced with great satisfaction, "and the northern wastes that lie beyond."

"Have you shown it to Jincin?"

"Why should I? He can barely read."

"It's the land of his birth!" she protested, not liking the sneer in his voice. "Surely he could supply information only a native would know—the flow of the ice in winter and the places elk herds gather during rutting season..."

He interrupted her mid-sentence.

"What do you know of ice and elk? Have you traveled in the north?"

"A bard travels everywhere! I told you the first night that we treasure the old stories, tales that date back to the years of before. I cannot read your maps, but I've climbed the smoking mountains and hunted elk on the tundra, watched the flights of egrets as they depart the valley of the moon to bathe in the waters of the Tellas where it meets the warm gulf waters to the south."

Sometime during her speech she turned to face him, waiting for his reaction. It came immediately and with unexpected violence.

One moment she stood before the fire; in the next she was hurled to the floor, flung there by an arm that hit her in the small of her back. She fell hard, her arms flung up to protect her face. The breath knocked out of her for a moment, she'd barely recovered her wits when she found herself under attack. Swatting madly at her skirts and petticoats, he shouted words she couldn't understand. Not until the smell of burning wool met her nostrils did she understand that her skirts were aflame. In that same moment, he switched to the southern tongue.

"Roll, damn you! Cover your face and roll!"

More frightened than she had ever been in her life, she rolled over and over until she ran up against the bed. Something was thrown over her, and Sandur was on top of her again, snuffing out the live embers with a blanket. Acrid smoke filled her lungs, and she coughed, hearing him panting above her. Then it was over, and she was sobbing, her cheek pressed against his chest as she was gathered up into arms that trembled as they held her.

"What a dolt I am, building up the fire and letting thee stand so close! Thou art safe now, safe, dost thou hear? Hush, Alyssa, thou wilt make thyself sick with crying. Hush, now, the danger's past."

In time her tears ceased, yet he continued to hold her tightly, as if she were a child come running to him with a cut finger or a bruised knee. When he released her at last, the soft "thou's" and "thee's" disappeared. For a moment she mourned their loss, feeling herself forced to say farewell to someone she'd only just met.

"Come, let's assess the damage. Are you hurt?"

Sitting upright, she pushed away the blanket to search through the scorched remains of her skirts. Pushing away her hands, he made his own inspection.

"Your gown is ruined. The petticoat prevented your legs from being burnt. No doubt you'll be bruised from the fall. I was too rough, I fear," he added apologetically.

"What of your hands?"

"I hadn't thought to look," he admitted with a trace of embarrassment. A short pause followed. "A few burns, none of them serious."

"And the cell?"

"Smokey."

Something in the way he pronounced that single word struck her as immensely funny. A giggle escaped her. He emitted a tentative chuckle, and suddenly they were laughing uproariously, rocking back and forth on the stone floor like people struck suddenly mad.

Recovering her wits, she asked, "Should we knock on the door and alert a monitor?"

They'd all been taught the special knock that requested outside assistance. Reserved for cases of direst emergency, it would summon the Nineteenth Mother as well as the monitors on night duty and allow immediate entry into the cell. The moment she suggested it she wished she could call back the words. She wanted no strangers here, no witnesses to her stupidity.

"They could do nothing but chide us for carelessness."

"Could we keep it a secret?"

"The only evidence is your dress and the blanket."

"And the burns on your hands."

"The burns are easily explained—a mishap with a smoldering log. Explaining the dress is more difficult."

"I've an idea!" she crowed with a sudden flash of inspiration. "We'll simply bundle it up in the blanket. You can write a note to the laundry explaining that we had a cooking accident, grabbed the first thing that came to hand to clean up the mess and ruined my gown in the process."

"And if they catch us in the lie?"

"Then we'll admit to it."

He chuckled at that.

"You'd make an excellent trader."

"And you make an excellent friend."

She wished she could cradle his burned hands in hers; instead, she made do with saying softly, "You need no lessons, Sandur. Only a friend would blame himself for my carelessness. And only a friend would feel remorse for hurting me at the cost of saving my life."

He stood up abruptly, brushing off his clothing.

"We must get to work. Strip off those clothes while I open the window and sweep the ashes back into the hearth."

She pulled herself up from the floor and searched for the handle of the wardrobe.

"I'll request another gown from the supply rooms."

"Have them find something not quite so ugly."

She froze at the wardrobe door.
"Was it ugly?" she asked, struck suddenly self-conscious.
The broom was wielded with unusual vigor.
"It was poorly made, and the color did not suit you."
"What color should I ask for?"
There was a long silence before the broom whisked against the floor once more.
"What you will," came his noncommittal reply.

THE NEXT EVENING, a waist-high screen appeared at the hearth. When she questioned him, fearful he'd revealed their secret, he reacted as if stung, replying huffily:
"Friends keep their word, and I kept mine. I simply informed Pentaur that I required a screen."
"Does everyone always obey your commands?" she teased, amused by his high-handed treatment of the hapless monitor whom she guessed was routinely insulted by Sandur's thoughtless arrogance.
"It wasn't a command," he replied indignantly, but upon hearing her dubious sniff, admitted slowly, "at least I didn't intend it as one."
She forgave him on the spot, unable to gainsay his thoughtfulness. Sometimes she saw him as a precocious child, plunging forward without thinking, heedlessly pursuing his newfound quest for friendship as if it were a butterfly drifting on a breeze.
As she was to learn to her eventual dismay, Sandur was not a child but a man of so unforgiving a nature that an inconsequential gesture on her part caused him to cast their burgeoning friendship aside without a second thought, leaving her more miserable and alone than the early days when indifference was her sole companion.

THEY'D SAT FOR hours talking in front of the fire. Now it was time to disrobe in the icy northwest corner where the wardrobe stood. If her gown hadn't been new, she might have flung herself fully clothed into the enormous bed and buried herself under the covers.
But the gown was dear to her, the fabric selected by a group effort, each woman examining the wool and pronouncing it practical and warm, yet soft to the touch and pleasing to the eye. There was some disagreement as to its color. Ulkemene likened it to the lilacs that grow wild among the orchards of New Agave; Zuniga was insistent that it was the exact shade of dawn

breaking over the southern seas. Becca, voted the finest seamstress by popular acclaim, drafted the pattern and did most of the draping while others assisted with the handwork. Alyssa hemmed the skirt and sleeves herself, laboring over the small, even stitches her grandmother demanded of her, the old woman accepting no excuse for a task poorly done.

The style was a simple one, the bodice fashioned with long darts and the bias-cut skirt falling into natural folds. The sleeves were slightly gathered at the shoulders, narrowing as they reached her wrists. Five days in the making, she'd worn it tonight for the first time, half-expecting a comment from Sandur. None was forthcoming, although he seemed unusually animated over their meal. She put her disappointment aside, content to hear Dorian's critique of the latest map and the outcome of the day's wrestling match.

As she unlaced the sides of the gown and pulled it carefully over her head, she found herself imagining Sandur's appearance. That he wore his hair unbound she'd learned from Vlatla, that his chest was wide and his arms strong she knew from the evening of the fire. Other than his height, which she figured to be a handbreadth more than her own, he remained an enigma, a shadowy figure she named Sandur but who had no features, no substance. His scent clung to his pillow in the morning, the shadings of his voice told her when he was troubled, amused, or weary, but try as she might, she couldn't create a face she could safely label "Sandur."

She doubted he was handsome, if for no other reason that neither Lynsaya or Vlatla had said so. That same reasoning implied he wasn't homely. It would be a strong face, she decided, a face not easily forgotten.

"Alyssa?"

She learned early on that he lay awake until she took her place beside him in the bed. She puzzled over this behavior until the morning she stumbled over a stool, sending what proved to be a candlestick rolling about the floor. For some reason he insisted on keeping a candle burning each night next to his side of the bed. Doubtless her movements cast shadows that disturbed his ability to sleep. Once she lay beside him, he seemed to relax, although sleep always came slowly to him, and his rest was often troubled.

"Come to bed, Alyssa!"

Clearly he was annoyed at her dawdling, and she decided to forgo braiding her hair. As she crawled beneath the covers he grunted and rolled over on his side.

"Are you cold?"

"I've been cold for five moons," he snarled.

"Is it always warm in Endlin?"

He grunted in the affirmative.

"Just warm or truly hot?"

"By the four winds!" he roared. "How am I to sleep if you chatter away like a kaka bird?"

Unrepentant, she pulled the blanket under her chin.

"It might help if we imagined being warm."

"I've not that much imagination."

"Then I'll begin," she announced, laughing softly to herself when he groaned aloud and pounded his pillow.

"Imagine yourself lying in an open meadow beside a dusty road, the insects humming, the sun high overhead. On the opposite side of the road stand vineyards, the grapes plump and ready for harvest. The air is sultry, warm breezes from the south promising even hotter weather for the next few days. Beads of sweat appear on your forehead, and you wipe them away with the back of your hand. The grass on which you lie is cool and slightly damp, a welcome relief from the heat rising from the road . . . ."

She wove the tale as she'd been taught, filling it with the sounds, smells, and sights of summer, sights seen last by a child, still cherished by a woman. She knew this particular meadow well, having lain there many times in her youth, gathering dreams on lazy afternoons when the world stands still, hushed by the heaviness of summer's heat. The bedclothes warmed, the fire hissed, the breathing of the man beside her slowed and deepened, and she lay in her grandmother's meadow, watching a spider weave its web . . .

She woke to the sound of his moans. Disoriented upon waking, she found her bearings with difficulty. The bed shook, the walls echoing his hoarse cries as he wrestled with a night demon. Creeping toward him she reached out, fearful she might wake him. Her hand brushed against the smooth planes of a closely-shaven jaw. Running her hand up toward his temple, she pushed coarse stands of damp hair away from his face, murmuring softly to him as she brushed away the nightmare.

In time he quieted, his flailing arms falling to his sides, his head resting again in the damp hollow of his pillow. With a bravery she didn't know she possessed, she drew him toward her. He never woke, but came willingly, his shoulders and back covered in a cotton fabric smelling faintly of cinnamon. When she pulled his head down to rest on her breast, he uttered a weary sigh and nestled close.

She lay awake for minutes or perhaps for hours, his body heavy against hers, his muscles flaccid, his sleep that of a warrior who rests after a battle unto death. Sleep came gradually, her eyes falling shut, her head nodding as his warmth permeated her gown, enveloped by his scent and the streaming hair covering her like a spider's web . . .

"WHAT DID YOU do to me, woman?"

Someone was shouting at her, spittle spraying against her face.

"What spell did you weave last night?"

Two hands, twin vises, gripped her shoulders, pressing her down into the mattress. There was no time to wonder what possessed him, no time even to think. She opened her mouth to speak to find she had no tongue. His words were like blows—cruel words against which she had no defense.

"Is this your idea of friendship?" he raged, "To seduce me in my sleep? To make me lie with you against my will?"

She whispered a denial, knowing that nothing she said could be heard over the sound of his rage.

"Never approach me again, woman!" he screamed at her, "I'll not be polluted by your touch!"

Something died inside her. The hands on her shoulders shoved her brutally aside, and she careened out of the bed, landing awkwardly on her hands and knees. Tears filled her eyes, tears of pain for her scraped knees and palms, angry tears at this ruthless madman and his outraged pride.

"Three more days," she promised herself grimly, *"Three more days, and I'll rid myself of this friendless prince of Endlin, this great fool of a man who goes berserk at a blind woman's touch."*

"SHE WILL REJECT him."

"You said they were progressing."

"So they were."

She-Who-Was-Magda sighed, weary unto death.

"Did he hurt her?"

"Aye. He's cruelest when he's frightened, and she frightened him badly."

"Is it over then?"

"I cannot tell. She broke through thirty years of barriers in less than thirty days. I would not have guessed it possible."

"Might she forgive him?"

"Perhaps, but only if he does what he has never done before."

"What is that?"

"Make a decision based not on tradition, duty, or logic, a decision he knows is rash and even dangerous, one based solely on what he, Sandur, feels he must have."

"Then you have hope?"

Esslar's sigh was as heavy as hers.

"Some hope, but also a nagging fear."

"Which is?"

"That he will wait too long and find her gone."

Chapter 14

Days of Choice

THE OLD WOMAN seemed to nap, a thick rug draped about narrow shoulders, her head nodding against her chest, hands clasped loosely in her lap. The window behind her seemed a solid sheet of ice crystals, the braziers arranged around the library creating little more than an illusion of warmth. Shivering, Sandur pulled his cloak closer about him. As he did so, the old woman lifted her head.

"Welcome."

The study tables with their rows of benches were shoved aside, pushed against the walls to create a central area empty but for two chairs facing one another. The arrangement was intimate, suggesting an absence of barriers, yet retained a certain formality. She made no gesture toward the empty chair, seemingly content that he should stand. Once her head lifted, her eyes never left him. Without preamble, she began.

"As you know, I spoke to Alyssa earlier today."

He opened his mouth to interrupt.

"She chose not to continue your joining."

For two hours he'd waited as the male ernani came and went according to their turn, readying himself for battle, eager to countermand even the slightest suggestion that he rethink his decision, impatient to vent his anger, demanding that the next woman they offered him be unblemished.

For thirty days Alyssa plotted and schemed, eager to capture his affections, playing her game of supposed friendship, revealing her true purpose when he'd awakened to find himself in her arms, her hands entwined in his hair, his mouth at her breast, a triumphant smile on her face. To his requests for explanation she made no answer, to his accusations she turned away, confirming by her silence the truth of her intentions.

Intent on rejecting her with the impassioned speech he'd perfected over the past three days, never once did he consider he might be the one rejected.

"We are in agreement, then," he replied evenly, intent that the old woman not think him surprised.

"So be it," she said, her decree final, absolute, as though a door had suddenly swung shut. Anxious as he was to escape the cell, suddenly he wanted nothing else but to confront Alyssa, to demand the reason for her choice.

"I need never see her more?" he asked, determined that this old woman not pity him.

"The Rules of Preparation are quite clear; your joining is ended." She paused, considering him a moment before continuing in a gentler vein. "Your paths may cross again, but later, much later, when both of you have found more suitable partners."

A vivid image came to mind, another ernani taking his place in the high-backed chair, his laughter mingling with hers in the tiny cell. Shaken, he sank into the empty chair, no longer resentful of the sadness in the Nineteenth Mother's eyes. For the first time he found himself at ease in her presence. They sat together in the quiet hush of the library, both lost in private woes, private regrets. A leafless branch scratched mournfully at the window.

"Will you continue on the Path?"

He nodded, unwilling to speak lest he find himself tongue-tied.

"A new partner will be chosen for you in the next few days. Until that time, you'll reside with the others in the Hall of Men."

"Others?"

"Men who share your situation." With a sigh she added, "You aren't alone in this. Rarely does the Day of Choice come and go without producing change of some sort."

Rising to his feet, he stumbled toward the door and the new joining promised him.

"Go in peace. You begin anew, as will Alyssa. As for the memories," she addressed his departing back, "they will fade in time."

As he moved toward an uncertain future, of all the painful memories haunting his past, the one he feared would never fade was the vision of Alyssa in her amethyst gown.

WRESTLERS HEAVED AND grunted, bodies slick with sweat, twisting and straining on the mat. The match was equal, both men undefeated in the middleweight tournament now underway. A crowd gathered around the ropes.

Dictys leaned against one of the padded walls, his hands stuffed in his belt, listening to the crowd's enthusiasm as they shouted out encouragement, voices raised, gesturing as they urged on their favorites.

"Take him down, Eddo!"

"Hold fast, man!"

"Watch his legs!"
"Salaris, he's yours!"
Something in the ferocity of their cries struck a warning note in his brain, and Dictys drew himself up to attention. A sixth sense that had never failed him came into play, the short hairs standing up along the back of his neck.

A five-year veteran of the Legion, Dictys might be new to his position as Head Trainer, but this room was a second home to him, having trained here himself during the moons of his Preparation. Likewise, the majority of his trainers and monitors were former ernani, all of them handpicked, experts in their particular fields and eager to serve. Duty in the Maze was a hazardous yet necessary step if one hoped to rise through the ranks, for these steamy rooms that stank of male sweat were the proving ground of some of the finest Legionnaires in memory. Here Rama, a name already legend, taught an entire generation of swordsmen. Here, too, the redoubtable Prax underwent his stint as monitor to no less than the great Kazur. Galen, the current Commander, served as Head Trainer for seven years, the hair-raising tales of his tenure a staple of Legion lore.

The mission of the trainers and monitors was a simple one: train bodies, build stamina, teach the ernani to defend themselves, and keep them safe. The first three requirements were easily enough accomplished; the fourth had always been, and ever would be, the most trying. Without it, their job would have been easy; with it, duties became more complex, judgments more difficult. Tempers flared easily here, grudges becoming vendettas in the blink of an eye. The air rang with the clang of metal, grunts, shouts, and the occasional scream. It was the screams that made duty hazardous and insured them double pay. Injuries were common, most of them bruises and sprains. In former, less frugal times, healers worked rotating shifts to insure that help was always within hailing distance.

Dictys found no solace in the fact that he was responsible for twelve men while his predecessor looked after more than a hundred. Understaffed by at least three trainers and denied a healer, he'd drilled his men repeatedly in emergency procedures, earning a nickname in the process. "Flint Eyes" they called him when his back was turned. He'd stifled a chuckle the first time he'd heard it, pleased at their choice and proud they thought he merited one.

You've need of toughness, he thought to himself, for these ernani are a special breed. Wild, proud, often unmanageable, they quarreled continually among themselves despite the punishments he meted out with as much fairness as he could muster. He'd learned to turn a blind eye toward some infractions, coming down hard on anything that might result in injury. The weather didn't help. The skies cleared yesterday, although after ten days of snowfall the arena was a morass of melting snow and frozen mud. While the staff shoveled, he devised the wrestling tournament as a means to keep the ernani occupied, promising the winners the right to choose their partners for swordplay—a risky venture, but one he hoped they all might survive.

His eyes flicked to the bout in progress, marking the trainer who served as referee and the burly monitors posted to keep the onlookers off the ropes. Satisfied that all was proceeding as planned, he made a quick survey of the other trainers involved in various practice sessions on the fringes of the wrestling ring. Finding them, too, busily engaged in their work, he had just begun to chide himself for an over-active imagination when he heard the scream.

Later, one of the monitors informed him he knocked three men to the floor in his haste to cross the room; at the time he was aware of nothing but the scream and the heart-stopping fear that he would come too late.

Then he saw Sandur.

His blouse ripped open at both shoulder seams, he crouched astride a half-naked body lying stomach-down on the wrestling mat, his forearm wedged tightly against the man's windpipe. While once the downed man screamed, now he could only struggle weakly, his eyes popping nearly out of his head.

"Release him!"

Seeing no sign that he'd been heard, Dictys jumped the ropes. Taking a firm grip on an unruly mass of hair, Dictys jerked Sandur's head back, and with his other arm applied an expert headlock. When Sandur released his hold on the ernani's throat, Dictys pulled him up and away as another trainer appeared. The transfer went smoothly, the trainer forcing Sandur's left arm up and back until his hand lodged against his shoulder blade. Since further struggles might result in a broken arm or a dislocated shoulder, Sandur quieted, head down, breathing fast and hard. Judging him to be tamed, at least for the moment, Dictys crouched beside the downed ernani, a man named Pwyll.

A scuffle broke out behind him. Turning just in time to see a dark-skinned hand move smoothly to the trainer's belt, Dictys glimpsed a flash of metal as Sandur freed the dagger from the trainer's sheath. Time stopped, the trainer standing frozen, eyes glued on the blade as Sandur tossed it lightly from hand to hand, daring him to reclaim it. Without any prompting from Dictys, the trainer spread his empty hands wide in a gesture of appeasement, moving backward careful step by careful step, until he retreated behind the ropes.

Reminding himself that a knife is an easterner's weapon of choice, Dictys swore softly in pure disgust. Sandur held the knife with every indication of expertise, his knees bent and his weight low to the ground, his attention never wavering from the trainers and monitors who, obeying Dictys' silent summons, were closing in around him, forcing him into a corner of the ring. For the first time, Dictys got a good look at Sandur's face. With a sinking feeling in his gut, he realized this was far more than a grudge match between warring ernani. Chest heaving under the ripped, sweat-drenched shirt, nostrils flaring, eyes wide and slightly glazed, Sandur was the elegant eastern prince no more. Like a maddened beast, he lashed out at the tormentors holding him at bay.

"*It's your own fault,*" Dictys reminded himself silently. "*If you'd kept hold of him you might have calmed him down, and he'd never have grabbed that accursed knife. Well, old son,*" he sighed as he hitched up his breeches, "*it's time to earn your pay.*"

Swiftly considering the best strategy for attack, he decided to go in low and hope Sandur was more off-balance than he seemed. *He'll have time for one pass before I can grab his knife arm.* Just as Dictys was resigning himself to being sliced by that gleaming blade, a warning voice assaulted his thoughts, a grimly furious Pentaur taking him to task.

"Call them off! Look at his face, man! Would you risk him turning the knife on himself?"

And then that same voice spoke aloud, calmly and reasonably, as if discussing something of no more consequence than the weather.

"Give me the knife, Sandur."

Pentaur took a few paces forward, halting at the ropes, his hands extended palm up.

"Come—no—closer!" Sandur snarled, eyes darting wildly from side to side as the trainers continued their approach. Dictys frowned, then, drawing a deep breath, made a decision. Pentaur knew Sandur better than anyone; if he wanted to go it alone, so be it. With a jerk of his chin, he ordered his men out of the ring and backed away himself.

"You're tired and must rest."

A dazed look came over Sandur's ravaged face, a look of such desolation that Dictys winced to behold it.

"She . . . the old woman . . . she lied to me."

Dictys could barely hear these mumbled words, but Pentaur heard.

"Did she?" Pentaur asked, climbing calmly over the ropes.

"She . . . she said the memories would fade."

The monitor was perhaps five paces away, out of knife range but moving slowly forward.

"Perhaps you should talk to her . . ."

"No!"

Dictys tensed at the pain contained in that wrenching cry. Before him stood the reason he would never be a monitor. Only a select few had the fortitude to deal directly with an ernani on a day-to-day basis. Pentaur was such a one, a veteran of fifteen years in the Maze and a favorite of the Nineteenth Mother. Dictys had envied him that closeness until today.

"You've no wish to hurt me, Sandur."

The hand holding the knife began to tremble.

"Give me the knife, and we'll go to the baths."

The knife lowered.

"I . . . I want . . ."

"What do you want?"

Sandur's face was a twisted mask of pain.

"I . . . I want . . . H'Esslar."

The knife fell to the mat, brown fingers gone limp. Pentaur draped an arm around his charge's shoulders.

"Come to the baths. I'll bring Esslar to you."

Pentaur spoke as if to a child. Once over the ropes, Sandur's body sagged toward the floor. With no apparent effort, Pentaur swung him up into his arms and made his way slowly through the hushed crowd, a pathway clearing for him as he carried his burden toward the swinging doors and the baths that lay beyond.

The ernani stood with heads bowed, eyes hooded.

"One of you must know what set him off," Dictys began slowly, aware that none of these men would inform on a fellow ernani, although he remained hopeful that the seriousness of Sandur's actions might cause someone to come forward. "Why did he go after Pwyll?"

"Pwyll's a fool!" Yossi spat.

A chorus of muttered agreement rose around him.

"How so?" asked Dictys, not overly fond of Pwyll himself but doubtful he deserved so harsh a punishment as death.

"He teased Sandur, even after we told him to hold his tongue."

Tibor's face was dark with disapproval. Pharlookas, his great bulk looming over the marsh-dweller's shoulder, nodded agreement.

"Teased him about what?"

"Being unmated," Pharlookas rumbled from somewhere deep in his chest.

"Four of you are unmated since the Day of Choice, Pwyll included," Dictys pointed out. "Why would Pwyll provoke Sandur when he shares his situation, and why should Sandur take it so hard?"

The western giant threw Dictys a pitying look.

"Tibor, Pwyll, and me, we're in the Hall of Men by choice. It's different with Sandur."

Dictys made no attempt to hide his amazement, stunned that close-mouthed Sandur would discuss so private a matter.

"Sandur spoke to you about this?"

Yossi shot Dictys a scathing look.

"Speak to us? He's not said a word for five days!"

"Then how do you . . .?"

The Head Trainer was interrupted by the other mountain-dweller, Kokor, a man who rarely spoke but when finally moved to speech, expressed himself with a rare sense of authority to which the others usually responded. If it could be said of these ernani that they had a leader, that leader was undoubtedly Kokor.

"He mourns for her," Kokor stated simply and unequivocally. "Pwyll taunted him, boasting that Alyssa would soon be his."

Dictys nodded, sick at heart. This might have been prevented, he reflected dismally. With a small measure of foresight I might have barred all sessions between the unmated ones. I warned the Council of the change I've seen in Sandur, but the Nineteenth Mother counseled patience, and I lacked the courage to gainsay her.

"Who is this Esslar?" Eddo boomed from the back of the crowd.

"Our Searcher," Kokor answered. Fixing Dictys with a measuring stare, he asked, "Will Sandur be punished?"

A mutinous rumble followed on the heels of Kokor's question. Dictys found himself confronted by ten pairs of angry eyes. Think quick, old lad, or you'll have a riot on your hands. He considered his options: call for help, go by the book, or improvise. Given the uniqueness of the situation, he chose improvisation.

"Pwyll will recover. I'll take no action since you agree Sandur was provoked. But the rules prohibiting attacks on Maze personnel are strict. He landed no blows, but he disarmed one of my men and threatened us all." They were calmer now, listening as he reasoned with them. "What do you advise?"

Kokor stroked his moustache.

"On no account should he be beaten."

Dictys had seen the scars covering Sandur's back and shoulders, ugly pink welts on brown flesh, and was as unwilling as the ernani to watch Sandur endure another flogging.

"Let Esslar decide what's best," Kokor suggested. "He's a good man and fair. We've no right to judge Sandur," he added almost angrily, "for all of us have yearned to see our Searcher again."

"Aye, you've hit on it, man!" Pharlookas muttered, the others either grunting or nodding their heads in solemn agreement.

"Why didn't you say something?" asked Dictys, amazed at the emotions unleashed by Kokor's confession. "We aren't here to torment, but to help. If you've a reasonable request, and surely this is reasonable, the Council will grant it."

With consummate dignity, Kokor replied, "We did not know."

They did not know.

How stupidly we've handled them, Dictys raged, isolating them from the ones who know them best. We sent the Searchers to the farthest reaches of the known world to find a new breed of ernani, yet we treat them like the ernani of old. They've no candidates from Pelion to smooth the way, as I had when an ernani in my class would stop me in the arena or the dining hall, asking questions they'd never consider bringing to a staff member. The Searchers are their bond between home and Pelion, yet we forbade their presence, thinking the ernani would be best served if they left everything from the outside world behind.

"I'll take your request to the Council. As to Sandur, I'm in agreement that Esslar should judge his guilt and decide his punishment."

A slow smile spread over Kokor's face. Pharlookas mustered a short word of thanks. Even Yossi, who made no secret of his dislike for anyone occupying a position of authority, nodded grudging approval.

"Now then," said Dictys, clearing his throat, eager to give his charges something to remember about this day other than the incident that nearly destroyed what little regard they held for him. "The arena is muddy, but negotiable. The sky has cleared, the sun is bright, and we've two more hours until the trumpet sounds. What say you, ernani?" he bellowed, hands on hips, "Does anyone remember how to string a bow?"

A chorus of cheers met his challenge and they were off, hurrying to dress in the antechamber, the trainers streaming behind them, grabbing up the archery gear, urging them to make haste.

Alone in the training room, Dictys stepped over the ropes and picked up the knife where it lay forgotten on the mat. Idly, he tested the blade. The razor-sharp edge sliced through the thick callous on his thumb as if it was butter. He sucked the cut distractedly, the taste of his own blood all too familiar.

You've much to learn, old son, he mused. A moment longer and it would have been your throat instead of your thumb, all because you trusted your brawn before using your brain. The Nineteenth Mother said something of the kind to him the day she offered him the job.

"We are not born leaders, Dictys. We become them. One mark of a leader is the measure of trust they inspire; another is the degree to which they trust their followers."

Pentaur trusted that Sandur would not attack him just as Kokor trusted Esslar to decide Sandur's fate. What is this trust that saved one and perhaps two lives today? Dictys answered with the lesson he'd just learned: Trust is the faith that we are not alone, that others share our condition in the world.

And so Dictys left the hallowed precinct of Rama, Prax, and Galen; of Luxor the Wolf and Strato the Bear; of Legionnaires like Hume, who sacrificed their lives that others might live; of Phylas and Flavius, who walked into the hell that was Agave of their own free will—men who put their faith in humanity before their skill with weapons. Slaves and sons of slaves, ernani and sons of Pelion, each learned the lessons to be taught within these walls. Not the least of these was the lesson learned today.

THE TILES OF the bath ran with moisture, the air steamy, dense, nearly impenetrable. Through the haze Esslar could just make out a form slumped on one of the benches built into the walls—Sandur, clothed now in a loose cotton tunic and regulation breeches. The warm, moisture-filled air reminded Esslar of Endlin, causing him to wonder if Sandur felt stronger here, free of the cold for the first time in many moons.

As he drew closer, he saw the wet ropes of Sandur's hair hanging like a necklace of water snakes and shuddered at the image, pushing it away, back into the recesses of his mind where he kept visions that might, or might not, come to pass.

At his approach, Sandur turned his head to regard him. Circles of exhaustion lay under his eyes like bruises, the angles of his face so pronounced that he appeared half-starved, gaunt cheeks recessed under jutting cheekbones and an unshaven jaw dark with stubble. While the earring gleamed, the eyes were lusterless, blank and staring. *As if he's blind*, Esslar realized with a start.

"They tell me you've hurt someone and threatened others with a knife. Is it true?"

A weary nod was his answer.

"Had you cause?"

Again, a listless response—a half-shrug and a shake of his head.

Frustrated, Esslar considered how to proceed. Pentaur's summons caused him to hope for the first time in many a day. Somehow he must spark a response for they were nearly out of time.

"You requested my presence, ernani. What do you want?"

The slumped form straightened at the sharpness of Esslar's tone. The healer took heart. *For once this wretched clansman training will stand me in good stead.*

"I want to leave this place."

"No one keeps you here. You've known this since the night we spoke on the riverbank. Simply ask Pentaur, and he'll escort you to the bronze doors."

With that, Esslar turned to go, sad that it had come to this, yet oddly resigned. Sandur's departure, always a possibility, might be the best choice for all concerned. *With Sandur they played with fire. Why risk losing almost as much as they hoped to gain?*

"Don't go!"

Esslar closed his eyes.

"Truly, I . . . I don't want to leave."

It was a grudging admission, but an admission all the same.

"Then I ask again, what do you want?"

"I want . . . I want a woman!"

Esslar heard the lie. Even so, the manner in which it was spoken infuriated him. Turning back to regard Sandur, who dropped his eyes to the floor, Esslar announced coldly, "Your new partner has been chosen. You're to be escorted to her cell tonight."

His former melancholy forgotten, Sandur sat bolt upright on the bench, his mood ugly, his temper held barely in check.

"What's this new woman like, H'Esslar? Is she deaf or perhaps a mute? Should I be prepared for a cripple?"

Ignoring the outburst, Esslar replied, "She's perfect."

The color drained from Sandur's face. Encouraged, Esslar began to elaborate, dredging up memories of last night's Council session during which he said not a single word, much to the confusion of everyone. Everyone, that is, save the Nineteenth Mother.

"Her name is Jaclyn, an ernani from the south. She resembles the women of Endlin, small-boned and dark-skinned with flashing black eyes. She's an avid reader with a distinct talent for languages."

"And . . . and Alyssa?"

"What about her?"

"Have you . . . have you seen her?"

Gathering his robes about him, Esslar sat down on the bench, leaning his head back against the tiles. At last the conversation could begin.

"What troubles you, Sandur? You pine for her, but ask for another woman in her place. You demand reassurances from the Nineteenth Mother that you need never see Alyssa again, yet this afternoon you attacked Pwyll for suggesting he might share her cell. What do you want, Sandur Kwanlonhon?"

"I . . . I want Alyssa," the Tehran's sa'ab confessed, "but I'm afraid."

"Afraid of what?"

The requisite spark had been struck. Lurching to his feet, Sandur paced back and forth, his hands thrashing the steamy air, his voice echoing hollowly against the tiles.

"You know our ways, our customs! Can you imagine her welcome in my father's house? Can you see him sneer? Hear the insults spoken to her face? I would bear it for her sake, but what of these gifts I must give? I might risk breaking tradition by joining without my father's permission, but I can't," he ground out the words between clenched teeth, "I won't be the father of a flawed child."

Esslar made no response, waiting for what he knew must follow.

"But this is nothing to the fear that she . . . that she doesn't return my feelings." He stopped pacing, face taut and body rigid. "I hurt her as I've been hurt. I was my father again—cruel, remorseless, seeing only what I wanted to see. And I . . . I fear I've lost her."

Sighing inwardly, Esslar posed the question a fourth time, praying it would be the last.

"Sandur, what do you want?"

Words tumbled out, brown eyes under jet-black brows burning with sudden urgency.

"I want you to arrange a private meeting between Alyssa and me. I know it's forbidden, that it breaks all the rules. Tell the Nineteenth Mother I made a mistake, tell her I lied, tell her anything, so long as you convince her that I must see Alyssa again."

Betraying nothing, indicating neither approval nor discouragement, Esslar considered the proposal.

"If she agrees, and I make no promise that she will, what makes you think Alyssa will want to see you? What if I ask and she refuses?"

Sandur's dismay confirmed Esslar's worst suspicions. The Tehran's sa'ab never considered the possibility of his offer being refused. Think again, Sandur, Esslar thought grimly. Harness that pride or lose her. Woo her with your usual arrogance, and she'll reject you as she did before.

"She'll agree," Sandur said at last, without conviction, Esslar noticed, and with a rueful shake of his head. "She'll agree if only to insult me to my face."

Satisfied that the euphoria of hope had been replaced with a harsher, yet truer, reality, Esslar rose and headed for the door.

"I'll do my best. Dry your hair, now, lest you catch a chill."

He added as an afterthought, "Don't forget to shave."

"She can't see me," Sandur protested. "What matter if I shave or not?"

Esslar never answered.

SHE STOOD IN poignant beauty before him, the memories he'd hoarded discarded since none of them compared with the loveliness of Alyssa in her amethyst gown, shining tresses hanging about her slender shoulders like a mantle wrought of molten gold. Despite his assurances to Esslar, he'd feared she might not come and held his breath as she stepped hesitantly over the threshold.

"Sandur?"

"I'm here by the window, to your left and about ten paces away."

A startled look came over her face. She opened her mouth to speak, then bit her lips. She's thinner, he thought, and a trifle pale. He cast about wildly for something to say.

"You spoke to H'Esslar?"

He'd forgotten the tiny crease that grew between her eyebrows when she was vexed. He'd also forgotten the sharpness of her tongue.

"I would think that was obvious, even to a great dolt like you."

He almost laughed, catching himself at the last moment, heartened by her insult. If he could provoke her so easily she must care for him a little. His worst fear was that she would be unfeeling, remote.

"Would you like to sit down? There's a chair here."

"I've no interest in sitting," she stated flatly. "I came to listen, not to chat."

If she was to listen, he must speak.

"I . . . I wanted to beg your pardon."

"To what purpose?"

"So you might forgive me." He could read nothing on her face. "That . . . that morning," he began awkwardly, "I was wrong to accuse you. The things I said, I regret with all my heart."

"And how, may I ask, did you make this remarkable discovery?"

"It happened the night after we parted. I . . . I was asleep," he confessed shyly, "dreaming of you, I think. Something woke me, and I . . . I was lying on my stomach, cradling the pillow in my arms, my cheek pressed against the place you would have been . . . and I knew . . . I knew . . ." he finished lamely, " . . . I knew you weren't to blame."

Sometime in the course of his speech she turned away. Her profile remained set, implacable.

"You say you regret the things you said. A person may regret their words and believe them still."

"Everything I said was a lie. Every word was false."

"Prove it," she demanded. "Prove to me that my touch won't pollute you."

Cringing under the lash of her tongue, he accepted its punishment as befitting his crime. He'd used her cruelly, and she had every right to call up those hateful words spoken in the madness of the moment.

He took his place before her.

"Here I am, Alyssa. Do what you will."

Her face tilted up, and a hand reached out to find his shoulder. He wondered if she could feel him trembling as a tapered forefinger crept up his neck and the side of his jaw, her touch no heavier than a moth lighting on a frond of lacy fern.

It was an odd sensation, but not an unpleasant one. Ten fingertips played over his face from his brow to his chin, tracing his eyebrows, his cheekbones, the line of his jaw. Her eyes were shut, an expression of intense concentration on her face. In time, her fingers stilled and dropped away.

"I forgive you."

Pushing him aside, she moved toward the door, her hands stretched out to find the latch.

Baffled by her behavior, since it was impossible that she could leave him, impossible for her to drift away like this, cool and silent, unmoved by his apology and indifferent to his need. Calling after her, he demanded the reason for her departure.

"You begged my pardon, and I forgave you. What else remains to be said?"

Not until that moment did he realize how badly he'd bungled the entire affair. She understood nothing of his purpose. A stranger accosted her in the Hall of Women, begging her to converse with someone she'd already begun to forget. Angry enough to grant any request that would allow her to speak her mind on a subject that wounded her deeply, she'd come to listen and was gracious enough to forgive. Now she was leaving, and there was nothing he could do except cast aside his pride and become a beggar for her love.

"Stay with me, Alyssa."

Her hands stilled in mid-air.

"Walk with me on the Path. Help me render up my gifts, for without thee beside me, I've naught worth giving."

She turned, face aglow.

"Tell me thy tales as we sit together in front of the hearth, the wind whistling through the cracks. At night, whisper in my ear of sunlit meadows and grapes plumping on the vine."

Her up-turned nose wrinkled as she smiled, her lips revealing teeth like rows of perfect pearls. He was whispering now, drawing her toward him step by step, a flush rising to her cheeks.

"Let thy face be the first thing I see each morning and thy breast my pillow each night."

As she came into his arms, he pressed her tight against him, burying his face in the lavender fragrance of her hair. Softly, he whispered his promise.

"We'll make the cell our kingdom by the sea, the bed our island, and float there while the tides ebb and flow about us."

His mouth found hers, and he had never tasted anything to rival the sweetness of her lips.

Suddenly she was laughing, peals of joy ringing out to celebrate their reunion. He swung her around the room, her hands clasped behind his neck, her amethyst skirts swinging about her ankles.

"Dost thou believe me now, nymph?" he asked as they paused to catch their breath.

"One question, prince," she said, cocking her head as she always did when teasing him. "If you answer correctly, I might be persuaded to enter this kingdom of yours."

"And what is that?"

"Do you like dogs?"

Mystified, but too busy admiring the color in her cheeks to puzzle over her meaning, he answered without thinking, "I had a pup once, the only friend I've ever had but for thee."

A hand reached up to caress his smooth-shaven cheek.

"In that case, Sandur Kwanlonhon, the prize is yours."

Chapter 15

Crooked Paths

THE LAST ROUTE charted, the final set of inventories inspected, a unanimous decision made concerning the construction of a new warehouse, the bi-weekly meeting of the Kwanlonhon elders approached conclusion. The atmosphere that day was, as always, formal and unfailingly polite. Grievances were aired, but with an eye towards propriety and rank. Differences in opinion were tolerated, although in true clan fashion, once the Tehran expressed his views, they immediately became the majority opinion. As was customary, the Tehran closed the session, offering a bit of unexpected news that jarred those assembled, causing several braided heads to wag, the most elderly member of the gathering actually pounding his fist on the table to signal his upset.

"It saddens me to announce this, but there would seem to be no more propitious time to do so. I've received word that another Assad frigate was boarded and sacked off the Pitanes."

If the Tehran was sad, no sadness showed. He sat, as was his right, at the head of the table, flanked on either side by his brothers, the princes Shakar and Tasir, select representatives of the ship-builders, pilots, traders, warehousemen, suppliers, and stewards seated in descending order according to age. Those seated near the far end of the table, among them Pischak Kwanlonhon, took a fatalistic attitude toward the Tehran's news. Not so the elders.

"This is an outrage!" sputtered the Tehran's revered and ancient uncle, Kasovar Kwanlonhon. "Two Assad ships reported lost in as many moons and the Synzurit flagship unaccounted for since early autumn! Not in my father's or my grandfather's time has the fleet suffered such damage!"

"There have always been pirates, uncle."

The Tehran's response, while mildly spoken, suggested boredom with reference to the past, an attitude shared by most of the younger members. Since verbal ridicule of an elder was forbidden, they made do with rolling their eyes, producing several long-suffering sighs the old man must have heard, but chose to ignore.

"Pirates? Bah! A handful of drunken smugglers who keep to the windward side of the farthest isles! This is altogether different, nephew, and decidedly more dangerous. The Pitanes lie on the main corridor between Tek and Endlin. Every vessel in the fleet uses that route for the return voyage from Salmydessus and points south."

"Calm yourself, uncle," the Tehran counseled, directing an indulgent smile toward his favorite uncle and former guardian, his reaction causing most of those present to dismiss the old man's tirade as proof of the onset of senility. "We all remember your navigation course," he was smiling broadly now, "especially those who, like me, had difficulty passing." When his jest drew a round of appreciative laughter, he smiled again, saying, "After all, uncle, they're Assad ships, and hardly worth . . ."

"My point, nephew," Kasovar protested, "is that it might have been a Kwanlonhon ship! So far we've been lucky—a single ship lost and no report of foul play—but our luck won't hold forever!"

To interrupt a Tehran in mid-speech was unheard of, and might have been considered mutinous if not for Kasovar's unique position within the clan. Forty-two years ago Kasovar received thirteen-year-old Manthur Kwanlonhon, the third son of his eldest brother, into his household for the purpose of training him for manhood. The last living brother of Linphat V, Kasovar was accorded enormous respect due both to his age (past eighty) and his position as teacher of navigation for the Kwanlonhon clan. Despite that respect, tension rose around the table as they waited for Manthur's reaction to what might be interpreted as a studied insult. To everyone's relief, Manthur lifted his eyes toward the ceiling, shaking his head as if to say, "Forgive him, friends, as I do."

Disaster averted, Prince Shakar posed a question of a more practical nature.

"How will the loss of the ship affect Assad credit?"

"Do you fear they might recall your notes, brother?"

Several clansmen shifted in their seats, all of them made uncomfortable by the Tehran's disdain for his elder sibling.

"The question has merit, brother."

Prince Tasir rarely spoke during clan meetings; when he did, heads shot up all around the table. More often than not, the fourth son of Linphat was the only person capable of cajoling Manthur out of his legendary fits of bad temper. Everyone breathed more easily when the Tehran nodded cordially before responding to Tasir's request.

"These are only rumors, of course, but if they're true, then the Onozzi as well as the Assad will be hard hit. It's common knowledge that they combined resources in an effort to recoup last year's losses. If, indeed, the *Zephyr* was a joint venture, its loss will affect both clans. Unfortunately, the Assad may not recover."

Shakar was not the only clansman visibly shaken by the Tehran's prediction. Gambling debts were one thing; the financial destruction of an entire clan would be an unprecedented event in the five centuries since Endlin's founding.

"Might I suggest we extend our loans to the Assad for an indefinite period at no additional interest?"

Open palms slapped the table in support of Tasir's motion. The Kwanlonhon's rapid rise to fortune brought with it the responsibility of insuring the continuance of the system that made their wealth possible. No one must say of the Kwanlonhon that they lacked generosity toward less fortunate clans. After the Tehran added his approval to the vote, the meeting was duly adjourned.

As the clansmen filed out, several fathers with daughters living in the Assad palace lingered to convey their gratitude to Tasir. By the time the room cleared, Tasir and the Tehran remained.

"May I have a word with you, brother?"

Tasir hesitated, then pulled the door shut and resumed his seat. Relations between them had been strained since the night of Sandur's beating. Tasir readied himself for a tongue-lashing, all too conscious of the fact that Manthur preferred his brothers to consult him privately before airing their opinions in public. Today the gods favored him, and instead of a frosty rebuke, he received outright praise.

"Your suggestion was a good one, and I thank you for it."

"If the winds blew otherwise, it's my belief the Assad would return the favor."

The Tehran nodded, somewhat distractedly, Tasir thought. So many worries—pirates who play havoc with our fleet, the ruin of the Assad. A tender pride rose up in Tasir at the thought of his brother's selfless labors on behalf of the clan. Without Manthur's leadership, it might be the Kwanlonhon rather than the Assad who teetered on the brink of bankruptcy. Instead, we're building more ships and warehouses. Difficult he may be, but he's led us to greater riches than any Tehran in memory. With those charitable thoughts in mind, Tasir resolved to think better of his brother in the future.

Having risen from his place at the table, Manthur wandered aimlessly around the room. Stopping at the map, he perused it for a moment before turning, rather abruptly, to face Tasir.

"What have you heard from Sandur?"

Six moons had passed without the name of his sa'ab being mentioned.

"Nothing," Tasir answered slowly, trying not to reveal his shock that Manthur evidenced interest in a son he had virtually banished from the citadel. "I asked him to write when he arrived at his destination. I've received no word from him as yet."

Long ago Tasir grew accustomed to the strange rigidity that sometimes overcame his brother's features, the dead eyes and frozen mask-like expression. After a short time, Manthur's eyes flickered back to life.

"I would ask a favor of you, Tasir."

"Anything, brother."

"You would have my gratitude if you composed a letter to my sa'ab telling him that I . . .," the Tehran seemed at a loss for words, ". . . that I've forgiven his disobedience and would have him return to the citadel with all due haste."

Tasir's heart swelled to bursting, fighting the desire to swallow Manthur in a hearty embrace. Not only would a show of joy be unseemly, he had no intention of revealing to Manthur how the prospect of Sandur's return affected him.

"Relate everything that's transpired during his absence, the increase in piracy, the rumors concerning the Assad, and stress that I need his help."

"Perhaps you should write him yourself . . .?"

"No!" Manthur said sharply, then repeated, more quietly, "No." He wandered over to his desk and peered out the window. "If he harbors a grudge against me, you are better suited to sway him."

"As you wish, brother."

Pushing back his chair, Tasir started for the door.

"I would prefer," the Tehran called after him, "if he thinks the idea of writing comes from you."

Tasir nodded, understanding Manthur's reluctance to admit his error. Not for the world would Manthur apologize to his sa'ab since for to do so would undermine the basis of his parental authority.

"My steward will locate a caravan heading west. I'll offer a hefty sum to insure its safe arrival."

"Give it to me when you're finished. My agents can have a letter in Pelion in thirty days."

So light was Tasir's heart that not until later did he come to wonder at the fact that his brother felt the need of quick communication between Endlin and Pelion. Several weeks later, he had the opportunity to examine the clan accounts, finding with a sense of foreboding he could not dismiss from his thoughts, not a single record of expenditure for agents employed as outriders between the Kwanlonhon citadel and a city called Pelion.

A fortnight later, a visitor arrived. As is often the case with uninvited guests, he brought unwelcome news.

AFTER A TOAST to the continued success of the clan, the first bowl of tea was drunk. As was customary, the concubines took no refreshment, plying

Prince Tasir's guest with sweetmeats and peeled fruit, their eyes dancing with excitement at the prospect of entertaining Fawaz, the foremost pilot of the Kwanlonhon, hopeful that he might entertain them with a story of the outside world. Fawaz won their instant approval by fulfilling their expectations without necessity of coaxing. Like a flock of scarlet birds, they fluttered about him, arranging their robes and folding the great wings of their sleeves as they settled at his feet, chattering gaily among themselves, jockeying for position with a nudge here and a prod there. Some continued to preen, kohl-lined eyelids lowered so as to observe the visitor more freely, all of them drinking in the aura of the sea which seemed to hang about him still, noting the effect of sun-darkened skin against the flash of white teeth as he spoke.

What wonders he has seen, they signaled to each other, speaking the wordless language at which they excelled — the arch of a plucked eyebrow, the pass of a hand across a rouged cheek, the delicate flare of nostrils, the subtle moistening of coral-stained lips. As he warmed to his tale, their combined delight became more voluble, the great room resounding with muted cries of wonder and delight. When at last the story ended, after refilling the porcelain bowls, they retreated to their apartments where they told and re-told his story, refining its details, practicing its nuances, so that tomorrow it could become a currency of sorts, to be traded for gossip with other concubines living within the citadel.

After their departure, the room seemed to shrink, stripped of its color and vitality. The two men sipped their tea, the younger one waiting respectfully for the elder to begin the conversation, the elder somehow loath to learn the reason for Fawaz's visit.

Tasir readjusted his position on the floor cushions. Placing his bowl on the low table upon which rested an elegant arrangement of orchids, he regarded the pilot from under hooded eyes.

"To what do I owe the honor of your presence, cousin?"

The bloodlines they shared were distant at best, fifth cousins to be exact. A look of gratitude appeared on the younger man's face as he, too, put aside his tea.

"Forgive my intrusion, prince. I knew nowhere else to turn."

The elder man nodded his permission for the younger man to continue.

"First, have you heard of Kasovar's retirement?" When Tasir seemed clearly astounded, Fawz added quickly, "I did not believe it myself. The old man is dear to me, having taught me my trade, so I made it my business to learn the truth of it. I found him this afternoon in a piazza, napping under a lemon tree."

"His reasons?"

"None I can understand. He pleaded his health, but he has never seemed so robust, and his memory is as sharp as ever." Tasir indicated agreement, motioning for Fawaz to continue. "When I prodded him, he said, 'It pleases the Tehran that I take my ease.'"

Prince Tasir's eyes bored into Fawaz for a long moment before lowering to the rug.

"More troubles you than the retirement of an old man. Speak your piece, cousin."

Heartened, Fawaz took a swig of tea, gulping down the sugary stimulant, feeling the need for sustenance before beginning his task.

"The Tehran summoned me yesterday. Since no contract's been offered me since the maiden voyage of the *Seahorse*, I feared I'd angered him in some way. I couldn't think how, since our profits were enormous. In any case, I bided my time, helping the younger ones with their studies. When the call came, I was relieved. Once I understood what he intended, I . . ." Fawaz hesitated, "I was frightened."

"How so?"

"He wants me to take Issur on his first voyage."

"Issur! He's an unbraided boy!"

With a sudden surge of energy, Tasir jumped to his feet and began pacing to and fro, nervously fingering the rings dangling from his left earlobe.

"Fifteen years old and a novice to the trade! Issur has no business aboard a trading vessel, especially with the dangers to be faced these days!"

Fawaz held his tongue while the older man fumed.

"I know the boy a little. He was a sickly infant and so has been pampered since birth. The rigors of such a journey might kill him—injury, illness, a storm at sea."

Tasir wheeled to face Fawaz.

"What did my brother say when he proposed the contract?"

"That he wants to test the boy's mettle. That he hopes this voyage will make a man of him."

"'Man of him,'" Tasir muttered. "The death of him, more likely."

"That was my opinion," Fawaz confessed, "until another idea came to me after our meeting, one that frightened me all the more."

No one understood Fawaz's fears more clearly than Tasir. To undertake the task of rearing a Tehran's son was difficult enough within the protective environment of the citadel; to take an untrained boy to sea might end in a disaster that would ruin Fawaz's career and dishonor his entire family. Yet there was something in the pilot's demeanor that awoke a deeper fear.

"Speak, man!"

"At first I doubted his sincerity. Now I think he spoke the truth. He truly cares for the boy and wants no harm to come to him. Yet for some reason, he's in a hurry to rush him into manhood. It made me wonder if . . .," Fawaz swallowed hard," . . . if he intends on raising Issur to . . . to another's place."

Even though Fawaz did not speak Sandur's name, it lingered unsaid, drifting in empty space between them. But Sandur is his sa'ab, Tasir protested silently, until his mind began to work, and he sat down hard. Struggling to retain his composure, he reached for the porcelain bowl with a shaking hand.

"What's the nature of the voyage?" he asked, settling back against the cushion to consider Fawaz's reply.

"To Nisyros and back, an easy jaunt if the winds blow true. The boy is to be assistant steward in charge of trading goods. He's to remain on board at all times. An apothecary will accompany us and share his cabin. I'm to select the crew myself—experienced seamen with no history of brawls or drunkenness. They're to be paid a handsome bonus if Issur returns uninjured and in good health."

"Are those the terms he offered when Sandur shipped with you?"

Fawaz raised mournful eyes to his host.

"No special provisions were made for Sandur. I checked with others who've shipped with him. They told me the same."

"You must accept the contract," Tasir stated flatly.

Fawaz sighed, nodded, and rose to go.

Nothing was said by either man that could not be repeated. Fawaz expressed worry over the care of the Tehran's second son. Prince Tasir, after his initial fears for his nephew were put to rest, supported his brother's decision as was his duty. Not until the final moment of their conversation did they touch upon a subject that, if overheard, might bring about their mutual disgrace.

"What else do you fear, Fawaz?"

The pilot stood braced for a swell, the deck heaving under his feet.

"That I'll never see Sandur Kwanlonhon again."

Alone in the great room, Tasir pondered the facts. Kasovar interrupted the Tehran in public; a fortnight later he was forced into retirement. Manthur's second son, a spoiled child being trained by Pischak, a sometime drunkard and an outright fool, was to be given active duty in the Kwanlonhon fleet some four years before his time. Sandur, the rightful heir, was to be lured back to the citadel with promises of forgiveness, while between Pelion and Endlin stretched a chain of agents unaccounted for in the Kwanlonhon financial records, and thus answerable not to the clan, but to a private employer, namely, Manthur, the most powerful man in Endlin.

These facts were enough to cause Prince Tasir to mutter aloud, "Oh, nephew, what have I done?"

"SO, MY FRIENDS, we progress!"

When a chorus of groans greeted this announcement, the Nineteenth Mother wagged her head at her Council, exasperated by their lack of enthusiasm although her eyes sparkled with good humor. They'd never seen her so vibrant, so alive, as if in the past few days she'd shed half of her seventy years.

"Think how much we've learned," she scolded them, "and in so short a time! Think you this world was created in a single day?" She shifted her attention to the thin, waspish woman on her left. "Remind us of our accomplishments, Symone."

Pulling a pencil from her meager bun and re-shuffling the papers in front of her, Symone reacquainted her colleagues with the newest changes to the ever-evolving Legislation for Preparation.

"Since the end of the first moon the following procedures have been implemented: The former policy prohibiting ernani from making statements of preference before being assigned their partners has been discontinued. The Nineteenth Mother's suggestion that those whose first joining failed be allowed to voice their preference for a second partner was approved. The success of Vlatla and Tibor, Draupadi and Pharlookas, Hanania and Jincin suggest that in the future it may be possible for those already mated to undergo Preparation."

"Hurrah!" Anstellan interjected, bringing on a round of smiles as their youngest member rejoiced at the prospect of being relieved of his least favorite duty.

"Next, all Searchers have been recalled to duty in the Maze and from this time onward will serve as advisors to the ernani. In addition, we recommend that the Head Trainer bar ernani whose joining has failed from competing with one another during training. Dictys has further suggested that Searchers be allowed to participate in decisions involving transgressions against the rules."

"What was decided concerning Sandur's punishment, Esslar?"

Recently returned from The House of Healing, Japhet was hearing most of Symone's report for the first time.

The Master of Mysteries seemed to dream, starting when Galen nudged him in the ribs.

"A private apology to Pwyll and a formal request for pardon delivered publicly to Dictys and his staff."

"He spoke it prettily," Galen observed with paternalistic pride, "with hardly a trace of his high and mighty airs."

"Pwyll's reaction?" Japhet asked with uplifted eyebrows. An answering snort from Dictys indicated that Japhet was not alone in his dislike of Pwyll.

"He's a bully and a braggart with not a friend to his name. I dragged Yossi off him yesterday, scratching and hissing like a wildcat, and received not a word of thanks for my trouble."

"Even if his behavior does not meet with our approval," Evadne stated calmly, "we are not his judges. There is room for us all, even the bullies and the cowards."

Evadne's defense of Pwyll brought a firm nod of approval from the Nineteenth Mother.

"It would seem Evadne's reminder is a timely one. We must guard against scapegoating, especially in so small a group. Instead of condemning Pwyll, we should look for some talent or skill unique to him, something worthy of admiration." A smile played about her lips as she turned to Evadne. "Perhaps Jaclyn can help us. Seek her out, Evadne, and advise us how to help him."

Evadne accepted the task willingly.

"Now, Anstellan," the Nineteenth Mother turned to the Master Hetaera, "why this gloomy face?"

Anstellan was by nature a cheerful person, blithe of spirit and unfailingly optimistic, yet it was with an extremely sour expression that he regarded her.

"I've made a mess with these ernani, Mother. If you care to name my replacement, you'll get no argument from me."

"Why assume the fault is yours?" she asked, a twinkle in her eye suggesting that she shared some private joke with herself.

"Where else could it lie?"

Instead of answering him, she observed, "You've grown too serious of late, Anstellan. Perhaps you should put your duties on hold and visit your House."

"Visit my House?" he repeated, clearly astounded.

"A suggestion only," she shrugged, an unusual gesture for the Nineteenth Mother of Pelion. "I have fond memories of your House, memories which do not fade with time."

A faraway look came over her, and she seemed to slip away from them, lost in some memory or another. All of them marked the peacefulness of her expression, a welcome change from the worry lines that had creased her brow during the past moon. In time, they dismissed themselves, leaving her to enjoy her private reminiscences. When she returned, it was to a room emptied save for a lone occupant in the chair directly to her right.

"Do they think me rude or simply in my dotage?"

"They believe you to be in remarkably good spirits. Evadne and Japhet, who have been concerned about your health, are reassured. Symone was flattered when you turned the meeting over to her. Dictys and Galen are busy thinking up ways to include the Searchers in daily activities. Anstellan, mystified by your advice, plans to cancel his appointments tomorrow afternoon so as to visit his House."

"You might have had a glorious career as a spy."

The Master of Mysteries shrugged off the compliment. A comfortable silence stretched between them, two people content to sit quietly together without the pressure of making needless conversation. When at last the

Nineteenth Mother opened her mouth to speak, Esslar had already divined her question.

"It is as you guessed. The search for Sandur begins."

"Ah," she sighed, "so soon."

Leaning back in her chair, she passed a veined hand over her face, as if brushing away the cobwebs of false hopes.

"What's your decision? Shall you tend the son or keep the father at bay?"

"Alyssa eases some of my worries. They walk the Path now, a crooked path, perhaps, but at least they're safely begun."

"Do Sandur's dreams persist?"

"Aye, all of them bad, some so full of evil I can barely refrain from interfering."

With a sad smile, Esslar met the Nineteenth Mother's troubled gaze.

"Sometimes I think we ask too much of him. Daily I ask myself if I could forgive someone who treated me in a like manner. Perhaps charity has its limits, although that thought troubles me almost as much as the fear of what Sandur may become."

"He needs time to explore his freedom, to send forth roots into the new soil we offer him. He will flourish here," her lips tightened with the force of her determination. "I know it," she struck the table with her clenched fist, "if only we can give him enough time!"

"Then you make my decision an easy one." Esslar placed his hand over hers. "I will release the son and take on the father."

She clasped his hand in gratitude, for she knew what she asked of him. She also knew, although she said nothing, that despite his doubts, this most charitable of men would forgive and forgive again, regardless of the cruelties he faced. No power of darkness would ever sway Esslar from the light.

"OUCH, WOMAN! Do you think my head is made of wood?"

"Would you prefer to finish this yourself?"

The threat worked, although he mumbled something uncomplimentary under his breath. Translating as rapidly as she was able (for she'd recently begun studying his language), she understood enough to retaliate in kind.

"If I'm slow, it's because you insist on turning your head to admire yourself in the looking-glass!"

As proof that she'd understood him rightly, he sulked a bit, muttering to himself this time in the southern tongue. Something about nagging, she realized, which infuriated her.

"If I nag, it's because I'm nearly done! Now, sit still!"

She'd approached the task lightheartedly, the suggestion entirely her own. Four hours later, her neck and shoulders stiff, her fingers cramped and aching from plaiting the hundred braids of a Kwanlonhon clansman, her temper shortened by his frequent fits of wiggling, she wished she'd never begun.

"How often must this be done?" she asked, beginning to understand why the women of Endlin had little time to labor over paper and quill.

"It will become easier as you grow more skilled."

So pompous an evasion was punished by a hearty tug.

"Not often!" he yelped.

Amused by his decision to sulk, she waited for him to settle back into position, his hips pressed against her thighs, the sideboards of the bed supporting her back, her skirts hiked up so that she could place her legs on either side of him. The closeness of his body was the single source of enjoyment to be derived from the entire evening. From time to time her hands brushed against the fabric covering his back, the heat from his body releasing a faint scent of cinnamon from the cotton fibers. His hair had been damp from his bath; now it was dry and difficult to work with. Her tongue caught between her teeth to help her concentrate, she began the last row.

"What didst thou do today, nymph?"

This style of address never failed to charm her. Softened by the intimacy of "thous" and "thees", here was a completely different voice than the imperious one with which he'd addressed her during the first moon. She wondered briefly where he learned such charm before putting that thought firmly aside.

"Let me remember," she murmured, casting her thoughts back over the day's events while her fingers finished another braid and tied it off with the piece of thread he handed her.

"I took a language lesson with Esslar in the morning, worked sums on the abacus, and helped Ulkemene with her lace. After the midday meal, Rauros and I played ball, and Lynsaya took him for a run."

The dog's tail thumped against the stone floor at the mention of his name, and he uttered a low whine, a sound that signified he was being scratched.

Lingering over her vision of the hound lying with his square muzzle resting on Sandur's thigh, dozing contentedly in front of the hearth, Alyssa's happiness was almost complete. She'd hoped they might become friends, never daring to dream that Rauros would offer his affections so quickly, or that Sandur would accept them quite so readily. Last night they'd rolled about on the floor, dog and man growling and panting as they wrestled each other to a stalemate and parted friends, the dog retiring to his water bowl, the man to his mug of sweetened tea.

"And thou, what didst thou do today, prince?" she asked, expecting him to laugh, unprepared for the sharpness of his reply.

"Do you mock me, woman?"

Spreading her hands so that they rested on his shoulders, she rested her cheek against his back. These were the moments that took away her happiness, small moments when he lashed out to hurt her. She'd never known anyone so thin-skinned, so easily angered. Teasing was a way of life in her family; childhood in the Kwanlonhon citadel must have been quite different. Saddened by his reaction, she sought for the right words with which to communicate her upset.

"Are you the only one allowed to speak so, Sandur? If that's your custom, you must tell me. I'm willing to learn your ways, as you will learn mine, but we are bound to make mistakes. Why must you always return hurt with hurt? Can you not simply tell me when I go astray?"

The bunched muscles beneath her hands relaxed.

"I didn't mean to bark at you." He took a deep, steadying breath. "Only a clansman speaks so, and only to certain members of his household. It's a sign of deep affection; so fathers speak to children and . . ."

" . . . and clansmen to their concubines?"

A prolonged silence indicated she'd guessed aright.

"I'm not your concubine, Sandur."

"I know this, Alyssa."

Two hands reached up and covered hers, the palms calloused and hard, a bandage wrapped around the right forefinger where he'd cut it with the knife. He'd done the same to her finger, kissing away the pain after he squeezed out the drops of her blood to mingle with his on the cloth they'd offered to the Nineteenth Mother the morning after their reunion. This was their first gift, a pledge for continuance offered up in gratitude that the rules of the Maze were not so rigid that they could not be bent.

"I'll not speak so again. You've my word on it."

"I cannot bear to give it up," she whispered fiercely into his braids. "Speak to me always as you did in the library, for those were the words that drew me to you and brought me joy."

Lifting her hand to his mouth, he kissed her palm, lips pressed against the tender flesh at the base of her thumb. Gently, she disengaged her hand and began to braid again. They sat in silence for a while, lost in private meditations. Securing the last braid, she reached back to massage a cramp in her neck.

"I've finished. What say you? Do you a feel a proper clansman now?"

Her fear that she would never again hear his tender mode of address was dispelled by the fervency of his thanks.

"Thou laughs at me, I fear, but thou hast taken away my shame. I am a clansman again, as I was on the day I was first braided, the day I attained manhood."

"Is it such a wondrous thing, Sandur, to become a man?" she teased him, catching her breath at the seriousness of his reply.

"Wondrous indeed, and all the more wondrous because thy hands make it possible."

* * *

ARRANGING THE PILLOW under his braids, Sandur watched under half-closed lids as she went about preparing herself for bed. Her second-best dress duly unlaced and drawn over her head, her hands found the peg inside the wardrobe and hung it beside the amethyst gown. Her form was half-hidden by shadows, for the room was dimly-lit by dying embers and a candle flickering on the small stool he'd drawn beside the bed. Familiarity with her nightly routine made it no less fascinating. She moved in darkness as if it were her dearest friend, her creamy limbs gleaming as her hands lowered to the basin and lifted to bathe her face and neck. Deftly, her hands located the cloth at its accustomed place on the drying rack. He found himself wishing he might be that cloth, dabbed gently at face and throat to wipe away the last traces of moisture from skin that rivaled the softness of the innermost petals of a full-blown rose.

The shift drifted to the floor to lie in a puddle about her ankles. As she reached for her nightgown, for a brief moment she shone before him in the moonlight, like a distant star winking on the horizon before dawn rises and it blinks out, hidden by the white folds of the gown descending to shield her from his view. Now she would attend to her hair, brushing it away from her forehead with long powerful strokes and then bending over at the waist, the tresses kissing the floor, a red-gold waterfall rippling as the brush passed over and down.

With a toss of her head, she stood upright again and began to brush more slowly, her face tilted up toward the window, her eyes seeming to look up at the moon, a thin crescent spilling its light into the cell and covering her with a silvery sheen. The rate of brushing slowed, then halted, and with a sigh, she replaced the brush on the metal tray. Before she could begin the next part of her toilette, he called out to her.

"Leave off thy braids tonight, Alyssa. Come to bed."

When she evidenced no surprise at his suggestion, he wondered if she guessed what this night held. *What must she think of me, so many nights of quiet slumber in the enormous bed with nothing more than a few kisses shared between us?* In her presence he found himself a boy again, unbraided and unmanned, unsure how to begin a bedding unlike anything he'd experienced in the citadel. The act of joining was simple there, uncomplicated by anything more than mutual need. A scratch at the door of his apartment, a graceful dance of garments being shed, a naked body reclining on a couch, perfumed and oiled, waiting expectantly for his touch. He knew nothing of wooing other than the provocative glances with which he might garner a woman's attention in a public place. With Alyssa, those signals were useless. He'd tried to tell her tonight when she'd finished braiding his hair. She'd smiled, pleased by his gratitude, unaware of what the braiding meant.

For years he'd anticipated the bringing-in of his first concubine, a three-day celebration attended by every member of the Kwanlonhon clan. In the days before her monthly flow they would have lived together chastely (since no clansman would bed a concubine until she proved she bore no other man's child.) Once her flow ceased, he would issue a formal invitation for her to braid his hair, and that done, would bed her nightly until she quickened with his seed. It was a civilized ritual, the rules understood by all concerned, yet here in the Maze there was nothing to smooth the way, no traditions on which he could rely. As she said, she was not his concubine, and although this must be a simple bedding, he was unsure how to begin.

The wardrobe door clicked shut, and she tiptoed toward the bed, perhaps believing him to be asleep. The mattress shifted as she slid under the covers, a sudden rush of lavender scent filling his nostrils. Her hair lay strewn on the pillow, her cheek nestled against her hand. When he cleared his throat, her eyes flickered open.

"You're awake?" she asked, "I thought you'd be fast asleep."

"I . . .," he began, wishing his voice was more steady, "I was watching you."

"Were you indeed?" A smile tugged at the corners of her mouth. "I thought you kept to our agreement. When did you break it?"

"The first night," he confessed.

Her smile deepened but she said nothing in response. Desperate now, he struggled for the right words.

"I watch thee because of thy loveliness. Thou art beauty incarnate, a dew-touched rose at dawn's first light, a pearl glistening on pink sands . . ."

To his dismay, this outpouring of flattery did not result in its usual effect. Rather than cooing her delight, as would any self-respecting concubine, she smothered a laugh. Propping herself up on an elbow, she cocked her head as she often did when she heard something that strained her credulity.

"What brings on these sweet words?"

Shyness overcoming him, he blurted out a graceless invitation a commoner would have blushed to speak.

"I would give thee pleasure, Alyssa."

Poetic descriptions of her beauty did not move her, yet this simple statement brought a flush to her cheeks and moved her to sudden action. He watched, amazed, as she swept aside the blankets and reached out for him.

He was unprepared for such passion, for breasts pressed urgently against him, for hungry lips seeking his. No concubine had ever attacked him so shamelessly, with hands moving restlessly over his nightclothes. He planned to begin slowly, sensuously, helping her remove her gown, arousing her with hands and lips, bringing her to the moment of pleasure as he was trained to do. The wildness of her need perplexed and troubled him. Then, to his horror, she lifted the hem of his blouse, seeking to touch his naked flesh. Twisting away, he retreated to the far side of the bed to rearrange his garments. His breath came unevenly as he fought for composure.

"It seems you are no virgin," he choked out when he could summon breath enough to speak. A shadow flew across her features as she pulled herself up to a sitting position, her arms wrapped around her knees, her hair tumbling about her shoulders.

"Does that matter?"

According to tradition, it made no difference at all; he'd witnessed her monthly flow and knew her to be untouched by any other man since entering the cell. Yet in his mind he'd always thought of her as a virgin. The discovery that he'd so completely misjudged her combined with the unceremonious manner in which she behaved unnerved him, sending everything into disarray.

"Nay, it matters not," he replied curtly, wondering whom she'd joined with and why she never told him anything about this man or, he reminded himself grimly, these men.

"Then why did you pull away from me so rudely?"

How dare she accuse him of rudeness when she'd attacked him like a common whore! His knowledge of prostitutes was limited to the tales the seamen swapped during the long watches. Even so, nothing else could explain the fact that she'd tried to remove his clothing. Disrobing was entirely a clansman's prerogative and unnecessary for a simple bedding. He had no interest in breeding, but in giving her pleasure. Did she think to untie his challah? A shudder ran through him at the thought of her boldness.

"Perhaps we should sleep now," he replied evenly, unwilling to put his disgust into words. She reacted as if he slapped her. Turning away, for he dared not witness the hurt he'd given her, he pulled the coverlet up around his shoulders.

Sleep did not come. After what seemed to be an age, she slid back down into the bed and lay still. The candle sputtered out.

Her voice spoke out of the darkness.

"I won't be treated in this manner, Sandur. You say one thing and act another. I'm not your concubine, nor am I willing to become one. Don't approach me again until you're ready to join with Alyssa; not a rose or a pearl, but a blind bard of Cinthea."

IN HIS DREAMS, Sandur was drowning. Borne on the tides of a winter storm, giant waves beat him into submission. The salt water stung his eyes, awakening the fire smoldering in the open cuts on his back. He struggled to keep his head above the surface, fighting for air, fighting for his life. His muscles ached, a cramp like the pincers of a crab eating at the flesh between his ribs. He was sinking now, drawn under the murky waters by a force he could not resist.

Just as he gave up hope, resolving to surrender to the power of the deep, a voice trumpeted forth.

"This is not your kingdom, nor shall it ever be! Get thee hence from the sacred city and learn we will not be trifled with!"

A tremendous roar rose up out of the deep, as though the monster lurking below screamed out in mortal fear, and Sandur was buoyed up, weightless again, to float on a calm sea, lulled by limpid waters.

"*Rest now*," the sea murmured to him, a voice he remembered dimly but could not place, a voice meriting his trust. The tides ebbed and flowed about him, and rocked in the cradle of the sea, he slept.

Chapter 16

The Gift to the Giver

PICKING OUT DICTYS from among a group gathered around the climbing ropes, Anstellan increased his pace from a walk to a jog. The last of the snow lay in great piles, the soggy ground squelching underfoot as he made his way across the field. Most of the men had shed their cloaks, enjoying the warmth of the late afternoon sun. All told, it was the oddest winter in memory—a fortnight of freezing temperatures and record snowfall followed by days warm enough for some of the hardier ernani to train bare-chested in the arena. Anstellan shook his head, certain that the weather mirrored the frequent vacillations of the ernani.

Reaching the climbing ropes, he approached Dictys.

"The foot races won't start for another hour. You're welcome to join us if you think you've breath enough," the Head Trainer drawled, eyeing him askance, obviously curious as to his reason for visiting the arena.

Ignoring the fact that he was being baited, Anstellan let his gaze rove across the arena before asking, "Where's Sandur?"

Cocking an eyebrow, Dictys jerked his head over to the archery field.

"He's in as foul as mood as I've ever seen. If you value your skin, you'll leave him be." His eyes narrowed. "What are you up to, hetaera?"

"Nothing at all. Merely an urge to take a short run and a need for company."

Glad he'd taken the trouble to exchange his robes for proper running gear, Anstellan tossed an innocent grin over his shoulder and headed for the line of archers in front of the straw targets, Dictys' disapproving glare burning into his back.

The ernani gawked as he jogged by. He hadn't planned to be quite so visible a presence. That was last night, when he'd worried over how to approach Sandur. Since he harbored not the slightest hope of luring him into his office for a repeat counseling session after the debacle of three days ago, he'd considered dropping by the library to interrupt Sandur's studies with Dorian. Dismissing that idea as overly formal and unfitting for what he wanted to communicate, he'd stumbled onto the idea of the arena, hoping this more casual atmosphere might be conducive to conversation.

As he slowed his pace to a walk, he passed Yossi and Kokor, who were involved in a heated discussion in the mountain language. At his approach,

Yossi looked up and frowned. Kokor eyed him warily, darting a nervous glance in Sandur's direction. Sandur himself seemed oblivious to anything but the target, pulling the bowstring taut, aiming with relentless intensity and releasing the arrow, his expression a sullen scowl. When the arrow pierced the third ring, Sandur swore nastily under his breath.

"Would you care to run with me?"

Sandur's jaw set. Without any interruption in the rhythm of his work, he pulled another arrow from the quiver slung over his back.

"What do you want?" he ground out between clenched teeth, "I thought our discussion ended."

Having primed himself for exactly this reaction, Anstellan forged ahead.

"I was unsatisfied with our session. I thought if you're willing, we might try again."

Wood creaked, the bowstring hummed, and the arrow slammed into the target, this time missing the inner circles completely and lodging in the far corner of the straw. With a filthy curse the bow and quiver were thrown to the ground. Sandur wheeled to face him, smoldering brown eyes showering him with sparks. Anstellan stood his ground. And then, quite suddenly, the anger was gone, replaced by a cynical shrug. Unfastening his cloak, Sandur tossed it next to the discarded quiver and bow. Removing a bit of string from his breeches pocket, he gathered his braids together and tied them at the nape of his neck.

"Since I cannot shoot, I might as well run."

Such was the admission of a man with no one to turn to and nowhere to go. Breaking into a trot, Sandur lead the way toward the track, his braids bouncing against his back. Anstellan followed, dodging some of the worst of the puddles in the muddy field. Upon reaching the track, they settled into a jog, moving to the outside lanes reserved for slow-moving runners.

As Anstellan made his first pass by the climbing ropes, Dictys glowered at him before turning to address Pentaur, who had appeared by his side as if by magic. On the second pass, Anstellan heard an inner voice caution, *"Remember Pwyll,"* and sent back a sober reply to the worried monitor, *"I'll not push him. You have my word."* By the third pass, the monitor had vanished. Dictys could be heard bawling profanities at a climber poised thirty feet above the arena, reluctant, perhaps, to begin his descent into the maw of hell.

By the time they began the fourth lap, both men were running easily. The stiffness in Sandur's jaw was gone and his head was up. Anstellan picked up the pace and Sandur responded immediately, throwing the hetaera a bemused glance as he closed the distance between them.

"Care for a race?"

A quick nod of the braided head indicated agreement.

"One lap?"

Another nod and they crossed over to the inner lanes.

"On my mark."

Four paces.

"Ready."

Four more paces.

"Go!"

It was good to run again, to feel his toes grip the track, his heart pounding and his arms pumping by his sides. Sandur moved immediately to the inside lane, Anstellan content to take his usual place behind the front-runner's right shoulder. Six years since his last race, yet it was as if he'd never left the track. Over the sound of his breathing and the air rushing past his ears, he imagined he heard his former trainer yelling encouragement as they rounded the final turn and flew down the straightaway. Just when he thought he could go no faster, he caught his second wind and pulled ahead. The fourth pole marker loomed in front of him, and his heart hammering against his chest, he passed it with a final burst of speed.

Bent over at the waist, hands braced on his thighs, he gulped down air like water, feeling slightly nauseous and sadly out of condition. One lap and he was exhausted. Sandur collapsed beside him on the grass.

"It--seems--," Sandur confessed between gasps, "I--can--neither--shoot--nor--run--today."

Anstellan dropped to his knees, too winded to laugh.

"Are all hetaeras so quick on their feet?" Sandur asked when he'd regained his breath. Anstellan shook his head ruefully.

"This particular hetaera used to run wind sprints every morning. Now I can barely manage a single lap and almost couldn't pass you."

There was something new in Sandur's face as he picked a blade of grass and rolled it between his thumb and forefinger.

"Why did you come?"

Instead of answering him directly, Anstellan posed his own question.

"Do you still need my help, Sandur? If so, I'm willing. If not, we'll part and say no more about it."

Refusing to meet his gaze, Sandur tossed the ball of grass away with a sudden gesture.

"Nothing's changed. We prepare our meals and tell each other what the day brought us. Some nights I work on the maps while she hooks lace; other times she tells a tale of her people, or I describe the lands she'll never see."

An infinite amount of sadness was contained in that last phrase. Staring moodily into the distance, Sandur continued.

"I was angry the day of our session, too angry to hear you or to say what was in my heart. It . . . it's new to me, this anger that wells up inside me, choking me. I was never allowed to express anger as a child. Now I think I'll never be able to control myself again."

"Are you angry with Alyssa or with yourself?"

"With her," and then, very low, "and with myself."

Sandur had shared a few sparse details, most of them sputtered out incoherently as he paced around Anstellan's office like a fugitive from justice, raving something about braids, about women who had no decency, ending with a quick exit and a slammed door when Anstellan posed the exact question Sandur had just answered.

"I said nothing's changed. I lied. There's no joy between us anymore."

For this proud prince of Endlin to offer such a confession freely and without prodding bespoke the measure of his misery.

"Have you spoken to her about this?"

"What can I say?" Sandur scoffed. "Shall I give her lessons in bedding while she ridicules me, having told me plainly my ways are not hers? Or should I bow to her will and play the part of a woman, a thought that fills me with disgust!"

Here was the crux of the matter, the same dilemma the other ernani faced in one form or another. All of them knew the mechanics of the sexual act, knew it long before they came to Pelion. Anstellan's job was to expand their knowledge, to convince them there were many ways of celebrating the body, to lessen fears and discredit former taboos. Some, like Becca and Sandur, had enough experience to appreciate the artistry of what he tried to teach them. Yet, as the Nineteenth Mother had warned him, customs concerning joining remained a highly sensitive matter.

"What is a woman's part?" he asked, honestly curious about the bedding customs of the clansmen of Endlin.

"To receive pleasure," came the brusque reply.

"What of your pleasure?"

Sandur frowned and shrugged, picking at the dry grass. When no response was forthcoming, Anstellan leaned back, pillowing his hands behind his head in order to consider the cloudless blue of the winter sky.

"Have you ever laughed in bed?"

"What is there to laugh about?"

"Has it never struck you funny that we build great mysteries around the simplest act imaginable, something every animal does purely by instinct?"

"We are not beasts."

"True enough, yet our ability to laugh distinguishes us from other animals. Perhaps you might try laughter." He let it sink in a bit before adding, "I've heard Alyssa laugh, Sandur. It's a lovely sound, one I treasure."

Sometime later Anstellan heard the grass rustle and guessed he was alone. Freed of his duties, he let his mind wander, musing over the events of the day, hearing again the laughter spilling out into the corridors from the classrooms of his House. An enormous booted foot descended near his shoulder, was followed by another of equal size, and he looked up into Pharlookas' troubled face.

"I, uh, I wondered if we might talk awhile?"

"Of course. How can I help?"

Much later in the course of his conversation with Pharlookas, Anstellan looked up at the sky and said, "Perhaps you might try laughter."

If long-cherished customs were to be obliterated, the ernani must learn that nothing subverts the tyranny of tradition quite so quickly as laughter, for to laugh one must set oneself free.

Heads turned all about the arena as the Instructor of the Maze let out a whoop and leapt to his feet, then set off running toward the gates.

"Likely he remembered something," Dictys observed to no one in particular, resuming his duties without giving the incident another thought.

THERE IT WAS again, that strange, scuffling sound, like something being dragged. Nails clicked against the stone floor as Rauros went over to investigate. What was Sandur up to? She heard the same sound when he entered the cell this evening. Curiosity gnawed her, but she said nothing, having resolved to cut out her tongue rather than reveal the slightest interest in his affairs. In an attempt to ignore whatever it was he was doing, she worked as noisily as possible, banging the pots and clattering the crockery as she dried and stacked the dishes. With a toss of her head to prove how little she cared, she draped the drying cloth over her shoulder and began returning each item to its rightful place.

The problem was she cared very much. If she hadn't, the past few days wouldn't have been so dreadful. Lately, she'd found herself wishing she could curl up at her mother's feet and tell her everything . . .

"WHAT A FOOL you've become, daughter, what an addle-pated fool! Cut out your tongue, would you? That's a pretty picture—mute as well as blind! Why not cut off your fingers or plug your ears?"

"He started it, mother! I'm not the one who stopped almost before we'd begun! And I'm also not the one who gives a fig about virginity, his or mine! How dare he say it doesn't matter and then roll over and go to sleep!"

"Child, child, you tire me with these excuses! It's a pointless game you play. You're in the right. He's to blame. What difference does it make when your feet are cold and you've nowhere to warm them? I would have thought you'd learned something from your time with Boal. "

"We were young, mother. Sandur is nothing like Boal."

"Nothing like Boal? I should hope so!"

"You never liked Boal, and you never told me why."

"It was important that I not like him. You were all of sixteen; he still had peach fuzz on his chin. If I'd liked him, you'd have lost interest. Young people need something to rebel against."

"That's ridiculous!"

"No more ridiculous than your recent behavior, feeling sorry for yourself when you should be attending to business. Did you and Boal never quarrel?"

"Of course we quarreled!"

"And you were always right and he was always wrong? Ah, she says nothing! By the horned moon of Tek, I never thought I'd see you at a loss for words! You've a golden tongue, Alyssa. Rather than cutting it out, put it to use!"

EVERY IMAGINARY CONVERSATION ended the same way, her mother scolding her for taking refuge in silence, a silence magnified by Sandur's refusal to say anything at all. Overnight the cell become a battleground with Rauros caught in the middle, whimpering in his sleep, as if their hostilities haunted his dreams.

All day she worried over how to begin. An apology was out of the question. Introducing an anecdote about her day was a possibility, but seemed childish somehow. She could broach the subject of Boal, but that smacked of confession, and if Sandur didn't offer a confession in return, she knew she'd be even more furious with him than she was now. She'd even dallied with the notion of confronting him, demanding the reason for his hasty retreat, but found herself too much of a coward to force the issue.

If truth be told, and it was only recently she'd forced herself to face the truth, Sandur frightened her. Not a fear he might physically hurt her so much as the danger she sensed inside him, dark places where demons hid. If, as she'd been taught, dreams were the mirror of the soul, then Sandur's soul was sorely troubled. Nothing else could explain the nightmares he suffered with disturbing regularity, groaning and crying out in his sleep, his limbs thrashing and his garments soaked with sweat. Night after night she evicted his night-demons from the cell, humming nonsensical words until he hushed, cradling him against her breasts and stroking his hair.

Holding him in her arms, the desire to see his face was almost more than she could bear, an enormous hunger no food could satisfy, a thirst no beverage could quench. If, for only a single instant she could regain her sight, she would spend that precious moment memorizing the features of Sandur

Kwanlonhon. A new-formed resolve followed that admission. If you are ever to see him, daughter of Latona, you must take another step along the Path.

"Alyssa, could you help me?"

Locating the direction of his voice, she took a step forward. Warm hands grasped hers, leading her to a place between the table and the door.

"Stand here. Now, crouch down." She felt what seemed to be a thick board. "Grab the edge." He was speaking directly in front of her now. "I'll raise my side first. When you have a firm grip, tell me, and we'll lift it together."

Whatever it was, the effort of lifting it waist-high explained why he'd been forced to drag it along the floor. Grunting out directions, he guided her to the correct place and together they swung it over the table and lowered it to rest. Rubbing her hands to ease the blood back into her fingers, she couldn't contain her curiosity any longer.

"What is it?"

"A present."

Tension lay underneath that cautious reply.

"What kind of a present?"

"You must judge for yourself."

Gingerly, she reached down to find a cool, moist surface beneath her fingertips. Walking her fingers over an irregular surface of bumps, she met a smooth expanse. She could make no sense of it until her fingers found a wide groove and followed its indentation along a series of meandering curves. The groove almost doubled its breadth from the point where she began, spreading out to form a series of shallower grooves that finally ended at the edge nearest her body.

"Could it be . . . a river?"

"The River Tellas and its southern tributaries."

Her fingers raced eagerly over the surface of the map. Ridges became the Sarujian Mountains, flat expanses the plains and grasslands of Lapith. He was coaching her now, moving her fingers to the spot along the river where Vlatla's people lived, the northern hunting grounds where Jincin and his tribe hunted caribou and elk. A tiny hole pierced in the side of a craggy mountain named Dragon's Tooth represented the cave where Yossi spent his youth.

He described the map as unfinished, an experiment in clay, a poor imitation of what he intended. There was pride beneath his modesty, boyish enthusiasm as he described Dorian's excitement and the Chartist's promise that more maps would be put at his disposal.

Through it all, her mind filled with a single thought, "Sandur has given me the world!"

"I took your advice and asked the other ernani for details. At first only Kokor and Tibor helped. Once the others saw what I was doing, they came forward with so many suggestions that it was all Dorian and I could do to revise the existing charts. In time I'll expand the map to the west and south."

"And the east?"

Her fingers told her the clay ended at the Sarujian Mountains.

"Later, perhaps."

Dismissing her misgivings at hearing this vague reply, her fingers found the valley in which they resided and moved due east.

"Where's Cinthea?" she asked, anxious to feel the furrowed fields of her homeland. He made a minor adjustment to her direction.

"It's so small!" she wailed, crestfallen to discover the insignificance of her village in contrast to the wideness of the world. "The scale must be wrong, either that or you're trying to trick me!"

"Nay, nymph," he chuckled, "'tis as big as your fingers tell you, a small village nestled among the provinces stretching between Pelion and Tek-By-The-Sea."

"Well," she sniffed, "at least it's bigger than Yossi's cave."

Hooting with unrestrained delight, he slapped his hand against his thigh. Inspired by his laughter, for there had been none in the cell for many days, she reached out, her arms stretched wide, searching through the mists for him, and suddenly, he was there.

"Dost thou laugh or cry, beloved?" he murmured into her hair. She shook her head, unable to speak since, as he said, her laughter mingled with tears. Time hung suspended, a wordless moment in which they made their peace.

"I would give thee pleasure, Alyssa, but . . .," he stammered, ". . . I don't know how . . . how to . . ."

Reaching up, she placed her palm over his lips.

"Let's make a pact, a promise that tonight there will be no past for either of us. Let us be like children with each other, free of worries and fears, able to enjoy one another without thought of any yesterdays or even of tomorrow."

A reckless abandonment came over him, a determination that with her help he could accomplish anything, even if it meant imagining a childhood he'd never known. Kissing her palm as a token of his pledge, he carried her to the bed.

They began with a game. Laughing up at him, cheeks flushed, eyes sparkling, she invited him to play geography, ". . . for you are a Chartist, are you not? And I will be your map."

Such revelries were new to him. Games he knew, but none like these, his hands playing over the landscape of her body, her breasts straining against the bodice of the amethyst gown. Her play was more assured than his, her eyes in her fingertips as she explored the hills and depressions of his chest and belly, searing touches that left tracks of fire on the skin beneath his clothes.

From time to time she murmured to him of the things she learned, giggling when she found a ticklish place between his ribs, a discovery more surprising to him than the well-spring of happiness unleashed by the sound of her laughter.

"Has no one ever tickled you, prince?" she teased, and then, sensing his answer, contritely begged his pardon, "Nay, say nothing, Sandur, for I forgot our pact."

He murmured to her as well of things she could not see—of the curve of her lashes against her cheek, of the creaminess of her skin, of the slenderness of her neck and shell-like perfection of each ear. Not long after, when his hands were drawn to the rounded hips he'd admired from afar, she whispered, "If you would explore those lands, you must undress me first."

Her disrobing became another game of sorts. Unfamiliar with hooks and laces, he fumbled and fumed until she took pity on him, offering instructions as his frustration grew into a fit of temper. When one of the laces snapped, he threw the frayed cording violently to the floor.

"Damn this dress! Will it never come off?"

A menacing growl answered him, a huge grey head appearing beside the bed, lips pulled back into a toothsome snarl.

"Softly, Sandur, softly," she cautioned, giggling all the while, "Rauros does not take kindly to angry words."

Placated by Alyssa's hand stroking his nose, the hackles along the dog's back lowered. In the next moment, Sandur watched, amazed, as Rauros leapt up onto the mattress in a single bound and settled on his haunches at the foot of the bed.

"Does he mean to watch?"

Peals of riotous laughter rang out against the stone walls, the mattress shaking with the force of Alyssa's mirth. Sandur glared at the huge hound, who matched him stare for stare.

"Alyssa, do something!" Sandur begged.

Her giggles redoubled, kindling his own, chuckles becoming outright laughter until, either reassured by their hilarity or simply bored, the dog jumped off the bed and returned to his basket by the hearth.

"Is he gone?" Alyssa asked breathlessly. When Sandur answered in the affirmative, she pulled the gown and shift over her head and tossed them carelessly to the floor. Turning to him with an impish grin, she explained, "We must not risk another interruption, or we'll never reach the end of our game."

At the sight of her beside him, naked and unafraid, her hair strewn carelessly over her shoulders and breasts, her limbs glowing like porcelain in the candlelight, he reached out to touch her. A hand was placed firmly in the middle of his chest.

"Remember the game," she reminded him, her hands fumbling for the hem of his tunic. Habit made him jerk away. Immediately, she withdrew, solemn with reproach. How could he disappoint her, denying her the only thing she asked of him? That he forget the past for a single night and free himself from old customs, old hurts . . .

Taking her hands in his, he guided them to either side of his tunic and lifted his arms. Life sprang back into her face. His tunic and breeches joined the amethyst gown, and they lay together on the enormous bed.

Now began a different game, one of give and take, part of it familiar, another part new and vaguely troubling. He'd never experienced the sensation of hands running over him, or heard a woman tell him his body pleased her. He should rightly speak those phrases; instead, he found himself struck dumb. Her slightest touch scorched his naked flesh, burning away the old, replacing it with something novel, something dangerous, a whole host of strange desires, all of them forbidden a clansman from time immemorial. Was this normal, he wondered helplessly, this delight in her touch, the pleasure of hands stroking his thighs, lips roving over his chest? Her sighs relieved some of his doubts. These same sounds issued from the throats of his uncle's concubines, their eyes demurely closed, politely avoiding any contact he did not initiate, content to receive pleasure without thought of reciprocation. Nothing in his experience prepared him for supple limbs wrapping themselves around him or an open mouth returning his kisses with such sweet enthusiasm.

Trained to put aside his own desire, he maintained control by keeping his attention on the signs of arousal—the panting breath and flushed skin, the upright nipples, the flood of moisture from between the thighs. Again he watched as a woman's body responded to his mouth and hands, yet for the first time he was uncomfortably aware of his own body's needs, hearing with unbelieving ears a groan escape his lips as her palm rubbed against his challah.

"Sandur," she whispered urgently, her fingers working at the knot of the thong tied about his hips, frantic fingers seeking to free him from the past. For one hope-filled moment he thought he could enter the land where Alyssa dwelt, a place that cared nothing for rules five centuries in the making. Hope took flight as a deep melancholy overcame him. With it came the realization that her childhood was not his. Gently, he disengaged her fingers.

"Thou must not untie my challah."

His sadness was reflected in her face.

"Listen, beloved," he whispered, taking her in his arms and stroking her hair to quiet her, "I would give thee pleasure, but I must not enter thy body."

"If you worry we might make a child, put that fear aside. I take the medicines they give me without fail."

Her soaring confidence grieved him, as did the shining face regarding him with perfect trust. So little she asked, yet so much. Medicines preventing conception had been tried and discarded by Sandur's people centuries ago. Mistakes were too frequent, concubines forgetful or careless, clansmen too easily seduced from the path of total abstinence that assured no unwanted child would be brought into the world. Her fingers stole up to stroke his face. At the tenderness of her touch, hesitation filled him. *Why do I persist in honoring a father who never gave me anything but pain?* Before he could answer, a vision smote him, that of a newborn babe being placed in his arms, a babe with blank, unseeing eyes . . .

"I take great delight in thee, this thou must believe."

"But what of your pleasure?"

"It is enough to see thee in ecstasy. Anything more is forbidden."

No tears met his denial, no entreaties or displays of wounded pride, just a heartfelt sigh as she searched for the bedclothes and pulled them up to cover her nakedness.

"I hoped our game would suffice, but I see we are not children and no amount of wishing can make us so." When he made no answer, she said, "You've never asked me about my blindness, Sandur."

"And thou, my beauty, felt the scars across my back tonight, yet made no mention of them. Thou speakest aright. We are not children, and to speak of certain things brings misery to the soul."

At the mention of the scars, tears flooded her sightless eyes.

"Who whipped you so cruelly and for what cause?"

Wonder filled him as she cried for him. Was this the measure of her devotion, that she could forbear tears for herself, but shed them freely for him? Touched by her concern, he summoned up old memories.

"The order came from my father; my uncle wielded the rod. As to the cause, I questioned my father's judgment. This is our way, Alyssa. My father is the highest authority in our clan, and his decisions rule my life. According to our laws, I failed in my duty. The punishment was just."

Sandur sought to control his anger as he spoke. He'd not reckoned with the fury of Alyssa, who burst from his arms like a hawk flies from the fist, beating her wings against the air to spring skyward, then plummeting to take her quarry in a single, death-dealing dive.

"What sort of justice is this? A son questions his father and is beaten until the blood flows? What kind of monster is he, to punish his child with no thought as to mercy or forgiveness?"

Like a vengeful siren she damned his father outright, sparing neither curses nor shouts, the oceans in her eyes tumultuous, her hair storm-tossed.

"Calm thyself, or the dog will be upon us again."

"I would set Rauros on your father and laugh as his fangs sank into his throat!"

So bloodthirsty a threat from the mouth of a naked woman brought a smile to Sandur's lips. When he pulled her down beside him, she came willingly enough, but not before issuing a challenge.

"You think I jest?"

"I doubt thee not! Thy rage sends shivers up and down my spine!"

A down-stuffed pillow smacked him squarely in the face. Before he could blink away the tears, another one found its target in the pit of his stomach and burst open, spewing feathers that danced upon the air. With a cry, he was after her. She might have been an eel, squirming and sliding over the feather-strewn bed, giggling madly as they tussled, giving in when he pinned her around the waist and hauled her back to the middle of the mattress. He'd just recovered his breath when a question was posed from beneath a curtain of red-gold hair.

"What do you see when you look at me?"

His first impulse was to tease her unmercifully. Still, there was something about her tone—a shyness, a reticence, that warned him to put all thoughts of playfulness aside.

"I see a sea-nymph born of the waters." A blush spread from her breasts to her cheeks. "This nymph is the color of pink-fingered dawn, her hair strewn about her shoulders like a golden net."

"Do you see no rose, then, no pearl?"

"I see Alyssa," he replied slowly, "a blind bard of Cinthea."

Wordlessly, she held out her arms to him.

The memory of what followed would live inside him forever—a silken head nestled against his shoulder, tears anointing his chest, a melodious voice telling the story of a girl who woke from a seven-day battle with death to learn the awful cost of her victory.

In the silence of the candlelit cell he damned himself a thousand times a fool. What guarantee did anyone have, even if they came perfect into the world, of a life lived free of imperfection? Was anyone more blemished than the Tehran's sa'ab, whip-scars on his back and hatred in his heart? Remorse turned his throat to dust. Why did it take him so long to realize that from the first day he entered the cell, perfection was always within his reach?

"Untie my challah, beloved."

Sightless eyes opened wide, seeming to look past skin and bone into a heart beating with a new rhythm, a drum throbbing wildly against his ribs.

"It is I who have been blind."

Her hands drifted down his flanks, and the challah fell away.

Delicate, oh so delicate, was their dance amidst the feather-strewn bed.

And so, as Sandur promised, their bed became an island floating on the waves, their cell a kingdom by an inland sea. And as Alyssa promised, the prize at last was his. For as the mariner cries out at the sudden sight of land, a joyous shout sprang from Sandur's throat as he found safe harbor in Alyssa.

Chapter 17

Battle Cry

THE CUSHIONED CHAIR stood empty. A stooped form, partially silhouetted by taper-light, cast a murky shadow against the stone walls of the tower chamber.

"Tell them, Commander."

"Aye, 'tis time they knew."

Shifting in their chairs, the council exchanged bewildered looks. A pall fell over the room.

"There's been a murder in the city."

Before anyone could react Galen barked, "I'll tolerate no ruckus here! The matter's in hand, an investigation's underway, and there's nothin' to be gained by weepin' and wailin'."

Symone's temper, always short-fused, flared white-hot, "I, for one, am not given to 'weepin' and 'wailin'! Give us the facts!"

Soldier and scholar locked wills. Theirs was a history of confrontation, the crusty Commander versus the acid-tongued Archivist. On this particular occasion, the soldier retreated.

"'Tis not a pretty tale, and 'tis a sadness to tell it. I meant only to spare ye."

For once, Galen's carefully cultivated west-country accent was stripped away, ample indication of the seriousness of his message.

"We guessed Manthur would search for the lad, which is why Esslar talked him out of writing to his uncle about his whereabouts. But money talks, and the Kwanlonhon arm is long, longer than any of us suspected. At first, questions were circulated among the moneychangers, requests planted in several ears for information about a foreign prince exchanging certain letters of credit for local currency. 'Tis my bet the Tehran believed he'd prevented Sandur from entering the Maze and thought the lad was hiding from him. If he could trace the money, the rest would fall into place."

"Lately, the past moon or so, he's switched tactics, probably figuring that if the letters of credit haven't been used, the next place to search is the Maze."

"Reports came in slowly, one of them from a non-adept laundry worker approached in a neighborhood shop by a foreigner searching for news about his nephew, who, so the story goes, was an ernani in the Maze who needed to be contacted about his mother's illness. We were lucky with that one—the laundry worker accepted the story as truth, asked a co-worker about procedure, and was referred to me. Once I explained the circumstances, he agreed to be read. The foreigner's accent was eastern, of that I'm certain, but somehow he got wind a search was on and high-tailed it out of town before we could question him."

"Our luck held. The next agent approached a monitor, an adept monitor at that."

The Commander's humorless laugh grated harshly against their ears.

"Imagine, if ye can, Pentaur accepting a hefty bribe for information concerning a certain ernani by the name of Sandur Kwanlonhon. Pentaur played the fool while he picked the man's mind clean. We located him a few hours later in an inn and gave him escort to our eastern borders. Given Manthur's record with those who fail in their duty, I doubt he'll return to his master anytime soon."

"These were his orders: Find Sandur and bring him home. Abduct him if necessary, bind him hand and foot if he'll not come willingly, but bring him home."

The weightiness of that proclamation hung over their heads, producing in all of them torpor, a sluggishness of mind and body.

"Delay no longer," ordered the stooped figure by the wall. "Let them hear it all."

The Commander roused himself with an effort.

"Today our luck ran out. We're still picking up the pieces, but it seems an agent finally located an informer, a non-adept kitchen-worker, a lass of just twenty-five who lost her position when we made cuts in our personnel."

"What have we done?" Evadne demanded. "What have we done that this madman brings murder to the sacred city?"

The Nineteenth Mother's robes billowed as she turned to face them, the shadow cast on the wall suddenly immense.

"We've done what we thought best and will continue to do so. Manthur is one of us, a transformed adept who walked the Path, a product of the Maze. He's broken every vow, yet I tell you, Evadne," she pronounced each word slowly and deliberately, "we made him what he is. A twisted adept, a madman, a monster—what matter the name we give his malady? He exists because of our failures, a warning that if we shirk our responsibilities, chaos will reign."

An odd expression came over Evadne's face, a mingling of relief and dread. When Japhet turned to her, a question in his eyes, she shook her head at him.

Lowering herself slowly into her chair, her hands gripping the arms, white-knuckled from the strain of supporting herself, the Nineteenth Mother gestured for Galen to continue.

"There's not much more to tell. According to her mate, she'd been troubled of late, depressed and nervous. We think she was approached in the marketplace, perhaps singled out as someone with a grudge against her former employers. Her mate defends her on that point; we may never know the truth of it. Many of her friends still work inside the Maze. One of them admits to telling her she'd seen a man with braided hair in the men's refectory. My guess is she arranged a meeting for the fifth hour after midday, when the markets are packed with last-minute shoppers, thinking, perhaps, she'd be safer in a crowd. Her body was found in an alleyway, stuffed into an empty bin, her throat cut. The murderer took care not to arouse her suspicions—we found the bribe money tucked safely in her apron pocket."

"If she gave them the information, why was she killed?"

"Tis an old game, and a crooked one. Maybe she turned greedy, wantin' more money to guarantee her silence. 'Tis more likely that he tried to enlist her aid for an abduction, and she panicked. The slash was from left to right, a clean, precise kill by a professional. She accepted the money and turned to go, thinking herself safe. He took her from behind."

"Have you found the murderer?"

"Not yet," came Galen's guarded response. "'Tis my hope we never do."

Symone nodded, understanding instantly that if the killer was caught, Galen's command would signal the stool should be kicked away, causing a hooded figure with a noose about his neck to swing slowly from side to side. It would be Galen's duty to oversee the first public execution in Pelion for over three hundred years.

Amidst the silence of the tower chamber, they mourned as one. None mourned as did the old woman, who relived another woman's murder, another knife sinking into tender flesh. Out of their grief rose Esslar's voice, his unexpected entry into the discussion catching them all off-guard. For the past few weeks he'd existed in a trance-like state, half in and half out of the world, going through the motions of physical existence while his thoughts lived elsewhere. Now, from beneath his robes, he produced a curved dagger with a serrated edge and placed it in the middle of the table. Cleansed now of any trace of blood, it glinted coldly in the candlelight. Cruel it looked to them, and sinister, a ghastly reminder that death was in residence among them.

"He wooed her with the Tehran's gold. At her first words, his heart leapt up, exultant that at last the Tehran's sa'ab had been found! It was not his intention to kill her, for he found her pliable, a useful tool he could train to fit his hand. When he saw her eyes widen with fear as she looked beyond his shoulder, he knew that he must kill. Someone saw her talking with a stranger—a friend, a neighbor, it made no difference—and he killed as he has killed many times before, without passion, without guilt, without thought."

"It's here," Esslar's forefinger traced the blade, "the Tehran's mission written in blood. The murderer fled, but as he dropped the knife, before it clattered to rest on the pavement, a single thought was his: 'I must tell the others. I must flee, but first I must spread the word.'"

Symone shivered, glad that it was Esslar's hand that touched the blade and not her own. The ability to read objects was a rarefied talent that she shared to some degree, but one she did not practice. Then another thought struck her, one that brought her hand to her throat as if checking for a rope.

In the next moment, Symone's life changed.

The Nineteenth Mother's voice spoke inside her head, a voice of such power that she gasped and closed her eyes, hearing not a conversation, but a command.

"So, Symone. Your prediction comes true. Soon Adrastus will scream his message from the rooftops, 'No foreigners in Pelion!' And the city will rise up against us."

Language ceased. Instead, a vision of a possible future appeared inside Symone's head, the colors blinding in their intensity, the shapes stark, the light harsh, unforgiving. There stood the residents of the city, the enraged citizens of Pelion amassed to storm the Maze. In their hands they grasped cobblestones pulled up from the streets; arms raised, they pushed forward toward the bronze doors. . . and then, before the tide of their anger could break against those triple-thick walls, the vision flickered, diminished, and dimmed.

Symone opened her eyes on the tower chamber, empty now but for the Nineteenth Mother, Galen, and Esslar. Sometime during the course of her vision, the others departed for destinations unknown, their empty chairs scattered forlornly about the room. Four of us, she lamented, the vision still throbbing, four of us against the entire populous of Pelion. No chance to train my successor as Kazur trained me, no one to take up my pen. I am the last of my kind, the last archivist of the last ernani to walk the Path. Upon reaching the bottom of her despair, she found bubbling there a wellspring of anger, a refusal to be the last hand to record the procedures by which a world could be transformed. As the anger rose within her, fanned by the vision of destruction, its flames burned away the fear and billowed her spirits as if they were sails, full-blown and pregnant with resolve.

"Guard your talisman well, Symone. Carry the vision inside you; I've borne it long enough alone. It's my gift to you—fuel to feed the flames of indignation and keep your anger alive."

The inner voice departed as the woman in black spoke aloud.

"Our tasks are clear. You, Symone, will alert the League of Independent Traders, counseling them to buy up extra food and supplies in the next few days. Urge them to flee the city quickly and quietly, before unrest spreads. Adrastus holds a bitter grudge against them. They, and all those not native born, will be the first to feel his wrath."

"Galen, advise the Maze personnel that they must either bring their families inside, flee the city, or live in fear of Adrastus' reprisals." Galen nodded. The Nineteenth Mother scrutinized him for a moment. "What were your orders to Dictys?"

"He's stationing extra units around the perimeters of the Maze," came the terse reply. "I recalled all cavalry patrols at dusk. They'll trickle back over the next few days and take up positions to safeguard our control of the northern gates. If worse comes to worse," he muttered darkly, "at least we won't be trapped."

The Master of Mysteries broke his silence.

"What would you have me do, Mother?"

"What you have done from the beginning. Protect the son; deny the father."

Troubled eyes lifted to meet hers. She answered him softly.

"We'll not abandon him, Esslar, this Tehran's sa'ab who may destroy us all."

Something in that tender exchange sparked a sudden flash of insight in Symone. The murder itself might have been a shock, but these three people suspected this might happen. Symone was party to a meeting begun twelve moons ago. Galen and Esslar were members of the Nineteenth Mother's confederacy from the plan's inception. If she had not passed the Nineteenth Mother's test, Symone, too, would have been dismissed with the others.

The black veil turned in her direction.

"Do not judge us harshly, Symone, or think we do not trust the other Council members. Their job is to safeguard the ernani while we take up the war outside the Maze."

"I've prepared them as best I can for what lies ahead. Evadne, gentle, trusting Evadne, who for sixty years believed herself safe from all that is evil, has learned the cruelest lesson of the three. The power of deception I've taught her, the smiling face that hides what lies within, for it was deception that brought about our downfall. Tonight she learned what she long suspected to be true. For years she's carried a single question inside her. `Why Japhet and I instead of Didion and Lara? How did they come to lose the Nineteenth Mother's trust?'

"Tonight she learned why I dismissed Didion and Lara from my Council. Because of them, Manthur's sickness went undetected. They meant no harm, but they broke their oath to me. Too eager they were to believe him cured, too disturbed by his actions to consider the cause, too fearful of visiting the dark places where his spirit hid. Forbidden by them to plumb those depths, new to my position and uncertain of my powers, I relied on their judgment. Trusting them, I unleashed Manthur on the world."

"Evadne will not fail as Lara and Didion failed. No falsehood shall elude her watchful eyes, for so she was named Evadne, that nothing shall evade her."

There was grim satisfaction in the Nineteenth Mother's manner, a relief at passing on a secret hidden for thirty years. Symone was struck again by her energy, an energy she had not possessed in many moons.

"To Dictys I've given a weighty gift, one he shouldered without complaint. As a leader, he had potential; compassion he sorely lacked. I chose him on my last visit to Cyme, then prepared him for his trial, one that might have cost him his life. He came away with a single scar, a small price to pay for the lesson that will keep my ernani safe under his flint-eyed gaze, for Dictys learned he is only as strong as those he gathers around him."

Symone had marked the change in Dictys herself, the persistence with which he fought for revisions of the rules, his determination that the Searchers be included in the inner workings of the Maze.

As she reflected on this, a strange sensation came over her. Something was beginning to resonate inside her mind, as if a tuning fork was being struck, its reverberations passing from the mind of the Nineteenth Mother to hers. Rather than fight against these new, unsettling vibrations, she surrendered herself to the pitch being struck, hearing the rest of the recital through her mind rather than her ears.

"To Anstellan of the winged feet, I gave back the laughter he'd nearly forgotten. With it I surrendered my youth and what was left of my desire."

The Nineteenth Mother's lips ceased moving. The tuning was complete. They existed in perfect harmony, two minds working as one. This was beyond the closeness of born adepts, beyond anything in Symone's experience. She was not so much inside the Nineteenth Mother's mind as she was an active agent in its processes. Understanding was effortless, graceful, a dance without necessity of music.

Their bond established, the harmony of their minds complete, the floodgates opened, spewing images and information that rapidly became a blur of perpetual motion. A glowing sun, a crescent moon, a whispering plain, blackened silhouettes—a myriad of images spun by with such rapidity that Symone could make nothing of them other than to register their passing. The whirlwind encompassing her slowed and finally settled on the figure of the Commander of the Legion. Galen gave no sign that he heard the thoughts filling Symone's mind. Frowning, he stared fixedly at the dagger lying untouched in the middle of the table.

"No one loves a fight as Galen does, yet still he hesitates. For this I value him all the more, for none shall fight for me but those who hate the thought of violence among us."

The Nineteenth Mother's thoughts focused on Esslar, pale and haggard, dream-filled eyes gleaming brighter than the tallow candles burning overhead.

"Here is a child of light born to fight the darkness. There have been none like him before, and perhaps none will follow. He came, as was promised, on a night without stars. Even now he wrestles with Manthur, keeping his thoughts always at bay."

Like a cloud racing across the moon, a shadow fell over Symone. As another mind reached out, intent on reading her thoughts, a frigid cold overcame her. Here was no light, no reason, only madness—a twisted mind greedy for conquest, intent on wresting from her all secrets, all knowledge, even the power of thought itself. As an icy darkness filled her, within that darkness she heard the scream of a tormented soul filled with a boundless hatred of everything that walks upon the face of the earth. Darkness piled upon darkness, sucking her toward the east—until, like a door being shut, the darkness was thrust aside, light and warmth restored.

"Day by day Manthur's power grows. His is an unrelenting hunger that will not be stopped until he has devoured the world."

The voice within Symone retreated gradually until she was left alone with her own thoughts. Even so brief a contact with Manthur's madness left her shaken. Her mind raced, sorting through what she'd learned. A voice cracked with age broke through her thoughts.

"We await your observations, Symone."

Three pairs of eyes fixed on her, three faces rigid with strain, willing her to speak.

"One thing remains unclear. Why does Manthur search for Sandur? Why not forget this son he hates and let him fade into oblivion, a traveler lost somewhere in the vastness of the west?"

Esslar answered.

"This was his first thought, the reason he allowed us to take Sandur to Pelion. Upon deeper reflection, he discovered his mistake. A sa'ab is a sacred trust. To report Sandur lost or dead would damn Manthur in the eyes of his people. He must be able to prove he has not been careless with his sa'ab. Thus Sandur must return to Endlin."

Slowly, carefully, Symone put the pieces together.

"Inside the walls we fight Adrastus for the purpose of establishing, now and for all time, the sovereignty of the Maze. Perhaps Manthur exacerbated the situation; in any case, it would have come to this—a war of independence that, if won, will assure the continuance of our promise to the Sowers despite political upheavals within the city itself. Inside the Maze, we fight to preserve the integrity of the Path, for if this class of ernani should fail, all our efforts will have been for naught."

As her thoughts leapt ahead, she became the favorite pupil of Kazur, the student selected to assist him with the editing of his monumental history of

Agave. Every factor pointed to the same awful eventualities. As the gift spread, Endlin would be threatened by the rebellion of its commoners as well as the gradual corrosion of its economic and political stability. Like Agave, Endlin would strike back, but Endlin was not Agave in terms of population, resources, or military potential. Endlin was no city of slaves, but an enormous empire based on the economic conquest of illiterate peoples. If the six clans brought the same initiative with which they explored the eastern seas to bear on military expansion, what havoc might they wreak on Pelion and its environs?

"Finally, we must correct a mistake of the past if we are to hope for a future. Manthur has put the transformation of the east thirty years behind schedule; if his power continues unchecked, his policies will influence the clans long after his death. Eventually the scales that balance the spread of the gift will tip again, and in a hundred years, we'll be faced with a war which, in all probability, we will not win."

The Nineteenth Mother bobbed her head up and down, indicating her pleasure at Symone's reading of events. Now she learned over the table, her expression intent.

"We pose a question in return. Establish priorities for us, Symone. What must succeed lest all else fail?"

So Kazur presented her with the single question comprising her final examination. Here is the data, Symone; give me your findings.

"Adrastus' cause must be discredited before civil war ensues. In times of strife, the Legion has traditionally supported the Office of the Mother over the secular arm of the government."

Symone lingered over that particular pronouncement, to be rewarded with an emphatic nod from the Commander of the Legion. Her assumption was correct. Galen would support the Nineteenth Mother. In turn, the Legion would stand firm behind the man who'd led them these thirty years. Her heart went out to him, knowing what the decision cost him, understanding how loathe he was to support a course of action that might pit brother against brother, father against son. Still, he was a product of the Maze, as were nearly two-thirds of the Legionnaires. Who knew better what would be lost than those who'd walked the Path?

"If we refuse to capitulate to their demands, in all likelihood the citizens will attempt to hold the Maze in a state of siege. Eventually," she continued, "the Legion will be forced to take up arms against the mob. Regardless of the actual victor, the resulting bloodshed will cause a breach between Maze and town that might never be healed."

"What would best discredit Adrastus and his followers?"

This was more difficult. Symone struggled to reply.

"Something without precedent. Something so heinous to every man, woman, and child who lives within the city that irrespective of their affiliations, either to guilds or Legion, they'll be revolted by the thought of what Adrastus promises."

"What event would be without precedent?"

A tiny set of knives stabbed between Symone's breasts.

"I . . . I couldn't say, Mother."

The old woman shook her head, impatient with half-truths.

"You've already said it, Symone! Whose existence affects all residents of Pelion from the moment of their birth?

Defeated by those unwavering eyes, Symone whispered, "Yours."

"What must I do to stop Adrastus, Symone? What must I do before protests become riots, riots produce a siege, and a siege brings the Legion forth to crush the populace?"

To contemplate the answer was difficult enough, to speak it aloud might endow it with a frighteningly logical inevitability, as if a Mother of Pelion existed as a commodity that might be spent. The individual who wore the black robes might be expendable; her office was not. No one except a Mother of Pelion knew the rite of selection, yet of this fact Symone was certain—the actual transference of powers always occurred between two living women. If the Nineteenth Mother's life was the fulcrum on which everything was to be balanced—the continuance of the Maze or the ruination of Pelion—Symone rejected it utterly. Not even the power of that all-knowing, all-accepting gaze could stay her tongue.

"Is Pelion's punishment to be robbed of your successor? Would you willingly become the last of your kind?"

"Ah, Symone," the Nineteenth Mother sighed, smiling at her younger self, "is it possible you think me so irresponsible?"

Irresponsible? Having just confessed the magnitude of her plans, including the preparation of every member of her staff, did the Nineteenth Mother merit the charge of irresponsibility? Shame filled Symone as her thoughts raced on, trying desperately to solve the puzzle, certain that a solution existed. She fashioned us specifically to her needs, each of us tried and tested, weapons forged to help her in this, the desperate ploy of a Mother who finds herself rejected by her people. I, too, have been molded, first by Kazur, now by her, although for what purpose . . . and then the world about her collapsed. The way lay before her, wide and beckoning, but Symone was sick with dread.

Her silent appeal rose upward, past the rafters and the roof of the tower chamber, shooting up toward the stars and the moon floating benignly on the sea of the night sky. Anguish filled her soul; lost and alone she looked into the soulful eyes of She-Who-Was-Magda. As had happened before, the tuning fork was struck, and they spoke mind to mind.

"I issued the call tonight. It came as no surprise when you answered. Everything rests within you now, untapped until my passing unlocks the secrets of the ones who came before."

"But I am unworthy!"

"I suspect all of us were. I, myself, am an accident of history, a limited adept who screamed aloud at the pain of transference. Yours was accomplished with little more than a growing sense of wonder, a flowering of the mind as you absorbed the combined memories of all who came before."

"Why must you do this?" Symone pleaded, earning a quick rebuke.

"You are not the only one who loves this city! I adore Pelion as I do life itself, and I will give my life willingly, even happily, if I can preserve what I took a vow to protect."

No more words were shared between them, although they lingered for awhile in harmony, the old woman grateful for the younger woman's company after thirty years of solitude. At last they parted to enter the waking world and take up their duties.

"It is accomplished. Symone will don the black robes."

Galen's usually ruddy complexion matched the whiteness of his beard. Stubborn to the end, he battled the inflexible logic of the Mothers of Pelion.

"Nothin's writ in stone. Ye canna deny yer presence may daunt'em, and we fear for naught."

"Of course," She-Who-Was-Magda agreed, anxious that Galen not grieve.

Overcome by emotions that robbed him of the crusty exterior that fooled everyone except his mate and the people now present in this room, Galen buried his head in his arms.

"How much time do we have?" Esslar asked quietly.

"Time enough," the Nineteenth Mother promised.

Esslar blinked back tears. A calm, unfettered silence descended on the tower chamber.

Four of us against the world, mused She-Who-Was-Symone, the Twentieth Mother of Pelion. A warrior, a mystic, a scholar, and one whose martyrdom might make all things possible.

FOR A HUNDRED years there had been Gatherings amongst the ernani; never had there been one quite like this. During the past week, the personnel of the Maze, from the men who hefted animal carcasses from the supply gate to the kitchens to the women who scrubbed laundry in enormous copper tubs, their arms elbow-deep in suds, from the greybeard who for fifty years had seen to the lighting of the torches at the blast of the evening trumpet to the bald-domed secretary of the Nineteenth Mother herself, talked of nothing else. The lucky ones found occasion to scurry up the stairs that led to the Hall of Gathering to catch a glimpse of the wonders inside.

At first it seemed pure chaos, as did the peculiar requests coming down the stairs with increasing frequency as the days wore on. "Might we borrow the largest cooking pot available?" brought guffaws from the kitchen staff and complaints from those designated to lug it upstairs. A fairly simple request for odd pieces of fabric brought on a diligent two-day search among the supply rooms and ended in a decision by the supply steward that every shelf merited a dusting. As the lists grew longer and more difficult to provide, the women requesting items unavailable in the store rooms, an exasperated Remy assigned a staff member as liaison to the ernani with frequent warnings that costs be kept to a minimum. Despite his fears to the contrary, the items sought were neither expensive nor particularly hard to find. Rushes cut from the banks of a stream, chunks of sandstone, goose and hawk feathers, hollow reeds, a length of brass tubing, and a garter snake borrowed from the butcher's son, were duly delivered, as were armloads of fragrant branches of pine and fir.

Speculation as to the exact nature of the ernani's plans ran wild, although the word being whispered knowingly among the majority of personnel was "theatrics." If questioned, the women would smile mysterious smiles, then continue their work, twelve pairs of hands busily plying needles, pounding nails and moving furniture, humming snatches of unfamiliar tunes as they worked. Additional tables were transported from the library to the dayroom. When their number totaled twelve, the idea of amateur theatrics was dismissed. It was the butcher's son who supplied the solution after turning over his pet to a woman who, much to his amazement, neither shrieked nor shuddered, but wrapped the snake around her wrist like a living bracelet of smooth green ribbon and thanked him heartily.

"It's a fair!" the boy announced with the breezy confidence of the young.

And a fair it was.

The idea, strangely enough, came not from Zuniga or Becca, the unquestionable leaders of the group, but from Ulkemene. Sweetly, with earnest longing, she described an evening entertainment that called up memories in all their minds. After much discussion, her suggestion was unanimously approved. Twelve tables became twelve booths, arranged around the walls of the dayroom with a central space left free for demonstrations. Some were decorated with the arts and crafts of the places the ernani had left behind, others were spare of any ornamentation save pungent boughs of evergreen, since it was these booths that would offer up samples of native foods and exhibitions in carving sandstone, feathering arrows, weaving rush baskets, tooling leather, and flute-making.

Until yesterday, everyone save messengers or those making deliveries were barred from the room, although every worker in the Maze found an opportunity to peek through the crack between the wide double-doors. Today, during the women's scheduled visit to the arena, the cleaning staff was granted admittance in order to clean and polish the wooden floors in preparation for the night's festivities. A single ernani remained in the dayroom, standing near the windows with her head bowed. Respectful of her privacy, the cleaning crew went about their work with quiet industry, eyeing her from time to time with frank curiosity. Some minutes later, the doors swung open and a man with many rolls of paper stuffed under his arm walked over to an empty table situated against the eastern wall. At his approach, what had seemed to be a grey rug let out a woof and sat up on its haunches, the woman turning to call out an eager greeting. When they saw her take a hesitant step forward, her arms stretched out in his direction, a welcoming smile on a lovely face marred by unseeing eyes, they lowered their heads to their work and tried not to stare as the man put her palm to his lips.

They'd all heard rumors about a blind ernani, most of them passed on by the food-servers in the women's refectory. None of them had ever seen her before, although news of the stories she told the women during the long winter afternoons sparked some interest among them. Full of life she seemed to them, and more than passing fair, graceful in movement and quick with a laugh or a jest. The dog, for indeed it was a dog despite its immense size, watched with ears upright as the pair began preparing their booth.

After a great deal of hammering, a frame was formed out of odds and ends of lumber. Next, the man selected several lengths of cloth from a stack near the door and began draping the fabric in a series of folds, attaching them to several upright posts with cross pieces attached at regular intervals. The woman assisted by handing him nails and holding up the cloth while he worked, both of them conversing in low voices. Once, the man swore loudly when the hammer hit his thumb rather than the nail-head, the woman laughing merrily as he placed his thumb in his mouth and glared at her.

At first they thought him stern and imperious of manner, for he frowned as he strode by them, his dark brows knitted with annoyance. In time they forgave his arrogance, their opinion tempered by his gentleness with her, the way he nodded thoughtfully when she voiced a suggestion and the ease with which they worked together. When the last fold was arranged to his satisfaction and he stepped back to admire his work, they looked up from the floor long enough to stare in amazement at what appeared to be a three-masted schooner in full sail. The tabletop served as a deck of sorts; behind it rose three poles rigged with ivory sails.

The ship completed, the man went to work unrolling the large pieces of parchment he'd placed on a nearby booth for safekeeping and tacked them to the frame he'd built. The dog accompanied his mistress over to the large cupboards against the western wall, waiting patiently as she pulled out a drawer and ran her fingers over what lay inside. When the cleaners looked up again, for they'd finished the floor and scattered over the room to dust window sills and sweep hearths, it was to see the table covered with a length of midnight-blue fabric upon which were arranged small pieces of white, hand-woven lace, resting like snowflakes on the ocean of dark cloth. One observer, who tarried near the eastern windows to wipe away some imaginary specs of dust from the sill, heard the woman ask softly, "Are you content?" and saw a flush rise to her cheeks as the man whispered his response in her ear. A sense of urgency seemed to overcome them as they hurried to replace the tools and clear the area around the booth. This done, they made for the door, the dog trotting contentedly behind them.

"They're maps," observed one fellow after the door was safely closed and they could talk freely among themselves, "and finely drawn, as good as the ones mounted in the Great Library."

"Cinthean lace!" crooned a cleaning woman, reaching out to stroke an impossibly intricate web of white threads. "Who would have thought it possible?"

"The price they'd fetch in the shops could feed my family 'til summer," another woman remarked candidly, "although despite the talent of her fingers, I'd not trade places with her for the world."

"He doesn't seem to mind," the first woman observed with a knowing smile, for she'd been young herself once and fancied she understood why they hurried to the privacy of their cell in the belly of the Maze.

They chatted among themselves for a time, wandering around the room to inspect the other booths, commenting on the objects on display.

"It's like the world in miniature," observed the man who had admired the maps. "See, they've arranged the booths according to the compass. The north wall is the Land of the Lapith; to the west is New Agave and the Western Ridge; south is Botheswallow and the Gulf of Swiasa; east is the Tellas River and beyond that, Endlin."

"I've heard they've been preparing food from all the different regions, everything from squirrel stew to stuffed plovers. One of them brewed some kind of liquor by boiling and condensing table wine."

A shudder passed through them at the thought of ruining good wine. The evening trumpet brought them quickly to attention, and they gathered up their brooms, mops, waxes and rags.

"Where's Mikel?" asked the first woman after counting heads and finding one of her crew missing. The others glanced around the room without much interest. The youngest of them, a good-natured lad who was particularly drawn to a booth displaying leather goods, answered without lifting his eyes from the hand-tooled saddle he was admiring.

"The last time I saw him he was over by the maps."

"Well, he's taken his things with him, so I suppose he's left for the supply room already. It's strange he didn't say anything," the senior member of the crew confessed to her co-worker of some fifteen years, "not like him at all."

They lit the fires before they left since the room grew chilly now that the sun had sunk below the horizon and would be icy cold by the time the ernani arrived after the evening meal. Later they would remember that Mikel was not waiting for them in the supply room when they arrived to put away their equipment. They shrugged it off at the time, anxious to head for home and families after a full day's work, forgetting everything but the threat of low-lying clouds heavy with snow.

None of them noticed, not even the man who praised the display of charts, that a narrow strip from the lower right-hand corner of one of the maps had been torn away by a careful hand. Even if he'd noticed, he would have thought it signified nothing other than a simple mishap in the unrolling and mounting of the maps on the wooden frame. And what difference did it make, all things considered, when every map bore the same, almost illegible scrawl? And who would think that the time-honored phrase of the craftsman would be enough to unleash the events to follow?

The sole person to realize the importance of that phrase hurried over the paved avenues of Pelion, the hood of his cloak pulled over his head against the falling snow, careful not to slip on the icy flagstones, his mood jubilant, his fingers repeatedly checking the inside pocket of his vest.

There, in the warm depository of that knitted vest, lodged a scrap of parchment ripped from the bottom of a finely-drawn, hand-colored map, a single line of script proclaiming, "Sandur Kwanlonhon made this."

Chapter 18

Letters in the Flame

RAUROS WHINED HIS misery, pressing his nose against her hand and rubbing himself against her skirts. Accustomed to accompanying Alyssa everywhere, he couldn't understand why he was being left behind.

"Can't we take him with us?"

"The hall will be crowded and noisy," Pentaur replied from the doorway. "We can't risk his reaction if someone should brush up against you by mistake."

Her fingers curling in the wiry coat, Alyssa knelt down to murmur farewell, promising a speedy return. When a moist tongue licked her cheek, guilt struck her hard.

"We need not go, Alyssa."

Surprised, she hesitated before dismissing Sandur's offer as mere politeness. Surely he must long (as she did) to enjoy the ernani's first evening of joint fellowship since entering the Maze! The rules did not require their presence; even so, everyone would be there, eager to celebrate the end of the rule of privacy. Shaking her head, for the lure of seeing her friends through Sandur's eyes was greater than her remorse at abandoning Rauros, she rose to her feet, ashamed that Pentaur had seen her tears and wondering if he thought her foolish. A familiar hand gasped her arm at the elbow, and she walked out of the cell and toward the Hall of Gathering.

LIT BY TORCHES, candles, braziers, and four blazing hearths, the Hall of Gathering glowed and hummed with activity. Outside, flakes of snow drifted past the face of the waxing moon. Inside, spring had taken up a brief but energetic residence, kindling vitality and a wealth of goodwill among the assembled ernani and their honored guests. If there were grudges against Pwyll, they were forgotten with the first sips of his native brew. Rather than dodging blows in the arena, Pwyll underwent an attack of another sort—one he showed every sign of enjoying—the men slapping him on the back, loudly voicing their appreciation and demanding his recipe. If Zuniga sometimes rode rough-shod over the women, they forgave her a hundred-fold as they watched her blue-black body, sinewy and supple as the snake with which she danced, gliding and swaying in a series of seemingly endless loops and circles. The room held its breath except for a single ernani who whispered intermittently into the ear of a woman who leaned her head against his shoulder.

No torch burned so brightly as Alyssa did that night. An hour ago she'd been tearful, a bad omen sparking Sandur's offer to remain in the cell. For days he'd dreaded this Gathering, picturing the pitying looks of the men as they beheld her blindness. That the men might pity Alyssa was barely acceptable—that they might pity Sandur was well nigh unendurable. With this in mind, he paused at the double-doors, wishing desperately they'd never left the cell, when Kokor strode up. Bracing himself, Sandur waited for the mountain man's reaction.

"You're late!" Kokor announced, placing an arm around the waist of a tiny, bird-like creature beside him. "This is Ulkemene," he said by way of introduction, adding with a welcoming smile, "and you must be Alyssa. I am Kokor of the Painted Caverns, who journeyed with Sandur from the east."

Try as he might, Sandur could discern nothing but honest interest in Kokor's expression, an interest Alyssa evidently returned.

"You're the sword-master, are you not?" she asked, her expression ripe with laughter.

"An advanced beginner at best," Kokor replied with his usual modesty, and a friendship was born.

Through the introductions and the many genial conversations that followed, Sandur watched the miracle of acceptance repeat itself. For forty passages of the sun across the sky he'd shunned Alyssa for no other reason than her blindness, yet these men, most of whom he considered uncivilized, even savage, accepted her without hesitation. If he read anything on their faces, it was an awe he shared at the radiance emanating from her, as if she, the one who lived in darkness, had become a source of light. Tendrils of hair floated around her upturned face, her braids a halo of spun red-gold crowning a head floating on the slender column of her neck. In the privacy of the cell, only hours ago, he'd lifted up the weight of her hair, still damp from her bath, and kissed the nape of her neck, running his lips over moist skin fragrant with lavender oil.

Earlier that afternoon, after they completed their work on the fair booth, they'd dogged Pentaur's heels like guilty children as he led them back to the cell, listening at the door until the bolt slipped into place and the monitor's footsteps faded away. Falling to the rug in front of the hearth, heedless of their clothing, they'd joined together with reckless abandon, achieving a quick, violent release, then lay panting as Rauros paced nervously around them, upset that they had not used the bed.

Perspiring and breathless from their exertions, a bath followed. Sandur went first, stepping into the tub while she brushed out her hair. To his initial surprise and eventual delight, she joined him. Could anything surpass the sight of Alyssa rising from the bath water, eyes closed, lips slightly parted, oval-nailed fingers gripping the sides of the tub as he moved beneath her, the smooth skin of her inner thighs rubbing against his flanks? By the time they finished, the cell was afloat, the hearth flooded, and the Gathering nearly upon them.

Pinning his hopes on the festive nature of tonight's event, he offered to help her dress, knowing before he did so he risked offending her. She could fend for herself, she informed him, her expression stormy and her chin held high. Exasperated as he was by her stubbornness, he controlled his temper, refusing to admit defeat.

"Why wouldst thou deny me such a simple pleasure?" To her answering frown he said, "Dost thou think because I may not braid my own hair, my fingers have no skill?" When she shook her head slowly, her expression hidden behind damp hair, he added, "Thou must trust me, Alyssa."

"I do, Sandur," she replied evenly.

To others it might seem a small thing—to accept help when none was requested; to Sandur it held immense significance. For the first time, Alyssa allowed him to help her in ways she could not help herself. As he worked, lacing the amethyst gown and draping the heavy folds of the skirt, he learned the joy of caring for someone other than himself, the intimacy a healer shares with a patient or a parent with a child, an intimacy he had never known. An azure scarf, embroidered with threads of spun gold, placed in his pack seven moons ago by a thoughtful servant, was draped across her breast and tied in a knot at her hip, the long silken fringes falling almost to her knees. When at last he finished braiding her hair and circled her to admire the shades of blue against lavender, the metallic fibers of the scarf accentuating the glints of gold in her hair, he bent down to kiss the nape of her neck, her fragrance filling his nostrils, her beauty a tonic to his misgivings of what this night might hold.

TAKING A TENTATIVE sip of Pwyll's brandywine, Sandur experienced a taste unlike anything he'd ever known—oaken-flavored sunshine, mellow and full-bodied. In their frenzy to repair the cell and dress, they'd given up hope of preparing a meal, both of them empty-bellied, their stomachs rumbling with hunger. Now they were stuffed, Sandur with Draupadi's rice-filled plovers and Alyssa with two bowls of Yossi's squirrel stew. A nudge in his ribs brought Sandur quickly to attention.

"What is Eddo doing?" Alyssa hissed at him between lips that did not move. Startled, Sandur looked toward the center of the room and nearly choked on his wine. Stocky, short-waisted Eddo looked a buffoon in the ill-fitting garb issued to all male ernani. Stripped to a clout wrapped around his loins, adorned with tattoos and feathered bracelets circling wrists and ankles, he seemed a figure out of legend. Everyone stood with mouths agape as he worked his magic, eating fire and spewing out tongues of flames, emulating the powers of his smoking mountain. As with Zuniga's dance, Sandur supplied a rapid description, enjoying the fire-eating exhibition all the more because of the wonder he read on Alyssa's face.

Eddo's demonstration finished, they wandered from booth to booth, tasting and browsing their way across the room. Pausing by a booth along the northern wall, Sandur watched Jincin carve a lump of sandstone into a sleek, blunt-nosed seal, its tail wrapped around its plump body like a house-cat napping in front of the grate.

The red-haired man looked up from his work, eyeing Alyssa from beneath his straight bangs (for the unruly hair and beard were trimmed now), and asked, "Want to touch?"

Alyssa's fingers trembled as Sandur placed them on the stone.

"A seal! A sleeping seal! Jincin, you're a master!"

"Aye, he is at that," Hanania observed proudly, appearing from the other side of the booth and nodding companionably to Sandur, "although he insists his father is a better carver."

"Take it," Jincin said haltingly. "I make another."

"I've nothing to give you in return!"

"If you've a piece of lace, I'll call it an even trade," offered Hanania with a sly grin. "Ulkemene's the only one who shows any promise as a lace-maker. By the time she finishes her first piece, we'll all be home again."

Sandur stood slightly apart as the trade was completed, overhearing an exchange between Alyssa and Hanania.

"Where will you and Jincin go after you leave the Maze?"

"We talk about it often, but we've made no decision. My mother's alone and her health is bad; a neighbor took her in when I left with the Searcher. I want to go with Jincin. His people are nomads, you know, and follow the caribou." A note of sadness entered her voice. "I've always fretted indoors and felt happiest under the open sky. His way of life would suit me, but my mother wouldn't survive the first winter."

Whatever Alyssa intended to reply was interrupted by the arrival of Pharlookas and a sharp-featured woman with the slender body of a boy.

"Hey, Sandur," the smiling giant boomed, "we saw your maps!"

"The ship is wonderful," the woman said, sticking out her hand. "I'm Draupadi of Droghedan."

Her palm was dry and hard, covered with horny calluses representing years of hard labor. Sandur returned the compliment.

"Your plovers were excellent. I am Sandur."

"Is it true you're a prince?"

He'd thought himself inured to forward women. Still, her boldness took him off-guard. Fearful he was being mocked, he drew himself up to his full height in order to stare her down only to be saved by Alyssa's quick wit.

"Do you doubt my word, Draupadi? Must a prince wear silken robes and jewels on every finger and toe?"

Draupadi sulked, running the tip of her shoe over the cracks between the boards of the hardwood floor.

"The princes in your stories always wear jewels. He's only got one earring, and it's ever so small."

"I've a blue diamond taken from the mines at Kilput," Sandur offered hopefully, unsure as to the direction of the conversation and decidedly uncomfortable at being the center of attention. Draupadi's skeptical gaze swept over him again.

"Why don't you wear it, then?"

Outraged that this chit should challenge him, he tensed and nearly exploded. Again, Alyssa saved the day, her face alight with fun.

"This particular prince doesn't wear his diamond on his finger. He wears it in his nose!"

Pharlookas let loose a belly laugh at the look of stunned disbelief on Draupadi's face. Hanania was nearly in tears, and even Jincin, who understood only a small part of the joke, was smiling broadly. Nonplussed by their amusement, although he guessed that Alyssa had kept him from making a fool of himself, Sandur was relieved when into the fray swaggered Yossi, with what looked to be a halter thrown carelessly over his shoulder. Beside him walked, or rather glided, a statuesque woman attired in a gown similar in cut and fit to Alyssa's. An embroidered headband circled her brow while her braids reached well below her hips.

Yossi was several years her junior, Sandur decided, although the difference in age seemed not to bother the mountain man at all as he proudly announced, "This is Becca."

Introductions were made all round. In the pause that followed, Sandur felt Becca's eyes upon him. He searched for something to say.

"What's the meaning of the halter, Yossi? I thought you had no use for horses."

The mountain man shrugged.

"Lynsaya traded it for one of Becca's gowns. I thought you might be interested in swapping it for one of your maps." A mischievous look came over him as he added, "It would look fine on Seal."

"Seal?" Jincin asked, obviously confused. Yossi provided an explanation as he handed over the halter to Sandur for inspection.

"Seal is Sandur's stallion, a big grey with silver dapples."

While Hanania tried (without much success) to explain "dapples" to Jincin, Sandur examined the halter. Finding the leather supple and fine-grained, the style unmistakably Lapithian, Sandur marveled at the craftsmanship, which exceeded anything he'd ever seen in the markets of the Abalone district.

"Lynsaya said to remind you that her tribe exports the rejects. They keep the best pieces for themselves."

Admiring the astuteness with which Yossi bargained, Sandur cemented the trade.

"Which map do you want?"

"The one with the route marked between Pelion and Botheswallow."

Swallowing his surprise, Sandur nodded.

"You are shocked, I think, that Yossi chooses my people," Becca interjected quietly. All around Sandur, conversation came to an abrupt halt. There could be no doubt as to whom she addressed. Alyssa stirred beside him, turning her head in Becca's direction, her fingers working at the fringes of the scarf, but made no reply. Feeling trapped without really knowing why, Sandur looked to Yossi for help, hoping the mountain man could control his woman's tongue. Here, too, he was met with silence.

Rescue came in the form of Dorian, one of the many teachers invited to the ernani's first Gathering. Light-footed as a rope-walker with the mobile face of a clown, he broke into the group surrounding Sandur and proceeded to shake everyone's hand while his mate, a moon-faced woman whose night-black hair bore a single streak of purest white, looked on, her eyes flicking from face to face. Affable and quick-tongued, the Master Chartist seemed perfectly at ease with his students, exchanging insults with Pharlookas and laughing out a protest when Yossi pressed a brimming bowl of squirrel stew into his hands.

"My stomach remembers mountain food only too well! Hot going down, hotter coming out—far too rich for an old man's digestion."

"When did you eat mountain fare?" Yossi demanded. "I thought you hailed from Pelion?"

Dorian darted a contrite glance at his mate, then shrugged and smiled.

"They've caught us, Fenja."

A confession followed, that of a Chartist entering the cell of a woman from the Eastern Isles, of friends made in the Maze (one of them, Altug by name, serving up squirrel stew at every opportunity), and of another first Gathering some thirty-odd years ago. Hungry for information, excited by the presence of two who had once been as they were, the ernani loosed a rash of questions with such rapidity that Dorian was forced to beg for silence.

"One at a time, one at a time! Have you no pity for a simple map-maker and a drummer?" His face softened as he registered their disappointment.

"You know it's forbidden to speak of the Path. We'll gladly tell you, though, of our lives once we left Pelion."

"Where is your island, Dorian?" asked Becca.

"First of all, 'tis Fenja's isle, although 'twas my home for twenty-five years. But to answer your question, Salmydessus lies seventy leagues south of Tek-By-The-Sea. There are forty-six islands to be exact, some no bigger than a strip of sand and a palm tree. We lived on Salmydessus proper, the largest and most populated island, until eight years ago."

"Why did you leave?" Yossi asked, a wistful look in his eyes, as though he strove to pierce the thick hazes which linger on the peaks of the Sarujian Mountains until well past midday. The Master Chartist hesitated, and something unspoken seemed to pass between him and his mate. They all sensed it, permission asked and granted in one instantaneous moment of communication. Fenja took over the telling of their tale, the accents of her native lands still heavy on her tongue.

"We lived there in great happiness and serenity. Dorian explored the surrounding islands, making the first detailed maps of the area, and together we taught my people to read and write the southern tongue."

As she continued, Sandur found himself remembering Salmydessus, a bow-shaped volcanic island with a deep natural harbor nestled in the bow's curve, an ideal spot for trading vessels to set anchor. The major export was a rare plant used as a fixative for dye, extremely valuable because of the difficulties of harvesting its berries at the exact moment of ripeness. Caught up in his training, he listed from memory their other trading goods: balsa, pineapple cloth, baskets and mats, the latter woven with the Salmydessian signature of three concentric circles surrounded by a square. His thoughts wandered until Fenja reached the conclusion of her tale.

"Everything ended five years ago. We had a single child, Haji, a boy of great promise who, when he reached manhood, wanted nothing else but to enter the Maze. We sent him to the mainland with a trusted friend. Some time later, both friend and son disappeared."

In the quiet that followed, everyone sensed the grief locked around Fenja's heart.

"Could the sea have claimed them?" Alyssa asked softly, the sound of her voice reminding Sandur that she'd not spoken in a long while.

"We know they made it safely to shore; one of my father's friends gave them food and shelter the first night. They left Tek-By-The-Sea the next morning, intending on journeying west, and were never seen again."

Fenja's eyes traveled from face to face until they came to rest on Sandur.

"Dorian searched for the better part of a year. All he gained for his efforts was a bit of gossip whispered to him in a tavern."

There was no need for Fenja to finish her story. The ernani saw it in both their faces: the mother's torment, her unwillingness to live among the places her son played as a child; the father's guilt, his inability to witness her unhappiness. Respectful of their grief, the crowd drifted toward more temperate climes than those of Jincin's frozen tundra, for they were chilled by Fenja's recital, hearing in it the pain of lost homes, lost lives. The colored maps bedecking the easternmost booth, once objects of veneration, reminded them of the vast distances which would separate them from their families, of children who might never know their grandparents, of friends they might never see again.

Only Alyssa seemed unmoved.

"What was the piece of gossip, Fenja?"

The black eyes of the one-time ernani from the Eastern Isles narrowed as she considered the blind woman of Cinthea and the unsmiling prince of Endlin. "Only this: 'Ask the Tehran of the Kwanlonhon.'" She stated it flatly, without emotion, before adding in a much gentler voice, "It's a hard thing to be raised to duty, is it not, Sandur?"

Before Sandur could reply, even before he could consider what answer he should make, whether to call the man in the tavern a liar or commiserate with them over the loss of their son, the Mistress of Ceremonies called for their attention.

"We've another hour before the torches are put out," Zuniga announced, her hands outstretched for silence. "One demonstration remains, and since it's of a quieter nature, we thought it should come last of all. When you've seated yourselves, we'll begin."

Chairs were drawn up hurriedly, although many preferred sitting on the floor. By the time Sandur looked around for Alyssa, she'd drifted away without making her excuses. Unsettled by Fenja's question, troubled by Alyssa's defection, he wandered over to a nearby booth and leaned against it, wishing this evening would end and end quickly.

The women began to chant, "A story! A story!" as Zuniga led Alyssa forward to take her place on a three-legged stool.

"In my homeland," Alyssa began, settling her skirts around her, "the bards gather each winter to recite the epics, the long poems that comprise the memories of the years of before. Tonight, I've chosen an excerpt from one of those tales, the story of a wanderer who journeys homeward after a ten-year absence."

The ernani murmured their appreciation of her choice, for who were they but wanderers, strangers in a strange land who yearned for hearth and home? Sensing their eagerness, the blind bard of Cinthea recited the opening phrases:

> Sing in me, Muse, and through me tell the story
> of that man skilled in all ways of contending,
> the wanderer, harried for years on end.

> Begin when all the rest who left behind them
> headlong death in battle or at sea
> had long ago returned, while he alone still hungered
> for home and wife . . .

Try as he might, Sandur could not concentrate. Moodily, he gazed out over the crowd, picking out the dark heads of Vlatla and Tibor, sitting cross-legged on rush mats, the marsh-dweller's arm draped around the river woman's shoulders. Kokor and Ulkemene, too, sat side by side, both of them intent on Alyssa's tale.

"Sandur Kwanlonhon?" someone said, and before he could turn his head to see who whispered in his ear, a piece of parchment was shoved into his hand. Staring at the handwriting, his first thought was to wonder how his uncle had found him. The soft pad of departing feet brought his head up. The messenger had vanished, lost in the crowd of servants, guests, and ernani surrounding the storyteller. Slipping behind a booth, careful that no one noticed him, he cracked the seal and spread out the parchment, reading it by the light of one of the braziers. A second reading followed, then a third and a fourth. When at last he lifted his eyes to stare out the casement windows situated on the eastern wall, a permanent chill embedded itself in his heart. The snow lay in drifts over the sleeping garden outside, for spring remained a wistful promise, and winter reigned outside the Maze. How long he stood there he never knew, although the bard finally reached the end of her tale.

> Now from his breast into his eyes the ache
> of longing mounted, and he wept at last,
> his dear wife, clear and faithful, in his arms,
> longed for as the earth is longed for by a swimmer
> spent in rough water where his ship went down
> under Poseidon's blows, gale winds and tons of sea.
> Few men can keep alive through a big surf
> to crawl, clotted with brine, on kindly beaches
> in joy, in joy, knowing the abyss behind:
> and so she too rejoiced, her gaze upon her husband,
> her white arms round him pressed as though forever.

But poetry is not life, and this wanderer's eyes were parched wastelands as he held the letter to the flames, watching it curl and convulse itself like the death-throws of a viper. At the sound of applause, Sandur started, then straightened his shoulders, answering Fenja's question in the deepest recesses of his soul.

"Tis a hard thing indeed to be raised to duty."

* * *

THREE PAIRS OF eyes watched the Tehran's sa'ab move through the crowd of well-wishers, shouldering his way past them as if he, and not the woman beside him, was blind. In that rigid face, the jaw set and the lips compressed into a thin line, Dorian and Fenja read the success of their mission. A personal request by the Nineteenth Mother brought them to the Gathering. Nothing else could have persuaded Fenja to enter the place where by everything that was just, her son should have received the greatest of gifts. The events of this wintry night strained her self-control to the breaking-point, for in each ernani, energetic and fearless, she saw Haji's youthful earnestness, heard him describe his best-loved dream, and felt the grief sweep her away to the dark places where she envisioned his limp, lifeless body shoved into a carelessly dug grave, his bones the food of jackals and crows, the promise of his manhood lost to her and to all the world.

Worst of all was the moment she recognized Sandur, for she had been transported to another Gathering, watching from the musician's platform as Manthur swung Aethra's frail body into his arms, reading in Aethra's eyes the sure and certain knowledge that tonight she and her prince of Endlin would render up their final gift. The Nineteenth Mother warned her, but even so, she was unprepared for the feelings of hatred aroused by the rows of tightly braided hair, the golden earring, the heavy brow and flared nostrils of Manthur's firstborn. It was Dorian who sustained her, maintaining an unbroken stream of private reassurances as she watched Sandur enter the hall.

"No matter what your eyes may tell you, he's not his father. That is our purpose, to make sure he'll not take Manthur's path."

"How can he not know what is common knowledge to all of us? Has he not eyes? Can he not see that he is the only one among them from the far east? Does he not wonder that in places as distant as Droghedan the name of Pelion is known, while in Endlin it remains unspoken?"

"He spent his boyhood in the harem, his youth on trading vessels. In the years since reaching manhood, he's passed five, maybe six moons on the mainland and never far from the Kwanlonhon citadel. Look at him. Look deep and show me what you see."

And so she looked, putting aside her hatred of the father in order to view the son. Her first impression was one of instant dislike, for in his hostile face and imperious manner she saw the clansmen of Endlin descending like locusts on her people, offering in exchange for their goods not the knowledge they craved, the books and charts that would enable them to travel, to learn, to improve their way of life, but barter taken from other lands. They produced nothing, these clansmen of Endlin, making themselves rich by denying others the learning that made their wealth possible. Sandur might not wear the silken robes of a clansman, but he was a clansman still.

Only when the mountain man (for so she identified the ernani with the topknot and mustache who reminded her of Altug) approached him, calling out a greeting, did she see his stiffness depart, and then, in the next moment, when the tension around his mouth relaxed and his lips curved upward in the haunting smile of Aethra of Pelion, could she see in Sandur anything other than the Tehran's sa'ab.

From that moment on she saw it all, the air of reserve which clung to him, setting him apart from the others. She saw as well, with stunning clarity, that he was frightened, shy of meeting the women and equally ill at ease with the men. Not for him the brashness of the one called Yossi or the hearty good nature of the giant named Pharlookas. Even the red-haired carver laughed with the group while Sandur stood tense and uncertain, unable to join in their games. Is this pride, she wondered, or has he never experienced the joys of fellowship? And then she heard the woman of Botheswallow's question and saw naked fear race across his features. There, in the bleakness of his eyes was writ a devastation that caused her to ask Dorian to intervene, anything to erase her vision of Sandur's pain.

He fears for her, the blind woman garbed in shades of lavender and blue, and well he should, Fenja thought with an inner shudder. Intuition told her that Sandur and Alyssa had never discussed their future, never brought up the painful subject of the life they would live beyond the walls of the Maze. His partner's silence spoke volumes, her slender fingers entwined in the long fringes of the gold-encrusted scarf as the others agonized over the same decisions Fenja and Dorian faced a generation ago. Fenja's knowledge of Endlin might be limited, but she could guess all too well what life would hold for a blind woman in the citadel of the Kwanlonhon. Shunned, spat upon, her presence a constant reminder of infirmities which threatened the clansmen's cherished notions of cultural and physical superiority, hers would be a miserable existence, ostracized and despised by every member of the six clans.

And so, in accordance with her mission, Fenja informed the son that his father was an accomplice to murder, not just of her child, but of countless children of countless mothers, of anyone who sought to leave the empire of Endlin and journey to a place called Pelion. She spoke the words without rancor or blame, her hatred of the tyranny he represented blunted by the certain knowledge that Sandur, too, would experience a grief not unlike her own. For in his face, so like his father's save for the sweetness of his mother's smile, Fenja read Sandur's tragedy and gave it a name. Duty, damnable duty, would be his downfall.

* * *

ONE OTHER PERSON in the Hall of Gathering noticed the departure of the Tehran's sa'ab, although he himself was careful to slink away unseen. As he made his way down the back stairs, dodging the other servants, keeping his face in the shadows, he rejoiced.

"No longer need I labor for these foreigners, these ernani who must be expelled from Pelion lest the walls crumble around us. We'll burn the maps and bar the gates, keeping ourselves safe from intruders who would steal away our greatness. Damn the ernani," cursed Mikel of Pelion, his pockets heavy with the unaccustomed weight of gold, "and damn the braided easterner most of all!"

Chapter 19

A Dog Howls

"Name?"

"Haji."

"References?"

"My father, Dorian of Pelion, a Master in the Guild of Chartists. My mother, Fenja, formerly of the Eastern Isles, currently a teacher in the School of Music."

Having scribbled away at the contract without bothering to look up, painfully aware of the line of prospective clients stretching across the snowy field and back toward the northern gates, the mention of a familiar name roused Labicus' curiosity. A trader's success depended on accurate maps, and Dorian was one of the few Chartists who'd mapped anything east of the provinces. Raising his head, Labicus took a long, speculative look at the man standing in front of the trading table marked "For Points East."

"Word has it Dorian's son disappeared some years ago."

"Mere rumor, I assure you," the fellow replied evenly. "The distances are such that I visit my parents infrequently. If you've heard of my father, then you know he teaches within the Maze. He thought it best for me to depart without delay."

Labicus nodded and resumed writing, silently ticking off information as his pencil flew. The folds of a hooded cloak might obscure this fellow's features, but after thirty years in the trade, Labicus prided himself on his powers of observation. Accent: definitely eastern in origin. Dress: an expensive fur-lined cloak, an absolute necessity for a thin-blooded islander forced to travel during the dead of winter. Character: aloof, yet polite. Reason for travel: the same as everyone else. Cursing Adrastus and the entire Guild Assembly, the scarcity of horses and the heavy-bottomed slate-grey clouds gathering overhead, Labicus blew on his fingers to warm them.

"Destination?"

"Tek-by-the-Sea."

Here was a departure! His hand was so accustomed to writing the names of Cottyo, Cinthea, and Cyme or leaving the entry blank, he'd almost given up asking the question. Fully half his clients had no particular destination in mind other than traveling as far from Pelion as their savings would allow. He'd sent his own family packing five days ago, a runner sent ahead to warn an old friend who'd retired to a spacious house in the west country that Labicus was calling in a long-standing debt. Some traders doubted the seriousness of the situation; not so Labicus. Exactly ten hours after the most recent (and perhaps final) meeting of the League of Independent Traders, Labicus strapped the last piece of baggage on his best pack-mule, re-checked the girth-straps on the saddles, issued last minute instructions to his youngest apprentice, and bade his mate farewell, trying not to notice the tears in her eyes.

"Come with us," she begged, hugging their three-year-old daughter as if she held life itself on the pommel of her saddle. "If it's as bad as you say, what will be gained by you staying?"

"I'm not staying," he repeated for the hundredth time. "None of us are staying."

By nature an undemonstrative man, he decided to ignore the inquisitive eyes of the apprentice and his eight-year-old son long enough to deposit a chaste kiss on his mate's cheek. "Others depend on me, others not so lucky as us. Anyone not city-born must exit the city on pain of death. They must go and I must take them. I'm doing what I gave my word I'd do."

He flattered himself it was the kiss that quieted her. Whatever the cause, she was dry-eyed when she reined her horse around and kicked him into a trot, gesturing for her son to follow. Labicus watched their departure from the battlements, scanning the dawn-lit skies for signs of snow, wondering how long it would be until he, too, could travel west.

The eastern routes being his specialty, to the east he must go, taking with him the frightened and the dispossessed. Such was the League's decision, and after hearing the testimony of the woman Symone, a representative of the Nineteenth Mother's Council, the decision was unanimous. Now he sat, a man of his word, booking passages for clients unused to travel, babes screaming in their mothers' arms, solemn-eyed children holding onto their fathers' hands, while Pelion crumbled about his ears.

"Baggage?"

"My own tent and gear."

"Animals?"

"A stallion and a pack-horse."

Damn it all, where had this foreigner found not one, but two horses? The league had most of the apprentices and half the journeymen out ransacking the countryside, buying up mules, donkeys, oxen, anything with four legs that could either be ridden, carry baggage, or pull a cart. Labicus tried not to think about the exorbitant fees the greediest of the farmers were demanding for their stock by reminding himself it wasn't necessary for this trip to turn a profit. If he could lay his hands on enough pack animals, at least those who walked wouldn't have to carry their baggage.

By force of habit, he searched the skies with a worried eye, hating the idea of undertaking a journey in mid-winter, especially with so many women and children in attendance.

"How many in your party?"

"Myself."

"What can you pay?"

A leather purse was tossed onto the table. Loosening the drawstrings, Labicus caught a glimpse of gold. This, too, was unexpected, a small fortune in hard currency, each coin stamped with the seal of the six clans of Endlin. Extracting five coins, as fair a price as any trader would have asked given the circumstances, Labicus pulled the drawstrings tight, holding out the purse so it might be reclaimed.

"Keep it."

Unsure of the foreigner's meaning, Labicus peered up into a pair of dark eyes gleaming in the depths of the shadows, a close-shaven jaw, and a stern, resolute mouth.

"Nay, friend, it's too much."

"My needs are taken care of. Use it for those who can't pay."

Speechless for at least three heartbeats, Labicus stammered out his gratitude to be cut off by a raised hand clad in a deep-cuffed leather glove.

"Thanks are unnecessary. When do we leave?"

"At first light."

A curt nod indicated understanding. Pushing his way through the crowd surrounding the table, his cloak pulled tightly about him, Haji disappeared from view, melding into a milling landscape of worried men and pensive women, all of them anxious to flee a city gone mad. The trader's meditations on greed and generosity in times of crisis ground to a halt as a bass voice spoke up from behind him.

"Who is he?"

"The son of a Chartist and a woman from the Eastern Isles," Labicus shot back over his shoulder, glad the Legionnaires were out in force today. If they'd done nothing else but assist the beleaguered apprentices with the task of herding people to the correct table for purposes of registration, he would have been grateful, although they did much more, including keeping the peace and lending some much-needed dignity to the proceedings. Not that Labicus didn't feel resentment at being spied upon. The League of Independent Traders was just that—free-traders beholden to no one, least of all the snooty craft guilds and their maniacal president. Still, what with the daily protests making havoc of the city streets, Adrastus' supporters screaming for the revenge of the murdered woman and the ousting of anyone not native-born, he'd rather put up with an occasional question concerning a client's background than face the prospect of harboring a criminal on the long road east.

Taking up a fresh contract, Labicus motioned the next person in line forward, his spirit gladdened by the purse he'd tied to his belt, relieved he need refuse no one passage no matter how meager their savings. The foreigner's gold made all things possible: extra beasts of burden, oats to feed them, the purchase of wagons and supplies, and maybe even some tents to shield the very young and very old from the elements. Would that I were as generous, Labicus thought with a touch of regret, forgetting, perhaps, that generosity is measurable in more ways than a purse filled with golden coins.

KICKING HIS GELDING into a trot, Labicus headed for a snow-covered rise off to the right of the trail. The line continued to advance, cart wheels bumping over the corrugated surface of the once-frozen road now turned to slush, conveying its occupants slowly, ever so slowly, over the rolling hills east of Pelion. With grim satisfaction, Labicus surveyed his ragtag caravan, proud of their progress in spite of himself. If someone bet him that a hundred city-bred soft-living civilians could survive the hardships of a poorly-provisioned mid-winter caravan, he'd have given the fellow ten to one odds they'd not last a week. While his clients might be city-bred, no one would guess it to look at them now. Twenty days on the road had toughened them, and not just their feet and their backsides.

Face after face passed him by—dirty but undaunted, hooded and wrapped against the bone-chilling cold and damp, the elderly nodding as they bounced along in high-walled carts, children walking beside their parents in the muddy rents that passed for a road. Everything that could have gone wrong had done so: a rash of broken wagon wheels, a dead mule, filthy weather, and a severe bout of belly cramps among the smaller children. A less motivated group might have given up in the face of any one of these difficulties. Instead, they converted crippled wagons into two-wheeled carts, butchered the mule, and learned to light fires with damp wood. If it hadn't been for the healer, who joined the caravan a few miles out of Cottyo, there might have been dead children as well as dead mules. Under the healer's supervision, the sick were identified and quarantined, protecting the healthy from contagion, then dosed with medicines until their strength returned.

When all was said and done, they'd performed admirably considering the misery of their situation. True, the journeymen assigned night duty reported sounds of weeping as they walked the pickets, although by morning there was never any evidence of tears shed in the privacy of the tents.

Hearing hoof beats approaching from the east, Labicus scrutinized the snowy landscape for a first glimpse of the rider. From behind a stand of leafless birch trees, a mounted figure emerged, black against the predominately white background. Generalities gave way to specifics—a half-grown youth with a shock of white-blonde hair riding a small-boned roan lathered with sweat. Labicus swore under his breath, wondering what scrape Macris had gotten into this time, half-expecting to see bandits hot on his trail.

The trader's hard-eyed gaze softened a bit as he appraised the boy's horsemanship. The three-year-old filly, Tulia, a cast-off of the Cavalry, had been deemed untrainable and sold for a pittance. In much the same way Labicus acquired the horse, he'd accepted the fourteen-year-old Macris as a probationary apprentice, a cast-off of his family, deemed unteachable and a menace to the community at large.

Labicus made the filly Macris' first hurdle, a testing ground for continuance in the apprentice program. The lad thought himself tough until he met Tulia. An expert in various forms of combat, she'd bitten, kicked, and thrown him, sending him hurtling over fences she refused, dumping him in rivers and streams before high-tailing it for the stable, her empty saddle bouncing against her hindquarters as she whinnied news of her latest victory.

More than once Labicus doubted his belief in both horse and boy, readying himself for failure at the same time he rooted for their success, seeing in both of them the audacity necessary to a trader and a mount. The proof of his belief was the sight of Macris riding hell-for-leather on the smooth-striding filly, both of them spattered liberally with mud as they swung wide to avoid the caravan. Catching sight of Labicus, the boy waved and shouted, then urged the filly up the crest of the hill.

Labicus' gelding shied and reared, made uneasy by the pair's rapid approach. Annoyed, but promising himself he'd not lose his temper, Labicus settled his horse.

"What news could possibly be worth the death of a good horse?"

With a lop-sided grin, Macris ran a gloved hand over the roan's steaming neck.

"Tulia's not near tired! We like a run, don't we, girl?"

As if to prove her rider correct, the filly tossed her head and blew out her nostrils, spraying mucous and muck all over Labicus' last pair of clean breeches. Raising his eyes to the heavens, Labicus heaved a sigh, praying for patience with the two of them.

"I asked for news, Macris, not excuses. Your first duty is to report. How fares the trail up ahead?"

The boy was definitely making progress. A year ago, the slightest correction, no matter how fairly spoken, would have been met with outright defiance. Today, a much sterner rebuke brought a deep flush and a hurried explanation.

"The river's flooded nearly to its banks, and the bridge hangs on by a hair. Haji says we can rig some ropes so the women and children can walk in safety, but thinks we shouldn't risk the weight of the stock or the wagons over the rotten timbers. He swam Seal across about a mile downriver without much trouble."

Clearly, the boy worshipped the easterner, his eyes shining with admiration. As his tale ended, he removed his gloves to wipe his nose with the back of his hand, then ran that same hand through his hair, causing it to stand, quite literally, on end. With an inward shudder, Labicus decided to overlook his appalling manners. Time enough to teach the boy how to use a handkerchief.

"I'd appreciate hearing Dymus' thoughts on the subject."

Instantly contrite at having overlooked the contributions of the forward scout, the boy's former hero and Labicus' most experienced journeyman, Macris added quickly, "'Twas Dymus who tested the bridge and found the downriver crossing."

"What about the wagons?"

The boy frowned.

"Dymus thinks the big ones will make it. Mostly, he's worried about the carts. Haji says . . .," the boy bit his tongue, ducking his head, sure of yet another correction.

The master trader sighed.

"Haji's a good man, but Dymus is a journeyman of our League. As an apprentice, you owe Dymus your allegiance and respect."

The boy nodded, shame-faced.

"I meant no disrespect. It's just that . . ."

The boy faltered, at a loss for words. Sternly, Labicus completed the lesson, one every trader must learn.

". . . that Haji is like no one you've ever met—proud, fearless, with expensive gear and a blooded stallion the likes of which you've never seen. Admire him, make him your friend if you've a mind to, but remember his path lies elsewhere. Such is the life of a trader, many meetings and an equal number of partings. A client can only be a friend in passing. A member of the League is a friend for life."

Lightening his tone, for the boy was beginning to sniffle, Labicus continued with the problem of the day.

"What did Haji suggest we do with the carts?"

Wiping his nose this time with a dirty palm (and smearing a wide swath of mud across his face in the process), Macris straightened in the saddle.

"He says he can build a raft sturdy enough to pole the carts across. Dymus was organizing the front riders into teams when I left. He needs more volunteers to help with the felling of the trees. He said to tell you this: we should camp this side of the river tonight and not attempt the crossing until full light."

Six hours of precious daylight wasted on the first dry day in over a week. Labicus shrugged away regret. He'd lived too long by the seat of his pants to waste time lamenting over events out of his control. Years ago he'd decided the only way a trader could keep his sanity was to turn obstacles into ladders.

"Macris, find another apprentice to send word on to Dymus that he needs to scout a camp this side of the river. Then, find Galva. The last time I saw her, she had her shoulder up against a wagon wheel stuck in the mud. Tell her to round up able-bodied men and escort them to the river. Next, send me the clients' representative . . . what's her name?"

"Kenuthia."

"Just so. Kenuthia." Labicus repeated, pleased with the boy's quickness for names and faces.

"What should I tell her if she questions me?"

"Tell her we're going to have a party."

"A party?" the boy squeaked, his sandy eyebrows rising into peaks.

"Aye, Macris, a party!" the trader bellowed, slapping the filly's rump with his reins. Tulia was up and away before Macris could ask another question, although, plainly, the young apprentice thought his master mad.

We need a party tonight, Labicus thought. He didn't need to see the river to guess they'd probably lose a few wagons during the crossing. He'd never before seen Macris frightened, but the boy had watched the foreigner swim his big grey across the angry river, and Dymus cross the half-rotten bridge, and he was scared.

We need something to lift our spirits, a pleasant memory to cushion the blow when the time comes for them to watch the few possessions they've brought away from Pelion float downstream in one of the lost wagons, or face the trail on foot because a team of oxen drowned.

Labicus also decided is was time to take Macris off probation and list him as an official apprentice in the rolls of the League of Independent Traders. The boy had proved himself worthy of the position since the day of their departure from Pelion. Clearly, he thrived on excitement, loved to travel, cared enough about the clients to be frightened for their safety, wasn't put off by foreigners, and, given time, would become a valued member of the League.

An elderly woman with grey in her braids started up the rise, her skirts befouled with mud up to her knees. Kenuthia, Labicus reminded himself. Time to plan a party, old girl, he thought as he dismounted, and stood waiting for her approach.

It's worth remembering that not once did Labicus picture his retirement spent in any other place than Pelion. Nor did he admit to himself that he, more than anyone, needed a break in routine, anything to spell his guilt at the hardships his clients endured on what became known in the lore of latter days as the Flight of the Innocents, a time when anyone not native-born fled the city in any manner possible. His was not the only caravan making its way along the trails that coldest of winters, nor was his the only one outfitted with dilapidated wagons, meager supplies, and farm animals unfit for the rigors they faced, being thin and out of condition after a hard winter. Frozen carcasses littered the trails leading away from Pelion, as did the dust of human ashes. Fully half the casualties suffered by those who walked the roads came from disease; the other half lost to floods, starvation, and marauders. Disinherited by their adopted home, those not native born fled with a few cherished belongings toward destinations unknown, putting their trust in a handful of traders like Labicus, Dymus, Galva, and the boy, Macris, to deliver them to sanctuary.

A HEMP BRIDGE stretched across the raging river, two of the thickest ropes rigged a little less than waist-high, running parallel to each other a shoulder's breadth apart. Galva made the first crossing, stepping confidently over the slatted timbers, her hands sliding along the ropes, her eyes trained on the boards under her feet, avoiding the places where the wood had rotted away. Once across, she waved gaily to those assembled on the western bank, then retraced her steps, moving like a dancer despite her clumsy boots, smiling encouragement at the women and children who shivered in the wind as though offering them a chance at great adventure rather than a death-defying walk over a bridge dangerously close to collapse.

The men were already across, having driven the wagons through the churning waters a mile downriver or swum the stock across, the horses and mules breasting the rushing currents with necks outstretched and ears flat against their heads, the slow-moving oxen bleating low in their throats, their eyes rolled back in their sockets, showing the white of fear. Once safely on the eastern side of the river, fathers and grandfathers manned the ropes, hauling the raft across the foaming waters while Haji and Dymus worked the poles. Once, twice, three times the raft crossed from bank to bank, until its final cargo of carts and supplies rested safely on the eastern shore. A single wagon, the last one to attempt the crossing, broke its axle on a hidden rock and was lost, the driver pulled to safety by the rope attached to his belt, emerging half-drowned and bruised after being battered against the rocks. Trapped by their traces, dragged downriver by the remorseless current as the wagon broke apart, the horses screamed out in terror, their cries mingling with the roar of the angry waters until, exhausted, they lowered their heads and drowned.

Thankfully, the women and children were spared the death of the horses. More than one man wept at the sight. The boy, Macris, stood with tears streaming down his dirty cheeks, his arms circled tight around Tulia's neck.

The filly whickered a mournful tribute to her less fortunate friends, her warm breath a steamy vapor in the frigid morning air.

"Come, boy," a stern voice ordered, "We've no time to grieve."

Wiping his face with his sleeve, Macris mounted, following the powerful hindquarters of the dappled stallion through the leafless trees and snow-laden undergrowth toward the site of the bridge.

A solemn procession met his eyes, women and children walking in single file, keeping at least a full body-length apart, the only sound the monotonous drone of the raging river. If the children cried, they did so quietly; if the women wept, their sobs went unheard. Like a line of penitents crawling toward salvation, step by agonizing step along the swaying bridge they marched. Some of the women wore slings across their bodies, infants tied between their breasts, young mothers searching for the best footing, refusing to lift their eyes toward their final destination lest they lose heart. Fathers, sons, and mates watched the ghastly pilgrimage with horrid fascination, clenching and unclenching their fists, helpless in their helplessness. From time to time the line slowed and halted—a child standing motionless with fear, a misstep bringing a woman to the brink of disaster as a board shifted beneath her foot. Each time, Galva was there, shepherding them on, making her way gamely on the outside of the hemp bridge, shuttling back and forth, her hair whipped by the wind, her hands gentle but firm as she pried a child's frozen fingers from the ropes and urged him forward.

Macris dismounted next to one of the huge elms supporting the ropes, mesmerized by the bridge-walkers, imagining himself traversing that fearful span, the ice-cold waters foaming and billowing underneath his feet, uprooted trees hurtling along like so many matchsticks, feeling himself drawn forward by the awesome power of the river. Dimly aware that Labicus and Dymus had come up behind him, searching out Haji for a quick conference, Macris held his breath as the end of the line neared the eastern bank.

The last two walkers were nearly across when, without warning, the bridge jerked and swayed, central supports snapping, timbers groaning, the middle section broken apart to hang at a crazy, impossible angle. Pandemonium erupted, the girl child nearest the bank knocked off her feet, wailing as the ropes stretched taut, the boards beneath her feet shifting and trembling with the strain of supporting the weight of the collapsed section. Before he could think, almost before he could breathe, Macris took a flying leap off the bank, landing on his hands and knees a few feet away from her. Wrapping his right arm around a rope to steady himself, he stretched out full length, trying to grab on to her, his reach falling short by at least two arms lengths. Having fallen to her knees, the child stared at him as if transfixed, huge brown eyes watching his every move like a new-born fawn surprised in her thicket by an intruder.

Behind him, over the hysteria of the child's mother, Labicus roared, "She'll not come to you, Macris! She'll not let loose of the rope! Keep your weight low, boy! Steady, that's it, steady on!"

Macris heard nothing except his master's voice booming out over the river's tumult, taking him inch by inch over the boards stretching between him and the child. He crawled on his belly, the splinters ripping his blouse, punishing his hands, fighting off nausea as the flapping bridge ducked and pitched beneath him. Later, he would remember nothing except the child's arms wrapped around his neck as he dragged her to safety and Labicus reaching out for him, the trader's burly frame the rock to which Macris clung, shaking from the aftershock of the rescue.

Over the noise of his racing heart, above the sound of rushing waters, a wild, weirding cry rose from the vicinity of the bridge. Once again, the cry was voiced—a low, muffled sob rising to a keening, high-pitched wail—no human sound, but the eerie, full-throated howl of a timber wolf baying at a distant, unreachable moon.

Macris' head flew up from Labicus' sheepskin coat, his first sight over the trader's broad shoulder that of Haji staring fixedly at the bridge. Macris blinked. When he looked again, Haji had disappeared.

Dymus would tell him everything later that night, how Haji went mad, ripping loose the ties of his cloak, pulling off his gloves and boots as he shouted for a rope, shoving anyone between him and the bridge away with brutal force, the snow-covered ground littered with his discarded belongings and those unlucky enough to have barred his path. Macris would see Galva spread-eagled on the near edge of the broken section, clinging like a drunken sailor to the hemp bridge, her arms almost pulled from the socket by the weight of the woman dangling beneath her. Half in and half out of the freezing water, the woman clung to Galva's forearms with both hands, her head thrown back as though searching the snow-laden clouds for a sign. Macris saw the hound as well, an enormous grey beast crouched dangerously near the breach, his great head reared back to repeat his mournful cry, as though he, too, begged for intervention.

No gods descended from the heavens, no divine hands reached down to lift the woman to safety. Instead, Haji jumped from the bridge, a daring leap into the churning water below, the rope tied to his waist unfurling like a lazy serpent, following the arc of his passage through the air and down into the chilly depths of the maddened river. Macris fought his way to the front of the crowd, straining for the sight of a dark head emerging from the foaming waters, watching with the hushed onlookers as Haji worked his way toward the woman, swimming strongly against the current, his progress slow but measurable. At last he reached her, grabbing her around the waist, his mouth open as he called out to her, his voice lost over the roar of the waters. Whatever command he issued was obeyed, for the woman released her hold on Galva, her head plunging beneath the surface of the water to re-emerge almost immediately, her arms flailed helplessly in the swirling eddies until they locked around her rescuer's neck.

One arm holding the rope at his waist, with the other Haji steered a course toward the eastern shore, dodging debris as the current threatened to drown them, or, when he'd fought his way closer to shore, to smash them against the boulders and uprooted trees littering the banks. Men ran to assist Dymus and Labicus, who hauled at the frozen rope hand over hand, their gloves torn to shreds by the time Haji found a footing and, lifting the woman into his arms, struggled up the icy bank, the soles of his feet leaving crimson stains on the snow.

In the noise and confusion that followed, Macris saw the healer press something into Labicus' hand, heard Dymus utter a glad shout as Galva strode into view, and reached out reverently to pat the hound, who ignored him, his muzzle lifted to scent the wind, his soulful eyes searching the crowd.

Haji walked out of the gathered hordes as a ship-wrecked man walks out of the sea, sobered by his brush with death, the woman's body hanging limply from his arms. His garments, plastered against him, rained water. Wild, unbound hair streamed over his shoulders like a necklace of water snakes swarming in a brackish pool. The uncontested master of those hellish waters, he seemed to many worshipful eyes a triumphant river god, a long-dead deity emerging from a dream of yesteryear, a votaress of his order swooning in his embrace.

Ignoring the cheers of the people pressed around him, Haji strode hurriedly toward his tent. Macris knew the easterner as well as anyone in the caravan, better than most, in fact, having dogged his footsteps whenever Labicus wasn't looking. Labicus thought Haji proud, Dymus admired his breadth of learning, close-mouthed Galva offered no opinion other than following him constantly with her eyes. Whatever the ruling sentiment might be as to the easterner's character, Macris was sure of one thing that day. He would sooner face a score of Labicuses, each one more angry that the last, than face the fury burning in Haji's eyes.

DUMPING HIS LOAD unceremoniously onto his sleeping robes, Sandur pulled the tent flap shut and fell to his knees, working feverishly at the knotted muffler wrapped around her neck, tearing at the shabby cloak wrapped around her limbs rather than throttling her as she deserved. Mindless with fury, shaking with the cold, his fingers stiff and uncooperative, he spewed profanities as he attacked her clothing, growing angrier by the minute as layer upon layer, each of poorer quality than the last, came away.

Rags, she wears rags, he fumed, the cast-off leavings of a beggar child! Patched breeches, twice-darned socks, a baggy sweater with gaping holes at the elbows, even her boots were second-hand, the soles worn paper-thin, the laces frayed and knotted. Working himself into a towering rage, Sandur threw item after item against the tent walls, cursing with every breath.

"Does she live?"

Startled out of his tantrum, he flung a blanket over her, shielding her body from the trader's curious gaze. Furious at being interrupted, he wished Labicus and every interfering soul on the face of the earth to the bottom of the ocean floor.

"Leave us," he snarled, earning a surprised frown from the master trader.

"Come now, Haji," Labicus began amicably enough, crouching down beside him, "this is best left to the women. Let me summon . . ."

"Get out or I'll throw you out."

It was not a threat, but a promise. In his present mood, he could have gutted the trader and eaten his entrails raw. Labicus backed away with all possible speed, pulling the tent flap shut behind him.

Alyssa stirred, moaned, and retched. Grabbing a cloth from his trunk, he turned her head to the side as she vomited up the river water she'd swallowed, then wiped her face clean. Renouncing any feelings of pity for her half-drowned state, he tossed aside the blanket and went to work, rubbing life back into her clammy flesh with a rough cloth, working over her from toes to crown, watching as her lips gradually lost their bluish tinge. Dry at last, her skin rosy and warm to the touch, he piled blankets on top of her sleeping form, trying not to notice the way her eyelashes curled against the curve of her cheek.

A throat was cleared behind him.

"We appreciate your efforts on her behalf, but . . ."

Reluctantly, Sandur turned to face his accusers, resentful of their presence while at the same time acknowledging their rights. How could he blame them for their common decency, their persistence in protecting an unconscious woman from the unwanted attentions of a strange man?

"She's my mate."

Labicus, Dymus, and an elderly woman wrapped in a ragged shawl stared at him with jaws gone slack. Labicus recovered first, stroking his beard thoughtfully, his eyes flicking to the sleeping robes and back to Sandur. The woman peered anxiously at the golden head resting on the pillow, venturing doubtfully, "Alyssa never mentioned a mate."

"We met in the Maze."

This grudging admission brought about a distinct change in the atmosphere. The woman nodded slowly, corroborating his claim, a look of something like wonder erasing some of the weariness etched on her face. Dymus and Labicus exchanged glances, the younger man stifling a grin, the elder suddenly brisk and business-like.

"The healer sent these." Labicus tossed an oilskin packet at Sandur's feet. "You're to steep them in boiling water and let her breathe the vapors. We've lit bonfires. We camp here tonight."

Quickly and quietly, they filed out of the tent.

Fatigue settled over Sandur like a dense fog. Teeth rattling in his head, he stripped to his challah and dried himself, almost too weary to go through the motions of lighting the brazier and tossing the herbs into a pan of water. His body ached from the bruises around his throat to the torn soles of his feet, his shoulders stiff from poling the raft, the skin around his waist chafed and sore, rubbed raw by the rope. A distant memory of sunlit meadows beckoned him to the pallet; the promise of warmth caused him to crawl under the blankets and press himself against her. Like the summer sun, she warmed him, dispelling the cold, the damp, the days and nights of awful loneliness, the hollow ache of remorse.

As afternoon faded into evening, the camp bustled noisily about the richly caparisoned tent, the curious who came too close warned away by a menacing growl from the dog standing watch. Accepting an offering of bones with a regal nod, the sentinel cracked them open with immense white teeth while the children, standing a safe distance away, watched in awed silence. When at last the camp slept, the dog slept too, his belly full, curled on the ground near the bonfire's companionable glow.

All dogs dream, whining and quivering in their sleep, eyes moving beneath half-open lids, muscles atremble, nose atwitch. What did he dream, Rauros the Brave, on the eve of that fate-filled day? An endless procession of chickens on the boil? A hunting expedition, perhaps? The thrill of catching rabbits on the run? Of long-dead ancestors, his wolfish kin gathered on the high plains to serenade that serenest of majesties, the moon?

Did Rauros dream as his mistress did, of the angry river below, of plunging into icy nothingness, of futility and fear? Or did his dreams resemble those of Sandur—a single image relentlessly repeated, a tick without a tock, time frozen on a riverbank, Alyssa poised above the raging river?

If dreams are the stuff of memory, let us hope the memories of beasts are blessedly short, daily events forgotten, washed away into oblivion, each day a blank slate to be written upon with new chalk, no erasures, no mistakes, no cloudy residue left to mar the surface of experience. Let us hope Rauros' dreams were gentler than those of his masters, perhaps nothing more than the soothing repetition of his name, a name like the sound of rushing waters.

Chapter 20

Sacrifice

As ADRASTUS MARCHED toward his destination, a plaza near the northern gate, he took a certain amount of pride in the fact that it was exactly six moons ago that he'd informed the Nineteenth Mother that the Maze must be closed. Perhaps it struck him as ironic justice, a stroke of fate, as it were, which gave much-needed approval to his actions; perhaps he was simply superstitious. Whatever the reason, he believed himself to be in the right and organized the march on the Maze as a fulfillment of what he considered to be the proper destiny of Pelion. As the people grew in number, fists raised in the time-honored gesture of protest, Adrastus' face settled into grim lines, his step firm, his bearing stiff, uncompromising—a man bent on establishing his role in history.

The crowd itself was made up of those who supported Adrastus' cause—an end to the Maze—but also a larger issue, namely, the closing of the northern gate to anyone not born and bred in Pelion. The murder of Lisle, a former worker in the Maze, her throat slit, her body stuffed into a bin, her murderer never found, had so destroyed their faith in the Legion's ability to protect them that they were eager to shut the northern gates tight. No more Maze meant no more strangers among them.

Since the dimly remembered siege of Pelion, an event that occurred thirty-odd years ago and ended with the quick retreat of the surrounding army, the populous of Pelion, who believed themselves safe within their walls, faced the threat of personal danger. Lisle's death brought them face to face with fear and its accompanying emotion, fury. For the first time in centuries the people of Pelion were no longer placid. Several hundred worthy citizens left the central marketplace and set off toward the northern part of the city, marching shoulder-to-shoulder through the narrow streets behind Adrastus, determined to put an end to anything that might threaten their sense of well-being.

They'd already held two rallies in the marketplace in preparation for this day of days, shutting down all commerce and putting everyone on notice that they were a force to be reckoned with. Their boycott of foreign-owned businesses sent those not native born running for the hills, or so they liked to congratulate themselves, dimly aware that the League of Independent Traders was escorting hundreds of men, women, and children out of the city in the middle of one of the worst winters on record.

Their destination today was the oldest plaza in the city. In the early days, during the construction of the Sanctum, this area served as a stone-yard run by the Guild of Masons. As time passed and work began on other sites within the city (the Greater and Lesser Libraries, the House of Healing and Guild Hall), the stone-yard was moved to a more central location. As a parting gift, the stone-cutters left behind a wonderfully intricate pattern of paving stones laid over the surface of the plaza, a subdued, yet accurate representation of the night sky over Pelion. If one stood in the exact center of the plaza on the longest night of the year (if the longest night corresponded with the dark of the moon), the concentrated starlight would bounce off the polished, mica-flecked paving-stones below, striking them at such an angle that the entire plaza seemed a celestial mirror in which the heavens could view its reflection. Given the fact that this night was usually bitter cold, sometimes marred by moonlight, and more often than not cloud-covered, most residents considered themselves lucky if they were able to view this phenomenon once or twice over the course of their lives. No matter the season, the plaza was a favorite place for lovers' trysts in the evening hours, couples wending their ways among the constellations, lost in the stars while rooted to the stones.

The Sanctum itself stood on the north side of the plaza, a broad bank of wide steps leading directly from the plaza to the enormous bronze doors forged three hundred years ago by Houras, a Master of the Forge, the founder of the Guild Assembly and its first elected President. Perhaps believing the Sanctum deserved an atmosphere of quiet contemplation, the city-planners kept the streets and alleyways leading into the plaza narrow and unfit for more profit-minded enterprises. Two and three-story row-houses sprang up along the remaining three sides of the plaza, forming a subdued, genteel neighborhood far removed from the hustle and bustle of the market district or the primarily commercial plaza facing Guild Hall.

Longevity being a valued commodity in Pelion, few, if any, of the houses facing the Sanctum's plaza had undergone any major changes since their construction three centuries earlier. Assuredly renovations had been made, windows cut and glass panes installed, rotted timbers replaced, new plaster spread, tiled roofs supplanting those of thatch; but on the whole, the plaza was unaltered save for the height of the plane trees and the grooves worn into the stone steps leading up to the Sanctum.

The newest addition to this part of the city could barely be seen beyond the Sanctum's imposing facade. If one stood on either the eastern or westernmost edges of the plaza, choosing a spot free from overhanging branches, and craned one's neck almost to the breaking point, one could just catch a glimpse of the grey, triple-thick walls of the Maze. Compared to the high-roofed Sanctum, with its graceful lines and lofty sense of spacious grandeur, the low-slung Maze seemed insignificant and even homely—a blunt line of windowless walls decked with squat turrets overlooking the nearby northern gates. Like a shy child hiding behind its mother's skirts, the miniature fortress concealed itself behind the bulwark of the Sanctum, as if to say, "Come no closer," while the Sanctum pledged in return, "Fear not, I will protect you."

There was, in those days, a single public entrance to the Maze. A hallway branching off from the narthex of the Sanctum led to an enormous set of doors depicting an abstract sunburst worked in highly-polished bronze, the life work of Aidan the Younger. Although these doors were similar in size to the exterior doors of the Sanctum (some twenty feet high with a span of nearly equal dimension), they were rarely opened except to admit those chosen to walk the Path of Preparation. Cognizant of their primarily ritual purpose and at the same time confronted with the problems of daily traffic, Aidan the Younger's solution was to design a much smaller door, cunningly wrought so as to be almost invisible to the naked eye, hidden in the farthest right-hand corner of the glowing sun.

Through this door Magda passed that morning, bowing her head to walk under the low portal, ignoring the protests of those gathered on the other side of the door.

"Obey my wishes," she reminded them, not unkindly. "Let no one pass."

Swung shut by unseen hands, the opening vanished, becoming just another part of the smooth plane of the immense bronze doors. Stepping back, she surveyed the bronze sun that offered a burnished welcome to all who entered. Determination urged her on, out into the daylight, out into the dazzling brilliance of the sun-filled plaza. The voices of the whispering plain added their encouragement. *"Not yet,"* they had murmured to her for thirty years. Today they set her free, her education at an end. *"Now!"* they chanted, their choir swelling inside her head. *"Now!"*

Magda swept down the hallway, her maturation complete. Thirty years ago she'd hesitated on another threshold, a guilty woman confronting her failure as a mother. Today she strode confidently toward her destiny—to save one child by reclaiming the affections of another. Both children were much-beloved: one born of a five-century long past, the other of a dimly-perceived future; one a spoiled adolescent, mean-tempered and aggressive, the other an infant being weaned from the breast, fretful and difficult to pacify. Siblings born of a common goal, their quarrel was a century in the making, a hundred years of jealousy, slights, and misunderstandings simmering into the full boil of outright rebellion.

Even so, her step was light, for she was Magda again, her immense mental powers surrendered to her heir, Symone, leaving her a limited adept. Esslar and Galen knew the truth. Remy kept his suspicions to himself; and Symone, terrible actress that she was, fearful of giving away the secret before it was time, went into hiding in the Great Library. "Until I'm needed," she told Magda, turning away from the older woman, fearful her stoic mask might crumble.

Everything was in readiness. The crowd milled about the plaza, a few of Adrastus' followers prying up stones from the courtyard. They waited impatiently for her appearance, expecting trumpet fanfares and drums signaling the approach of the Legion, there to protect the Nineteenth Mother from any who might do her harm. So the Legion had done for centuries, and so (Adrastus promised his followers) they would do today.

Down the halls of the narthex Magda trod, hearing the murmur of the crowd like so many bees in a hive, until she revealed herself to them, an old woman attired completely in black, walking alone and unaided. Having abandoned her veil, her hair, grey and coarse, thin and lifeless, fell down her back. *"Here I am,"* she thought grimly, *"grown old as one day all of you shall grow old."*

Their expectations thwarted by the sight of an elderly woman with not a single Legionnaire in sight, the crowd buzzed its surprise. They had marched; now they meant to riot. But against a single antagonist?

Adrastus recovered first, speaking to her in a clear voice, obviously desirous of being heard by everyone occupying the plaza.

"What trick is this?"

"No trick."

Even without her full powers, Magda was a strong speaker, commanding attention to the degree that the crowd quieted, intent on hearing every word.

"You lie."

"On the contrary, I speak the truth. Six moons ago I warned you the Maze will endure, must endure. Now I tell you why."

A wave of expectation swept through the plaza. Here was news from half a millennia ago, information privy to none but the Mothers until today's revelation. Small wonder that some scoffed while others sighed.

"The building of the Maze was the First Mother's promise to the Sowers."

"Preposterous!" snapped Adrastus. "Are you this desperate, that you make up rumors, old wives tales designed to frighten us?"

"My purpose is not to frighten you, but to reveal the truth."

"The Maze is barely a hundred years old; the city is nearly six hundred. How, then, could the First Mother make such a promise to the Sowers or to anyone else?"

Instead of answering Adrastus' question, Magda took a deep breath and began to recite what was immediately recognizable to many in the plaza as an ancient text. There were no scholars present in the plaza that day, but city-dwellers learned to read by studying the history of the city, some of it written in an archaic version of the southern tongue.

Time stopped as Magda spoke, telling them a story they had never heard before, revealing to them a time when the Sowers, having rescued their ancestors from a doomed world, lived and worked among them. Many noted that Magda's voice lacked the strength it had possessed in former days, but they chalked it up to her advanced age. Even so, her audience of noisy, rowdy citizens grew quiet so as to listen with unusual attentiveness, struggling as they did to hear every word of this previously unknown tale.

> And the First Mother said: "Stay, for we are nothing without you."
>
> "We have tarried longer than we intended," said the Sower known as Singer, a favorite of the First Mother as she was to him.
>
> "What of the gift you promised? One that will prevent us from destroying this world as we did the one called Earth?"
>
> Singer went silent until it seemed he might not speak again. Then he said:
>
> "Build a maze. There will your descendents go to be transformed. There they will learn to speak heart to heart, mind to mind, unto the thousandth generation."
>
> "How should we build it? We know nothing of mazes."
>
> "You have books, do you not?"
>
> The First Mother, a lover of books, nodded and said: "We do."
>
> "Build it," Singer said, "and all will be as I have promised. Build it," he repeated, "and we will come again."

Here it was, the secret of a former age, shared for the first time with the people of Pelion by the Nineteenth Mother in the public square nearest the Maze.

Some believed, some did not. Some became enraged, hating the thought of non-humans amongst them.

Adrastus asked, "They will come again?"

"So the one called Singer promised."

"Singer? What sort of name is that?"

Magda kept her temper, knowing this man's mocking tone sought to strike a spark in her, hoping to discredit her in front of the crowd.

"The old texts tell us that before the Sowers rescued our ancestors, they did not know music. Some believe that our songs convinced the Sowers we were worth saving. The one who called himself Singer was the first Sower to address the First Mother. It was he who promised us the Gift."

"This being from another world promised to save us from future destruction?" Adrastus was wagging his head, rolling his eyes, working the crowd, making them doubt as he doubted, disbelieve as he disbelieved.

A raucous voice erupted from the crowd: "Who needs saving?" It was answered by several shouts of "Not me!" and general laughter.

Aware she was being held up for ridicule, her only weapon was truth, and truth she continued to speak:

"He made no such promise."

The crowd was becoming unruly, turning away from her, bored with the fine points of her argument, eager for action. Still, she persevered, although she was beginning to mourn the loss of mental powers she had taken for granted for some thirty years. It was only now, alone in the square facing Adrastus and his mob, that she could recognize her weakness. She had been so sure she could persuade the crowd. Now she struggled to be heard.

"The Singer's promise was this: Build a Maze, make it possible for everyone to walk the Path, and the Sowers will, in the fullness of time, return."

"Return?" Adrastus reared up his head, his alarm spreading like wildfire among his followers. "Why need they return? If the Maze is the magical place you say it is, turning us all into 'adepts,'" Adrastus sneered the word, "why should the Sowers return?" Dismissing her with a wave of his hand, his voice rang out over the plaza.

"Could it be they return in order to take from us all we have accomplished? Are they the rulers of the universe, seeding the planets so that in time they can return to reap the harvest of our goods, our lands, our myriad achievements?"

Magda was in control of the crowd no longer.

"Is this what we 'prepare' for? Are we animals? Beasts bred to the Sowers' design?"

The roar of the crowd answered his question, causing him to turn his back on Magda, who felt herself shrink away from Adrastus as if she was a not-too-bright student being dismissed by a teacher. Anger flared within her to be quenched by painful recognition. Had she not felt this way as a limited adept in the presence of full adepts? That wretched night at the House of Healing when she learned Aethra would die? Hadn't it hurt to be condescended to by all of them? The Higher Healers? Even the Eighteenth Mother herself?

And in that moment, as the crowd began to mill around Adrastus, the noise increasing, the colors swirling, Magda began to understand that the fault did not lie in Adrastus and his followers, but in the Keepers of the Maze.

Our fault, she thought. We brought this on ourselves. We've loved our secrets from the beginning. No honesty, no openness between us and the citizenry. Even when the greatest of our hopes was proved true in the Maze, when the first couple achieved Transformation, we said nothing, explained nothing. Perhaps there was some reason for secrecy in the beginning, but not now, not eighty years after we proved that what the Sowers promised could actually come to pass.

Here was something everyone in the city could have, should have, celebrated. Embracing one another, we could have taken pride in what we achieved. We should have become Pelion the Great, Pelion who shall save the world! Not Pelion, a walled fortress in the south who keeps its true purpose hidden, who distrusts strangers and locks its gate up tight every night.

And there it was, the answer springing out of her consciousness. Bring down the walls! We must share everything with the people and bring down the walls!

Only then did she remember that in her present state, she could not share this information with her successor. This was her punishment, to know how everything could be put to rights, but be unable to share it with others.

Turning helplessly from one citizen to another, her hands reaching out to grasp a shoulder, an arm, trying to make someone pause and listen to her, her attempts were shrugged off, frowning faces turning away from her, dismissing her mumbled pleas begging them to "Listen, please, listen!"

"Keep your hands to yourself!" one man cried and pushed her forcefully away from him, causing her to lose her balance and fall to her knees. Struggling to rise, she felt the press of many bodies as they streamed past her in their rush toward Adrastus, the man of the hour, who was urging them to march with him to the bronze doors, his staff of office raised, gesturing for them to follow him up the stairs and through the narthex of the Sanctum, crying, "Come, citizens! Bid the Maze goodbye!"

When her efforts to right herself caused another man to stumble, he uttered a curse and kicked her out of his way, never looking back to see what damage he'd done. The kick took her down to her knees again, sending her sprawling forward to land on her hands, crawling another step or two before collapsing on the stones, her heart banging against her broken ribs. A crush of bodies surrounded her, boots, shoes, and slippers stepping on her hands, her arms, her hair. Fighting for air as the dust of passing feet enveloped her, she felt a tide of panic rising, her pulse racing, frantic at the thought of not being able to breathe, until a voice near her ear, advised quietly and calmly:

"*Stop fighting.*"

It wasn't a voice she recognized.

"*Time to give everything up.*"

It was such a novel idea, she who had never given up, that she decided to embrace this anonymous directive, the last one she would ever hear, for she was dying now. This was why she had come to the plaza on this day, at this hour, taking her final walk in the bright sunshine of a winter's day. She need take only two, three, four more breaths, her ancient heart would stop, and she would have accomplished exactly what she set out to do.

"*Time to go*," the voice said, and She-Who-Was-Magda agreed.

Hers was a little death, but a welcome one, as the crowd hurried past, bent on destroying the one place capable of ensuring that their world was indestructible.

On marched the crowd, men and women united in purpose, until, and many spoke of this later, a single voice cried out: "Bring her with us! Bring the Nineteenth Mother to the Maze!" No one ever identified the speaker, but many took up the call, the crowd slowing around Adrastus, causing him to hesitate and look about, searching for the tall figure of a woman dressed entirely in black, expecting her to stride forward and reveal herself, steeling himself for her contempt, remembering how she had spoken to him of Gwyn, the mere mention of the woman he abandoned in the Maze like a knife thrust between his ribs.

He slowed, as did the crowd, noting as he did so that voices formerly raised in triumph were dying about him, a general hush spreading over the plaza. Hoods of cloaks were being drawn up and over individual heads and shoulders, some citizens dropping to their knees, others prostrate on the cobblestones. On Adrastus went, forced to slow his pace as he moved through a crowd turned suddenly into statues, looking into faces seemingly set in stone, hands pulled up to shield their eyes from something they could not bear to see.

He stood in the middle of the plaza now, the place he had last seen the Nineteenth Mother and felt triumph rise inside him, knowing he had defeated her and glorying in it, remembering how he had lifted up his staff and moved deliberately toward the Maze, the crowd streaming behind him . . .

Until, looking down, Adrastus recognized the crumpled robes of deepest black and locks of grey hair partially covering a face of deep-wrinkled skin gone suddenly slack. Her mouth open, her eyes unblinking, staring at nothing, she lay curled on her side, no longer tall and mighty, but small, dusty, defenseless, and dead.

For a moment, he could not fathom it, the sight of the Nineteenth Mother of Pelion dead at his feet. Mothers of Pelion did not die in public squares, trampled by a mob of angry citizens. Such things simply did not happen, could not happen . . .

And in that moment, Adrastus contemplated the unqualified failure of his plan to close the Maze, for he saw bitterly and completely that nothing would happen now, that everything he'd planned ended with the tremendous calamity of this event.

He saw as well, or thought he saw, a being he had never seen before, dark-winged and bird-like to the waist, with burning holes where eyes might have been. It seemed to Adrastus that the figure acknowledged him with a simple bow before lifting off from the cobblestones directly into the air above the plaza. Wings flapped once, twice, and the being disappeared.

All this happened in the blink of an eye, and a quick blink at that. Looking down, Adrastus registered the Nineteenth Mother's body still crumpled at his feet and realized in the part of his mind that was still functioning, that he would take this vision out and examine it repeatedly, year after year, and never understand what he had seen. It was, finally, the only problem that Adrastus the champion wrestler, the mighty engineer, would never solve. Nor could he ever shed the feeling that the bow being offered him was neither ironic nor blameful, but held within it a certain woeful air, as if to say, "If not you, Adrastus, then another," signifying that Adrastus' role was to do exactly as he had done, a thought which first woke vehement denial, and then, with the passage of time, brought a certain sense of peace.

Yet still, the impossible had happened, and a Mother of Pelion lay still and silent on the stones. The plaza had become a tomb, its citizens mourners, and there was no sound save an occasional sob. Quietly, so quietly that it took some time to put a name to the sound, they heard unshod hooves on stone and looked up to find a small cart that might have held fruits and vegetables pulled by a long-eared, mild-eyed donkey. At the shaggy head of the beast walked a man clad in a regulation Legion uniform, his brown cloak held together at the neck with a simple bronze clasp. He looked neither right nor left, but led the donkey carefully through the crowd, people making way for him, quiet, respectful, grateful that he had come and so absolved them of the task of moving the Nineteenth Mother's body to the Sanctum, and from there, to the flames.

For they had killed her. They had not meant to do it, but this they had done, remembering her entreaties to them to listen, turning away from her, pushing her away none too gently. More than one remembered kicking away something in their path, a sense of treading on something underfoot, but to a man (and a woman) they rejected those memories as somehow false. No one meant to hurt her, after all, this ancient woman who seemed more frail and fragile than they had ever seen her, which set them to thinking about when, exactly, they had seen her last. The Blessing of my grandchild, my son, my daughter. The last Gift I gave, when she placed my offering on the altar. Who will bless the newborns now?, they asked themselves. Who will say the rite of remembrance? Some asked a greater question: How shall the city survive?

It struck them, too, as they watched the Legionnaire pick up her body and place it on the blankets spread on the floor of the cart, that they had seen her but rarely. She was not one to flaunt her position. Yes, she would appear at the northern gate occasionally, surrounded by a troop of hard-eyed Calvary soldiers escorting her on a tour of the southeastern province, but it was rare that one saw her anywhere on the streets or in the markets . . . and so they began to remember her thirty-year reign, a widow who owned a small fabric shop until suddenly becoming the Nineteenth Mother. "Magda" someone said, a white-haired fellow who claimed to have known her in her youth.

And so it went as the donkey clip-clopped, sure-footed over the cobblestones, his burden light, the Legionnaire walking beside the cart, head bowed, respectful of the crowd's grief, blaming no one, questioning no one, carrying out his duty as he had been instructed until the humble cortege passed out of sight, and the crowd stood frozen no more, but began to shift slowly, stiffly, from the horizontal to the vertical.

Those who thought to look for Adrastus found him standing where the cart had been, staring down at his feet, his staff of office abandoned nearby, never to be reclaimed. He had not participated in her death, but everyone blamed him as much as they blamed themselves. He would never hold office again, nor would he remain in his beloved Pelion. He departed the Maze all those years ago because he could not bear to leave Pelion as Temenus willingly left with Gwyn, returning to Cyme with their new gift, a gift Adrastus disdained yet coveted, for if he could not have the gift, he would see to it that no one else did. He was not asked to leave the city, but leave he did, unable to bear the whispers and frowns that surrounded him, the leader of the Maze Riot, a misnomer since the rebellion he planned never came to fruition, but so it came to be known, damning his name and reputation forever.

For the rest of his long life, living in melancholy exile, he would revisit the memory of the alien figure with the burning eyes, wondering if he had seen one of the mysterious Sowers standing watch on the day the Nineteenth Mother died.

THE PLAZA STOOD empty, twilight transformed into blackest night with stars twinkling on high. There were no clouds, no moon, only starlight illuminating the paving-stones cut and set by the hands of ancient stone-cutters, turning the entire plaza into a blazing mirror of the heavens over Pelion. Not a single citizen enjoyed the sight. No star-gazers, no lovers old or new. Word had spread, many mouths to many ears, and the inhabitants of the walled city slept restlessly under a frigid, brilliant sky.

She is dead. Having killed our mother, we must learn to live as orphans.

For three days the city mourned until, on the fourth morning at dawn, they were awakened by a woman's voice speaking inside their head.

"I am She-Who-Was-Symone, the Twentieth Mother of Pelion."

Thus, the so-called Maze Riot ended with but a single casualty, and in the centuries that followed, never again did the people of Pelion question the right of the Maze to exist.

"WHERE'S MY DIAMOND?"

Such was Alyssa's awakening. No salutation, no welcome, not even a kiss, just a rough hand shaking her shoulder, a rougher voice barking orders.

"I know you're awake! Now, where's my diamond?"

Stretching and yawning, she rolled over onto her stomach, pulling the pillow under her breasts.

"What's the hour?"

"Damn you, woman, I'll not be put off! Practice your charms on someone less gullible. I asked you a question, and I demand an answer!"

"Your diamond, as you so rudely put it, is with the rest of my things. If you'll hand me my clothes, I'll return it to you without delay."

"I burnt them."

She'd never heard him sound so smug, so infuriatingly pompous. Not trusting her ears, she repeated slowly, "You burnt my clothes?"

"I burnt your rags," he corrected her savagely, "since what you call clothing was nothing more than an assortment of tatters."

Plainly, he was furious with her, certainly not the reaction she'd anticipated after waking in the middle of the night to the pungent smell of herbs and the familiar contours of his body next to hers. She lay awake for at least an hour, basking in the lovely warmth of the thick blankets, careful not to disturb his rest although she'd been unable to resist touching him. Her fingers found the same Sandur who'd slept beside her in the cell with one puzzling exception—an empty hole in his left earlobe. She'd fallen asleep pondering the loss of his earring to wake and find him gone, the sounds of the sleeping camp all around her. Now she faced a different Sandur—foul-tempered and decidedly unpleasant. Vexed at his bad manners, she refused to be bullied.

"My clothes weren't chosen with your approval in mind. If memory serves, you forfeited your right to consult with me over my wardrobe."

"And if my memory serves, I left you an extremely valuable blue diamond and a letter of credit, thus making you the wealthiest woman in Pelion!"

"Thinking, no doubt, you could assuage your guilt by making me rich!"

"Guilt has nothing to do with it."

"On the contrary, guilt has everything to do with it! Did you really think I'd pawn your diamond or live off your father's letter of credit? Did it soothe your conscience to think of me living in luxury, surrounded by servants, leading the same boring, useless existence as your concubines!"

She hadn't known how angry she was until he pushed her past the point of no return. How dare he flee the Maze in such a cowardly fashion, leaving her to enter the cell at the evening trumpet and find him gone, no warning, no discussion, no explanation, not even a note, just a square of parchment and a multi-faceted stone! His belongings had vanished as well—maps, books, halter, clothing—nothing left save the silken scarf he'd draped over a peg in the wardrobe.

"I have no concubines," he pointed out stiffly, hiding behind logic, a typically masculine ploy that exasperated her almost past endurance.

"Whether you do or don't is a matter of complete indifference to me," she sniffed. "In any case, I'll be delighted to return your belongings."

"If it's a matter of complete indifference to you, why did you follow me?"

"Follow you?" she snorted. "What gave you that idea?"

"If you weren't following me, why did you join this particular caravan? And why take such pains to hide from me? Were you afraid I'd send you back to the Maze where you belong?"

Such insolence was beyond bearing. Determined to set him straight, she sat bolt upright, pulling the bedclothes over her breasts, and gave him the tongue-lashing he deserved.

"I'm traveling with this particular caravan because I met Kenuthia in the lines outside the northern gate. When she offered to let me join her party, I jumped at the chance. As to hiding from you, don't flatter yourself!"

She felt better than she had in weeks, giving him the rough side of her tongue, dripping sarcasm all over the bedclothes.

"How, exactly, do you think I could hide from you even if I knew you were here? Spy on you from behind a tree when you weren't looking? Hide in a ditch when you were? Or, could it be that so mighty a prince doesn't deign to notice the poor folk on foot? Perhaps the prince has been gallivanting around on horseback, ignoring those who must walk."

Another thought struck her.

"And where, may I ask, was the illustrious prince of Endlin the evening before last, when the entire caravan gathered to share food and drink, to sing and to dance? I was there, as was Rauros. Where were you?"

After a long, obstinate pause, he muttered, "Here."

Surprised, since she'd not known anyone crossed the river before yesterday, she filed that information away.

"So, without eyes to see you and never hearing anyone mention your name, how, exactly, did you come to the brilliant conclusion I was following you?"

"If you aren't following me, where are you going?"

Thanking her mother for her training, Alyssa rolled her eyes. Surely this was the most tiresome, irritatingly suspicious man she'd ever met!

"I'm going where you're going—home! I've relatives and friends, my work as a bard, people who love and cherish me. Where else should I go but Cinthea?"

He made no answer, seeming to pace randomly around the tent. His route gave her a sense of the dimensions of the tent, twice the size of the one she shared with six adults and four children. He'd stayed here alone the night of the party, hauling his gear across the river on the horse Yossi mentioned and setting up his tent, keeping himself removed from the others as he always did.

"If you scorned my gifts, what did you use for money?"

"I traded my gown for traveling clothes. Labicus told me there was money enough for those who couldn't afford to pay the travel fees. I sleep with Kenuthia and her friends and entertain the children in exchange for food."

"Your amethyst gown?"

She nodded, saddened by the loss of so precious a belonging. After a short pause, during which he seemed to be rummaging about, a tin plate was thrust into her hands.

"Here's a biscuit, a boiled egg, and hard cheese. Don't worry about Rauros; I fed him at first light. There's a kettle of tea, a pitcher of milk, and an empty mug on a platter near the brazier, about three paces in front of you. Be careful of the brazier; it sits on a tripod and isn't particularly well-balanced. There's a comb and brush on top of my trunk to your left."

A blast of cold air invaded the tent.

"Where are you going?" she called after him, confused by the hastiness of his departure.

"To find you something to wear."

SANDUR LEANED AGAINST the center pole, his arms across his chest, watching her struggle into the new clothes. He might have helped, but couldn't bring himself to touch her. The slightest touch and his defenses might crumble.

She was pulling on the woolen stockings now, grey lambs-wool covering her calves and knees, ending mid-thigh, thick enough to keep her dry and warm, as would the heavy petticoats and cotton camisole. The dress came next, the best one he could find, bought with a sack of rice, dried fish and dates, and two bottles of Cymean wine. No one wanted gold. Food was the preferred medium of exchange. Everyone was hungry it seemed; the woman who supplied the dress seemed delighted with the exchange. The boots were the most difficult purchase since footwear was dear. Finally, Galva took pity on him, stuffing a pair of scarred riding boots in his hands and pocketing the gold with a tight smile, shrugging off his thanks.

Everyone seemed to look at him differently, or perhaps he was the one who had changed. As he wandered through the camp, stopping by cook fires to make inquiries, scratching at tent flaps in search of an extra shawl, a spare petticoat, he saw how Alyssa lived—sleeping in a cramped tent with ten other unwashed bodies, telling stories for her bed and board, wiping the noses of the dirty-faced children, helping the harried women stretch food enough for five to feed ten hungry mouths. Every word she spoke was true—every accusation, every sneer, every jibe. Wrapping his sorrow around him like a shroud, he'd wallowed in self-pity, comforting himself with visions of Alyssa ensconced in luxury, ridiculously proud of the fact that he'd left her rich and well-cared for, certain the Nineteenth Mother would prevent her from leaving the Maze given the riots and protests in the streets.

"Where else should I go?" she'd demanded, her face flushed with anger as her hair tumbled wildly about her shoulders. It never occurred to him that she might yearn for friends and family, for those who cherished her as he proved he did not. Word by word, she stripped away his vanity, exposing his conceits, and then, when his pride lay in broken shards at her feet, confessed that she'd parted with her dearest possession rather than accept so much as a coin from his hand.

Her head emerged from the neck of the gown. The bodice was a trifle tight, the waist somewhat roomy, the sleeve length perfect, as was the skirt. He'd been careful to find one she could lace by herself.

"What color is it?"

Crisply and evenly, her deft fingers pulling the laces tight, she addressed him for the first time since he'd reentered the tent. Rauros was there when he returned, being fondled by his mistress, polishing her cheeks with an eager tongue. There was a certain novelty in being jealous of a dog.

"The gown is blue. The shawl is grey, as are the stockings. I couldn't find a cloak; no one will part with one. You can wear one of mine. It will drag the ground, but since you'll be riding, it won't matter. I've an extra pair of gloves to protect your hands."

"And what, pray, will I ride?"

She was angrier than he had ever seen her, angrier even than she had been upon waking, a bright red spot burning on each cheek.

"My pack-horse. He's soft-mouthed and gentle. He'll think himself well-off since you're considerably lighter than my gear."

"What happens to your gear?"

"Labicus agreed to haul it in a supply wagon."

Her hands went to her hips.

"What makes you think I'll ride your pack-horse? Since you burned my clothes, I'm forced to accept these. I neither need nor want your charity." Before he could respond, she cut him off, demanding, "Did you bring my things?"

"On the pallet next to Rauros."

Her pack was pitifully light, handed over to him by Kenuthia, whose poker-faced stare made him feel like a thief absconding with stolen goods. Kneeling on the rumpled bedclothes, she untied the pack, pulling from its depths the azure scarf. Untying a loose knot, she smoothed the silken fringes away, revealing a tin he recognized as one used to hold spices in the cell. Prying off the lid, she removed a rolled piece of paper, then tipped the tin until a diamond fell into her palm.

"Here's your diamond, your letter of credit, and your scarf. Take them."

Sandur shut his eyes at the sight of his gifts being thrown back in his face. She wanted nothing of his, no reminder of their time together, no memories of a foreign prince who left her without a word of explanation, without even a farewell.

"I'd planned to send them to you once I reached Cinthea. You've saved me the trouble."

Even to his own ears his voice sounded queer, as if he were being strangled.

"You don't understand. My uncle writes that my father needs me. I've no choice. I must go back, but I couldn't—can't—take you with me. I didn't want to leave, couldn't bear the fact of leaving you, of never seeing you again." The ache in his throat increased. "I didn't say anything because I couldn't find the words. I hoped the gifts would speak for me. The diamond is my most precious possession, my uncle's gift to me upon reaching manhood. I . . . I wanted you to having something of mine, some token, something to remember me by . . ."

"But you took nothing of mine," she interrupted, "nothing to remind you of me! I searched through all my belongings, thinking I would find something missing. Everything was untouched, exactly as I'd left it!"

Her voice became quiet and deadly in its intensity.

"Can you imagine what it was like, Sandur? To walk through that door, to sense nothing different about the cell, going about my usual tasks, wondering why you were late, not realizing the truth until I found your things gone and a piece of paper I couldn't read? I ran to Evadne at dawn, certain you'd left me a note. Can you imagine the humiliation of listening as she read a letter of credit drawn on the clan of the Kwanlonhon, duly signed by your father? What was I to think, Sandur! What was I to think?"

She was weeping now, tears rolling down her cheeks, her shoulders shaking, the dog crouching miserably beside her, staring up at Sandur with baleful eyes.

"But I did take something."

Slowly, he pulled out a chain from under his fleece-lined jerkin, the metal links warm from the heat of his body. Kneeling beside her, he opened the silver locket he'd traded for the piece of pink coral he'd worn about his neck since boyhood. Patiently, he straightened out her clenched fingers, set aside the diamond, and placed the locket in her open palm.

"What... what is it?"

"Thy hair, thy golden hair."

Her sobs quieted as she fingered the strands he'd stolen from her brush. Disturbed by her nearness, he straightened and backed away.

Her head still bowed over the locket, she asked, "Why did you leave?"

"As I said, I received a letter from my uncle Tasir, pleading for my return."

Retreating to his trunk, he sat with his forearms resting on his knees, willing her to understand.

"Can you imagine what it means to me, Alyssa, to have my father need my help?"

"The same father who ordered you beaten?"

"That is our way," he explained wearily, "and I am his sa'ab. Duty is bred in our bones. You cannot know what it means to be a sa'ab, the firstborn child of your father. My entire life has been spent readying myself to take his place as Tehran. Once you asked me why I return hurt for hurt; now I try to change this about myself. I go not because of any love I feel for him, but in spite of my hatred."

"Yet you would leave me behind."

Hardening himself against her misery, he said, "I cannot take you with me."

Her head came up.

"If the call of duty is so strong that you must leave the Path, so be it. Nonetheless, I require an explanation of why we must part. If you're ashamed of me, tell me to my face."

"You cannot go," he repeated forcefully, willing her to be silent. "I'll escort you to Cinthea, then I'll travel on alone."

"And if I follow?" she asked, her eyes still bright with tears. "Rauros can track you to the ends of the earth. What's to prevent me from making my own way to Endlin?"

He was across the tent before she could draw another breath, digging his fingers into the soft flesh of her shoulders, resisting the urge to shake her until her teeth rattled.

"Put that thought out of your head! If I must hire guards to keep you in Cinthea, I will do so!"

"No one in Cinthea would detain a bard against her wishes, certainly not the daughter of Latona! You're not the only one with power in the land of your birth!"

"You must not do this, Alyssa!" He was begging now, fear making him stammer. "You can't know ... can't imagine ...!"

"Then tell me! Explain it to me!" she raged, wriggling out of his grasp.

"I'm not one of your mindless concubines, sheltered in a palace, ignorant of the world! I've been struck blind, orphaned, and robbed of my inheritance. I've begged for my supper from door to door. What is so terrible that you can't bring yourself to speak it aloud?"

She rubbed the places where his fingers bruised her. Nothing would satisfy her but the truth. Warnings, intimidation, pleading—to all these she turned deaf ears. He'd hoped to spare her. She left him no choice. As cruelly as he could, in the harshest terms possible, he explained why she must not follow him to Endlin.

"In the citadel, you would live as an outcast. Even if I gave you my protection and brought you into my apartments, all would shun you. The servants wouldn't prepare your food or launder your garments, since my father will most probably forbid them to touch anything of yours. The plates from which you take your meals, the pillow on which you rest your head, would be considered unclean. You'd not be allowed to leave my apartments without me by your side. Since I must travel, sometimes for six moons at a time, you'd be trapped inside my rooms, friendless and alone."

Rigid and white, she nodded for him to continue.

"There are no medicines to prevent conception in Endlin. If, through my carelessness, your womb should quicken, I would have to file an appeal to the Equerry, asking him to grant your offspring immunity from your pollution. If the court ruled that your child could, contrary to my father's wishes, become my sa'ab, the babe would be allowed to live if perfectly formed. If not," he swallowed hard, "I would be duty-bound to smother it with my own hands."

She was trembling now, as was Sandur.

"Since none of the concubines would be allowed to help you with the birthing, I would pay for apothecaries to attend you. As most of them are inept, you would most probably suffer a difficult and dangerous delivery. Once the cord was cut and the child was pronounced blemish-free, my sa'ab would be placed in my arms to receive a name, then hurried away to the harem, where you could not follow. There, ayahs and wet-nurses would attend its needs. Nothing would change after the babe was born, except your misery and mine as I'd watch you grieve."

From all around them rose the sounds of the camp, a mother calling for a toddler who strayed too far, Labicus overseeing the loading of the wagons, the rush and scramble of last-minute packing, an elderly man's quavering voice demanding assistance from Dymus, children's conversations as they grubbed in the snow, bridle chains jangling, an infant wailing, a cow lowing—all the humble sounds of a domesticity they could never share.

She knelt, pale and silent, lost in reverie.

"I never knew how difficult it must have been for you that first night," she said at last. "You touched me, do you remember? I reached out my hand, and you took it in yours."

"I remember," he whispered, wishing desperately they could be transported to the haven of perfect peace and privacy that was the Maze. She rose to her feet, his necklace clutched in her hand.

"Give me a lock of your hair."

Unable to deny her anything given her mood, he unsheathed the dagger hanging at his belt and quickly severed several strands. Clutching them in her fist, she took a few steps toward the brazier.

Mystified as to her purpose, he watched, amazed, as she freed the strands of her hair from the locket, entwined them with his own, and cast them onto the coals. Tongues of fire consumed the woven plait greedily, the tent filled with the acrid smell of burning hair, the smoke drifting up through the center opening toward the morning sky. Before he could question her, she smiled, lips quivering a bit, the first smile he'd witnessed since the day of the Gathering.

"We offer the third gift."

"But we've left the Maze . . ."

The daughter of Latona raised a hand to silence him, a blaze of certainty lighting her face from within, her sightless eyes opened wide.

"I've always believed in two things—my dreams and things I can hold in my hand. Two nights ago I dreamt of you; yesterday I heard you call out to me over the noise of the river. Two days ago I held a diamond between my fingertips; last night I held you as you slept. Twice we've parted; twice we've been reunited. I've come to believe we belong together. That we walk the Path wherever we go, whatever we do, and the gift we seek will come to us in time."

She took a deep breath, gathering up her courage.

"I go to Endlin. I go of my own choice, in full knowledge of what I may find upon my arrival." She cocked her head, always a sign of uncertainty, before adding, "May I ride your pack-horse, or must I walk?"

The folk of the caravan thought Haji brave, jumping into an icy river with a rope around his waist. What would they think of Alyssa of Cinthea, stepping toward the brink of a far worse fate with no rope to pull her to safety, only her dreams, things she could hold in her hands, and her belief in Alyssa and Sandur, together. Would they deem her foolhardy, innocent beyond belief, or simply possessed? He hardly knew what to call her himself, this woman who looked at him as though she saw him reflected in some inner eye.

"May I be lost at sea," he growled deep in his throat, sounding like Rauros when he frightened strangers away, "if any harm should come to thee."

Clansmen swore on the heads of their children; lacking children, Sandur swore the ancient oath of those who ply the seas in fragile vessels tossed like twigs between waves reaching up like giant fists to pummel them about. He knew of what he swore: gales blowing him off course, doldrums becalming the waters, the sails flapping aimlessly for weeks at a time, tempestuous storms and treacherous shoals. Capricious as the sea might be, Sandur faced its dangers head on, schooled in its fickleness, its immense and awesome unpredictability. As a sailor he swore, a challenge issued to any and all who stood between him and a blind bard from Cinthea.

Quiet descended, the man standing tense, poised to do battle, the woman silently cursing the darkness in which she dwelt, striving with every fiber of her being to see him, to pierce the gloom and read whatever might be written on his face. And then, as the sun breaks triumphantly through snow-laden clouds, Alyssa smiled.

Reaching up to caress his stubbled cheek, wild, wind-tossed locks barred her path. "Your hair is a disgrace! A lion's mane, no less! And where is your earring?"

"All in good time, nymph," he teased, no less relieved than she to put aside thoughts of the future, "all in good time."

The mention of time brought back the immediacy of their situation. The tent stood in shambles while outside Labicus could be heard braying orders at the top of his lungs.

"We must clean up this mess and pack. By the way," he added with a well-timed thrust, knowing how much she hated a mystery, "thou must remember to call me Haji."

"Haji?" she repeated, then emitted an ear-splitting squeal, wagging a forefinger in his general direction. "No wonder no one ever said your name! And you accused me of following you? As if anyone would follow the likes of you, you lout, you dolt, you good-for-nothing . . .!"

How good it was to tease and be teased! Re-packing his trunk, Sandur listened with a grateful heart, egging her on with surly grunts and mumbled complaints, trying not to laugh until, unable to control himself any longer, he whooped aloud. A decidedly devilish look came over her.

"By the way, Haji," she cooed with infinite sweetness, lingering over the unfamiliar name as she shook out the bedclothes, "I've never ridden a horse before."

Groaning inwardly, he managed an equally pleasant reply.

"Then it will be my pleasure to teach thee."

Devilment lingered in her face.

"Also, Haji, I don't sleep with strangers."

He started to object, then remembered the cramped quarters inside Kenuthia's tent and the group of men and women gathered around the old woman's campfire as they broke their morning fast. Several of the men were young and not bad-looking.

"Alyssa," he asked, biting back his jealousy, "who exactly was living in that tent?"

She dropped to her knees, busily folding blankets. "All in good time, Haji," she replied airily. "All in good time."

Caught in his own trap, he swore aloud. Shoulders shaking beneath the grey shawl, she dissolved into a fit of helpless merriment. Rauros wagged his tail, romping around her prostrate form, emitting a series of high-pitched barks as he joined in the fun.

Happier than he had been in ages, perhaps happier than he had ever been in his life, Sandur set to work.

Chapter 21

The Sign of the Gull

A SHIP'S PORTER LOUNGED by a food stall on the side of the road, trying not to burn his mouth on the skewer of grilled fish he'd just purchased with two copper coins dug from the pocket of his baggy, roll-cuffed breeches. A woven hamper with wide leather straps, the tool of his humble trade, lay empty and abandoned at his feet, proof he'd gotten no work that morning down at the wharves. The sun was high overhead, broiling the seven hills of Endlin to a crisp, uniform brown, a fortnight since the last rainsquall and not a cloud in sight. Naked above the waist, barelegged from the calves down, a pair of ragged sandals on his feet, the porter's skin was nearly the color of his charred fish. Rivulets of sweat poured down the middle of his back, making a v-shaped pattern of moisture at the waist of his breeches. Like most natives, he seemed oblivious to the heat and wore his wide-brimmed straw hat at a jaunty angle, ogling the women who passed by.

Small, wiry, with the flat, hard muscles of one who works long hours on few rations, the porter devoured his midday meal with every evidence of enjoyment, smacking his lips after swallowing the last morsel and licking the skewer clean. Using his breeches as a napkin, he ran his eyes over the crowds, squinting against the glare and the choking dust unsettled by passing feet.

"Waiting for someone?" the owner of the food stall inquired as he reclaimed the skewer, speaking from boredom rather than any real interest in the affairs of a lowly porter. The midday trade was disappointing, perhaps a sign that he should move his cart to another location. The traffic was usually heavy between the southern road and the Abalone district, village people scurrying to the markets with their wares, sometimes a few travelers up from Tek, tourists mostly, or those with clan business. Today was no exception, but for some reason (perhaps the fact that his fish wasn't as fresh as it might have been), he'd waited on a mere handful of customers.

"A friend," the porter replied easily, flashing the owner a white-toothed grin. "He's late, though. Always is. Always was."

Grunting his commiseration, since nothing irritated him quite so much as waiting for his usually tardy woman, the food-stall owner busied himself with wiping the skewer clean.

"Where's he from?"

"Tek," the porter replied, intent on searching through his pockets for another coin. "How much for a glass of tea?"

Casting a quick glance at the empty basket and the numerous rents in the porter's breeches, the food-stall owner weighed the price of a hard-earned copper against the fact that the tea was no longer cold and, having been brewed the day before, was somewhat rancid and must be thrown out at day's end. Added to his decision was a businessman's sure and certain knowledge that nothing scared prospective customers away more quickly than an empty food stall. The longer the porter lingered, the more business he might attract.

"On the house."

Ducking his head, shy with thanks, this grin wider than the last, the porter took a healthy swig of tea and resumed his former pose, leaning comfortably against a pole supporting the awning and gazing out over the southern road. The food-stall owner noticed the porter ignored anyone on horseback or riding in a conveyance; his interest centered on the pedestrians. He considered asking another question about the porter's friend, again, not so much out of curiosity as boredom, then decided, on a whim, to venture onto another topic.

"What news from the docks?"

"Nothing much," the porter threw back over his shoulder, his speech as indolent as his manner, his eyes busy with the crowd. "An Onozzi frigate two days overdue. Nobody's worrying yet, or at least that's the official story."

The food-stall owner scowled as he wiped the counter clean. Prices were sky-high in the city, speculators bartering with frantic haste, everyone certain a late ship meant a lost ship.

"There was some work for the Kwanlonhon, but the steward didn't choose me." The porter paused a moment, no doubt reflecting on the hard life of a working man, before adding, "They're moving into a new warehouse, a nice one, too, clean and dry with high ceilings to keep down the heat."

"Damned lucky, the reds," the food-stall owner sighed, adopting the street lingo commoners used when reflecting on their betters.

"Aye," the porter agreed between sips of tea, "damned lucky."

Conversation came to a halt as the porter's head shot up. The food-stall owner thought him a singularly lethargic young man and was unsurprised to learn the exacting stewards of the Kwanlonhon had overlooked him. This opinion was reversed when the porter sprang into action. Grabbing up his basket by the straps, dodging pedestrians with easy grace, he approached a dust-begrimed stranger, pulling him into a fierce bear hug. In the next moment, the two men were walking side by side, arms locked, heads bowed in earnest conversation. Pouring out the last few mouthfuls of warm tea onto the thirsty soil, the food-stall owner watched as they headed toward the Abalone district, wondering only briefly how a lowly deck porter chanced to make a friend in faraway Tek.

"I hardly recognized you!" the porter exclaimed, taking in skin tanned to the shade of old leather, smooth-shaven cheeks, and a head of coal-black hair. Only Esslar's eyes were the same—doe-brown, dream-filled eyes belying the fierce black eyebrows above.

"I could say the same of you," Esslar offered with a gleam of rare humor. "Your costume smells, uh, quite authentic."

"And my accent?" the porter asked eagerly, probing unashamedly for a compliment and receiving a rueful laugh in return.

"Better than mine, I fear, being sadly out of practice."

"We'll soon have you jabbering away like a native. We've got the slang down pat."

Esslar smiled at the porter's boast before lowering his voice to the tones of conspiracy.

"Tell me everything."

The porter, also known as Phanus of Pelion, rushed to comply.

"They arrived yesterday, a little before sunset. We might have missed them but for the dog. San . . .," catching himself, the porter continued more carefully, ". . . he wasn't what I expected."

"How so?"

"I thought he'd be easy to spot even in disguise, that he wouldn't be able to hide the carriage, the angle of the chin. Also, we weren't prepared for pedestrians. He must have ditched the horses, afraid the stallion might be recognized. Anyway, they came in on foot, no jewelry, no braids, not a hint of silk, just a modestly dressed young couple and a large dog. He's smart, very smart," the porter nodded his approval. "Wrapped her hair with a length of dark gauze so its color wouldn't draw undue attention. The clansmen at the gates didn't give them a second glance."

"They're staying in the harbor district?"

"Where else could they go?" the porter asked, bewildered by his friend's reaction, which bordered on alarm. "It was either an inn or the citadel, and it's clear he has no intention of announcing his arrival to his father."

"You're right, of course," the traveler sighed. "I should be thankful he's heeded our warnings."

"Don't worry so much, Esslar. He booked rooms at The Nesting Gull, the best inn in the district. She'll be safe there, especially with the dog for protection."

"Is Lampon with them?"

The porter nodded. "She's not budged from the room since their arrival. He ordered a light supper in their rooms and had hot water carried upstairs, took the dog out at dawn, and carried the morning meal up to her on a tray. Lampon took over at breakfast. I grabbed a short nap at the shop before coming to meet you."

"You've done well, Phanus."

They continued without conversation, the Legionnaire basking in Esslar's praise, the healer reminding himself he must not let his private worries cloud the judgment of his helpers. The fact that Phanus and Lampon survived here for a full year without arousing suspicion proved their expertise. As limited adepts they were perfect for this type of work, quick-thinking and resourceful, two of Galen's finest.

"What news of home?"

Steeling himself, the wound still too raw to be handled, Esslar forced himself to answer, sensing the uneasiness with which Phanus posed the question.

"The Guild Assembly disbanded. Adrastus resigned and left the city in disgrace. There's much confusion, much discussion, calls for a different kind of ruling council, one not limited by craft affiliations or guild standing, perhaps with members-at-large. Most seem to want a mixed body, including representatives from the Legion and the League," he added darkly, "that is, if the Legionnaires and the traders will ever forgive them."

Phanus took it like the soldier he was, setting his jaw against any show of emotion. "And the traders?"

"Too early to tell. Too early even to guess."

"Whose caravan did you join?"

"Labicus, a Master Trader who specializes in the eastern route. We were lucky, I suppose, to lose so few."

Esslar bore no resemblance to a man who considered himself lucky.

"Three children to a bout of measles, a stillborn babe, and a feeble old woman who ought never to have left Pelion. One man lost in a flash flood, his body never found; another whose heart stopped when he tried to free a wagon stuck in a ditch. I warned him not to do the work of a much younger man the first time he came to me complaining of chest pains. Labicus forbade him to help, but it did no good . . ."

The healer's voice trailed off, the death toll left incomplete. They walked on, mourning private losses, while around them the steady stream of traffic leading toward the Abalone district grew in size and volume. As they approached the fabric market, their progress was interrupted from time to time by people trying to move against the flow. Phanus side-stepped them or shoved them aside if they came too close, keeping a firm grip on Esslar's arm, always mindful of his role as bodyguard.

"No one recognized you, not even . . . him?"

"Only the dog," Esslar confessed with the hint of a smile, "on the day I joined the caravan. He rode with the forward scout, heedless of everything save his own misery; she sensed nothing, not even when Rauros woofed at me and wagged his tail in greeting."

"Did Labicus suspect anything?"

Esslar seemed about to answer in the negative, then spoke dreamily, as was his habit when considering the inexplicable.

"I thought not, until the day we parted in Tek. He's not adept, you see, but he possesses an extraordinary ability to judge a person's character, to guess who will panic and who will not, to know which tent to search first when a sack of meal is stolen. He sensed a lie in me from the beginning, but was so thankful to have a healer he refrained from asking questions. When I took my leave of him, he looked me straight in the eye, saying, `Look after them, healer.' It was a strange thing to say, especially when I was careful to have no contact with them, and they'd departed the day before."

They walked more quickly now, matching the pace of the crowd, listening to the rapid chatter of merchants hawking their wares, drawing prospective clients into their shops. Multi-colored canopies protecting their wares billowed in the steady off-shore breeze. As they reached the top of Abalone Hill, the harbor shone like a flat, blue disc below them, anchored vessels bobbing like so many corks on a fish line, their pennants fluttering like slender, pointed fingers—the blue of the H'ulalet, the green of the Synzurit, the yellow of the Effrentati, and the red of the mighty Kwanlonhon.

"No Assad or Onozzi."

"The Onozzi flagship, *Albatross*, is overdue. Two Assad frigates, the only two in their fleet not lost or disabled, shipped out in tandem a fortnight ago. If they don't return with cargos intact, rumor has it the Assad will be no more."

"And *Seahorse*?" asked Esslar, his gaze riveted on a schooner moored alongside the Kwanlonhon dock, her decks swarming with workers.

"She's undergoing repairs from storm damage suffered on her last voyage to Nisyros. She limped in a week late, four hands lost at sea, washed overboard when a storm hit. Quite a scene when she docked. The Tehran himself came down from the citadel to meet her. Lampon saw him passing out bonuses to the crew with his own hands."

When Esslar seemed about to reply, a muttered warning cut him off.

"Keep your eyes on the road."

Phanus kept their pace unhurried as they approached a round-bellied tea merchant engaged in a loud disagreement with an unsatisfied customer. As they passed a decrepit shop with a small, hand-lettered sign in the window, Phanus swore softly under his breath and sauntered on, passing a sponge dealer and a rug merchant.

"What's amiss?"

"A note on the door. An irate customer, no doubt, furious at finding us closed for the second day in a row."

Avoiding the shoppers surrounding them with a practiced eye, Phanus dodged to the right, turned down a side street, walked three blocks more, then doubled back to an alleyway off the main thoroughfare. His companion made no comment, matching him stride for stride, content to be led, posing no distractions. Coming to a halt at a door on the alley, Phanus produced a key from a cleverly hidden pocket in the waistband of his breeches. They entered the cool, dark interior of the bookshop.

Phanus wasted no time in throwing his headgear onto the table while grabbing up a robe to cover his porter's disguise. Taking a deep breath, he strode to the front door, opened it with calculated disinterest, removed the note and, without reading it, closed the door, locking it behind him.

"It's from the Equerry," he explained briefly, running his eyes swiftly down to the signature. "Good," he sighed, looking up at Esslar with a relieved grin. "I feared it might be from Lampon."

Esslar nodded, glad Phanus and Lampon had heeded his warning to refrain from using inner speech unless an emergency made shared communication vital.

Responding to a call for limited adepts put out by the Nineteenth Mother some years ago, this mated couple volunteered for a long-term mission in the east knowing how high the stakes might be. Totally invested in becoming indistinguishable from thousands of commoners who lived and worked among the seven hills, they'd mastered the Endlinese language and harbor slang, worked the docks in countless jobs, even signed on for a voyage as first and second mates so as to learn on-board protocols. For the past six months, they'd alternated roles as book-shop clerks and harbor district spies, aided, no doubt, by the fact that they might have been twins, these small-boned, dark-skinned men with keen eyes and ready smiles.

Worried that even their small adept gifts might be sensed by the Tehran of the Kwanlonhon, Esslar was relieved to hear Phanus' report that neither he nor his partner had sensed even the slightest touch of Manthur's mind. Written communication was a bother to those with adept skills, although Galen had remarked, with his usual gift for understatement, "Better a bother than a dead agent."

Another thought came to Esslar's mind as he swatted dust from his cloak. "What do you make of the Equerry, Phanus?"

Esslar's host was already rustling up a meal, tearing apart a wheel of bread and spearing pickled cucumbers from a crock with the tip of his dagger.

"He's a tough old bird, typically Synzurit, crotchety and ill-tempered. That place," a lifted eyebrow indicated the room beyond the canvas wall, "is his sanctuary. Sometimes he lingers for hours, the guards lined up outside the front door to insure his privacy."

"Any special interests?"

"Anything and everything to do with legal procedures. The last shipment left him drooling, especially when he found a copy of the judicial system adopted by the Agavean Session."

"What does his message say?"

"Just as I guessed—instructions as to how lazy shopkeepers can best show proper gratitude to illustrious patrons. He'll be back the fourth hour after midday," Phanus pulled a face, "at which time he'll probably lambaste me in person."

"By the time he arrives," Esslar laughed, accepting the trencher of sun-dried fish, pickled cucumbers, rice balls, and dates, "you'll be asleep in the back room. I'll wait upon him as a cousin of yours recently arrived from Tek. You're to turn over all the shop business to me."

A sober-faced Phanus nodded, relieved by Esslar's instructions. No longer chained to the shop, he and Lampon could better attend to their other duties.

"Rest," Esslar ordered between bites. "I'll wake you at dusk."

"One more thing." Phanus poured out a pitcher of water into a basin. "The Equerry hates the reds with a passion."

Esslar shrugged, unimpressed. "He's Synzurit."

"It's more than that," Phanus insisted, washing off the dirt and sweat from the road and privately resolving never again to complain about the occasional cold winter in Pelion. "Everyone knows the Synzurit resent the Kwanlonhon's rise in fortune. That's old news. This is different, something personal."

Esslar stopped eating.

"If there are reds in the shop when he arrives, he won't enter until they leave. If one comes in while he's browsing, he's out in the next moment, cutting him dead as he departs." Phanus yawned, his voice fading away as he stretched out on the narrow cot. "It's more than simple resentment. He's angry, deeply angry, about what I don't know. Something unjust, I think. Something . . . unfair . . ."

Gentle snores filled the tiny room as the healer chewed out of habit, the bread turning to sawdust in his mouth.

So the Equerry knows. He's put it together, just as we have, but he's powerless to act. Did he read the copy of the contract I filed in his court? I would have done so, even if it were marked private, especially if I was already suspicious of the Tehran of the Kwanlonhon. Unjust, Phanus said, unjust and unfair, this from a man who studies law, our law as adopted by the Agavean Session. What would he say if he saw Sandur's back?

We must watch over the Tehran's sa'ab, for his life is worth less than nothing in the city of his fathers. We must watch over them both, for I see the light begin to shimmer around them, proof that they approach the beginning of the end. Let them be as One, and let it happen quickly, quickly, or I fear all will be lost.

So the Master of Mysteries began the long watch, munching thoughtfully on the future, unaware that beyond the limestone wall, the Tehran's sa'ab, the subject of his prayers, began his final voyage.

"YOU'LL NOT TARRY?"
Everything Alyssa feared for him, for herself, for their lives together, was contained in that question. Lately, he had to remind himself she was blind. It was uncanny, the way her eyes seemed to track his every movement within the rooms they made their private sanctum. Strange though it was when he thought about it, since leaving the Maze they'd tried to recreate the cell every step of the way. First the tent, now the Inn of the Nesting Gull; in each we hide from the world. But I can hide no longer.

"I'll return as soon as I can."

Nodding, she turned away, her profile lit by the ruddy gleam of the candles burning brightly by their bedside. Her hair, a stream of molten red-gold running down her back, blended with the over-robe of patterned gold embroidered on amethyst silk. Pink pearls bedecked her earlobes, the only jewelry she'd ever owned, worn to please him on this night of nights.

He knew the source of her trouble, and it was not just the thought of the coming interview with his father. In the past few days it had become increasingly difficult to leave her, if only for a moment. Yesterday, as he left the inn to deliver a note to Tasir's steward, he'd felt slightly nauseous, with a peculiar light-headedness accompanied by a faint ringing in his ears. When he mentioned it to Alyssa, she admitted experiencing similar symptoms. They decided it was the food, since they ate from the same bowl, feeding each other despite crumbs on the bedclothes, unwilling to give up the bed for the table. Now, his stomach in knots at the thought of leaving her, he doubted their diagnosis.

Many things had changed in the past two moons—things for which Sandur barely had words. He, who from childhood feared the dark, fell asleep in Alyssa's arms without need of candle or brazier. The bad dreams vanished, swept away by the warm breezes blowing along the eastern shore. Instead, they found they shared their dreams, something neither of them could explain, although Alyssa seemed convinced it was some kind of portent, whether good or evil she could not, or would not, say. Gone, too, was his fear of fathering a child. Nightly, his seed found a resting place within her womb; daily, he watched for the signs of the sa'ab-to-be. Alyssa said nothing, as reticent as he was to speak her hopes aloud, yet her tears told him everything when she woke one morning with blood on her shift. He held her close, crying inside himself at the sight of those rust-colored stains.

Shaking away his sickness, he grabbed up his cloak.

"Let me fix the clasp."

Rauros' half-opened eye gleamed red as he lay curled on his pallet at the foot of the bed. Throwing the cloak over his shoulders, Sandur bent his head to watch her nimble fingers work the clasp of solid silver, the oil of lavender he'd bought her in the marketplace blending with the smell of the sea. Her hands lifted, drifting up to touch his newly-braided hair, the diamond implanted in the crease above his nostril, the earring restored to its rightful place, then floated down to linger over the four layers of gold-encrusted silk. Upon reaching the dagger hilt thrust in his sash, her hands flew away as if burned.

"You are much changed, I think, from the ernani I met in the cell. What would Draupadi make of you, I wonder?" Her lips curved in a half-smile. "Perhaps she would finally be convinced that you are, indeed, a prince."

"Thy prince, Alyssa."

Her brows knit, her mood suddenly intense.

"You must remember," she said, dismissing his finery with a wave of her hand, "I see nothing of this. To me you are simply Sandur, not your father's son, not a future Tehran, not even," she added softly, "a prince."

He left the inn, hurrying toward his appointment. The city, cooled by the night breeze off the water, slept around him, the tang of salt heavy in the air. The shell path rose up before him, crunching underfoot, the limestone cliffs chalky white as black waves crashed beneath them. A light beckoned him, a stab of brightness leading him to his destination . . . and all the while, in his mind's eye, he envisioned the candles in their chamber sputtering out one by one, gutted by the humid breezes drifting in the bedroom window, plunging Alyssa into darkness. A wave of nausea overcame him.

Fighting the desire to turn and run, he drew another picture in his mind—Alyssa waiting patiently for his return, a white lady glowing redly in the flickering light as Rauros napped at her feet. It was to this vision he would return again and again in the hours that followed; that, and the words that set him free, "To me you are simply Sandur."

ROBES SWIRLING RESTLESSLY about his feet, Manthur paced the confines of the great room as a leopard stalks its cage, countering tedium with indefatigable energy, constantly in motion, weaving a monotonous pattern into the deep-piled rug. Head bowed in concentration, the furrows across his forehead and alongside his nose plowed deep into the ocher soil of his face. Never have I seen him so tense, thought Tasir, trying to dismiss his growing apprehension. A harsh voice ripped across the room, shattering the silence of the empty apartments.

"Why must I meet him here? My study is more private."

"You read the note yourself, brother. I know no more than you. Rest assured we will be alone. My steward has arranged everything."

Silence reigned again, Manthur never altering his course. Time passed tediously, a snail borne along on a tortoise's back.

"Tell me again what your steward said."

Tasir stifled a sigh before repeating the oft-told story, remembering all the while that the ninth hour approached.

"He refused to believe it was Sandur, even when I hinted as to his identity. He said the man who approached him was unquestionably a commoner, rough of manner and short of speech. His face was partially hidden by a hood pulled low over his forehead. He wore no jewelry of any kind. He was taller than most commoners; other than that, he bore no resemblance to Sandur."

The Tehran gave no sign that he heard.

The sound of footsteps brought both men's heads up. Turning in unison, they faced the tiled archway leading from the exterior entrance to Tasir's apartments. A cloaked figure paused under the arch. The steward who accompanied the visitor bowed and took his leave. A hand appeared from beneath the cloak, a silver clasp flew open, and the robe fell in a pile at the feet of the Tehran's sa'ab.

It was as though time, in a fit of unexplained nostalgia, reversed direction. This was not Sandur, but Manthur, a beloved brother returning home after a five-year absence. So Manthur stood thirty years ago, darkly tanned and impeccably groomed, as highly-strung as a prize stallion, eyes moving swiftly over the room before coming to rest on his father. Manthur's return had been joyous, impossibly poignant, their ailing father weeping at the sight of the son he never thought to see again. Time and distance turned the son into a man, and so it was with Sandur, who bore no resemblance to the nephew Tasir last saw bleeding on the carpet, his slender body writhing under the blows of the bamboo rod. This was another man, heavily muscled about the shoulders and chest, his wide-legged stance confident, aggressive, his palm resting lightly on the jeweled hilt of his dagger.

"Do you come armed into your father's presence?"

Tasir's vision crumpled, his hopes dashed by a father who shed no tears at the return of his sa'ab. Something died in Sandur's face as well, anticipation turning to wariness, a feeling of danger stalking the room.

"I come as all must come who speak the name of Pelion."

"Is that an accusation of some kind? Something squawked in your ear by those who hope to turn you against me?"

Sandur threw back his head, the oil lamps hanging overhead casting a faint reddish halo over his braids.

"That is fact, father, told me by those who've suffered at the hands of your agents. At first I didn't believe; since then I've gathered proof. Dorian, who lost his son outside Tek; Lynsaya of Lapith, who heard her attackers discuss between themselves the fees they're paid to waylay travelers journeying west. If this is not true, then why, of all the ernani, was I the only one from the eastern shore?"

Tasir was quickly lost, not understanding Sandur's accusations but believing them as he watched his brother's expression change from cold dislike to glowering rage.

"That black bitch fed you these lies! Give me one shred of evidence that what you say is true! Or have you become your grandmother's boy, sucking hatred from her withered dugs?"

Sandur went rigid, whether from insult or shock Tasir couldn't be sure. The hand gripping the hilt of the dagger trembled.

"Grandmother?"

A cruel laugh signified Manthur's disbelief.

"Grandmother?" Manthur mimicked in a shrill voice, spitting out venom with practiced aim. "Don't insult my intelligence. Why do you think she wanted you, stole you from me? Why do you think she sent you back? Are you to be my assassin? Is that her plan?"

The voice that made Tasir quail brought an opposite reaction from Sandur. Eyes narrowing into slits, nostrils flaring, he stood his ground against the earth-shaking fury of his father.

"Think what you may, she spoke no word against you, nor did she reveal our kinship. As to sending me back, I left the Maze of my own accord."

"Why would you do such a thing if you fear for your life?"

Manthur's sneer went astray, for Sandur never flinched.

"I came because you need me, or so my uncle wrote."

"Need you? Need you?! What need have I for someone who believes me guilty of crimes I didn't commit?"

Sandur continued as if he had not been interrupted.

"I came, too, to claim my inheritance and to stop you from persecuting those who would enter the Maze."

Manthur's humorless laughter set Tasir's teeth on edge.

"Is it possible you are so naive as to think yourself the next Tehran? You? A puling, sniveling, half-witted coward? Have I ever treated you with anything other than disdain? Have I ever shown you the slightest kindness, revealed by a look or a word anything except my complete disgust at what you've become?"

This was beyond dislike, beyond malice, beyond reason and even beyond imagination. With this speech, Manthur broke every rule governing Endlin for five centuries, a rule that guaranteed an unbroken line of perfect, priceless children, to the end that every sa'ab was a treasure to be cherished by the father. For Manthur to hate his sa'ab was to turn his back on duty, on order, on existence itself. Tasir reeled under the lash of Manthur's tongue; Sandur stood firm, his speech clipped, exacting.

"I've done nothing to earn your disdain. I am your sa'ab and your heir by right of birth. Not once have I failed in my duty. Come what may, I am your luck..."

Whatever Sandur intended to say was lost under a rising wail of maniacal laughter. Flecks of foam flying from his lips, his face contorted into a twisted mask of madness, Manthur screamed out his hatred in a voice that shook the citadel.

"My luck? My luck, do you say? If you be my luck, why fear hell itself, for there I've dwelt since the hour of your birth! My luck died with my true sa'ab—a stillborn daughter, not you, you spawn of the devil! A murderer you were born and a murderer you remain!"

"How am I a murderer?"

Manthur pushed out the words between sobs of rage.

"You--killed--the--one--who--bore--you!"

"Then my mother . . . Aethra . . . is . . . ?"

"You will not speak her name!" Manthur snarled, his lips pulled back in a feral snarl. "You're not fit to wear it on your tongue!"

Father and son reached stalemate. Here was the reason for the loveless boyhood, the beatings, the years of studied neglect. Sandur gripped the hilt of the dagger, his face haggard, old beyond his years. Bracing himself for bloodshed, too appalled by Manthur's ravings to offer his support as was his duty, Tasir decided he would not interfere, that he would allow nothing to come between Sandur and his revenge. As he made that decision, one formed with the agonizing knowledge that the Kwanlonhon clan would be forever shamed by a patricide, another Sandur stood before them.

With a deep sigh, the Tehran's sa'ab loosed his grip on the dagger. Reaching up, he found the pendant hanging from a silver chain around his neck. Clutching it in his fist, he began to speak, understanding and compassion writ on his face.

"So this is why you persecute those who would walk the Path. You walked it yourself, my mother by your side. When you lost her, you lost everything." A shadow flew across his features. "I understand this fear, for I, too, have felt it—the fear of losing my other self, my Alyssa. If you cannot share the gift with my mother, no one shall have it. And for this, you blame me."

"Alyssa?"

Sandur smiled at his uncle's question, a smile of such unexpected sweetness that Tasir gasped aloud. Was this possible, his nephew speaking a woman's name as tenderly as a caress?

"Aye, Alyssa. She waits for me, and I must be off."

Moving with a sudden burst of energy, Sandur wrapped the cloak around his shoulders as he spoke.

"I shall write a formal letter to the Equerry rescinding my right to succeed you as Tehran. My possessions and my portion of the clan revenues I leave to Tasir. You'll never see me more," his features hardened, "although I give you fair warning. Call off your agents or I'll make it my business to hunt them down. I have friends now," he smiled again, relishing the thought, "and they'll join me in my fight. Leave Pelion to its own devices."

To this admonition, simply made but heartfelt, Manthur made no reply. Tasir called out to the retreating back of his nephew.

"What will you do? Where will you go?"

Sandur wheeled to address his favorite uncle.

"I don't know, nor do I care. I walk the Path, uncle, and I go where it takes me. Don't grieve for me, for I've found happiness and more than happiness. I shall miss the sea, but I've learned how wide the world is and what a tiny part of it we inhabit."

In this way, the Tehran's sa'ab took his leave, relinquishing the duties for which he was bred, those same duties which once served as his sole reason for existence. He came expecting forgiveness. Finding none, he asserted his rights. Those rights denied, his sole course was revenge, to punish the one who ruined his youth and betrayed his hopes for the future he was promised. Yet, that night Esslar's story was re-written. At last the old pattern was broken: kindness offered instead of piling hurt on hurt; good given in exchange for evil; charity rendered by one much abused; the dagger rejected for the contents of a locket strung on a silver chain.

HIS THOUGHTS A chaos, dimly aware of the movement of Tasir's lips, Manthur heard the screaming of his mind. The world around him receded, leaving nothing but a wall of hatred surrounding him, choking him, sending him reeling down a hallway, any hallway, since any he took would deliver him to the room where vengeance waited. Somehow he found the door, pushing his way past the groveling steward, slamming it behind him.

Vengeance sat in his master's favorite chair, his calfskin boots resting lazily on the ottoman, cleaning the dirt from under his fingernails with the tip of a curved dagger with a serrated blade. He barely looked up when madness swept into the room, barely started as the door quivered on its hinges, the frame threatening to break asunder. What better face could vengeance have than this one—smooth, well-fed, self-assured, the face of a bored child, an idle woman, an indifferent man?

Something in his quietus soothed Manthur, perhaps the air of nonchalance with which he flicked away the final particle of dirt and resheathed the dagger. This was expertise, this the hallmark of deadly craftsmanship. Chaos gave way to cunning, the pieces on the game board arranged and re-arranged, moves tested, rejected, new strategies put into play. All the while vengeance sat napping.

"You had him followed?"

A closed eye fluttered open, an eyebrow arched. A pained expression implied that Manthur's question bordered on insult.

"There is a woman . . ."

A flicker of interest, a slight rearrangement of boots on the ottoman.

"A woman called Alyssa . . ."

A nod indicated the name would not be forgotten.

"She will be nearby, perhaps in the harbor district, perhaps in a village on the outskirts of town."

A faint sigh. More agents to hire, more work for everyone.

"Kill her . . ."

A suggestion of a yawn, covered politely by an open hand.

". . . but kill her in the presence of my son."

Both eyes flew open. A look of grudging admiration.

"It must be public, the more public the better."

A sharp pain stabbed Manthur behind his right eye.

Vengeance spoke, his voice like gravel shaken in a tin cup.

"And your son?"

The pain was back, this time behind the left eye, a hole being drilled from the back of his head into the cavity of his skull. Inadvertently, his hands went to his temples, trying to rub out the sound of the drilling, an incessant clamor ringing between his ears.

"After he has witnessed the killing . . ."

The urge to scream was so great he bit his tongue, the blood curdling in his mouth before he swallowed.

". . . he must disappear without a trace."

Registering disappointment, vengeance chanced a suggestion: "Surely there's a simpler solution?"

"No!"

Manthur's head was a throbbing mass of agony, the effort of speech so extreme he could barely manage the slightest of whispers.

"He must live, don't you see? Live with the picture of her death always before him."

Vengeance nodded once, twice, his enthusiasm growing as his imagination leapt ahead. Invigorated by the elegance of the plan, for nothing suits vengeance quite so well as variations on a theme, he rose to his feet.

"My fee?"

The pain redoubled, alarms shrieking out protests, warnings that he still might find redemption, that all might be forgiven.

Through gritted teeth Manthur whispered,"Perform the deed as described, perfectly and without omission, and you may name your fee."

And with that, Vengeance was gone.

SPIRITS WERE HIGH in the tavern of The Nesting Gull. The Onozzi ship sailed in on the evening tide, bringing with it an almost hysterical urge to offer up toasts to her pilot and crew, every able-bodied seaman in the district raising a glass in their honor. The tavern, a more respectable establishment than most due to the presence of the inn overhead and the fact that the brothels were located several blocks away, was crowded, but not unusually so given the lateness of the hour.

The tavern itself was built slightly below ground-level, dug-in, one might say, with the inn rising three floors above. Even on the hottest day the ground floor remained cool, if a bit moist, both because of its location and the fact that the kitchen (in true Endlinese fashion) was detached from the building proper. A narrow passageway linked the kitchen to the tavern and the dining room, located directly behind the innkeeper's desk and to the right of the tavern's separate entrance. All told, it was a convenient arrangement, allowing a free-flow of traffic between tavern, inn, and kitchen.

Besides guests of the inn, the tavern enjoyed a regular clientele of dockworkers, ordinary seamen, merchants, and tradesmen, a fairly well-behaved group, although overly fond of singing drinking songs until the wee hours of the morning. As much as their caterwauling annoyed the innkeeper, especially when guests complained (and rightly so) that sleep was a near impossibility until well after midnight, the tavern keeper was often heard reminding his business partner that things could be worse. Their customers might sing at the top of their lungs, arms draped over shoulders as they swayed to the tapping of their boots and sandals against the scarred wooden floors, but they rarely killed one another in fits of drunken rage. Breakage was common, as was brawling, since like all establishments catering to the seamen's tastes, rough and rowdy customers were fundamental to prosperity.

This particular night, every chair was taken, every bench along the planked tables lined with amiable rows of buttocks, many customers forced to stand alongside the bar where the tavern keeper watched the tap with one eye, the other on the coin-box. By midnight, the din was overwhelming, customers shouting at one another over a chorus of male voices raised in a sea-chantey, most of them hoarse with drink and decidedly off-key. The heat generated by so many unwashed bodies pressed against one another, combined with the sour smell of vomit and ancient urine, was a touch oppressive, although no one seemed to mind, perhaps because seamen are accustomed to cramped conditions below deck. Whatever the reason, neither temperature, odor, or noise seemed to bother the clientele of The Nesting Gull, all of them celebrating the return of *Albatross* while adding certain unprintable remarks concerning the recent acts of piracy that made their profession twice-dangerous since now they must face the capriciousness of man as well as that of the sea.

Given the general confusion of the proceedings, it was a stroke of luck that Phanus happened to catch sight of Sandur making his way through the crush around the bar.

Having nursed his bowl of rice wine for several hours, Phanus downed it in a single gulp, waved his empty bowl at his companions at the table, and headed toward the bar. By the time he reached his destination, pushing his way with steady determination through the welter of shouting drunkards, he observed, with some dismay, that Sandur was engaged in earnest conversation with someone Phanus had never seen before. After five nights spent studying the regulars, he knew them all down to the table they frequented, their preference for rice wine or pale ale, and their favorite topics of conversation. This man, with his hearty laugh, smiling countenance, and constantly moving eyes, didn't match any of the descriptions Lampon supplied of newly arrived guests, nor did he appear to be a commoner. As tall as Sandur, whose height set him a head above most of the crowd, the man's dress lent no clues as to his profession, although Phanus noted that his knee-high calfskin boots were Lapithian in style and worth a tidy sum in hard coinage. Edging nearer, he strained to hear their conversation over the tumult of the crowd.

"... a nor'wester blew her down beyond Salmydessus, out into open seas. The pilot despaired since they were off the charts. Finally, they reached a sargasso sea ..."

"Sargasso?" Sandur interrupted, frowning at the unfamiliar word.

"Gulfweed," the man explained with a patronizing air, "which convinced the pilot they'd passed into the Gulf of Swiasa. The clan trader on board was at wit's end, a coward no doubt, afraid of his Tehran and anxious to return home with all possible speed. So, sad to say, they never went ashore to prove the pilot's theory correct. Once the nor'wester blew itself out, they tacked their way west, then north again, and made it back three weeks behind schedule."

Clearly, Sandur was interested, even excited, by the man's recital, although Phanus had only the dimmest notion why. A rapid examination followed, Sandur firing questions, all of them answered by the stranger with an unruffled air of expertise. As the conversation progressed, Phanus' fears abated.

Sandur's interest in cartography was well known, as was his friendship with Dorian the Chartist. Relaxing a bit, Phanus ordered another bowl of wine and leaned with his back against the bar, listening to Sandur with one ear while studying the crowd, all the time wondering what happened to Sandur in the citadel last night.

Assuredly, Sandur returned a different man from the elegantly robed clansman Phanus followed through the limestone gates, past the Abalone district and up the northern road to a private entrance on the west wing of the citadel. Something of import transpired, of that Phanus was certain. Simply dressed now in tight-legged breeches and a loose-fitting cotton blouse, woven sandals on his feet, his hair freed of its braids and tied at the nape of his neck with a piece of cording, Sandur might have been a tradesman enjoying a night on the town rather than the son of the most powerful man in Endlin. Gone, too, was the brooding look in his eyes, replaced with something resembling contentment.

Lampon commented on the change this evening when they'd met in the tavern to share a meal and discuss the day's events. For the first time since they'd arrived, the woman accompanied Sandur out-of-doors, spending the day touring the city, the dog on her right, Sandur on her left, Lampon trailing discreetly behind. They'd strolled for hours, taking their midday meal near a famous vista overlooking the harbor, Sandur talking constantly, with great animation, Lampon reported, as though he sketched out plans for her approval. The woman, too, seemed excited, nodding her gauze-covered head from time to time, sometimes intervening with a question or a comment, sometimes laughing aloud.

"They reach the end of the Path," Lampon remarked between spoonfuls of shark stew sprinkled liberally with pepper sauce. "Esslar says it won't be much longer, a matter of days, maybe hours."

So close are we, thought Phanus, so close to success, before turning his attention abruptly to his charge, who was making his excuses as he picked up a tray with two glasses and a bottle of what looked to be imported wine.

". . . and so you must excuse me. I've been overlong in returning, and she must wonder what keeps me."

The smile on Sandur's face tightened as the stranger threw a friendly arm around his shoulders. No one else would have noticed the signs of his discomfort, a flinch as the stranger touched him, a slight widening of the eyes. Phanus recognized them, as do all who have worked in the Maze and witnessed firsthand the reaction of someone in the first stage of Transformation to the touch of anyone other than their mate. Sandur swallowed hard, trying, without success to shrug off the detaining arm. The stranger cajoled him to stay awhile longer, pulling him away from the bar over to a table beneath a window with a great show of affability. Sandur demurred, face strained, lips tightening into a thin line. Then, just as Phanus decided to rescue him from what must have been torture, especially at this vulnerable stage of Transformation, a woman's voice, a clear contralto floating above the riot of the tavern, called out.

"Haji?"

What followed was a series of impressions flashing rapid-fire in front of his eyes. Later, with Esslar's help, Phanus would sort them out, putting them into some kind of recognizable order. At the time, however, he was only aware of bits and pieces, a string of events flashing by him with the swiftness of arrows being loosed from a series of bows.

First, a woman descending the staircase, arrayed in a fortune of silks, hair unbound, hands sliding along the balustrade as she made her way tentatively down the last flight of stairs. The sound of her voice as it rose above the singing seemed nervous, unsettled, not the same voice that had laughed aloud that afternoon. Pale of face, seeming to float rather than walk, her robes billowing about her, she paused, obviously dismayed by the pandemonium confronting her descent.

Then came Sandur's greeting, cut-off as the arm around his shoulder transferred to his throat. Immediately after, Sandur struggling as the men seated at the table under the window rose as one to grab him, pinioning him at arms, waist, and thighs, unmindful of his frantic attempts to free himself.

Next, the instantaneous knowledge that he, Phanus of Pelion, one of the Legion's finest agents, had been duped, and badly so. One of the regulars lounging against the bar, someone Phanus shared a drink with just last night, drew his dagger and made his way deliberately up the staircase.

No one in the tavern was aware of what Phanus was witnessing, no one except Sandur, ashen-faced, a hand fixed over his mouth, staring wildly at the woman on the staircase, straining against his captors like a man gone mad while they laughed and joked, to all appearances a group of life-long comrades playing a harmless trick on a friend.

The man with the dagger passed the woman on the staircase, then turned and grabbed her wrist, wrenching it up behind her back. The woman cried out in surprise and fear, her free arm flailing the empty air. He must have tightened his grip, for she became immobile, her face frozen as he leered over her shoulder and whispered something in her ear.

Then, from nowhere, the furious snarl of a wolf. A streak of grey bounding down the stairs. A human scream. A dagger clattering down the steps. A spray of bright red blood shooting out of a jugular vein to spatter against amethyst silk. The woman's wail as she was thrown forward by her attacker's death throws and tumbled down the stairs. The giant hound standing over his kill, massive jaws shaking the limp body as the singing changed to cries of alarm, heads lifting, fingers pointing toward the stairs.

Forcing his way through the crowd toward the steps, cudgel raised, Phanus hurried toward the crumpled pile of amethyst silk only to find someone there before him. The flash of metal, a blade gleaming as a hand reached for a white throat. Phanus' cudgel smashing down. The solid thud of leather against bone. Another man on top of him now, the woman trapped beneath. Silk ripping, the woman struggling to free herself, sobbing all the while. The sound of his own voice as he dropped the cudgel and reached for his knife, calling to her in the southern tongue as he dodged a lightning-swift slash to his gut.

"Run, ernani! Run!"

A wiry coat of iron-grey flashed over his head, the hound leaping him and his attacker in one ferocious bound, the sounds of growing panic as customers scurried toward the exits, ducking for cover, streaming from the tavern, crying out in fear of the hell-hound loose inside.

Defending himself against the dancing knife, calling on every practice session with Lampon, every dirty trick Galen had taught them, unable to see either Sandur or the woman, Phanus heard the dog growl over the sound of his panting.

Seeing an opening and taking it, he stabbed deep in the gut and twisted the knife, intent that this man never fight again. Staggering toward the bar, looking everywhere for the woman, he met a tide of people fleeing the bodies littering the ground. Here, too, was the smell of blood—sweet, nauseating, unmistakable.

Sandur was on the floor, wrestling with three men, his blouse ripped halfway off his body, fighting silently, a gag stuffed in his mouth. Three more men stood frozen, eyeing the wolfhound crouched before them, lips pulled back to reveal blood-stained fangs, the hackles along the beast's back and shoulders standing straight up, stiff and unafraid.

A menacing movement from the man in the middle—the stranger with the calf-skin boots. The dog leapt forward; a blade slashed upward. The hound's death cry, almost human in its agony, rose to the upper-registers before dying away in a soft, barely distinguishable moan as his body crashed to the floor.

The sound of running footsteps behind him. The realization that he was too late to dodge the blow.

Then, blackness.

GROGGY, HIS EYES smarting as he reached up to explore the lump on the back of his skull, Phanus struggled to his feet.

The tavern was empty but for the dead. One body lay sprawled on the stairs, the throat ripped out, the face frozen in an eternal grimace of white-faced fear. Another lay at the foot of the stairs, the hilt of Phanus' knife sticking out of his gut, his eyes open, staring at the ceiling with a look of child-like surprise.

No time to spare, mindful that the clan guardsmen must be already on their way, Phanus retrieved his weapon, then set about searching the bodies for distinguishing marks, jewelry, coins, anything that might aid him in the search to follow. Ignoring his throbbing skull, his mind went into report mode, registering the facts as he had been taught.

Empty pockets except for a few coppers with which to purchase drinks. An assortment of new and used clothes probably purchased that morning in the market. Prying off a worn sandal, he found smooth white soles belying the footgear and garb of a common deck-worker. Routine took over as he made a careful sweep of the area, pausing to kneel by the pool of blood beside the hound and pulling the dagger free. Testing the balance, noting the steel was hand-tempered, it struck him as odd that so valuable a weapon had not been reclaimed. Something nagged at his memory, but he put it away, intent on the area around the table. No sign of blood on the floor, shards of glass from a broken wine bottle scattered underneath the table, but no blood. A twisted length of twine, the end frayed from being cut with a dull knife and the end discarded as the binding was complete. It began to make sense. Sandur, face down on the floor, resisting the men who were tying his hands behind his back. No plan to kill him, then, but to gag him, bind him fast, and take him, where?

Seven men, maybe more, escorting a bound and gagged captive out of the tavern with all possible speed. Both exits had been crammed with bodies, people spilling out onto the unlit street. His attention flew to the passageway leading to the kitchen. That's the way I'd choose, no traffic to speak of, a clear path to the alley and beyond. Shoving the abandoned dagger into his belt, Phanus was half-way down the corridor when he stopped dead.

It was a classic situation, one much debated in his studies at the Legion's academy. How do we decide whom to protect? All things being equal, whom do we serve? His first impulse came from his gut, his blood up, his mind set on finding Sandur and repaying those who'd played him for a fool. Also, seven against one were unwinnable odds. The woman might have been followed, but he had his doubts . . . until he remembered she had no eyes with which to see and nowhere to run.

Cursing the entire stinking world in which he found himself, Phanus set aside his fears for the Tehran's sa'ab. Running out the nearest door, his ears rang with Galen's advice, "All things bein' equal, ye must help those least able to help themselves."

By the time the clansmen and their contingent of guards arrived at the tavern of The Nesting Gull, Phanus was long gone. Hurrying along the moonlit path of crushed shells, he searched for a terrified woman, blind and alone, in the infamous harbor district where any woman, be she commoner or whore, was considered fair game.

Chapter 22

Beacon of the East

THE MOON, LIKE a skiff cast adrift in a starry sea, drifted in and out of high-flying clouds. Waves slapped against the pier's moorings, muffling the slither of silks and the slip-slide of sandals as a veiled silhouette moved on cat-feet, embraced by the night.

Hugging the edges of the deserted wharf, Ridha made her way past the warehouses to be greeted by watchdogs sniffing her perfume. High-pitched whines emerged from collared throats as they strained against their chains, anticipating the tidbits secreted in her robes. Willing co-conspirators after their feeding, they whimpered their gratitude as she passed them by, the friendly shadows converging again, enfolding her in a dusky sheath. Mists that smelt of the sea enveloped her in flowing draperies; moist night breezes caressed her cheeks through the filmy layers of her veils.

Light was her enemy; the clear light of day a call to reckoning, candlelight spilling out of an open window a reminder of her shame. A creature of the night, flitting from one shadow to the next, she was happiest when undetected, unconnected to everything she once knew. Here, in the hours before dawn, where the dark sea beckoned, her spirit found repose.

In time she moved more warily, the safety of the deserted wharf left behind, the crowded taverns looming up ahead. A door flew open, startling her, the voices inside quarrelsome and ugly. A bulky shape, hurled out into the street, landed with a grunt at her feet. Shrinking against a wall, she heard the sounds of retching, smelled the sour stench of vomited ale, then breathed easier as the drunken sailor crawled away on hands and knees to collapse belly-down, his face mashed against shells and sand. Moving on tiptoe, careful not to brush against him, she traversed the street, anxious to avoid discovery.

For a while she traveled undisturbed, by-passing an enclave of street whores, the poorest of prostitutes, most of them middle-aged or older, their former beauty lost to the ravages of time and hard living. Once they'd commanded respect, even admiration, their names on the lips of the customers who frequented the brothels they called home. But all flesh grows weary given time, and these women were weary unto death. "Finished for the night, dearie?" one called after her. Making no sign that she heard, Ridha hurried on.

Directly in front of her came a distant shout, vague calls of distress, and then a group of guardsmen brandishing torches, a prelude to unwelcome confrontation. For a moment she deliberated, balancing the danger of a deserted alleyway against the promise of discovery, and slipped into the alley.

Here were no stars or moon, nothing to help her find her way through the gloomy passageway of over-hanging eaves. The smell of offal and rotten fish added to her melancholy. Running her fingers over rough stucco walls, she felt her way tentatively through the darkness. So intent was she on listening for any indication she might be followed, she stumbled over something in her path.

Fighting to maintain her balance, readying herself to flee, a half-stifled sob from a woman's throat made her kneel down, bringing her level with the huddled figure at her feet. "Fear not," Ridha whispered. Reaching out, her hand met silk. "Nay, I'll not hurt thee," she murmured, certain now that the woman had been brutalized. Sighing, she pulled her into her arms.

"Thou must tell me what happened or I cannot help. Canst thou walk? Where dost thou live?"

Despite her soothing tone, the woman's trembling did not cease. A stream of foreign words poured from her mouth, all of them unintelligible. For a moment Ridha despaired, then listened with a different ear, one she thought forgotten.

"Come," she said, helping the woman to her feet. "I shall find thee a home."

They moved slowly along the deserted alley, for it was late now, just a few hours before dawn. The foreigner stumbled from time to time, but kept moving forward, trusting her rescuer, who threw her outer robe over the woman's silks and held her close.

They passed through the clans' checkpoint without incident, the clansmen on duty bored and contemptuous of women who worked the streets of the harbor district. Up the crushed shell pathway they walked, up into the deserted Abalone district with its shuttered shops and folded awnings.

Turning down an alley, Ridha stopped in front of a door. Fearing to knock, she scratched once, waited, then scratched again. After what seemed to be ages, the door opened a crack, a stern-faced stranger with a bandage wrapped about his head peering out.

"H'esslar?" she whispered, all the while searching the man's countenance for some semblance of welcome. Something flickered in his eyes as he looked beyond her to the woman hovering in the shadows. The door swung wide.

Stepping aside, she watched as the man who opened the door approached the foreign woman, his head bent as he whispered something in her ear, something that seemed to calm her, for she accompanied him willingly over the threshold.

Relieved that her duty was done, she was about to slip away into the shadows when she found herself being pulled inside, the fellow with the bandage offering no explanation or apology as he closed the door behind her and slid three bolts into place.

What followed seemed a dream. Swiftly, yet with infinite care, the foreigner was escorted to a cot, the man with the bandage grabbing up a pitcher, a basin, and a sponge. Another man, whose presence she did not notice until after she entered the room, knelt beside the cot. The foreign woman seemed to understand their intent, for she made no move to resist them when they removed her bloodstained robes. She swayed and would have fallen if they had not held her upright, shivering in a fine linen shift, staring blankly at nothing as a steady stream of tears rolled down her cheeks. They cared for her tenderly, as men care for daughters or sisters, lowering her to the cot and washing her blood-smeared hands and face. Finally convinced she bore no hurt, they urged her to drink from a tin mug and eased her head onto a pillow. The man with the bandage on his head pulled a chair to the side of the cot, settling into it with a weary sigh. The other man turned, wiping his hands on a clean rice-sack.

"You bring us what we could not find. Welcome, Ridha."

Confusion filled her upon hearing the voice of H'esslar, for she could not reconcile this stranger with the memory of a pale-skinned bookseller she knew a lifetime ago.

Shrinking away, drawing her veil across her face, a gasp escaped her as he smiled. Despite the tanned complexion, the night-black hair and smooth-shaven jaw, no man had ever smiled at her as H'esslar did, nor had anyone ever looked at her with such penetrating eyes, eyes that looked deep, more deeply than she could bear. Horribly aware of the change in her appearance, of the gaudy robes clinging to her body, of the crusts of paint on her lips and cheeks, she turned away, walking blindly toward the door.

"Much has changed since last we met. There's sadness in your eyes."

"You, too, have changed," she said when she could find her tongue. "Time has not been kind to either of us, I fear."

"You've left the citadel."

He did not pose it as a question. She answered as if it were, hoping she could change his welcoming smile to one of disgust, intent that he know how far she'd fallen so he might not be contaminated by her filth.

"I am a whore now, the first whore of a famous brothel."

On she rushed, eager for him to punish her as her father had punished her, damning her to a life of depravity and disease. Her sole moments of peace were the few hours before dawn when she escaped the brothel to stand poised on the edge of the pier, gazing longingly into the waters of nothingness. Each night her courage failed her. Yet each night she returned.

"My price is high, the highest in the city since no other brothel boasts a former concubine to a Kwanlonhon prince. They say men whisper my name in their sleep. 'Ridha the Magnificent!' they chant as they wait their turn, 'I want none but her!'"

His response came slowly.

"The red robes did not bring about your dreams?"

"My dreams? Say rather my father's dreams."

Bitterness coursed through her.

"They brought me nothing but loneliness and lies."

"You did not . . . care . . . for Shakar?"

"Care for him? I never saw him. He has no interest in anything but gambling. As to children, he could give me none. I left the citadel a virgin, thinking my father would dissolve the contract. But I was naive," she said, embittered by anger and shame, "too naive to understand that if Shakar's failure became common knowledge, the Kwanlonhon would ruin my father's business and his reputation among the other merchants. Thus, he refused to bring the case before the Equerry. Instead of Shakar, it is I who am dishonored, the cast-off sa'ab of a disappointed father."

By the time she finished speaking, she was angry no longer. Fool that she was, she'd thought to make H'esslar understand, forgetting that a foreigner could never comprehend the price she paid for her freedom. Wearily, she reached for the bolts, wishing she'd never come. Now she would have nothing of H'esslar left to treasure, not even the memory of their last meeting.

"Stay."

Unbelieving, she turned, finding in his expression no blame, no disgust, no hint of disapproval.

"You are more fair than I remember and more brave than fair. Have you no worth, you who would take a stranger under your protection, someone to whom you owe nothing?"

"But H'esslar, I am a . . ."

"Are you?" he countered swiftly, his gaze seeming to search her soul. "I think not. If you thought so little of yourself, you would have ended your life long ago." The fine lines around his eyes crinkled as he smiled. "Stay with me."

How many times had she dreamed of hearing these words on his lips? H'esslar, who among all the men she had ever known, was the only one who touched her heart. Was it possible he wanted her as a man wants a woman? Or was this a pledge of friendship, an offer to be treasured yet not the one she longed for?

His smile dimmed, his mood more serious now.

"I need your bravery, Ridha. I make no other claim. If that is enough, then join me in my work."

So be it, she decided, casting disappointment aside. He offers friendship; more than this he cannot give.

"What is your work, H'esslar?"

Weariness overcame him, such weariness that she longed to offer him the solace of her arms.

"So much to be done I fear to begin. To prevent her," he indicated the woman sleeping on the cot, "from going mad. To help him," he indicated the man with the bandaged head who nodded at his post, "remember what he longs to forget. To keep myself," he confided with a shy smile, "alert and unafraid. And most importantly," the smile became a frown, "to find someone who is lost." Noting her confusion, he cautioned, "Some things I can explain; others I cannot. You must take my offer on trust."

She took it on the strength of her love for him and never once, in the days and nights to follow, did she betray her feelings or regret her choice.

ALYSSA WANDERED THROUGH a nightmare not of her making.

Her body, bruised and sore, was somehow removed from her, existing not as her body but as that of a stranger. It lay cold and still while she wandered through the grey mists of half-remembered dreams. Only when the hands touched her did she return, hands bringing her back to the body on the cot. Too weak to escape them, they bound her to reality, to the ones who hovered over her—Esslar, the sweet-voiced woman, and the two men whose names she did not know.

Time and time again their presence called her back from the brink of madness—a spoon held to her lips, a comb working its way through the tangles of her hair, a blanket tucked around her shoulders. Once they made her walk. They could not grasp that she was dead, having died in the tavern the moment Sandur died, for only death could prevent him from coming to her aid. Rauros was dead as well; otherwise he would be beside her, his nose pressed against her hand, his tongue wiping away the tears that slid down her cheeks. Her mind balked at imagining the manner of their deaths in the horrid tavern where some men sang while other men died. Instead, she imagined her own death, resentful when hands called her back to a life that held no allure.

Lately, she'd begun to wander further and further away from the body on the cot, leaving it without regret, even thankful to be free of its confines. A voice inside her head urged her on. *"Find him!"* the voice kept repeating. *"Find Sandur!"*

She found him easily, without effort. Her mind reached out, and he was there, as substantial as the coarse hair between her fingers when she pulled the braids tight, the cadence of his laughter, his weight as she lay beneath him. Every memory was intact, although the one she mourned over longest was Sandur reborn after his visit to the citadel. A different person returned to her that night, light-hearted, almost giddy, a carefree boy rather than the stern-faced sa'ab of the Kwanlonhon's Tehran.

But the voice inside her head was not content.

"Search him out, Alyssa. You've shared your dreams, have you not? Find him in those dreams! Find Sandur!"

Hating that voice and the demand it made of her, she left the chambers of memory and journeyed into the land of dreams. At times she thought she found her mother, Latona the Dreamsayer, to whom no dream was unreadable.

"The realm of water..." her mother divined with her last few breaths, *"... things that float on the surface of the sea."*

The Nineteenth Mother was there as well. *"Search for Sandur,"* the old woman insisted, although sometimes it sounded as though she said, *"Search for sight."* The two grew muddled in her head—Sandur and sight, sight and Sandur, like the notes of a half-remembered chord.

And so she searched, sending out her dreams like setting free so many pigeons from their coops, flying on the currents of despair but flying all the same into the grey mists, losing her way more often than not to be brought back to consciousness by the hands of her caretakers.

Snatches of their conversations made no sense to her.

> "Word is out. His formal robes were found when they searched the inn, also maps and books inscribed with his signature."
>
> "Manthur denies knowing anything about his sa'ab's whereabouts. They're calling it a kidnapping and waiting for a ransom demand."
>
> "And Tasir?"
>
> "Nothing yet."

> "*Seahorse* is ready to sail: bilges scrubbed, sheets and lines newly rigged, holds stocked with provisions. Not a hint as to her destination."
>
> "Any word of Fawaz?"
>
> "He's made several trips to the inn. Lampon's convinced he's conducting a private investigation. Let's hope he's discreet."

"I've decided. When the time comes, Ridha will go."

"But the danger if she's discovered!"

"We've no other choice. None of us know the inside of the citadel as she does. She has the courage to offer; we must find the courage to accept."

As the days passed, measured by hands shaking her awake or lulling her to sleep, the voices inside her head grew more impatient, insisting she fight her way past the mists to whatever lay beyond.

"No one else can find him. You are so close, Alyssa, so close to everything you seek! Walk the path, ernani!"

A resonance was struck, its reverberations carrying her further than she'd ever dared go before.

"Hold fast, daughter."

The voice was her mother's, yet not her mother's. There were similarities of timbre and accent, yet the tone was somehow altered, suggesting a joyful serenity that she did not easily associate with Latona the Dreamsayer, a woman to whom joy did not come easily or often.

"The future forms a labyrinth through which all must walk. Hold fast, daughter of Latona."

This refrain pounded itself into her consciousness, reminding her that having walked a labyrinth once before, the thought of walking another one held no terror. As she thrust her thoughts onward, the mists seemed to clear, to part . . . and she was plunged into a world of the senses, a waking world unconnected with memory or dreams, a world that seemed to her as real as anything she'd ever experienced.

A sea bird's plaintive cry filled her ears, as did the sound of waves being sliced by a wooden hull. The ship rolled and pitched beneath her, sensations she'd never experienced before, each of them rich, full-bodied, as if she ate food she'd never eaten yet recognized the taste.

A single-mast sloop headed north by northeast, running under full sail on the empty seas near Nisyros. Part of her wondered how she could understand the ship's course with such clarity; another part accepted it without question.

Hinges creaked. Chains rattled.

"No use being sullen."

The scrape of a tin plate being slid along wooden flooring.

"Eat up."

The clatter of a plate being kicked away.

A stinging slap.

"Mind your manners."

The sound of retreating feet. Hinges creaking. A key being turned. The roll of the ship . . . and then she knew.

Her return was immediate, the mists crossed in the blink of an internal eye. Hands welcomed her back, the hands of a healer.

It was to Esslar she returned, Esslar and the woman, Ridha.

"He lives!" cried Alyssa, her shout a whisper, her voice rusty from disuse, like the hinges on the door to Sandur's prison.

HEADS TURNED AS three Kwanlonhon clansmen strode purposefully up the street, puffs of shell dust rising from beneath their booted feet. Despite the fact that the street was more crowded than usual (the gossipmongers busier than ever with the latest development concerning the abduction of the Tehran's sa'ab), a wide path cleared, allowing them to walk abreast. Hands raised to cover whispering mouths as they passed, eyes lowered in a show of respect.

"Prince Tasir."

"The pilot, Fawaz."

"Who's the grandfather?"

No one seemed to know, although speculation ran wild concerning the ancient clansman, frail and withered, his thinning braids turned white with age. Falal, the sponge dealer, settled the matter.

"Kasovar, brother to Linphat V," he announced with surprising certainty, causing Oman to raise his eyebrows but hold his tongue, a recent development on his part. On any subject concerning the Kwanlonhon, Oman kept mum.

Upon reaching their destination, the clansmen passed over the bookshop's threshold, the old man first as befitted his age, the Tehran's brother next, the pilot last of all. As the door closed behind them, the rug merchant voiced the general opinion of the merchants of the Abalone district.

"Two rings mean trouble."

As if by mutual agreement, the crowd around the bookshop dispersed. True, the Equerry was known to frequent those dilapidated premises, but on the whole its customers were stewards or junior clansmen sent on errands for their superiors. Two-ringed clansmen ventured out rarely, if at all, and then only on clan business in the harbor district.

"Bad business," Oman muttered under his breath.

"Maybe their luck turns at last," suggested the rug-merchant, gloating over the idea of the insufferably arrogant reds getting their comeuppance.

Or maybe they've come to find it, Falal thought to himself, having been close enough to the door to see who greeted the clansmen beyond the threshold. Though slow of speech and weak of opinion, Falal was far from stupid. As surely as he'd known the hand-lettered sign announced the nature of the merchandise to be found within, he recognized the black-haired cousin from

Tek as the bookseller who vanished the same day the Tehran's sa'ab left for the west.

He knew, too, that Oman's sa'ab lived within, having glimpsed her one evening while sweeping out his storeroom. As she slipped out the back door of the bookshop, dressed like a serving girl, he'd watched her fasten the veil across her face and scurry down the alley as though a pack of wild dogs nipped at her heels.

"Trouble brewing," was all Falal, the sponge-merchant, said aloud.

WHAT COULD HAVE gone badly did so.

First came the surprise appearance of Kasovar, which did nothing to ease the wariness of Lampon and Phanus, both of them furious that the terms of the meeting had been broken without discussion or a well-deserved apology from Tasir. Next came the look of shocked affront as Tasir recognized Ridha, the woman responsible for shaming his brother, Shakar. Her departure from the citadel in the dead of night, turning her back on the rank and luxury to which she'd been raised, was deemed an insult to every Kwanlonhon in Endlin. Then came the moment for Ridha to escort Alyssa from behind the canvas wall, at which time the room shivered around them in an icy pall of disbelief.

The clansmen stared at her with loathing, then averted their eyes, three generations confronted with the unthinkable. The silence of ultimate rejection reigned.

"What proof?" Tasir ground out, furious at allowing himself to believe, if only for an instant, the summons that appeared one night on his pillow. "He lives!" the message began, the rest of the words forgotten as his spirit leapt up, hopeful for the first time after endless days of self-recrimination.

"What proof would content you?" Esslar replied evenly, motioning Lampon and Phanus to their posts at the doors.

"Proof that this . . . this . . ." Tasir searched in vain for a word to describe the abomination standing before him, ". . . this woman is my nephew's concubine."

Much to Esslar's surprise, Alyssa joined their conversation. Using the simplest of words and phrases, she addressed Sandur's relatives in their own tongue.

"If you need proof, take these."

A diamond glittered in one palm; a piece of parchment lay in the other. When no one moved to take them from her, Esslar passed them along.

"He said I must keep them hidden in my robes whenever he left me alone," she explained

Tasir fingered the diamond while Kasovar squinted at the signature on the letter of credit. Fawaz was first to believe, leaning back against the bookshelves, his arms crossed on his chest, considering the pale-skinned woman with ocean-grey eyes. Wonder showed on the pilot's face, wonder mixed with sadness.

"He has nothing now. They've taken everything away."

The war against tears lost, silver droplets ran down her pallid cheeks. If they doubted her story, they did not doubt her grief. The diamond clenched in his fist, Tasir eyed the armed guard at the door before turning his attention to the bookseller who escorted Sandur to a place called Pelion.

"What do you want?"

"Your help."

After a lengthy pause, during which Tasir seemed to take Esslar's measure, the Tehran's brother sneered, "For what price?"

"I thought the life of the Tehran's sa'ab beyond price," Esslar snapped, eyes like dagger-points, no trace of the healer in the jut of his jaw or the stiffness of his backbone as he matched Tasir insult for insult.

Ridha stirred beside him, uneasy at the game H'esslar played with one unaccustomed to losing. Phanus, watching Esslar's transformation from his vantage point near the front door, realized the time for games was past.

"A reward is offered for knowledge as to his whereabouts or the names of his abductors. If you've any information concerning my nephew, I suggest you come forward, although you'd best hurry. When the ransom note arrives, you'll be too late."

Sapphire robes swirled as Tasir turned to go.

"There will be no ransom note. As to the name of his abductor, you know it already."

Silver braids swung about Tasir's shoulders as he turned to face his accuser.

"What do you suggest, book-seller?"

"What you've known since the night Sandur visited the citadel."

The truth hung unspoken between them, quivering in the dusty air.

"You ask for information; I give it freely," Esslar began, his attention riveted on the stony-faced prince. "Alyssa found the ship that holds him, a small sloop with a seven-man crew, seven of the nine who formed the attack against them in the inn. They docked in Nisyros two nights ago to take on fresh water and supplies. Their course is due east."

"Nothing lies beyond Nisyros," Kasovar interrupted, his age-spotted hands folding and re-folding the letter of credit endorsed by the nephew he trained to manhood. "To venture east of Nisyros is to lose oneself in the great void. No charts map its shoals or currents; no pilot has ever returned."

"Yet that is their course," Esslar insisted calmly, "on a ship with provisions enough for a single moon. Two explanations are possible. They are mad, or they have a clear destination in mind. I prefer to believe the latter."

"If what you say is true," Fawaz observed from his place against the book-lined wall, the colored maps and charts hanging over his head like so many slack sails waiting for the west wind to blow them out to sea, "what hope have we of finding them? I would search for Sandur even to the ends of the earth, but without charts to steer by, how should I find him?"

"I will take you to Sandur."

All heads turned to the blind woman.

"Impossible!" Tasir exploded.

"A woman on board a ship?" Kasovar protested, aghast at the idea of a female at sea.

"But lady," said Fawaz, waiting politely for his elders to finish, "you're blind!"

Sensing the good will underneath the pilot's declaration, Alyssa smiled, then laughed, a trill of sweet mirth dispelling the tensions of the afternoon. Fawaz's lips quirked. The old man with milky eyes frowned his disapproval, while a strange expression passed over Tasir's face as he remembered a well-beloved nephew who had laughed at fate before hurrying away to rejoin his Alyssa.

"She found him, and she alone must lead the way. I can offer no explanation, but I give you my word she speaks the truth."

"Faith between strangers is never easy," Tasir replied slowly, "and trust a bond forged after many moons. We have barely an hour to believe a blind woman can lead us to my nephew through unknown waters no pilot has ever explored." Pausing, he searched Esslar's countenance as a sailor scans the horizon for signs of land.

"You ask me to believe the impossible, book-seller."

This was the juncture, the crossroads at which two cultures met, both of them mature, wise in their areas of expertise, founded on ancient traditions. One prided itself on its far-flung trade routes, its exploration of strange lands, strange peoples. The other existed in happy seclusion, content to plumb the inner-workings of the mind. The world had grown too small to contain them both unchanged.

These were the thoughts coursing through Esslar's mind as he made his decision. Silently, he ordered Phanus to surrender his post and take Alyssa with him to the back of the shop. She went without complaint, leaning on the Legionnaire's arm. Ridha, who had not left Esslar's side, departed more reluctantly, darting worried glances at the three clansmen. This done, Esslar drew up a chair beside the elder clansmen, motioning Fawaz to come closer.

"We of Pelion have been given a gift, one we would share with the world." He chose his words with care, always mindful of his vows. "To speak of it freely is forbidden, but in simple terms, it allows us to understand the thoughts and feelings of others. It is not magic or a conjurer's trick, as was believed in centuries past, although there are some who use it to further their own purposes."

"Manthur . . .?" Tasir breathed, a question in his eyes.

Esslar nodded.

"In the city, they say he dabbles in sorcery. How else can the shrewdness of his guesses be explained?"

The clansmen exchanged glances. Tasir frowned, his brow puckered with doubt.

"If you have this gift, why can't you serve as guide?"

Esslar shook his head.

"It's impossible to describe the gift in a few simple words. Perhaps the best description is a note plucked on a single string. Every individual mind has a peculiar resonance. Alyssa and Sandur share a resonance between them, something we call attunement. Because their gift is not yet complete, she can find him only in the dreaming state."

Tasir pressed the point.

"But if your abilities are greater . . .?"

"If I attempted such a thing, one or both of them might lose their reason."

"And if they are not reunited?"

"You know the answer already," Esslar replied, to which Tasir nodded his head, remembering the madness of his brother. Yet, trader that he was, he understood that this negotiation concerned more than the life of Sandur. Curiosity drew him on. His demand had been met—information offered in exchange for trust, yet still he hesitated, unsure as to what this bookseller hoped to gain.

"Pelion would share this gift with us?"

"It is yours for the asking. Its source is the Maze, in the city of Pelion."

"What do you ask of Endlin in return?"

"That the clans combine forces to find the eastern passage."

Tasir's eyes widened.

"Myth!" Fawaz scoffed.

"The eastern passage!" Kasovar whispered reverently. "The ancient route of our forefathers!"

"To what purpose, bookseller?"

"To find what was lost. We've gathered knowledge of the years before the founding of Pelion. We have found ancient maps bearing no likeness to our world; our scholars have found mention of other continents. Your lore hints at the presence of lands far to the east, far beyond Nisyros. We've lost touch with the sea. You have not. This, then, becomes Endlin's rightful task—to find the forgotten worlds from which your forbearers sprang."

The clansmen weighed it between them, holding the future in their hands. Thoughts flickered past Esslar as he closed his eyes, a rainbow of impressions—skepticism, doubts, and fear. Having expected no less, he waited patiently, considering these clansmen of Endlin, descendants of others like the First Mother, chosen by the Sowers to settle this new world as the First Mother had been chosen. For reasons he could only guess, they built ships and sailed west to found a city, now an Empire, that like Pelion, valued knowledge salvaged from the old world. They, too, must share in the gift given by the Sowers. If they did not, all would be lost, of this Esslar was certain. With these thoughts in his mind, he sought and found tranquility.

At last he heard Tasir say: "What must we do?"

Releasing his breath, light-headed with relief, Esslar opened his eyes on a new world.

"Return to the citadel. Request an appointment with Manthur tomorrow. Ask him for a special favor—to take *Seahorse* on a quick excursion. Use as your excuse the necessity of checking recent repairs. In the meantime, Fawaz must hire a crew—the most trustworthy men available. Offer them double, even triple pay."

"But the cost!" Fawaz objected, ever practical in times of confusion. "Have you any idea of the cost of such a venture? We can't use clan funds without clan approval. Even if I can find a crew willing to sail with a woman aboard, how shall we pay them?"

"If the letter of credit isn't enough, what's the market rate for a flawless diamond?"

Kasovar cackled as he passed the letter of credit over to Fawaz.

"There is some justice in this, book-seller, that Manthur must finance the return of the one he would disinherit. Nay, Tasir," the old man declared when his nephew gestured for him to be silent, "I'll not hold my tongue! I've been silent too long. 'Twas madness to send Issur on that voyage, madness to dismiss me from my post!"

A twinkle shone in his milky eyes.

"Almost as mad as a man of my years giving up a soft bed for a hard berth! I thank you, bookseller, if a bookseller you be, for rescuing an old man from retirement. This will be my last voyage, and who could ask for more than a chance at mapping the eastern passage?"

"We've a more pressing problem, bookseller. What of my brother? If he reads my thoughts, we stand betrayed."

"Manthur is my responsibility. You'll find him changed, Tasir, of this I give warning. Take no notice and proceed as planned. Once everything is arranged, send word and we'll bring Alyssa down to the docks."

At the mention of her name, Tasir shifted uneasily in his chair.

"Has she strength enough to make this journey? I would not have her death on my conscience."

Esslar smiled.

"Sandur told me a tale one day, the story of the founding of Endlin. He mentioned six men by name, yet there were women aboard those ships. Their names are forgotten, just as you've forgotten the route of their ships. Perhaps Kasovar is right—it's time to remember the old tales. Alyssa is no less strong than they were; she will persevere."

"Once you find Sandur, let no one tend him but Alyssa. Give them a place of their own with a guard at the door. No one must disturb them for any reason."

Three heads bowed in solemn acquiescence. Rising to his feet, Esslar extended his hand, palm downward. Three hands descended to cover his, one deeply tanned by the sun, one with swollen knuckles and yellowed nails, the last bedecked with a square-cut sapphire set in a silver band.

"We give our word as Kwanlonhon of Endlin. May the four winds cease and the seas expire before our word be broken."

"I give my word as Esslar, citizen of Pelion. May our children's children remember this bond."

AND SO IT came to pass that they went down to the sea.

Kasovar's heart was lightest, tasting the tang of salt on his lips again. Fifty years ago he gave up the sea, called by his eldest brother to begin his duties in the citadel. His children were elders in their own right now, his grandsons fathering their own families, his great-grandchildren playing happily in the pools and fountains of the harem. Kasovar left the citadel without regrets, freed of his responsibilities since the death of his last concubine during the previous year's rains. Precious charts wrapped in oilskin accompanied him, a lifetime of learning borne in the sea chest the porters stowed in the cabin he would share with his finest student, young Fawaz, pilot of the *Seahorse*.

That same pilot went down to the sea more solemnly, helping Kasovar hobble up the gangplank, feeling the brittleness of ancient bones under the pressure of his fingers. Checking the rigging as he climbed aboard, his gaze drifted down to the deck and the forty men standing at attention. Fawaz acknowledged each man by name, from the ship's cook to the quartermaster, from the ordinary seamen to the cabin boy. Sternly he greeted them, as if to remind them of the reason they were being paid three times their normal fee.

Prince Tasir came next, sapphire robes gleaming under a breathless, dawn-lit sky, his tread heavy, his head bowed in thought. Not for him the exultation of Kasovar or the worries of Fawaz concerning the crew. His thoughts lay in the citadel, where Manthur kept to his rooms, having cancelled all clan business, even the regularly scheduled meeting of the council of elders. The Tehran's chief steward roamed the halls like a man bereft. When questioned by Tasir, he looked over his shoulder, fearful of being overheard, before confiding in the faintest of whispers, "He dances to music no one else can hear."

What awesome powers did this bookseller possess, to reduce Manthur to a smiling lunatic, his hands positioned as if he held a ghostly body close to his? Was this his fastidious brother, this man with robes awry and stubble on his jaw, his eyes full of dreams, humming an unfamiliar melody under his breath as he whirled about the room? Recognition flickered in his eyes as Tasir approached him, his confusion growing as Tasir voiced his request, to be followed by an indifferent shrug.

"Do as you wish, brother. Better yet, ask our father."

Ask a father thirty years dead? Shrug off a request for which there existed no precedent, then resuming his dance without embarrassment after biding Tasir a fond farewell? Cries of "Good journey, Tasir! Good journey, brother!" rang in Tasir's ears as he stepped onto the main deck of *Seahorse* and made his way swiftly to his cabin, too troubled in his mind to notice the sudden hush that followed on the heels of his departure.

Alyssa came down to the sea last of all, stepping lightly, every faculty concentrated on the unseen ship floating on the morning tide. As she ran her fingers along the rope stretched between the upright posts along the gangplank, the melody of the gulls became her private song, her excitement rising like the wild cries of the sea birds circling overhead.

A gruff voice apprised her that she'd reached her destination.

"Take my hand," the pilot ordered, and she reached out, meeting a leathery palm. Two more steps and she was aboard, the deck rolling slightly beneath her.

"Will it trouble the crew if I stay on deck until we leave the harbor?" she asked in a clear voice, sensing the presence of many people around her.

"Impossible," came the crisp reply. "We'll haul anchor and be towed away from the dock. Once we reach the mouth of the harbor, we must wait for a west wind to fill our sails. 'Twould be best if you retire to your cabin."

A breeze teased the veil covering her hair.

"Is this not the west wind?" she inquired with a coaxing smile, unaware that all about her the crew stood open-mouthed at the sight of her, veils and robes billowing as the wind obeyed her summons. Muffled entreaties grew as Fawaz hesitated.

"Let her stay!"

"A good omen!"

"She brings the wind!"

Once he worried they might mutiny against her; now he wondered if he could maintain his authority if he overrode her wishes.

"Let them believe in her." Turning, he found Kasovar by his side, his eyes shrouded by a whitish cast. "What harm can it do?"

Bowing to necessity, Fawaz led her up to the quarterdeck, where a chair was lashed to the mast. Here she would sit once they left Nisyros, a place to dream her way east while the first mate manned the helm and Fawaz used the compass and astrolabe to chart their course. She thanked him courteously, nodding vaguely in his direction, then turned her face toward the prow of the ship, her profile lit by the sun as it rose from its bed of clouds along the eastern horizon.

In due time the ship flew east, borne on the wings of the west wind toward Nisyros and the great abyss beyond.

In the tales of latter days, they would recall that the wind rose up at her approach, just as they would remember the color of her robes—a peculiar shade, neither pink nor blue but somewhere in between, the exact hue of the dawn-painted sky over the seven hills of Endlin, the colors of the Tehran's sa'ab.

Chapter 23

Always and Forever, the Sea

TWENTY-NINE DAYS BEYOND Nisyros and still no sign of land. Yesterday, a bird sighting, the lookout at the top of the main singing out the news, those on deck rushing port side to follow the petrel's flight. Long-winged, small-bodied, racing the wind on a parallel course with *Seahorse*, the petrel dipped and glided its aerial greeting before veering off to the north. Wings beating in powerful, downward strokes, the bird sped away, watched with envious eyes by the ship-bound crew.

Then, this afternoon, a mammoth coral shoal sighted off the port bow, several outcroppings reaching nearly to the surface. Excitement coursed over the deck as word spread, snaggle-toothed grins flashing in sun-burned faces as the crew went about their tasks with new-found energy. All of them, even the youthful cabin boy, were experienced sailors; four of them—the quartermaster, cook, first and second mates—shipped regularly with Fawaz. None of them, including their pilot, had ever sailed uncharted seas.

The bird and the coral reef rekindled hope after almost thirty days of monotonous seas filling an implacable horizon. Quarrels erupted with disturbing frequency since leaving Nisyros. Kasovar, either sensing the crew's nerves or experiencing a like feeling himself, took the pilot aside for a private conference below deck after Fawaz broke up an especially vicious fist-fight.

"Hard though it is to admit, we're little more than coastal traders. For centuries we've island-hopped up and down the coastline, never more than a few days from the next landfall, our greatest fear that a storm might blow us out to open seas. It's an odd feeling to be sure, this many days without sight of land, and one for which we're ill-prepared."

A man not given to fanciful airs, in the days since leaving Nisyros a peculiar feeling (one for which he could offer no explanation) overcame Fawaz at frequent intervals. His knew they were making steady progress over empty seas, the prow splitting the waves, the sails full-bellied as the wind blew steadily from the west. His charts told the same story, as did the unfamiliar stars beginning to appear overhead.

Yet often, especially during the periods when the blind woman dreamed on the quarterdeck, Fawaz found himself imagining the ship as stationary, held motionless by an invisible force, while the world rolled forward in an endless succession of cresting waves.

When the blind woman roused herself to consciousness, her hand gleaming eerily in the moonlight as she pointed out the direction they must follow, the vision would fade, replaced by a new one as he marked the appropriate course correction on his chart and ordered the first mate to nudge the wheel a few points to the north or east. Like a living being rather than an object constructed of wood, nails, pitch, and canvas, a slight shudder would run through *Seahorse*, and then, like a race horse responding to the rider's spur, she would gather herself up, timbers straining, and plunge ahead with a sudden burst of speed. More often than not, the wind would adjust its direction as well, wind and ship conspiring to bring them swiftly to their destination.

No one could have put Fawaz's apprehensions into clearer form than Kasovar. Rheumy-eyed he might be, also brittle-boned and short of breath, but four-score years had taught him how to wait. He, like Fawaz and the woman, became a creature of the night, haunting the quarterdeck from dusk to dawn, then sleeping away the morning, rising after midday to supervise the reeling of the log line and the turning of the sand-glass, recording information necessary to finding their way back home.

As chief trading representative of the Kwanlonhon, Tasir stood equal to Fawaz in rank. Early on, he made it clear that he had no intention of involving himself in the daily workings of the ship. The crew returned the favor by avoiding the Tehran's brother at every opportunity, taking cover whenever he emerged from his cabin to stroll the deck. Silks whipping about his massive form, silver braids tossed by wind and salt-spray, he would stand on the quarterdeck for hours on end, staring at the empty horizon as one studies an adversary.

From the first, Tasir presented a stony face to the woman's charms, refusing to have any contact with her and insisting that Fawaz confine her to her cabin. The voyage to Nisyros was a dreadful affair, the woman suffering from acute sea-sickness and Fawaz put in the unenviable position of over-riding Tasir's wishes, allowing her to come above deck in the hope her nausea might be quelled by breathing fresh sea air.

Once, after watching Tasir stalk back to his cabin, indignant at finding the woman above deck, Fawaz confided his frustrations to Kasovar.

"It's not her fault she's a poor sailor. What's to be gained by rudeness? The crew accepts her presence; why can't he?"

Rather than answering his question, Kasovar posed one in return.

"Why this sudden show of concern?"

When Fawaz shrugged and would have walked away, the old man became irritable.

"Say what you mean. You want Tasir to approve of her in order to justify your own feelings."

When Fawaz uttered a quick denial, Kasovar waved off his excuses as if swatting flies.

"Be careful, Fawaz. Tasir remembers what you seem to forget—she's blemished and so unworthy of your notice."

"Sandur forgot," Fawaz retorted, much more sharply than he intended considering his regard for his former teacher.

"That may be," Kasovar conceded, "but it's not your affair. Tasir is Sandur's rightful guardian. Let him deal with the woman as he sees fit. If you set yourself up as her protector, you'll put this mission in even greater jeopardy."

After considering Kasovar's warning, Fawaz resolved to keep a careful watch on himself. No longer did he engage the blind woman in conversation, nor did he make it his business to ease the discomforts of shipboard life. Assigning the cabin boy to look after her wants, he took pains never to be alone with her. Once they departed Nisyros, stopping overnight to take on fresh water and foodstuffs, she came nightly to the quarterdeck, at which time he made sure Kasovar stood watch with him. If the woman noticed a change in attitude, she gave no sign, but went about her duties serenely, never seeming more content than when she took her place on the quarterdeck each evening at sunset.

They were a fortnight out of Nisyros when Tasir came to Fawaz with an unsettling request.

"Have I your permission to interrogate the cabin boy?"

Clan procedure allowed a trading representative access to the crew at any time. Frowning, for this was the first time Tasir had approached him in a formal capacity, Fawaz ventured a question.

"Has he failed in his duties? I've heard no complaints."

"I wish to question him concerning the woman."

Obeying the warning signals flashing in Tasir's eyes, Fawaz gave a hasty nod and retreated to the quarterdeck. For the rest of the day he thought of little else, wondering what possible information the boy could offer concerning the woman in his charge. That afternoon, an hour before dusk, the answer came.

Summoned to Tasir's cabin by a nervous deck hand, Fawaz hurried below, almost tripping over the slower-moving Kasovar in his rush down the stairs. Like guilty children preparing themselves for a reprimand, Fawaz and Kasovar arranged their robes before knocking on the cabin door.

An oil lamp suspended from low rafters swung back and forth over Tasir's head, casting looming shadows on the paneled walls. Pacing the cramped quarters with his hands clasped behind his back, he announced without ceremony, "She carries Sandur's sa'ab."

Too stunned to form a reply, Fawaz stared at the floorboards, sending up fervent thanks to the wind gods that he'd heeded Kasovar's advice. The old man was quite clearly aghast, although he was first to recover, asking in a quavering voice, "Are you sure, nephew?"

Casting a withering glance in his uncle's direction, Tasir continued pacing, three steps to the right, three to the left, a study in perpetual motion.

"Have I not lived with concubines long enough to recognize the signs? Fawaz lacks experience. You and I, uncle, have no such excuse."

"What did the cabin boy say?" Fawaz asked.

"He confirmed what I suspected. Forty-two days have come and gone without a show of blood. What fools we are! Even the poorest sailor adjusts to a ship's motion in a matter of days!"

"Surely this must be some other man's child!" cried Kasovar.

Tasir stopped pacing.

"What man?" he demanded, eyes narrowed into slits.

"Any of the commoners on board!"

"Do you think me witless, uncle!" Tasir thundered. "Would I allow Sandur's concubine to lie with another clansman, let alone a commoner? Fawaz understood my wishes and comported himself honorably. No one has touched her since departing Endlin! On this I will stake my life."

Kasovar was desperate now.

"Then . . . then the bookseller!"

"Ridiculous!" Tasir snapped. "Why would he be so anxious to part with her if he enjoyed her favors? And why would she put herself and the child she carries in danger to find Sandur if he is not the father? You grasp at straws, uncle. The child is his."

"But it cannot be!" Kasovar wailed. "Such a thing is unnatural, unthinkable! She's totally unsuitable for breeding. The child will be flawed! You cannot allow it, Tasir! She must be stopped!"

"And how do you propose to stop her?"

Something in the way Tasir posed that question, gazing speculatively at his uncle, his voice soft as cat's fur, signaled danger. Fawaz resumed his contemplation of the floor. Kasovar stood dumb.

"Listen to me, uncle. No harm is to come to my nephew's concubine. From this day forward, every care will be given to her health and happiness. If the child is flawed, its life rests in Sandur's hands. I trained him to manhood. In his absence, my authority extends to his concubine and his sa'ab."

Kasovar nodded miserably before shuffling toward the door. When it closed behind him, Tasir sat heavily on his berth. Fawaz fidgeted, eyeing the door, unsure as to whether his presence was desired.

"You disapproved of the way I treated her."

The pilot's head snapped up.

"I, uh, I didn't understand . . ."

Tasir sighed.

"Nor did I." Keen eyes attached themselves to Fawaz. "You've never been a guardian, have you?" Fawaz shook his head. "It's a perilous undertaking to train a boy to manhood. Their failures reflect on your honor. Worst of all, they hurt. Manthur hurt Kasovar by making him retire; Sandur hurt me by choosing this woman."

A short pause followed during which Tasir fingered his earrings.

"I hated her on sight—initially because of her blindness, more recently, because I saw her as a threat to our closeness. I love Sandur as my own child, yet it is she who reaches out to him, she who leads the way."

Suddenly Fawaz understood the hours Tasir spent staring out to sea, the brooding melancholy that had so disturbed the crew.

"Only now do I begin to understand what the bookseller meant, yet the thought of a woman sharing this gift with Sandur, a blind woman at that, is beyond my comprehension. Then, today I learn she carries his sa'ab."

Fawaz posed the question he'd puzzled over since the moment Tasir announced the woman's condition.

"Why would she not tell us? She's a foreigner, to be sure, but Sandur must have told her our customs concerning the care of a breeding woman, especially if the child she carries is a sa'ab."

Tasir's lips twisted into a wry smile, a surprising development considering his former mood.

"It's my guess he told her everything, which is exactly why she's been so secretive. If she'd confided the truth beforehand, I'd never have allowed her to leave Endlin. Instead, I would have brought her bound and screaming to the citadel, where she would remain in seclusion until the child was born. If she'd said anything before reaching Nisyros, I'd have left her there despite the fact that we've almost no chance of finding Sandur without her help."

The prince shook his head in wordless admiration.

"She can't be more than two moons along. When I remember my concubines, whining and complaining, demanding constant attention from the first to the last, I wonder if Sandur hasn't chosen more wisely than I did."

"Will you speak to her concerning the child?"

"No. Nor must you. Now that he knows my intentions, Kasovar won't interfere, although he's never been one to hide his feelings. Luckily for us, he'll probably go out of his way to avoid her."

"What if the boy talks? He'll be quick enough to guess why you questioned him . . ."

". . . and smart enough to know I'll skin him alive if he breathes a word to anyone! In any case," Tasir added with a crooked grin, "I retripled his wages to keep him quiet."

Rising from the berth, he adjusted his robes.

"We must go above. If I keep you here any longer, the crew will fear for your life. After all," he said, only half in jest, "everyone knows two rings mean trouble."

In the days that followed, a peaceful truce grew between the blind woman and the clansmen of Endlin. How much she guessed was never clear to Fawaz. Under his direction, the crew rigged a series of ropes around the entire forward deck so she might walk in safety, Tasir's greatest fear being that she might stumble and bring on a miscarriage. To the news she was free to wander as she willed above deck, she spoke her thanks with a grateful smile but made no attempt to discover the reason behind the change in policy regarding her confinement in her cabin. On the pretext of dissatisfaction with the cook's efforts, Tasir was consulted on menus each morning. The cabin boy noted everything she consumed or pushed aside, and new dishes designed to tempt her appetite began to make their way to her table. Again, she made no comment, ate more heartily, and was even heard to laugh from time to time with the cabin boy who served her.

And then, one evening at dusk, when the air cools and sea turtles rise to feed near the surface, she told a story.

SHIPBOARD DISCIPLINE WAS necessarily strict, the days divided into regular watches, repair and maintenance, inspections and drills. Laziness was not tolerated, nor was insubordination or a slovenly appearance. Crew kept apart from clansmen; seamen of higher rank disassociated themselves from ordinary sailors. Yet despite the hierarchies of command, it was the custom aboard most trading vessels to relax these rules during the hour between the evening meal and the changing of the watch. Gambling was a favorite pastime, as was the singing of songs, either humorous or obscene, or laments of a sentimental nature dedicated to those left behind.

This particular evening, an enormous moon hung like a perfect pearl on an invisible chain, illuminating the sky to the brightness of day. The woman, as was her custom, took her meal in her cabin before appearing above deck. Breaking off a song in progress, an uncomfortable silence descended on the crew as she guided herself toward their gathering on the forward deck by means of the ropes.

"Why do you stop?" she asked, clearly uncomfortable with the awkward hush greeting her arrival. "Your music brought me here. Please continue."

The crew eyed each other nervously, searching vainly for a spokesman, until the cabin boy piped up in a clear treble.

"Our song's not fit for your ears, lady."

All of them marked the smile that lit her face at the boy's explanation, for indeed the lyrics were bawdy to a degree.

"The melody is lovely all the same. Sing it and I'll not take offense. After all," she reminded them, "I'm new to your language. I need to learn new words."

A round of guffaws greeted her jest. One brave soul boasted, "I'll explain them to you, lady, if you've a mind to learn."

She laughed aloud at that, color rising to her cheeks.

"Nay, sailor, but what say you to an even exchange? If you sing, I'll tell a story. If some meaning is lost in the singing or the telling, what does it matter?"

They chattered among themselves for a while, obviously intrigued by her offer if only because of its novelty. The first mate, the designated spokesman for the crew, rose to address the robed trio of clansmen assembled on the quarterdeck.

"What say you, Prince Tasir? Have we permission to sing for your concubine?"

It was an honest mistake. What else were they to think? Fawaz wore a single ring while Kasovar was clearly beyond the days of bringing in concubines. The color of her silks was a matter of speculation among them since by rights they should be red. Still, commoners rarely questioned clansmen, and it was with surprise that they heard the prince offer them a formal introduction to the woman with blind eyes.

"She's not my concubine, Osami, although she travels under my protection. Her name is Alyssa, from a land called Cinthea. As to the bargain she proposes, decide as you will."

Satisfied of their safety, the grizzled, bow-legged rigger began tapping out a rhythm on the tight-skinned drum clasped between his thighs. Others took up the beat with clapped hands, the cabin boy's sweet soprano sending the melody drifting above the bass rumbles of the chorus. The woman tapped her foot in time, a faint smile hovering around her lips as they sang of pleasuring, of flashing eyes and fluttering lashes, of dripping thighs and swelling breasts, of the heat of bodies joined together, sweating under a tropical sun. The tempo increased, the drummer's hands a blur, voices throbbing, ending in a triumphant shout.

Her burst of applause pleased them, causing one of them to ask, "Have you such songs in your land?"

"None quite like yours," she replied, "although we sing of much the same thing as we stomp the grapes at the end of harvest."

"Where is Cinthea?" another one called out.

"Far to the west, beyond the River Tellas."

None of them had ever heard of stomping or grapes or a river named Tellas, but they smiled all the same, proud that she addressed them as equals.

"Time for a story!" shouted the cabin boy, dodging a cuff from the quartermaster whose duty it was to teach him respect for his betters. Unrepentant, the boy grabbed up a stool and ran to the woman's side. Seating herself facing the wind, her unbound hair streaming off her shoulders, the moon a backdrop to her makeshift stage, the blind woman began her tale.

Simply, with graceful gestures, she told them a tale of the sea, of sailors like themselves in search of a great white fish. It took awhile for them to accustom themselves to the peculiarities of her accent, but as she promised, no one minded when she paused to search for an appropriate word or phrase, all faults forgiven as they recognized her artistry.

The sea she described was different than the one they knew—cold and rough, fraught with icy gales and giant sea creatures leaping out from under white-capped waves to threaten tiny boats commanded by a half-mad pilot with a wooden leg. Ahab, she called him, a two-ringed clansman if ever they had known one, ruling his crew with an iron hand.

With her, they mourned the death of the tattooed seaman who foretold his own demise, for no one understands superstition as do those who sail the seas. And when at last they clung with the boy to the wooden box in which his dead friend rested, they wept as she wept at the poignancy of innocence lost, at the cruel enigma that is the sea.

They sang of pleasure, she of duty and revenge, yet common ground was found between them. They went to their hammocks with full hearts that night, finally reconciled to this perilous journey through uncharted seas. From that night forward they clamored for her presence. Willingly, she took them with her to seas where sirens sang, where talking fish jumped into fishermen's nets, where fur seals frolicked on shores no human ever trod. They took her in turn to beaches of powdery pink sand, their drums beating out the rhythms of waves crashing against the shore. Island songs they taught her, songs gathered in many lifetimes of wandering the eastern seas.

Each night they bid her farewell as the watch changed, most of them unaware that the story-teller with sightless eyes guided their ship through the night, searching in her dreams for one who was, like them, a sailor of unknown seas.

Until, on the evening of the twenty-ninth day out of Nisyros, the blind woman awoke from her dreams.

SEAHORSE FLEW EAST, the only sound that of waves being split by the ship's prow, and the occasional creak, for a wooden ship is a living thing, constantly adjusting to the forces of wind and water. It was nearly dawn, the sand-glass in need of turning, the crew fast asleep in their hammocks below deck. Osami, the first mate, manned the wheel, while the cabin boy, Tama, slept in a curled-up ball at the blind woman's feet. Kasovar had gone below to search his sea chest for new quills.

"Fawaz?" the blind woman whispered.

He was at her side in an instant, bending over to place his ear near her lips, sensing she didn't want to wake the boy.

"We're very close."

"You've found him?"

"Hurry," she urged, sinking back into the chair, seeming to sleep again except for the tears leaking out from beneath her eyelashes and running down her cheeks.

Fawaz, never happier than when called to action, woke the boy with a firm hand, gesturing up to the top of the main mast. Rubbing sleep from his eyes, Tama scrambled up the rigging, small-bodied and dexterous with fingers and toes. Almost immediately, he loosed a jubilant shout of "Land!"

"Land!" repeated Fawaz, savoring the word as never before. In the next breath, Kasovar appeared at his side, the old man panting after his quick trip from below deck, speaking excitedly to his former student, reinforcing every command Fawaz thought to issue, bringing a smile to Fawaz's face as he watched his elderly teacher become fifty years younger.

"First, recall the boy and wake the crew. Second, send more experienced look-outs up each mast. We're far enough away to do this right," the old pilot counseled. "Give the island wide berth until we get our bearings, and keep an eye out for that sloop!"

"She's given us time to forge a rescue plan," Fawaz observed, for *Sea Horse* remained invisible, too far below the horizon line to be seen by anyone on the island.

The old man responded with a grudging nod toward the dreaming woman, "That she has, if she can be believed."

"She's guided us to an island in uncharted seas exactly twenty-nine days east of Nisyros, and you doubt her still?"

The old man blinked twice and changed the subject. "I'll get Tasir," he offered and disappeared below.

It begins, thought the pilot, filled with excitement and renewed determination as *Sea Horse* flew toward Sandur Kwanlonhon.

THE FIRST MYSTERY was the number of masts filling the skies above the newly discovered island. They thought to find one—the sloop that had transported the Tehran's sa'ab. The *Sea Horse's* look-outs called down this unexpected news to the three Kwanlonhon clansmen who stalked the quarterdeck, still blinded by the distance between shore and ship, dependent on the lookouts whose news floated down to them from above. Ships, they called out, many ships, some at the docks, others moored in the harbor.

If it hadn't been for the woman's warning, they might have sailed directly into the coral reef guarding the harbor of this tiny island, a thumbprint of sand with a scattering of dusty palm trees along the shoreline. The conical slopes of an ancient volcano, eroded almost beyond recognition, gave the isle an exhausted appearance. Once it had waged war with the elements, surrendering at last, beaten down by wind, water, and the passage of time.

In the pre-dawn light, the look-outs spied what looked to be wooden buildings close to the dock, spread out along the shoreline, news that brought the clansmen into a tight huddle. Finally breaking away from Tasir and Kasovar, Fawaz took up his position to address the crew, who had gathered below him on the main deck.

"Tama, escort the lady below."

Everyone watched as she rose from the chair and began her descent, amethyst robes rippling in the breeze as the dawn skies revealed themselves above banks of low-lying clouds. Fawaz waited until she was safely below deck before addressing them again.

"We won't be so fool-hardy as to reveal ourselves before studying the lay of the land. We'll continue due east, then come about and tack our way to the northern side of the island, where we'll search for a bay or inlet in which to hide."

Muttered grunts and nods indicated the crew approved the plan.

"As we get closer to shore, Kasovar will oversee the soundings. The pinnance needs readying as well. We've some reconnoitering to do tonight."

Fawaz paused to regard them, causing most the crew to shift their weight, made anxious by his unblinking gaze.

"No songs tonight. Once we drop anchor, Prince Tasir is in charge."

AS INHOSPITABLE AS the island seemed, it offered them sanctuary, providing a small cove surrounded by a thin crescent of beach on its northwest shore. A thick fog drifted in not long after they dropped anchor, wrapping the ship in a fine mist and providing cover for the three men sent to explore the harbor area on the southern coastline, the only place evidencing any sign of habitation.

It was the second hour after midnight, the pinnance having left *Seahorse* four hours ago, four hours in which Tasir felt himself grow old. The sharp-eyed cabin boy was first to sight the boat as it pulled around the point, alerting the others with an excited whisper. Tasir planted his hands firmly on the boy's shoulders, following the direction of the finger pointing out the boat's progress over blackened waves.

Once the pinnance was secured alongside, a rope ladder was lowered, and three men climbed aboard. Blankets were proffered to the first two, who were sodden and shivering, naked save for their challahs. Next came steaming mugs of sugary black tea.

Averting his eyes, Tasir waited until Fawaz had dried himself and was decently clothed before he began.

"Any trouble?"

"None."

Shivering in the coolness of the night air, for the sea was warm as soup, Fawaz sipped his tea, feeling the warmth spread out from his stomach to his goose-fleshed limbs. The swim from the pinnance to shore was long, the return even longer, since while waiting for the swimmers' return, Osami spied a light flickering nearby and rowed another hundred yards offshore.

Tasir began the meeting without preamble.

"Your report, Hamad."

Pulling his blanket up around his shoulders, Hamad (the strongest swimmer on board), shifted uneasily, mumbling something under his breath.

"Report!"

The entire crew jumped. Hamad cringed, licking his lips, darting nervous glances at those assembled around him.

"I checked the dock first, like you said, and I . . . ," his voice dropped to little more than a whisper, "I found the lost ships."

For a moment nothing could be heard on deck except the slap of waves. The lighting of oil lamps forbidden and the moon shrouded in fog, not even the sharp-eyed cabin boy could discern Tasir's reaction to Hamad's news. His voice emerged from the darkness, speaking calmly and reasonably to the terrified sailor.

"Tell us exactly what you saw."

"At first I couldn't figure it," Hamad began. "Too many ships for a place no one has ever heard of. Then I recognized *Zephyr*. I served on her once, four, maybe five years ago."

"The Assad frigate lost in the Pitanes?" Tasir interrupted, to which Hamad nodded eagerly, encouraged by the prince's interest. He'd feared he wouldn't be believed.

"Aye, prince, *Zephyr* and more! The Synzurit flagship no one's seen since last autumn, a H'ulalet schooner reported lost six moons ago, and others, many others, most of them rotting hulks, stripped of their timbers, the ribs bare, like skeletons."

Shivering, he pulled the blanket tighter. The crew stirred uneasily, muttering among themselves, unclear as to how Hamad's findings affected their mission. They'd been hired to find the Tehran's sa'ab; no one mentioned the possibility of pirates. A new voice spoke out of the fog, that of Fawaz the pilot.

"That explains the condition of the docks, most of them newly built. The buildings are constructed of wood as well. Lacking trees, they must have used the ships as a ready supply of lumber."

Had he been alone, Fawaz might have wept. The pride of the Endlinese fleet reduced to a graveyard of floating ruins.

"What buildings?"

Fawaz played for time, trying to cushion the blow.

"There's a compound built close to the docks. Most of the buildings are warehouses, built tight and dry with no windows and locked doors. They're arranged around a larger building, a sort of dormitory, with a kitchen and laundry around back. I got fairly close to the windows on the harbor side although I couldn't risk a look inside since the lamps were lit. I could hear the rattle of the dice cup as they placed their bets."

"How many?"

"Nine pairs of sandals lined up outside the door."

"I saw a light," Osami interjected, "moving around west of the docks. I couldn't make out much through the fog, but I saw what looked to be shacks."

Fawaz braced himself. There was no easy way to say what must be said.

"Those are the slave quarters."

Before anyone could react, he rushed on.

"I counted ten shacks, all of them chained shut. They're poorly built compared to the warehouses. I got close enough to one of them to peer through a crack between two warped boards."

If only he could take Tasir aside and whisper to him privately of what he'd seen, men lying in their own filth, half-starved, moaning in their sleep.

"I counted twenty, which means there must be close to two hundred of them. They'd need at least that many to build the docks and warehouses."

Fawaz prepared himself for the next question.

"Sandur?"

"I didn't see him."

Tasir made no response.

"Are they clansmen or commoners?" demanded Kasovar.

"I couldn't say. Most likely some of each."

Somehow he couldn't bring himself to relate all that he'd seen: bruises, whip scars, sunken eyes in gaunt, unshaven faces.

Tasir took charge again.

"What about guards?"

"One made the rounds not long after I'd swum ashore. That must have been the light Osami saw."

"Was he armed?"

"A knife only."

"This makes no sense," Kasovar interrupted. "It would be impossible for ten men to wreak such havoc. How could they overwhelm an entire ship's crew, forty men at least?"

"Agreed, uncle," Tasir said, "unless these are the rear guard, left behind to safeguard the booty and keep order among the slaves. They're very sure of themselves," he observed bitterly, "and why shouldn't they be? The island's small enough that a runaway could easily be recaptured. Even if they rebelled against their captors and managed to fight their way to the docks, once they stole a ship, without charts or logs, where could they go?"

Silence greeted his question. He'd expected no answer.

"We must work fast. If we tarry, the others may return. They suspect nothing and so will be careless. We'll go ashore at dawn and travel overland. With luck we'll reach the other side of the island before midday and take them unaware. Travel light. The cook will issue rations and water. Kasovar, you'll be in charge in my absence. You, boy, will look after the woman until we return."

Crestfallen but obedient, Tama voiced no objections.

"Have you forgotten your promise?"

A startled murmur rose from the crew as the blind woman, a ghostly apparition born of the fog, appeared.

"Have you forgotten your promise to Esslar," she repeated, "that I alone must tend him?"

"We'll bring him back to you," Tasir promised with unusual gentleness. "We must travel fast, too fast for you to follow. And there will be fighting, of that I'm certain."

"The boy can take me in the pinnance. Once the danger's past, he'll row me ashore."

"You cannot go," Tasir stated more forcefully, annoyed that she dared question his orders. "I forbid it." Perhaps regretting his tone, he attempted to reason with her. "You've waited this long, a few more hours won't matter."

"In the space of a few hours we might lose him. His strength is nearly gone," she stated simply, "as is mine."

"Think of what you risk," came the reproving reply.

"I must go," she insisted, "just as you must honor your promise."

What followed was without precedent, for Tasir Linphat Afaf Kwanlonhon, hereditary prince of the most powerful clan in Endlin, let his judgment be swayed by a woman. Rather than locking her in her cabin, an action well within the scope of his authority, he sighed and said, "So be it."

TAMA HELPED THE woman out of the pinnance, noticing as he did so violent fits of trembling wracking her slender frame. The sun stood at its zenith; the sand burned underfoot. Still she shivered, her skin waxen in the harsh light of day. Tama watched her as they listened to the attack, hearing the screams of men fighting for their lives. Prince Tasir's orders were simplicity itself—no quarter given. Tama supported this decision, as did the rest of the crew, but sitting in the pinnace, facing the pale-faced woman, he admitted to himself he was glad he'd played no part in the slaughter.

Fawaz was there to meet them, his outer robe torn and bloodied, the fire of battle still burning in his eyes. When he attempted to take the woman's arm, she shrank away from him, adding with an apologetic smile:

"The boy knows my ways. Let him be my guide."

Tama placed her hand on his shoulder. Long ago he'd learned her reticence at being touched. At first it hurt his feelings, for he kept himself cleaner than most and was always respectful of her position as a clansman's concubine. In time he accustomed himself to her ways and she to his, the secret of the child an unspoken bond between them.

As he followed Fawaz up the beach, he was grateful for her blindness, glad she was spared the sight of lifeless bodies being dragged across the sand to be tossed into a careless heap. Nor could she see the cut bleeding over Osami's forehead, or the makeshift bandage wrapped around the drummer's hand.

"What is it, Tama?" she whispered.

"Many are injured," he whispered back.

A faint sigh escaped her as they walked on.

The worst was not behind them, for now they drew near the huts. Here the sand was littered with slaves who'd emerged from their ramshackle prisons, many of them with tears streaming down their faces. Some were too weak to walk and crawled on hands and knees. Tama had never seen men like these, bearded and filthy, teeming with lice, their bodies thin, their stomachs swollen. Though she could not see, her ears were sharp, sharper than his, he felt sure. A fierce surge of protectiveness caused him to wish her deaf as well as blind, anything to prevent her from hearing the sounds of their misery.

Hut after hut they passed, following the stiff-backed pilot, until at last Tama caught sight of blue robes rifled by the offshore breeze and heard the sound of splitting wood.

Ignoring the chains on the door, members of the crew were prying apart a wall of one of the huts. Tasir stared grimly at the shack as it was dismantled. Fawaz took his place next to Tasir, motioning Tama forward. The opening grew wider, each board cast aside with a curse as the seamen worked at a frenzied pace, calling out warnings to those inside to stand aside, until at last, the opening was complete. Prisoners emerged. Like skeletons on review they passed by, squinting in the harsh sunlight, until the hut was finally emptied.

A malaise seemed to overcome both Fawaz and Tasir, the former staring blankly over the sun-bleached landscape, the latter regarding the woman closely, as if judging her reaction to unwelcome news.

"This is the last hut," Tasir explained quietly, his eyes never leaving her face. "I fear we've come too late."

"There are some . . ." Fawaz began hoarsely, clearing his throat before continuing,". . . some shallow graves behind the huts. Osami found them while scouting the perimeters before the attack. We'll start looking there."

The woman shook her head. Turning away from their grief, she reached out for Tama.

"Take me to the place where the others are gathered."

Something in her tone gave him the courage to obey. Ignoring the clansmen, he led her to the place where the crew was handing out food and drink to those newly freed from their prisons. At their approach, those alert enough to wonder at the sight of a woman walking among them grew silent, following her progress as Tama picked a path through their recumbent forms. Heads lifted as she passed, more than one hand reaching out to brush against the gold-encrusted silk of her robes as if to reassure themselves she was no phantom. Crisply, clearly, she addressed them, defiance in her carriage, in the angle of her chin.

"There is a man among you, a clansman called Sandur."

Brows furrowed, beards were scratched, cracked lips repeated the unfamiliar name.

"Perhaps you know him as Haji."

A hush descended. Head after head bowed, eyes stubbornly downcast. Finally, a scarecrow of a man stretched out on the sand, clothed in filthy tatters that might once have been silk, pulled himself up to a sitting position.

"I know of whom you speak. A prisoner the guards called Haji arrived a fortnight ago."

A mumbled murmur of assent confirmed the clansman's words, for a clansman he remained despite the ravages of slavery. What had he been, Tama wondered, before the pirates boarded his ship?

"He lived in my hut. We thought him mute since he spoke to no one. The guards singled him out for . . .," he hesitated, searching for the right words, ". . . extra duty. They took him away in the evening. Often, he'd not be returned to the hut until dawn. They came for him again last night. I've not seen him since."

"Who speaks of my nephew?" Tasir demanded as he shouldered his way through the crowd gathered around the woman.

The man rose to his feet with difficulty, swaying slighting at the effort of standing upright. As he did so, Tama saw him as he once had been, haughtily requesting a formal introduction before addressing a clansman of unknown rank.

"Whom do I address?"

"Tasir Kwanlonhon, son of Linphat V, brother to the Tehran."

The clansman's eyes narrowed as he studied Tasir. A tense silence ensued, during which he seemed to make a decision.

"I am Rassad, second son of Nayeem, Tehran of the H'ulalet, pilot to the schooner you see in the harbor, boarded by a Kwanlonhon ship on the open seas. The clansman in charge ordered most of my crew flung overboard. The rest of us were brought to this island a year ago."

"What ship?" Tasir thundered, a storm cloud settling on his brow as he rushed to uphold the honor of his clan.

"Fair Breeze."

Tasir controlled his temper with an effort.

"We lost *Fair Breeze* over two years ago. We've received no word of her since. I sit as an elder on the Kwanlonhon council. As such, I can assure you we have no connection with these pirates. If they use our ship, they do so without our knowledge or consent."

The H'ulalet pilot stood his ground.

"Then answer me this, Tasir Kwanlonhon. There are two hundred of us here, another four hundred drowned or buried behind the huts. Not one of us is Kwanlonhon, nor are any of the ships rotting in the harbor. If they are not Kwanlonhon, why does their pilot wear Kwanlonhon robes and fly a white pennant from the main mast, luring us to help a stranded ship in open waters, then boarding us to murder our crews and plunder our holds?"

A mutinous growl rose from two hundred parched throats.

"We are sick and weak, but still we listened as the guards joked among themselves. 'One more blow for the Tehran,' they sneered as they plied their whips. 'Be careful with that, slave, or you'll have the Tehran to answer to!' they jeered as we labored in those accursed warehouses."

Rassad's voice had risen during his speech. Now he passed a shaking hand over his haggard face and said more quietly, "You must forgive my rudeness, Prince Tasir. We have reason to thank you for our release."

Tasir stood as one struck dumb, bleakly surveying the pitiful survivors strewn at his feet.

"Rassad H'ulalet," the woman urged softly, "please tell me of Haji. Where might he be found?"

"Sometimes," the H'ulalet pilot said with obvious reluctance, moved by the sight of her unexpected beauty, "they would select a group of us for burial duty and march us over there," he pointed to a desolate stretch of rocky beach, "where we would find corpses. Try that place. He might be there."

* * *

THEY FOUND HIM near the sea. The force of the incoming tide was tremendous as it pounded the rocks strewn near the shore line, waves crashing and breaking, spewing spray and foam high into the air. The wind had changed, blowing steadily now from the northeast, forming the burning sand into patterns of innumerable ripples. Like living things, the ripples crawled slowly, relentlessly, toward a body lying half-buried in the drifting sand.

His skin was as black as the sand was white. Here a hand emerged, encircled by a leather thong strapped to an iron stake. Here a shoulder broke the surface of the sand; there the unmistakable curve of a buttock; further down, a calf, the heel of a foot. Flat on his belly he lay, his head turned away from the wind, protected by the recess of his out-flung arm. Scabby crusts bore witness to the cruelty of the guards who nicked his scalp as they hacked away his hair.

His body lay lifeless, stretched taut by thongs at wrists and ankles. High above their heads a lone gull circled, voicing its mournful cry above the monotonous drone of the rising surf. Sea, sun, sand seemed to merge, the waves pummeling the shore into submission, the sun a fiercely glowing stone in a hazy sky, the sand a burning blanket radiating scorching heat.

On that blanket the woman knelt, working patiently at the knots, slender fingers working deftly, delicately, as if she labored over lace rather than the rough leather straps binding him to the stakes. As each limb was freed, she brushed away the powdery sand clinging stubbornly to his sun-baked flesh, crooning to him under her breath. He gave no sign that he heard her, even when she eased his upper body onto her lap and cleaned the sand from his lashes with the hem of her sleeve. From about her waist she untied an azure scarf worked with threads of gold. It billowed in the wind as she floated it down the contours of his chest and belly, falling into folds as she draped it about his loins.

Stroking his bearded jaw, she bent her head, her hair an awning shielding him from the remorseless sun, and kissed his lips, whispering to him of cool meadows and dewy fields, content to hold him forever, her lips pressed tenderly against his sun-blistered flesh.

The two men who accompanied her on the long trek across the bleached sands stood like stones. The wind whipped their silks into frenzy, their braids streaming out behind them as they bore witness to the trials of the Tehran's sa'ab. They saw what the woman did not—the positioning of his body so he might offer no resistance to those who raped him, the bowl of water set just beyond his grasp, a constant goad to his raging thirst. The plight of the prisoners moved them to pity; Sandur's treatment assured retaliation.

No words passed between them. None were needed. Here they pledged themselves to action.

"SANDUR," SOMEONE CALLED. "Sandur," the voice repeated, more urgently this time, "you must wake!"

The voice came too late. Sandur died one night in a tavern, a raucous drinking song his death-knell. As a sailor he swore and as a sailor he died, his lifeline cut as he fled the sinking ship to plunge headlong into the white-capped waves of a tempest-tossed sea. Allowed no farewells, he gave himself up to the sea, the breath leaving his lungs as he sank down into the lower depths, called to rest at last, thankful for an end to everything. Soon he was little more than a shell of what had once been Sandur, cleaned and polished by countless grains of sand, the roar of the ocean soothing to his ears.

Memory was his companion as he drifted out to sea, memory and her sad-faced sister, regret. Memory sustained him as he sank; regret caused him to dream of a grey-eyed woman whose name he couldn't recall. Sweet-voiced, tremulous, they sang him out to sea, the sound of their singing drowning out the grunts of the rutting guards. Greedy hands turned him this way and that, holding him fast despite his struggles. Bruised by their roughness, he ached and sometimes bled. Yet eventually the pain would subside, soothed by the power of dreams, and he would escape, sent sailing on a whispering breeze. There he would find the enchanted seas he had once known in a place called the Maze, a place without pain, without sorrow, a place where he could rest.

A cool hand stroked his temples, and he was lost in memories again, remembering another hand, another caress.

"Have I come so far to find you've forgotten me?" he was asked with infinite sadness. "Have you no word for the one left behind?"

He was done with words. None had crossed his lips since the night of his capture. Like a beast they bound and gagged him; like a beast he went silently to slaughter. Words would bring him back to the body tied to stakes on the burning sand. To speak would revive the thirst that had driven him almost mad.

Water dripped into his mouth, cool sweet water dribbling down his chin. He swallowed by reflex. The voice spoke again, begging for his return.

"Come back to me, Sandur."

Sandur is dead, he screamed inside himself, the hated son of a hateful father is dead! Why disturb his remains? He's better off dead, friendless brute that he was. Let him be forgotten.

"Why can you not forgive yourself? What have you done to deserve such punishment?"

Disembodied voices rose around him, a chorus of raucous sailors singing a drinking song. He tried to stave off the vision, whimpering as she called out for him, seeing her on the staircase, a blade hovering near the slender column of her throat.

"I live, Sandur."

He feared this to be true even as he struggled to free himself from his attackers. Darker visions appeared, things much worse than a quick death. What would become of her? How many men would accost her as she stumbled blindly down those unlit streets? How long until they robbed her of everything she possessed? He promised to protect her, yet now she wandered cruel streets lost and alone, a blind beggar to be shoved rudely aside, a pitiful prostitute to be used and discarded, a mad woman mumbling to herself in a foreign tongue, reciting stories no one understood. Having betrayed her trust, he deserved nothing less than death.

"Esslar cared for me in your absence; Fawaz brought me to your side. Have they labored in vain, all these who risked their lives for you?"

He wondered at this new punishment called hope. Having no defense against it, he felt his head break the surface of the water and gasped for breath. Blinking away salty tears, his vision cleared.

The glow of an oil lamp met his eyes. Encircled by that halo of light, a hazy form took shape, indistinguishable at first, the outlines growing solid as he strained to bring the world into focus. Hair, a red-gold waterfall fell in thick waves around a serious face with a tiny frown etched between delicately upswept brows. A pink lip caught between white teeth, and finally, large grey eyes surrounded by sooty lashes.

A finger traced the tracks of his tears.

"What do you see, Sandur?"

She lay beside him, her limbs entwined with his, on a narrow berth draped with silken sheets. His body was a mystery to him, clean and oiled, smelling faintly of cinnamon, bearing no resemblance to the one left behind on the beach. They lay on their sides facing one another, his loins pressed against hers as she stroked his ribs and flanks, her cool white hands awakening what he thought extinct.

"Do you feel it? The roll of the ship?"

Recognition dawned and with it, confusion. What sort of dream was this, to feel the movement of waves beneath him when he lay facedown, half-smothered by drifting sand? He'd found peace in other dreams, but never with her by his side. Always, he'd been alone, abandoned, borne along by a magnificently indifferent sea.

"Speak my name, Sandur."

One word would free him. One word would bring him back to life, and he would again be Sandur. Speaking that single word aloud would begin everything anew, yet still he hesitated. What if he spoke, and the phantom vanished? Should he risk the loss of the oblivion he craved only to wake to the noise of the surf, the punishing glare of sun on sand?

"Speak for life."

He understood in that moment how desperately he yearned for death. Existence was reduced to a single equation: speak and live; keep silent and die. If he embraced death, he would never be hurt again. If he chose life, he must accept all its consequences, even the chance that he might awake on a desolate beach, the forgotten son of a monstrous father, the beloved of one whose trust he'd betrayed.

"Alyssa?"

With the utterance of her name, he was reborn, delivered from his watery grave by a grateful cry. Covered with her kisses, anointed by her tears, he let himself float on the tide of her joy.

Questions began to filter though his mind.

"Where . . .?" he whispered, watching her smile as she settled his head more comfortably on her breast.

"*Seahorse*. This is the cabin you shared with Fawaz, is it not?"

If it was, it resembled no cabin he remembered. True, the dimensions were familiar, cramped and low-raftered, but she'd made it cozy and comfortable. The paneled walls were polished to a high sheen and smelt faintly of lemon oil. Bright rugs covered the tiny floor-space between the berths and a sea trunk lay open, its contents spilling out onto the rug, her robes and underthings, spools of thread and pieces of lace, her brush and comb, scarves for her hair, the vial of lavender perfume he'd bought her in the marketplace. On the berth across from them rested a basin and ewer, soaps and body oils, drying cloths, and a tray of what looked to be food and drink.

"How long . . .?"

"Three days since we found you," she said, tightening her arms around him and kissing the crown of his head. "Fawaz and Tasir carried you here on a stretcher. No one else has seen you except the cabin boy who brings me whatever I require. I tended you myself," and then with attempted lightness, "and you were a surprisingly good patient."

As he rested for a while without speaking, he began to build a past. They found him on the beach, naked and helpless, and made every effort to spare his pride. Tasir, a patrician unused to physical labor of any kind, helped Fawaz carry him to the ship. And Alyssa never left his side.

Deciding from the roll of the waves that the ship wasn't under sail, he asked, "Where are we moored?"

"Ever the chartist!" she laughed, her gaiety unforced. "We're anchored in a cove, they tell me, on the north side of the island. Except for the cabin boy, the cook, and your great uncle Kasovar, we have the ship to ourselves."

"Where are the others?"

The laughter died on her face. Sensing her unwillingness to reply, he tried to reassure her. "Thou can speak of it, Alyssa. I am myself again."

"They . . . they lay a trap."

Her mouth clamped shut, signaling that he would learn no more from her until she judged him fully recovered. Yet one question remained.

"And the . . .," his voice caught, " . . . the guards?"

A shadow flew across her features.

"The ones who hurt you are dead. They're buried near the remains of those they tormented. They are dead," she repeated gravely, "and you live." A hand caressed his brow. "You must put it behind you, beloved. Already the bruises fade, or so Tasir tells me. I cleansed you of their filth. There's no lasting hurt except the memory of what they did. In time, that, too, will fade."

Lassitude swept over him, an exhaustion so great he felt himself melt into her arms. As he closed his eyes, her fingertips brushed against his scalp.

"My hair . . .," he began woefully.

" . . . will grow," she assured him, although her tone suggested amusement at his concern over so trifling a matter. "Until then, my fingers shall enjoy a much deserved rest."

Cocking open an eye, he regarded her more closely. As though she sensed his gaze and wished to avoid it, she reached for a blanket at the foot of the bed and wrapped herself in it.

"I must tell Kasovar you've awakened."

Bustling about the tiny cabin, she found her robes and dressed quickly, turning away from him as she did so. He was the modest one, retaining his challah despite her blindness and the privacy of the cell. She'd always been flamboyant about her nudity. Now she hid from him. Gradually he became aware that she was chattering on about his great-uncle.

" . . . and sometimes he stands just outside the door, spying on me, I suppose. Of course," she added, with a trace of all too familiar wickedness, "I've shocked him on more than one occasion. He thinks me quite shameless by now."

"What reason has he to disapprove of thee?" he demanded, amazed by his great-uncle's behavior.

When she made no answer, he reached out his hand and latched on to her robe, pulling her toward him. She came easily enough despite the weakness of his grip.

"What hast thou done that Kasovar finds thee shameless?" he repeated, refusing to be put off.

"He thinks you're shameless as well. No, not shameless," she amended quickly, sensing his frown, "but certainly failing in your responsibilities to the clan."

She was teasing him. Or was she? He knew her moods better than his own, yet he'd never seen her quite so animated, nor so stubbornly intent on making him guess the reason for her excitement. His eyes swept over her again, searching for clues, finding her as he'd left her that night in the inn, pink pearls embedded in her earlobes, robes of amethyst and gold tied loosely at her waist . . .

"My sa'ab," he whispered, his throat gone dry as desert sand.

Her correction came in the next heartbeat.

"Our child."

He did not say it. He shouted it aloud. A croak it was at best, hoarse and raspy from disuse, but it was unmistakably his voice, that of Sandur Kwanlonhon, crying out the news to anyone within earshot that the prodigal had returned.

Soon after, his shorn head resting on her silk-clad breast, she whispered into his ear the rhythmic meters of a poet as blind as herself.

> Few men can keep alive through a big surf
> to crawl, clotted with brine, on kindly beaches
> in joy, in joy, knowing the abyss behind:
> and so she too rejoiced, her gaze upon her husband,
> her white arms round him pressed as though forever.

Chapter 24

Judgment Day

FIVE TALL SHIPS sailed majestically into the harbor that day, pennants fluttering on the morning breeze. In solemn procession they sailed, five vessels crammed with treasure, riding low in the water as they swung around the point, rolled their canvases, and glided smoothly into port.

Beacon fires used to alert the city of a ship's approach were lit the previous evening up and down the coastline. By the time dawn broke, the first ship was sighted by the harbormaster, and a crowd gathered on the docks—primarily clan stewards and a bevy of porters eager at the prospect of employment. When a second and then a third ship sailed into view, a general rush ensued, emptying the markets and causing Falal the sponge dealer and Oman the tea merchant to shrug their shoulders, lock their doors, and hurry down to the docks. With the arrival of a fourth and then a fifth, a near riot developed, for not since the arrival of the clansmen five centuries ago had one day seen five three-masted, fully-rigged merchant ships sailing in procession into the deep, blue-water harbor of Endlin.

Gossip rose on the morning tide, originating in the harbor district, making its way up the shell path and beyond the limestone gates, spreading quickly to the markets of the Abalone district until it reached the palaces and citadels built high atop the seven hills.

"*Seahorse*!" the Kwanlonhon rejoiced, ecstatic at the thought of already bulging warehouses filled to the bursting point. Ninety days ago was her last sighting in Nisyros, and they feared her lost. Now, as they glimpsed her slim, graceful lines rounding the point, they nodded their heads wisely and smirked, "An excellent pilot, our Fawaz! How foolish of us to worry!"

Their delight was nothing next to that of the Assad, who rubbed their eyes in disbelief as the second ship (the first of three ghost ships) sailed into port.

"*Zephyr*!" they exulted, checking their excitement when red robes were spotted on the quarterdeck. "Who is this grandfather?" they muttered, disquiet filling them at the sight of an elderly, white-haired pilot standing near the helm. "Not an Assad," they agreed among themselves. "No, most assuredly, he's not one of us."

Tehrans, too, came down to the docks that day. One of them was Nayeem H'ulalet, who for twelve moons had mourned the loss of his second son. That morning he uttered a prayer of thanks to the wind-gods as the missing schooner sailed into view and cried aloud as he caught sight of a familiar figure on the quarterdeck. Later, as the schooner came alongside the H'ulalet docks, Nayeem wondered to himself, "Where are his formal robes?" A feeling of foreboding passed over him as he took in the hollows under his son's eyes and the threads of silver shot through his once night-black hair. Not until he crushed Rassad to his breast, feeling his fragility through the rough clothing of a common seaman, did the anger begin to grow — anger that his child had been mistreated and a private resolve that someone must pay.

Sheer incredulity filled the Synzurit clansmen as their flagship glided into view. Consternation followed as their eyes flew past the crew assembled on the forward deck to find something so unexpected that more than one of them questioned the balance of his wits.

"A woman?" they sputtered, "A woman aboard a Synzurit ship?"

As their minds began to function again, their attention centered on the man standing beside her on the quarterdeck. Again they questioned their powers of reason, for although the ragged crew obeyed his orders, he wore neither robes nor jewels, and his hair was cropped like a common criminal. If it had not been for the Equerry, who rarely frequented the docks but for some reason decided to come today, they might have stood there for hours, bickering in distinctly Synzurit fashion over the stranger's identity.

"Sandur Kwanlonhon, the Tehran's sa'ab," the Equerry stated unequivocally, ending any possibility of further discussion.

While the Synzurit fretted over this unexpected piece of news, the Equerry turned his attention to his clan's flagship, ruminating over the odd patches of different colored wood running along the stern, repairs that suggested the original planking had been recently replaced with new timbers. Before he could fully consider his findings, a cry arose as yet another ship sailed into view.

"*Fair Breeze!*" crowed the greedy Kwanlonhon, dancing up and down, clapping their hands in gleeful anticipation. "We thought her lost, but Tasir brings her home!"

As the schooner docked, the sounds of their celebration died in their throats, replaced by an awkward silence and avid curiosity, every eye trained on the rows of shackled prisoners gathered on the forward deck. Hands raised to cover open mouths as Tasir strode down the gangplank, eyebrows drawn together in a ferocious scowl. Brushing aside the compliments of his fawning kinsmen, he shouted orders over his shoulder to the first mate.

"Post guards while I'm gone! No one to board without my express permission!"

A line of hard-eyed crewmen appeared along the starboard side of *Fair Breeze*, hands on knife-hilts. Backing away, puzzled at being prevented from beginning their tasks, the Kwanlonhon stewards waved away the disappointed porters, who chattered uneasily among themselves. Fawaz had issued similar orders after *Seahorse* docked, forbidding them to come aboard despite the obvious richness of his cargo. The other docks were already a flurry of activity, workers swarming over the decks of the Assad, H'ulalet, and Synzurit ships. Why this reticence at unloading what was the rightful property of the Kwanlonhon?

Answer came in the form of the Equerry, flanked on either side by Prince Tasir and Fawaz. Behind them streamed a large contingent of Onozzi and Effrentati clansmen, among them a gold-robed Tehran, Yodhat Onozzi. With a steely edge to his voice that brooked no denial, Prince Tasir addressed the Kwanlonhon's chief steward.

"Vacate the docks immediately. Take with you any and all Kwanlonhon clansmen. Wait for me at the limestone gate."

Turning deaf ears to their protests, he addressed the Equerry, speaking in a loud, clear voice, intent that everyone should hear and understand.

"The men in shackles are responsible for sacking the clan fleet. I surrender them to you for trial and punishment. If you'll accept our assistance, my first mate, Osami, and the rest of my crew will escort them to the city gaol. They've grown accustomed to their jobs as jailers in the past two moons."

When the Equerry accepted his offer with a thoughtful gaze and a quiet word of thanks, Tasir inclined his head respectfully to the Tehran of the Onozzi, inviting him and the chief steward of the Effrentati to approach.

"The cargos of *Seahorse* and *Fair Breeze* are yours."

When the hubbub greeting his pronouncement died down, he spoke again and with such sorrow that those around him felt his desolation.

"Your ships were found, but were beyond repair. These cargos are meager recompense for your loss. Take them with our humblest apologies."

Yodhat Onozzi replied courteously, "The Kwanlonhon, too, suffered at the hands of these pirates. Since *Fair Breeze* was found, surely her cargo is rightfully yours."

"With all respect," Tasir stated forcefully, "you know not of what you speak." A bleak note entered his voice. "The Kwanlonhon have lost nothing but their honor."

With that, he turned on his heel, Fawaz at his side, both of them striding purposefully toward the limestone gates and the citadel that lay beyond.

Turning so he might observe their swift retreat from the docks, the Synzurit Equerry was surprised to discover his personal physician standing a respectful three paces to his right.

"So, H'Esslar, you are right again."

"I hoped I was wrong."

"The lost sa'ab and the lost ships," the Equerry muttered to himself, bent on remembering a conversation he'd half-forgotten. "This doesn't bode well for the Kwanlonhon."

"Does it not?" the healer responded dreamily, his attention riveted on a couple making their way down the Synzurit gangplank, the woman moving with some awkwardness as the man walked beside her, clearing a path for her with a healthy disregard for anyone's safety save hers.

"Where do you suppose they'll go?" the Equerry wondered aloud, voicing the thoughts of all who noticed the woman's blindness. "She'll not be welcome in the citadel," he mused, eyes trained on the swelling of her womb, "nor, I would guess, will Sandur. Manthur would never countenance a Kwanlonhon child being born of such a woman." He pursed his lips before adding, "Although I understand he is much changed of late."

"Indeed?" the healer replied, distracted this time by the sight of a raven-haired woman, a commoner of rare beauty who rushed forward to embrace the pregnant woman before welcoming the Tehran's sa'ab with a shy smile.

As if caught napping, the healer started. Recalling the Equerry's question, he hurried to answer it.

"My friends have found a place for them to stay, a modest house in a residential district. They'll be safe, never fear."

It occurred to the Equerry that he should inquire as to how a commoner came to be on such intimate terms with a Tehran's sa'ab. At the last moment he decided to forbear, not so much out of politeness, but in his haste to begin the task at hand. His health had improved fourfold since being introduced to the healer, as had his temper and, happily for all concerned, his manners. Good digestion breeds good humor, and he'd never felt quite so ready to tackle the work which lay before him. Tightening his sash around his slimming girth (for he'd dropped two stone on the dietary regime H'esslar prescribed), he patted what remained of his belly, then summoned his cortege of guards with the practiced flick of a plump, bejeweled hand.

"One request, lord, if I may be so bold."

The Equerry halted, eyebrows raised in mild surprise.

"When you question the prisoners, ask them about a foreigner who wears calfskin boots."

By the time the Equerry thought to demand an explanation, the healer had vanished into the crowd.

THE EQUERRY COURT of Endlin, established by Linphat the First in the fourth decade after the arrival of the founder's ships, sat at dawn. Even at this early hour, chosen for its relative coolness, the heat and high humidity of late summer was enough to wilt even the crispest silks as the clan elders gathered in the Court Pavilion.

Built of white limestone quarried from the cliffs lining the northern coastlands, the Pavilion was the only public building in Endlin in which clansmen and commoners mingled freely, although not always by choice. Here suits were heard, complaints registered, and judgments rendered by magistrates trained in local law, or if the magistrates could not agree, by the Equerry himself. By tradition, the court sat three days a week: one for suits between clansmen, another for those between commoners, a final day reserved for cases involving both commoners and clansmen. Also by tradition, court proceedings were closed to anyone not directly involved in the case at hand.

This day was different, both in the earliness of the hour and the fact that the Equerry had summoned the ruling councils of the six clans. That he did so without offering an explanation raised many eyebrows in the palaces and citadels scattered about the city, causing more than one elder to scratch his nose and finger his earrings as he turned the matter over in his mind. Creatures of habit that they were, no clansmen enjoyed the prospect of the unexpected. Even so, they arrived promptly on the hour, gathering in groups around the steps of the entryway, bowing and nodding as they greeted one another in hushed voices.

As was the custom for formal events, the members of each council exchanged the outside robe for the one which announced their clan affiliation. This change in attire symbolized their unity, a visual statement of their clan's solidarity. The result was startling, especially when they began to take their places in the courtroom. By the time the Tehrans arrived (since by custom they entered last of all), six phalanxes of elders sat in six banks of vibrant colors—Onozzi orange, Synzurit green, H'ulalet blue, Assad purple, Effrentati yellow, and Kwanlonhon red—waiting expectantly for the approach of the magistrates.

Six in number, one magistrate for each clan, they were attired in their clan's formal over-robe tied with a sash of spotless white. Elected for terms of five years, most of them were of an advanced age and selected for their fairness and discretion. It was something of a rarity to see them gathered as one body since by custom they heard cases in groups of three, a system which evolved over the years to relieve the burden placed on the Equerry. Linphat the First heard every case in former times. With the growth of Endlin and its rapidly expanding territories, it became impossible for a single man to manage the affairs of the Court.

It was not unheard of for a magistrate to become an Equerry, although since an Equerry served for life, the chances were slim that an elderly magistrate would outlive his superior. The last time this occurred, some seventy years ago, one Nazur Kwanlonhon, beloved of the commoners for the excellence of his racing stables and respected by his peers for the breadth of his learning, was chosen as Equerry after serving a single term as magistrate. Elected at the remarkable young age of forty-two, his tenure as Equerry resulted in important changes in court procedures, among them a growing reliance on written contracts and the beginnings of a discrimination between criminal and civil suits, primarily in regards to punishment. Still, all in all, the legal code of Endlin remained as harsh as it was swift. Thieves lost their hands, liars their tongues, rapists their testicles, and murderers their heads, all sentences carried out immediately and without possibility of appeal. Civil cases resulted in either stiff monetary penalties, various terms of exile, or outright banishment. Not for nothing had the saying "cruel as a day in court" come into common parlance among the inhabitants of Endlin, for mercy seemed in short supply in Equerry Court.

The magistrates, having settled themselves on the cushions arranged on the second level of the central dais, sat in dignified solemnity. They alone were party to the testimony of the prisoners delivered by Prince Tasir to the court, just as they were the only witnesses to the sessions held between the Equerry and the men freed from slavery by the crew of *Seahorse*.

Once the general euphoria generated by the return of the lost ships dissipated, rumors flew through the city, rumors ugly enough that a junior steward of the Kwanlonhon clan was attacked in the Abalone district by unknown assailants and severely beaten. Since that day, the Kwanlonhon kept close to their citadel. Then, a week ago, a single-mast sloop, the type used for recreational trips to nearby isles, docked at the Kwanlonhon pier and was immediately impounded by order of the Equerry. There was much gnashing of teeth among the proud Kwanlonhon over the Equerry's inexplicable behavior, yet also flurries of doubt, for it seemed that their Tehran had abandoned them.

Locked in his study for days at a time, Manthur's frequent absences brought clan affairs to a grinding halt. Everything was in a muddle, the stewards tearing their hair over his refusal to inspect cargo lists or approve the financial transactions necessary for maintaining Kwanlonhon credit, the pilots grumbling that not a single trading contract had been awarded in over four moons, the ship-builders driven to distraction by requests for payment from their suppliers. With Tasir's return, they turned to him for aid, confident of his abilities to either spur his brother to action or assume leadership himself.

But Tasir, too, had gone mad. True, he did not dance alone, humming a single, unrelenting tune under his breath for hours on end, but he was mad all the same, often departing the citadel before dawn and not returning until long after dusk, ignoring his concubines and, worst of all, failing in his fatherly duties. His children pined for him even as his concubines sighed over the dark circles under his bleary eyes. Gossip had it he cried in his sleep and woke drenched in sweat. "Night demons," said the apothecary, prescribing a foul emetic that smelt of tar and fish oil. "Worry," said his favorite concubine, who went to his bed without waiting to be summoned. "Grief," said his eldest brother, Rahjid the Wise, wagging his head in commiseration before taking up his reading where he'd left off.

Even stranger rumors circulated in the plazas and private apartments of the Kwanlonhon citadel, most of them initiated by a series of requests forwarded to them by the Equerry, again, without a word of explanation. Red-faced stewards huffed and puffed down the steep northern road, their bellies shaking like tart quince jelly, the ledgers wedged under their arms offered up to the Equerry like so many tributes to the commander of an unlooked for invasion.

Kwanlonhon pilots, too, every pilot granted a contract in the last five years, made a similar pilgrimage, although since pilots were by nature a tight-lipped breed, the foolish few bent on prying out their secrets were met with icy stares. Poor Pischak Kwanlonhon returned from his daylong interview with The Equerry to spend the next week in an inebriated stupor. And, perhaps strangest of all, Fawaz, the darling of the entire Kwanlonhon clan, had disappeared.

But a darker cloud hung over the Kwanlonhon citadel, darker even than the Equerry's mysterious investigation of their affairs, Tasir's nightmares, or the unnerving behavior of their Tehran. The insults of the Synzurit, their ancient rivals, burned their ears. The H'ulalet spit in the dust as they passed. So virulent was the Assad's hatred that former daughters of the Kwanlonhon forbade their fathers to visit them out of fear for their lives. Yodhat Onozzi, once an ardent supporter of everything to do with the Kwanlonhon, demanded the return of his sa'ab, Vavashi, on the grounds of a breached contract. Even the Effrentati, the mild-eyed, temperate Effrentati, renowned for their shrewdness as investors, sold their shares of Kwanlonhon stock at a loss and canceled the lease of the land on which the newest Kwanlonhon warehouse had been built. The council of elders scrambled to buy back the stock and dismantle the warehouse, but the effort cost them dearly, as did the loss of face.

All this the Kwanlonhon suffered without knowing why.

SUCH WAS THE mood of the courtroom that morning — rife with discord, bordering on violence. Duty brought them together as one body, discipline kept their tempers cool and their faces composed. Five hundred years of tradition brought them to their feet to greet the Equerry's approach with a respectful obeisance. Yet even as they bowed, the Kwanlonhon asked silently, "Why?" while the remaining five clans vowed just as vehemently, "Someone must pay."

The Equerry's face, bland, expressionless, a dark moon suspended above the pristine whiteness of his robes, offered no hint as to his thoughts as he took his place on the upper-most level of the three-tiered dais. His plump hands with their short, pudgy fingers were stripped of rings. He sat cross-legged, as did everyone in the courtroom, his robes arranged in perfect folds. Even the pattern of his braids was neutral, a hundred plaits newly woven by his concubines last night. A clansman bred as all present had been bred, today he put aside his name as well as his clan affiliation. Today he was not Balafel, second son of a Synzurit prince and an Effrentati woman he had never known. Today he was, quite simply, the Equerry of Endlin.

He was also, despite the placid demeanor he maintained throughout the proceedings, a different man than he had been a few short weeks ago. For he knew, with an inner dread that kept him sleepless for many nights, that what began today might rip apart the fabric of his world.

"BEFORE I CALL the first witness, we must settle a matter of some importance. According to law, commoners are excluded from the court when the matters discussed concern clan affairs. As it happens, a primary witness, a clansman by birth, refuses to testify unless a commoner is allowed to attend this session."

The Equerry ran his eyes over the hushed assembly, gauging their mood before proceeding.

"The testimony of the witness in question, Sandur Kwanlonhon, is vital to the case. The commoner, H'esslar, is a trained physician and a man of loyalty and tact. He has given me his word that nothing discussed today will leave this court. Therefore, it is my recommendation that his presence be allowed. It is my further recommendation that Sandur Kwanlonhon, although not a voting member of the Kwanlonhon's elder council, be required to hear all testimony."

A brief recess was called, during which time a low buzz ran through the courtroom. The recess over, Nayeem H'ulalet rose to his feet.

"If Sandur Kwanlonhon does not testify, what will be lost? Why compromise the integrity of the court when we have witnesses numbering in the hundreds?"

Braided heads nodded in agreement. Nothing filled a clansman with more loathing than the thought of their private affairs being bandied about by commoners and seamen, beggars and whores.

"If Sandur Kwanlonhon does not testify, this court will end in chaos and justice will not be served."

Nayeem blinked, then issued a grudging reply.

"I speak for the H'ulalet. Admit the commoner and require the presence of the Tehran's sa'ab."

The other Tehrans seconded Nayeem's motion, with the exception of Manthur, who sat as he had since his arrival, his expression blank and unreadable, swaying slightly as if to the rhythm of drums. When he made no move to answer, a subdued Prince Shakar rose to speak for his brother.

"The Kwanlonhon say aye."

A rustle of silk greeted the entrance of the Tehran's sa'ab, followed by a loud rumble of complaint. Omitting the respectful obeisance before his father demanded by the rules of filial duty, he took his place on a cushion placed to the right of the magistrates on the lowest level of the dais. Added to his sins was his informal dress, dark-red breeches and a white linen tunic with flowing sleeves, the garb of a common tradesman rather than a prince of Endlin. They forgave him his lack of braids, but eyed him with disapproval all the same.

He sat quietly, his forearms resting on his thighs, his hair combed back straight from his forehead and tucked neatly behind his ears.

His companion, the physician known as H'esslar, seemed more at ease, sending an appraising glance over the assembly before taking his place beside the Tehran's sa'ab. No one noticed that as his eyes swept over the courtroom, they rested for a fraction of a second on the Tehran of the Kwanlonhon, just as no one noticed Manthur's startled frown or heard him whisper, "Where hast thou gone, my beauty?"

To no one's surprise (except for the Kwanlonhon), the first witness called was Prince Rassad H'ulalet. As the highest-ranking clansman among the hostages, it was fitting he be allowed the privilege of speaking first. Everyone but the Kwanlonhon had heard his tale from his father's lips. Rassad had put on flesh in the past moon, but an air of fragility clung to him, as if a strong gust of wind might blow him away. The bringing-in of his first concubine had been celebrated a week ago, a gala occasion attended by every prince in Endlin save those who wore red robes. Nevermore would he pilot a vessel, he who was once the finest navigator in the H'ulalet fleet, for Nayeem swore never again to be parted from the son he almost lost.

Bearing a strong resemblance to his father, from his hawk nose to the leanness of his jaw, Rassad took his place at the foot of the dais, directly across from the six golden-robed Tehrans, and began his tale. Though oft repeated in the past few weeks, it lost none of its horror in the telling. The strain of reliving the murder of his cousins, the screams of the crew as their hands and feet were bound before being thrown overboard, the endless days of starvation, thirst, and back-breaking toil, showed in the pallor lurking beneath his olive skin. As he reached the end of his tale, he hesitated, seemingly indecisive. Then, after throwing an apologetic look in his father's direction, he straightened his too-slender frame.

"I must speak here of the kindness of Prince Tasir. We were treated with every courtesy upon our release, fed and clothed with the best supplies the Kwanlonhon possessed. Despite my illness, I was consulted on all decisions concerning the capture of the pirates. Although many of the hostages assisted Tasir and Fawaz in their ruse, repairing the shacks and posing as slaves and guards to lure *Fair Breeze* into port, the bulk of the fighting was undertaken by the Kwanlonhon and their crew."

His testimony ended, he executed a formal obeisance to the Kwanlonhon and resumed his place at his father's side. When Nayeem refused to meet his son's eyes, Rassad bowed his head. A flurry of whispers flew over the courtroom, everyone conscious that by publicly acknowledging his debt to the absent Tasir, Rassad had fulfilled his duty despite his father's wishes to the contrary.

"The court calls Djaras, steward of the Assad."

Clansman after clansman entered the courtroom, telling their stories much as Rassad had done, re-living the capture of their ships, their confinement in the black depths of the storage holds and finally, their emergence from that stinking hell into a life of slavery. As the Equerry questioned them, a pattern emerged, so that by noon the Kwanlonhon sat sick-at-heart, hearing from mouth after mouth the same scenario. Their Tehran appeared unaffected, or rather, disinterested, and seemed to sleep, a twisted, half-smile on his lips.

From Salmydessus up the long corridor to the Pitanes, from Nisyros to the north to the tiny island of Ofu to the south, at every point along established trade routes, *Fair Breeze* preyed upon her sister ships. Lured by the white pennant flying from the main mast, they ran to her like eager children, arms outstretched with offers of assistance, to find themselves held prisoner by clansmen wearing vermilion robes. The Equerry quizzed them unmercifully on this point, but they stood firm. Yes, they were Kwanlonhon robes and no other. Yes, the pilot's braids and nose jewel appeared authentic. Yes, the initial boarding was correct down to the last detail of ship-board procedure, from the first bow of the Kwanlonhon pilot to the moment his knife cut the throat of the chief trading representative.

After a break for midday refreshments, the prisoners were called. Freshly bathed, though denied razors with which to shave their beards, the men were hustled into the courtroom under guard, standing in chains at the foot of the dais. Questions came at them from all directions, the magistrates involving themselves for the first time in the proceedings. The Kwanlonhon magistrate pushed hardest, demanding that they name the day of their first outing and furnish information as to how *Fair Breeze* came into their possession. Who recruited you? How were you paid? Who gave you information as to scheduling and routes?

They quailed before him, stammering out their answers in the hope that they might yet save their lives, some of them kneeling, shackled wrists lifted heavenward as they pled for mercy. Yet, in truth, they knew next to nothing. A stranger approached one of them in a hostelry the night before he sailed on *Fair Breeze*, offering a year's wages if he mutinied. Others were recruited in various taverns within the harbor district. As to the routes, none of them could read a navigation chart or use the astrolabe and compass. As they spoke, similarities emerged. They were men without familial ties, most of them newcomers to Endlin, hailing from the coastal areas or faraway isles.

By late afternoon, a final witness, the man who posed as the Kwanlonhon pilot, remained.

IF NOT FOR for the growth of beard along his unshaven jaw, he might have been a clansman, this tall, well-formed gallant with waist-length hair who sauntered into the crowded courtroom, regarding those assembled with an insolent sneer. The elders eyed each other askance, squirming uncomfortably as he spread his legs in the typical clansman stance, his arms crossed over his chest. Enjoying their discomfort, his lip curled into something like a snarl.

"State your name and place of birth."

"I am Cassis, a native of Endlin. Unfortunately," he added, mocking them with his perfect manners as he bowed, "I've been denied my braids and a razor. With proper robes and a bit of gold dangling from my ear, the woman who gave me birth says I resemble the clansman who visited her regularly in the harbor district, although," his voice hardened, "his visits ceased when he learned he'd fathered a child."

"Abomination!" roared one of the elders, others echoing his cry as they faced what had always been their worst nightmare. For generations the clansmen of Endlin guarded their seed like a sacred treasure, denying fully half their sons the right to father children, turning a blind eye when those same sons sought forbidden pleasure outside the walls of their palaces. Now their sins came home to roost in the form of this whore's offspring who so easily passed as one of them.

Tossing back his head, Cassis proclaimed, "I've been called worse than that, old man!" his taunt bringing several clansmen to their feet, fists raised.

A sharp rebuke from the Equerry brought order to the teeming courtroom. "Enough! Turn your minds to the testimony offered."

An impudent smile clung to Cassis' lips.

"Begin at the beginning," the Equerry prompted sternly. "Omit nothing."

By the time Cassis finished his tale, the clansmen would have much preferred his death on that remote island by a Kwanlonhon dagger. Instead, they were treated to a catalogue of their failings. Raised in the squalor of the harbor district, where his looks belied his parentage, Cassis turned to a life of crime, joining a gang that preyed on those foolish enough to enter the harbor district unarmed. Early on he learned to ape the manners of the clansmen who guarded the limestone gates, studying them from afar, listening to their manner of speech, mimicking their imperious manner and perpetual sneers. Once, on a whim, he stole four second-hand silk robes, bribed a prostitute to braid his hair, pierced his ear, and succeeded in passing himself off as a junior steward assigned warehouse duty. It began as a lark, an envious young man imitating a style of life denied him. It became something more when one day, some five years ago, a foreigner approached him in a tavern, asking if he'd be interested in turning his prank into a livelihood.

"At first, I was annoyed at how easily he'd seen through my disguise. Later, I thanked him for the sharpness of his eyes. It was he who trained me as a pilot. We studied together for a full year, he coaching me in everything from table manners to trade routes. My first ship was a small sloop with an eight-man crew. He posed as a passenger and critiqued me along the way. Once he thought me ready, he booked us passage on *Fair Breeze*. The rest was easy," he shrugged, his contempt clear.

They heard of the sacking of *Fair Breeze* with inward shudders, imagining the decks slick with blood as the crew, bribed with the foreigner's gold, mutinied against their Kwanlonhon lords. Naked bodies sank under the waves as Cassis donned the red robes of a Kwanlonhon pilot to begin his first voyage as a pirate sailing under false colors. The rest, as he said, was easy, especially when the foreigner revealed to him the location of what would become their secret base of operations, a desert island twenty-nine days east of Nisyros. He swaggered a bit as he boasted of his conquests, reveling in the riches that lined his pockets, the respect with which his crew regarded him, the ease with which he'd boarded ship after ship, slitting the throat of the first clansman foolish enough to offer him rice wine in the privacy of his cabin. Bitterness took over as he recounted his capture, a similar strategy employed against him as he sailed into port to find everything as he left it until the moment he descended the gangplank and felt Fawaz's knife-point pressed against his throat.

Questions came thick and fast, Cassis answering them with an expression of acute boredom on his handsome face.

"The foreigner's name? Olimpoor, I called him, although he admitted to having many names."

"Once I took over *Fair Breeze*, I met him on the island. He'd show up with new schedules and trade routes, and we'd plan the next raid."

"His transport was the sloop on which I trained. His crew was always different. Some of them would stay behind to become guards or members of my crew. As good as the plan was, we often suffered losses during the boarding, and I was always in need of fresh men, especially those who could pass themselves off as Kwanlonhon traders."

"Describe him? As tall as I am, with a round face and short brown hair. Pale, like the Lapithians are pale, although he speaks our language like a native. He carried a curved dagger with a serrated edge, a curious weapon unlike any I've ever seen. His clothes were those of an ordinary seaman except for a pair of expensive calfskin boots."

When the Kwanlonhon magistrate took up the interrogation, Cassis became increasingly irritable when asked for details.

"I never asked him why! Why should I? Isn't it obvious what he was after? He took a fourth of everything, preferably in gold. If we were short of gold, he'd load up the sloop with silks and spices."

"Why a Kwanlonhon ship? How should I know? I assume he chose *Fair Breeze* because she was fast and handled easily in rough seas. What difference does it make? The Kwanlonhon, the Assad, the H'ulalet—they're all the same!"

"The last time I saw him was six weeks after we took the Synzurit flagship. For once he came without charts. He left a prisoner behind and a couple of new men."

"Identify the prisoner? Impossible. Without your braids and robes, you look alike."

Now came the Equerry's final question, the Kwanlonhon holding their breaths as Cassis frowned and shook his head.

"Aye, that's true enough," he began slowly, "I heard it mentioned from time to time among the guards. 'The Tehran this' and 'The Tehran that.' I never gave it much thought. After all, we've little reason to love you. Perhaps the guards said it to punish the slaves with words as well as blows." He shrugged. "I, myself, have no knowledge of any dealings with a Tehran, although it wouldn't surprise me to learn you've a traitor in your midst. Clansmen will sell their much vaunted honor for a single copper coin."

With a strangled curse, Nayeem jumped up from his place, his sons hanging on his robes in a desperate attempt to prevent an outright attack on the witness. The false pilot invited his approach, a queer light shining in his eyes as the maddened Tehran leapt forward. Violent quarrels broke out, the magistrates shouting for order as the Assad streamed toward the bank of red robes. Fights erupted along the fringes of the Kwanlonhon section, the Effrentati caught between the Assad and the Kwanlonhon, their swirling robes a clash of purple, yellow, and red. Threats and the vilest of profanities echoed against the limestone walls until, when all was chaos, a voice ordered, "*Stop!*"

Later they would wonder who spoke, although they decided, quite wrongly, that the Equerry had exerted his formidable powers as an orator.

Never moving from his cushion, the Equerry sat as if carved from a block of marble, his eyes shut against the madness of his kinsmen. Yet no human voice could have spoken so mildly and still be heard over the uproar of thundering male voices. Trained to obedience since childhood, the clansmen heard and obeyed, dropping upraised fists, and like a herd of disobedient children, sulked and pouted their way back to their cushions.

The courtroom sweltered, the torrid heat of late summer nothing to the white-hot flames of the clansmen's anger and voluble frustration. For ten hours they listened, discovering what they thought to be true had no basis in fact. Threats became mutters, curses whispered under their breaths as they resumed their places.

The Equerry cleared his throat. One hundred braided heads jerked to attention, two hundred ears trained on the words spoken by the man robed in white.

"This session is ended. We begin again at dawn. As you ponder today's events, ask yourselves this question."

His eyes narrowed as he surveyed their uplifted faces.

"Why did we never band together to discover the truth of these disappearances?"

His gaze lingered on the Tehran of the Kwanlonhon. Finding nothing there but a smile of supreme indifference, it traveled swiftly to the man with cropped hair who sat with head bowed, the knuckles of his clenched fists white with strain.

"Tomorrow's testimony will be difficult for us all. Until that time, hold your tongues and settle your tempers. You are dismissed."

"HOW FARES SANDUR?"

"He mends slowly, but he mends."

"I wasn't referring to his health."

"Nor was I."

The Equerry stirred impatiently.

"Will he testify or not?"

"I don't know. He asked me to come and I came. He left without speaking. It's difficult for him to be away from her for long periods of time."

"He's with her now?"

"Yes."

"Well guarded?"

"Yes."

Portly though he might be, the Equerry could move with deceptive speed when under duress. He did so now, bounding to his feet and walking rapidly to the small window of his private study through which he could see the lights flickering among the seven hills.

"Any word from Fawaz?"

"None."

"And Tasir?"

"He will come forward only if ordered to do so."

"Which will make him a hostile witness and so work in Manthur's favor." The Equerry wheeled to face the healer, slamming his palm down hard against the top of the desk.

"Damn you, H'esslar! You're responsible for this mess! If I hadn't pursued the matter of the calfskin boots, we could have written off the whole thing as bad business, hung the pirates, decapitated Cassis, and licked our wounds in peace. The Kwanlonhon would be hated for a generation or so for no other reason than their accursed good luck, but the Synzurit have been hated for hundreds of years, and it's done us no lasting harm. As it is, I've a key witness reluctant to testify, a phantom who escaped that blasted boat despite my every precaution, and a prince so racked with guilt he spends every hour of every day trying to make reparations to the families of those lost at sea. Word has it he's squandering his fortune, cries in his sleep, and worst of all, neglects his children . . ."

A quiet voice interrupted him.

"But you would still have the problem of Manthur." The healer shook his head sadly. "Do you think it would end there? The facts argue otherwise. Regardless of resentment over the Kwanlonhon's so-called 'luck,' it will take years for the others to recover what they've lost, while the Kwanlonhon retain the largest fleet. Have you forgotten that your own laws make the new island a Kwanlonhon possession for the next hundred years? A desert it may be, but its discovery offers the possibility of new explorations to the east. Who knows what treasures may be found there? That is why Manthur smiles. He thinks himself invincible."

"Perhaps he is," came the morose reply.

A silence descended, drifting in with the evening tide to hover over the wine-dark waters of the deserted harbor. The healer rose from his cushion and walked toward the door.

"Trust in the truth," he said in parting, and was gone.

"At what cost?" the Equerry asked tonelessly of the empty room. Are we strong enough to hear the truth, he wondered to himself, and most importantly of all, having heard it, are we strong enough to do what will be required of us?

Finding no answers, he turned to a well-thumbed book lying open on his paper-strewn desk. There is a certain justice here, he mused to himself before becoming engrossed in his translation, that I study a book of law written by one Kazur Kwanlonhon, son to Nazur, uncle to Manthur, great-uncle of the Tehran's sa'ab. Could this be the source of the Kwanlonhon's good fortune, since they alone have journeyed west?

His musings forgotten as he wrestled with a particularly difficult passage, it didn't occur to him, as it did to Esslar of Pelion, that Balafel, too, would write a book, and that the first case he discussed in what would become a classic study of Endlinese criminal justice, would be the one which began tomorrow at dawn.

Chapter 25

Testament

LIKE TWIN SERPENTS they lay entwined, carved ivory and polished teak, his cheek on her breast, her womb nestled against his loins, floating as the child floated within her, lulled by the rhythmic beating of two hearts. The scent of night-blooming jasmine wafted through the open windows, the gauze draperies seeming to breathe as languid gusts of an offshore breeze cooled their damp bodies.

The bed, too, was draped with close-woven gauze, protection against mosquitoes and midges during the humid days of late summer. This room was all they could have wished for after the cramped quarters aboard the Synzurit flagship. Large and airy, with what Sandur assured her was a breath-taking view of the harbor, it was perfect for their needs. Phanus and Lampon lived in an adjoining room, and although no one ever spoke of it, she guessed there was more to their presence than a simple wish to escape the heat of the windowless bookshop in the Abalone district. Ridha never issued a like complaint and seemed content enough to remain in the bookshop with Esslar, who was teaching her to read. They were frequent visitors, especially during sultry summer evenings when the cicadas whirred in the almond trees.

Alyssa smiled to herself. Health returned, and with it, the sharing of their dreams. Sometimes she fancied she could see again, or rather, that she could see through Sandur's eyes. Tonight, when he came to her, throwing open the door to their bedchamber, heedless of Ridha's presence, sweeping her into his arms to bury his face between her breasts, she thought for a moment she had seen herself—a candle-lit figure draped in loose robes turning to him with arms outspread, a smile of welcome on her lips, while a dark-haired woman who must have been Ridha lowered her eyes and hurried out the door. The newness of the experience both elated and unnerved her, causing her to doubt her senses, until his almost frantic need for her pushed away all other thoughts.

Sensing his restlessness, for it seemed he could not sleep, she brushed away the creases on the ridge of his brow.

"The wind shifted," he said. "Perhaps the worst of the heat is over."

"At last!"

"Is it so hot, then?" he tugged a lock of her hair for emphasis. "Perhaps thou should remember thy dunking in the river and count thyself lucky."

Carefully, he shifted their position, turning her on her side so that her hips fit snugly against his loins. Now he could stroke her belly at the same time he supported her back. Contentment filled her as she relaxed against him.

As was often the case when she lay abed, the babe stirred inside her womb. As her grandmother liked to boast, the women of her family were disgustingly fertile, birthing babes more easily than a hen lays eggs. After a childhood spent among a myriad of pregnant aunts, childbearing held no mysteries for Alyssa. For Sandur, the gradual changes of her body were a constant source of curiosity and delight. As the babe kicked more strongly, he chuckled softly to himself. Heartened by his mood, she broached a subject much on her mind.

"Do you remember how you introduced yourself to me that first night in the cell? `I am Sandur Manthur Linphat Kwanlonhon,' you said, the words rolling off your tongue like honey."

"I remember," he said, sounding remote and disinterested. Discouraged, but hopeful of eliciting some kind of response, she began to think aloud.

"In Cinthea, a child usually takes its mother's name. There are exceptions, of course, especially when honoring one no longer among us. Latona is a well-respected name in Cinthea—one I'm loath to have die with my mother. Then, of course, there are your family names, that of father, grandfather, and clan. That would mean four familial names plus a common name, which seems a bit much, don't you think?"

Again, there was no response. Holding her impatience in check, she ventured on, working out the puzzle in her head, half-aware that his arms had fallen away from her.

"Perhaps we should compromise and use Kwanlonhon Latona as the familial name . . .," she thought for a moment, ". . . or Latona Kwanlonhon. Then, after the birth, we can decide on a . . ."

"No child of mine will bear the Kwanlonhon name."

She knew every nuance of his voice, having heard him roar with anger, sneer with disdain, and curse with a fluency that left her breathless. She knew him to be arrogant, vain, and immensely stubborn, but never had she heard him speak like this. So a judge will speak when rendering a verdict or a king declaring war on a rebellious province. It was a voice out of the epics she memorized in her youth: inexorable, doom-ridden, tragic.

That he hated his father came as no shock to her. She shared that hatred every time she ran her fingers over the scar tissue that lay like serpent tracks over his back. But to extend that hatred to a clan that also counted Tasir and

Fawaz among its members, men of nobility and intelligence, filled her with alarm. And what of the great Kazur, the founder of the Agave Session? Symone spoke his name with special reverence during the study sessions with the female ernani. Was not Kazur a Kwanlonhon as well? Confused and equally distressed, she steeled herself against his temper.

"Why not?"

The answer was long in coming, the body beside her rigid.

"Because it holds no honor."

Honor. Duty. Obedience. By-words of the clan. How tired she was of these words and their everlasting power over him! Honor meant superiority over others. The call of duty meant leaving her behind. Obedience was the lattice-work of scars on his back. How had such decent words become distorted, destructive, even inhuman? Frustration filled her at his refusal to recognize their true meanings.

"Let me understand this. Tasir, Fawaz and Kasovar broke every rule imaginable to steal *Seahorse* from under your father's nose, risked their lives and reputations to find you with the result that two hundred slaves were freed from a miserable existence, yet the Kwanlonhon have no honor. Tasir placed me, a blind stranger, under his personal protection, taking every care for my health despite the fact that the idea of me carrying your child disturbs him deeply, yet he has no honor. Fawaz, who searches even now for the man responsible for kidnapping you, has none, nor does Kasovar, that frail old man pushing himself to the limit so as to bring us all safely to port. I suppose you, too, have no honor, having rescued me from certain death, not to mention the rafts you built, the wagons you lifted out of the mud, and the money you gave so that people like me might escape Pelion!"

"Thou mustn't . . .," he interrupted, to be cut off as she sat up abruptly, incensed that he should forestall her attempts to understand him.

"I must not what? Excite myself? Worry about things you refuse to discuss? Am I a fool, then, having retired my brain when I began to breed? Is that why you haven't said a single word about the trial? By the horned moon of Tek!" she exploded, her mother's favorite oath rising easily to her lips, "are you really so stupid as to think that the failings of one man are enough to rob your entire clan of its so-called honor? If that's so, your notion of honor is hopelessly flawed and deserves destruction. Honor isn't pride, Sandur. Let me make this perfectly clear—this child and all who follow will bear the Kwanlonhon name. By this action, we honor all the nameless women who have ever lived in that damnable citadel, women whose children never knew them as mine shall know me!"

Her voice rose to its height, both in pitch and volume. Not for nothing had Latona taught her to project. She did so now without apology, not caring who heard her through the walls of their bedchamber.

"If you can't bring yourself to discuss what's going on in the courtroom, I'll endure your silence. But don't you dare demean yourself in front of me! I would never share my life with a dishonorable man, nor would I allow such a man to father my children. When you demean yourself, you demean me, and I won't stand for it, do you hear?"

"I hear," he said at last, and though he said nothing more, she knew she'd won. Victory brought no elation, but rather a vague sense of guilt. So sad he was, and so silent. Sliding back down beside him, she blinked back angry tears.

The silence stretched between them until, at last, he whispered low, "Kwanlonhon Latona."

The experiment must have pleased him because he repeated it, adding wistfully, "May she be like thee in every way."

Since the first moon of her pregnancy, Alyssa became more and more certain the child she carried was a girl. None of her aunts ever reported experiencing such a phenomenon. She put it down to wishful thinking since she would dearly love to have a daughter. A son would content her, but somehow it seemed fitting that Latona, the renowned dreamsayer of Cinthea, should lend her name to her first granddaughter. Now it was as if Sandur had read her mind.

"What makes you think we have a daughter?"

Sandur replied, "I see her in my dreams."

Before she had time to consider this proof that they were sharing their dreams, Sandur of Endlin, who rarely (if ever) apologized, blurted out, "I held my tongue lest I upset thee. We ... do not ... cannot ... "

Taking a deep breath, which seemed to steady him, he continued more slowly, explaining yet another incomprehensible tradition.

"We do not discuss things of a worrisome nature in the presence of a woman who expects a child, especially a sa'ab. To do so is considered a breach of manners, since nothing must disturb the harmony of the child within the womb. For a servant or a visitor to do such a thing would be discourteous; for a father, it is unthinkable. Thou must believe me, Alyssa. I never meant to hurt thee with my silences."

She'd thought him secretive; instead, he'd behaved as any well-bred clansman should behave around a pregnant woman. For her sake, he faced everything alone. And she accused him of neglect.

"Pardon me, Sandur," she said, sounding nearly as contrite as she felt, "for the roughness of my tongue."

"Nay, thou wert in the right."

"Then will you forgive me for screeching at you?"

"Aye," he replied equally as solemnly, "although thou must beg Phanus' and Lampon's forgiveness for waking them in the middle of the night. Tell them thou hast no brain since thou art breeding."

She gave in to merriment, glad at being teased by one whose laughter seemed to have abandoned him during these endless weeks of waiting. His breath warmed her cheek as he curled himself around her.

"I call her Aethra."

"Hmmmm?" he murmured sleepily, his lips next to her ear.

"In my dreams I call her Aethra."

His arms tightened briefly around her in wordless gratitude, then loosened as he fell slowly, gradually, to sleep.

While the father slept, the child took up her dance again.

PISCHAK, CHIEF SHIPPING clerk and member of the Kwanlonhon council of elders, shifted uneasily before the dais, darting nervous glances about the courtroom. The distinctly greenish undertones of his complexion testified to yet another night passed in drunkenness.

" . . . if you have any knowledge of the foreigner who wore calfskin boots, the man known as Olimpoor?"

It was the second time the Equerry had posed this particular question. Pischak mumbled something under his breath.

"Repeat your answer for the court!"

The Equerry's command cracked like a whiplash. Pischak's head jerked up, the whites of his eyes streaked with broken veins.

"I never met such a man."

"Then for whom did you prepare the sloop?"

The foreign physician attending the Tehran's sa'ab stirred restlessly on his cushion. At that same moment, Manthur frowned, rubbing his temples as if they pained him. For the first time that morning, Pischak's eyes came into focus.

"I, uh, I prepared it for the Tehran. I did not think to question his orders."

"Describe those orders."

"I was to make sure it was always stocked with provisions, a certain amount of coinage, and, uh, several changes of clothing."

"What kind of clothing?"

Pischak surveyed the packed courtroom and swallowed hard.

"Kwanlonhon formal robes."

A low rumble began, like the sound of summer thunder that brings no rain.

"To your knowledge, did your master ever board the sloop in question?"

"Never," came the prompt reply, an expression of profound relief spreading over the witness' face.

"Is the sloop you were shown eight days ago, the one impounded by my order, the same sloop for which you were responsible?"

"It is."

The Equerry pursed his lips, squinting a bit as though balancing a scale.

"To your knowledge, is any other vessel in the Kwanlonhon fleet subject to the Tehran's personal commands?"

A pause, much shifting of feet, and then, when confronted with the Equerry's eyebrows uplifted in a show of patent disbelief, a sudden rush of assurances.

"Nay. Of this I'm certain. Only the one."

The examination continued, the pupil having learned to answer the teacher without evasions.

"Would it surprise you to learn that having interviewed every pilot who sails for the Kwanlonhon, not a single one of them admits to piloting the ship in question?"

Before Pischak could form a response came a bevy of questions, each more fearsome than the last.

"Would it also surprise you to learn I can find no ship's log? That according to the Kwanlonhon records, the sloop doesn't exist? What would you say if I brought forth witnesses from among those same Kwanlonhon pilots who will testify that they've seen this sloop moored at many ports, and one will swear he saw it being unloaded one night on the Kwanlonhon pier?"

Large beads of sweat broke out on Pischak's forehead. The Equerry pressed on.

"How do you explain this? You're the chief clerk of your clan, a post you assumed four years ago. How is it that a ship carrying Kwanlonhon cargo isn't listed in your ledgers?"

Sensing Pischak's growing resistance to his question, the Equerry's demeanor softened.

"Come now, Pischak. Everyone makes mistakes. It's clear you've never had any dealings with the man known as Olimpoor. Answer one more question, and you can resume your place."

Gazing longingly at the empty cushion the Equerry indicated, Pischak stammered, "He, uh, asked me not to include the sloop or its cargo in my records. He said, uh, he said it was used to spy on other ships. He needed it to bring him information he might use to, uh, our advantage."

The Equerry was smiling broadly now, a benign smile promising forgiveness and above all, an end to the torment of testifying.

"And what did you ask of him in return?"

The Kwanlonhon elders leaned forward to hear the confession mumbled by their shame-faced kinsman.

"Membership on the council of elders and the guardianship of his second son."

"You are dismissed."

Pelion Preserved

The red sea parted as Pischak stumbled forward, each man pulling his robes aside lest they be polluted by his touch. In silence, the elders let him pass, faces impassive. Head after head turned away as he slunk by, a leper in their midst, until he reached a cushion shoved to the back of the Kwanlonhon section.

Yet no one rose to accuse Manthur, not even the hate-filled Assad or the vengeful Nayeem H'ulalet. Deeper and deeper the Equerry probed, yet still there was no evidence linking the Tehran with a single act of piracy. Pischak had shown poor judgment, but he followed his Tehran's orders. Who could deny that this sloop, this so-called spy ship, might be the reason for the Kwanlonhon's rapid rise in fortune and something every clan wished they possessed? They despised Pischak not for his deeds, but for his avarice and lack of dignity. His behavior shamed them as surely as if he had robbed them, and for this he would never be forgiven.

Their opinion of Manthur was a different matter entirely. After all, a Tehran was more than the leader of a clan, more than a purveyor of good business or a bringer of wealth. In this society, a Tehran was the father of his clan. Under Manthur's guidance the Kwanlonhon prospered. What if his methods were unorthodox? What if he traded the guardianship of a lesser son for a promise of secrecy? If a father raises a perfect child, what matters his means of doing so? If anything, their respect for Manthur increased.

All this ran through the Equerry's mind as he watched the nervous tic twitching in Manthur's clenched jaw.

When Pischak's sobs quieted, the Equerry of Endlin called his last witness.

PART OF ESSLAR grieved with Sandur as his name was called; another part continued to work at the hopeless task that had brought him here. Maintaining his vigilance against Manthur's repeated attempts to control the testimony was sapping his strength. Somehow he wrested Pischak away from the fingers of the Tehran's mind; now he must be on his guard lest Sandur be his next target. In a fit of sudden desperation, he opened a channel to the south, finding his friends assembled and waiting, their thoughts flowing toward him as he became the living conduit by which the Council of Pelion maintained its watch.

They knew the potential for failure was greater than that of success.

"Find Olimpoor!" Galen spat the name like a curse. "*Produce Olimpoor as a witness or we've naught!*"

But Olimpoor was dead, executed three days ago by Fawaz in a remote village south of Tek-By-The-Sea. Helpless to prevent Fawaz's revenge, bound as they were by their vows of non-intervention, they sat together in the tower chamber, mourning the loss of the only witness capable of linking Manthur with his misdeeds. No one blamed Fawaz, least of all the Commander of the Legion, although Olimpoor's demise brought all their plans to ruination.

Now they turned, as did the Equerry, to Sandur. They did so with profound regret, none of them willing to increase his misery, all of them worried by the melancholy hovering over his troubled soul. Esslar worried most of all, sitting night after night in the house Phanus and Lampon guarded with their lives. How many evenings had he watched, awestruck, as Alyssa spun a protective web around her wounded mate? Her touch was as deft as any healer as she wove her spells while the cicadas whirred in the almond trees and an occasional shooting star streaked across sable skies.

Last night she'd helped Sandur reach the final step. Esslar sensed it this morning in the darkness of pre-dawn as Sandur picked his way through the crowds gathered on the steps of the Court Pavilion. In his mind's eye he'd seen an aura glimmering about that shorn head, the same halo of light he'd seen envelop countless ernani in the final stages of Transformation.

"*One more step, my friend,*" She-Who-Was-Symone counseled her Master of Mysteries. "*One more step and they will be One.*"

"*Give us Manthur,*" Evadne/Japhet urged. "*Give us the madman. We are ready.*"

With a grateful sigh, Esslar surrendered Manthur to their care, feeling as he did so his heart lighten and his spirit take wing.

"*Remind him he is not alone,*" Anstellan advised, Galen adding solemnly, "*And watch yer back.*"

And then there was only Sandur, bloodless lips pressed tightly together, dread written in every line of his darkly handsome face as he readied himself to accuse the one who gave him life.

AS SANDUR ROSE to his feet, he thought only of her. With her full breasts and swollen belly peeking out from under a filmy curtain of unbound hair, she might have been an earth spirit like those found in the Cinthean epics she recited for him at night, like them, a symbol of life's propensity for renewal. He found himself remembering an engraving he'd once seen in one of his uncle Rahjid's storybooks. A woman girt in silver mail held a flaming sword in her hands, a halo of brilliant light surrounding her head. As a child he'd always turned that particular page as quickly as he could, anxious to escape her probing stare. There had been some vagueness about what the woman warrior demanded of him; Alyssa's demands were clear-cut. He must stand witness so Aethra Kwanlonhon Latona might speak her name as proudly as he once had spoken his.

A hand reached out for his, a healer's hand, with square-tipped fingers and neatly trimmed nails. The gesture surprised him since Esslar rarely touched anyone unless to heal them. A tingle ran though him as their flesh met.

"*Fear not.*"

Sandur flinched, momentarily startled, and the hand was quickly withdrawn. Soon he was too involved with the task at hand to worry over the fact that Esslar spoke to him with lips that did not move.

The court room blurred before his eyes, the banks of brilliant hues merging into a glowing mass of vibrant color. Rather than trying to clear his vision, he sent up thanks that no single face emerged. It was easier not to see, to be blind, as Alyssa was blind, to the ugliness of the world. The thought of blindness soothed him, then lent him inspiration. Let me be blind, he prayed. If I must do this thing, let me be spared the sight of their faces. And it seemed a voice, a woman's voice, spoke within him, saying, "*So be it.*"

Enveloped in darkness, his fears dissipated. This was Alyssa's world, full of smells and sounds: the hacking cough of an elder; the fishy scent of the morning's catch wafting on a stray breeze; the faraway footfalls of palanquin-bearers running over the crushed shell road. His other senses sharpened, compensating for his lack of vision. To his right he felt Esslar's reassuring presence, to his left he heard the magistrates rearranging their notes. From above him came the strong scent of citrus-oil soap, and from that same place, the Equerry's voice.

"Tell us of your abduction from the Inn of the Nesting Gull."

Sandur answered as if caught in a dream, the events he described shadowy, unreal. The sound of his voice surprised him. Confident, he sounded, confident and at ease, the words flowing from his lips as if he had rehearsed them.

When he finished, the Equerry ordered, "Now tell us of your journey to the island."

Again, the words rose up effortlessly, springing from him as a school of flying fish leaps above the waves. His blindness became a shield, protecting him from the chains bolted to the cabin walls, from the hands fondling him as they stripped away his clothing, all the while testing the smoothness of his flesh, the firmness of his muscles, the texture of his hair. He stood outside himself, watching as the foreigner in calf-skin boots knelt to cut the string of his challah, hearing the mocking laughter as he struggled against the shackles, trying to hide his nakedness.

"Sandur," the foreigner purred close to his ear, "why do you hide from me?"

A faraway voice brought him up short, voicing objections to his testimony.

"You were registered at the inn as Haji, a merchant from Tek. The hostages knew you as Haji, as did all the guards. Did you reveal your name to Olimpoor in the hope he might ransom you?"

Sandur revealed nothing. On the contrary, he clung to Haji like a drowning man, for if this foreigner learned his name, he might be killed outright. If he were thought to be a wealthy merchant, he might buy his freedom with the promise of future rewards. If he was known as Manthur's son, the sa'ab of a great and powerful Tehran who would never rest until his son's abductors were punished to the full extent of the law, Olimpoor might panic and slit his throat.

"Why, then, did he believe you to be Sandur rather than Haji?"

Because of the scars. Because Olimpoor knew exactly where to look and exactly what he would find. Fingernails traced the network of raised welts on his back lazily, possessively, while his jailor crooned, "I see your father loves you well. He boasted to me that I would find the proof of his love engraved in your flesh. And it is lovely flesh, indeed . . ."

The chains rattled as he jerked away, fighting off panic, until a familiar voice brought him back to the present.

"Show us."

He heard the wave of protests, outraged demands that the rule of modesty not be violated. Grimly amused that they considered this an immodest request, Sandur turned his back to them. What did they know of violation, these sheltered elders of Endlin who had not left their palaces in a score of years? When his fingers fumbled at the fastenings of his blouse, Esslar was there, pushing his hands aside, helping him out of the fine linen and standing beside him as he listened to the shocked gasps of the crowd. He found himself thinking of Alyssa again, glorious in her nudity, unashamed . . . and he was being dressed again by Esslar.

"Why were you beaten?"

For voicing a reasonable request. A thirty year old man, an expert in navigation, ship-building, and trade, forced to beg for the right to ply his craft. A humble plea that he be allowed to return to sea, the only place he'd ever known peace. For this he was scourged until the blood ran in waves down his back. All in the name of obedience.

"Could anyone else have told Olimpoor about the scars?"

Sandur asked himself that same question as the sloop sailed east, overwhelmed by the consequences if his fears proved correct, coming at last to the same ghastly conclusion as those present in the Equerry's court. It was to protect his privacy that Tasir agreed to wield the rod, and no apothecary was summoned to treat his wounds. Shakar rose as witness, as did Rahjid. A plaintive sigh ran through the courtroom as if issued from a communal throat.

But the tale was only half-told.

"What else did you suffer because of your father?"

He'd told no one, not even her. It was enough that she nursed his hurts while he lay senseless. She knew, but she said nothing, an act of such charity that he almost wept, so great was his relief that he need not put his degradation into words.

When the words came, they came with awful slowness, the labor of pronouncing them almost more than he could bear. An uncontrollable trembling seized him as he relived the first rape, the one that left him moaning on the cabin floor. "It will grow easier in time," Olimpoor assured him as he re-fastened his breeches. "If you resist, it will hurt all the more."

Olimpoor lied. Every time was worse than the last, his ears ringing with the cries and curses of the guards as they cast lots for him each night. Long before they reached the island he stopped eating, starving himself in the hope that their interest might fade. As punishment for this act of defiance, they fed him by force and hacked off his hair. Day after day he would rest in the slave quarters, the other captives eyeing him askance, all of them aware of why he alone was never called to work in the blistering sun. His was night duty, and he cursed the night.

Only Rassad tried to break through the wall of self-loathing he built around himself, offering him a tattered shred of silk with which to cover himself. If not for Rassad's gift, he might have gone mad. The distinctive azure of the H'ulalet, faded by constant exposure to the sun, rotted by salt-water, that most pitiable of challahs became his lifeline with sanity. He hoarded it like a miser, terrified the guards might find it and take it away. Such a small thing, to be able to cover one's nakedness, but without it he was a whore, and with it he was someone who was once called Sandur.

A commotion in the court room brought him back to his place in front of the dais, his vision flooding forth as if a dam burst within him, colors and shapes cavorting wildly, mouths open in angry shouts, eyes blazing, fists raised as a great wall of bodies rushed toward him. And then, just as the horde of clansmen reached the foot of the dais, he understood that they came not for him, but for his father.

Before Sandur could react, he was shoved roughly backward and might have fallen if Esslar had not reached out a steadying hand. The mob seethed around him—faces distorted, lips curled into snarling grimaces, nostrils flared, braided manes flying—a pride of enraged lions jockeying for the kill. Somehow, Esslar maintained his place beside him, pulling him away from the center of the milling pack, until, with a final push, they were free of the press of bodies. Delivered up onto the steps of the dais, they watched, sweating in the festering heat, as the pack milled below them. The magistrates were on their feet, as was the Equerry, gazing down at the sea of many-colored robes converging around Manthur, swallowing him up like a many-headed monster, the floor a mass of writhing, twitching, quivering silk.

A triumphant shout rose from the center of the commotion. The silken sea parted to reveal Nayeem H'ulalet, his hands entwined in Manthur's braids, the Tehran of the Kwanlonhon on his knees, his head jerked up at an impossible angle to reveal his throat. The H'ulalet had led the charge, followed closely by the Assad. Now they pushed the others back, forming a barricade of blue and purple robes between the Kwanlonhon and their Tehran.

"A knife! Give me a knife!" Nayeem bellowed, struggling all the while to maintain his grip, his knee pressed cruelly into Manthur's back. At his command, twenty H'ulalet hands slapped twenty empty sheaths before remembering that their weapons were stacked outside the entrance of the pavilion.

An unsheathed dagger clattered noisily down the limestone steps.

"Kill him, Nayeem. Kill him and have done."

Shocked into silence, the clansmen of Endlin stood mesmerized by the sight of the Equerry's dagger, its hilt adorned with sparkling Synzurit emeralds, its naked blade glimmering in a stray shaft of afternoon sunlight.

"Why do you delay? You came with your mind set on murder; do as you please."

Nayeem stared at the knife thrown just beyond his reach, then searched the faces surrounding him until he found the one he sought.

"Give me the dagger, Rassad," he begged. "Hand me the dagger, son."

When Rassad made no move to do so, Nayeem continued in a quieter voice, falling by habit into the liquid cadences of Endlinese affection. Desperately he pleaded, uncaring that the others heard him speak his innermost feelings aloud.

"Dost thou think I do this for myself, Rassad? Can a father do less than avenge his child's hurt?"

Rassad beheld his father with anguish.

"I would not have thee be a murderer, father, not even for my sake."

For a moment time stopped. And then, while the clansmen of Endlin held their breath, Nayeem released his hold. Manthur slumped forward, his forehead touching the floor. Ignoring his presence, Nayeem stepped over him and into the outstretched arms of his son. They stood for a long moment, the slender prince of the H'ulalet embracing his grieving father. Nayeem had no greater desire than to protect his child from life's hardships; his son held fast to another truth—that by experiencing those hardships, he had at long last earned the right to countermand his father's wishes.

Order replaced disorder, the subdued H'ulalet making their way back to their cushions. Manthur crouched abandoned on the floor, golden robes askew and braids mussed. The magistrates returned the dagger to the

Equerry and resumed their places while the Equerry himself remained standing, regarding the courtroom with what appeared to be satisfaction and even a touch of pride. When everyone was seated, he glanced down at the pile of golden robes huddled at the foot of the dais.

"Manthur Linphat Afaf Kwanlonhon, the time comes for you to address us."

Glaring at the Equerry, a disheveled Manthur picked himself up from the floor. No one could deny his air of regal disregard as he calmly rearranged his garments, pulling his robes into a semblance of order and re-tying the embroidered sash at his waist. The face might be lined, the tangled braids liberally sprinkled with grey, but the figure was unchanged, flat of stomach and broad of chest, a mirror to the son who stood only moments ago stripped to the waist, revealing pink-tinged scars on his muscled back.

"I refuse to testify. Not a single shred of evidence links me with the charge of piracy. Either produce this so-called Olimpoor, whom I doubt exists except in the twisted mind of a commoner who parades himself as one of us, or let me be on my way."

It seemed the voice of reason spoke until its spell was broken by the Equerry's sneer.

"You surprise me, Manthur. I hadn't thought a brilliant tactician like yourself could so completely misjudge your situation. It's never been my intention to accuse you of piracy. As you've so neatly observed, I lack the evidence to do so."

A worried murmur ran through the courtroom. A thin smile appeared on the Equerry's face—contemptuous, humorless, deadly.

"Perhaps you've forgotten the old laws, the ones written by the first Linphat when the clans were formed. He wrote, 'No crime is so great as that of a parent who raises his hand against his child. No punishment is too severe for one who harms or assists others in the harming of his progeny. Death should be a gift to one such as this, a gift denied him until his pain equals that of his victim.'"

"There might be some among us who would forgive you for the beating, although Shakar and Rahjid testify that it was unwarranted. None, I think, will forgive you for providing your sa'ab's abductor with the means of identifying him. You and you alone brought Sandur to harm, of this there can be no doubt. According to the old law, your punishment will be twenty strokes with a split bamboo, after which you'll be stripped, shackled in the gaol, and raped nightly for a period of two moons. Perhaps we'll institute the drawing of lots to select your tormentors. Perhaps we'll rely on volunteers. Most assuredly, we'll shave your head. In time, I'm sure death will be welcome."

A resounding roar of approval greeted the Equerry's sentence, two hundred palms slapping the floor signaling their bloodthirsty delight. How could they have doubted this best of Equerries, a Synzurit to the marrow, his ruthlessness a credit to the best traditions of his clan? Only the Tehran's sa'ab shuddered as the Equerry outlined the last days of his father's life; only the healer bowed his head.

The Equerry was not finished. He'd recited the law of his fathers, but it was not the law as he had come to envision it. He knew, as did the Council of Pelion, that Manthur's death would solve nothing. The wounds he dealt his kinsmen would fester for generations, then erupt in another limb of the body politic. The germs of Manthur's ideas, his lust for power, the spy ship, the financial ruin of the Assad, the destruction of the clan fleet, would eventually putrefy and rot the core of Endlinese culture. The Equerry had heard, as had everyone assembled in the courtroom, the rumors concerning Manthur's sorcery. As a life-long skeptic, he disbelieved them, yet he believed with all his heart that given Manthur's success, another clansman would succeed as Manthur had succeeded, whether sorcerer or not. As Cassis said, everything was accomplished too easily to be dismissed as the work of luck or magic.

If the law was to be re-written, Balafel Synzurit must become a surgeon, cutting a tumor away from tender flesh. Justice was a hard mistress, yet he pined for her as he had for his first concubine, the vessel of his longed-awaited sa'ab. And so he began, his scalpels sharpened by years of study and experience, his nerves steady and his eye true.

"However," he continued, "if you agree to answer my questions and plead guilty to the charge of piracy, I might be persuaded to spare you the horrors you perpetrated against your sa'ab."

Something glimmered in Manthur's eyes. At the same time, the courtroom erupted with angry cries and demands for immediate punishment. At the top of the dais, the Equerry shouted down his detractors.

"This is my right by law! Would you punish him without learning what remains hidden? What do we lose by offering mercy?"

When at last he could be heard above the uproar, he cried out to Rassad H'ulalet,"What say you, Rassad? I put it in your hands. Would you hear Manthur's testimony?

After studying the face of the Tehran's sa'ab, who met his gaze without flinching, the H'ulalet prince replied slowly, "None suffered as Sandur did. Let him decide."

All attention centered on the Tehran's sa'ab, for they pitied him, this child of woe. Every failing, whether real or imagined, was forgiven during his testimony: his rudeness toward his father, his bizarre mode of dress, even the rumors that he awaited the birth of his sa'ab by a blind foreigner unsuitable for breeding. Prince Rassad had been strangely silent on the subject, as had the majority of the hostages. When questioned about the blind woman, they would change the subject or walk away, never denying the truth of the rumors, but refusing to add to them. The few that talked seemed reluctant to do so. One of them, a young Assad steward named Djaras, confessed to his guardian that he found the woman appealing despite her blindness, a shocking admission dismissed by his uncle as the result of stress brought on by his nephew's imprisonment. Still, the memory of that youthful confession lingered on in the minds of the elders, especially those who had from time to time considered offering their daughters as worthy vessels for Sandur's sa'ab.

As it was, although they pitied Sandur, they were secretly disgusted by his testimony. He was damaged goods now, no matter the wealth of the Kwanlonhon. Not a single clansman gathered in the courtroom would dream of mixing his bloodline with someone who had been molested by commoners, regardless of the circumstances. They knew that sons denied the right to father children went whoring in the seamen's district or coupled with other males, but they never thought to question a system that produced a Cassis and would, by extension, deny Sandur the right to father a child.

Later they would nod their heads wisely, mouthing one of many platitudes that passed for wisdom among the clansmen. "A man's luck is his sa'ab," they would cluck, caught between envy and regret. For without a moment's hesitation, the Tehran's sa'ab spoke up in a voice pitched to carry into every corner of Equerry Court.

"Let him speak."

Chapter 26

The Last Tehran

MANY PRESENT IN the courtroom that day knew Manthur's father, Linphat V; a few remembered his great-uncle, Nazur. The Kwanlonhon family resemblance was strong—a heavy brow, slightly flattened nose and sensuous mouth. Here, too, was the Kwanlonhon flair for rhetoric, the insolent grace of thought and expression, supremely confident, superbly prepared to meet any challenger. Manthur Linphat Afaf Kwanlonhon was, for all intents and purposes, the perfect embodiment of Endlinese manhood at its most mature, physically flawless and mentally alert.

Single handedly, he'd reversed the fortunes of his clan, bringing them in one generation to the pinnacle of prosperity and power. The Kwanlonhon had always been learned men, renowned for their gifts with languages, their reverence for books and study. Historically, they'd shown a lack of interest in amassing the fortunes so dear to the hearts of the greedy Synzurit or those subtlest of negotiators, the Effrentati. Manthur changed everything in a mere three decades, expanding their fleet, encouraging exploration, revising trade routes, even daring to send his sa'ab west of the Sarujian Mountains in search of new markets for Kwanlonhon goods. Not a single clansman present in the courtroom that day ever thought to question his actions, for was not power its own reward? Given the events of recent weeks, they struggled to overcome their natural tendency to overlook the means in favor of the ends. Manthur, a master orator at work, made their task no easier.

"Why the Assad?" he drawled with a disdainful glance at the banks of purple robes from which the question arose. "Why not the Assad? They're hopelessly inept when it comes to business, and their ship designers are the worst in Endlin. They borrow heavily between trading seasons, straining everyone's resources without so much as an apology for their bad judgment and laziness. Why should we be forced to bear the burden of their stupidity? Why not simply put them out of their misery?"

Receiving no answer, he shrugged, a graceful gesture executed with perfect feline indifference.

"They fell like the over-ripe fruit they are, bloated and fly-blown. Once I discovered they've not varied a trade route in five generations, I was able to predict exactly where they'd be on any given day at sea. Such lack of enterprise deserves destruction."

Dismissing the Assad with a careless wave of his hand, he turned next to the Onozzi, who glowered back at him from their cushions.

"Of course, the Onozzi were a different matter, especially when they decided to help the Assad." He paused a moment to reflect. "It surprised me," he continued, "to discover they'd joined forces, risking their own financial well-being in order to keep the Assad afloat. I'd spared them up until then, especially since Yodhat came so willingly into the fold, borrowing more than he could possibly repay. When I was finally ready to call in his debts, he'd be forced to declare the Onozzi bankrupt."

His face darkened as he considered Yodhat Onozzi, who squirmed under his gaze.

"Once I learned Yodhat's intentions regarding the Assad, I took steps to correct my oversight. We took the first Onozzi ship a fortnight later."

"But you offered me those loans!" Jumping to his feet, Yodhat looked around vainly for support. "I never asked for a single one! You said I needn't worry about repayment, that you'd be satisfied with collecting interest! You said . . ."

"I said," Manthur interrupted, "that if you offered your sa'ab to Shakar, I'd support you in any financial endeavor you chose. It was a test, a test you failed."

"A test?" Yodhat quavered, confused in the face of Manthur's blistering scorn.

"A test of character. What kind of father are you, Yodhat, to hand over your sa'ab, a lovely girl of nineteen summers, to a man three score and one? Shakar's gambling debts are common knowledge. A few discreet bribes to the mid-wives would have completed the picture. He's not fathered a child for fifteen years, yet you went forward with her bringing-in and now have the gall to commence court proceedings to dissolve her contract! Once I knew the measure of your ambition, that you would sacrifice your sa'ab for an alliance with the Kwanlonhon, I gave no more thought to the Onozzi."

A shaken Yodhat resumed his seat, his followers shocked into resentful silence as they considered Manthur's reasoning. They thought him finished, but he was not.

"The H'ulalet were a more difficult problem."

The bank of blue robes stiffened, looking like nothing so much as a wave poised to crash against the cliffs below the Kwanlonhon citadel. Manthur considered them carefully before allowing himself a small, tight-lipped smile.

"It took awhile for me to decide how to proceed against them, if for no other reason than that they've always been conservative in their dealings, no outstanding debts, a corner on the tea market, a preference for small ships and short jaunts. Cassis happened upon the first H'ulalet vessel by accident. Once he'd done so, my plan fell into place."

Only now did Manthur's eyes meet those of Nayeem H'ulalet, his voice softening to a mocking purr.

"It was the reverse of the Onozzi, you see. Yodhat loved too little; Nayeem too much. The loss of Rassad nearly destroyed him, sending him into a lengthy depression. What, I asked myself, will happen if another child of his ventures forth and disappears? How long until he stops sending out his sons altogether, depriving them of trading experience and undermining the confidence of his clan? My sources told me plans were underway to send another son out at the end of this moon. I gave Olimpoor the order the next day—any H'ulalet vessel with Nayeem's issue on board must be sacked. Sooner or later, his melancholy would drive his clan to revolt. When the time came, I would make my offer, to join our fortunes with those of the H'ulalet if they rid themselves of a Tehran so faint-hearted he couldn't bear the loss of a lesser son."

"What father would not mourn the loss of a child, even that of a lesser son?" thundered Nayeem, rising from his place. "And what father blames another for his grief!"

"You forget I am a lesser son," Manthur countered bitterly, "and as such I know of what I speak! Did my father try to stay me when I sought permission to leave Endlin? He wept, yes, but sent me along without regret. At sixteen I knew I was better suited than Rahjid to become Tehran. But Rahjid was my father's sa'ab, while I was merely a third son, to be used as my father thought fit. Is this not the way of the clan, to dispense its lesser sons as needed?"

A brooding silence filled the room. Nayeem sat down heavily, his vision clouded with the specters of all the sons who were not sa'abs. Rassad, his favorite since birth, far outshone the talents of his eldest brother, yet he could never be Tehran.

Up to this point, the Equerry allowed Manthur to proceed as he wished, listening closely to the tenor of the discussion, marking the ease with which Manthur handled himself, wondering at the quickness of his mind, the acuity of his perceptions. Everything he said struck at the heart of clan tradition: the buying and selling of daughters, the rejection of more gifted sons in preference of the sa'ab, the stupidity borne of pride that allowed the Assad to make bad business decisions to the detriment of every clansman in Endlin. From his vantage point on the highest level of the dais, he watched as Manthur systematically stripped the civilized veneer from clan society. He despises us, the Equerry decided, more surprised by this discovery than anything he'd learned in the time spent gathering information for the express purpose of exposing Manthur as a traitor. He despises us to the degree that he would destroy us without a qualm.

He thought Manthur a madman; he began to see him as something quite different, something both great and terrible.

"What of the Effrentati, and my clan, the Synzurit?" he asked, readying himself for battle as Manthur shifted his attention to the upper level of the dais.

"Arson for an Effrentati warehouse," Manthur replied almost casually, seeming not to hear the horrified gasps of the assembly, "the fires to be set by an ambitious Synzurit in my pay."

A ripple ran through the Synzurit enclave, each man stealing sidelong glances at his neighbor, wondering if the traitor sat next to him. Manthur smiled, amused by the furor he'd created.

"My plan included his eventual discovery and capture, but not until the other clans fell to the Kwanlonhon. I wasn't in a hurry, you understand. I discovered the location of the island east of Nisyros ten years ago. I was fully prepared to wait ten more."

A mocking smile twisted his lips.

"It might interest you to know that the original discovery was made by a Synzurit pilot blown off course two hundred and fifty years ago. I was browsing through some of my great-uncle's books one day when I came across the entry in an old ship's log. The Synzurit sent out a secret exploration several moons after the pilot reported his findings. With typical quick-profit mentality, they dismissed the island as worthless since it offered no immediate financial gain, then sold the book to my great-uncle two hundred years later for a single silver coin."

The studied insult stung, as did the knowledge that regardless of Manthur's fate the Kwanlonhon would retain its legal claim to the island for the next hundred years, during which time they could charge enormous docking fees or simply declare the island off limits to any ships but theirs.

"Once the feud between the Synzurit and Effrentati was in full swing, I would step in as peace-maker, earning the gratitude and trust of both parties. Then only one person would stand in my way."

Something in the way Manthur tilted his head, one eyebrow raised as he calmly described the course of history as he envisioned it, caused the Equerry to ask, equally as calmly, "Me?"

His reward was unexpected—an expression of genuine admiration from the Tehran of the Kwanlonhon.

"I always knew you were the only person capable of appreciating my plans! They," Manthur dismissed the assembled clan elders with an indolent wave of a manicured hand, "have no imagination. You, on the other hand, have always been of a scholarly frame of mind, which made you a dangerous adversary. I'd almost resigned myself to waiting for you to die, having considered several alternatives in the meantime. Assassinating an Equerry," he announced with a wintry smile, "is a tricky proposition. When Olimpoor's talents came to my attention, I realized I needn't wait after all."

Strange though it was to look into the face of the man who had planned his murder, the Equerry couldn't stop himself from probing Manthur's motivations.

"What would be gained by my death?"

"You surprise me," Manthur rebuked him, not unkindly. "What else but your position?"

"But you're a Tehran! There exists no higher rank in Endlin! You speak of lesser sons. I, myself, am one of these, as was your Equerry kinsman, Nazur. Why should you desire a post only a lesser son might fill? What power do I have that you lack?"

"You overlook the obvious. After your death, I would seek office with six clans under my control, their fortunes mine to do with as I willed. Once I made my desire known, the clans would elect me unanimously, as would the commoners, their votes paid for out of my private coffers. As Equerry, I could enact laws, punish offenders of those laws, and guide Endlin to its natural destiny!"

"Which is?"

Manthur's jaw was twitching again, a habit the Equerry noticed throughout the testimony as one that signaled deep unrest.

"The destruction of Pelion!" Manthur proclaimed, his expression glassy-eyed, transfixed, victorious.

"To conquer her southeastern provinces and bring her to her knees, her borders swarming with our troops, her supplies cut off, her people reduced to eating vermin. To pull down her walls stone by stone, to dismantle her libraries, press her populace into servitude, and set about ruling the West!"

On he raved, the appearance of sanity carefully preserved, as if, the Equerry found himself speculating, someone or something labored to keep him sane, preventing him from plunging headlong into screaming, foaming, lunacy. This impression was further substantiated when the Equerry stole a look in H'esslar's direction. Expecting to find condemnation written on those placid features, for it was H'esslar who provided the means of trapping Manthur, he saw a man lost in some private trance, slack-jawed, blank-faced, eyes clouded and unseeing. A vague sense of worry filled the Equerry as he turned his attention back to Manthur, wondering if those assembled shared his ignorance as to the nature of this place called Pelion.

But the clansmen of Endlin could not be bothered with details. Ah, what victories Manthur promised them! What glories he described! What clansman's heart did not beat faster at the thought of an entire world at their feet? Their eyes shone at his promises of new lands to explore, pristine seas where their ships might roam at will, fresh markets for their goods under yawning western skies. His call to arms, littered with names as unknown to them as Pelion, names like Droghedan, Swiasa, Botheswallow, became a litany of sorts, drudging up from the reservoir of their shared past and the ambitions of their fore-fathers. As he spoke, another veil was torn from their eyes, and they blinked, blind puppies anxious for the teat, shamed by their complacency, angered at having lost the knack of curiosity. How did it come to be lost, the urge to venture out into the vastness of the great unknown? To discover what lay beyond?

On he spoke, exhorting them to reclaim their greatness as it had been in the days of Linphat the First, when the empty seas beckoned them forth, and each moon brought with it the discovery of yet another pink-beached isle. When did they agree to settle for less, to become little more than merchants, their ships plying identical routes year in and year out, their sons drilled in uniformity rather than the individuality necessary to those who would make their mark on the world? When had they decided that safety was preferable to risk? When, they asked themselves, had they forgotten how to dream?

The Equerry felt it too, the rush of future expectations coursing like strong spirits through his veins. With his kinsmen, he grieved over time wasted and opportunities lost. Like them, he pledged himself to change. Even as he pledged his support of Manthur's dream, another thought brought him up short.

Some of the clansmen were on their feet by this time, their expressions a match to the Tehran, who stood with arms outstretched, head thrown back, urging them on, trumpeting his vision of exploration and conquest, his excitement contagious, his madness more seductive than any voice of reason could hope to be.

Yet reason, that most steadfast of friends, stood by the Equerry of Endlin, who summoned his own particular brand of majesty to combat that of the Tehran of the Kwanlonhon.

"What threat does Pelion pose to us?"

His question might have been shouted down had not another voice immediately echoed him, a bass voice booming out over the braided heads of the clansmen of Endlin.

"Answer the question, brother! What have we to fear from Pelion?"

There, at the back of the courtroom, silken robes fluttering about his bulk like liquid sapphires stood Prince Tasir, his chest heaving as though he'd sprinted the distance from the citadel to the Court Pavilion. Ignoring the furor his appearance produced, he marched down the aisle until he stood but a few feet away from his brother, confronting him with a countenance of doom.

Later, Balafel Synzurit would record that at this point in the proceedings, Manthur Kwanlonhon had suffered no equal in terms of self-possession or prestige. His testimony destroyed the credibility of every Tehran, overwhelming them with his scorching ridicule. Yet here stood one whom Rassad H'ulalet honored for his humanity, someone who returned the stolen booty and lost ships that were his by right of conquest, who delivered up the prisoners for questioning when he might have killed them all. One who held justice above the honor of his clan; one who weighed duty against truth and chose truth; one who rejected obedience in favor of compassion.

Could this be why H'esslar had persuaded him not to insist that Tasir testify? Had the healer thought it necessary that Tasir be exempted from the proceedings, untainted by the testimony offered, and if so, why should Tasir arrive now, at the exact moment of his brother's triumph? Another hurried glance at H'esslar revealed his return to consciousness, his once dream-filled eyes fixed on Tasir with the raptness of a hawk.

"What have we to fear?" came the thunder-crack of Tasir's scorn. "What could we suffer at their hands in comparison to the havoc you have wreaked these thirty years? Should we fear for our fortunes, which you have manipulated to bring about our ruin? Should we fear for our children's futures, you who spend your offspring like water? Or would Pelion deprive us of our freedom to explore, as you have forbidden everyone who ventures west, employing agents to murder those who defy your unwritten commands? What have we to fear of Pelion, brother, we who have feared you for so long? Will their reign be more tyrannical than yours, their policies more cruel?"

Tasir's unleashed fury built to a roaring crescendo.

"What could anyone possibly do, brother, to surpass your cruelties? Will they betray our trust, loot our ships, torture our sons, murder our kinsmen in cold blood? What more could anyone do to effectively destroy Endlin than you yourself have done?"

With every word the memory of the court proceedings that had brought them to this point came crashing back, dispelling the swelling tide of hysteria. Manthur stripped away one veil; Tasir removed another. Yes, they had gone astray, but was this the man to lead them, this self-proclaimed fanatic and unnatural father?

Reason came flooding back, old memories jarred by Tasir's tirade. Their ancestors were explorers, not warriors—sailors of repute, not soldiers for hire. What cared they for sieges or forced marches? For that matter, what cared they for land? Should they leave their darlings, their ships and their children, to venture forth on foot, they who loved nothing better than the roll of the deck beneath their feet, the salt spray coating them with brine, the sun-swept seas which acknowledged no paltry rules of ownership?

And in that moment, as they contemplated the oceans which had always been their home, the clansmen of Endlin entered a new age. Slowly, with great difficulty, for nothing is so difficult as birth, they rejected the call of the last Tehran.

Great and terrible he stood before them, destroyer and deliverer, for after Manthur nothing would ever be as it was. With mixed feelings they viewed him, for they looked at what might have been at the same time they worried over what might come to be. It was the measure of Manthur's greatness that he did not shrink from the moment of his defeat. A lesser man might have done so, feeling the hysteria dissipate and skepticism claim his supporters. He had not moved from his spot at the foot of the dais.

Now he addressed Tasir, saying lightly, as if in jest, "I had not bargained on your eloquence, brother."

Embracing his fate, he shrugged and smiled, lifting his insolent gaze to the Equerry, the man whose position he had coveted.

"It would seem my testimony is finished. Pronounce your sentence, Equerry, and deliver me from this place. The stench of so many cowards gathered in one room turns my stomach."

They turned deaf ears to his insults, confident of their choice now that Tasir had made them see Manthur for what he was. The intensity of their regard must have irritated him, for he turned on them as does the tiger held at bay, cursing and spitting, malevolent to the end.

"My curse on you and your children's children! May your ships founder and your women miscarry! May the winds spew you forth into the void and may you die unmourned and unavenged!"

Unmoved, they averted their eyes. The Equerry spoke, every syllable as crisply pronounced as if he had written these words long ago and recited them now from memory.

"Manthur, son of Linphat, for the crimes you perpetrated against the clans of Endlin, I do hereby expel you from the office of Tehran. For the betrayal of your clan's trust, I remove your name from the rolls of the Kwanlonhon, your possessions and revenues to revert to your heir. As punishment for your acts of piracy against commoners and clansmen alike, you will be publicly executed tomorrow at noon, your head severed from your body."

"Pischak Kwanlonhon, I find you guilty of conspiracy and hereby banish you to the island east of Nisyros for a period of five years. At that time, your Tehran will decide in what capacity you may best serve the Kwanlonhon, although you are never to serve on the council of elders again. During your absence, the care of your children and concubines shall revert to your brother, Bhakar. The guardianship of Manthur's second son, Issur, shall revert to Prince Tasir."

Summoning the guards with a crisp nod, the Equerry watched as Manthur was marched out of the courtroom. He went quietly, his rage spent, humming a simple dance tune under his breath. To no one's surprise, Pischak sobbed as he was led away.

The Equerry's recital continued.

"Cassis, commoner of Endlin, for his many acts of piracy and murder, will be taken from the gaol tomorrow at noon, at which time he shall hang by his neck until he is dead."

"As to his accomplices, they will labor in the shipyards for a period of three years without pay, rebuilding the ships they sank while being trained as ship-building apprentices. During that time, they will be fed, clothed, and furnished with building supplies and tools by the joint council of elders."

"Shakar Kwanlonhon, I hereby declare all concubines received into your household in the last fifteen years restored to their fathers with dowries intact. I also rescind your right to bring more concubines under your roof."

"Yodhat Onozzi, I deliver you to the judgment of your clan, although I caution you that should your indebtedness increase, your creditors will be invited to initiate legal proceedings against you."

"I also declare that as of this day, the clan of the Assad forfeit their rights to borrow on credit. At such time that I am convinced of their good faith, I will restore those rights. Also, let it be known that since the Assad suffered the greatest losses, the first two ships completed by the former pirates will be theirs."

"I hereby confiscate the following Kwanlonhon vessels: *Fair Breeze, Eye of the Storm, Crimson Sky*, and the schooner currently under construction in your shipyard to be distributed among the remaining four clans as recompense for their losses."

For the first time he surveyed his audience. Not a single voice had raised in protest, even when he took from the Kwanlonhon four of the finest ships in their fleet. Satisfied that the lesson Manthur taught had been truly learned, he turned at last to the one who sat silent all this time, perhaps unaware that he alone had made this victory possible.

"Sandur Manthur Linphat Kwanlonhon, I declare you Tehran by right of lawful succession. As custom decrees, you are granted leave to address the joint council of elders. What say you, Sandur? How may we welcome you as our newest Tehran?"

He expected some show of feelings, either pride or dread, unsure as to how this newest Tehran would react to the circumstances of his election. Sandur's expression offered no clue as to his feelings, although he started at the sound of his new title. As he rose to his feet to address the court, sunlight illuminated his shorn head, unruly locks suddenly ablaze.

"I ask for the life of my father."

At first the Equerry feared he had not heard aright. He knew what Sandur would request since the day he saw him standing on the quarterdeck of the Synzurit flagship with a blind woman at his side. From the moment Sandur allowed Manthur to testify, the Equerry readied himself to perform an act contrary to every belief he held dear, an act that might further incapacitate the already beleaguered Kwanlonhon. Their fortunes had suffered a severe blow today, but that would be nothing to their loss of prestige if their Tehran's first child was born of a blind concubine. He worried that if he honored Sandur's request, he might spark another, and this time unstoppable, rebellion. Yet somehow he could not bring himself to deny anything to Manthur's cast-off sa'ab, even if it meant attending the bringing-in ceremony of a flawed concubine to the citadel of the Kwanlonhon.

"I ask for the life of my father."

How is this possible? the Equerry asked himself, disturbed to the core of his being. His judgment of Manthur was fairness itself, an easy death in exchange for willing testimony. Manthur welcomed his demise even as the Equerry pronounced the sentence, a strange calm descending over him, the spark of madness absent from his eyes. Balafel's temper rose as he considered the already voluble reaction of the elders, up on their feet again, gesticulating and buzzing like a nest of irate hornets. Damn this sa'ab, he thought, will he bring the citadel down around his ears? First a blind concubine, now an unwarranted plea for mercy? Has he no understanding of the delicacy of his situation?

"If I understand you aright," he began ponderously, "you ask the impossible. I cannot remit your father to your custody since he is no longer a Kwanlonhon and has forfeited his rights to live within the citadel where you, by law, must abide. Do you suggest he remain shackled in the gaol for the remainder of his days? If so, I ask you to consider that your father might prefer a quick death to a life of imprisonment."

A chorus of approval greeted his reply. The newly-appointed Tehran of the Kwanlonhon did not back down.

"You misunderstand me. Having worn shackles myself, I have no intention of letting my father end his days in a gaol." Readying himself, Sandur forged ahead. "If you grant me custody of my father, I will abdicate in favor of my uncle Tasir . . ."

Before he could finish, Tasir was halfway up the steps. The court strained to overhear while they argued, the uncle's half-whispered harangue delivered with fearsome tenderness, the nephew shaking his head, his lips curved in what seemed to be a smile. Although party to their exchange, the foreign physician gave no hint as to the substance of their debate. He seemed, in fact, to sleep. Finally, their little drama concluded, uncle and nephew turned to face the Equerry of Endlin.

"I support my nephew's request that my brother be delivered into his custody."

A stunned silence greeted Tasir's first announcement, a joyful cry his second.

"And, if my clan will have me, I accept the office of Tehran."

Chapter 27

The New Age

NOTHING WAS AS Balafel Synzurit thought to find it.

He was partly to blame, having never really come to grips with the more mysterious elements of the trial. This was uncharacteristic of him considering his usual mental rectitude, although a forgivable failing considering the upheavals generated by recent events. Also, to be fair, he was summoned under false pretenses, which is not to say he was tricked so much as lured, for in truth, no one, not even Esslar, knew what would transpire that night. As it was, the Equerry of Endlin scanned the invitation, sent the messenger flying back up the hill with his acceptance, and spent the rest of the day in a state of exhilarated anticipation.

Arriving promptly on the hour, he instructed his palanquin bearers to return at midnight and hurried up the walk with nothing more in mind than entering into one of the many discussions he'd come to enjoy with the physician from a place called Pelion. That this city to the south, long thought to be a myth, did in fact, exist, was no longer debatable; that its existence might have any lasting effect on his tenure as Equerry seemed highly unlikely, or more to the point, so far beyond the realm of possibility that, if questioned about future relations between Endlin and Pelion before that night, he most probably would have replied, "None of consequence."

The destination to which he hurried (for he disliked tardiness in himself almost as much as he despised it in others) was one of the many modest residential districts nestled on the slopes of Endlin's seven hills, the crest of this particular hill reserved for the Effrentati enclave. The house, which bore the same diffident air as its neighbors, suggested a certain shabby gentility, unremarkable in any detail save for a double row of almond trees shading the tiled walk leading up from the street to the arched entryway. Modesty he could appreciate; shabbiness seemed inappropriate considering H'esslar's position as the Equerry's personal physician. Still, he mastered his disapproval, reminding himself that a foreigner's oddities deserved forbearance on his part.

His first look inside, when the outer door flew open at his knock, was even more unsettling. Passing the portal, he found himself in a tiny antechamber, cool and dark, inhabited by a man and a woman, both of whom rose to their feet to greet his arrival, the woman with face downcast, as was proper, holding in her hands a book, her forefinger inserted perhaps a third of the way into the pages, as though she marked her place. If this was not shock enough, the Equerry looked into the face of someone he thought dead.

"Fawaz!"

"Greetings, Equerry."

Considering the trouble the missing pilot had caused, eluding Balafel's agents by sneaking out of the city in the dead of night, the least he could do was feign contrition. Instead, he offered a polite but cursory greeting and gestured toward a draped doorway beyond the antechamber.

"They're expecting you. I'm to pass you through."

Taking in the cushions scattered randomly over the floor, the trays of half-eaten food, numerous bowls and eating utensils, and a stack of clothing and personal belongings piled in the corner, it occurred to him that here was something even odder than the sight of a woman who gave every indication of having been interrupted in the process of reading a book.

"Are you living here?" Balafel asked, trying to hide his dismay and doing a bad job of it. How could Fawaz, the most celebrated pilot in Endlin since his bold venture into unknown waters, prefer this squalor to the luxuries of the Kwanlonhon citadel?

"For the time being," came the unruffled reply. "Phanus and Lampon are needed within, so I offered to watch the door."

"Will you accompany me inside?"

"H'Esslar prefers that Ridha and I remain here."

The woman's name sparked immediate recognition. A certain tea merchant in the Abalone district, one Oman by name, filed papers yesterday for the return of his sa'ab's dowry from Shakar Kwanlonhon. This must be the daughter whose fate Oman bemoaned with copious tears and loud lamentations. Balafel inspected her more closely. Her robes, although fashioned out of third-grade silk, were elegantly cut and draped, embroidered with a single row of tiny silver fishes along the long lapels of the pale green outer robe. Her hair unbound, her face unveiled, she was lovely enough to ignite desire in a body the Equerry considered far too old to participate in the pleasures of the flesh.

Realizing that his mouth hung open, he feigned a yawn. Thankfully, the woman did not lift her eyes from the floor. Blustering a bit, embarrassed that Fawaz might have caught him gaping, he made for the doorway, hearing the pilot's last set of instructions as he pushed aside the drape.

"At the end of the hallway, turn left. The door is unlocked."

Not a man given to eavesdropping (although the agents he employed were experts in that discriminating art), something made him pause just beyond the drape, ears trained on the conversation already in progress.

". . . because he found you beautiful, I suppose. Why else would he stare so?"

"He's a clansman. He sees only a commoner."

"Have you forgotten that I, too, am a clansman?"

She must have shaken her head, for he said, "I'm flattered that for a moment you were able to forget."

And then, after a prolonged silence, "What are you reading, Ridha? I wanted to ask before but didn't want to disturb you."

"A book of stories a child might read."

"Would you read one aloud while we wait?"

"I make so many mistakes."

"Please. It will help pass the time."

A sigh, perhaps the demure nodding of a head, and the whisper of silk against a cushion. Then, her voice, softer than clouds drifting out to sea.

"Long ago, in a distant land . . ."

The carpet muffled the sound of Balafel's retreat.

He had hardly recovered his equilibrium when he found himself walking down a corridor, all the doors along it shut fast, one with what looked to be a newly-installed bolt mounted on the outside. As he paused at the end of the hallway, cooking odors wafted by—peppers fried in garlic mingled with the succulent odor of roasting pheasant. While his stomach rumbled, a reminder that his mid-afternoon snack had been forgotten, he found his good humor revived by the prospect of refreshments. Pushing the last door on the left with a gentle shove, it swung open on well-oiled hinges.

Here was yet another room showing every sign of hard use. Bare walls, mismatched furniture, several low tables littered with writing materials and books, a plethora of cushions spread haphazardly over the worn carpet, two uncomfortable-looking cots, a cracked basin and ewer—everything suggested that whoever had taken up residence here took no interest in the niceties of civilized existence. A single oil lamp burned overhead, valiantly attempting to disperse the murk of evening.

Quickly deciding that this was the most dismal room he had ever occupied, the next thing that struck him was that never before had he experienced such silence. Once the door swung shut behind him, it was as though the world beyond this room ceased to exist. Somewhere a woman stumbled over unfamiliar words in a children's storybook; somewhere a cook labored over a fire; somewhere pedestrians were returning home from the market district, strolling past almond trees, perhaps reflecting on the welcome coolness of the night air; here there was nothing except an otherworldly silence, a hush of eerie anticipation exactly geared to raising his gooseflesh.

Four men sat on four cushions staring at yet another door that seemed to open into an adjoining chamber. What they waited for he did not know, but they waited as though their lives depended on it. That H'esslar could sit motionless for what might have been hours, or even days, came as no surprise; that his two cohorts could match his stillness seemed plausible if only because Balafel considered H'esslar a man of extraordinary talents who would not willingly endure the company of lesser men than himself. That the newest Tehran of Endlin, one Tasir Kwanlonhon, sat as they did, cross-legged on a cushion, shoulders straight, eyes focused on a closed door, gave Balafel pause.

Disappointment struck him hard, for he'd thought to engage H'esslar in an evening of learned conversation. Instead, he found himself surrounded by four unsmiling men who stared raptly at nothing. The need for escape became insurmountable.

He might have turned and fled, if at that very instant, H'esslar had not said,"Greetings, Balafel. You are in time."

ESSLAR CONCEALED HIS amusement at the Equerry's look of shocked surprise. For the first time in Prince Balafel Synzurit's sixty-plus years, a commoner addressed him without employing the honorifics due his rank. Forming his inward laughter into a welcoming smile, Esslar rose to his feet in order to soothe his guest with a rapid exchange of pleasantries.

"You honor us with your presence. The evening meal is nearly ready and promises to be something of a masterpiece. Tasir supplied us with his personal cook since it seems he finds our efforts in the kitchen sadly wanting."

As the conversation progressed, Phanus and Lampon cleared off the tables with military efficiency. Tasir gestured to a place beside him with a friendly wave of his hand, and Balafel calmed himself, eager to forget his earlier distress.

The food arrived almost immediately, a sumptuous repast served on the cheapest of pottery, but no one seemed to mind. Balafel was himself again, pompous and patronizing, yet unquestionably brilliant, entertaining the others with tales of trials whose participants were long dead but not forgotten, every detail stored in the warehouse of his keen legal mind. Phanus and Lampon left off their general dislike of clansmen in order to engage the Equerry in serious debate, their prejudices tempered by their admiration of Balafel's achievements in Equerry Court. Clansman he might be, but they warmed to him and he to them, although he could not hide his astonishment that commoners could converse so readily about complex legal matters. Tasir, too, seemed more relaxed than usual, although Esslar caught him casting surreptitious glances at the inner door several times during the course of the meal.

Esslar himself only half-listened to their discussion, although he was careful to join in occasionally if only to mollify his illustrious guest. In the recesses of his mind, he listened with a different ear.

"Everything is as it should be; we can do nothing more until the moment comes for them to cross over."

"Is it enough?" Esslar worried, his thoughts sprouting wings, speeding toward the northwest tower where they were met by She-Who-Was-Symone. "There are only three of us, and Phanus and Lampon are without experience. If only there were some women among us."

"I am here," proclaimed Gwyn of Cyme, rocking her youngest grandchild to sleep.

"And I," affirmed Valeria, wide-eyed and wakeful in her mountain stronghold, her promise echoed by sloe-eyed Vlatla and Lynsaya the Fair.

"We are here," sang out a female chorus, Hanania and Becca, Draupadi and Ulkemene, their four part harmonies like wind chimes set in motion by a sudden breeze. "We come to guide her steps, to bring her to the other side."

"I come for Sandur," declared Altug, faithful to the end, his pledge seconded by Kokor and Yossi, Pharlookas and Tibor, Eddo and Jincin, each of them remembering friendships forged and not forgotten.

Pentaur offered a silent vote of support, as did flint-eyed Dictys, linking their minds with Esslar even as Anstellan's thoughts raced eastward with the wind.

Yet another mind joined his, Galen come to witness the completion of what they began so long ago.

"Aye, healer, 'tis me, come to help his lordship take the leap."

They were assembled, transformed ernani and caretakers of the Maze, their bodies scattered over the wideness of the world, their minds reaching out toward two who hovered on the brink of change.

Esslar closed his eyes, and it began.

THE PRINCE AND the bard entered the shadow lands as they always did, riding the high curl of an endless wave before plunging down, down, into the warm seas of shared dreams. This time they found themselves transported to a darkened plain, voices whispering around them like meadow grass stirred by a restless wind, like the murmur of the fountains of Pelion, like a susurrus of surf against a stony shore. The sky above them was indescribable in the depth of its blackness. Rising from the horizon, a pale sun and a paler moon sailed along an arched curve to take their place above their heads. Here there were no stars, only faint streaks of sunlight viewed through ever-shifting clouds. This sun did not warm, nor did this moon, a delicately wrought crescent of hand-rubbed silver, seem likely to alter its complexion as did its sister in the waking world. Unalterable, eternally fixed above the whispering plain, two heavenly bodies converged in space and time.

A sudden urge rose within them to pierce the darkness, to make sense of this fantastical vision, which filled them with a strange kind of hope. A trembling seized them as the darkness parted, leaving in its wake a faintly glowing path. Or, they wondered, had it always been there, its quivering light pulsing like a heartbeat, obscured by the darkness of their doubts?

"*Walk the Path.*"

This was not said so much as sung, whispers coalescing into a chorus of half-remembered voices. The path beckoned, stretching out into the distance. As they moved forward, it began to spiral, to twist and reverse itself, each turn, each convolution taking them deeper into the tangled web of a maze. On they journeyed, knee-deep in memory's fog, past childhood fears and adolescent longings, past the specter of blindness and the cruel blows of a leather strap. On they rushed, anxious for adulthood, hurrying toward the moment when they could enter the darkened cell. On impulse, they reached out for one another, causing them to wonder why they had never noticed the tingle that ran through their flesh as their hands met. It had always been so, even from the first night of their meeting, yet it took them unaware. Memories came fast and hard as they traversed the path, smoke filling their lungs, letters dancing in the flames, until, at last, a hound bayed mournfully under a pale winter sky.

A barrier loomed before them, a broken bridge hanging over a torrent of icy waters, yet they met it unafraid.

Gone now was the shared sense of anticipation which marked the early stages of their journey. Each step took them deeper into darkness, the man reluctant to continue, the woman insistent they proceed. Shackled to the cabin wall, he cried out for her, discovering that she had been with him then as now. He'd never been alone, nor had she, not even in the fetid alley, where she muffled her sobs lest they betray her. Heartened by their discovery, they weathered the first stormy separation and the second of mutual despair, convinced that if they persevered, darkness must give way to dawn.

It seemed they traveled a lifetime over the whispering plain, the path unwinding gradually before them, marking their quarrels and discords, their triumphs and delights. Understanding grew within them, half-formed as yet, the thoughts coursing through their minds beginning to shimmer even as the darkness shimmered around them, the depths of the blackness no longer a frightening, but a comforting, even a calming, presence. With this revelation came the discovery that this labyrinth, which initially seemed devoid of life, was in fact a reservoir of human experience. Tendrils of thought embraced them, slender fingers outstretched to guide them forward, the path widening and straightening until it seemed a highway of incalculable breadth. And then, just when they began to fear they were doomed to wander perpetually under this alien heaven with its curious sky, their journey ended.

The path was no more, vanishing even as they perceived their final destination across a seemingly bottomless abyss. There, on the far shore, brilliant as though lit by a thousand universes of suns, moons, and stars, was the place promised them, he by a master of mysteries, she by a sayer of dreams. Perched on the brink of discovery, they did not falter so much as pause to contemplate the awful slowness of their journey. How many times had they traveled over this same path, taking one step forward, only to lose faith and travel three steps back? Had there ever been two so blind as they, hampered not by eyes that fail to see, but the blindness of the soul which fears to hope? When, they asked themselves, had they ever truly believed?

And in that instant between question asked and answer given, they leapt as one across the void.

BALAFEL WAS IN mid-sentence when, quite unexpectedly, H'esslar raised his palm, signaling silence. Flashing a particularly unsettling glance in Balafel's direction, he rose abruptly to his feet. The Equerry's irritation at being interrupted was quickly forgotten in his attempt to decipher exactly what H'esslar's look boded, and then, to apply equal diligence in discovering why the other inhabitants of the room were joining H'esslar in a rapt contemplation of the inner door. Tasir hunched forward on his cushion, lips pursed, fingering his earrings with a nervous frown. The two commoners seemed to have stopped breathing.

The meal was splendid, the food excellent, the conversation sophisticated, the wine superb. Mixing with foreigners had never been Balafel's forte, yet, upon serious reflection, he couldn't remember having spent a more enjoyable evening. H'esslar seemed somewhat preoccupied, dropping out of the conversation from time to time for no discernible reason, then picking up where he left off as though the interruption never occurred. If Tasir noticed these lapses, he gave no sign of it, and Balafel, schooled to politeness since childhood, followed his lead.

H'esslar's raised palm, however, could not be ignored, nor did it appear that anyone expected him to do so. As they continued to stare at the inner door as if their combined wills could cause it to open, Balafel found himself in the unenviable position of wishing it would remain closed until he could vacate the room.

"Stay, Balafel. This is for you."

The latch-key turned, the inner door swung open, and a figure stepped forward out of shadow.

Clansman that he was, Balafel's attention was instantly claimed by the generous curve protruding from beneath robes of amethyst silk. Five, no, six moons along she was, carrying the child high and proud, not so big yet that she had lost her grace or the lightness of her step. Everything about her gleamed with the luster of the pearls dangling from her earlobes. Hair, skin, eyes, even the oval nails peeking out from the billowing sleeves of her robes, spoke of health, contentment, and even, he considered with a growing sense of wonder, a sense of elation.

Something nagged at him, something he'd forgotten, until with a startled gasp, he ran his eyes back up her body, past the glorious swelling of her womb, past the fullness of her breasts, to rest upon her radiant face.

Thrown off balance, trying to maintain his equilibrium, he heard H'esslar break the awed silence that greeted her entrance into the room.

"Balafel, this is Alyssa, a bard of Cinthea. Alyssa, this is Balafel Synzurit, the Equerry of Endlin."

Ocean-grey eyes danced beneath winged brows, her glowing smile full-blown, triumphant.

"Welcome to our home, Prince Balafel. Accept our apologies for not greeting you in person."

As she moved forward, her hand outstretched in greeting, someone stepped out of the shadows behind her, his palms resting lightly on her shoulders. For a moment Balafel couldn't place him, since this smiling stranger bore no resemblance to the grim-faced sa'ab who'd testified in his courtroom. For that matter, everyone was smiling, even the usually sober-faced Tasir.

Balafel's irritation grew as he considered the prank they played on him. Clearly, this woman was an imposter, although she might have been a twin to the blind woman he'd seen at the dock. It was common knowledge that Sandur's concubine was blind. Wasn't it for her sake that he abdicated? Uneasiness changed to hurt when Balafel realized that H'esslar, whom he considered a friend, was behind this senseless mockery.

"Is it your custom," Balafel ground out, sounding as affronted as he felt, "to make a fool of an invited guest?"

"Not a fool. A witness," Tasir replied.

Surprised, for he had not addressed Tasir, Balafel swung to face him.

"Are you party to this shameful jest?"

"Jest?" Tasir's gaze narrowed. "I see no jest. Look again, Balafel. This is Alyssa, who is blind no more."

For once, words, which had always been his stock and trade, failed Balafel Synzurit. With Tasir's confirmation of the woman's identity, his world turned topsy-turvy. Knees wobbling, his brow broken out in beads of sweat, he collapsed, landing heavily on a cushion.

"Gently, Balafel, gently. Here, drink this."

H'esslar raised a bowl of water to his lips. Impatiently, Balafel waved it away.

"You did this? You can cure blindness?"

A rueful smile tugged at H'esslar's lips.

"I'm a master healer, a curer of many ills, but the gift of sight is not mine to give."

"Then, how . . . How . . .?"

"I cannot tell you how. Even if I could, you wouldn't believe me without proof. This is why I invited you here tonight, so you might witness firsthand what few have ever seen. You know our secret now, and with it goes an equal measure of trust. You must swear, Balafel, on the lives of your children, never to reveal what you witnessed tonight."

"What have I seen?" he protested weakly, sensing that a favor was being asked of him that he could not fulfill.

"Two have become one—one mind, one heart, one pair of eyes shared between them," a woman's voice whispered inside his head. *"Why this fear of the miraculous, Balafel of Endlin? Didn't you preside over just such a change only days ago? Is not all change remarkable, containing within it the stuff of miracles?"*

What followed seemed part and parcel of a dream. He sat quietly on his cushion, musing over the miracle of shared consciousness with a woman who, he felt certain, possessed extraordinary gifts. Gradually he became aware of the others, but made no move to join them, content to watch as Tasir embraced his nephew. Nor did it seem odd to see the newly-appointed Tehran of the Kwanlonhon take the woman's hand in his and whisper something in her ear, causing her eyes to blaze with sudden happiness. Like a play it seemed to him, the final scene of a fabulous romance in which he had played a minor part.

Only later, much later, after the couple retreated into their bedchamber, was he left alone with Tasir, at which time he finally mustered the wherewithal to speak.

"Fawaz?"

"He's asked my permission to accompany them to Pelion."

"Your best pilot?"

"He will be a better one after time spent in the place they call the Maze."

"Who else knows?"

"Only Kasovar. He does not approve, but will say nothing out of respect for me."

"And what of you, Tasir? How does this figure into the affairs of the Kwanlonhon?"

"We'll devote all our resources to finding the eastern passage. This was my promise to H'esslar when he supplied us with news of Sandur. Even if

I had not witnessed the proof of his claim, I would have kept that promise, since I believe it to be the only means of reclaiming our honor."

"And the woman, Ridha, the tea-merchant's sa'ab?"

"She goes as well."

"A commoner?"

"You sound surprised, old friend. Did you think only clansmen would receive this gift they speak of? Soon they'll all go, seamen and sa'abs, commoners and concubines. They might have gone before if Manthur had not put a stop to it upon his return."

"What happened to him there? Must we fear others might return as he did?"

"H'esslar says no. It seems Manthur's woman died in childbirth, which drove him mad. This is Sandur's fear, I think, and one which worries him mightily."

The door to the hall swung open, and Phanus entered with a tray, on it a pot of orange-spiced tea, Balafel's favorite. H'esslar followed behind him.

"Sandur has no cause for worry. The story has been rewritten. All will be well."

This said, H'esslar settled himself on a cushion and poured three cups of tea. They sat in silence for a while, a comfortable silence this time, sipping their tea and pondering the future.

"He would have made a fine Tehran," Balafel mused aloud.

Tasir cleared his throat.

"I've thought of making him my heir."

"He would not accept," H'esslar said quickly, "and you must not offer. They could never live as your customs demand; to do so would destroy them."

Tasir brooded for a while.

"I shall miss him."

H'esslar's response was an enigmatic smile.

"How does Manthur fare?" Balafel asked with some trepidation, earning a frown from Tasir and a sigh from H'esslar.

"He lives in the room across the hall. Phanus and Lampon take turns watching him during the day. He is quiet enough, lost in dreams of yesteryear. Once in Pelion, members of my guild will reawaken him. It's our hope that the balance of his reason can be restored. He'll never be the man he was, but neither will he bring harm to himself or others."

Tasir's response, when it came at last, was bleak.

"When do you leave?"

"As soon as the babe is old enough to travel."

"Will you help the woman . . .," biting his tongue, Balafel tried again, mindful that he not insult his hostess. "Will you help Alyssa with the birthing?"

When H'esslar nodded, Balafel was off and running, his professional curiosity aroused.

"The first child can be difficult. My sa'ab was a breech, as was my brother's second daughter..."

So involved was Balafel in supplying a detailed description of his sa'ab's birth, from the first pangs of labor to the cutting of the cord, he failed to notice H'esslar's considerable amusement. "I forgot how involved a clansman is in childbirth," the healer remarked, not without a certain amount of admiration. The spark of an idea glowed in his eyes. Growing suddenly intent, he leaned forward on his cushion.

"Let me ask you something, Balafel. Will you serve as mid-wife to Endlin? Will you help your people give birth to a new age?"

The question did not surprise Balafel so much as put everything into perspective. Here was the reason behind his presence here tonight, not just to witness a miracle, but to pledge his support to something that could remake the world. The analogy of childbirth struck a chord with him, since he considered his participation in the births of his children among the finest hours of his existence. True, he was a skilled mid-wife, better than many of the women of his household, but to give birth to a new age!

"What would you have me do?"

H'esslar shook his head.

"It's for you to say what should be done. My involvement in your affairs ends tonight. The future rests with you."

The decision was his, to hinder or to help.

It would have to begin slowly, a few changes here, a few there, nothing to arouse undue suspicion lest he betray H'esslar's secret. Some customs would be harder to change than others, especially when the thought of women being taught to read and write turned his blood to ice. Still, it was time for a change. He felt it in the courtroom, had even pledged himself to change without knowing exactly what changes should be enacted. Exploration, yes, certainly a revision of the laws governing inheritance, perhaps a more lenient position regarding the rights of commoners . . .

And Prince Balafel Synzurit, who found nothing as he thought to find it, yet who gloried in the vision of what might be, took up the burden of change.

Reluctant to break the silence, which had become a treasured friend, he said quietly, "I will do what I can."

In a cluttered room, over sips of spiced tea, the new age began.

Epilogue

Pelion Preserved

OVER THE CREAKS of the harnesses came the shouts of the overseers, entreating them to pull for their lives. Pull they did—forty teams of horses, mules, and oxen straining forward, digging their hooves into the earth, muscles bunching under gleaming hides, their handlers urging them on with cries and whistles, the onlookers joining in with their own cries of encouragement as the beasts labored in their traces. The ill-tempered oxen grunted complaints while the mules and horses worked mutely, webs of sturdy ropes stretched taut behind them.

A grating noise was heard, the sound of loosened mortar giving way, and a section of the wall tumbled forward, several tons of hand-hewn rock crashing to the earth with a tremendous thunderclap, a billowing cloud of dust rising up toward the sky to the shouts of the assembled populous.

Once the dust settled, the handlers loosened the ropes and moved the teams off, clucking to them with promises of good rubdowns and an extra measure of oats. Everyone had a job, from the children who worked as water carriers to the elderly women in charge of the huge out-door kitchen where goats and chickens roasted over charcoal fires. Men and women swarmed among the ruins, sweating in the hazy heat of late summer, their hands wrapped with lengths of cloth or encased in heavy gloves necessary for protection against stone cuts. White teeth flashing in brown-skinned faces, they sang while they worked, or called out well-meaning jibes to one another as they pried stones apart, stacking and sorting them under the supervision of the stonemasons. A group of engineers were already surveying the next section scheduled for demolition, eyeing the watchtower over the northern gate and discussing with the architects the feasibility of converting it into a free-standing structure that might serve as a memorial to the great wall-builders of the past.

Busy as they were, they can be forgiven for not noticing when a wraith-like figure, standing somewhat apart from the others to observe the proceedings, lurched forward at an awkward trot, her long, pointed nose sniffing the air as she hurried toward a hilly rise just east of the Cavalry stables. If they had, they might have gawked at the sight of her, veil askew, black skirts flying up to reveal skinny legs and knobby knees, although no one would have been so ill-mannered as to laugh out loud. They had, in the course of time, become attached to the Twentieth Mother rather as one comes to appreciate an eccentric aunt, wincing a bit at her idiosyncrasies but cherishing her all the same.

They knew she was there, of course, for she came down from her tower room quite often these days, strolling around the roped-off work sites with an inquisitive gleam in her eyes, stopping from time to time to interrogate the engineer in charge or to strike up a conversation with the newly-elected First Speaker of the Greater City Council, a certain Briseis, who appeared to be as fascinated as she was with the toppling of this first section of city walls and who set aside time from his busy schedule to make a daily tour of the site. They formed an odd couple, the gangling, pinch-faced woman and the stout, red-faced man, as they ambled among the fallen ramparts along the eastern quadrant, pausing now and again to converse, although more often than not they walked silently, heads bowed in silent communion.

Briseis had not arrived as yet that day, although if he were present, he, too, would have joined her madcap spurt up the hill, panting from lack of breath, eyes trained toward a distant cloud of dust. With her, he would have stood with his hand shielding his eyes, straining to see the caravan wending its way through the rolling hills.

Squinting, for she was becoming increasingly near-sighted, She-Who-Was-Symone counted heads, ticking off her fingers one by one, before losing sight of them as they disappeared behind another hill. When they reappeared, nine riders with packhorses strung along behind them, the pace of the caravan increased, perhaps because the leaders caught sight of the north tower. As they drew closer, a stray shaft of sunlight bounced off the dappled hindquarters of a grey stallion. All her senses trained on the scene being revealed before her, the Twentieth Mother became quite still, intent on witnessing the end of a tale begun long ago.

Cresting the last rise, they reined in their steeds. She took in each travel-weary face, each sweat-stained garment, noting that the babe slept contentedly in her mother's arms, a few reddish curls escaping a tiny cap of exquisite Cynthian lace. The father's countenance was fixed, inscrutable, lips pulled taut over his teeth, remembering, perhaps, the last time he traveled this road. An elderly man, his braided hair streaked with grey, slumped forward in the saddle, his expression listless, drained; his twin escorts, tanned to a rich mahogany brown, held themselves as ramrod straight as if on cavalry parade. The easterners rode three abreast, one man in the purple of the Assad, the other in the brilliant vermilion of the Kwanlonhon, both of them supremely indifferent to the black-robed woman poised to greet them. The woman riding between them peered out shyly from beneath a cloud of filmy veils in shades of palest green, like the tender shoots of fiddlehead ferns as they push their heads up through the soil in early spring.

Last of all, pulling up slightly to the rear of the party, came the healer, his tattered cloak bleached to the color of old bones, his features etched by seemingly permanent exhaustion.

Her vision clouded by a surge of unexpected moisture, the Twentieth Mother blinked sentiment away. Raising her hands to the heavens, she proclaimed the time-honored words of greeting.

"Welcome to Pelion."

CONSULTING A SLIP of paper for the third time, She-Who-Was-Symone took a sharp right, bumped head-long into a pedestrian, muttered a quick apology, and hurried on, sensing rather than seeing the man's astonishment. She gave an inner shrug. *If they think me peculiar now, imagine their surprise when they discover just how outrageous I can be.* A shiver ran between her shoulder blades, and she smiled, not unpleasantly, in anticipation of the years to come.

The directions, written in Remy's distinctive scrawl, were confusing to a degree, especially as this section of the city was unfamiliar to her. It crossed her mind that she should hail a passerby and request assistance, but she decided against it, if for no other reason than she was irritated by her ignorance. *The Seventeenth Mother, knew every street, every byway. What's your excuse, Symone?*

Well, I never pushed a vegetable cart for one thing, but then it's doubtful that She-Who-Was-Meliope knew where to find Mycene's Commentaries *or the first draft of Houras'* Preface to the Guild Constitution. Comforted, she dodged two small children running ahead of their parents, turned left at the next corner, and found herself facing a row of houses.

Given that Pelion was designed as a walled city, building space had always been limited. As a result, the vast majority of residential dwellings were constructed with common walls on either side, stacked together like so many loaves of bread, or in this case, identical three-storied boxes with a single dormer window on the third floor. This particular row, crammed between what looked to be a sizeable inn and a smallish park, were unique in that each house (of which there were exactly twelve) were painted in bright, almost garish hues, each one a different color, as though the owners were bound and determined that their abode be distinguishable from its neighbors. The effect was jarring to say the least, although helpful in her case since Remy had written "the blue house on the end."

Crumpling the slip of paper into a ball, she shoved it into a pocket and bounded up the steps. Even though autumn had officially arrived, a potted geranium by the front door refused to admit summer's end, reaching out hungrily for a taste of early morning sunshine. Symone rapped once, then twice, fidgeting as she waited. After a third knock, the top half of the door swung open.

The woman who greeted her must have been interrupted in the midst of baking, for her stout waist was encircled by an enormous apron, her plump forearms, pudgy hands, and double chins dusted with fine white powder. If she was surprised at finding the Twentieth Mother on her doorstep, she gave no sign of it. Smiling amicably, she swung wide the bottom half of the door so Symone could step into the hall. A floury forefinger pointed toward the side stairs.

"You'll be wanting the top floor."

"Is he in?" Symone asked.

"I thought he was expecting you!" the woman exclaimed, obviously taken aback. "He's had so many visitors of late. Not that I mind," she added quickly, afraid perhaps, at being thought inhospitable.

It was on the tip of Symone's tongue to inquire as to the nature of these other visitors. At the last moment, she decided to hold her peace. Starting up the stairs, she concentrated on her errand. By the time she reached the first landing, she was deep in thought, remembering how she came to be here and wondering what sort of welcome, if any, she would find.

IT BEGAN INNOCENTLY enough, a stray comment from Japhet at the conclusion of a briefing session concerning Manthur's progress in the House of Healing.

"What do you hear from Esslar these days?" he asked, looking around absent-mindedly for his cloak.

Her pen paused in mid-stroke.

"I thought he was with you."

"With me?"

"At the House of Healing."

"I've not laid eyes on him since the last full Council session."

Taking a deep breath, she reviewed the facts.

"He said he needed to rest. Anyone could see how tired he was. When he asked to be excused from our regular sessions, I agreed."

Japhet frowned.

"And you've had no word of him since?"

"None."

Anyone with lesser powers of observation might have missed the regret with which her reply was spoken. Not so Japhet.

"If his absence troubles you, why haven't you done something about it?"

On the surface, it seemed simple. As a member of the Council, Esslar was hers to command. A single thought would summon him, for Esslar was nothing if not obedient. But Symone wanted him to come of his own volition. Part of it was pride, false pride on her part, although it seemed of great consequence at the time. Should she admit to Japhet her sense of inadequacy when it came to Esslar of Pelion? She knew better than anyone how different she was from her predecessor, and who had been more devoted to the Nineteenth Mother than Esslar?

"I hoped," she said at last, "that when he was ready, he would bring me his troubles."

Japhet considered her for a moment. Suddenly it struck her that Japhet, as High Healer, might be familiar with the sickness Esslar suffered during his youth. It was even possible that he'd consulted on the case. Perhaps Japhet should be the one to ...

But Japhet was already shaking his head.

"It's not a relapse. If it was, he'd have been unable to hide it from us during the last Council meeting. He opened his mind in order to share his impressions of the easterners, and although I sensed more than his usual number of barriers, there were no symptoms of adept melancholia."

"More than his usual number of barriers?"

This time it was Japhet who was slow to respond. When he did so, he gave the distinct impression of hiding something.

"Talk to Anstellan. He's better suited to this sort of thing than I am."

"What sort of thing?" she called after him as he beat a hasty retreat. Finding his cloak on the peg where he'd left it, he ducked through the door, leaving her more puzzled than before.

Finding Anstellan proved to be no easy chore. Soon the bronze doors would open on yet another class of ernani, which meant the entire Maze was in an uproar. His office was empty of everything except clutter. When she questioned his assistant (an apprentice hetaera whose name Symone couldn't recall) as to his whereabouts, she looked up long enough from the paperwork she was sorting to suggest with a fetching smile, "Try the library, Mother," before immersing herself again in her work.

The library yielded nothing, as did the dayroom, the solarium, the kitchen, the laundry, the supply rooms, and the dormitories. Neither did the scores of people running hither and yon, who, when questioned, would shrug their shoulders before scurrying away, intent on more pressing problems than a missing hetaera. She'd almost given up when she passed Dictys on the stairs.

"Anstellan?" she queried, not really expecting a response given the Head Trainer's harried expression.

"Arena," he barked, and hurried on about his business.

Finding her way with some difficulty, her visits to the arena infrequent at best, she swung open the wooden gate.

A running man seemed dwarfed by the vastness of the arena, which stood deserted but for him and feeble sunshine filtered through occasional clouds. Years ago, she'd attended one of his races, hearing the crowds scream their adulation as he rounded the last turn, the other runners left far behind as he flew toward the finish. "Stel-lan! Stel-lan! Stel-lan!" they chanted, urging him on to yet another triumph, another in a long line of victories.

Today he ran alone, the stands empty, yet she experienced the same exhilaration that had filled her then as she watched him approach the straightaway. Part of it was the perfection of form, the effortless grace of his body in motion; a greater part was the joy with which he ran.

He was slowing now, his strides shortening, his back and shoulders glistening in the cool afternoon air. Running a hand through sweat-dampened curls, he trotted over to a bench situated along the sidelines and began to wipe himself down. As he raised the cloth to dry his hair, he saw her. She was too far away to read his expression, but it seemed to her that he froze for a moment before reaching for a robe and starting toward her at a brisk jog, tying the loose ends of the belt around his waist as he ran. Before he reached the gate, she had only the briefest of moments to wonder why he, too, was hiding something.

"How did you find me?" he asked, his lips quirked at the corners, looking very much like a truant schoolboy.

"Dictys," she replied, to which he smiled outright.

"I guessed it was him. No one else knows I run here. If they did, I'd never have a moment's peace."

"What disturbs your peace? Esslar, perhaps?"

There it was again, the same expression that had come over Japhet this morning—haunted, oddly furtive. Why are they shielding Esslar, she found herself wondering, and why am I the enemy?

"Japhet visited me this morning," she began briskly, attempting to hide her impatience and doing a poor job of it, "at which time I discovered that neither of us has seen Esslar since the Council session a fortnight ago. Japhet suggested I talk to you. Something about sensing more barriers than usual...?"

She broke off, expecting an immediate explanation, only to find herself the object of intense scrutiny. Then, so suddenly that she was momentarily startled, Anstellan gestured toward the open field.

"Will you walk?"

Wordlessly, she did as he requested, aware of the tension between them although uncertain as to its cause.

"What do you know of the easterners?" he began, casually enough, but not so casually that she mistook it for an idle question.

"Only what Esslar shared with us."

"What were your impressions of them?"

As they strolled, she summoned up images and pieces of conversation concerning their long march to Pelion.

"That the men are much like Sandur—stubborn and immensely proud. That Fawaz, being a pilot, is more comfortable with decision-making than Djaras. That Esslar approved Djaras' candidacy because of his youth and the ease with which he accepted Alyssa's blindness. That both of them are quick to anger and prone to insolence toward anyone they consider of lesser status than themselves."

She might have gone on if she'd not been interrupted in mid-thought.

"And the woman? Ridha?"

These impressions were more difficult to recreate, as though a dimming fog surrounded the figure of the woman who lived in Esslar's thoughts. It was disconcerting to realize she'd not noticed it before, the moody sense of melancholy that clung to Esslar's every thought concerning the woman chosen as the first representative of the commoners of Endlin.

"Truly, she is magnificent," observed Anstellan with an oddly detached air, adding, "yet what will become of her?"

"She will enter the Maze, of course," Symone retorted with barely controlled impatience, earning a startled glance from the Master Hetaera.

Quickly recovering his equanimity, he said, "I think not," and walked on.

A memory nagged at her as she hurried to catch up with him, something she'd seen but subsequently dismissed. The caravan's arrival, the clansmen of Endlin arrayed in all their glory, the woman a shining star between them . . . and there it was. Jealous glares exchanged between the Assad steward and the Kwanlonhon pilot as they eyed the woman who paid no mind to their attentive glances, but rode sad-faced and pale, as if she, like the healer in his tattered cloak, hovered on the brink of imminent collapse.

"If Fawaz or Djaras don't suit her, perhaps another ernani will," she ventured tentatively, sensing rather than seeing the quick shake of a close-cropped head.

"No ernani will ever suit Ridha the Magnificent."

"It makes no sense, Anstellan. Why would she undertake such a difficult journey if not to enter the Maze? "

The Twentieth Mother came to an abrupt halt. Anstellan turned to face her, regarding her with unusual solemnity. She waited, fearful of what she was about to hear.

"She came because she would not be separated from Esslar. He encouraged her to come because he believed her to be sincere in her desire to walk the Path." Anstellan shook his head ruefully. "It's ironic, isn't it, that Esslar, the most sensitive of us all, could be so easily fooled?"

She-Who-Was-Symone made no reply.

Anstellan didn't seem to expect one.

"He read her thoughts during the first few days of his arrival in Endlin, later, only when necessitated by his mission. After she came to live in the bookshop, he cut himself off from her entirely. Those are the barriers Japhet mentioned. As her affection for him grew, he found it painful beyond bearing. The trip was hellish for them both, Esslar maintaining a careful distance, Ridha forced to endure the jealous posturings of Djaras and Fawaz."

Shaking his head again, he trained his eyes on the empty rows of bleachers.

"Having learned of her decision not to enter the Maze, Esslar feels betrayed. He won't see her, nor will he read the notes she sends to his lodgings. Worst of all, he thinks himself disgraced, having broken his faith with you."

"His faith with me?" Symone repeated tonelessly.

"That was the plan, was it not? That he would bring back the first woman from Endlin to walk the Path?"

This was not Anstellan's business, nor did she think it expedient to discuss plans that had no bearing on his duties. Instead of answering his question, she asked one of her own.

"I take it you see them both frequently, if not daily. Is this so?" When he nodded, she continued, "Ridha knew Sandur and Alyssa before and after Transformation. In your conversations with her, has she ever commented on the change? Surely she senses the difference in them, especially when Sandur lends Alyssa his eyes."

A rapt look came over him, the same look she knew she wore when she retrieved a memory from the vast storehouse of her mind.

"She asked me once if Esslar had ever lived within the Maze. When I answered that he had not, she seemed puzzled. Alyssa shared with her what information she can, for she, too, wants Ridha to walk the Path. They are great friends, although Ridha tends toward shyness in Sandur's presence. It's difficult for her to think of him as anything other than a Tehran's sa'ab. Still, I sense a certain curiosity on her part when they're together."

Symone considered the evidence, deciding that this woman of Endlin was as astute as she was beautiful. She senses that Esslar, Sandur, and Alyssa share something that sets them apart. From Alyssa she's discovered the source of that difference, yet Esslar has never walked the Path. It's no wonder she's confused. But is she brave, Symone wondered, turning the matter over in her mind. What would Ridha dare to be like them? And what would I dare to ensure her entrance into the Maze?

"Where is he?" was all she said aloud.

"You plan to visit him?"

Anstellan posed the question cautiously. Too cautiously for Symone's taste.

"What would you have me do?" she demanded, her temper roused and her tongue sharp-edged. "Should I let him pine away in solitude? Is the thought of a visit from me so odious that you would put me off? Do you think I would purposefully add to his troubles?"

Anstellan was instantly contrite.

"I hesitate because it's important that you go to him of your own accord. If Esslar senses the least encouragement on my part, he will think himself twice betrayed. That was my promise to him, to reveal nothing unless asked."

She weighed the matter, mollified by his response, yet remained troubled that he had not come to her. Friendship was one thing, loyalty to his vows another. No matter how innocent their intentions, Lara and Didion's affection for Manthur blinded them to his sickness, producing near-catastrophic results. If Anstellan was to remain on her Council, she must be able to trust him.

"I am not Magda," she said, watching him flinch at the mention of her predecessor's name, "yet I am the mother of my people. As such, I must care for them, all of them, as I see fit."

A flush rose to his face, for though she spoke more kindly than was her custom, he perceived the severity of her rebuke.

"If you want my resignation, I will comply, of course."

She knew what it cost him to utter those words. It was Anstellan's devotion to the ernani that brought him so quickly to the core of the mystery of Ridha and Esslar. Without his expertise in matters of the heart, Symone might have eventually stumbled onto the solution, arriving too late to intervene. As it was, there might still be time.

"I want you with me, Anstellan of the wingéd feet."

It had been She-Who-Was-Magda's name for him. Symone spoke it purposefully, hopefully, willing him to look on her with new eyes. His jaw tightened. And then it came, his barriers against the interloper who assumed the duties of one he adored cast aside, inviting her to know him whole, to share with her his fears for two who passed their days in quiet desperation.

In the merging of their minds, the first of many they would share, Anstellan saw the future the Twentieth Mother envisioned, and cried aloud in joy. At the top of the landing she paused to clear her mind. Regardless of its outcome, this interview would be unique to her experience. Taking a deep breath, she pushed open the door.

That Esslar had not sensed her presence in the house was immediately apparent. He was reading by the window, a book spread across his lap. As she crossed the threshold, he stared hard at her and thrust the book aside, not seeming to care when it fell to the floor with a dull thud.

She wondered how best to approach him, whether to cajole or chide or play the part of friendly confessor. She should have known he was past games, past confession, almost past hope.

"No pity," he stated flatly.

"Pity never crossed my mind," she replied with equal candor.

Having closed his mind to her the instant she entered the room, he erected a wall impervious to her probing. So be it, she thought to herself. We'll do this the hard way.

She was glad he didn't offer her a chair since it left her free to roam about. While he stared moodily out the window, as if by disassociating himself he could make her disappear, she inspected her surroundings, running her hands over the mantelpiece of the fireplace, noting that it had been recently dusted. The room itself was much as she expected—a hermit's lodgings, stark and spare, scrupulously clean, three of the four walls covered with bookshelves, the floors newly swept. The fourth wall was dominated by the dormer window under which he sat, the morning light spilling over the simple oaken table that served as desk and dining place, a plate of what looked to be freshly baked scones and a jar of preserves sitting on a varnished tray, the cutlery clean and untouched, the tea unpoured, the napkin folded.

"Do my lodgings meet with your approval?" he asked with the polite disregard of a perfect stranger.

"Austere, but passable," she replied, continuing to browse at her leisure, fingering leather spines along a shelf of books, occasionally pulling out a volume to inspect the title page, enjoying the esoteric nature of his collection. He must have begun it as a child, for there were illustrated storybooks mixed among assorted medical texts, histories, diaries, plays, and several well-worn foreign dictionaries.

Passing a wardrobe and a brassbound chest, she found herself at the foot of the narrow bed, the quilted coverlet drawn up neatly over the pillow, the bedside table bare but for a slim volume of poetry and a candle. He reads himself to sleep each night, she found herself thinking, and makes his bed immediately upon rising. Even at this early hour he is washed and dressed, keeping to a careful schedule in the hope that the empty days will pass more quickly.

"So," she began boldly, "you've decided to be a martyr. It's an interesting choice."

"Has it occurred to you that I don't relish your interference?"

"Has it occurred to you that I don't relish being ignored?"

He met her gaze and held it.

"Stop baiting me."

"Only if you explain yourself."

Interpreting his resentful silence as acquiescence, she seated herself on the chair opposite his side of the table, where she studied him from under half-closed lids.

Even at forty, he retained the appearance of youth, his trim figure that of a much younger man. His hands were his most arresting feature—long, square-tipped fingers with small knuckles, the hands of a surgeon. And then there were his eyes, twin pools of incalculable depth. Deeply tanned from the journey, his temples brushed with silver, she could well imagine why Ridha the Magnificent preferred Esslar's dignified maturity to the youthful beauty of Djaras or the muscled brawn of Fawaz.

"There's nothing to explain. Ridha will change her mind in time, of that I'm certain."

"That's your diagnosis? A passing fancy? A girlish whim?"

His jaw clenched, but he would not rise to the bait.

"Well," she announced with a great show of satisfaction, "I, for one, am relieved. Anstellan led me to believe the situation was far more serious. It seems he's mistaken. If you, who have known Ridha longer than anyone, are convinced that this is merely an infatuation, who am I to disagree?"

Leaning back in her chair, she beamed her approval, watching him wince under the lash of her tongue.

"Her misery will pass soon enough. She's young, after all, and the young heal quickly. Sooner or later, her thoughts will turn to other, more important matters. If you judge her aright, she'll eventually seek entry, if not this year, then the next."

In the towering silence of his grief, he sat dejected and forlorn, unable to meet her eyes.

"I thought you felt something for her. Since you do not, I can only compliment you on your tolerance."

"Tolerance?" he repeated, confusion robbing him of his carefully orchestrated calm.

She continued as if she had not heard him.

"It must have been trying. After all, how could someone twenty years your junior, a mere child, consider herself a prospective mate for a man of your years and experience? One has only to consider the disparity between her education and yours. She is barely literate, while you, well, we both know the extent of your learning."

She waited for the dam to burst.

"No one should know better than you," he ground out between clenched teeth, "that age has nothing to do with wisdom!" His voice rose. "You'd not dismiss her so casually if you'd seen her in Endlin. She risked imprisonment if she'd been caught sneaking Alyssa out of the harbor district, death for entering the citadel in order to deliver my message to Tasir. Are these the actions of 'a mere child'?"

He might have continued had she not interrupted his tirade with a quiet observation.

"Yet you find her childish in her affections."

When he made no reply, she pushed her advantage.

"She may be wise beyond her years and courageous to a fault, even so, she is mistaken in choosing you. Djaras and Fawaz worship at her feet, yet it is you she wants. You refuse to see her, return her letters unread, yet still she persists. Are these the actions of someone whose feelings will change in time?"

His defenses crumbled, his face a mask of pain.

"Now," she ordered gently, for she was learning to be gentle, she who had always been quick to criticize and quicker to condemn, "explain yourself. Tell me why Ridha must live alone and unhappy to the end of her days."

He was on his feet now, wandering aimlessly about the sun-filled room. "I would think you could guess without asking," he announced bitterly, "especially if you consider the extent of my gifts."

"It's not unheard of for an adept to mate with a non-adept," she reminded him. "Unusual, perhaps, not impossible."

"But I am unique, am I not? A Master of Mysteries?"

Spreading his arms wide, he turned to face her, inviting her to applaud his folly. When she made no move to do so, his arms dropped to his sides, his shoulders slumped in a posture of defeat. He was quieter now, reflective, as he described his doom.

"My gift is such that it cannot be turned on and off. Even with all my barriers in place, I sense the subtlest shifting of her moods. Were I to brush my fingers over one of her letters, I could read them without breaking the seal, not just the words, but every thought passing through her mind as she put pen to paper."

"As to joining," his voice thickened, "the thought of touching her, of being touched by her, is more than I can bear. In her presence I am continually at war with myself. Here, at least," he indicated the room, "I find some semblance of peace."

A thought seemed to strike him, for he paused for a moment, considering his tormenter.

"You call it martyrdom. I call it survival, since no other choice exists. My vows make it impossible for me to confess the nature of my gift. Even if you gave me permission to explain, and she, in turn, agreed to be read, how long could she endure the loss of her privacy—every thought known, every emotion laid bare—while she could sense nothing in return? How long until the unevenness of our mating filled her with resentment and me with despair?"

Mistaking her silence for agreement, he returned to his chair and, with a calmness that worried her far more than his recital of defeat, poured two cups of tea. The shadows shortened around them as the rising sun cleared the tops of the plane trees lining the city streets. She'd never tasted better scones, moist and packed with currants. Esslar ate by habit, she with greedy gusto, savoring the sticky sweetness of the raspberry preserves. When the plate was empty and the teapot dry, She-Who-Was-Symone judged the time right to continue.

"Have you ever wondered," she asked, willing him to concentrate on something other than his misery, "how, in the fullness of time, we should finally become One?"

Ignoring his bewilderment, she continued as she began, working through the equation with her customary care for details.

"Over the course of the next centuries, other cultures, other continents will be discovered. Some of them, like the Cintheans, may already be influenced by latent adepts. It's even possible that there are other Mazes in existence, for I'm not so proud or so foolish as to believe that we possess the only way to walk the Path."

"Another Maze?" he echoed, visibly shaken by the thought.

"Perhaps," she shrugged, "perhaps not. The point I'm trying to make is that everyone must receive the gift."

As she intended, she owned his undivided attention. Pausing for a moment, she wondered how much she should share with him. She'd let Anstellan see the merest glimpse of the future. Even so, he'd been overwhelmed, unable to do more than loose an inarticulate shout. It was important that Esslar retain his ability to reason.

"The first couple was composed of a male ernani and a woman of Pelion. Now ernani walk the Path side by side. Evadne is convinced that non-adept couples already mated will achieve Transformation as well. Those desirous of sharing their lives with others of their own gender, all permutations of human companionship, over time, these, too, will receive the gift."

He was with her now, leaping into the future, on fire with the visions that filled her dreams night after night, reminders that this was only the beginning of what would eventually come to be.

"Everyone," he whispered, awed by the grandeur of a promise capable of transforming an entire world.

"Everyone," she repeated softly, "including Ridha of Endlin."

She let it sink in for a moment, enjoying the spark of hope in his eyes.

"An experiment," she cautioned with an uplifted forefinger, "and only after I speak with her quite frankly. She must understand and accept, as you must, the risks involved. If you cannot achieve Transformation, neither of you will be better off than before."

"There are other considerations as well," she continued, intent that he consider the full significance of what she proposed. "If she is to attune her mind successfully to yours, it follows that you must have no contact with other adepts. This means you cannot serve on the Council, nor will you be able to practice anything except the rudiments of healing. If Ridha agrees, you and she must live in the Maze as all the ernani do, abiding by the rules, enduring Dictys' frequent bouts of ill-humor, relinquishing your privacy, even giving up your books for the first moon."

The sterner she became, the wider his smile. By the time she ran out of warnings, he was laughing.

She wagged her head at him, which only increased his mirth. Throwing dignity to the winds, she joined in, enjoying with him the picture of Esslar of Pelion, child prodigy, expert healer, Searcher of Souls and Master of Mysteries, grunting and sweating on a wrestling mat, grappling with an ernani half his age.

"Tell her," he said when their laughter died away, "that I have dreamt of nothing else since the day of our first meeting."

Embarrassed by the depth of his feelings, she gave a curt nod, aware of the irony of an aging celibate like herself being cast in the role of matchmaker.

As she shifted the subject to less personal matters, he leaned forward in his chair, intent on the latest developments in the ongoing business of the Council. As she hoped, it was as if he had never been gone, as if the previous fortnight was a nightmare from which he had, at last, awakened. He was himself again, considering everything she said with an air of studied reserve, dreamy-eyed, deeply thoughtful, a genius at work.

They chatted until noon, at which time the landlady informed them of the presence of a visitor below.

"Has Sandur made any progress?" Symone asked as the landlady lumbered noisily back down the stairs.

Esslar's pained expression revealed that he had not.

"Twelve moons since Transformation and still he hesitates."

"I understand that he's been contacted by Dorian . . ."

"And a spice merchant," Esslar interrupted wearily, "a dealer in imported teas, a horse-breeder, and yesterday, a representative from the mines at Kilput."

"You predicted this would happen," she reminded him as she rose to go, gratified that Sandur's unexpected arrival coincided so exactly with her plans. "You said it yourself, 'Nothing comes easily to Sandur.'"

Bending down to retrieve the fallen book, she held it out to him.

"You can do no more for him," she stated firmly, formally absolving him of the responsibilities he had borne so long. "The time has come for them to make their own way in the world."

Aware of the difficulties of a healer faced with the prospect of abandoning his patient at this most crucial of junctures, she softened her tone, the book suspended in the air between them like an unspoken promise.

"Set him free, healer. Be his friend, but a counselor no more. It's time."

As his resistance faded, she wondered if he, too, sensed the presence of She-Who-Was-Magda? Did he experience, as she did, the appreciation rippling steadily toward them, its source a darkling plain devoid of oceans, yet even so, encompassing them in liquid warmth, the grandmother's gratitude as tangible as the book being passed from Symone's hand to that of the healer.

"So be it," said Esslar, his smile touched by sadness.
They said no goodbye. None was necessary. She left as she came, scurrying down the stairs, already intent on the next address, the next interview, determined that the past be quickly put to right so that the future, her future, might commence.

In time, She-Who-Was-Symone, who had never been a patient woman, became one. She would learn tact as well, she who had always been quick to criticize and quicker to condemn. "Stone by stone" became her motto that year, the year they began pulling down the walls around Pelion.

THE PUP'S TONGUE scrubbed Alyssa's cheeks, his sturdy body wriggling with the energetic wagging of his tail. A cheerful fellow, even-tempered and eager to please, he had doubled in size in the past few weeks and, if appetite had anything to do with size, promised to be nothing less than gargantuan. He was teething now, as was Aethra, and derived enormous satisfaction from gnawing shoe-leather. That he consistently chewed her slippers rather than Sandur's boots amused her greatly, causing her to credit him with innate good taste and a highly developed sense of self-preservation.

On the morning of her daughter's first birthday, Alyssa awoke to find a basket by her side and within it, a tightly-rolled ball of silver-tipped fuzz. How Sandur had obtained a wolfhound, a rare and costly breed this far south, remained something of a mystery, although Jincin and Hanania were undoubtedly involved. Her eyes filled with tears, she stroked the sleeping pup until Sandur confessed in a subdued whisper, "I had not thought to grieve thee." Sensing his distress, she managed a smile, touched that he went to such lengths to please her.

She was unsurprised by his decision to dedicate his share of the Kwanlonhon fortune to charitable concerns. His natural generosity, coupled with his refusal to parade his wealth, caused him to insist on anonymity in giving. As a result, Pharlookas never guessed that his three-year apprenticeship at the Forge was financed by his friend, nor did Draupadi possess the slightest suspicion that her acceptance into the Potter's Guild was due to extensive renovations currently underway on the dome of Guild Hall.

Certainly no one except Alyssa, Dorian, and Fenja knew the source of the funds donated for the construction of a new home for the Chartists. Dedicated to the memory of Haji of Salmydessus, it would be the first building constructed outside the perimeters of what was already known as the Old City. Alyssa alone was privy to the relief with which Sandur put Haji to rest.

Despite the enormity of Sandur's yearly revenues, they lived simply in the house he inherited from his grandmother, a five-room apartment above a fabric shop located around the corner from the central marketplace. Alyssa adored it on sight, from the dusty antique furnishings to the sadly peeling walls, from the sun-filled kitchen blanketed with cobwebs to the neglected garden with its dilapidated grape arbor and overgrown banks of climbing roses. To Sandur's initial amusement and eventual dismay, he was pressed into immediate service since nothing would content Alyssa until the house was cleaned and aired, the furniture oiled, the chimney swept, the linens laundered, the upholstery brushed, the floors scrubbed, and the kitchen set in perfect order.

To his grumbling she turned deaf ears, content that he should work and work hard. Day in and day out he hauled furniture, beat rugs, trimmed hedges, split kindling, and replaced roof tiles, falling to sleep each night almost before his head touched the pillow. In the wee hours of those crisp autumn nights, the child nursing at her breast, Alyssa would consider the next day's chores, thankful that She-Who-Was-Magda had supplied the means by which her grandson could be kept from brooding.

Attacking each task she set him with ferocious industry, he would hack away at the waist-high weeds for hours, the rhythmic sweeping of his scythe measuring off yet another day spent in inner turmoil. Since their arrival in Pelion, he had cut her off from his thoughts, lending her his eyes when she had need of them but maintaining his distance, making clear without words his need for solitude.

She thought to stave off time, for surely time was her enemy, each hour bringing him closer to acknowledging his lack of purpose. This was her greatest fear, that with the passage of time he would come to regret what he'd left behind in Endlin. They returned to Pelion for two reasons: to deliver his father to the healers and to attend the blessing of their child. These things accomplished, with wealth enough to last a lifetime, what must Sandur do?

Part of her wept for him; another part recognized that he must forge his future on his own. When the last particles of dust were swept away and the copper-bottomed pots shone bright, she cast about for new diversions, anything to keep him occupied, only to learn that others, too, shared her concern.

Pharlookas appeared on their doorstep late one afternoon, a bearded giant inviting Sandur on a visit to the Legion training grounds.

"I need exercise," he declared with a twinkle in his eyes, "and I can think of no man I'd rather wrestle to the ground."

Dorian came next, worrying over the latest dispatches from Botheswallow, expressing hope that Sandur might be able to decipher Yossi's contribution to the continuing exploration of the southern lands.

"The lad's got a good eye for detail," Dorian admitted with a rueful grin, "but between you and me, he's never quite mastered the notion of scale."

Soon after, a note arrived in the morning post:

> Horse-breeder for the Calvary wants Seal for stud.
> Also interested in the importation of eastern stock.
> Please advise.   Galen

Requests for Sandur's expertise proliferated. Dictys' eldest sister, a dealer in spices, was in search of a partner, preferably one with firsthand knowledge of wholesale suppliers in the east. Pentaur's second cousin wondered if Sandur might be interested in learning the ins and outs of the tea trade. Anstellan's mother's next-door neighbor seemed to think it likely that her nephew, a representative of the Kilput mines, would profit from a meeting with a former clansman of jewel-hungry Endlin.

He went without comment, tending Aethra in the mornings so Alyssa could resume her duties telling stories to children in the Lesser Library. After the midday meal, he would wrap himself in a cloak and stride off toward his appointments in the business district, his stiffly measured footsteps ringing ominously against the entryway tiles. Each passing day found him grimmer, more remote, an unhappy phantom of his former self.

And then, last night, as she lay wide-eyed and wakeful, thinking him fast asleep, a low voice broke the stillness of the night.

"Thee must tell them to stop."

Startled out of her reverie, she lay quietly in the hushed house, listening as an internal clock ticked off the hours of their lives together.

"They want to help, Sandur. Is that so bad?"

"Bad?" he repeated blankly, as though baffled by her question. "Nay, not bad." Drawing her to him, he touched her hair. "Thee must understand, their friendship is a miracle to me. Yet the more they try to help me, the more lost I become."

She nodded assent, feeling his muscles tighten as his arms locked around her, clinging to her as a drowning man clings to a timber on a tempest-tossed sea. Content to be his anchor, she waited out the storm of his unhappiness.

"We cannot continue like this much longer," she said when he was calm again, "me, sick with worry; you, sick with doubts. I yearn for thee, Sandur Kwanlonhon," she whispered into the darkness, "and the loss of thy thoughts is more than I can bear."

"Dost thou think I do not share thy loneliness?" he replied with fearsome tenderness, confessing an anguish of spirit equaling her own. "I walk a score of paths each day, none of them to my liking, yet even so, each one brings me back to thee. If not for that, I would have given up long ago."

"Can't I travel with thee?" she asked with a quaver in her voice, remembering his last voyage without her. She closed her eyes, suddenly exhausted. Her head found its accustomed resting place on the pillow of his chest, his arms wrapped snuggly about her shoulders, shielding her from the cool night air. Sinking into slumber, she thought she heard him say something, but could not summon energy enough to concentrate.

Upon waking the next morning, she remembered the word he spoke as she floated on the currents of her dreams.

"Perhaps."

ALYSSA WAS GAMBOLING on the parlor floor with Calibros, playing assorted games of fetch, when she heard the familiar tread of boots in the entryway. The pup must have heard them as well since he emitted a series of high-pitched yaps.

The hinges on the parlor door squeaked.

"Greetings, nymph!"

A hand reached down to pull her to her feet.

"What news?" she asked, sensing in the enthusiasm of his welcome a change of sorts. He left at midday without stating a destination. Now it was mid-afternoon and nearly time to wake Aethra from her nap.

"Only that we must hurry. Ridha will be here in a moment. Where's thy cloak?"

"Ridha?" she called after him, totally at sea, hearing his laughter echoing down the hallway. How long it had been since she'd heard that laugh, joyous and deep-bellied, the same laugh that charmed her in the cell.

A cloak was wrapped around her shoulders, a pair of riding gloves stuffed impatiently into her hands.

"Sandur, I'll not budge from this spot until you tell me exactly what you're up to!"

But he was laughing again, attaching a leash to Calibros' collar and pushing her, gently but firmly, toward the entryway. "Hast thou no imagination?" he teased when she balked at the top of the stairs.

The downstairs door opened, and Ridha was running lightly up the steps, the scent of jasmine hovering in the air as she passed them by.

"Where are we going?" Alyssa demanded, almost at her wits end, to hear him announce, with a confidence that took her breath away.

"To a new life."

SANDUR LET HIS eyes rove slowly over the landscape, sensing Alyssa's delight as she absorbed the beauty of the countryside. A lush autumnal haze embraced the hills east of the valley of the castle, the leaves of the hardwood trees trembling like living flames, a stray breeze rifling them until they tumbled down in brilliant disarray to carpet the earth in intricate mosaics of crimson and gold.

The pup frolicked blithely in the falling leaves, leaping up to catch them on the fly with the tip of his nose. His excitement knew no bounds when, purely by chance, he flushed a hare. With a joyous yelp, he was off, scrambling with mad abandon after the wily hare. Tearing over the ground, dodging this way and that, the hare led the pup a merry chase, until, bored by the ineptness of his pursuer, he disappeared down a convenient hole, leaving Calibros to whine and dig half-heartedly around the site of his playmate's unexplained departure. Sandur whistled him up, pleased when the pup responded without delay, and threw the ball toward a distant stand of birches.

He'd found this place a few days ago when he'd visited the Calvary headquarters with Pharlookas. Deciding that Seal needed exercise, he refused Galen's offer of companionship and headed out on his own. Not surprisingly, he'd been drawn toward this spot by the sound of running water. Following a meandering stream which grew in size and energy until it plunged downward into a deep pool surrounded by water-hungry willows, he remembered thinking that this would serve him as a place to swim and dive. Today it seemed an appropriate place to imagine a future.

From time to time, his eyes strayed to the woman sitting beside him on the blanket he'd spread on the bank of the pool. She seemed serenity itself, her profile touched with fire as the sun began its descent behind her right shoulder. Sharing his sight with her was second nature to him now, a service he rendered without harboring the least resentment, a right she claimed without shame or painful humiliation. In truth, he loved nothing better than lending her his eyes, if only because she helped him see the world anew.

In the beginning, she wanted to see as he saw, her hunger for shapes and colors fifteen years in the making. As time passed, she made a pact with the darkness, finding in it, perhaps, the comfort of long companionship. His eyes were hers when they traveled or when she knelt at the cradle to kiss Aethra goodnight. In an upholstery shop, she matched colors and textures with the vision he lent her. In the privacy of their home, she preferred to manage as she always had, deftly negotiating the furniture he arranged to her specifications, crooning softly to the babe as she gazed blindly through the window, as though, he often thought, having seen the view once, she preferred to imagine it as she pleased.

Night after night, her head resting on his heart, he wrestled with himself, closing his eyes against a known reality in order to imagine, as she did, a new and better world beyond the window. No matter that any imagination he might have once possessed had been beaten out of him at an early age.

Somehow, he must leap into an unimagined future, and this time he wore no rope around his waist.

Realizing he was holding his breath, he expelled it in a sigh.

"So," she said, turning to face him, "what is this new life, and when does it begin?"

"After the winter thaw. As soon as the roads are passable."

A myriad of expressions flew over her face—surprise, panic, excitement, and then, stronger than any of the previous emotions, a rush of sudden curiosity.

"Where will we go?"

"South, I think," he said with studied nonchalance, "if for no other reason than to help Yossi with his maps." Enjoying her puzzled frown, he added quickly, "We could just as easily head north. Or west, for that matter, although I thought we'd wait until Pharlookas and Draupadi finish their apprenticeships and can travel with us."

"Why not to the moon, for that matter?" she asked, cocking her head as she always did when moved to sarcasm.

Stifling the urge to laugh, for she was working herself into a rare fit of temper, he replied with a sorrowful air, "I've no map."

Her lips quirked, and suddenly, she was smiling.

"Then you must make one!"

"I thought to do so. But only if you come with me."

And with a single touch of his palm to her shoulder, she saw it all, everything he imagined about their future together.

Alyssa felt a pang of regret at what she would give up—stability, security—then dismissed them with a smile and a shrug. Had she not given up these things the day she left her mother's house? If she retained any worries as to Aethra's future, she relinquished those as well. Could a clansman of Endlin be anything less than devoted to his children's well-being?

And so their pact was made on that day of days in golden autumn when they looked toward an imagined future and pledged themselves, a blind woman and a scarred man, to cross and re-cross the known world, bringing with them pilgrims desirous of finding a city that once was the stuff of myth, but now was open to all, a blossoming place called Pelion the Great.

"You must bring everyone," the Twentieth Mother insisted.

And so they did.

Appendix I

The Rise of the Eastern Republic

For those interested in reading more about the formation of the Eastern Republic, we reprint this introduction from Bettina/Hiroji's history of seventh century Endlin, *The Rise of the East*. [Great Library of Endlin, 920 A.T.]

"If your taste should run to fact, then turn to the book written by the Endlinese Equerry Balafel Synzurit. There, in a masterly prose style that a host of legal minds have since copied, you will find a detailed report of the decisions made that fateful summer, when the clansmen of Endlin rose as one body to pledge themselves to a new beginning. Laws are not rewritten in a single day, nor are the habits of five centuries abandoned with a casual farewell, but the Synzurit Equerry's account provides a thoughtful discussion of the major decisions made in the days and nights which followed hard upon the trial of Manthur Kwanlonhon, decisions which evolved into the grand benevolence with which Endlin forged a lasting partnership with its sister territories, forming in the decades which followed the great Eastern Republic, which stretched from the foothills of the Sarujian Mountains to the farthest flung isles, from wind-whipped Nisyros to the sultry Sargasso Sea.

If you prefer your history in poetic mode, consult the text of Tasir Kwanlonhon's inaugural address to the joint council of elders, a speech still recited annually on the first day of trading season, when the spring rains drape the seven hills in robes of brilliant emerald and searing pink, and the Endlinese fleet takes to the sea. On that day of days, citizens toss onto the waters the first blossoms of the flowering almond trees planted in what was once the province of whores and drunkards and is now a verdant park surrounding the Maritime Academy. Founded by a descendant of Rassad H'ulalet, it is the only school of its kind in the old world, open to any and all who share the ancient clansmen's fascination with anything and everything to do with the sea.

Because of two Kwanlonhon clansmen, Tasir and Fawaz, we speak now of the old world and the new. It did not come to pass in their lifetimes, nor in the days of their immediate successors, but come it did, almost a century later, when the eastern passage was discovered by a ship bearing a white pennant with a crescent moon and an eight-pointed sun embroidered in threads of bright silver and dull gold.

That same ship, whose prow came to rest on the edge of the new world, was piloted not by one, but by two. One stood at the helm, the other on the limestone cliffs of Endlin, their navigation swift and sure under strange stars. Its mission accomplished, that goodly vessel, christened *Pride of the East* for its maiden voyage, the ship on which rested the hopes of the old world, returned as the mating gull does to the nest, escorted by the easterly breeze sailors love best, the breeze which whispers above the sibilant song of cresting waves, '*Home.*'"

Appendix II

Excerpt from *Tyrants Among Us*

"... [For] in the years that followed the removal of Manthur Kwanlonon from his position as Tehran, he became known as "The Destroyer of Endlin."

Centuries later, when historians began their careful revisions of the period, they would dub him "The Last Tehran," a title more fanciful than accurate since the last person to actually bear the title of Tehran, a certain Lazlo Onozzi, would die of old age a hundred years after Manthur Kwanlonhon's testimony in Equerry Court.

Given the nature of most historians, their interest in Manthur Linphat Afaf Kwanlonhon, the so-called Destroyer of Endlin, becomes understandable when viewed in perspective. Like the vast majority of tyrants, Manthur's crimes were considerably less important than the rebellions they begot. Given this view, Manthur emerges from history as the last Tehran to wield absolute power and the first to undergo trial by his peers.

One suspects the historians of admiring Manthur rather more than he deserved, the result, perhaps, of a diary written by an Effrentati magistrate who heard Manthur's testimony first-hand and copied it down from memory some twenty years later. The consensus among historians is that by this time, due no doubt to the social upheavals already underway in Endlin, the magistrate in question was experiencing an all too frequent disease among the elderly, in short, an acute case of misplaced nostalgia for bygone days. One bold (albeit overbearing) critic went so far as to dismiss the Effrentati diary as a work of pure fiction, representing the yearnings of a die-hard conservative for a return to traditional values, among them autocracy, xenophobia, and the subjugation of women.

A more moderate stance was taken by a behaviorist, who found in the Effrentati diary what she believed to be a vastly more important truth, namely, that Manthur Kwanlonhon, the infamous Destroyer of Endlin, was as charismatic as he was conniving. Rather than damning the Effrentati diarist as a fascist or a fool, she suggests that he accurately documents what must have been Manthur's tremendous appeal to a group of immensely conservative, tradition-bound elder statesmen. The miracle, as the behaviorist is quick to point out, is that despite their admiration, they were able to condemn him for the tyrant he was."

[Excerpt from *Tyrants Among Us*, by Isa of Orfu, The Great Library of Endlin, 1018 A.T.]

About the Author

Anna LaForge read Tolkien's *The Lord of the Rings* at fourteen, Asimov's *Foundation Trilogy* at sixteen, and LeGuin's *The Left Hand of Darkness* at eighteen, at which time she decided that she, too, wanted to create new worlds. Born in Philadelphia, she has lived throughout the country, from urban centers in the Midwest and Northeast to tiny Andrews, Texas. A former executive director of several not-for-profit arts organizations, she divides her time between teaching and writing.

The first book of her Maze series, *The Marcella Fragment*, was published in June, 2012, followed by *Agave Revealed* in June, 2013 and *Pelion Preserved* in January, 2016.

Anna's books are published by Newcal Publishing.

Connect with Anna LaForge online:

Twitter: twitter.com/annalaforge
Facebook: facebook.com/annalaforge
Her website and blog: annalaforge.com

CPSIA information can be obtained at www.ICGtesting.com
Printed in the USA
LVOW07s0021170216

475347LV00004B/301/P